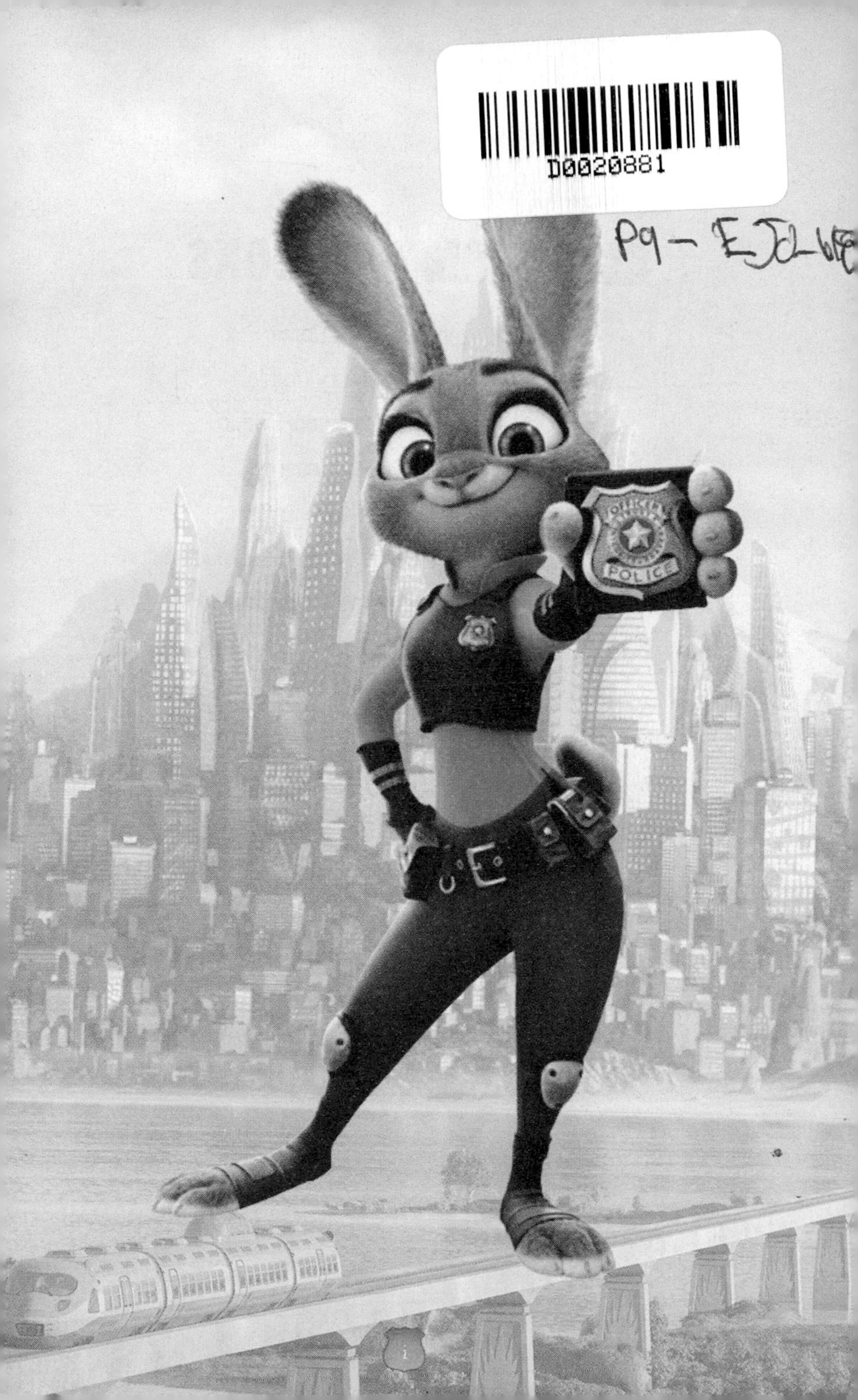
POLICE

ALSO FROM JOE BOOKS

Disney Frozen Cinestory Comic

Disney Cinderella Cinestory Comic

Disney 101 Dalmations Cinestory Comic

Disney Princess Comics Treasury

Disney*Pixar Comics Treasury

Disney's Darkwing Duck: The Definitively Dangerous Edition

Disney's Frozen: The Story of the Movie in Comics

Disney Big Hero 6 Cinestory Comic

Disney*Pixar Inside Out Cinestory Comic

Disney*Pixar Inside Out Fun Book

Disney Gravity Falls Cinestory Comic Volume One

Disney*Pixar The Good Dinosaur Cinestory Comic

Disney*Pixar The Good Dinosaur Fun Book

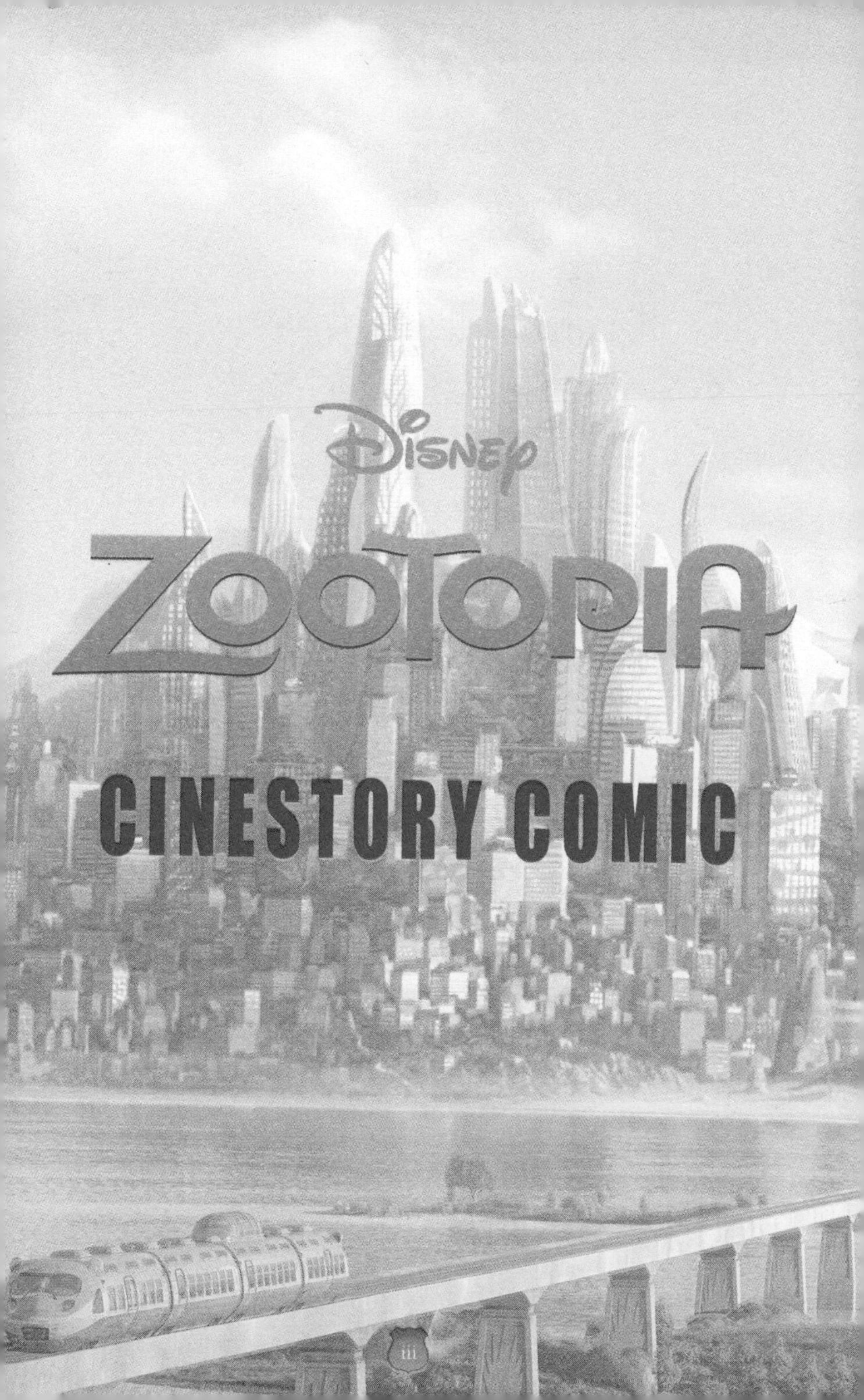

Disney Zootopia

CINESTORY COMIC

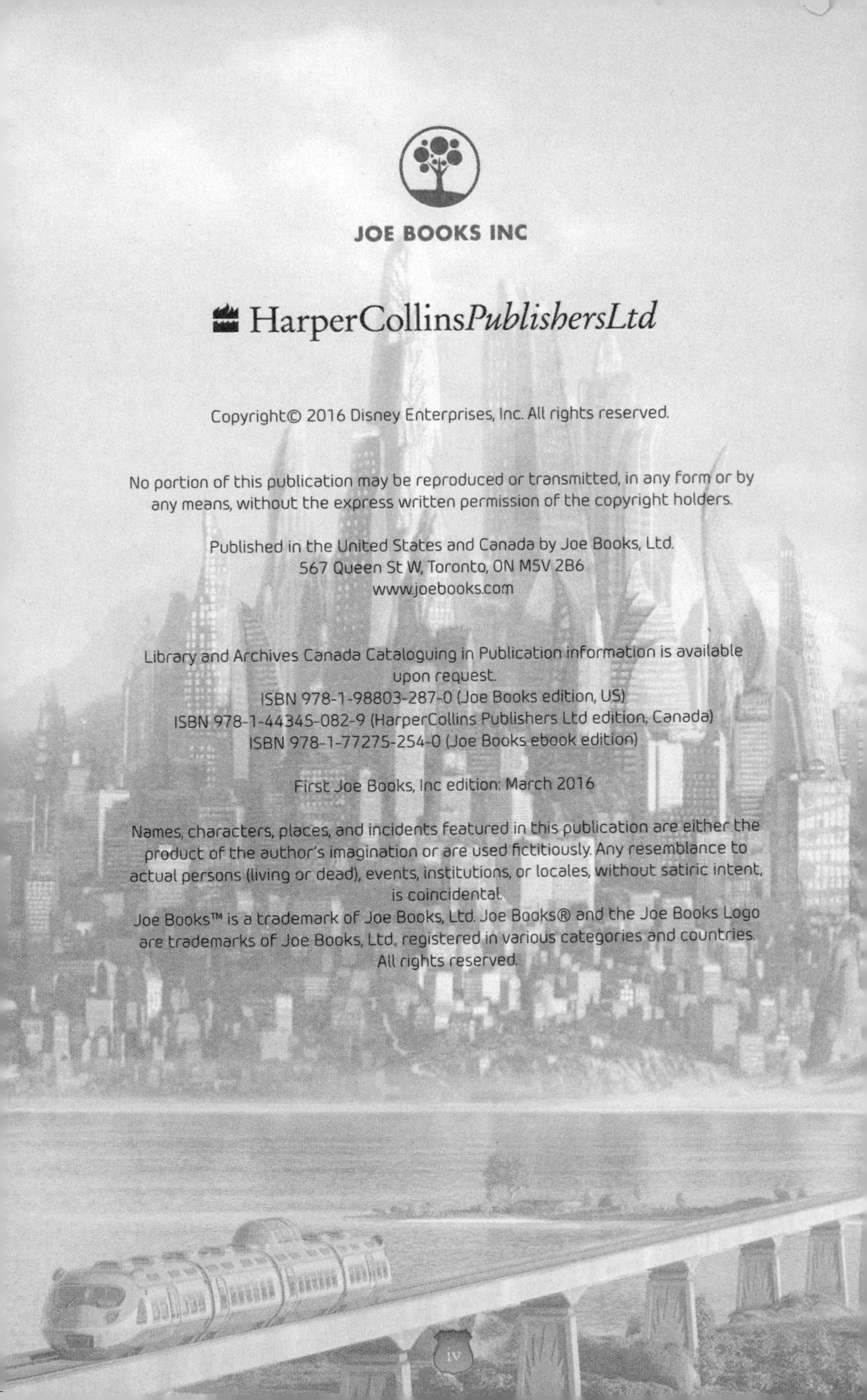

JOE BOOKS INC

HarperCollins*PublishersLtd*

Published in the United States and Canada by Joe Books, Ltd.
567 Queen St W, Toronto, ON M5V 2B6
www.joebooks.com

Library and Archives Canada Cataloguing in Publication information is available upon request.
ISBN 978-1-98803-287-0 (Joe Books edition, US)
ISBN 978-1-44345-082-9 (HarperCollins Publishers Ltd edition, Canada)
ISBN 978-1-77275-254-0 (Joe Books ebook edition)

First Joe Books, Inc edition: March 2016

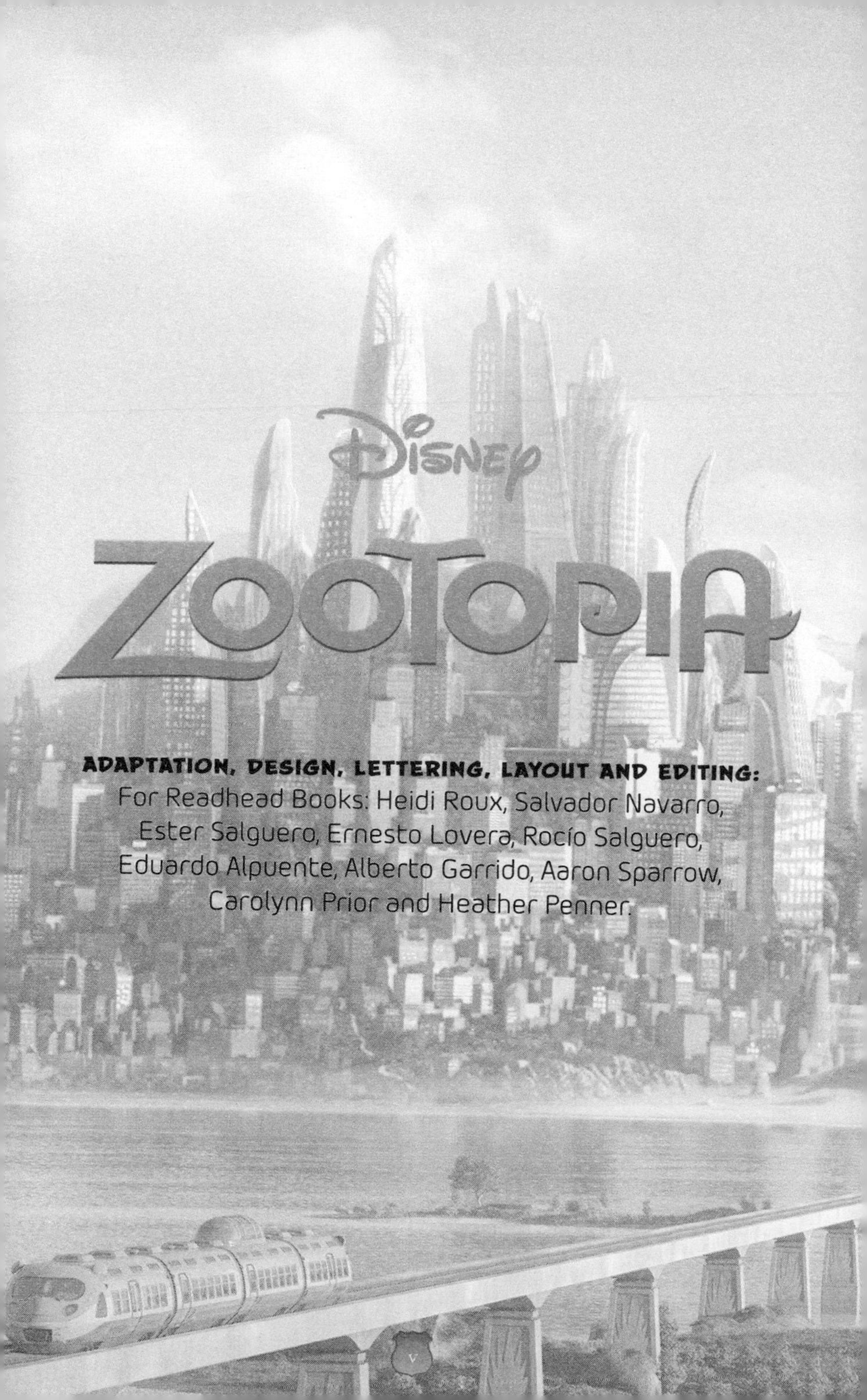

Disney Zootopia

ADAPTATION, DESIGN, LETTERING, LAYOUT AND EDITING:
For Readhead Books: Heidi Roux, Salvador Navarro, Ester Salguero, Ernesto Lovera, Rocío Salguero, Eduardo Alpuente, Alberto Garrido, Aaron Sparrow, Carolynn Prior and Heather Penner.

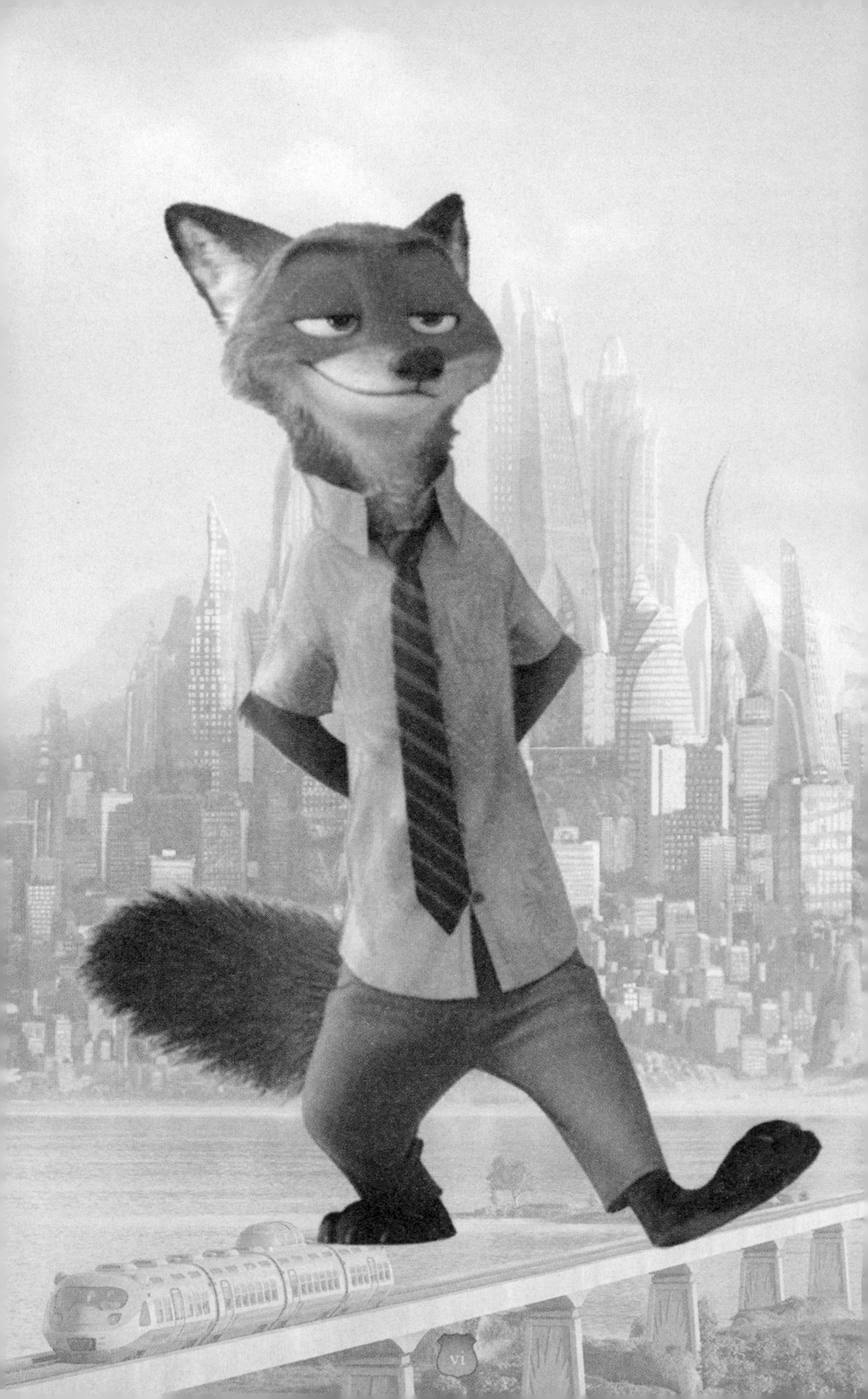

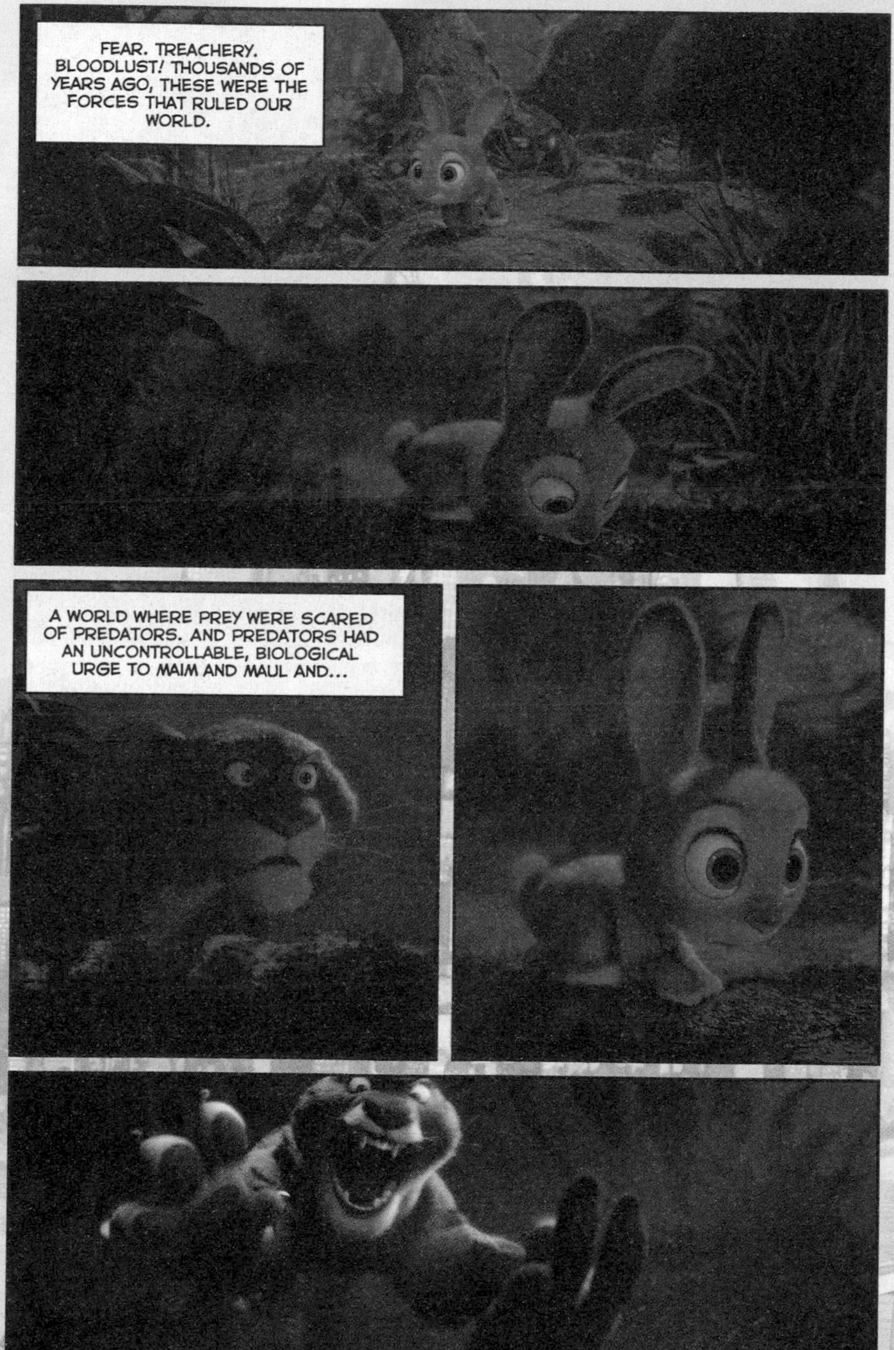
FEAR. TREACHERY. BLOODLUST! THOUSANDS OF YEARS AGO, THESE WERE THE FORCES THAT RULED OUR WORLD.
A WORLD WHERE PREY WERE SCARED OF PREDATORS. AND PREDATORS HAD AN UNCONTROLLABLE, BIOLOGICAL URGE TO MAIM AND MAUL AND...

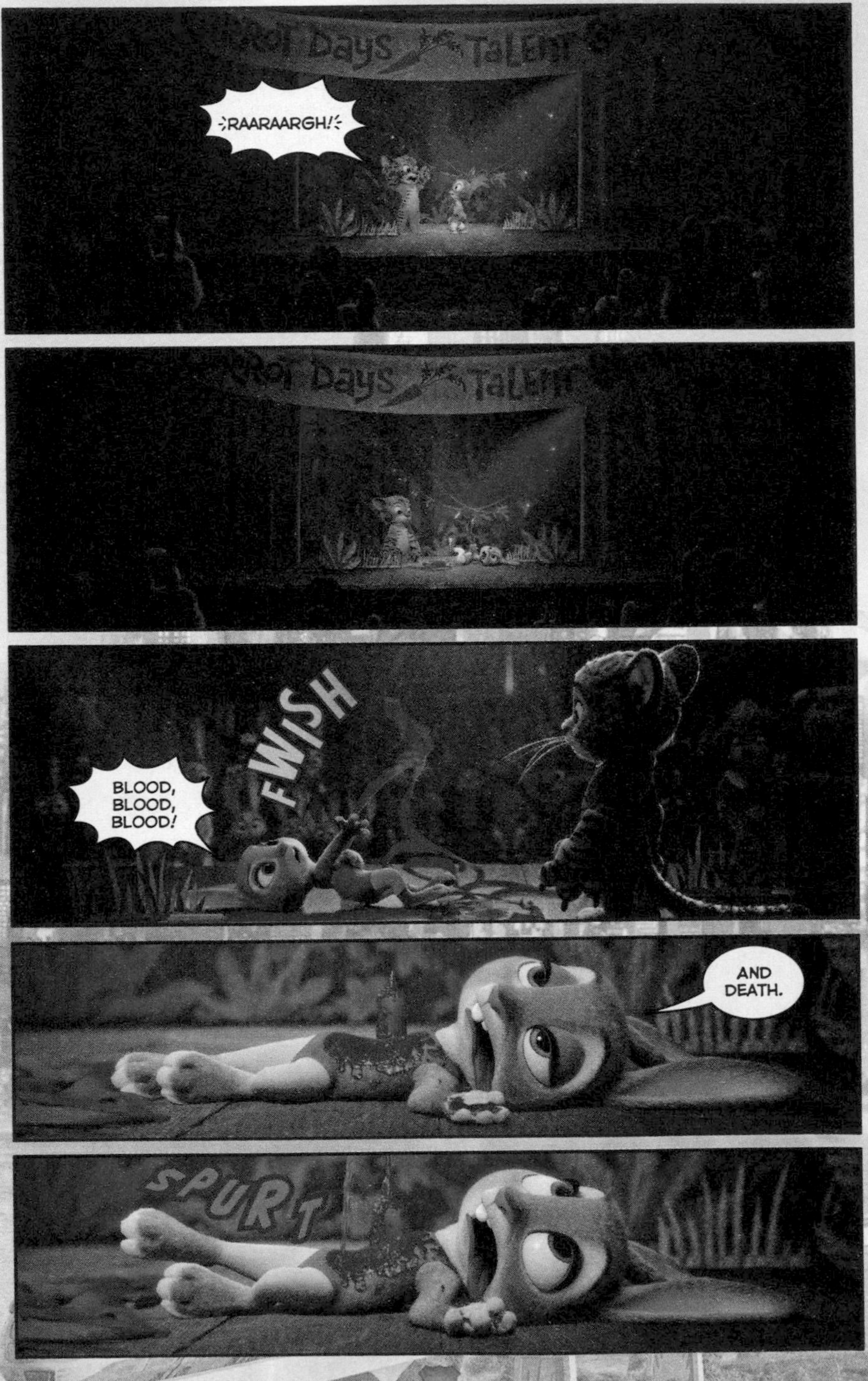
RAARAARGH!
BLOOD, BLOOD, BLOOD!
FWISH
AND DEATH.
SPURT

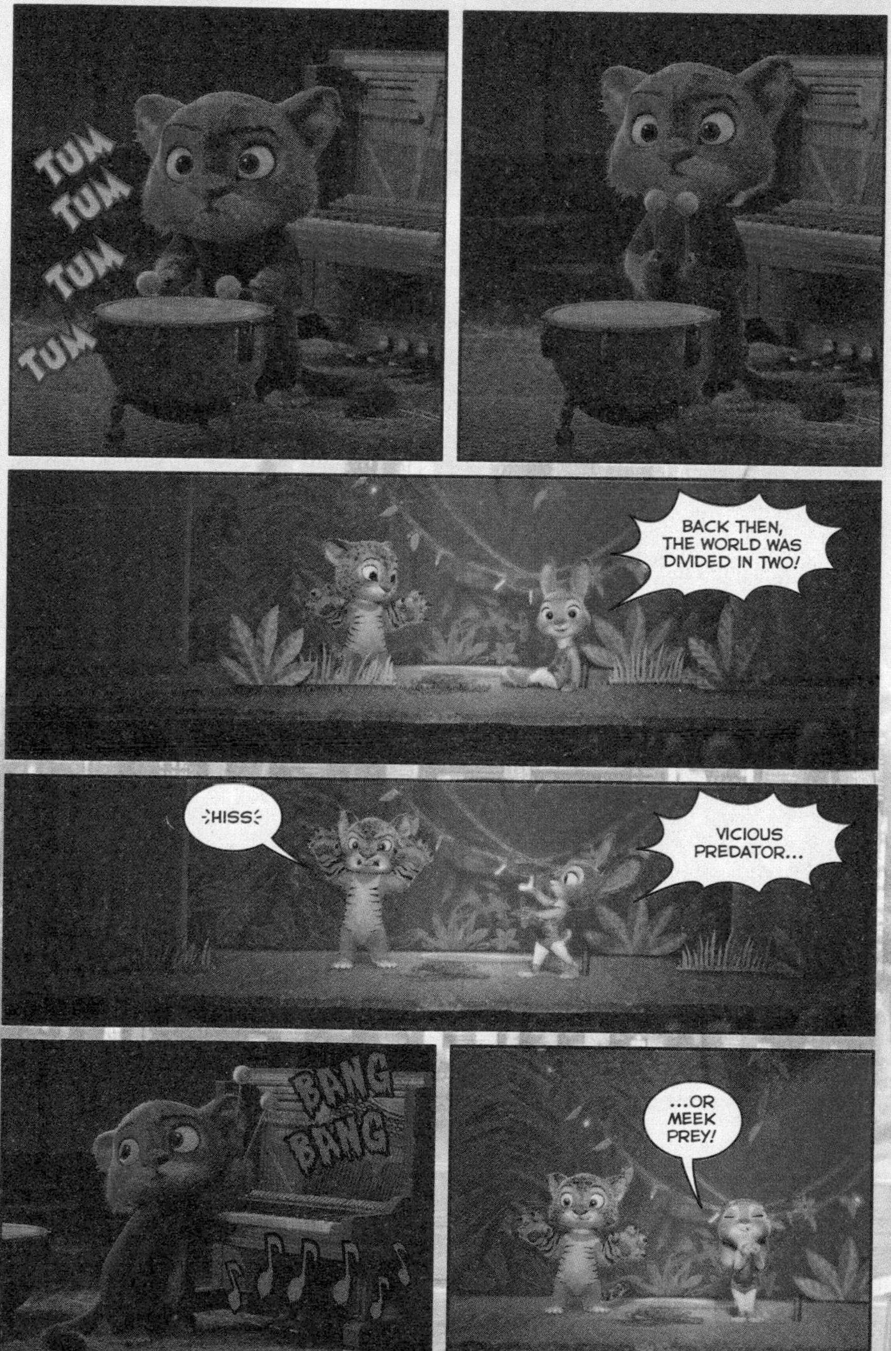
TUM
TUM
TUM
TUM
BACK THEN, THE WORLD WAS DIVIDED IN TWO!
HISS
VICIOUS PREDATOR...
BANG
BANG
...OR MEEK PREY!

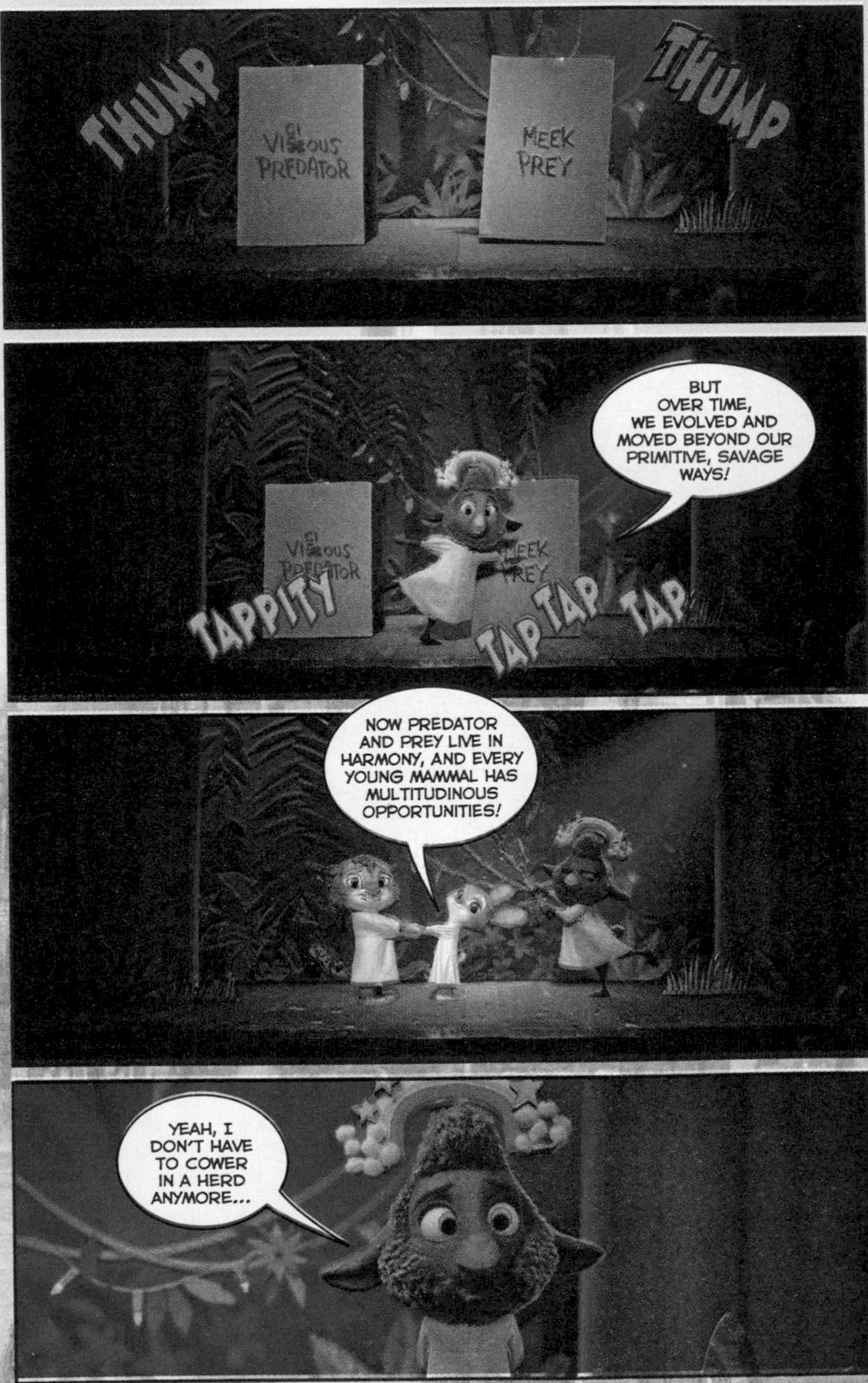
THUMP
VICIOUS PREDATOR
MEEK PREY
THUMP
BUT OVER TIME, WE EVOLVED AND MOVED BEYOND OUR PRIMITIVE, SAVAGE WAYS!
TAPPITY
TAP TAP
TAP
NOW PREDATOR AND PREY LIVE IN HARMONY, AND EVERY YOUNG MAMMAL HAS MULTITUDINOUS OPPORTUNITIES!
YEAH, I DON'T HAVE TO COWER IN A HERD ANYMORE...

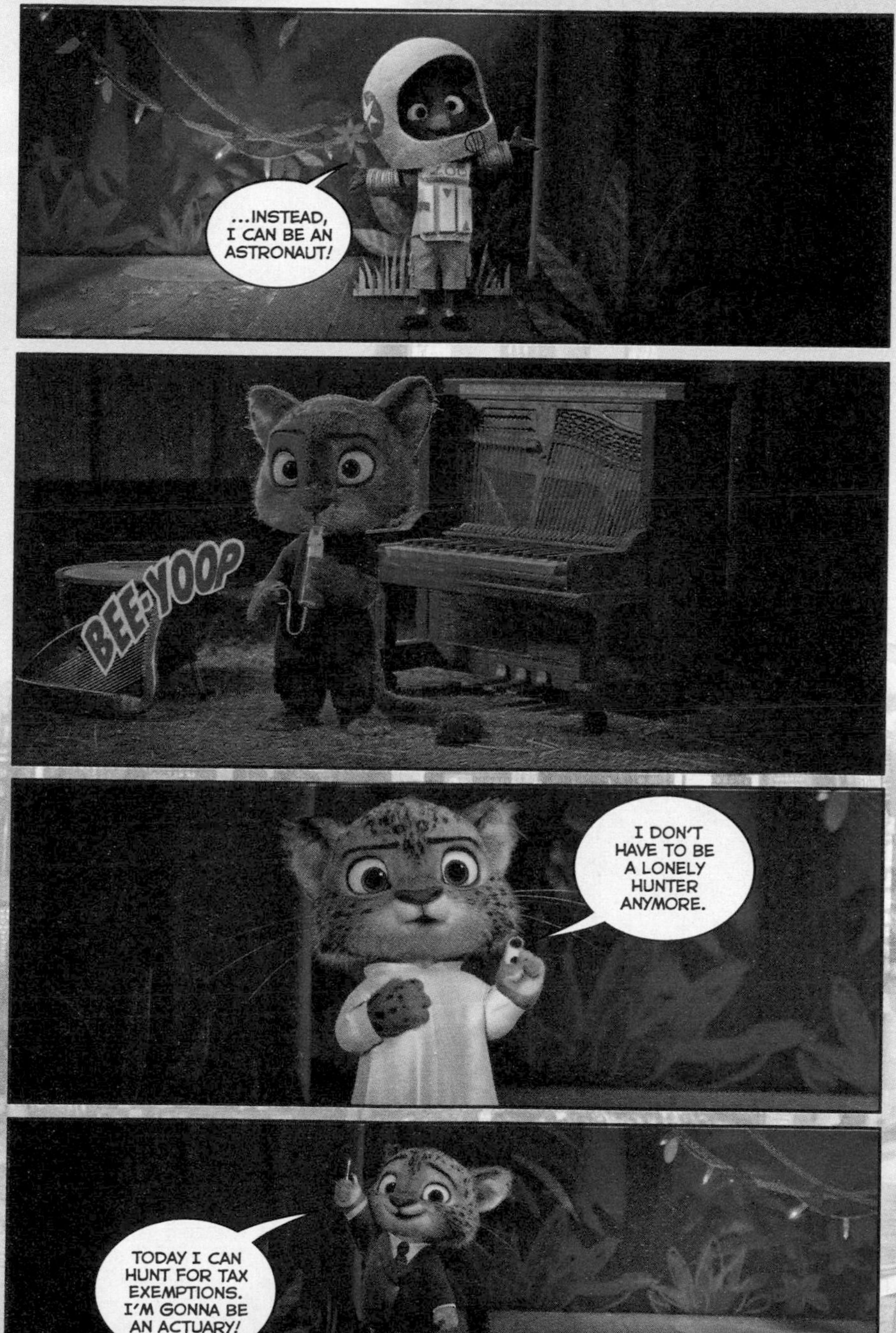
...INSTEAD, I CAN BE AN ASTRONAUT!
BEE-YOOP
I DON'T HAVE TO BE A LONELY HUNTER ANYMORE.
TODAY I CAN HUNT FOR TAX EXEMPTIONS. I'M GONNA BE AN ACTUARY!

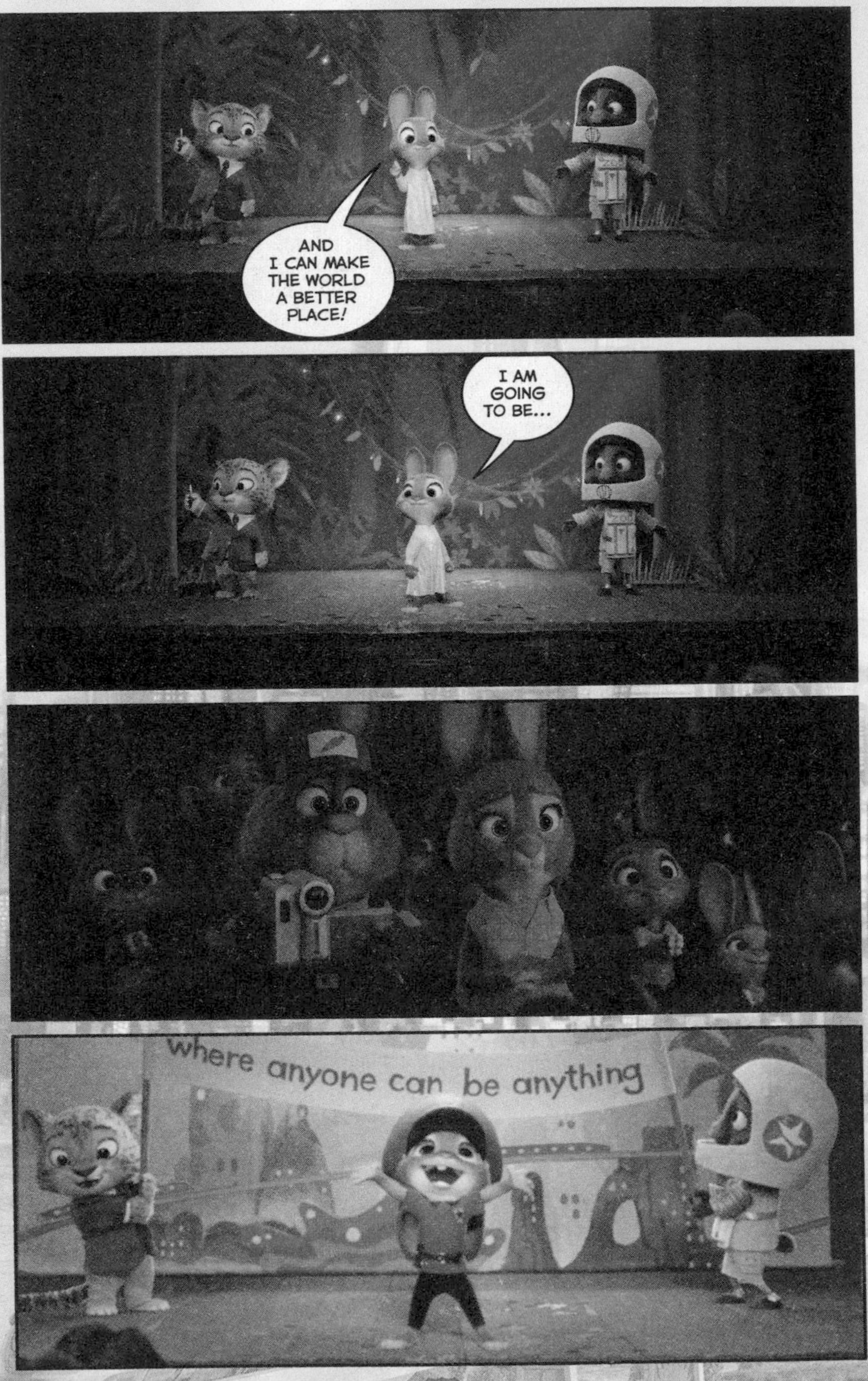
AND I CAN MAKE THE WORLD A BETTER PLACE!
I AM GOING TO BE...
where anyone can be anything

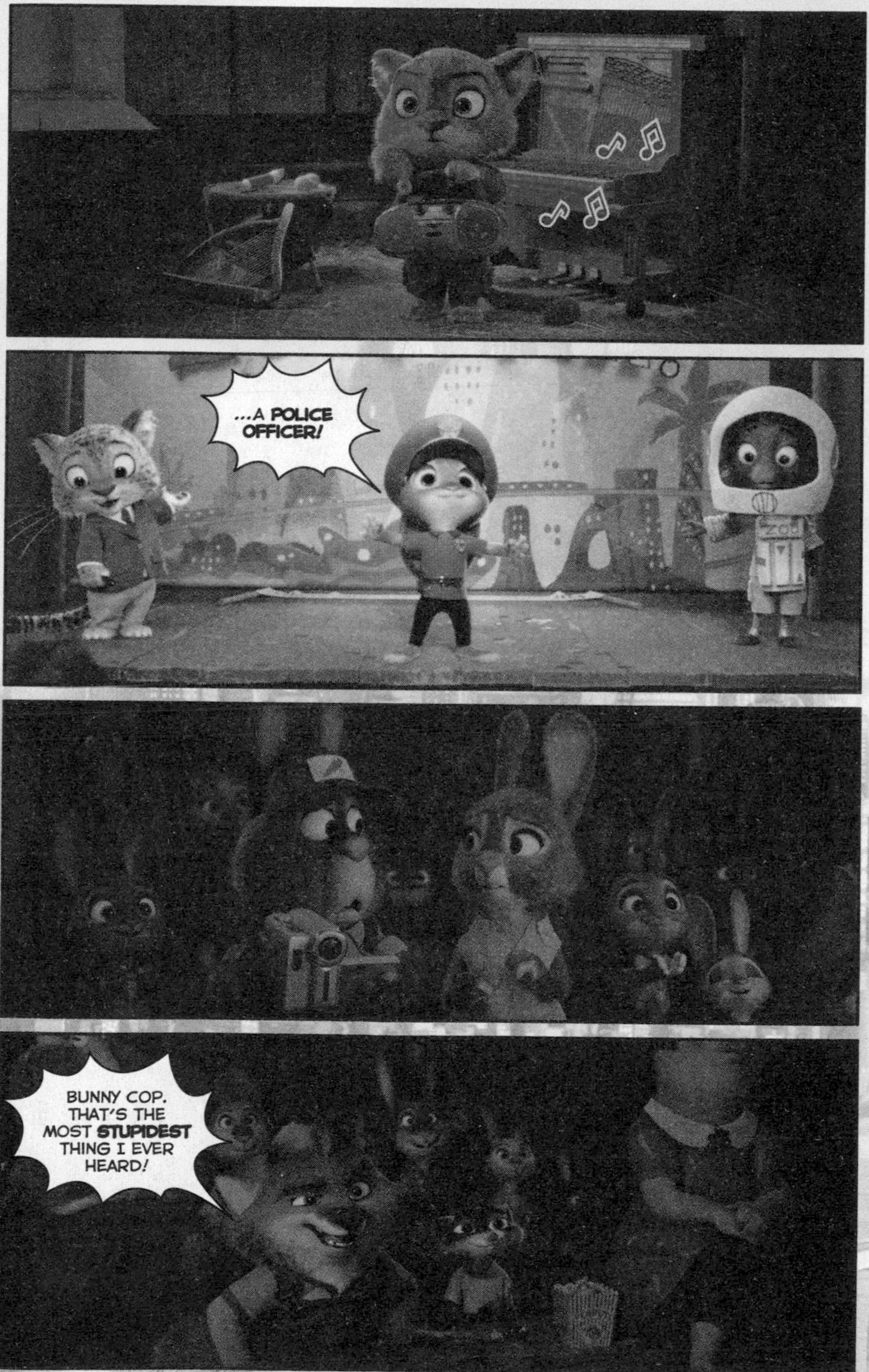
...A POLICE OFFICER!
BUNNY COP. THAT'S THE MOST STUPIDEST THING I EVER HEARD!

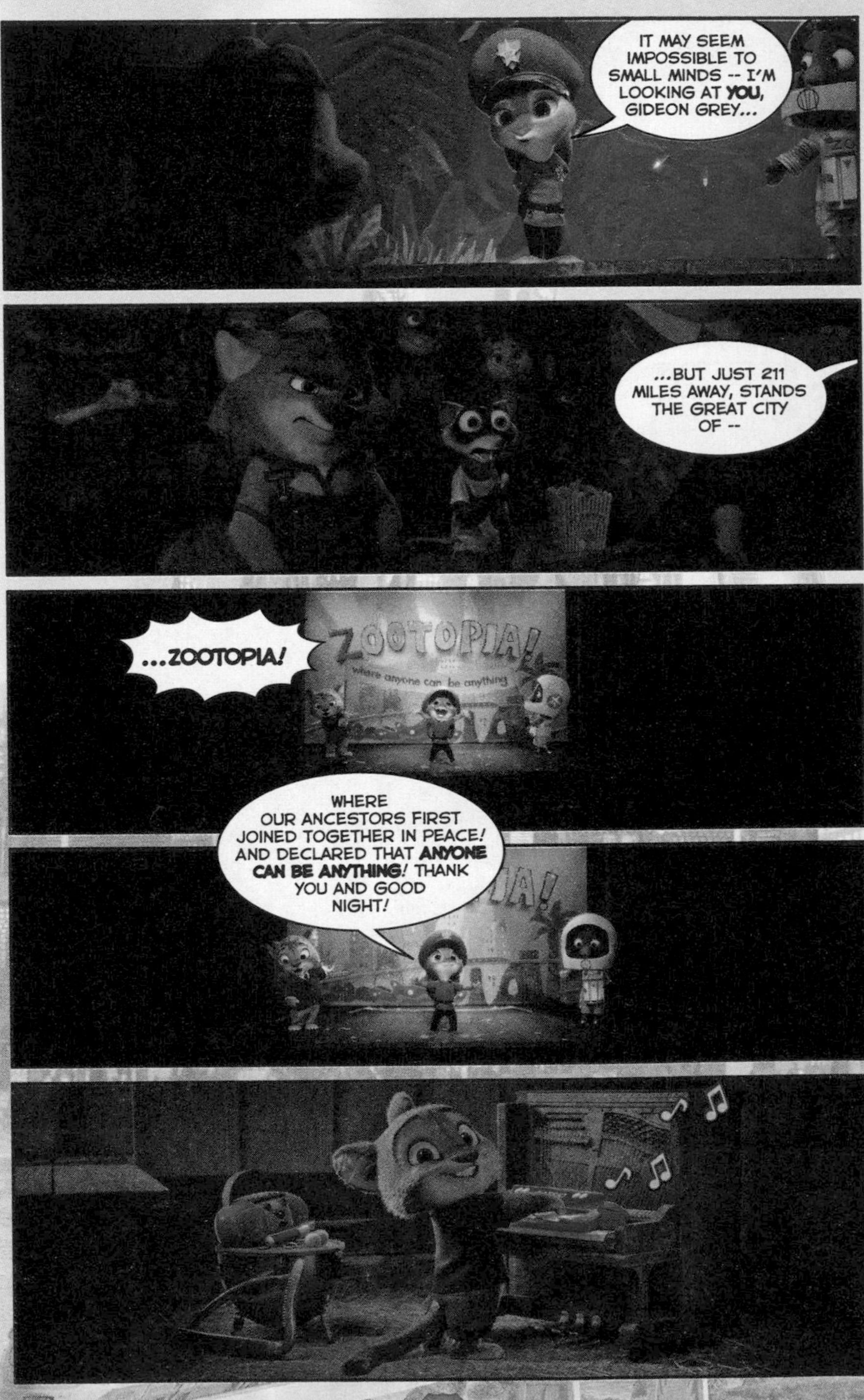
IT MAY SEEM IMPOSSIBLE TO SMALL MINDS -- I'M LOOKING AT **YOU**, GIDEON GREY...
...BUT JUST 211 MILES AWAY, STANDS THE GREAT CITY OF --
...ZOOTOPIA!
ZOOTOPIA!
where anyone can be anything
WHERE OUR ANCESTORS FIRST JOINED TOGETHER IN PEACE! AND DECLARED THAT **ANYONE CAN BE ANYTHING**! THANK YOU AND GOOD NIGHT!

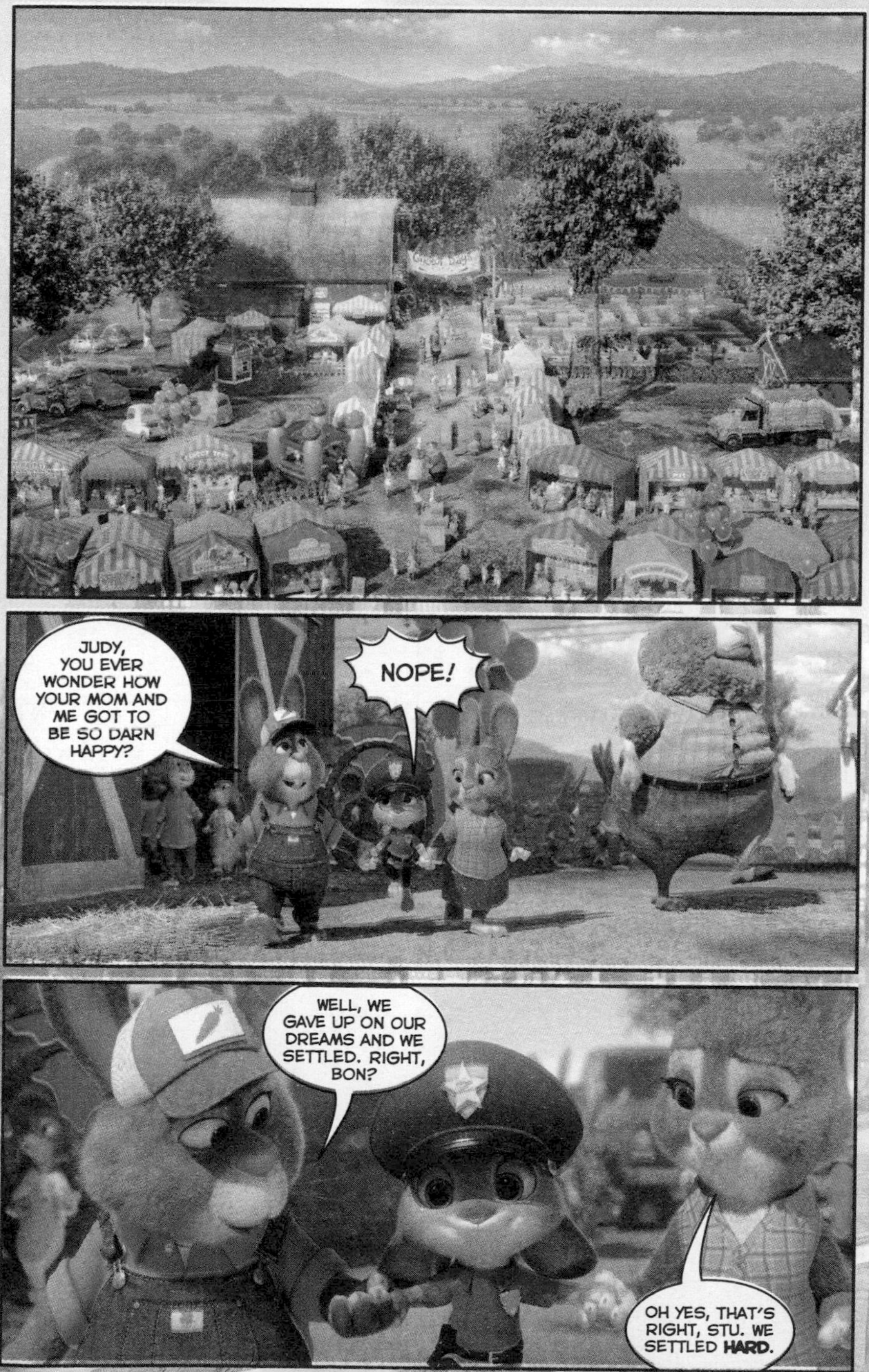
JUDY, YOU EVER WONDER HOW YOUR MOM AND ME GOT TO BE SO DARN HAPPY?
NOPE!
WELL, WE GAVE UP ON OUR DREAMS AND WE SETTLED. RIGHT, BON?
OH YES, THAT'S RIGHT, STU. WE SETTLED **HARD.**

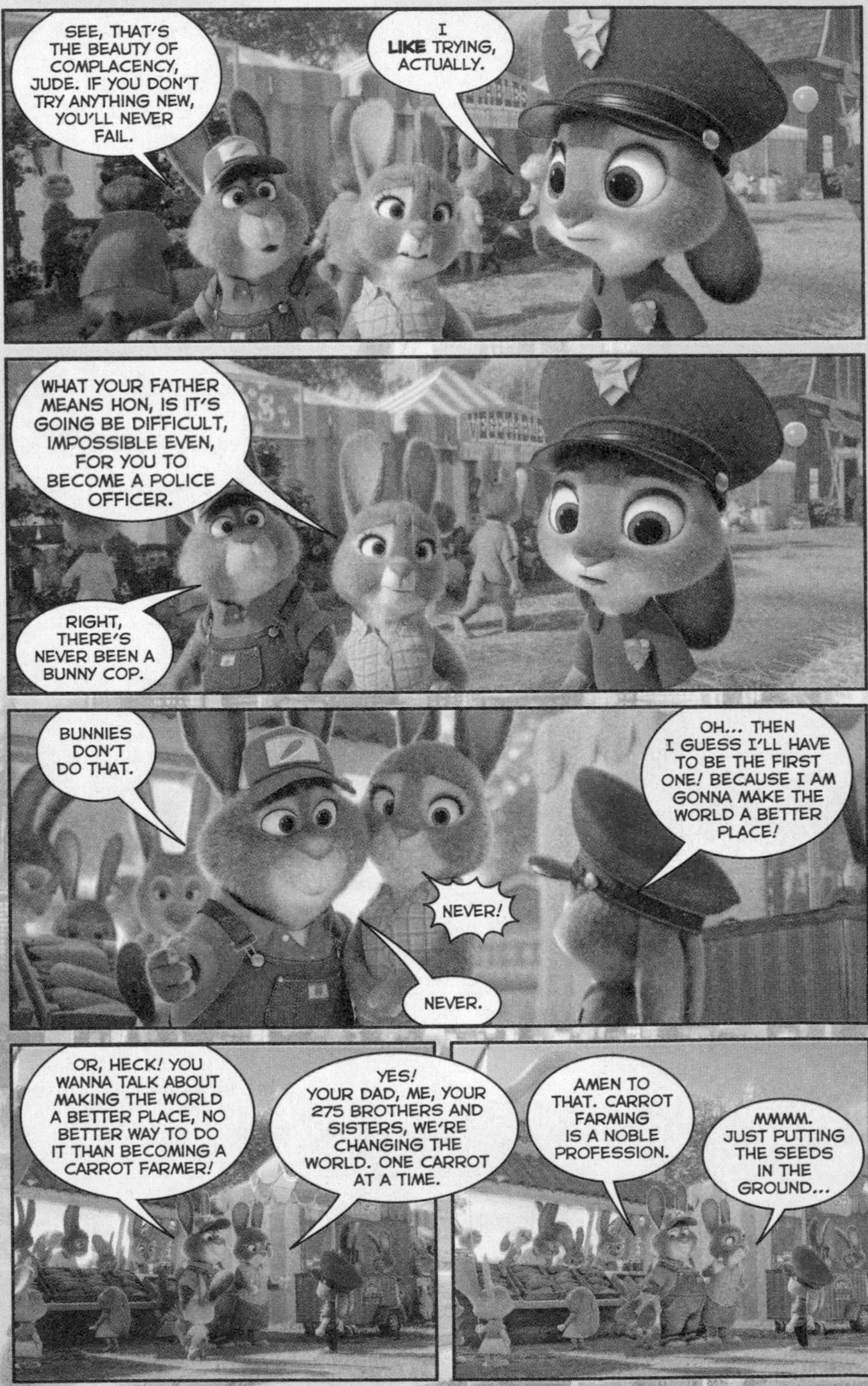
SEE, THAT'S THE BEAUTY OF COMPLACENCY, JUDE. IF YOU DON'T TRY ANYTHING NEW, YOU'LL NEVER FAIL.
I **LIKE** TRYING, ACTUALLY.
WHAT YOUR FATHER MEANS HON, IS IT'S GOING BE DIFFICULT, IMPOSSIBLE EVEN, FOR YOU TO BECOME A POLICE OFFICER.
RIGHT, THERE'S NEVER BEEN A BUNNY COP.
BUNNIES DON'T DO THAT.
NEVER!
NEVER.
OH... THEN I GUESS I'LL HAVE TO BE THE FIRST ONE! BECAUSE I AM GONNA MAKE THE WORLD A BETTER PLACE!
OR, HECK! YOU WANNA TALK ABOUT MAKING THE WORLD A BETTER PLACE, NO BETTER WAY TO DO IT THAN BECOMING A CARROT FARMER!
YES! YOUR DAD, ME, YOUR 275 BROTHERS AND SISTERS, WE'RE CHANGING THE WORLD. ONE CARROT AT A TIME.
AMEN TO THAT. CARROT FARMING IS A NOBLE PROFESSION.
MMMM. JUST PUTTING THE SEEDS IN THE GROUND...

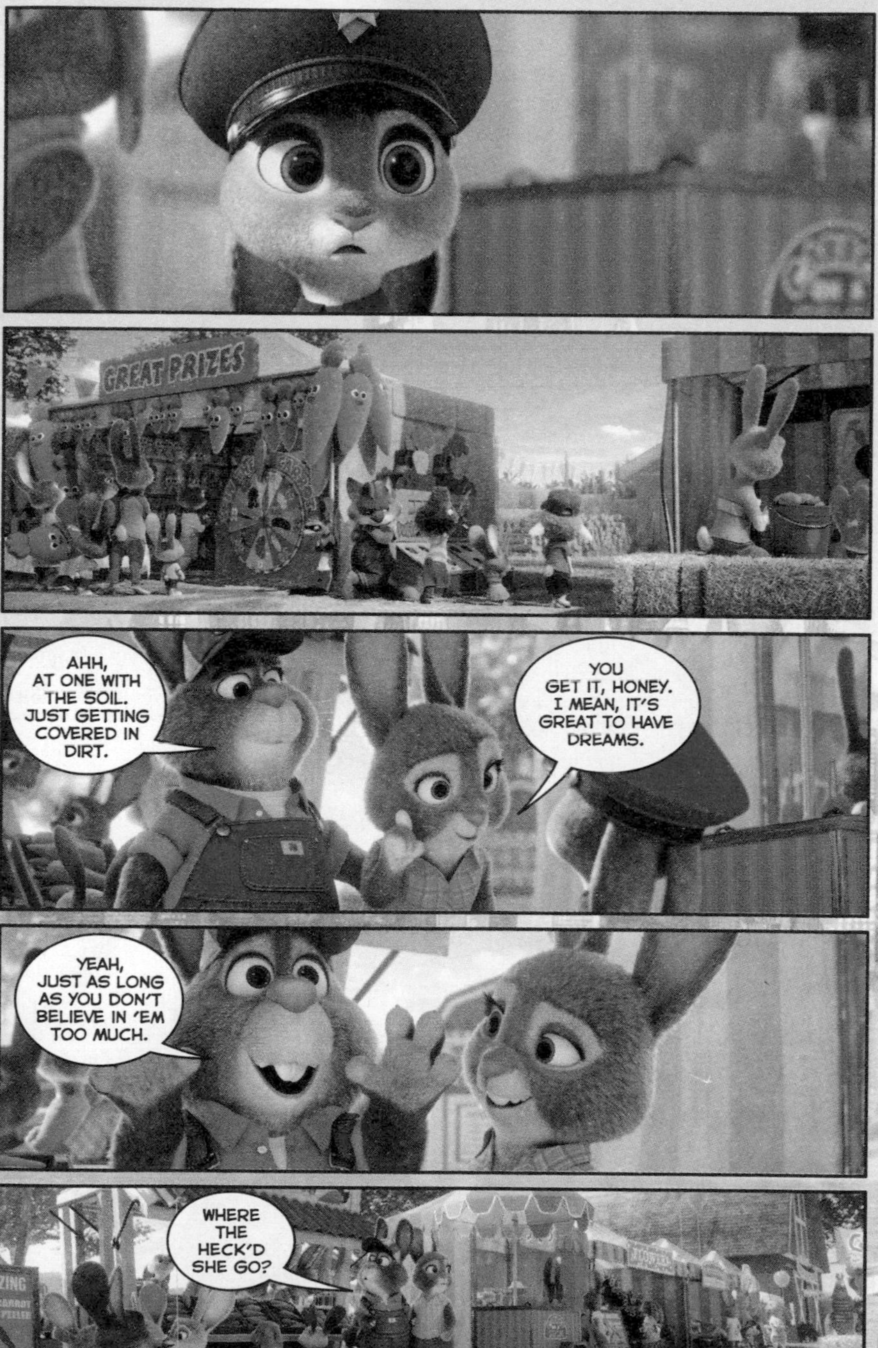
GREAT PRIZES
AHH, AT ONE WITH THE SOIL. JUST GETTING COVERED IN DIRT.
YOU GET IT, HONEY. I MEAN, IT'S GREAT TO HAVE DREAMS.
YEAH, JUST AS LONG AS YOU DON'T BELIEVE IN 'EM TOO MUCH.
WHERE THE HECK'D SHE GO?

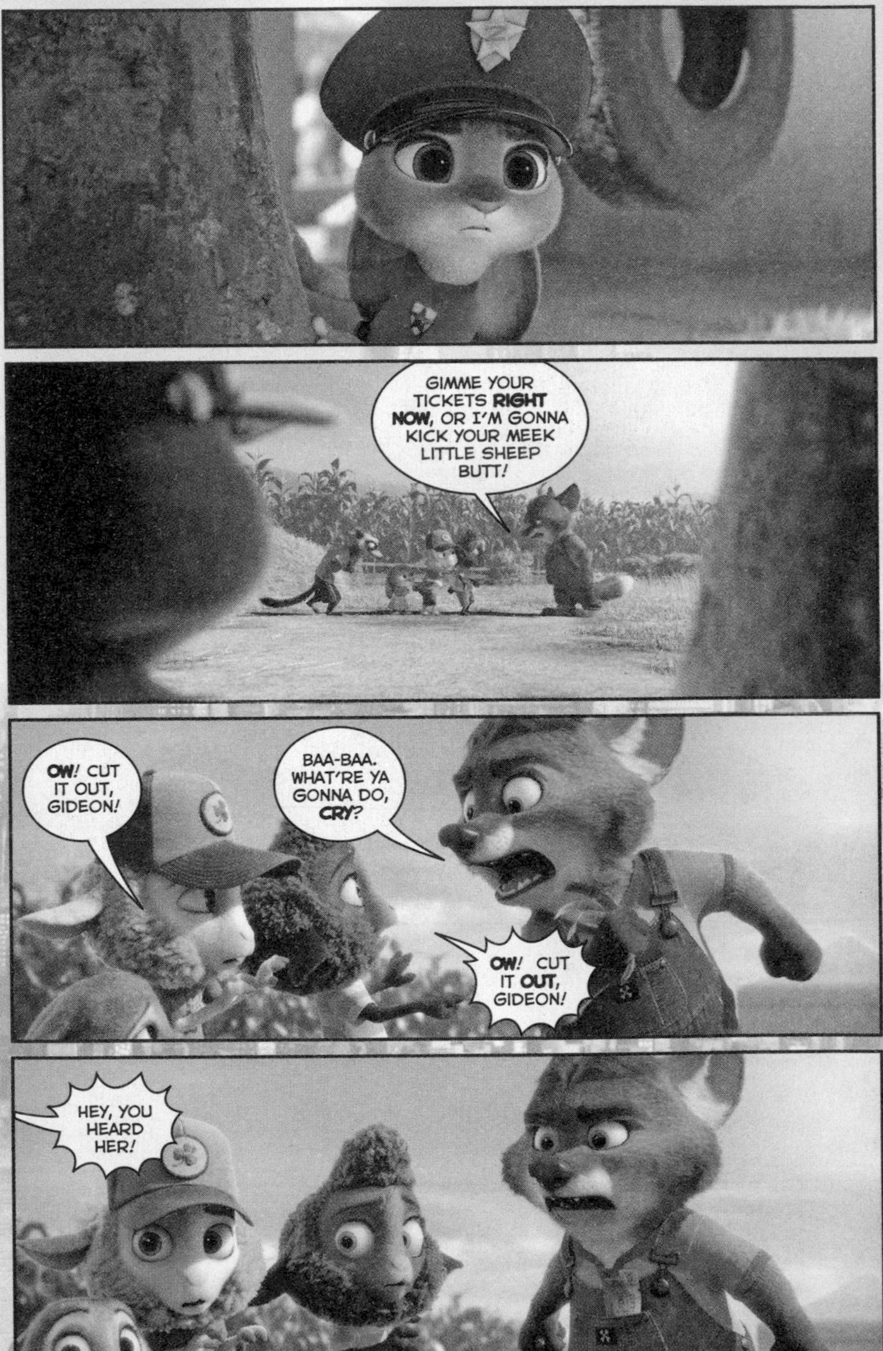
GIMME YOUR TICKETS **RIGHT NOW**, OR I'M GONNA KICK YOUR MEEK LITTLE SHEEP BUTT!
OW! CUT IT OUT, GIDEON!
BAA-BAA. WHAT'RE YA GONNA DO, **CRY?**
OW! CUT IT **OUT**, GIDEON!
HEY, YOU HEARD HER!

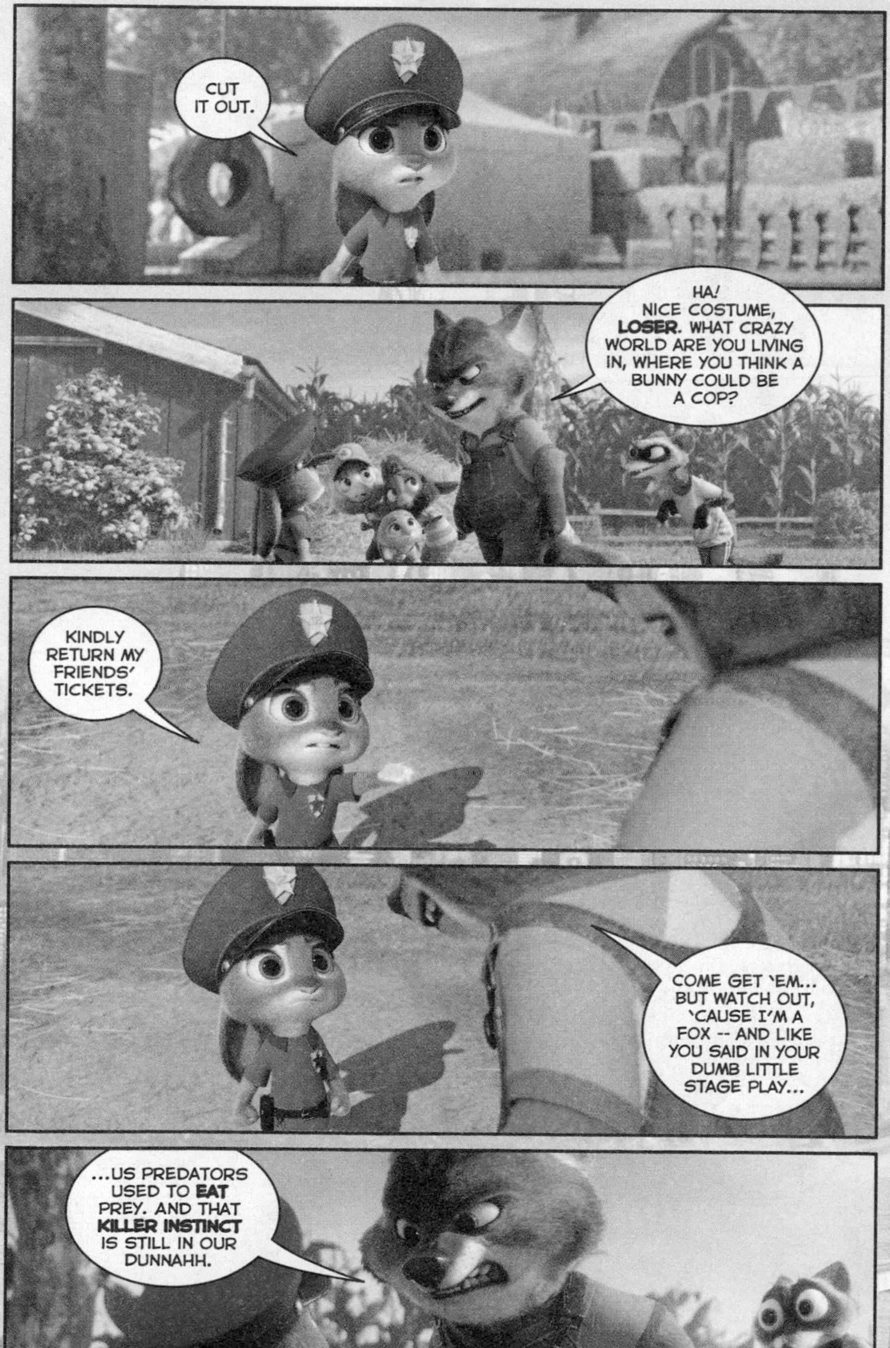
CUT IT OUT.
HA! NICE COSTUME, **LOSER**. WHAT CRAZY WORLD ARE YOU LIVING IN, WHERE YOU THINK A BUNNY COULD BE A COP?
KINDLY RETURN MY FRIENDS' TICKETS.
COME GET 'EM... BUT WATCH OUT, 'CAUSE I'M A FOX -- AND LIKE YOU SAID IN YOUR DUMB LITTLE STAGE PLAY...
...US PREDATORS USED TO **EAT** PREY. AND THAT **KILLER INSTINCT** IS STILL IN OUR DUNNAHH.

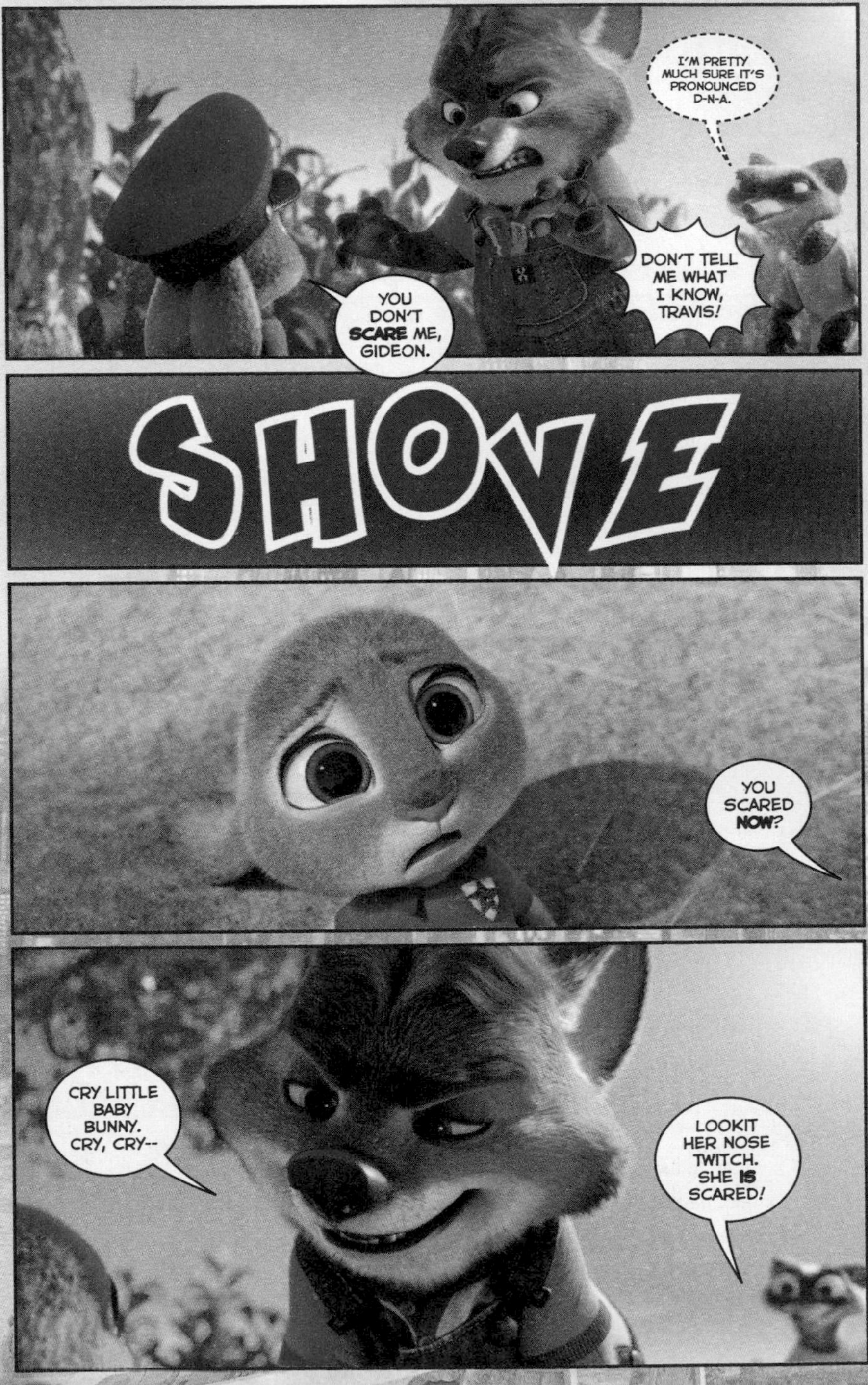
I'M PRETTY MUCH SURE IT'S PRONOUNCED D-N-A.
DON'T TELL ME WHAT I KNOW, TRAVIS!
YOU DON'T **SCARE** ME, GIDEON.
SHOVE
YOU SCARED **NOW**?
CRY LITTLE BABY BUNNY. CRY, CRY--
LOOKIT HER NOSE TWITCH. SHE **IS** SCARED!

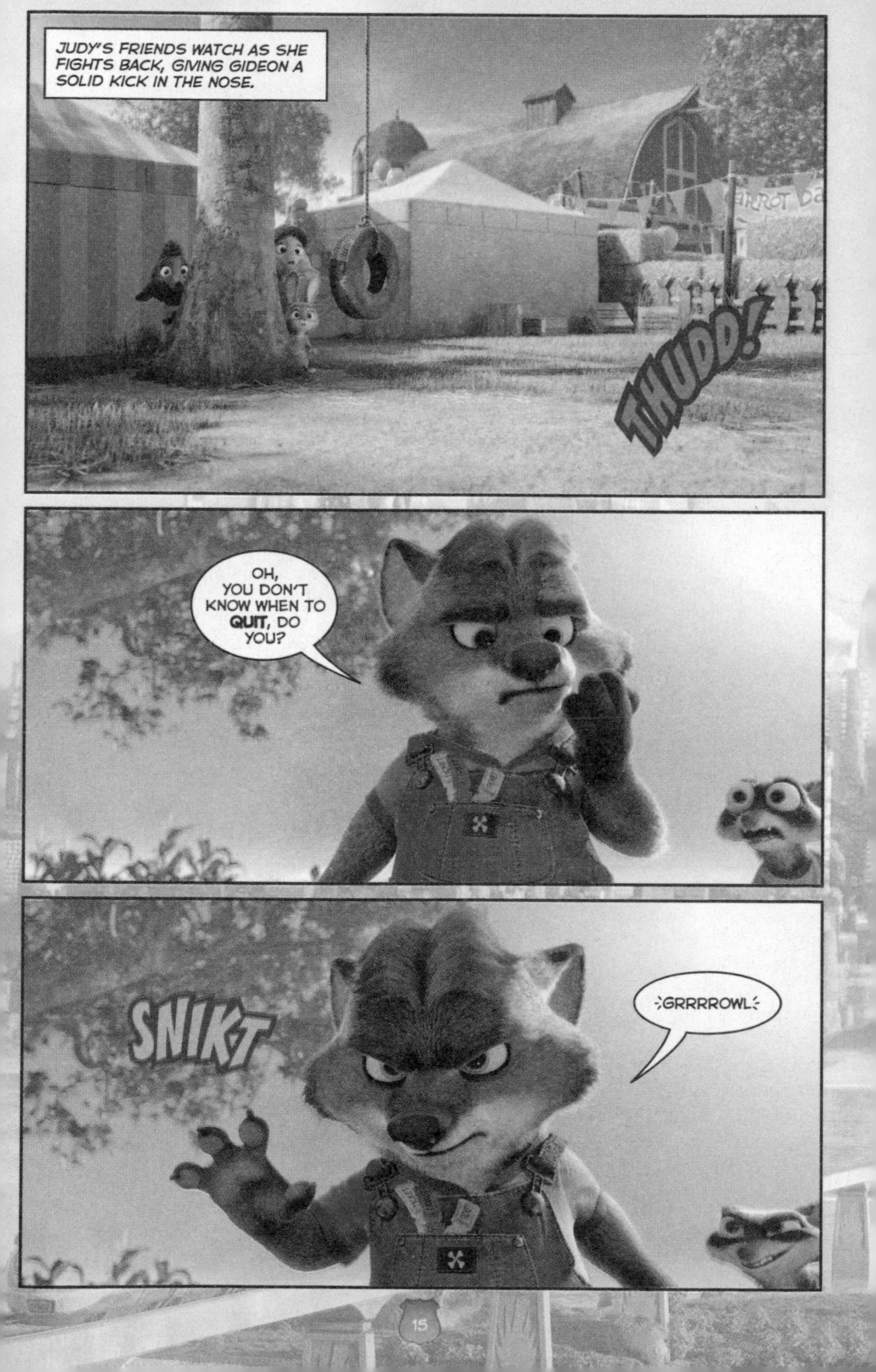
JUDY'S FRIENDS WATCH AS SHE FIGHTS BACK, GIVING GIDEON A SOLID KICK IN THE NOSE.
THUDD!
OH, YOU DON'T KNOW WHEN TO **QUIT**, DO YOU?
SNIKT
GRRRROWL

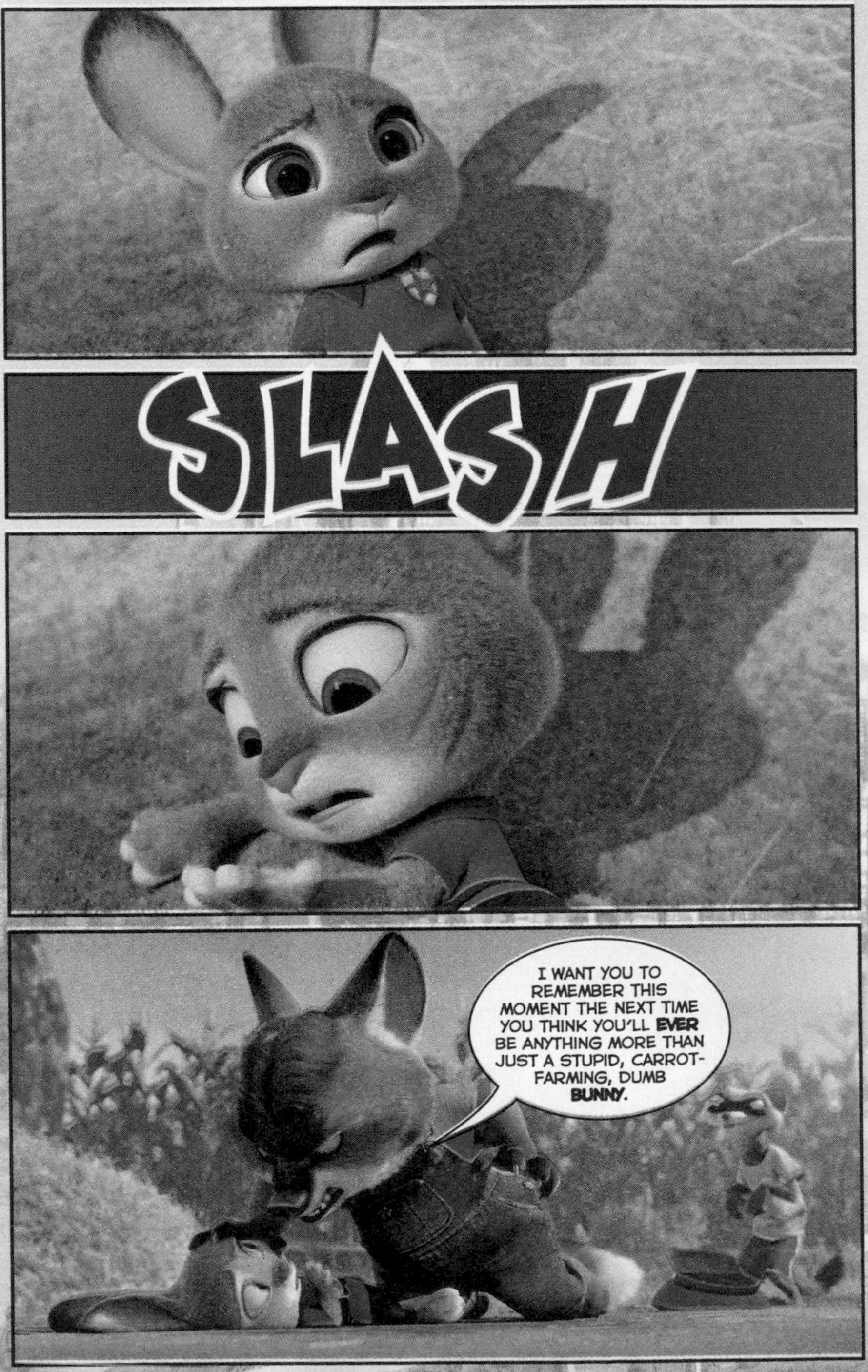
SLASH
I WANT YOU TO REMEMBER THIS MOMENT THE NEXT TIME YOU THINK YOU'LL EVER BE ANYTHING MORE THAN JUST A STUPID, CARROT-FARMING, DUMB BUNNY.

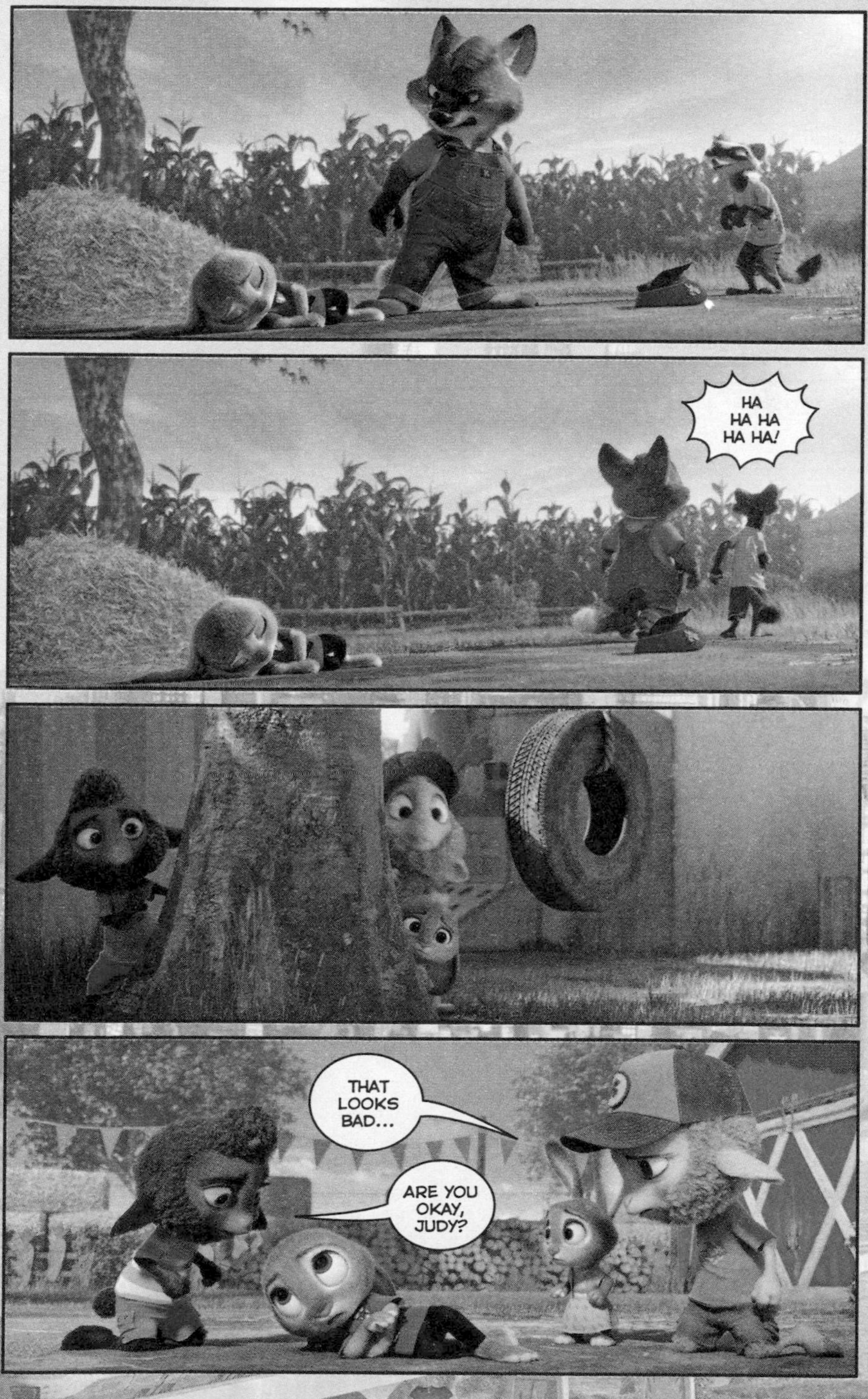
HA
HA HA
HA HA!
THAT LOOKS BAD...
ARE YOU OKAY, JUDY?

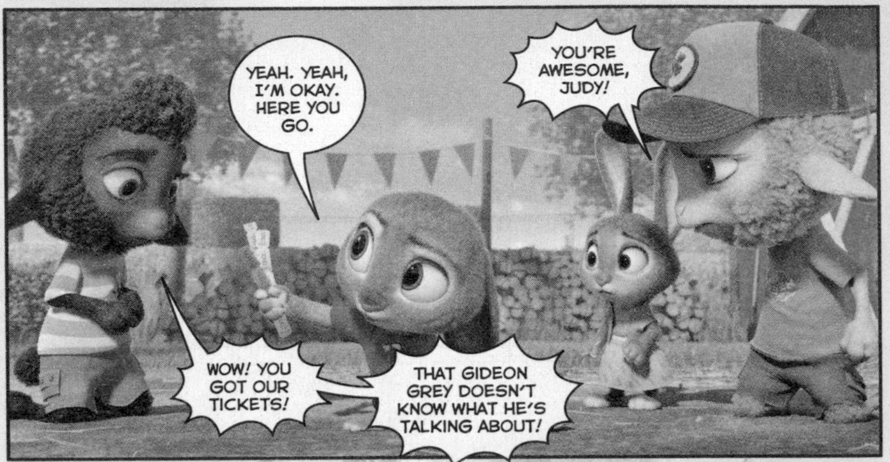
YEAH. YEAH, I'M OKAY. HERE YOU GO.
YOU'RE AWESOME, JUDY!
WOW! YOU GOT OUR TICKETS!
THAT GIDEON GREY DOESN'T KNOW WHAT HE'S TALKING ABOUT!

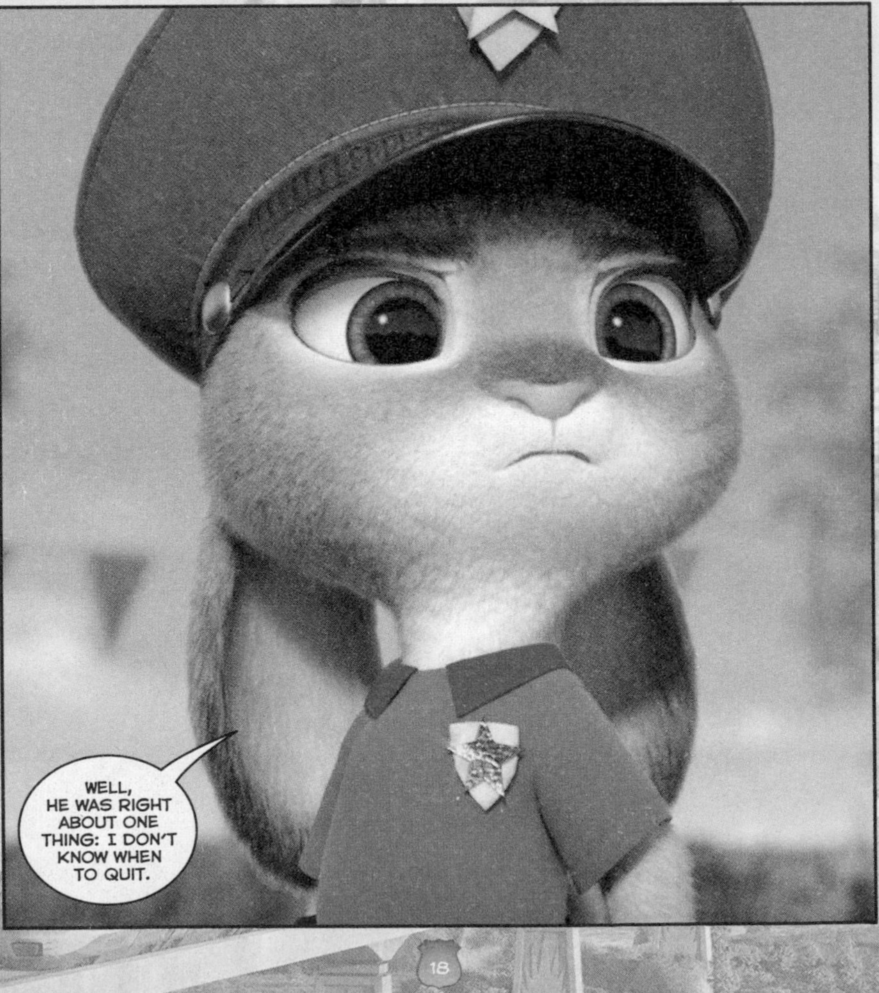
WELL, HE WAS RIGHT ABOUT ONE THING: I DON'T KNOW WHEN TO QUIT.

ZOOTOPIA POLICE ACADEMY

LISTEN UP CADETS! ZOOTOPIA HAS 12 UNIQUE ECOSYSTEMS WITHIN ITS CITY LIMITS --

15 YEARS LATER

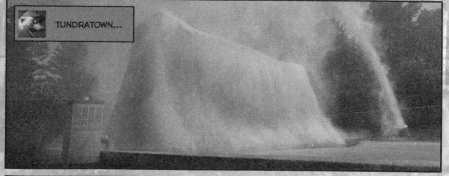

TUNDRATOWN...

SAHARA SQUARE...

RAINFOREST DISTRICT, TO NAME A **FEW**.

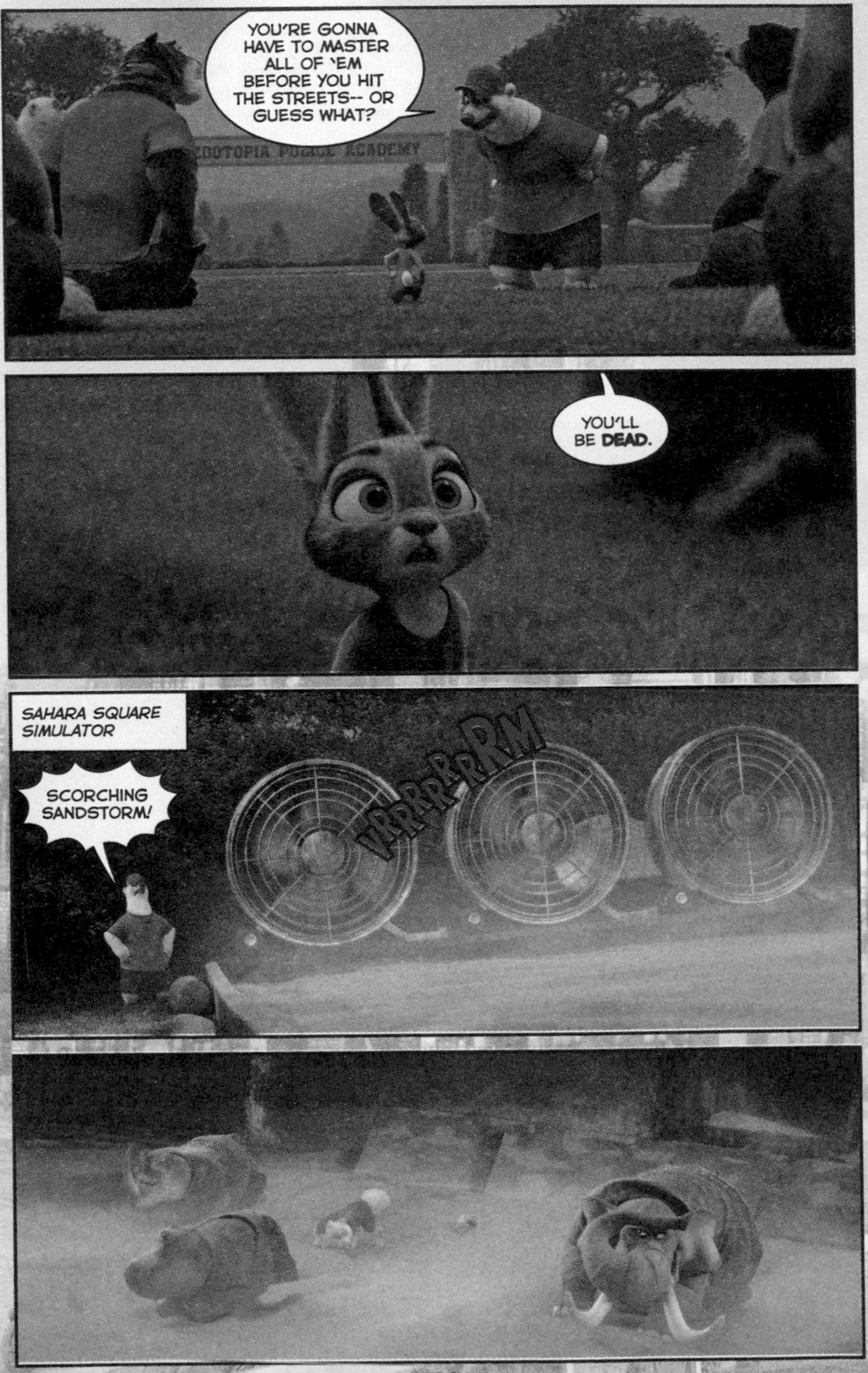
YOU'RE GONNA HAVE TO MASTER ALL OF 'EM BEFORE YOU HIT THE STREETS-- OR GUESS WHAT?
YOU'LL BE **DEAD.**
SAHARA SQUARE SIMULATOR
SCORCHING SANDSTORM!
VRRRRRRRRM

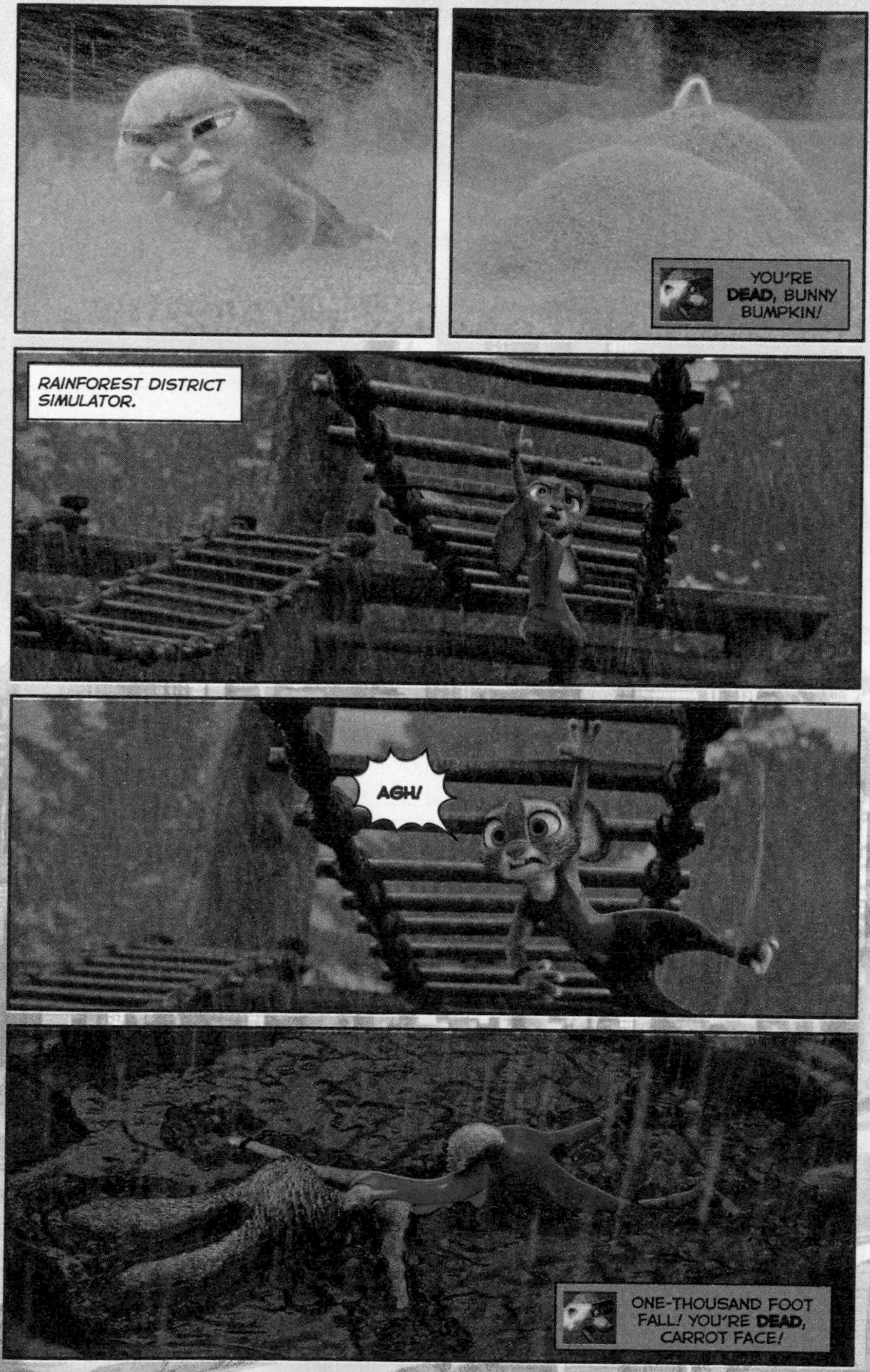
YOU'RE **DEAD**, BUNNY BUMPKIN!
RAINFOREST DISTRICT SIMULATOR.
AGH!
ONE-THOUSAND FOOT FALL! YOU'RE **DEAD**, CARROT FACE!

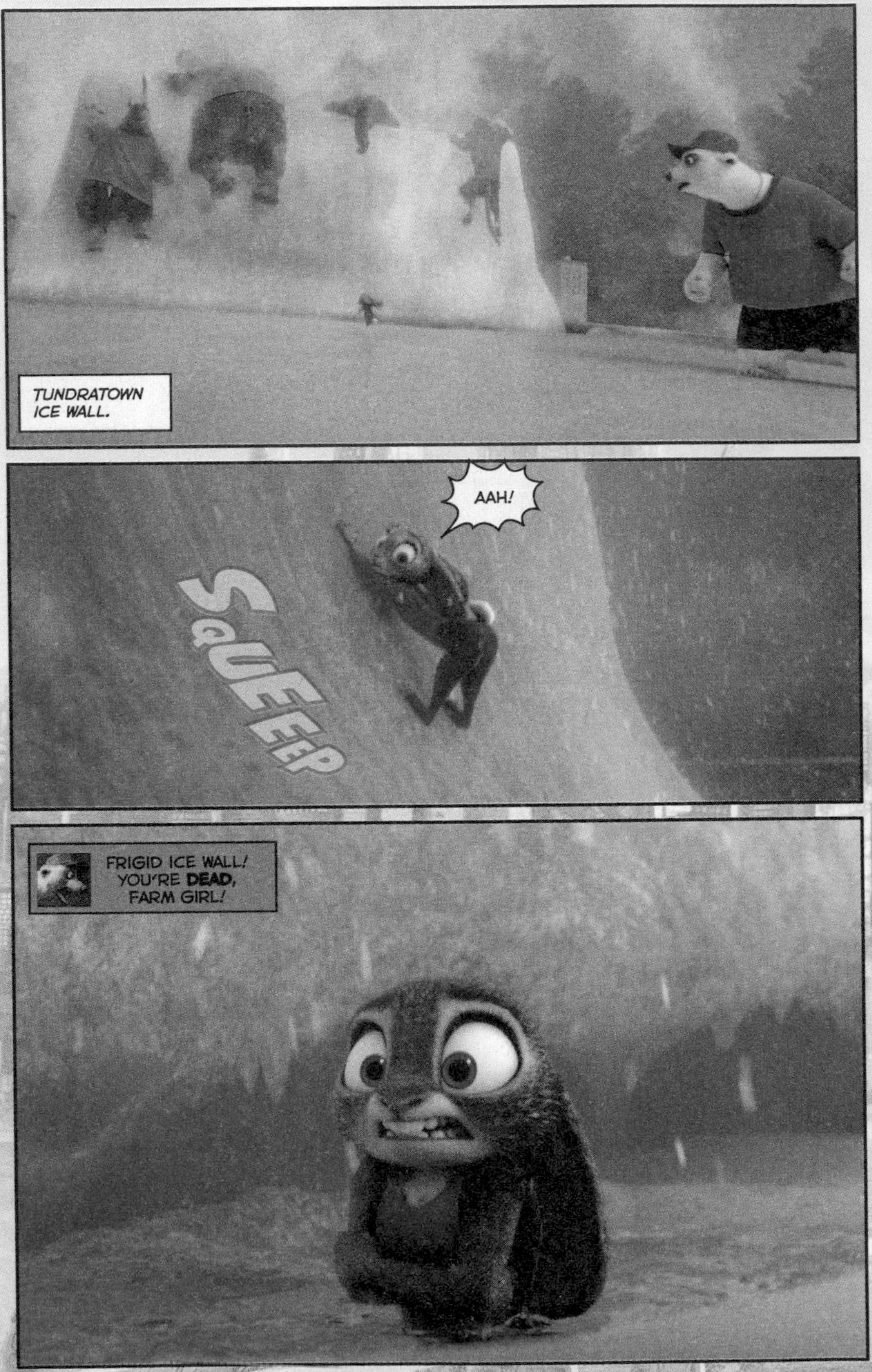
TUNDRATOWN ICE WALL.
AAH!
SQUEEEP
FRIGID ICE WALL! YOU'RE **DEAD**, FARM GIRL!

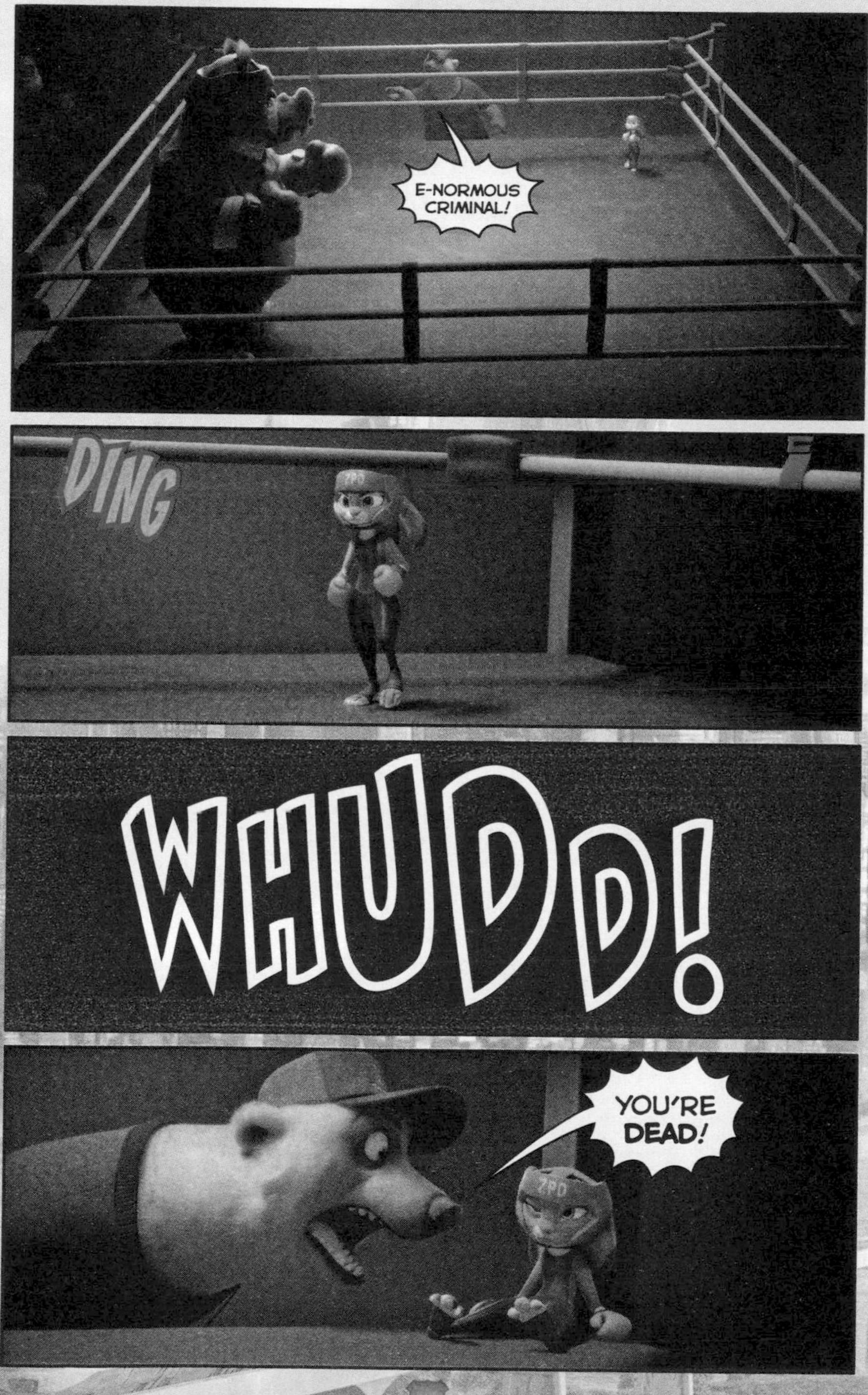
E-NORMOUS CRIMINAL!
DING
WHUDD!
YOU'RE DEAD!

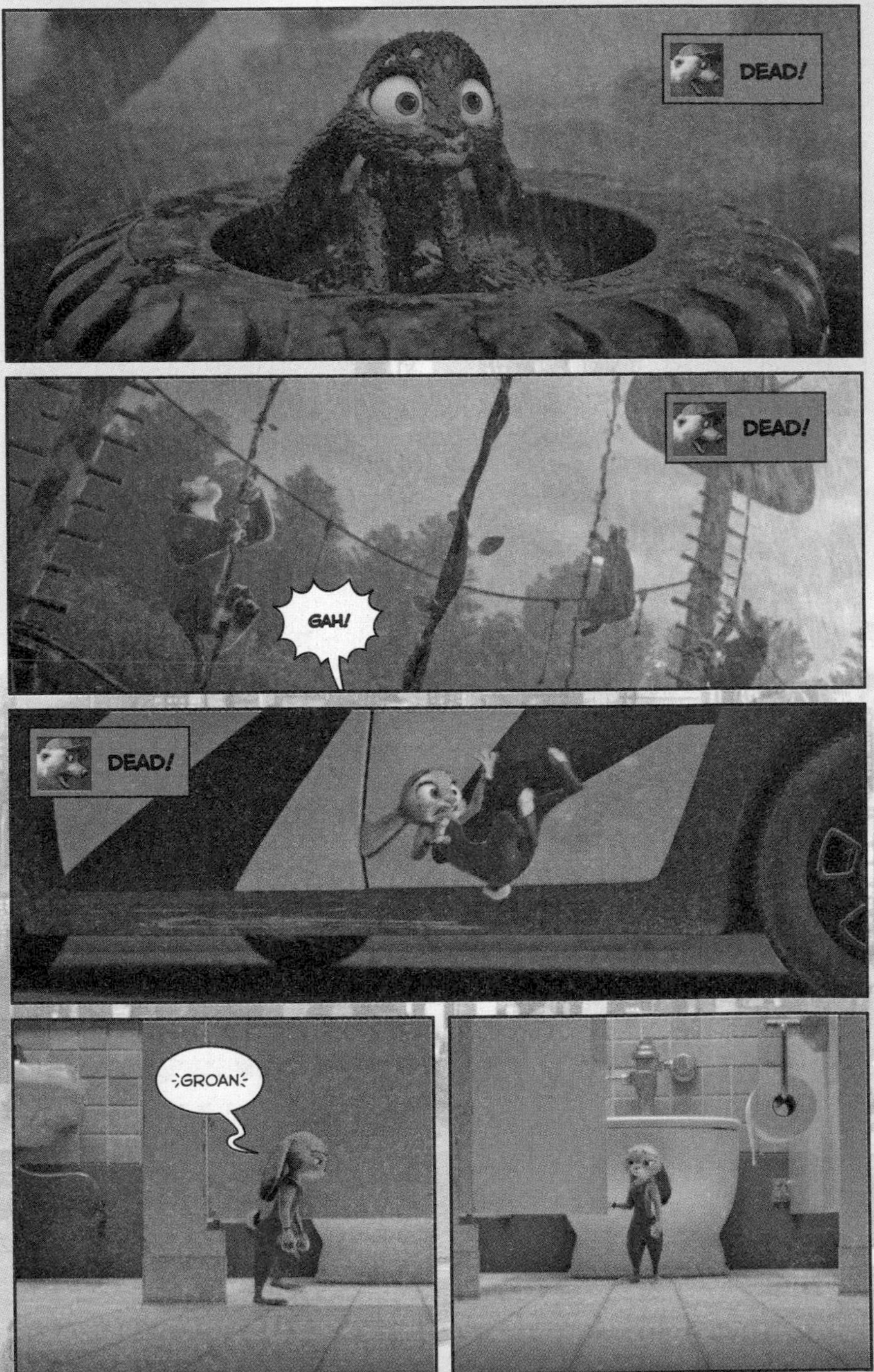
DEAD!
DEAD!
GAH!
DEAD!
GROAN

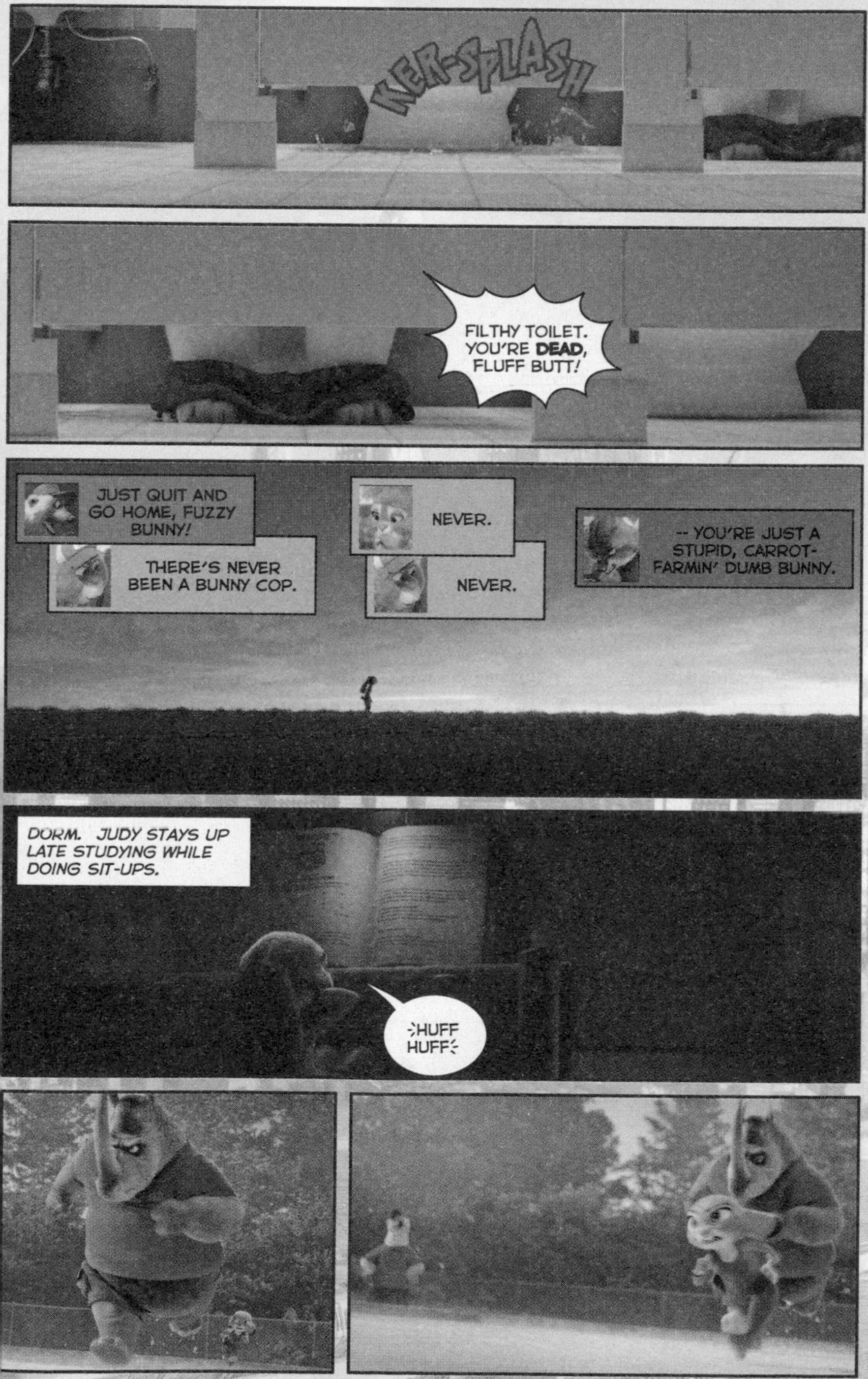
KER-SPLASH
FILTHY TOILET. YOU'RE **DEAD**, FLUFF BUTT!
JUST QUIT AND GO HOME, FUZZY BUNNY!
THERE'S NEVER BEEN A BUNNY COP.
NEVER.
NEVER.
-- YOU'RE JUST A STUPID, CARROT-FARMIN' DUMB BUNNY.
DORM. JUDY STAYS UP LATE STUDYING WHILE DOING SIT-UPS.
HUFF HUFF

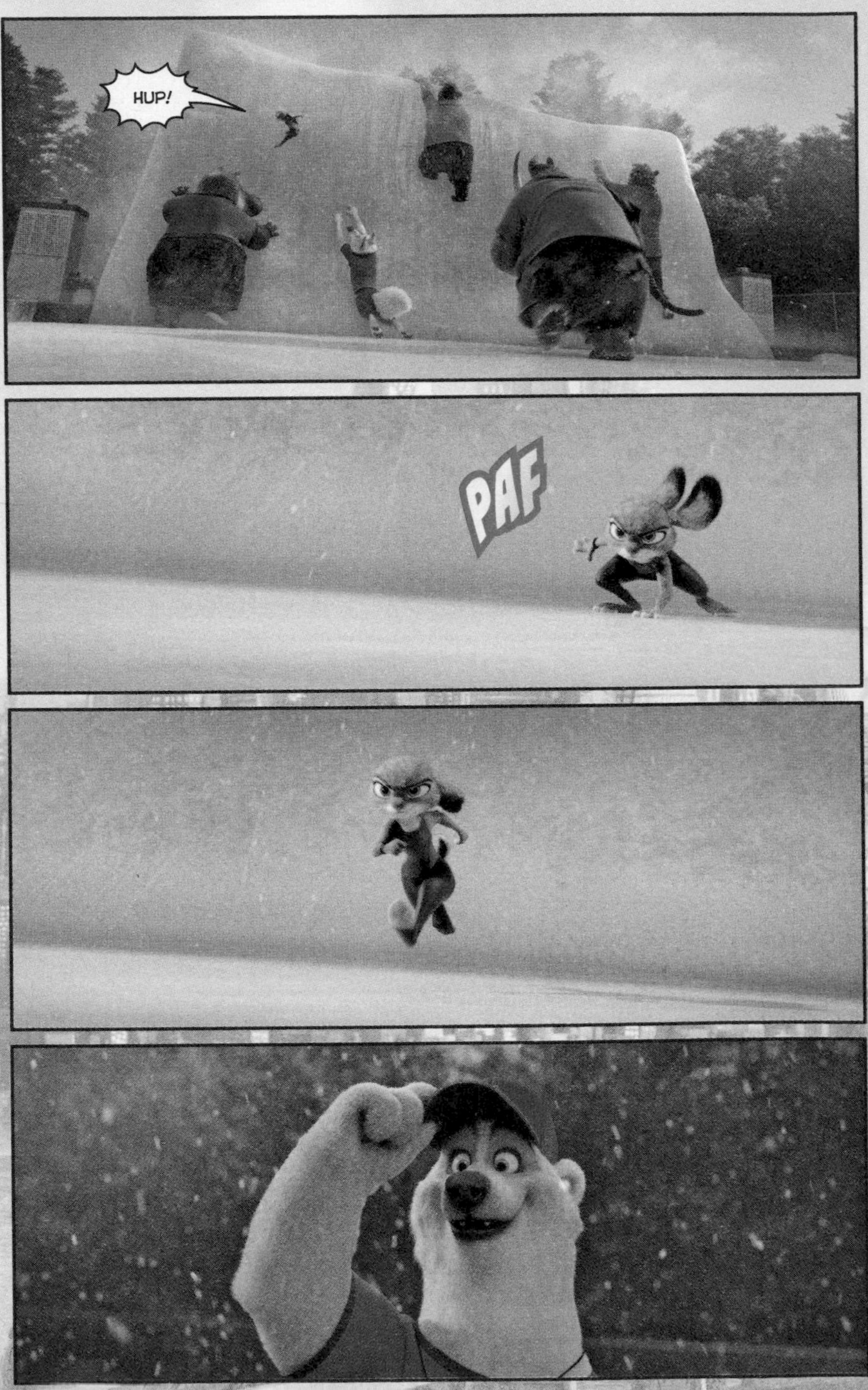
HUP!
PAF

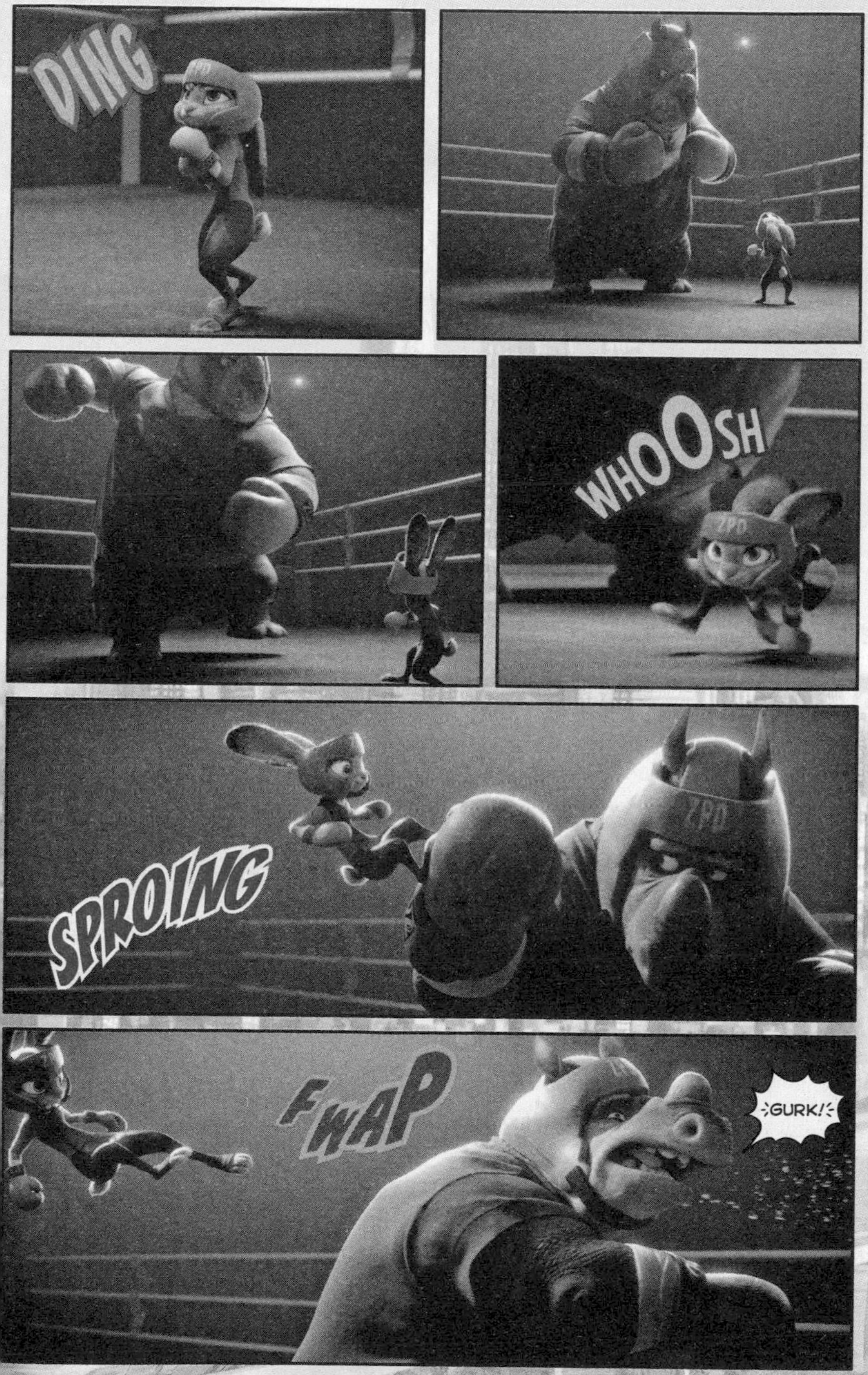
DING
WHOOSH
SPROING
FWAP
GURK!

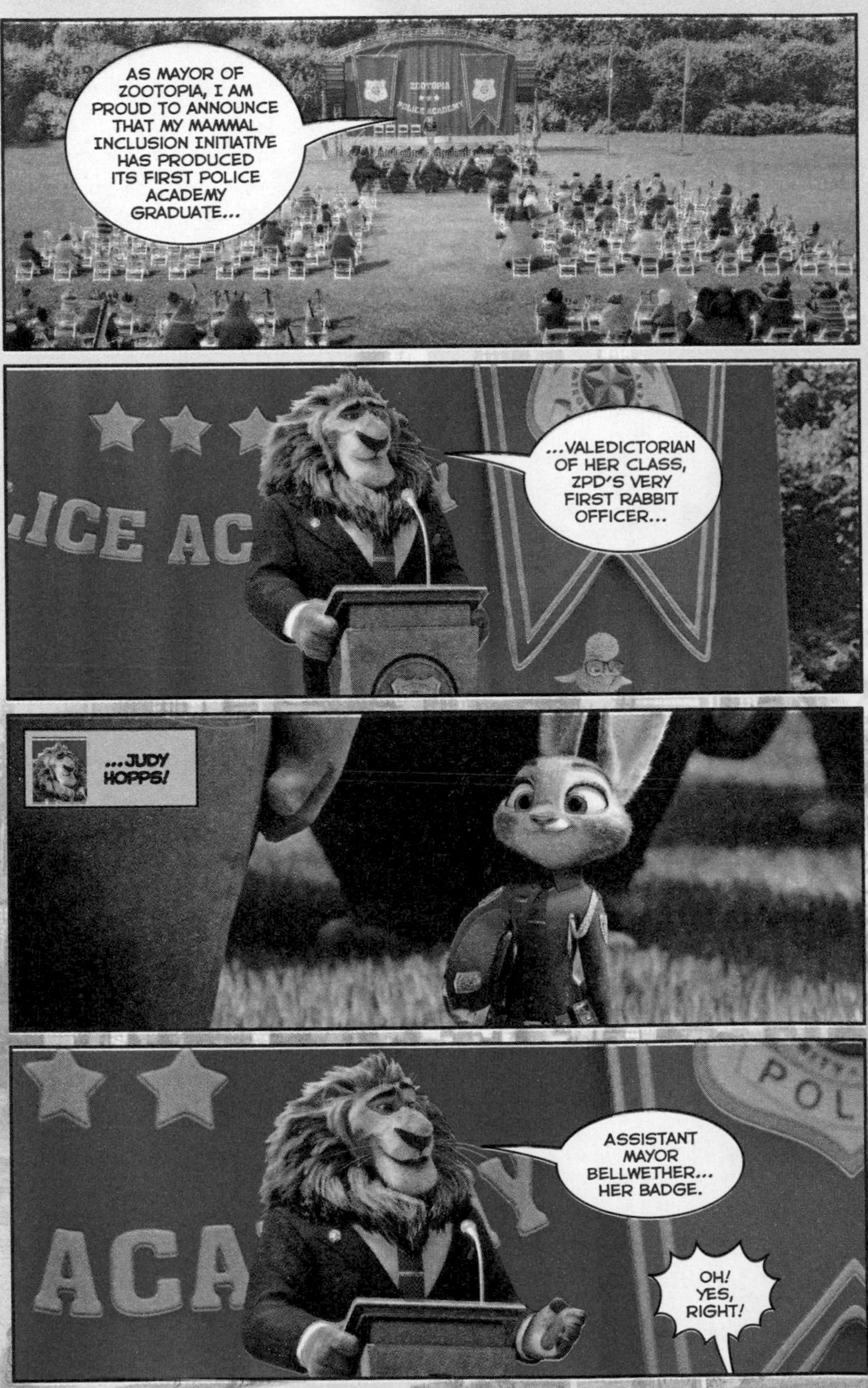
AS MAYOR OF ZOOTOPIA, I AM PROUD TO ANNOUNCE THAT MY MAMMAL INCLUSION INITIATIVE HAS PRODUCED ITS FIRST POLICE ACADEMY GRADUATE...
...VALEDICTORIAN OF HER CLASS, ZPD'S VERY FIRST RABBIT OFFICER...
...JUDY HOPPS!
ASSISTANT MAYOR BELLWETHER... HER BADGE.
OH! YES, RIGHT!

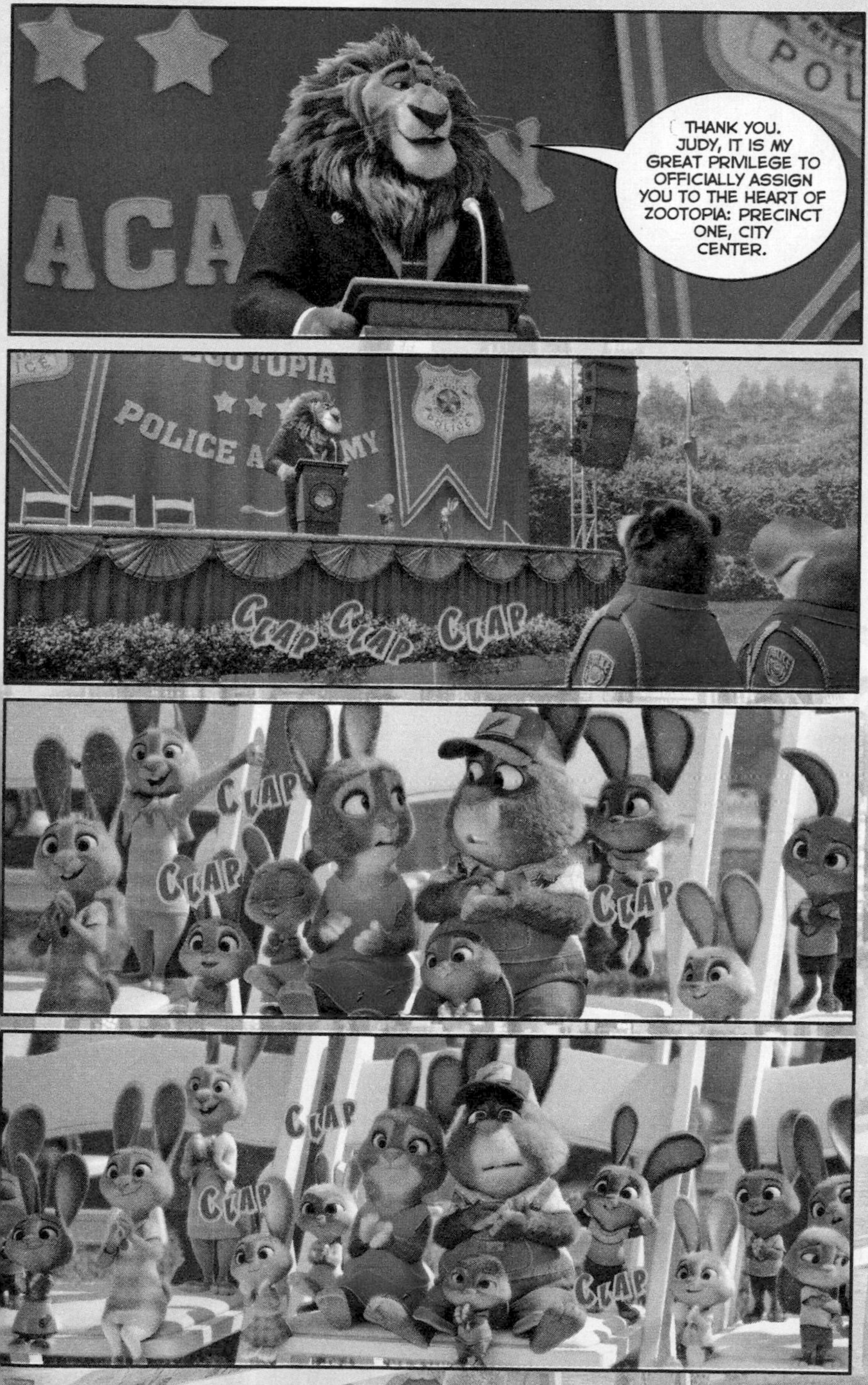
THANK YOU. JUDY, IT IS MY GREAT PRIVILEGE TO OFFICIALLY ASSIGN YOU TO THE HEART OF ZOOTOPIA: PRECINCT ONE, CITY CENTER.
CLAP CLAP CLAP
CLAP
CLAP
CLAP
CLAP
CLAP
CLAP

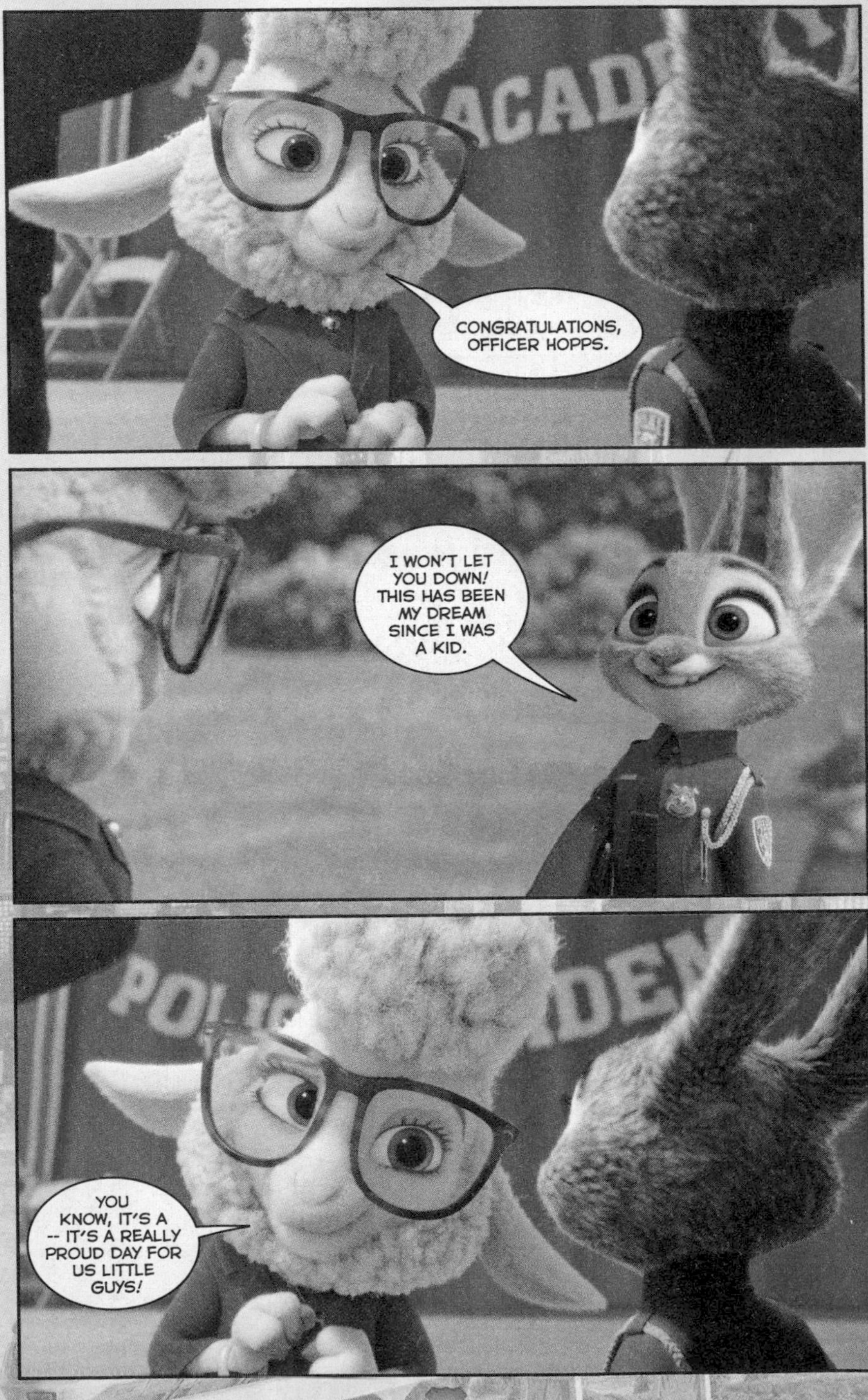
CONGRATULATIONS, OFFICER HOPPS.
I WON'T LET YOU DOWN! THIS HAS BEEN MY DREAM SINCE I WAS A KID.
YOU KNOW, IT'S A -- IT'S A REALLY PROUD DAY FOR US LITTLE GUYS!

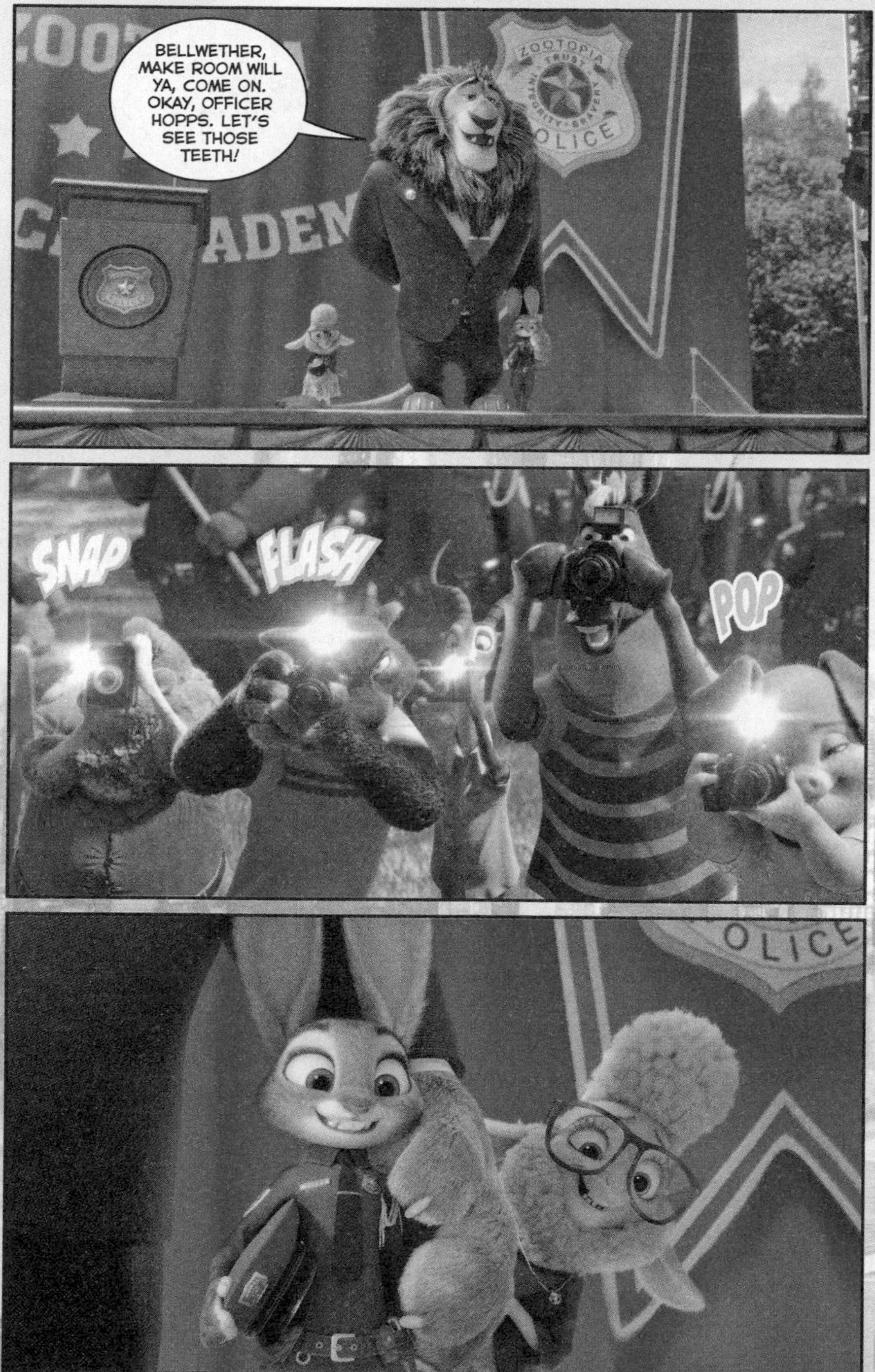
BELLWETHER, MAKE ROOM WILL YA, COME ON. OKAY, OFFICER HOPPS. LET'S SEE THOSE TEETH!
SNAP
FLASH
POP

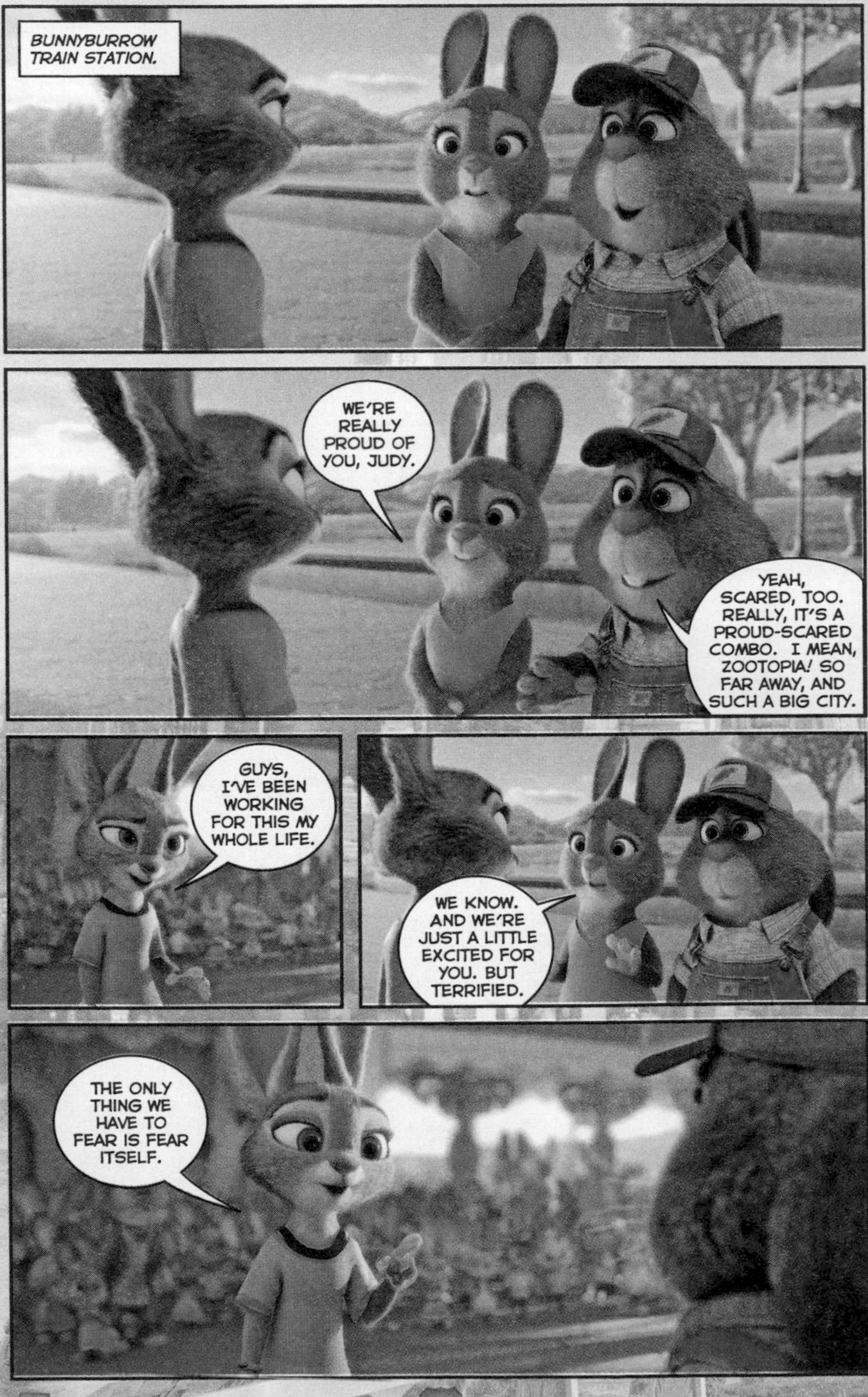
BUNNYBURROW TRAIN STATION.
WE'RE REALLY PROUD OF YOU, JUDY.
YEAH, SCARED, TOO. REALLY, IT'S A PROUD-SCARED COMBO. I MEAN, ZOOTOPIA! SO FAR AWAY, AND SUCH A BIG CITY.
GUYS, I'VE BEEN WORKING FOR THIS MY WHOLE LIFE.
WE KNOW. AND WE'RE JUST A LITTLE EXCITED FOR YOU. BUT TERRIFIED.
THE ONLY THING WE HAVE TO FEAR IS FEAR ITSELF.

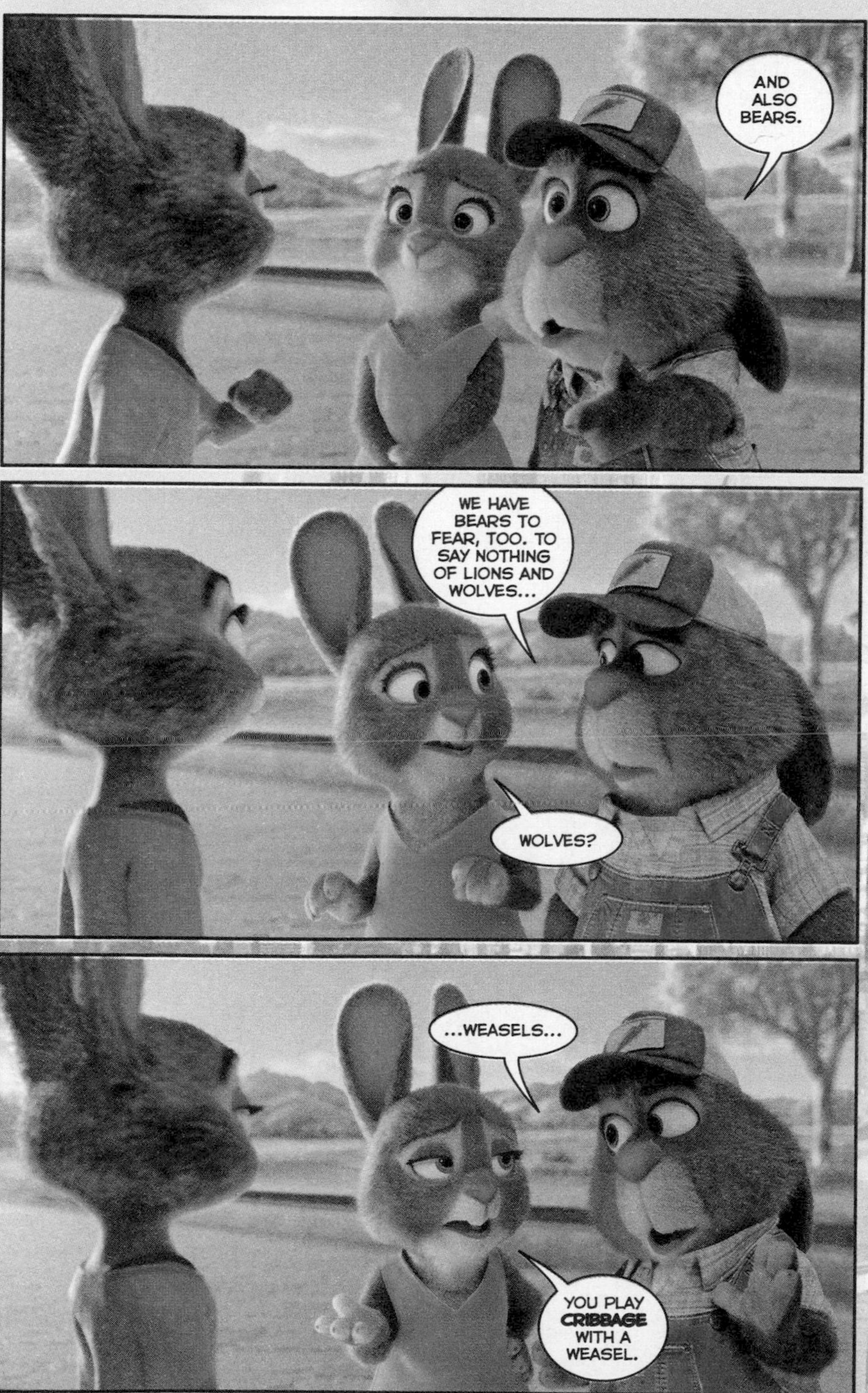
AND ALSO BEARS.
WE HAVE BEARS TO FEAR, TOO. TO SAY NOTHING OF LIONS AND WOLVES...
WOLVES?
...WEASELS...
YOU PLAY **CRIBBAGE** WITH A WEASEL.

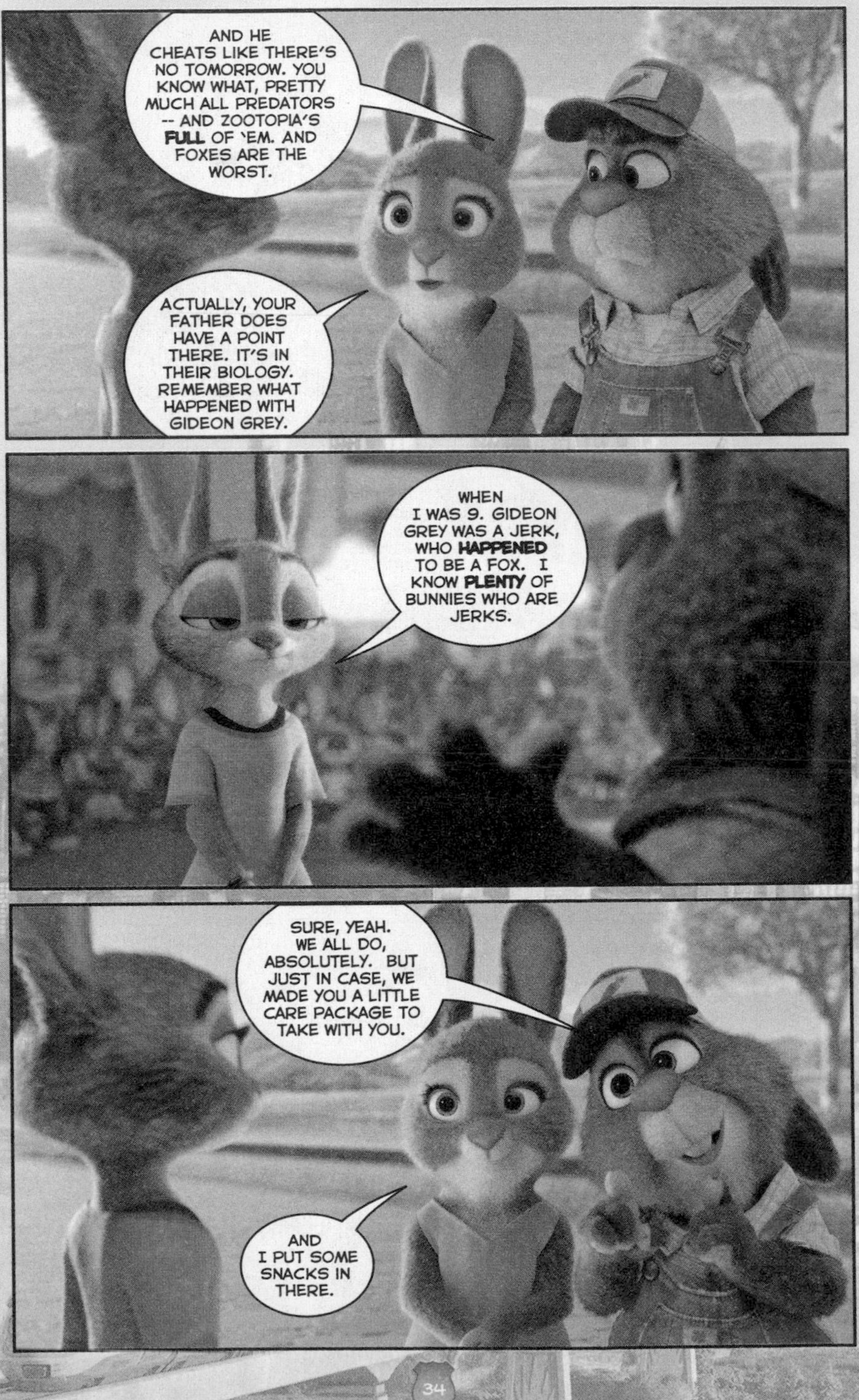
AND HE CHEATS LIKE THERE'S NO TOMORROW. YOU KNOW WHAT, PRETTY MUCH ALL PREDATORS -- AND ZOOTOPIA'S FULL OF 'EM. AND FOXES ARE THE WORST.
ACTUALLY, YOUR FATHER DOES HAVE A POINT THERE. IT'S IN THEIR BIOLOGY. REMEMBER WHAT HAPPENED WITH GIDEON GREY.
WHEN I WAS 9. GIDEON GREY WAS A JERK, WHO HAPPENED TO BE A FOX. I KNOW PLENTY OF BUNNIES WHO ARE JERKS.
SURE, YEAH. WE ALL DO, ABSOLUTELY. BUT JUST IN CASE, WE MADE YOU A LITTLE CARE PACKAGE TO TAKE WITH YOU.
AND I PUT SOME SNACKS IN THERE.

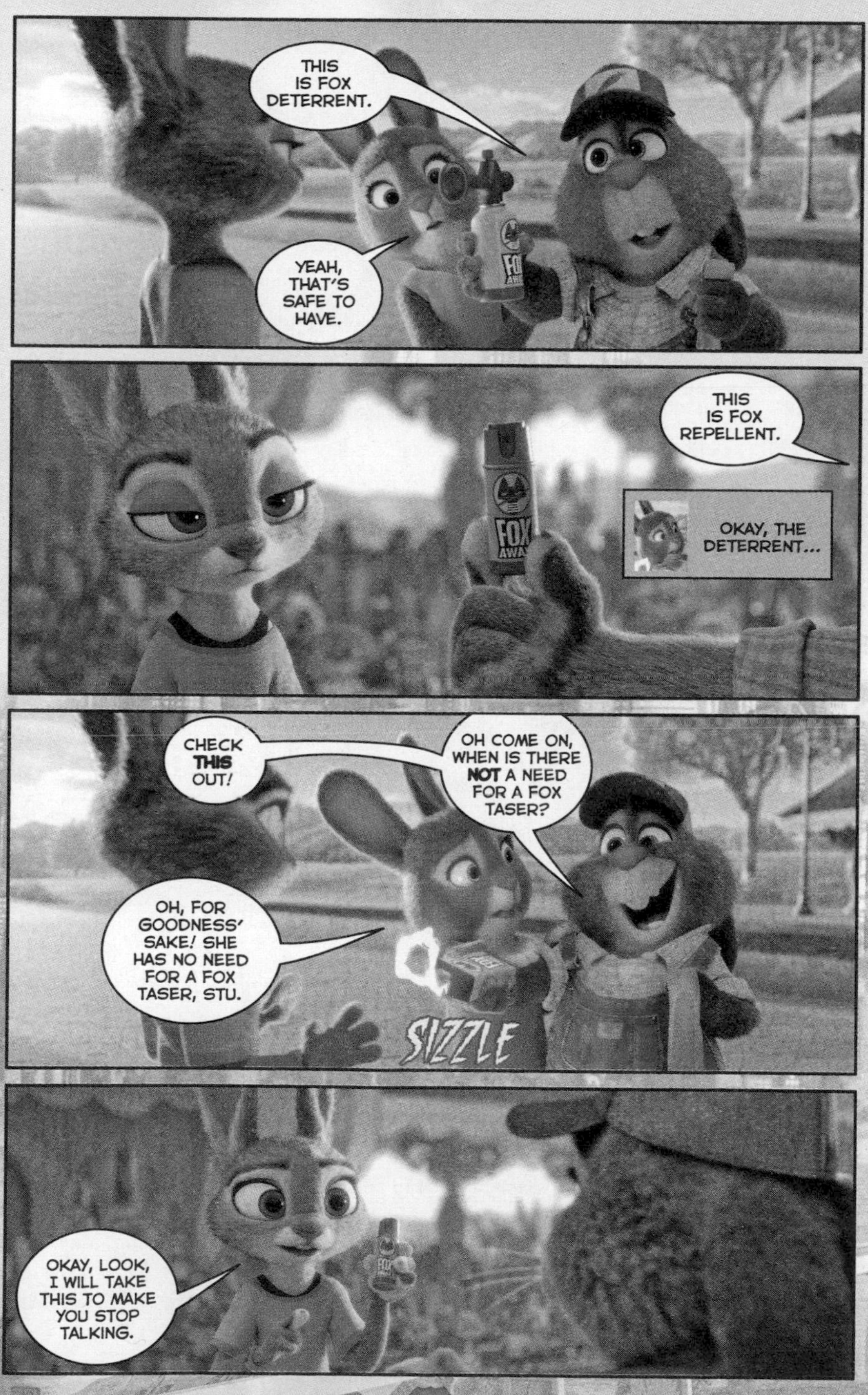
THIS IS FOX DETERRENT.
YEAH, THAT'S SAFE TO HAVE.
THIS IS FOX REPELLENT.
OKAY, THE DETERRENT...
CHECK THIS OUT!
OH COME ON, WHEN IS THERE NOT A NEED FOR A FOX TASER?
OH, FOR GOODNESS' SAKE! SHE HAS NO NEED FOR A FOX TASER, STU.
SIZZLE
OKAY, LOOK, I WILL TAKE THIS TO MAKE YOU STOP TALKING.

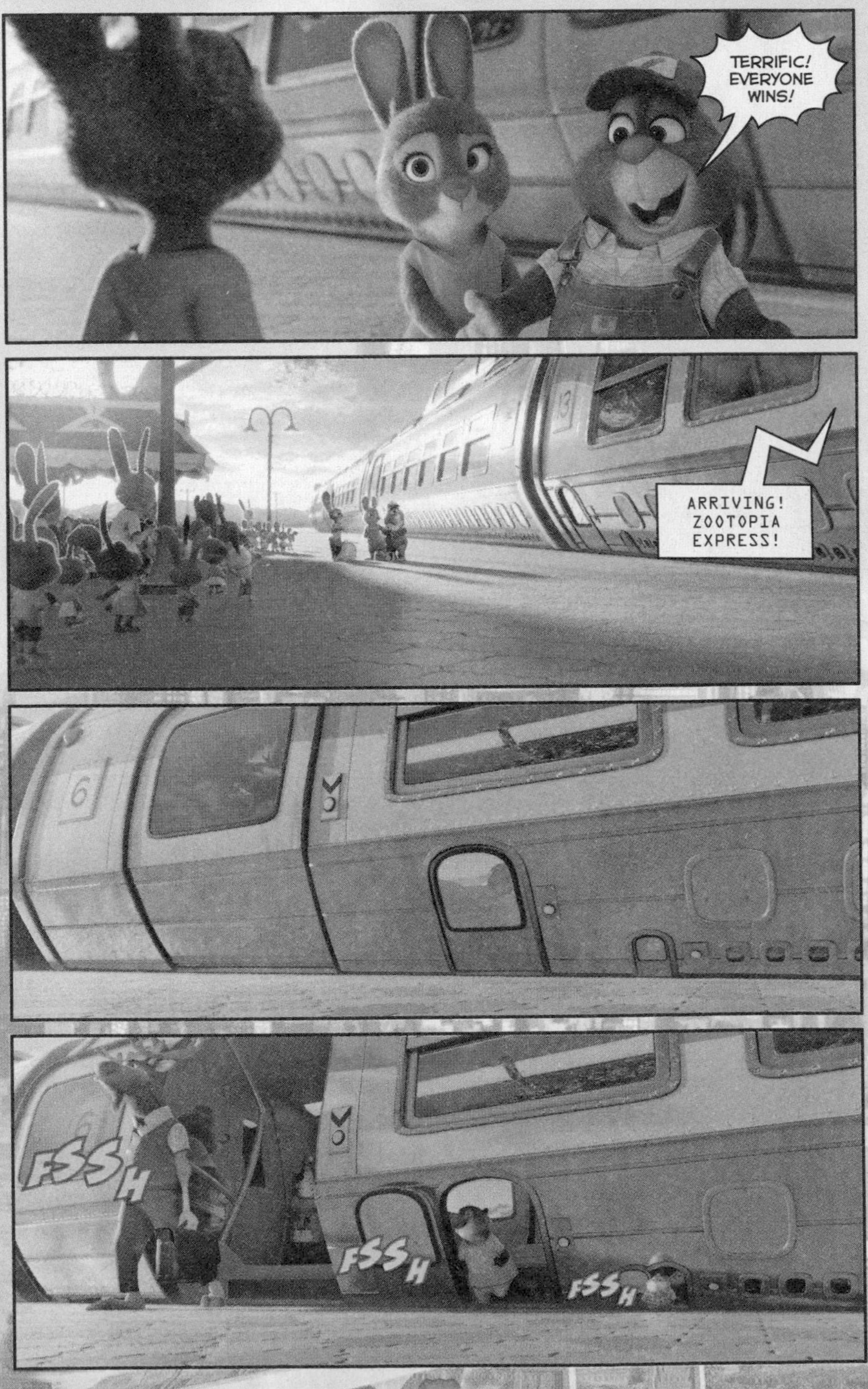
TERRIFIC! EVERYONE WINS!
ARRIVING! ZOOTOPIA EXPRESS!
FSSH
FSSH
FSSH

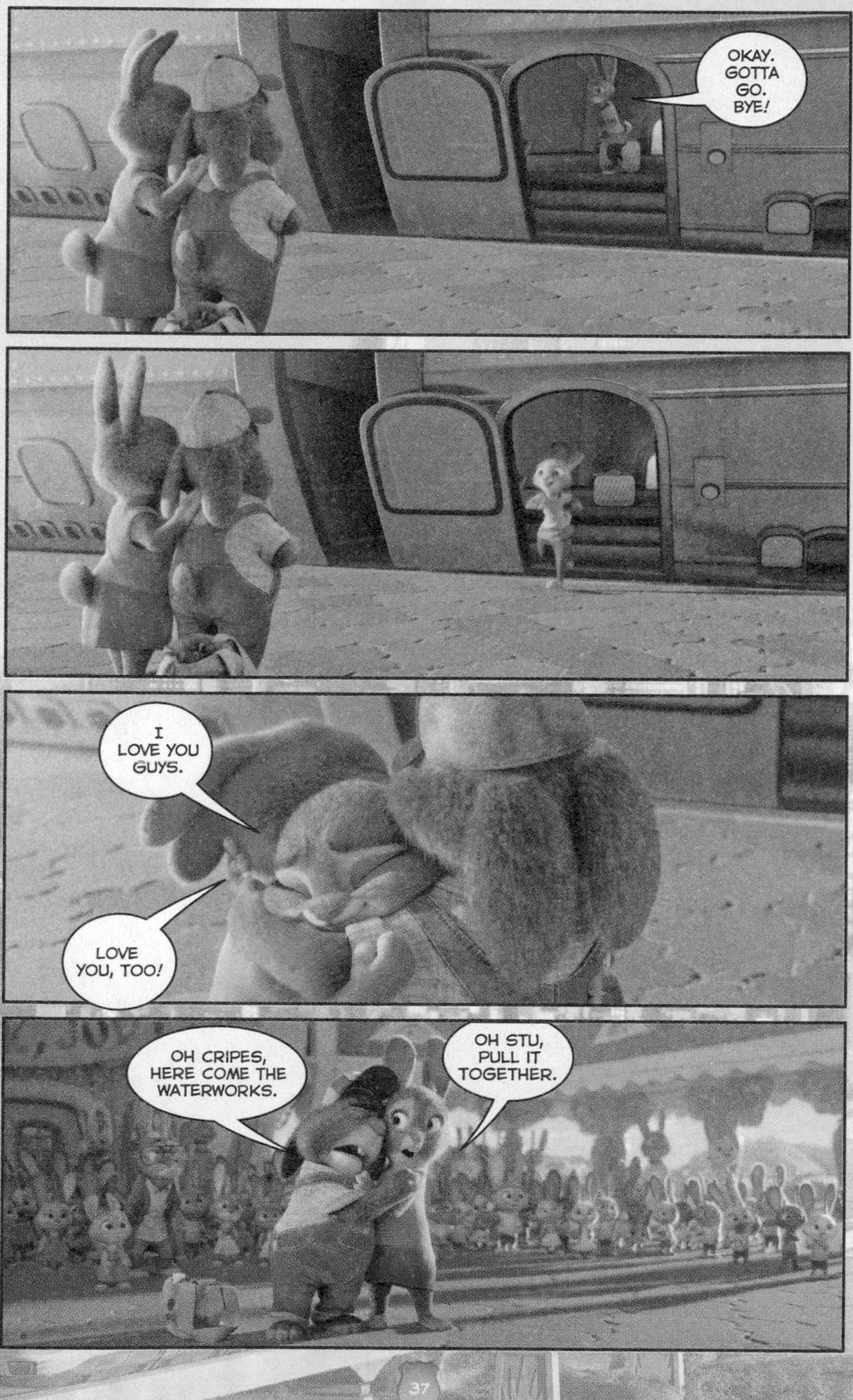
OKAY. GOTTA GO. BYE!
I LOVE YOU GUYS.
LOVE YOU, TOO!
OH CRIPES, HERE COME THE WATERWORKS.
OH STU, PULL IT TOGETHER.

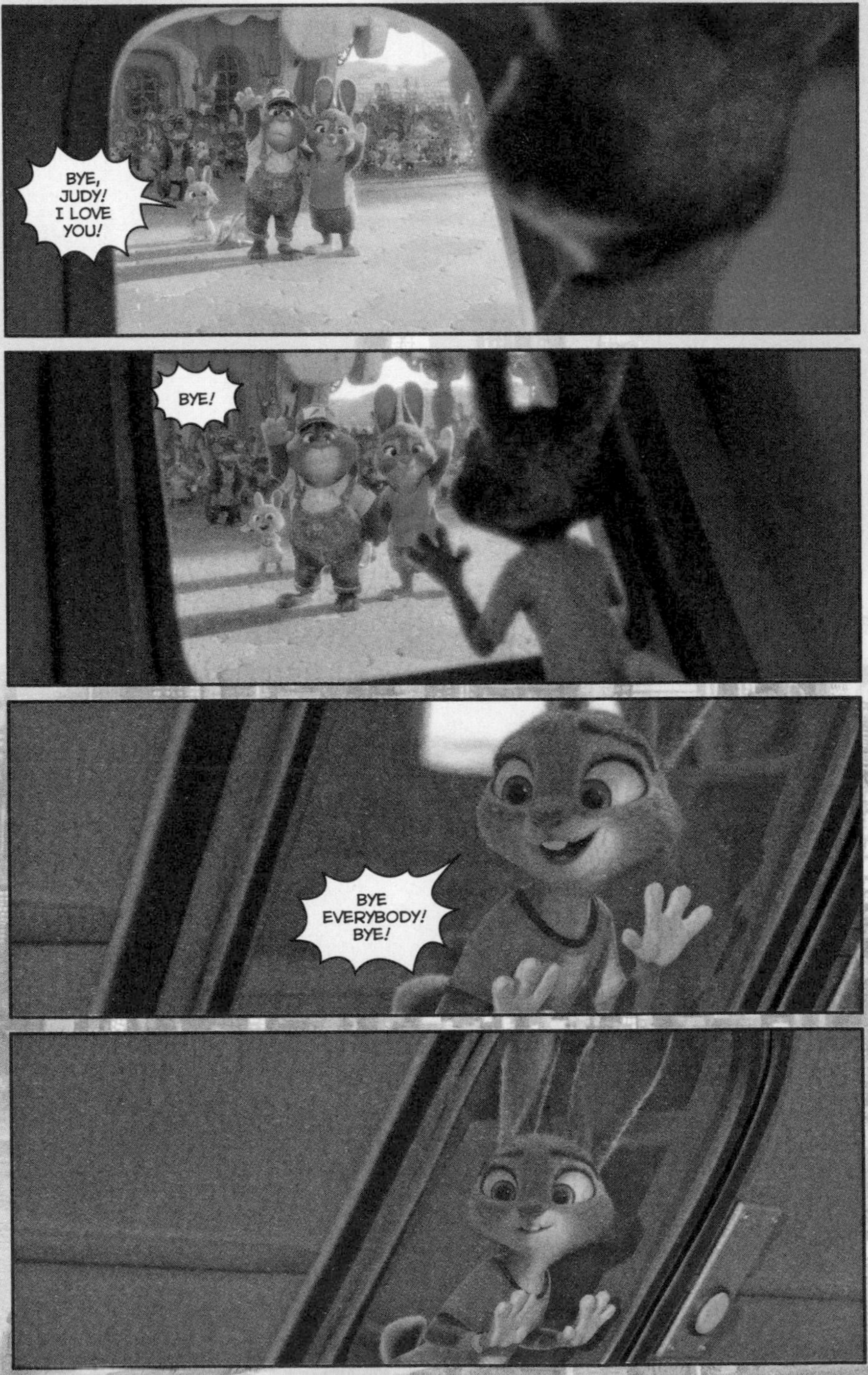
BYE, JUDY! I LOVE YOU!
BYE!
BYE EVERYBODY! BYE!

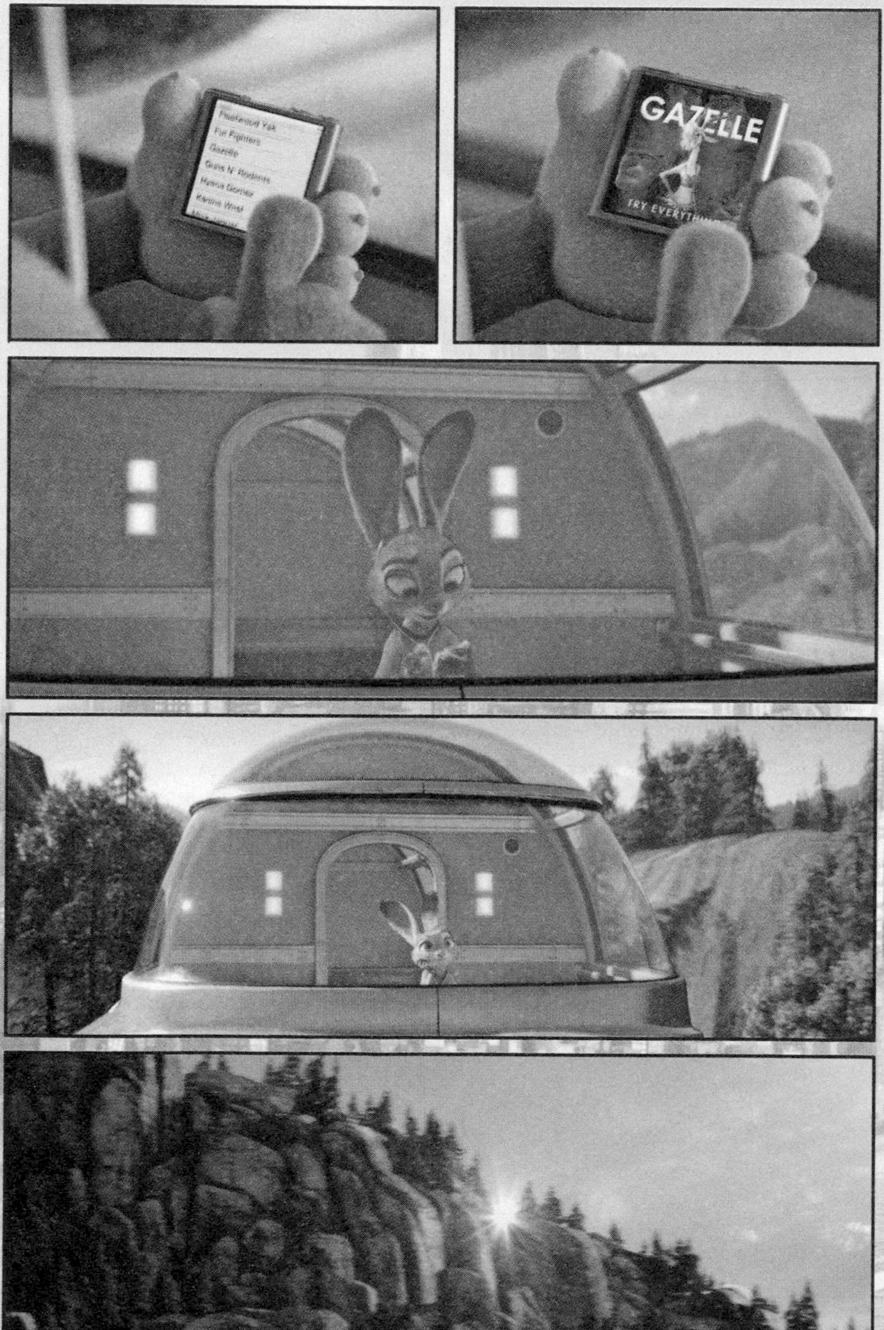
Fleetwood Yak
Fur Fighters
Gazelle
Guns N' Rodents
Hyena Gomez
Kanine West
GAZELLE

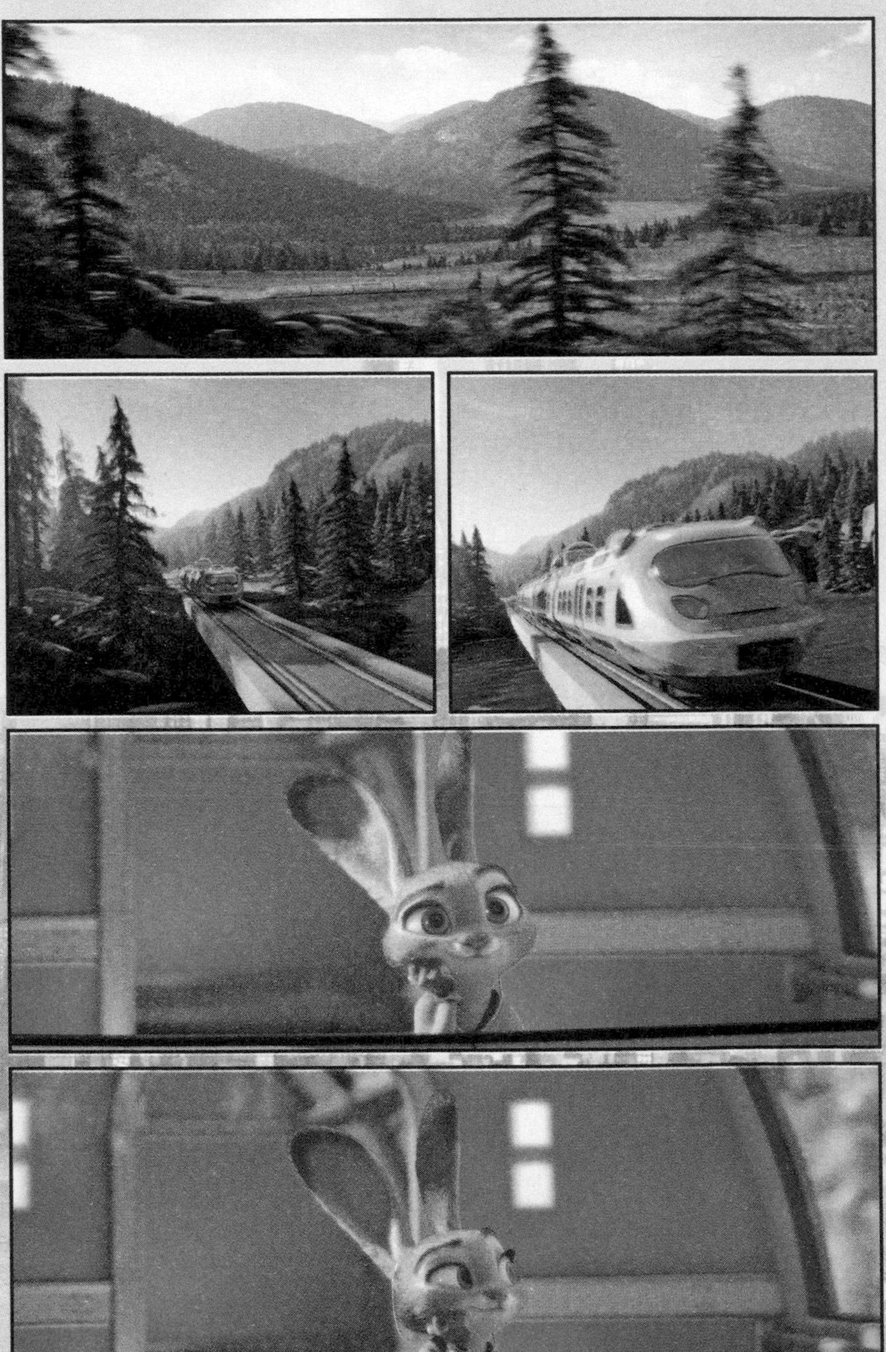

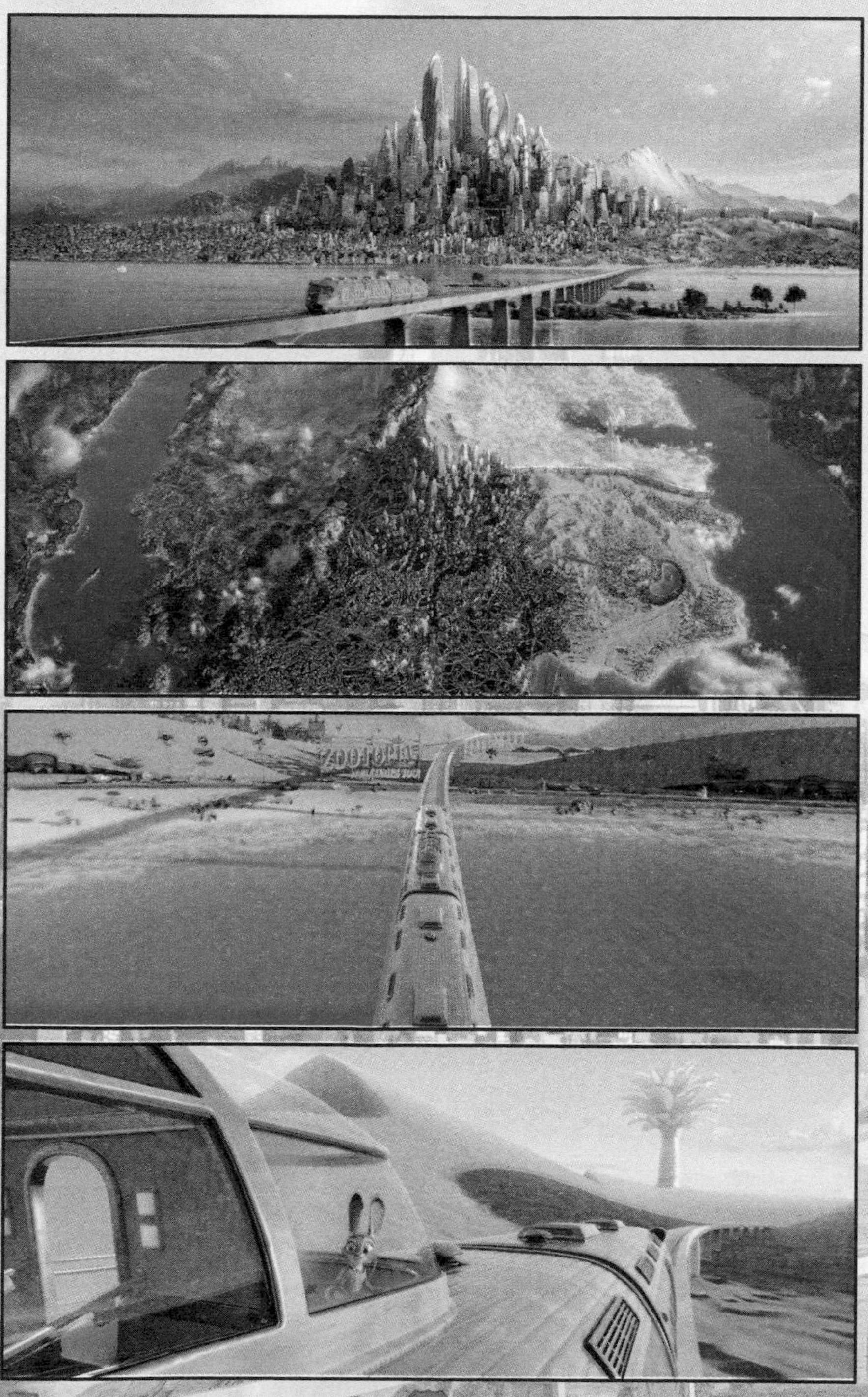
ZOOTOPIA

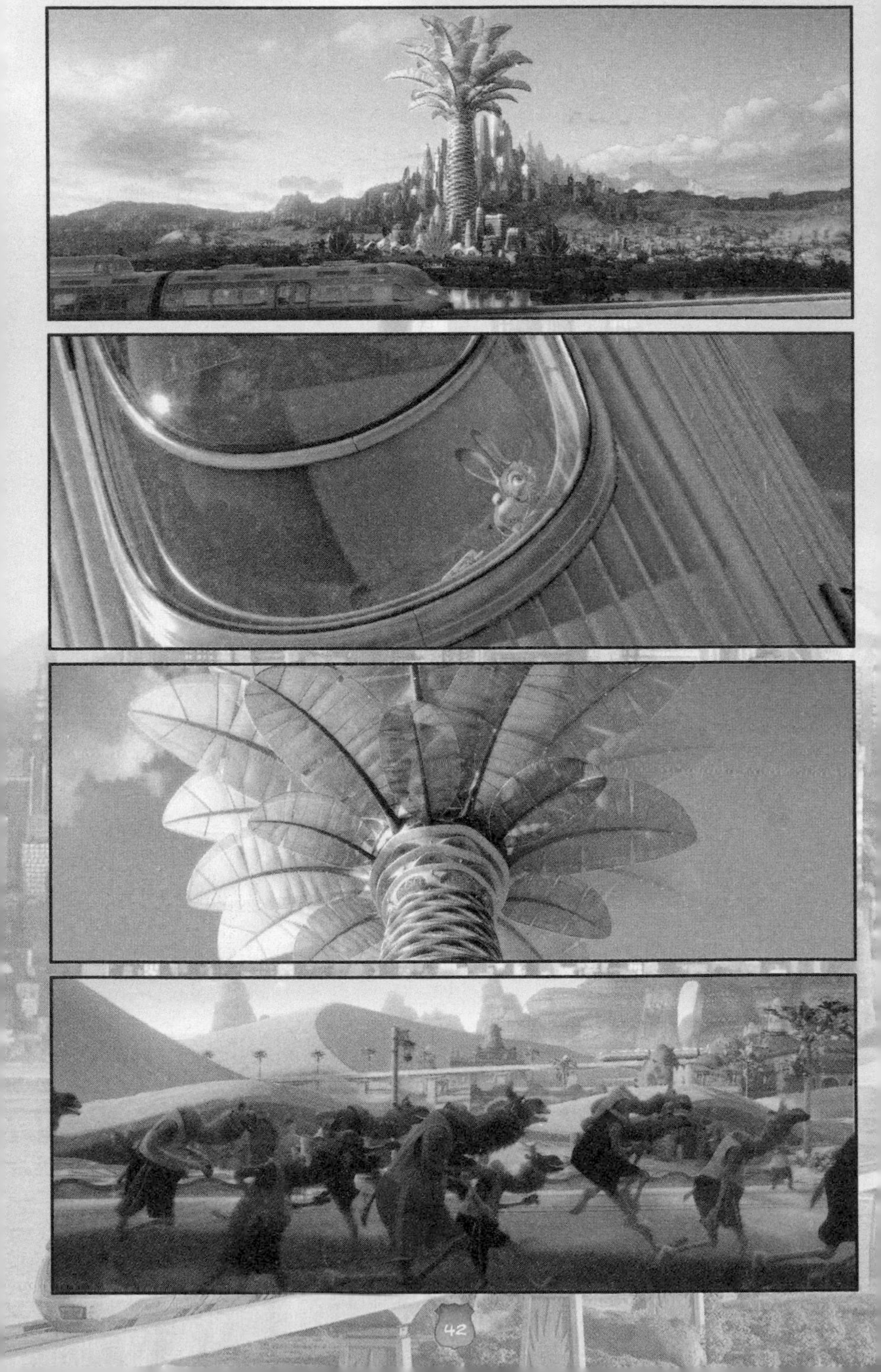

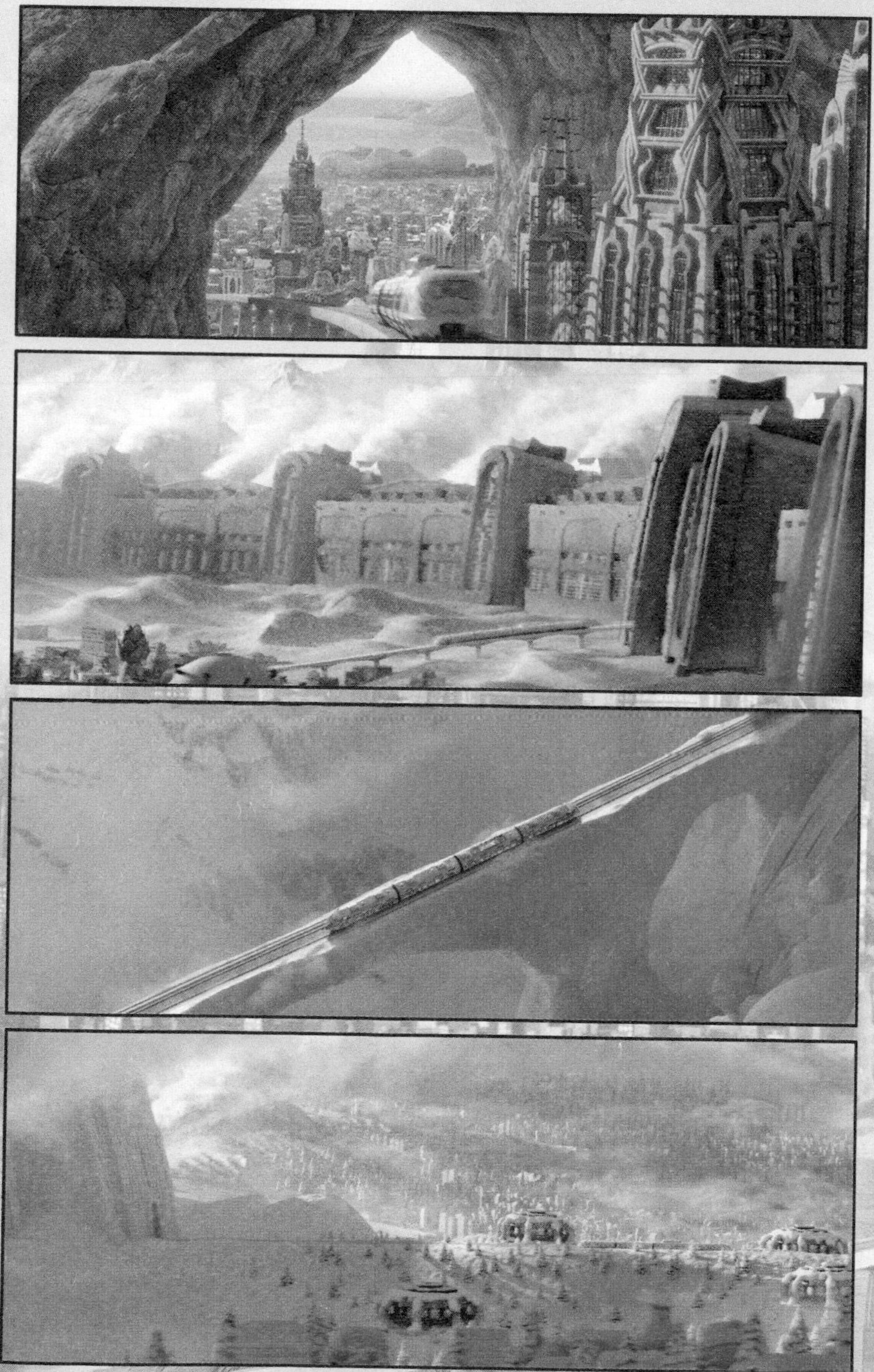

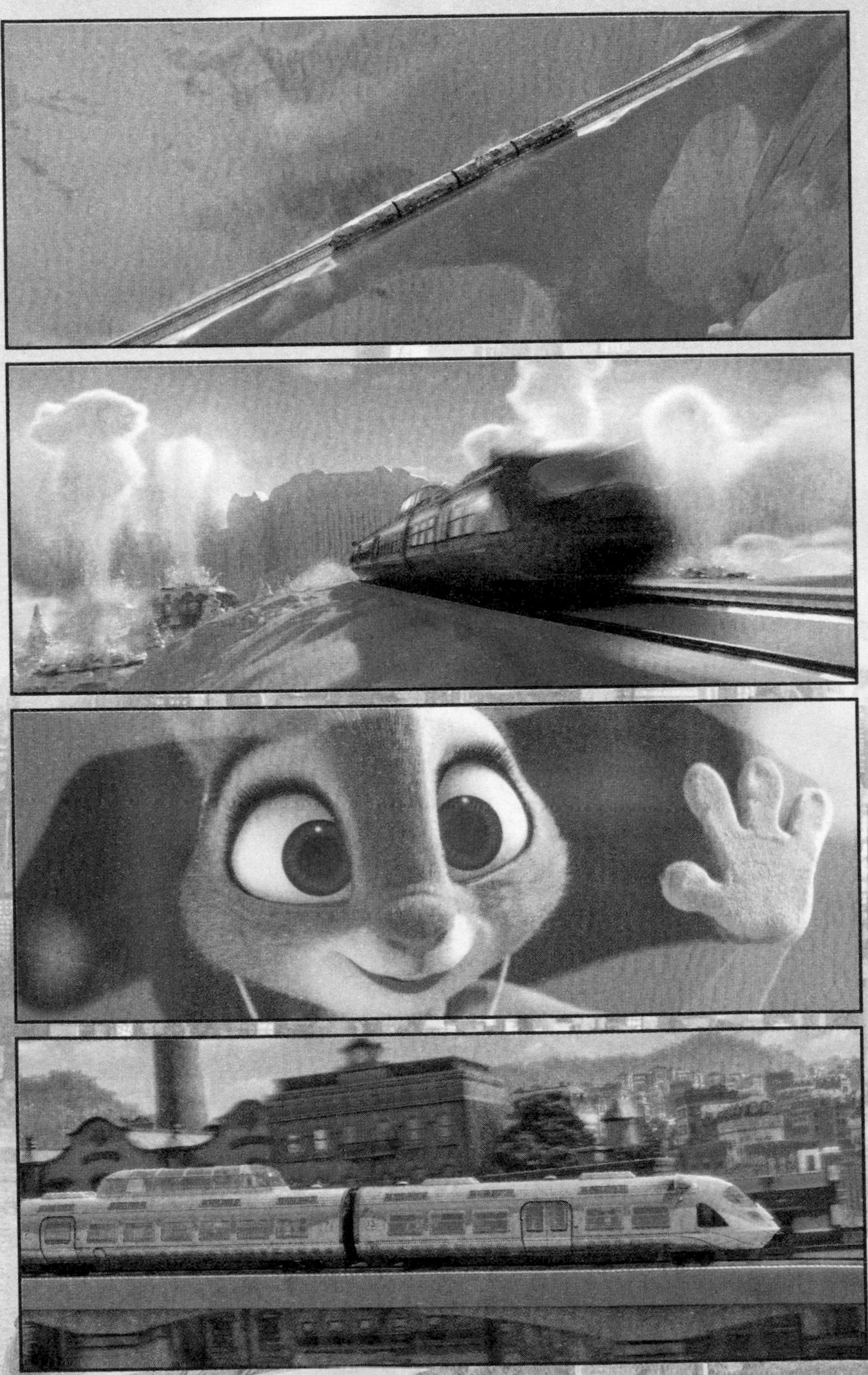

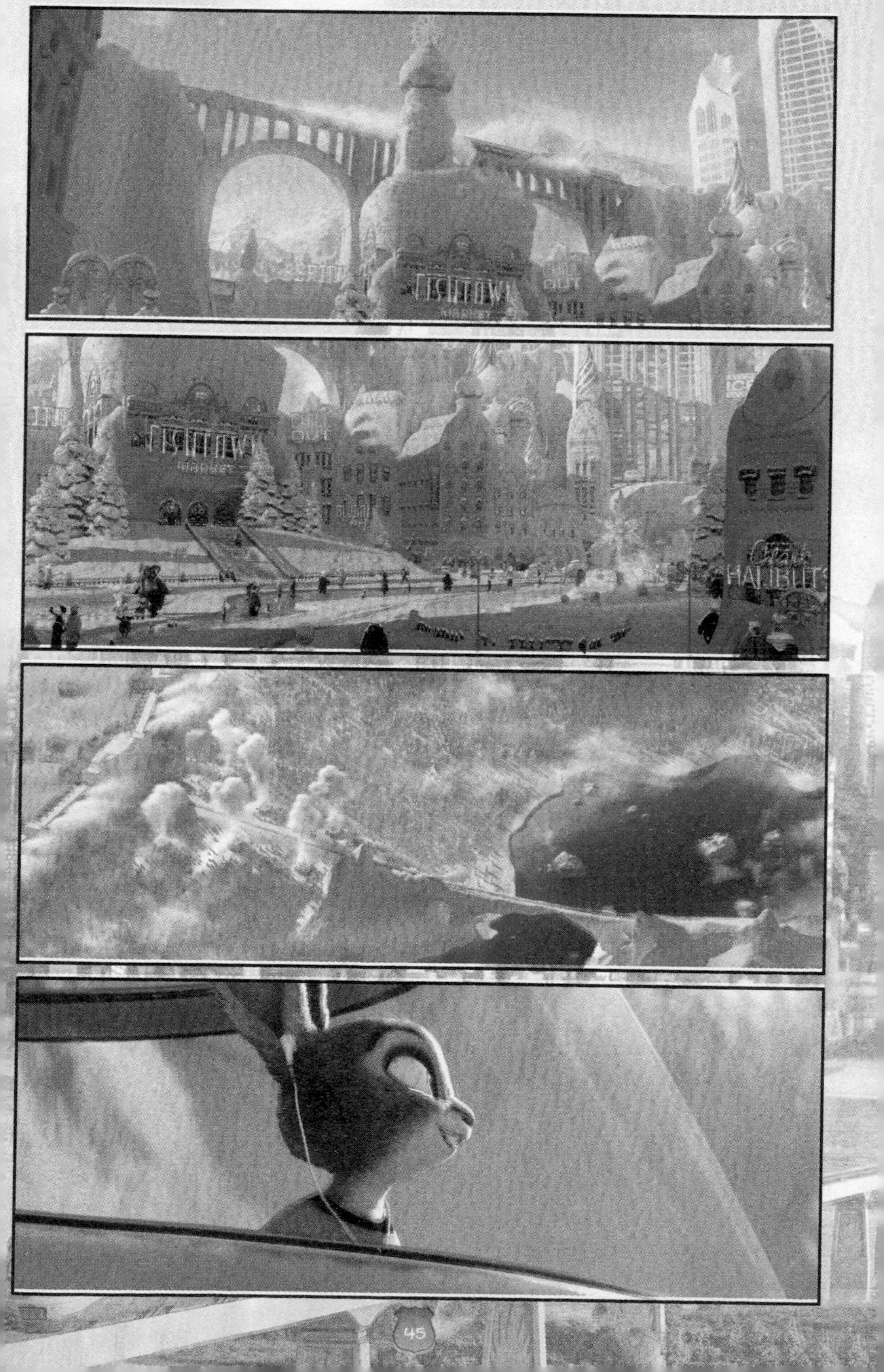

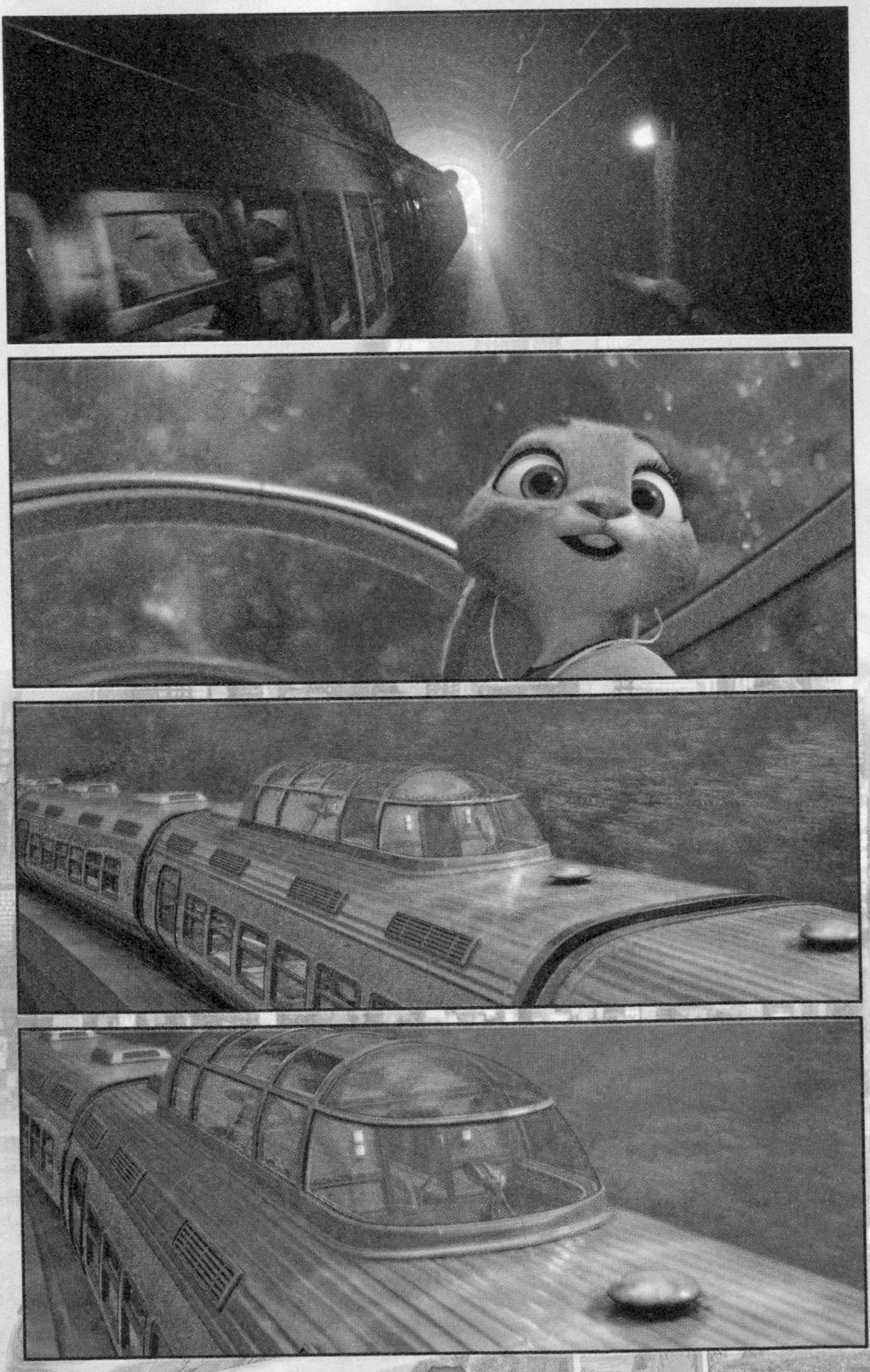

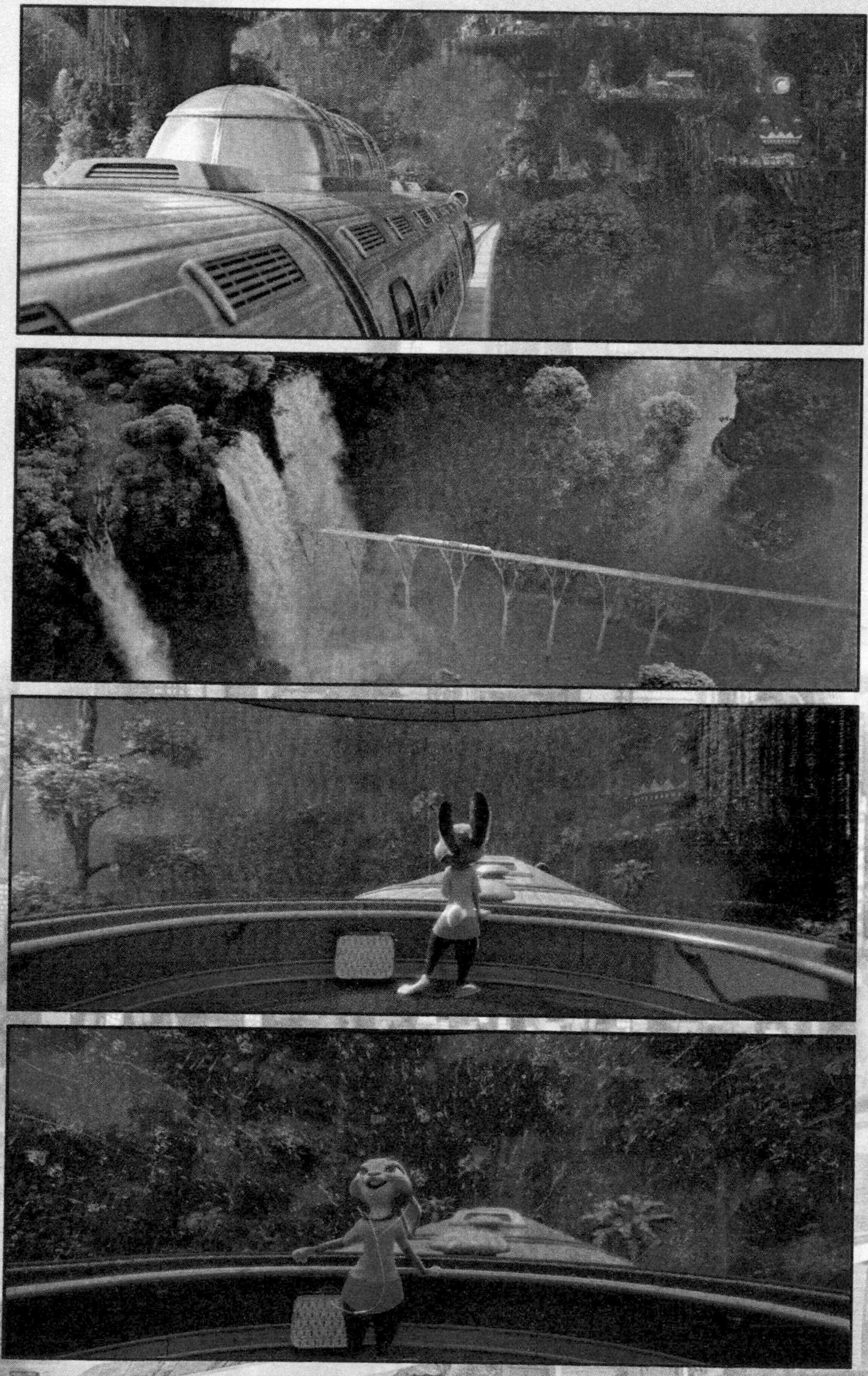

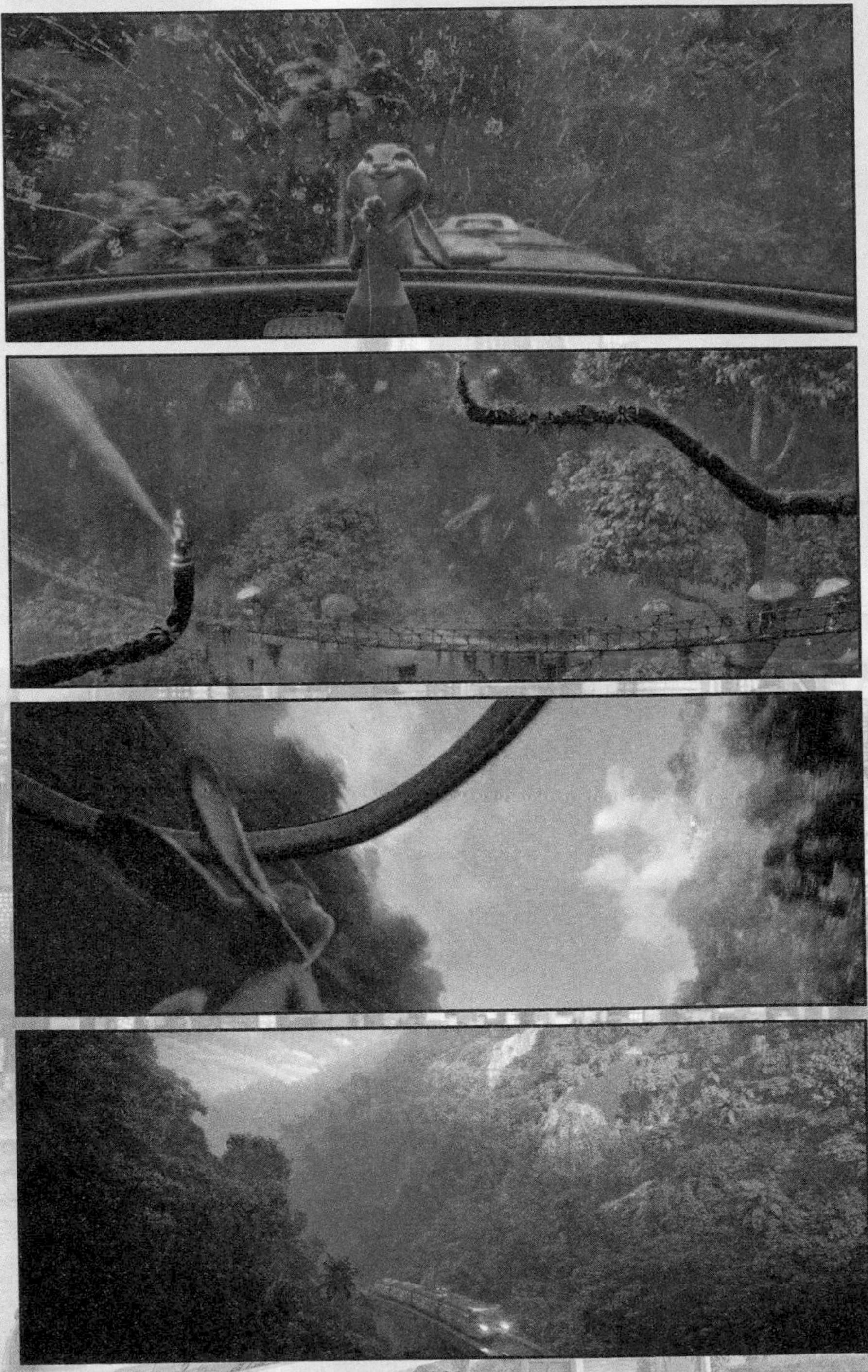

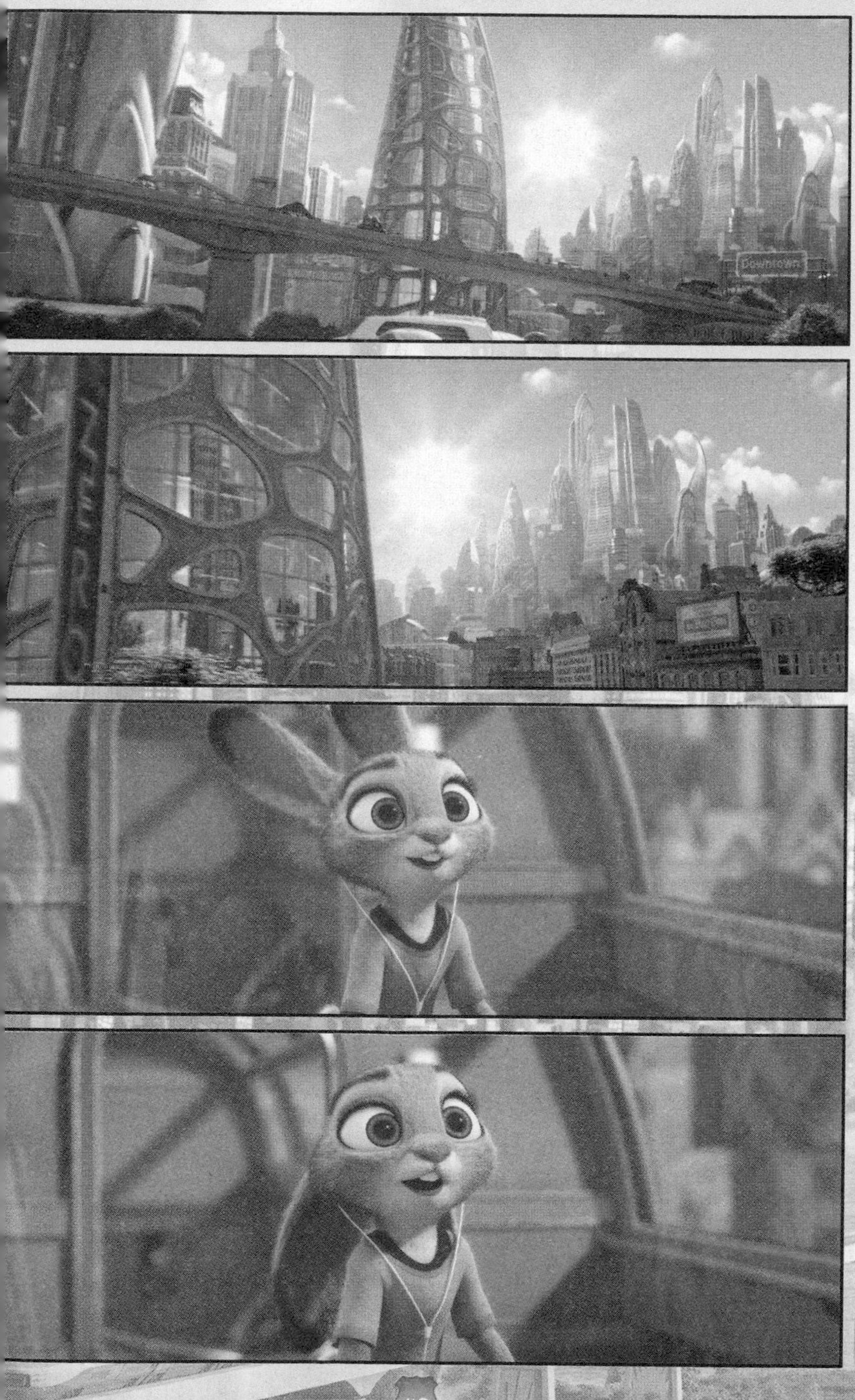
Downtown

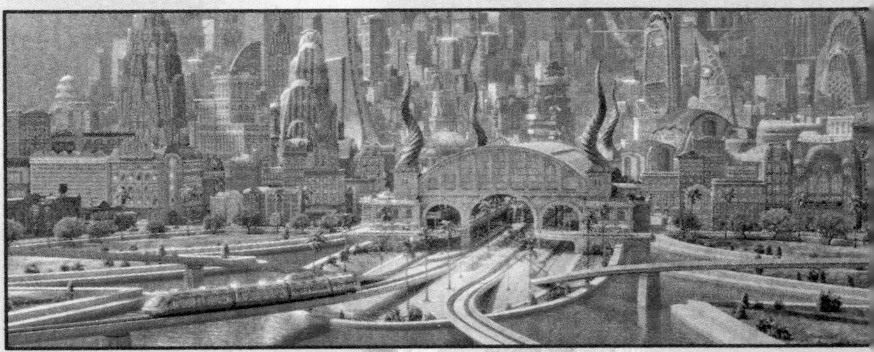

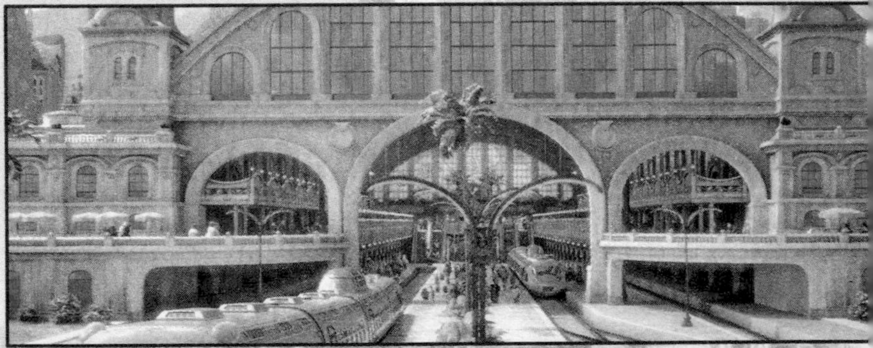

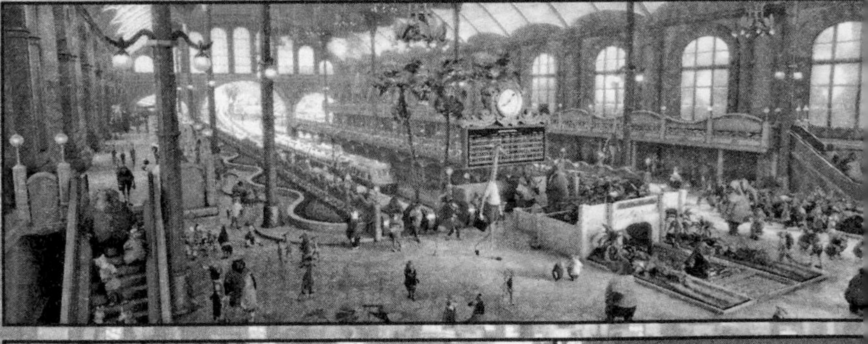

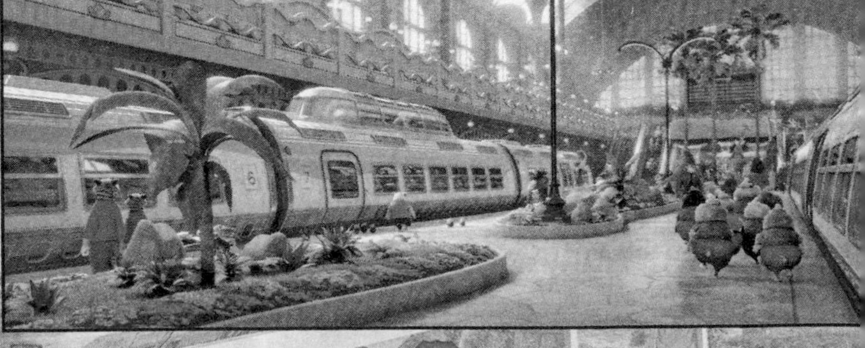

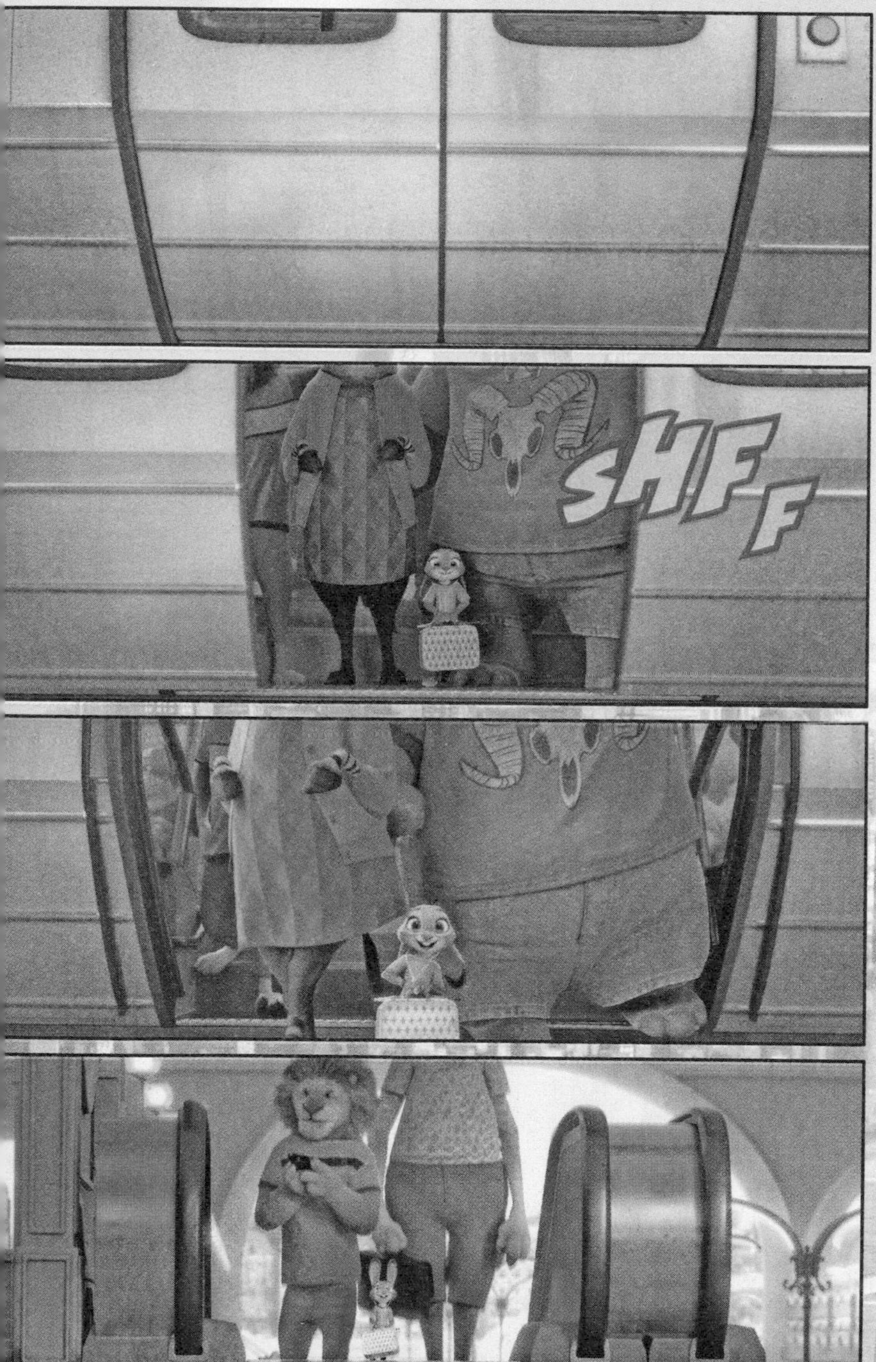
SHFFF

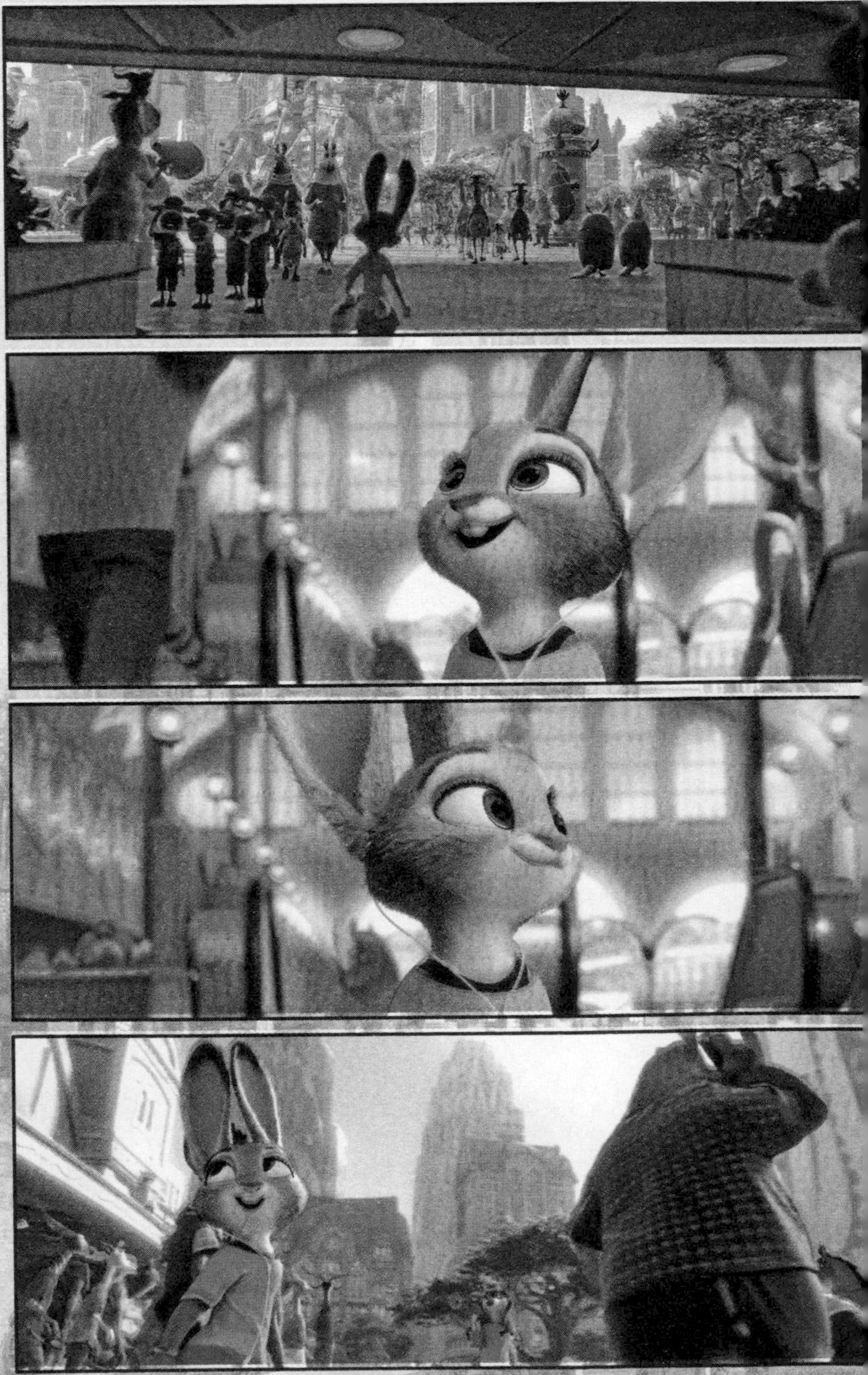

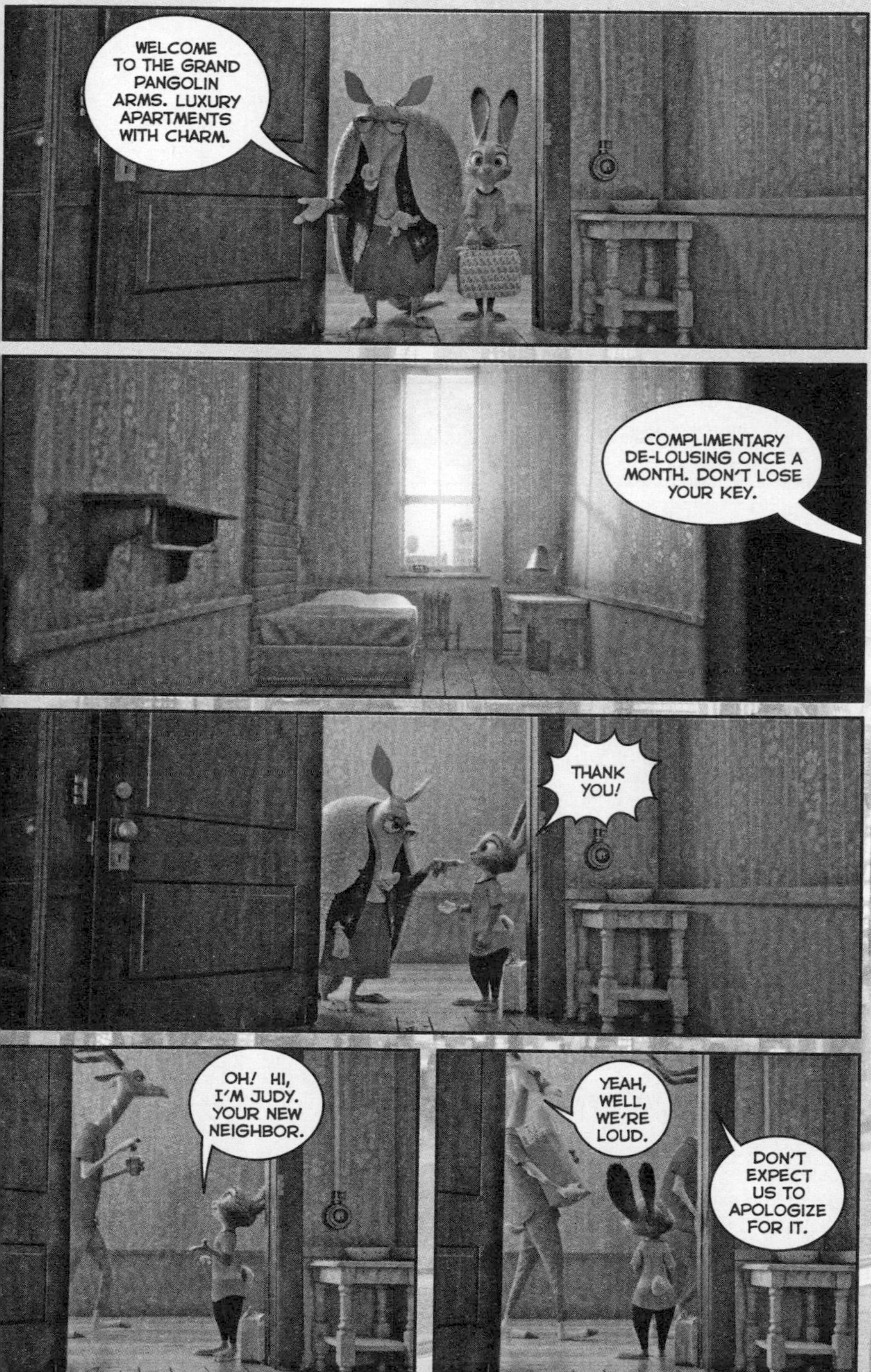
WELCOME TO THE GRAND PANGOLIN ARMS. LUXURY APARTMENTS WITH CHARM.
COMPLIMENTARY DE-LOUSING ONCE A MONTH. DON'T LOSE YOUR KEY.
THANK YOU!
OH! HI, I'M JUDY. YOUR NEW NEIGHBOR.
YEAH, WELL, WE'RE LOUD.
DON'T EXPECT US TO APOLOGIZE FOR IT.

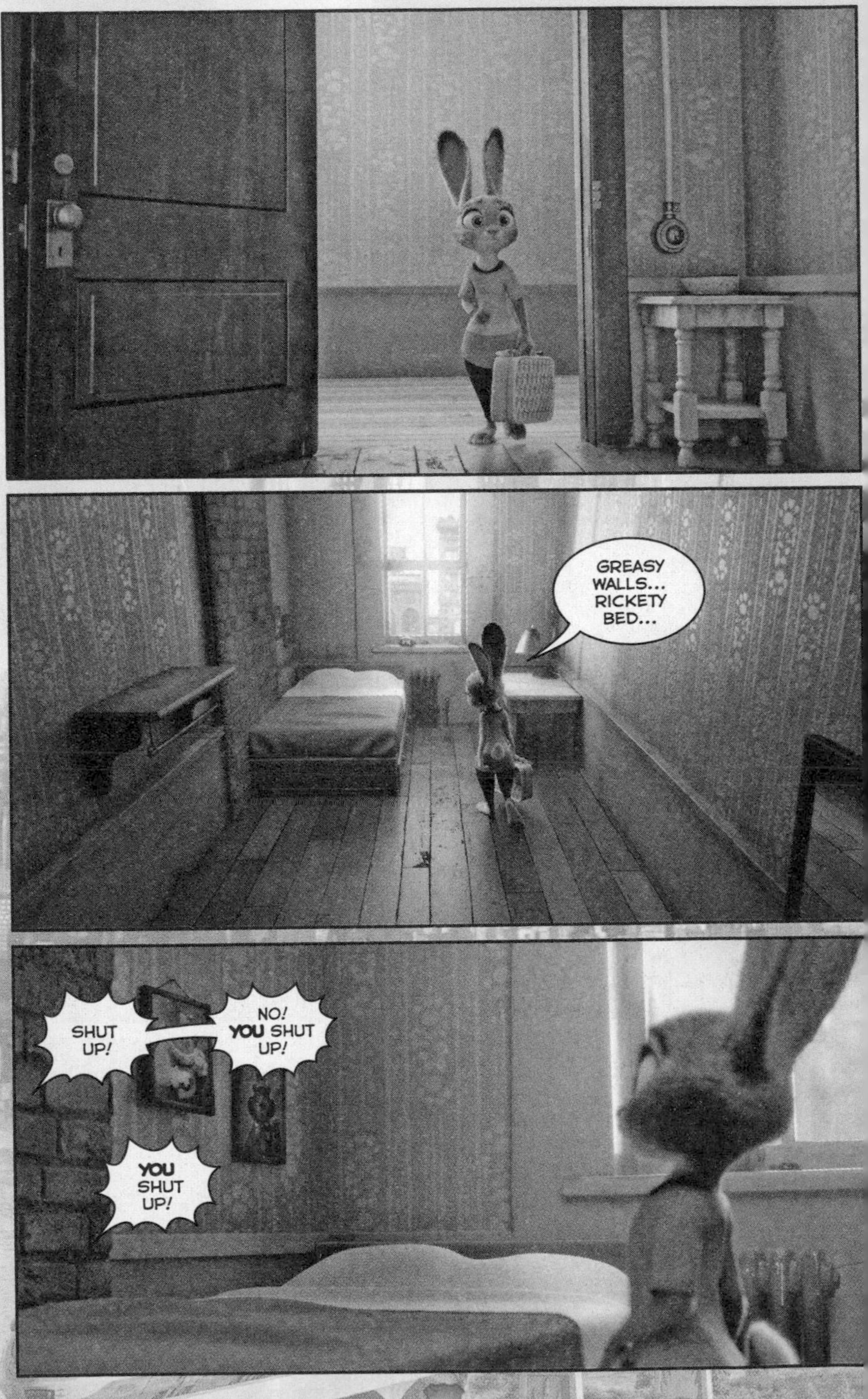
GREASY WALLS... RICKETY BED...
SHUT UP!
NO! YOU SHUT UP!
YOU SHUT UP!

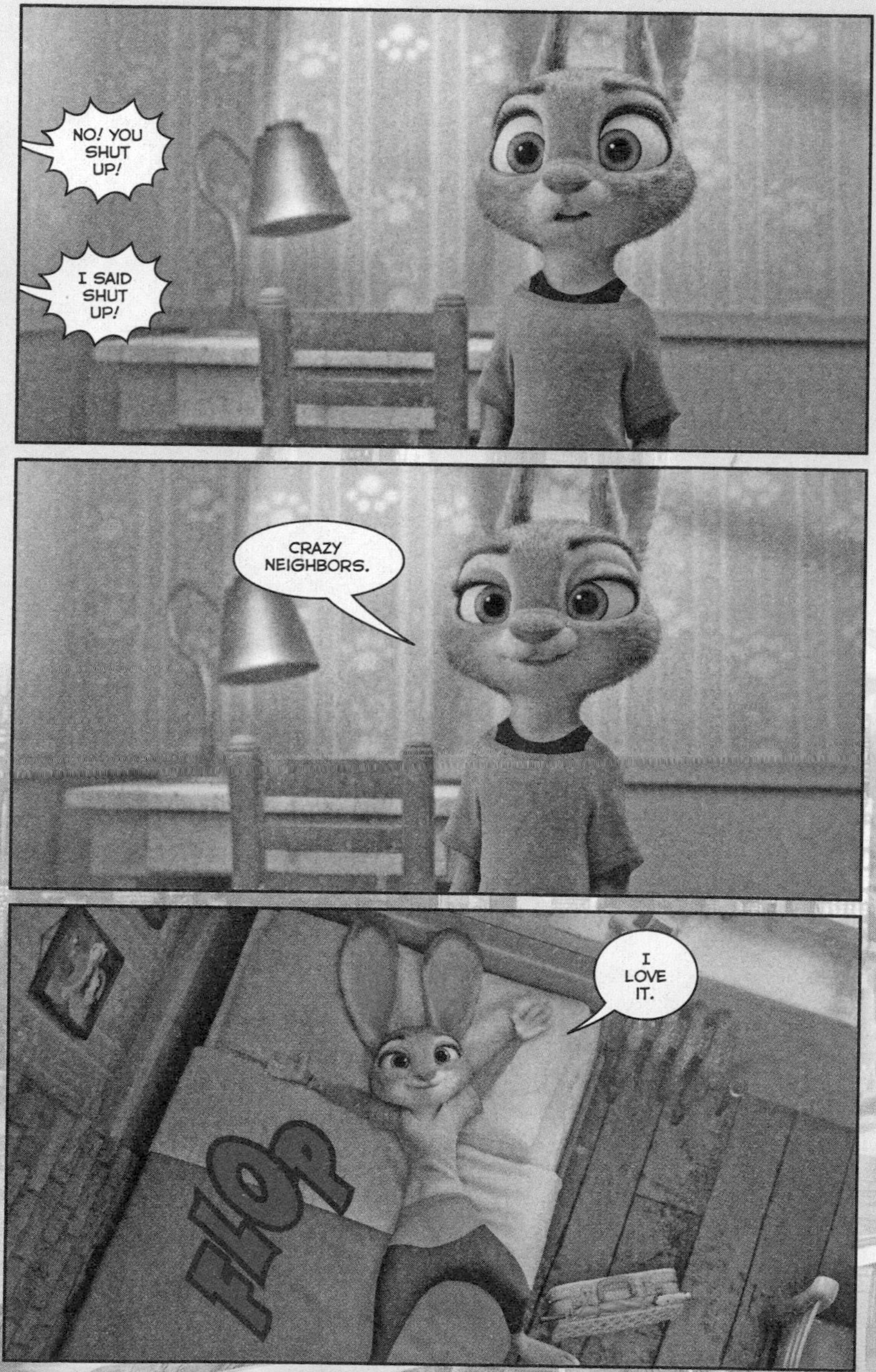
NO! YOU SHUT UP!
I SAID SHUT UP!
CRAZY NEIGHBORS.
I LOVE IT.
HOP

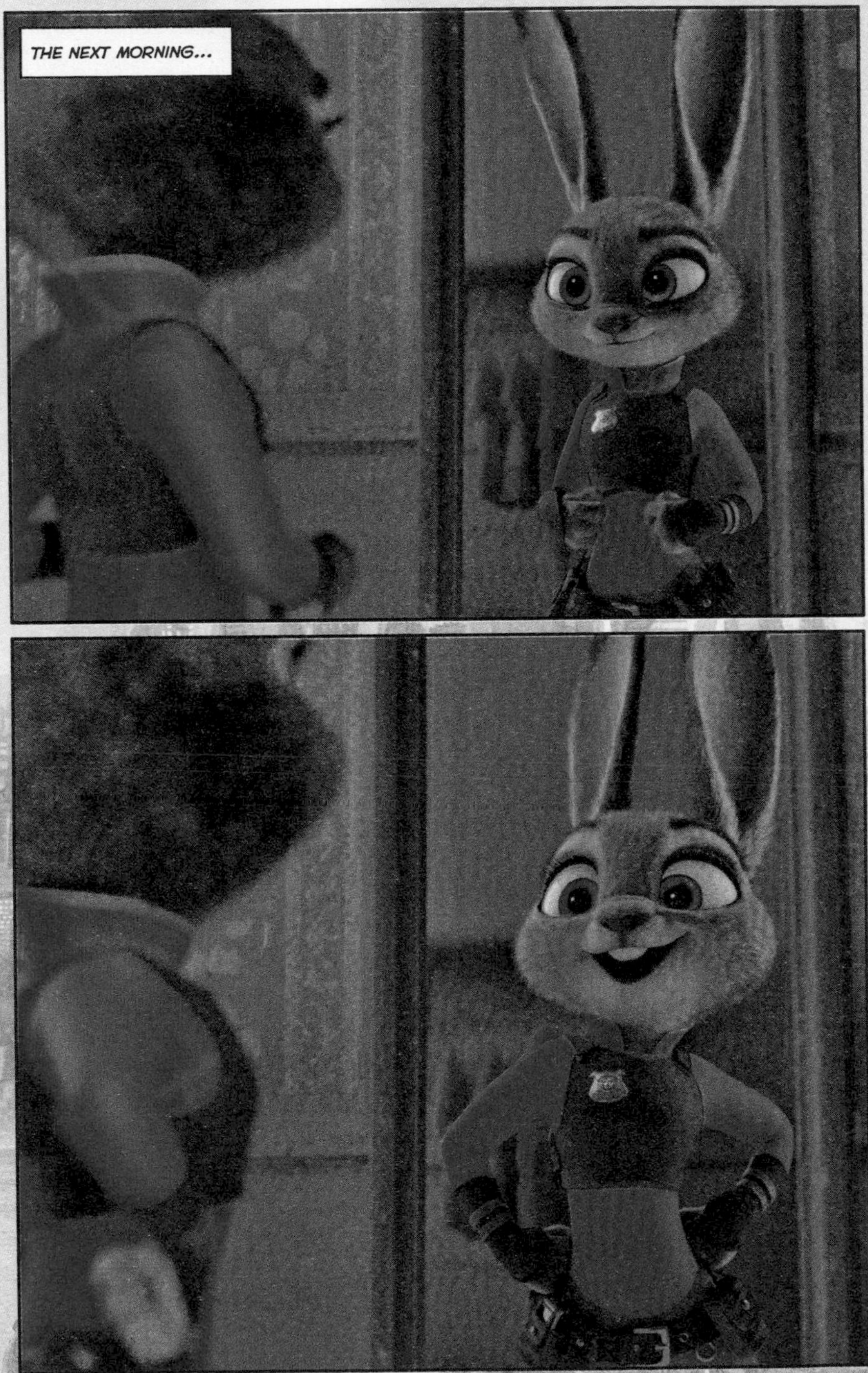
THE NEXT MORNING...

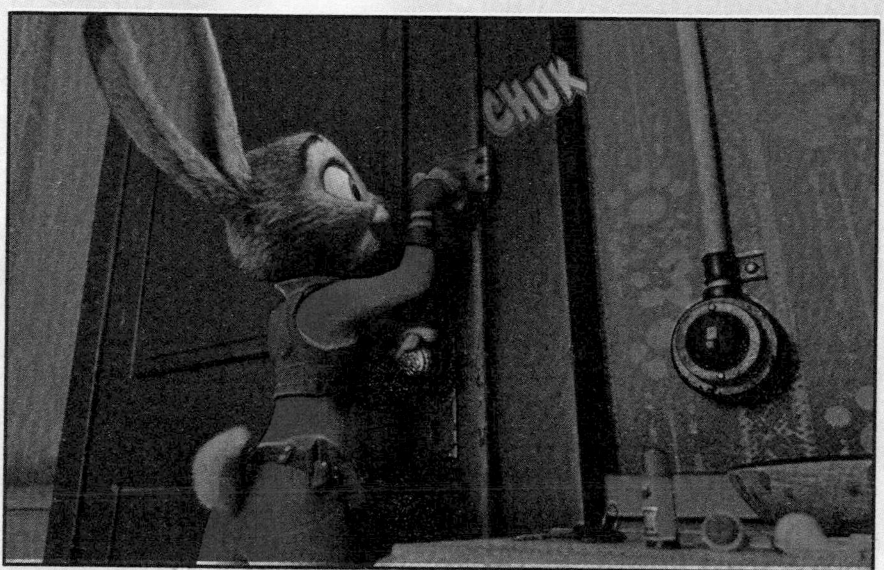
CHUK

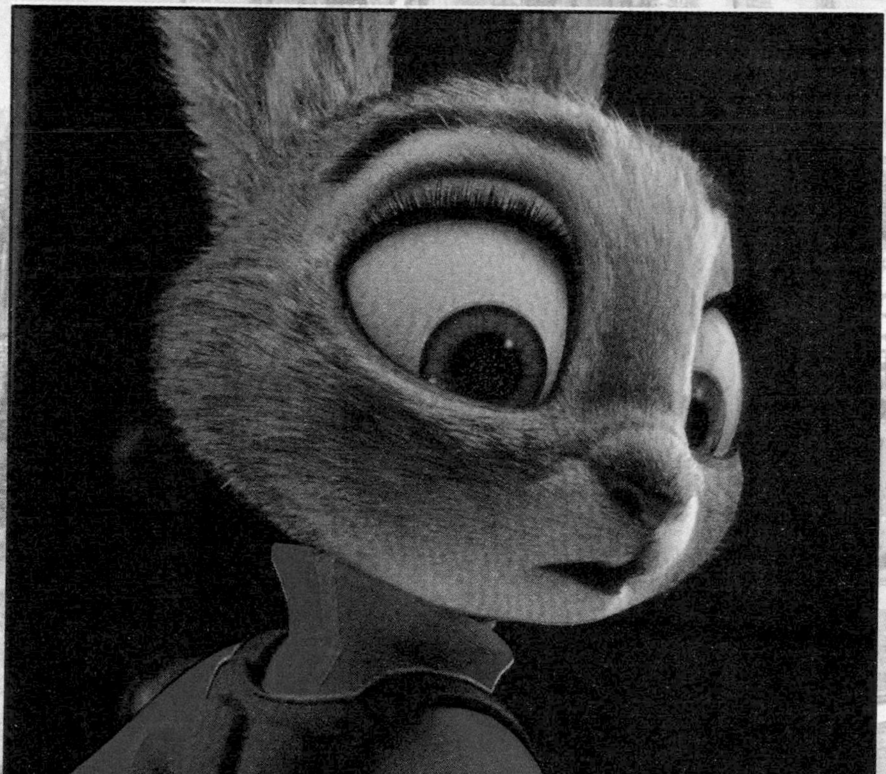

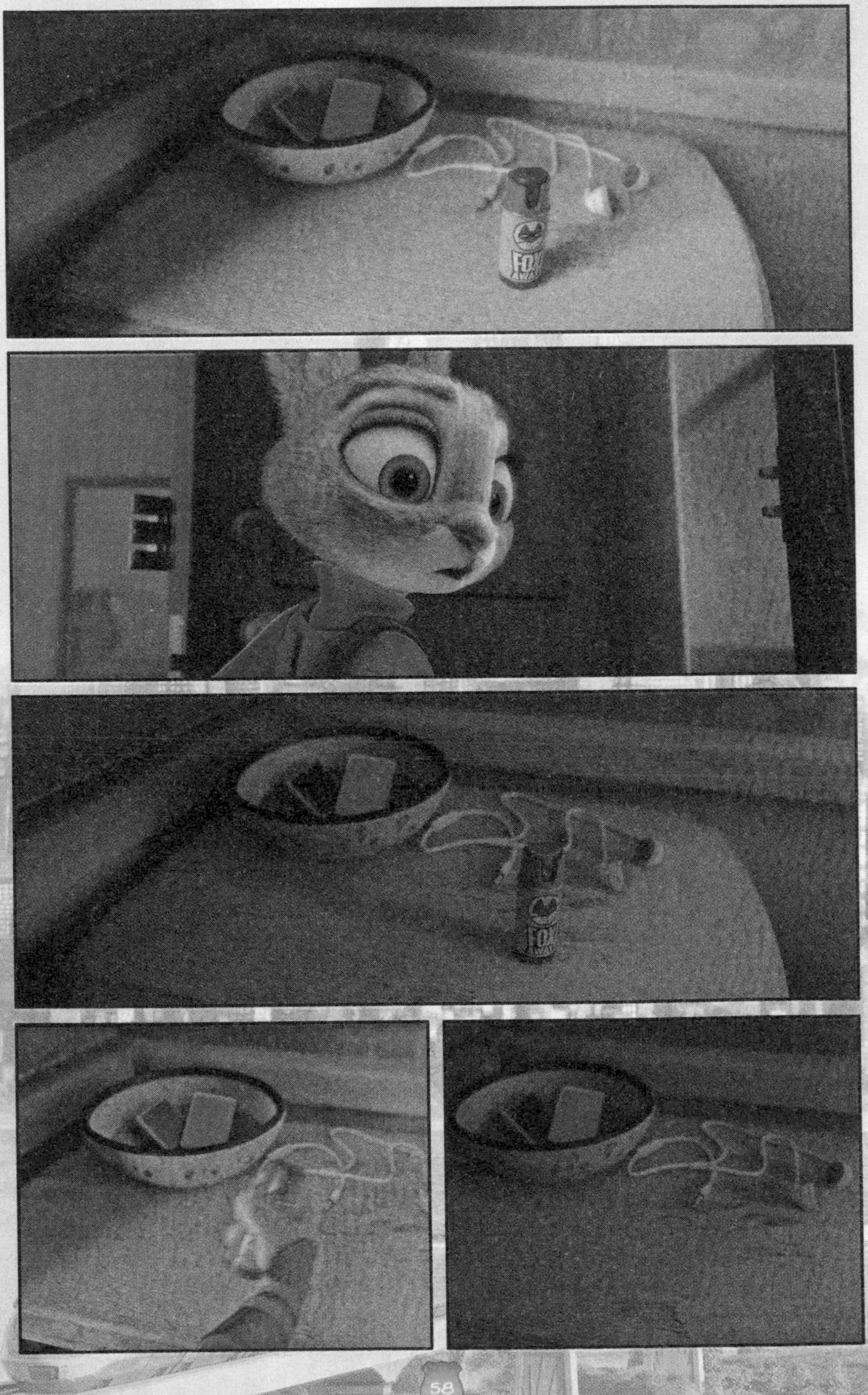

COME ON!

HE BARED HIS TEETH FIRST!

LUCKY CHOMPS

'SCUSE ME! DOWN HERE? DOWN HERE.

LUCKY CHOMPS

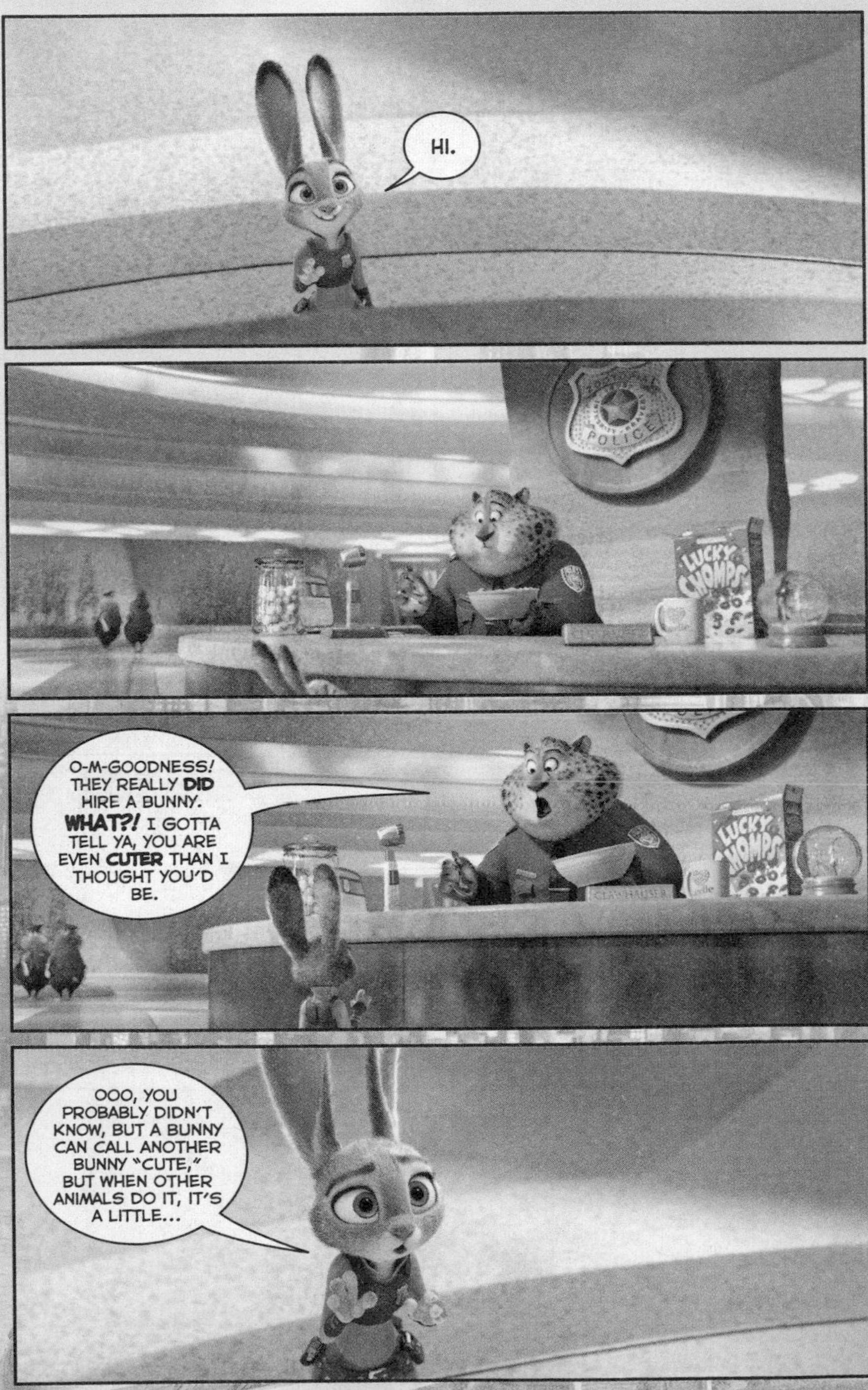
HI.
POLICE
LUCKY CHOMPS
O-M-GOODNESS! THEY REALLY **DID** HIRE A BUNNY. **WHAT?!** I GOTTA TELL YA, YOU ARE EVEN **CUTER** THAN I THOUGHT YOU'D BE.
LUCKY CHOMPS
OOO, YOU PROBABLY DIDN'T KNOW, BUT A BUNNY CAN CALL ANOTHER BUNNY "CUTE," BUT WHEN OTHER ANIMALS DO IT, IT'S A LITTLE...

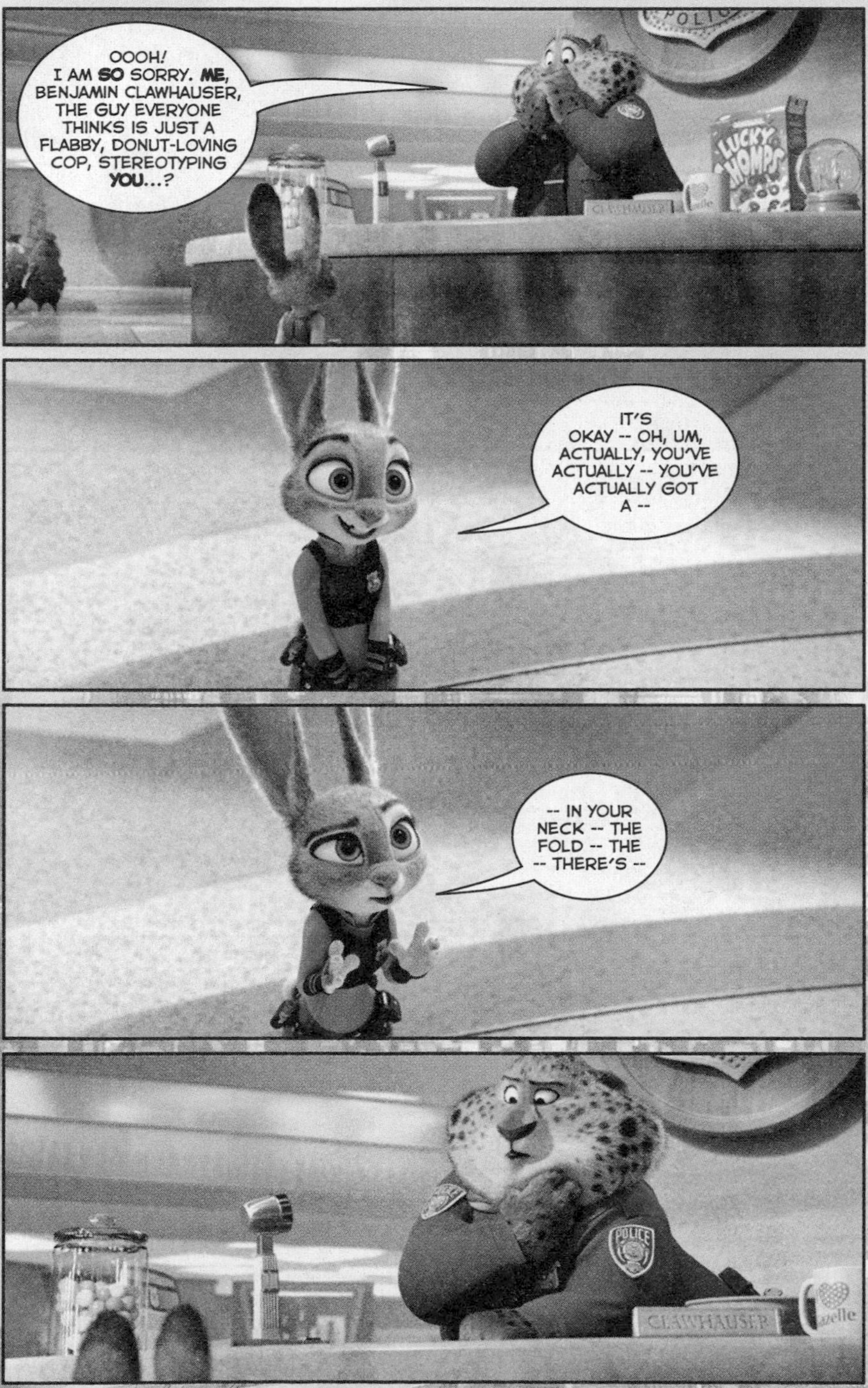
OOOH! I AM SO SORRY. ME, BENJAMIN CLAWHAUSER, THE GUY EVERYONE THINKS IS JUST A FLABBY, DONUT-LOVING COP, STEREOTYPING YOU...?
IT'S OKAY -- OH, UM, ACTUALLY, YOU'VE ACTUALLY -- YOU'VE ACTUALLY GOT A --
-- IN YOUR NECK -- THE FOLD -- THE -- THERE'S --
CLAWHAUSER

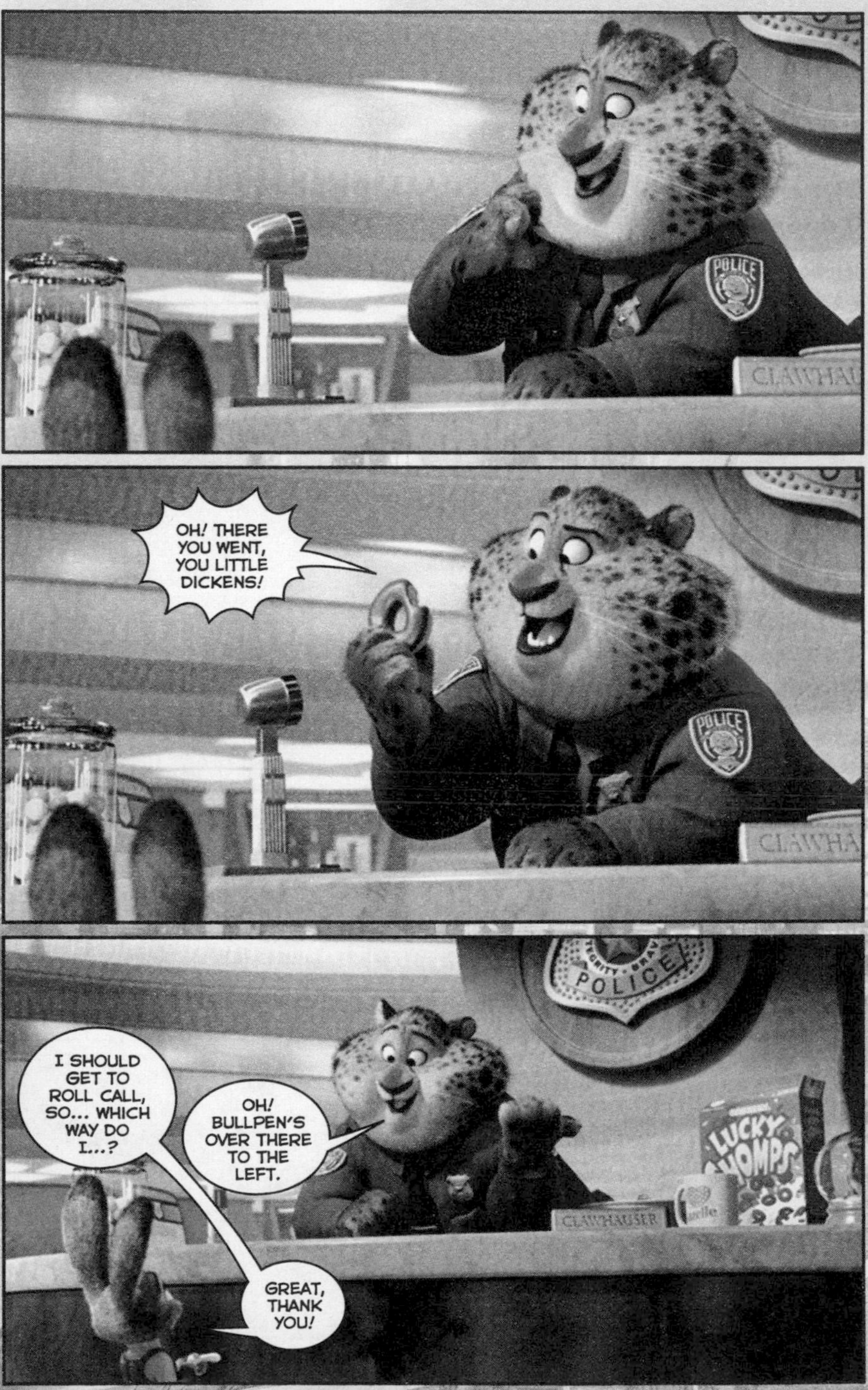

OH! THERE YOU WENT, YOU LITTLE DICKENS!
POLICE
I SHOULD GET TO ROLL CALL, SO... WHICH WAY DO I...?
OH! BULLPEN'S OVER THERE TO THE LEFT.
GREAT, THANK YOU!

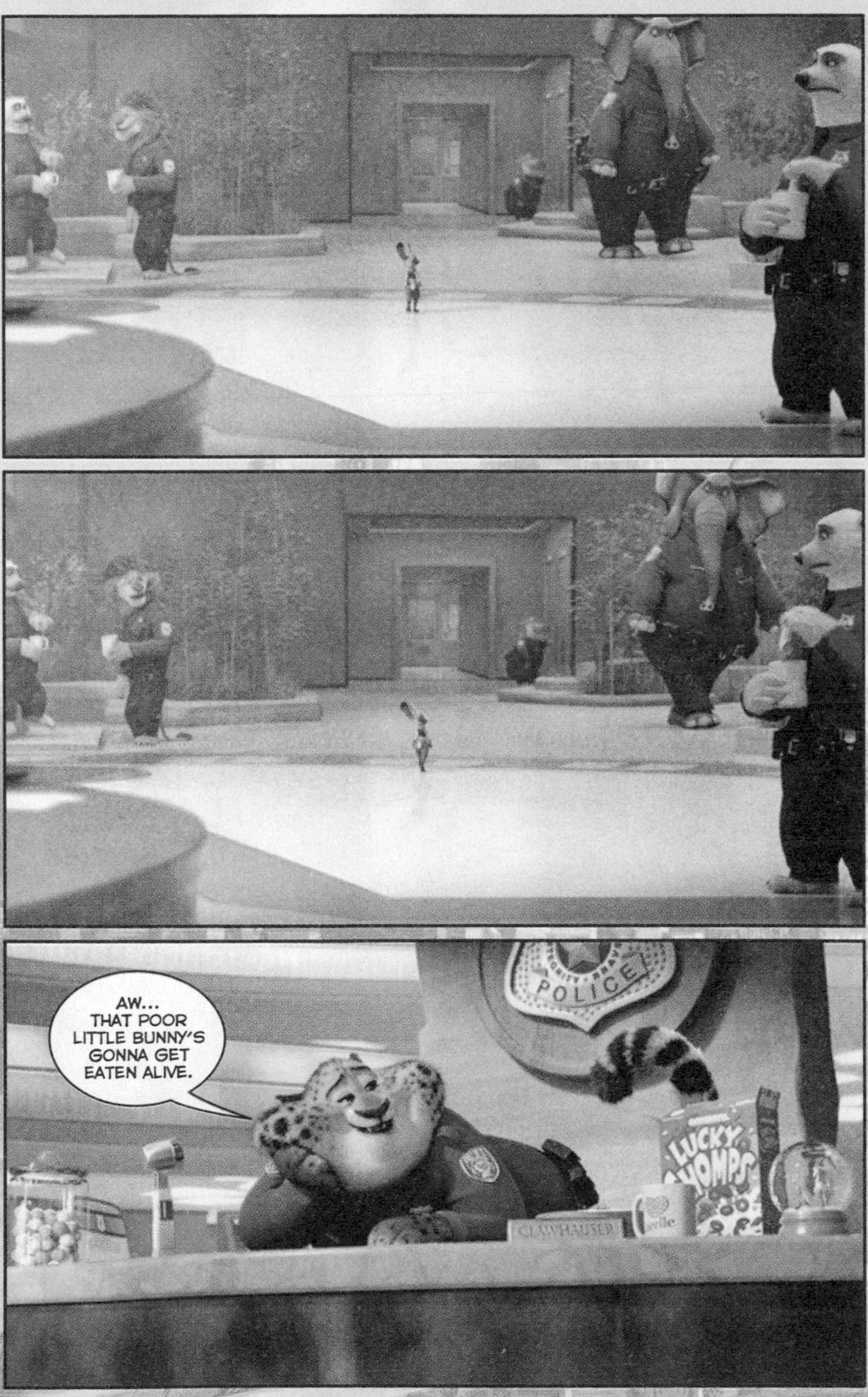
AW... THAT POOR LITTLE BUNNY'S GONNA GET EATEN ALIVE.
POLICE
LUCKY
CLAWHAUSER

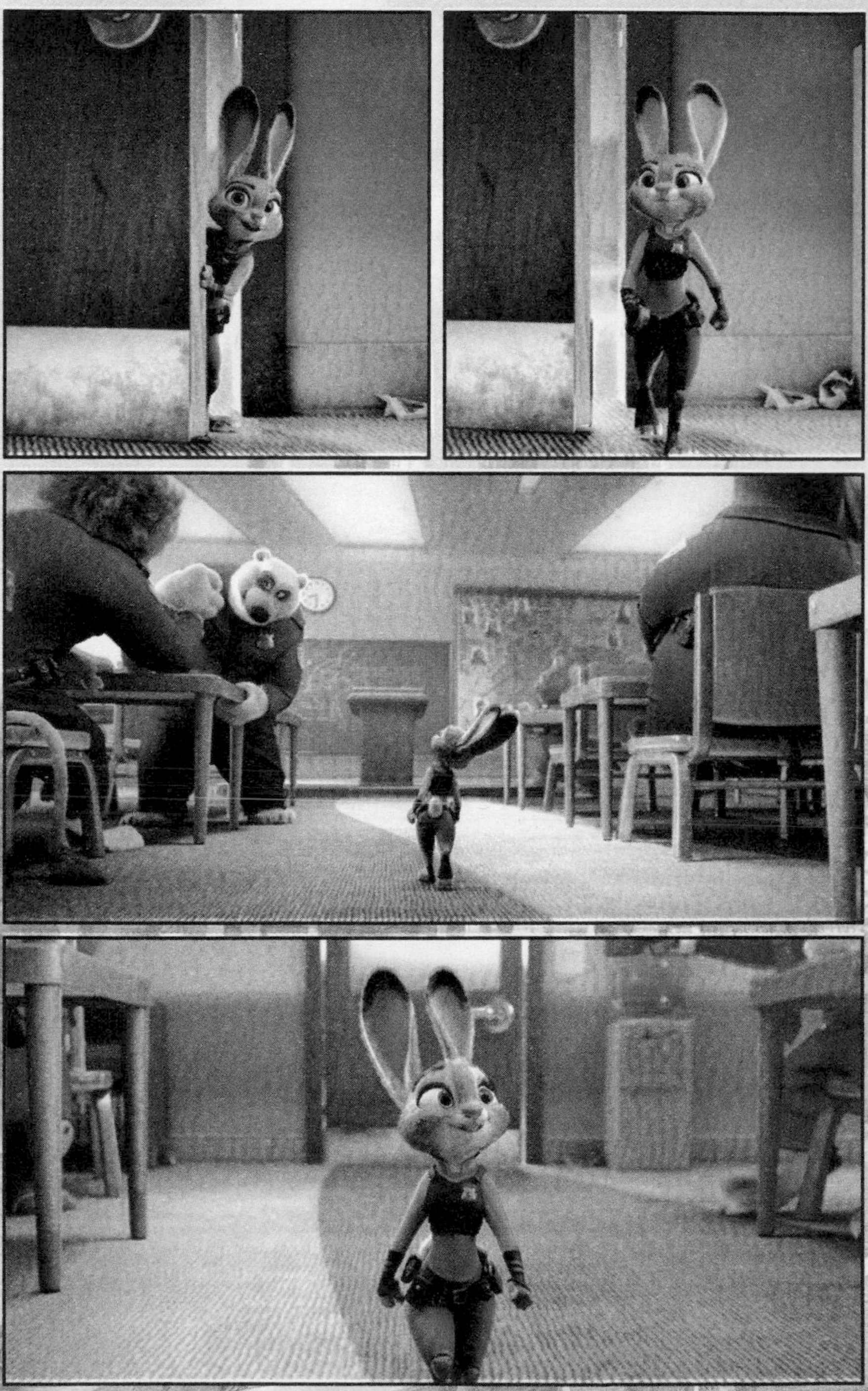

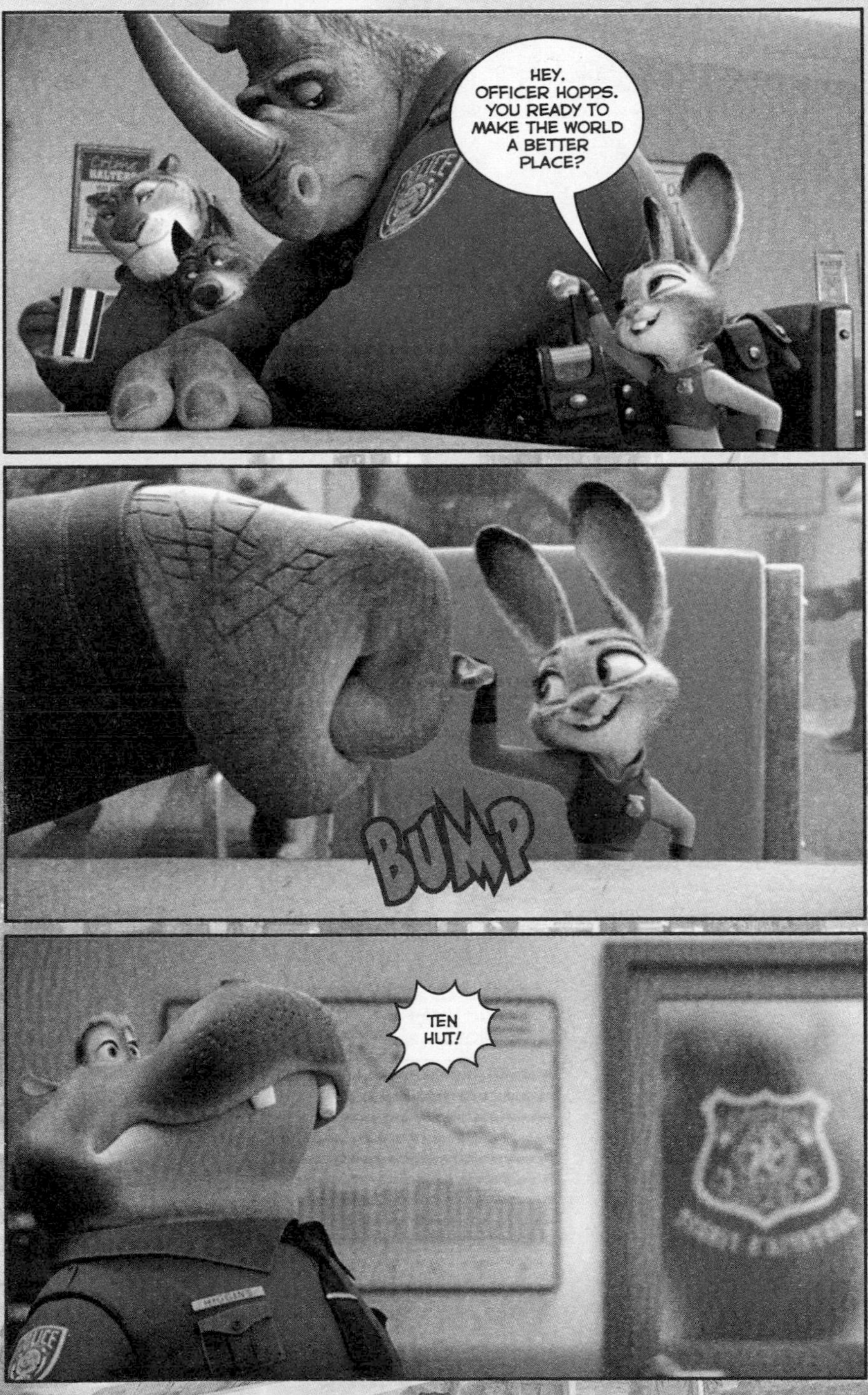
HEY.
OFFICER HOPPS.
YOU READY TO
MAKE THE WORLD
A BETTER
PLACE?
BUMP
TEN
HUT!

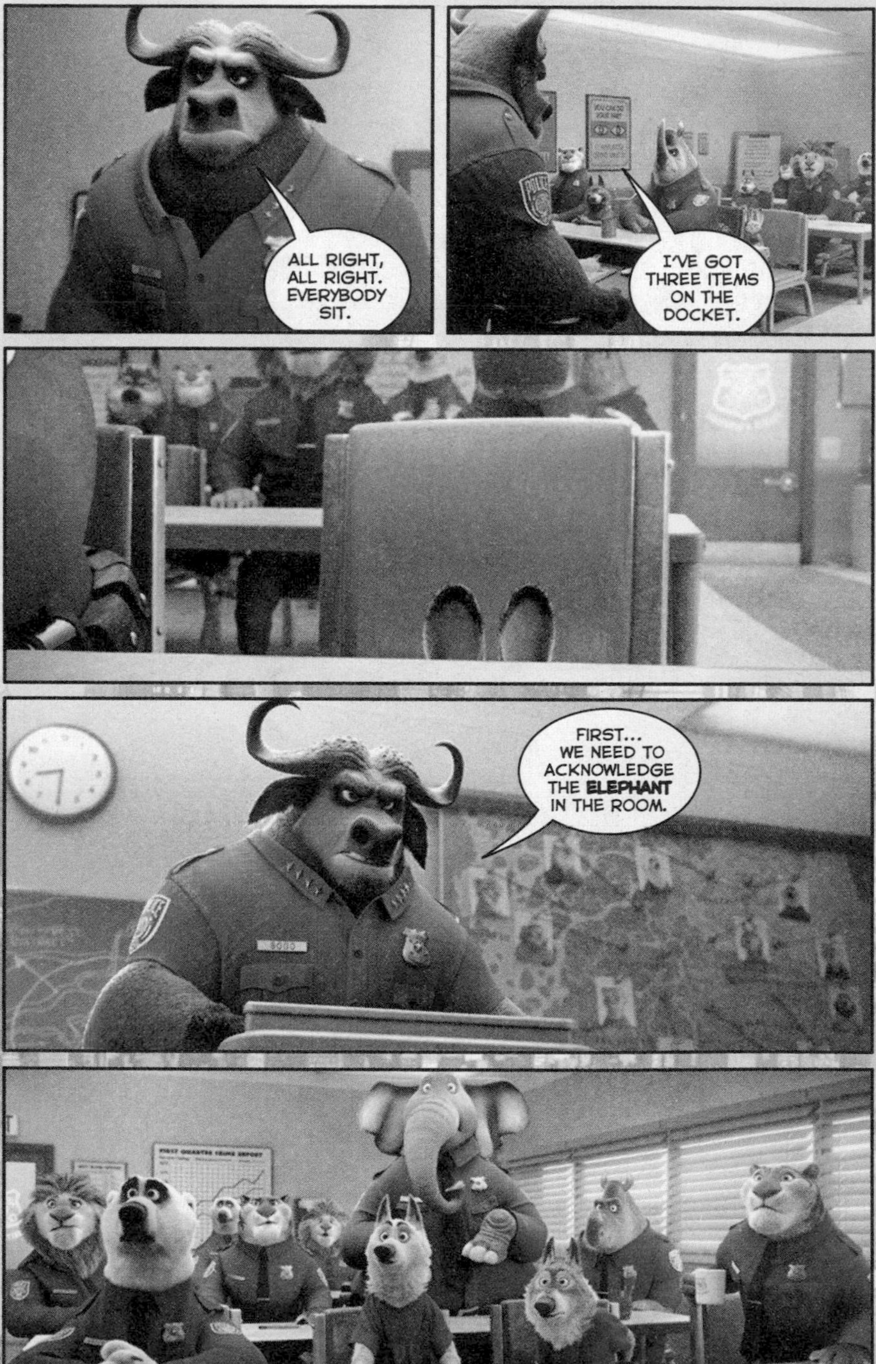
ALL RIGHT, ALL RIGHT. EVERYBODY SIT.
I'VE GOT THREE ITEMS ON THE DOCKET.
FIRST... WE NEED TO ACKNOWLEDGE THE **ELEPHANT** IN THE ROOM.

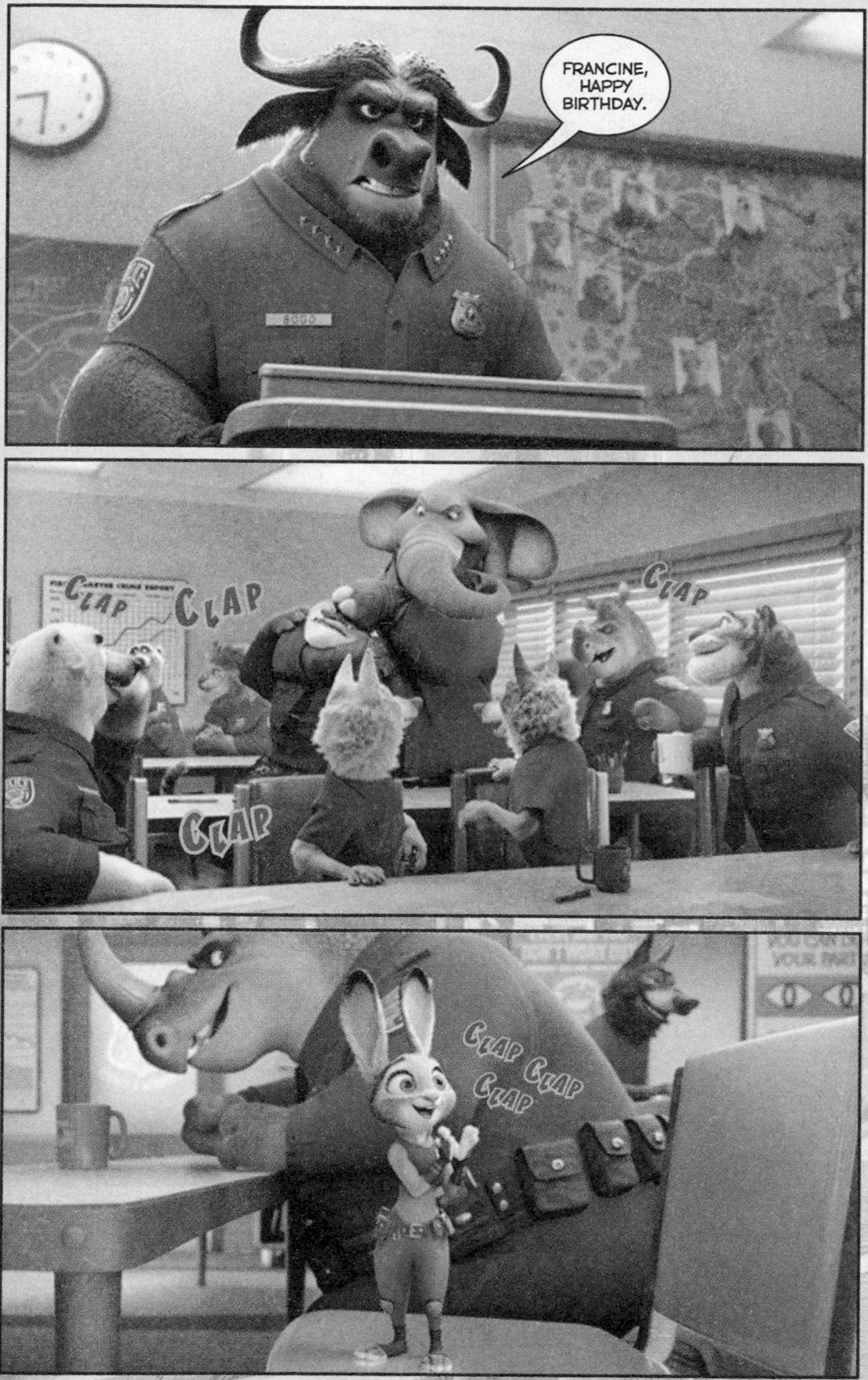
FRANCINE, HAPPY BIRTHDAY.
CLAP
CLAP
CLAP
CLAP
CLAP CLAP CLAP

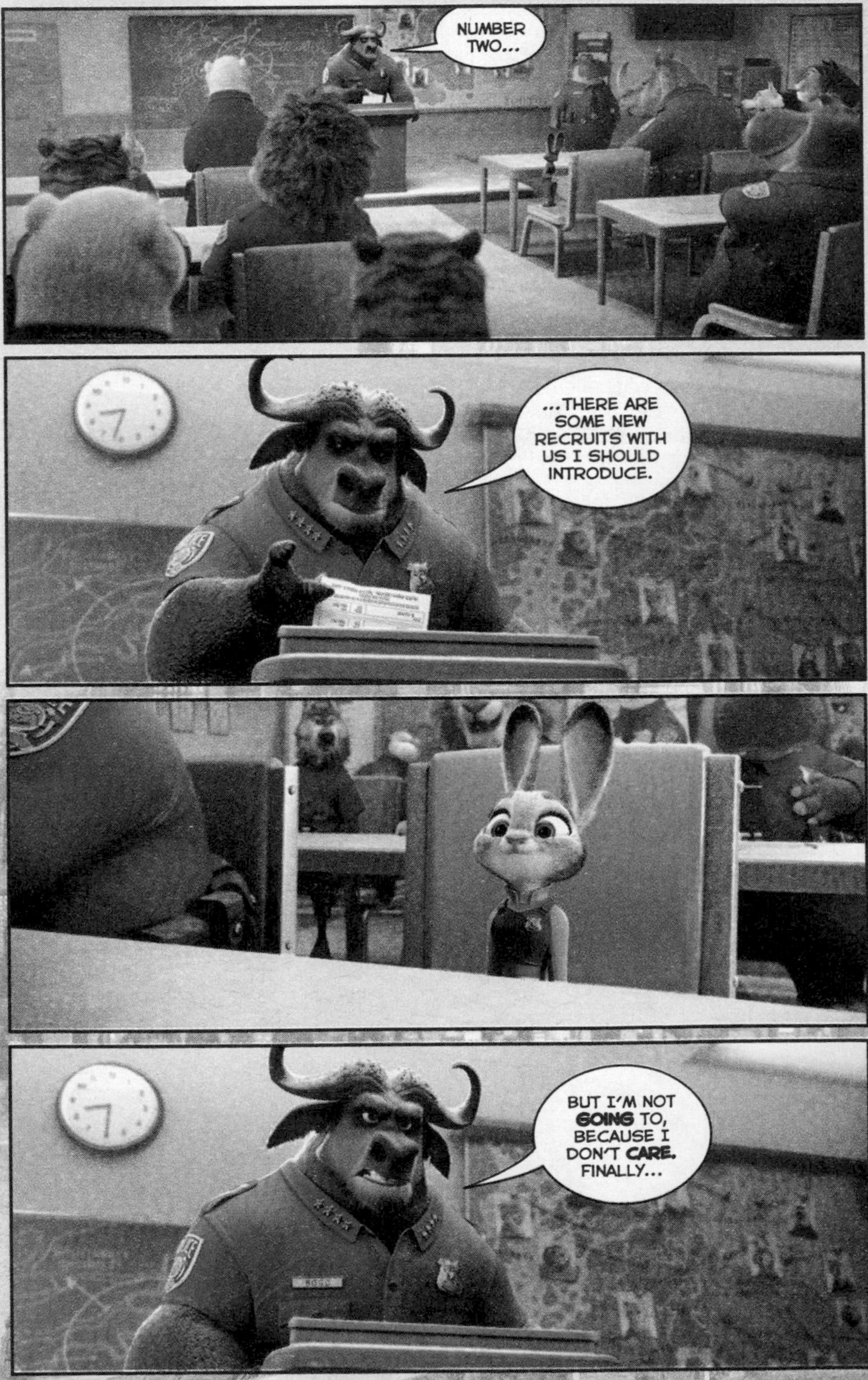
NUMBER TWO...
...THERE ARE SOME NEW RECRUITS WITH US I SHOULD INTRODUCE.
BUT I'M NOT **GOING** TO, BECAUSE I DON'T **CARE**. FINALLY...

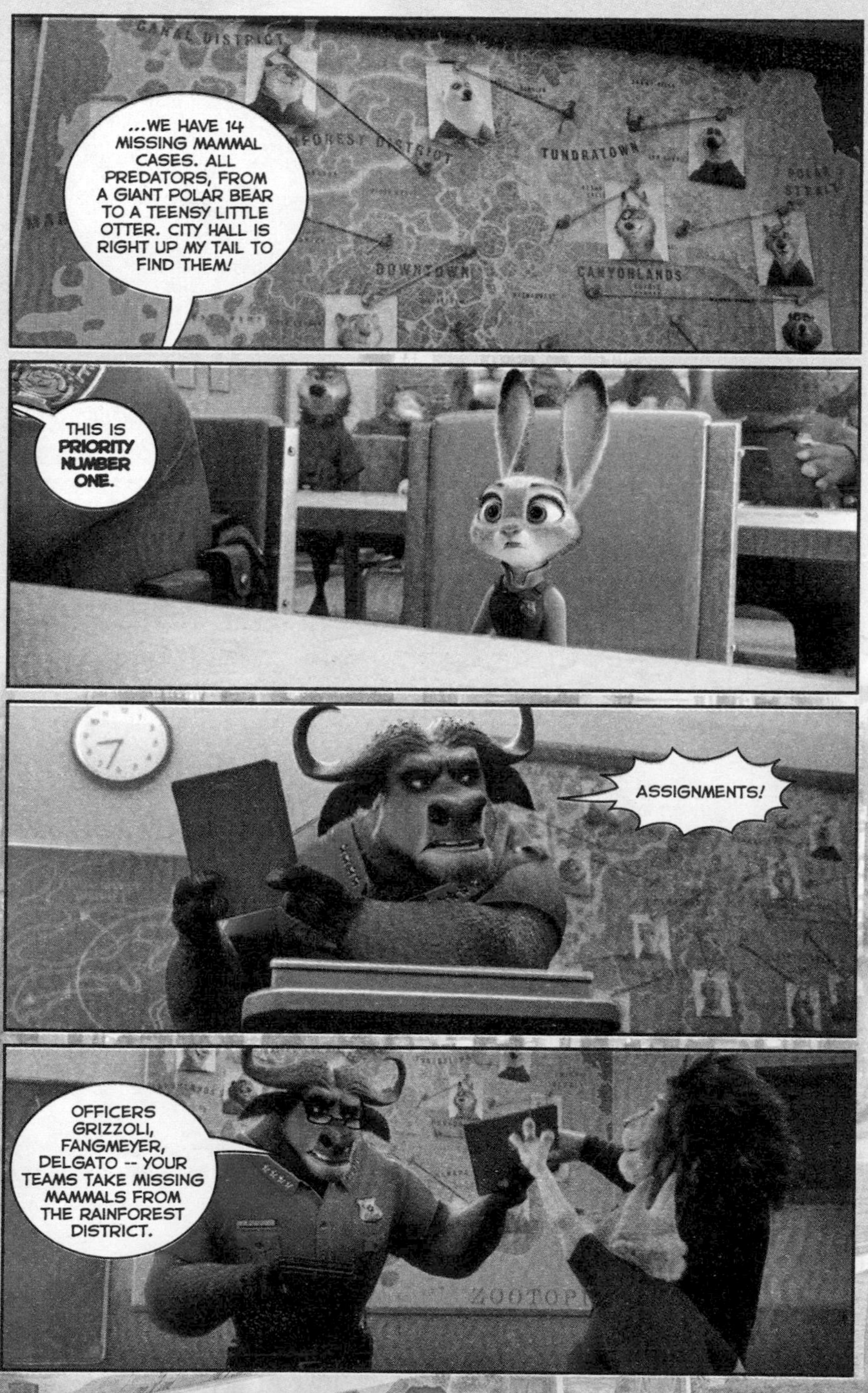
TUNDRATOWN
CANYONLANDS
...WE HAVE 14 MISSING MAMMAL CASES. ALL PREDATORS, FROM A GIANT POLAR BEAR TO A TEENSY LITTLE OTTER. CITY HALL IS RIGHT UP MY TAIL TO FIND THEM!
THIS IS **PRIORITY NUMBER ONE.**
ASSIGNMENTS!
OFFICERS GRIZZOLI, FANGMEYER, DELGATO -- YOUR TEAMS TAKE MISSING MAMMALS FROM THE RAINFOREST DISTRICT.

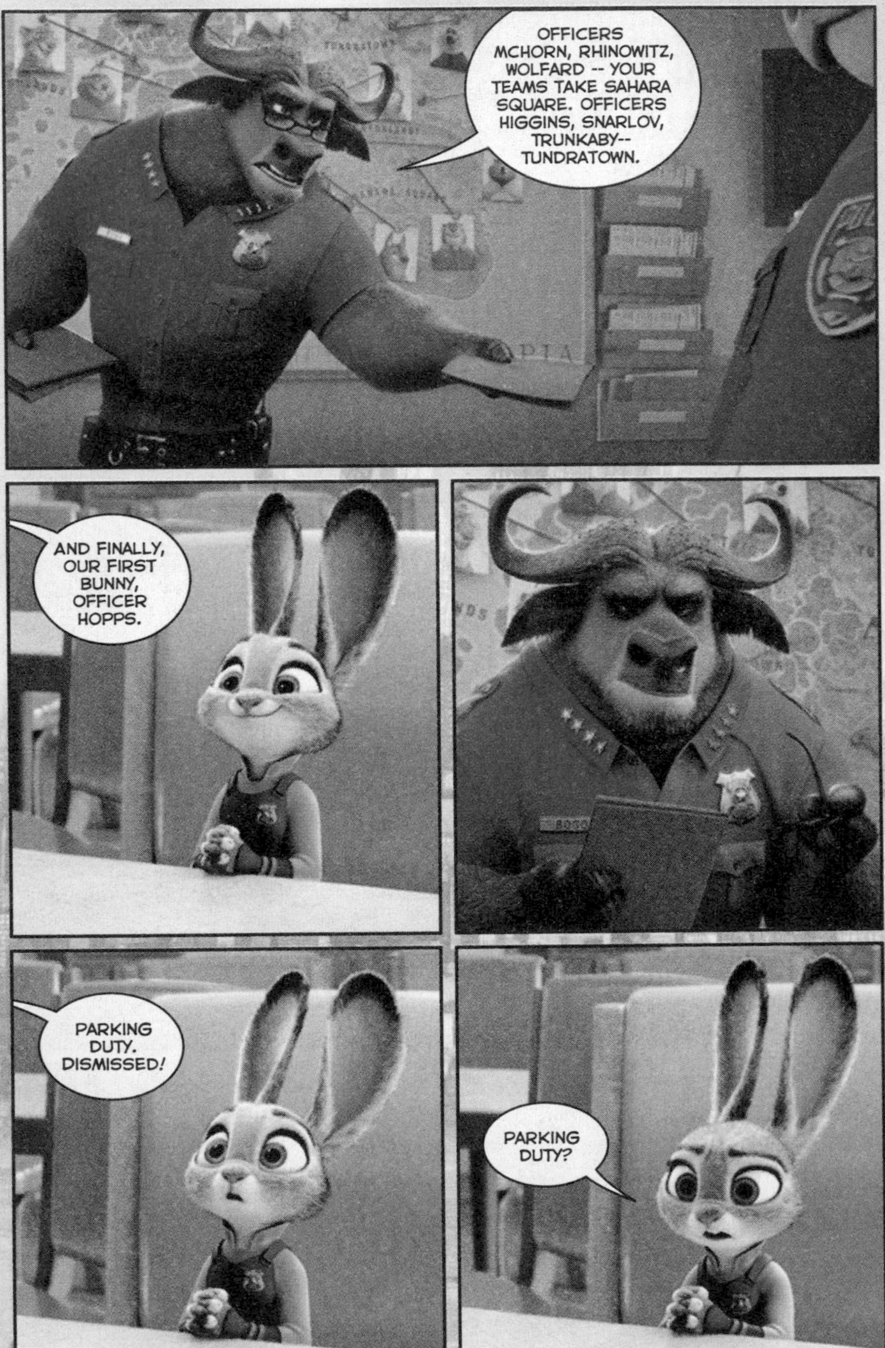
OFFICERS MCHORN, RHINOWITZ, WOLFARD -- YOUR TEAMS TAKE SAHARA SQUARE. OFFICERS HIGGINS, SNARLOV, TRUNKABY-- TUNDRATOWN.
AND FINALLY, OUR FIRST BUNNY, OFFICER HOPPS.
PARKING DUTY. DISMISSED!
PARKING DUTY?

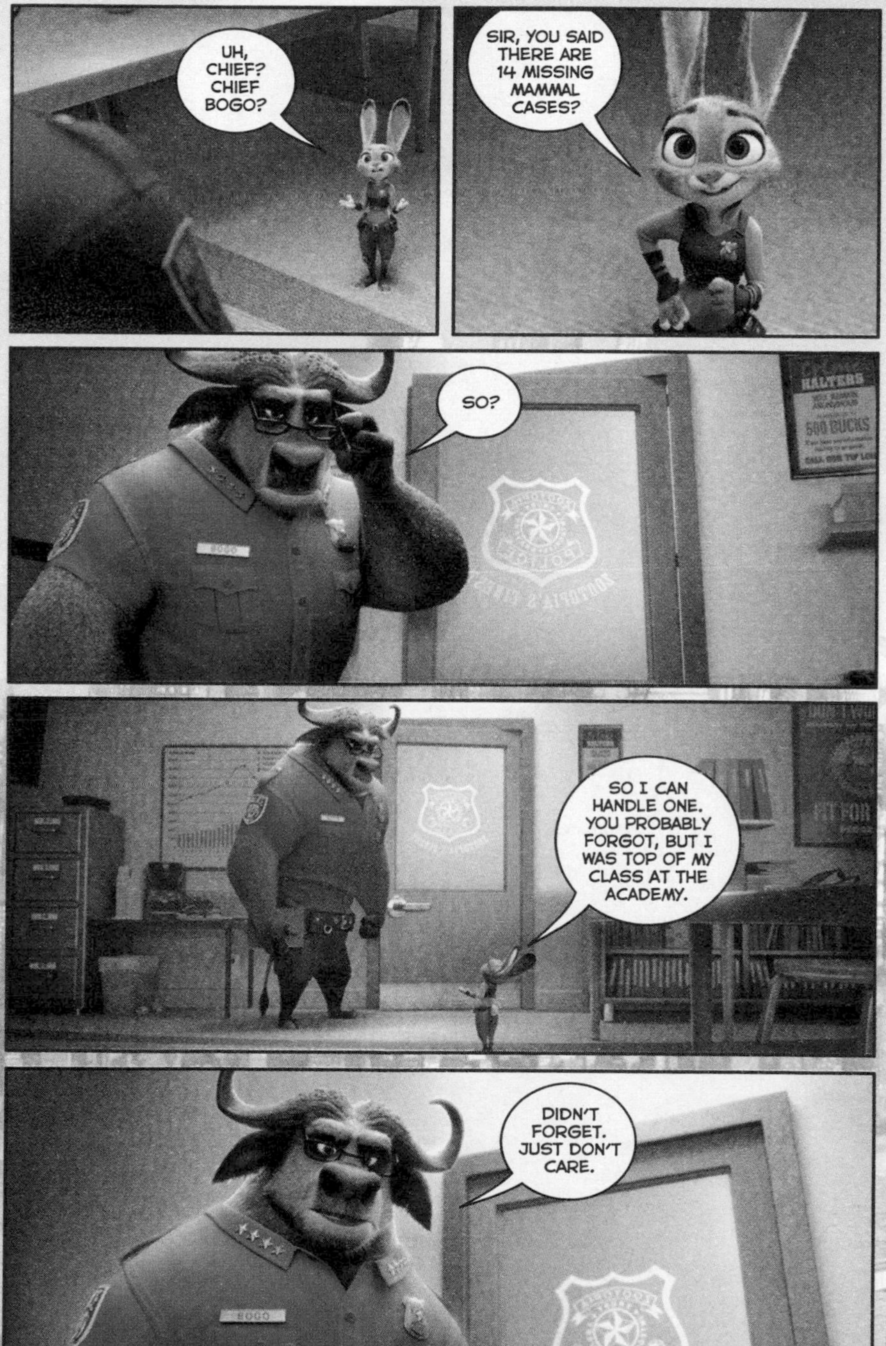
UH, CHIEF? CHIEF BOGO?
SIR, YOU SAID THERE ARE 14 MISSING MAMMAL CASES?
SO?
SO I CAN HANDLE ONE. YOU PROBABLY FORGOT, BUT I WAS TOP OF MY CLASS AT THE ACADEMY.
DIDN'T FORGET. JUST DON'T CARE.

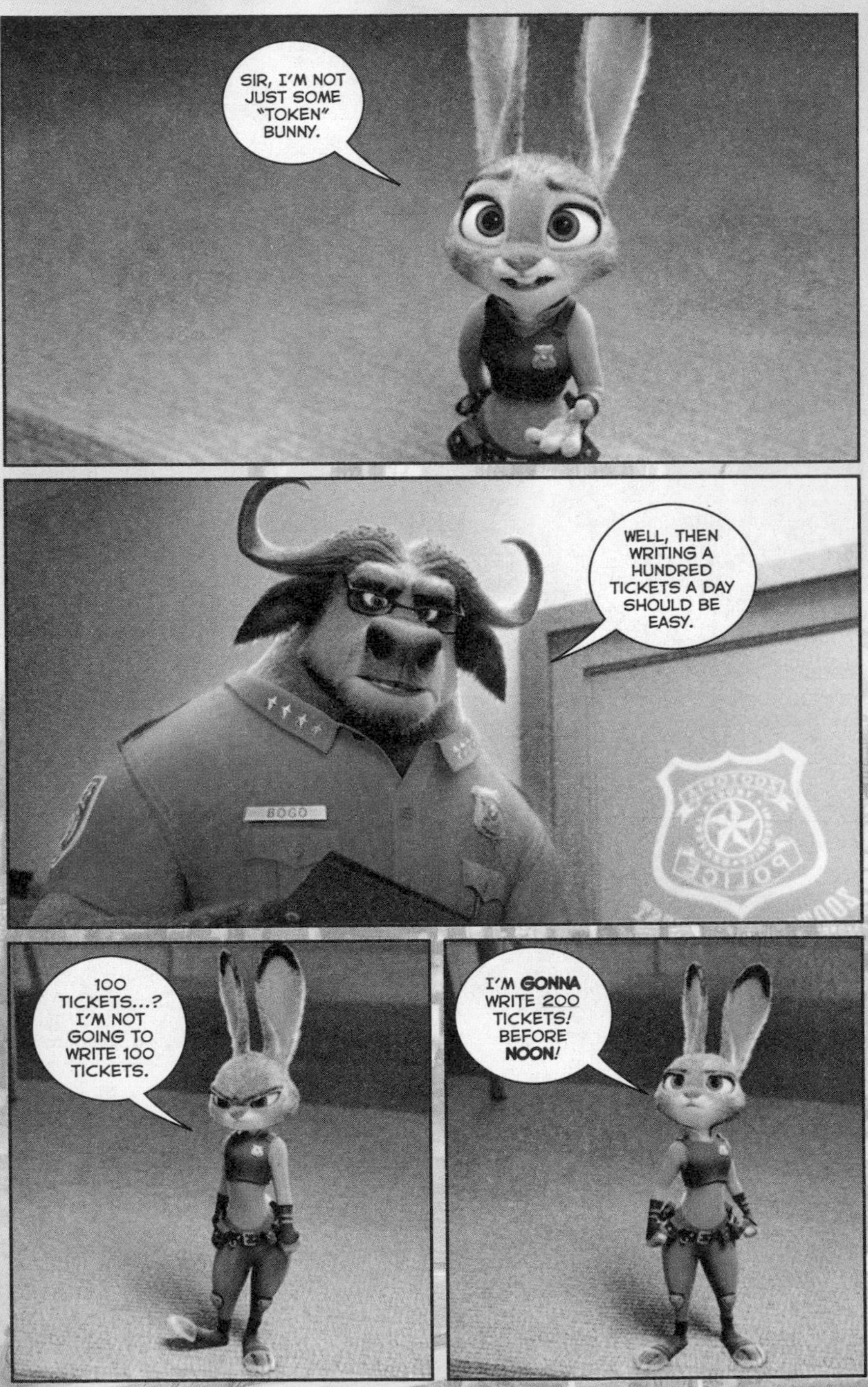
SIR, I'M NOT JUST SOME "TOKEN" BUNNY.
WELL, THEN WRITING A HUNDRED TICKETS A DAY SHOULD BE EASY.
BOGO
POLICE
100 TICKETS...? I'M NOT GOING TO WRITE 100 TICKETS.
I'M **GONNA** WRITE 200 TICKETS! BEFORE **NOON**!

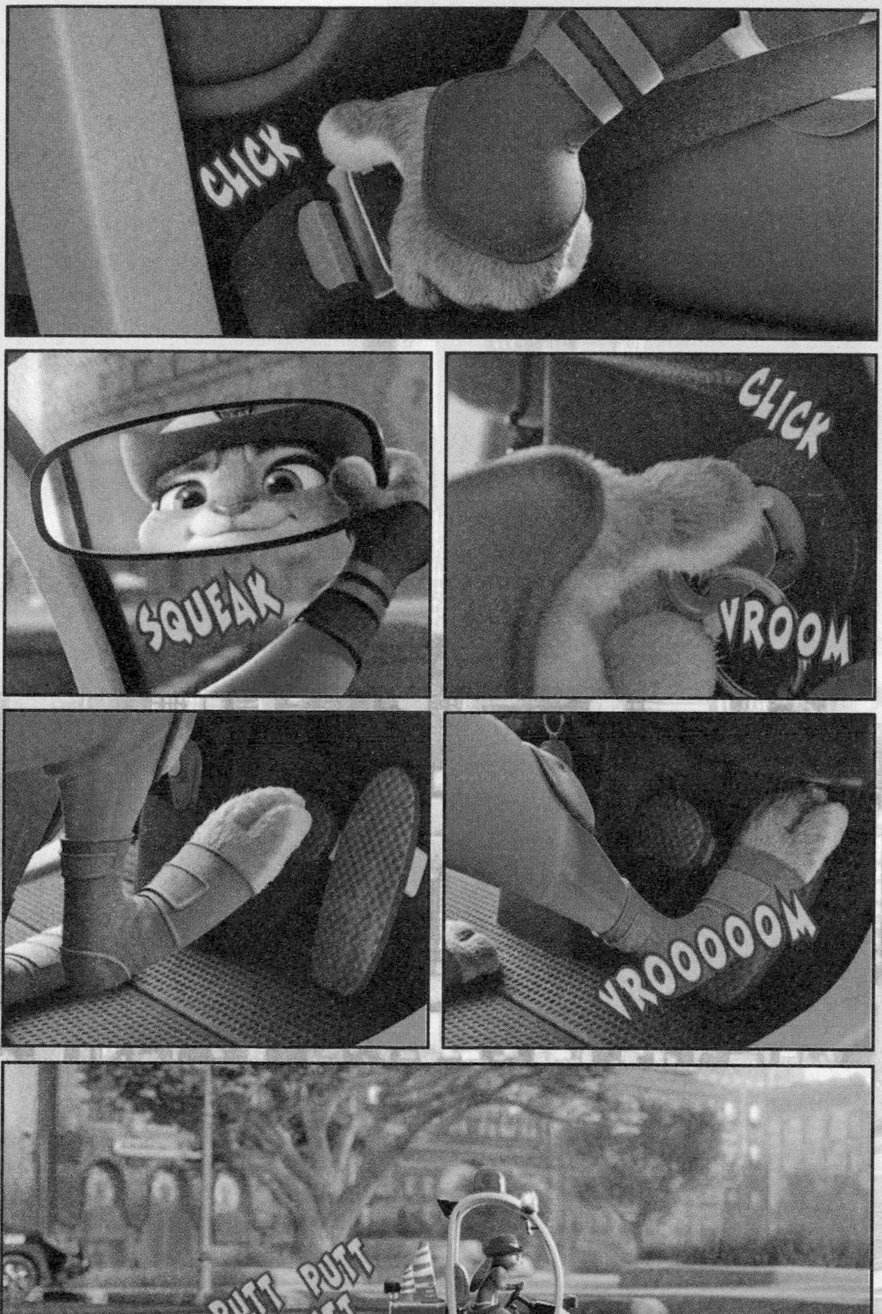
CLICK
SQUEAK
CLICK
VROOM
VROOOOOM
PUTT PUTT
PUTT PUTT

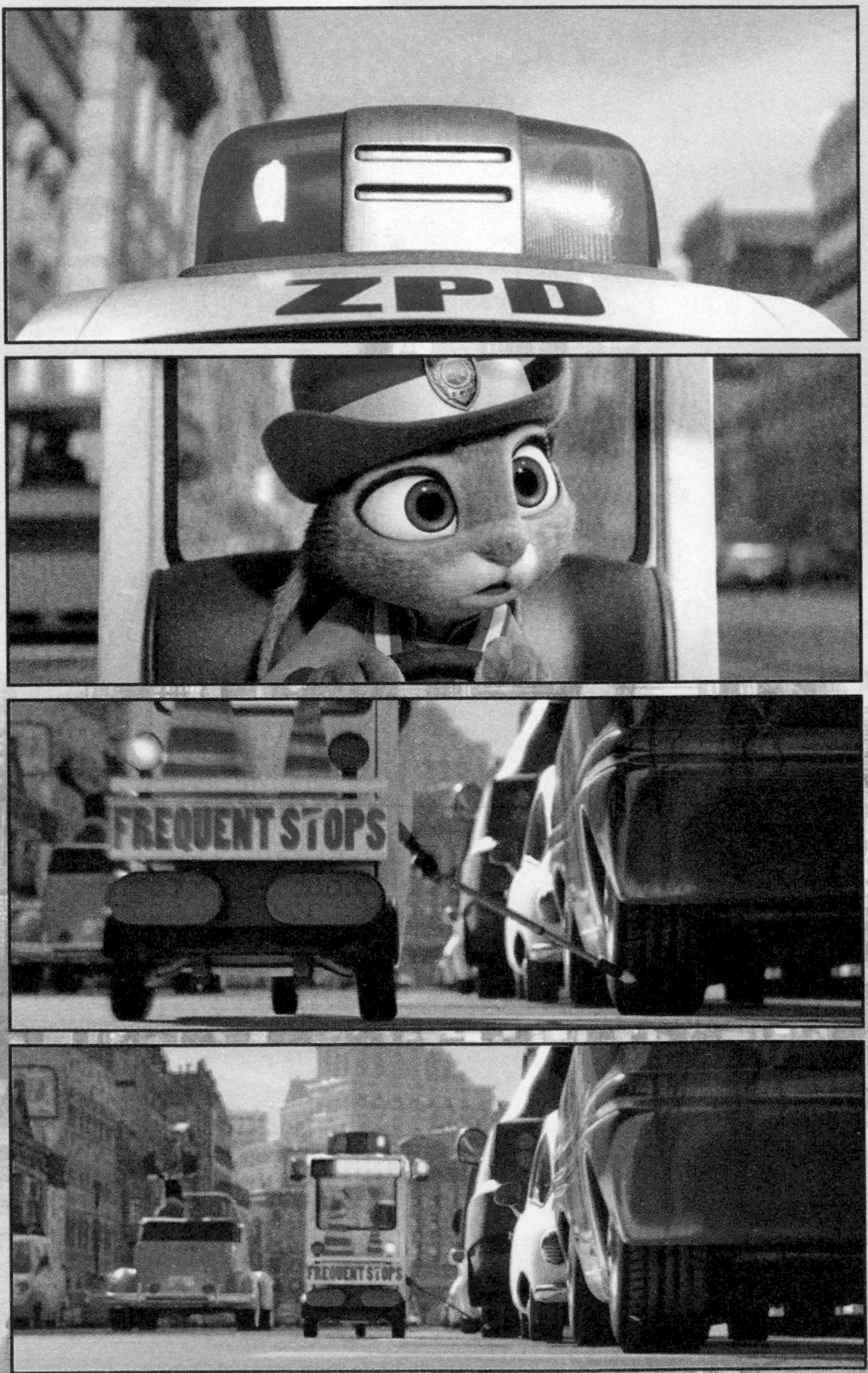
ZPD
FREQUENT STOPS
FREQUENT STOPS

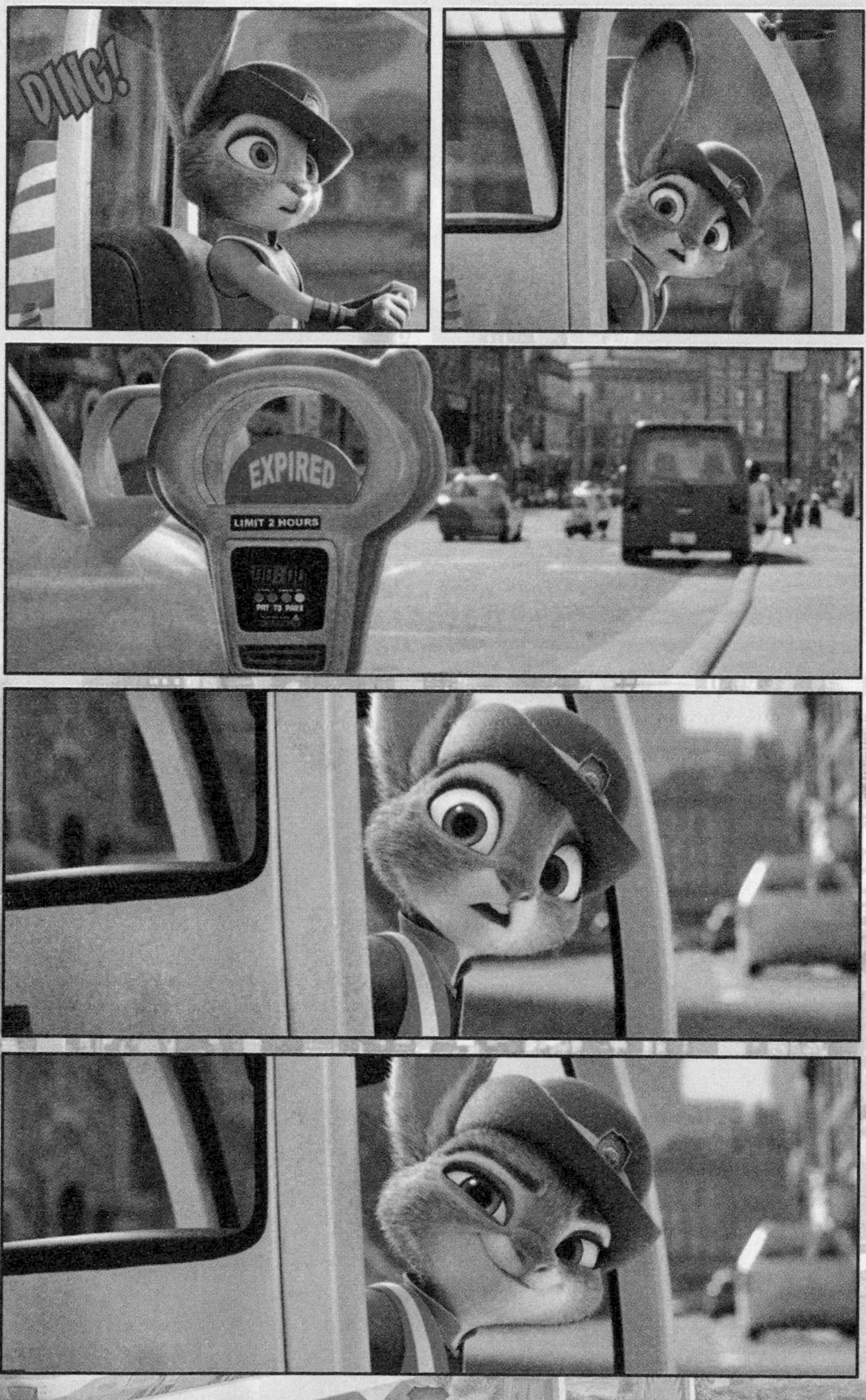
DING!
EXPIRED
LIMIT 2 HOURS
PAY TO PARK

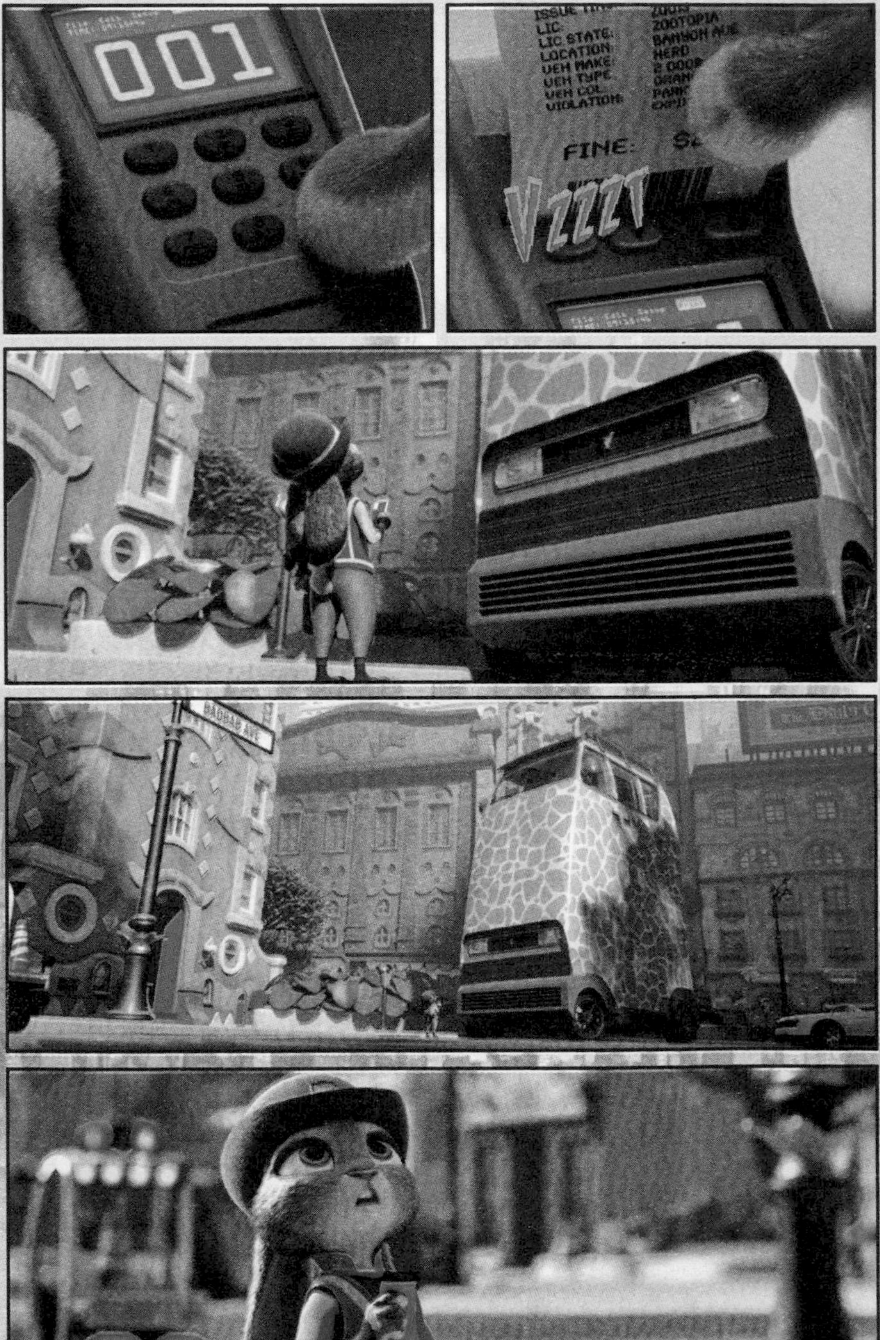
001
ISSUE
LIC:
LIC STATE:
LOCATION:
VEH MAKE:
VEH TYPE:
VEH COL:
VIOLATION:
ZOOTOPIA
HERD
FINE:
VZZZT
BAOBAB AVE

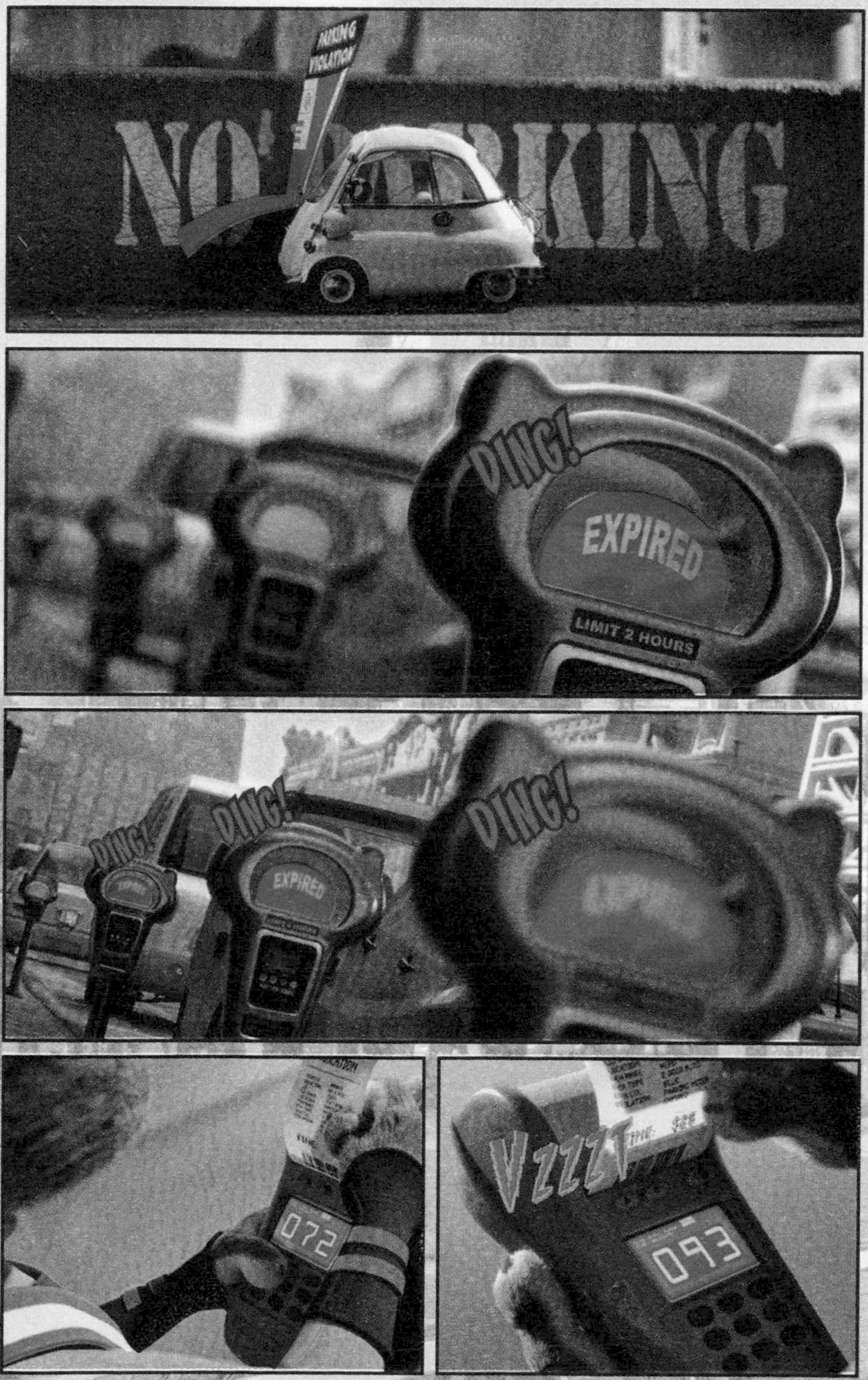
PARKING VIOLATION
DING!
EXPIRED
LIMIT 2 HOURS
DING!
DING!
DING!
EXPIRED
EXPIRED
072
VZZZT
TIME:
093

DING!

EXPIRED

EXPIRED

EXPIRED SNOUTFITTERS EXPIRED

200

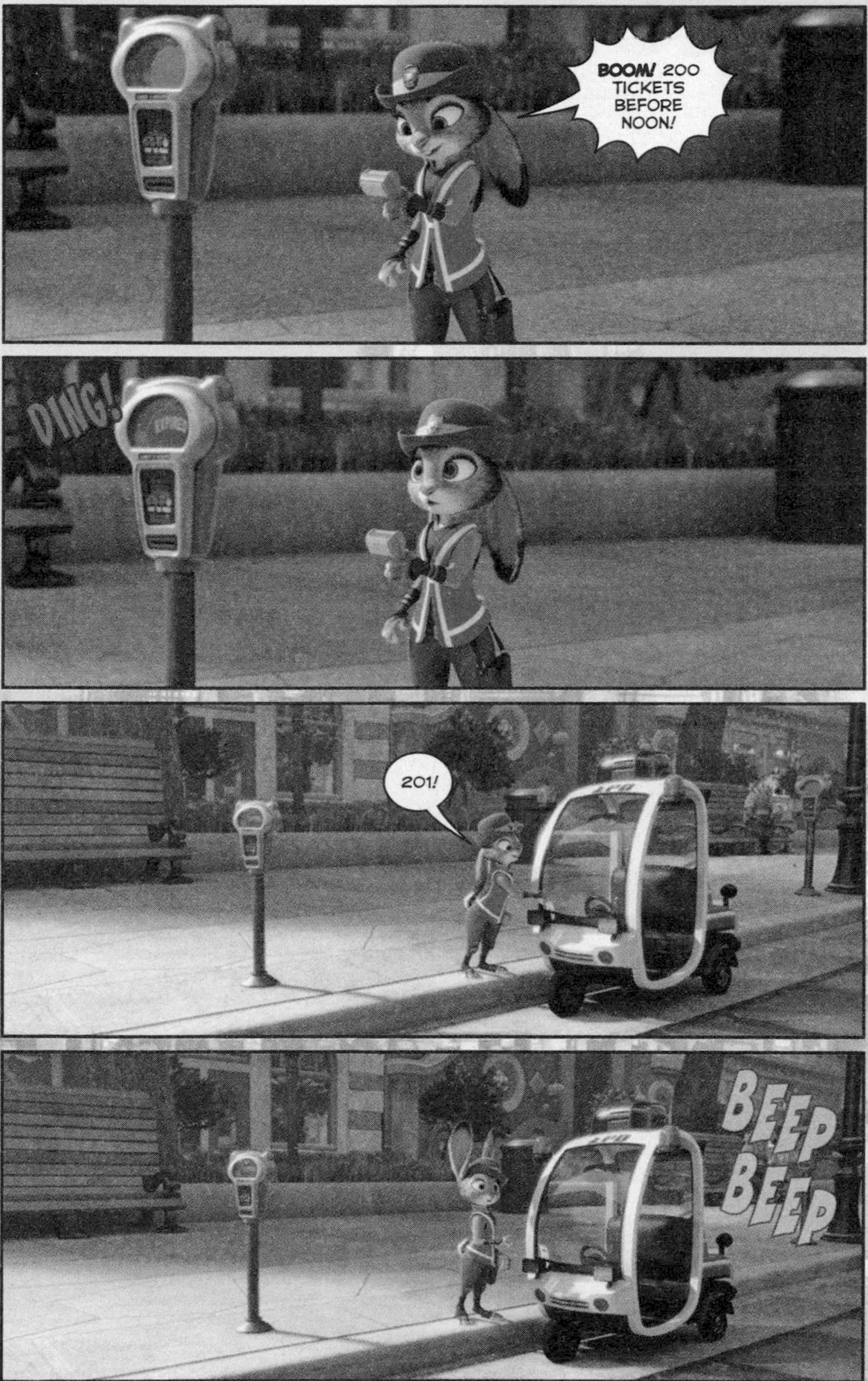
BOOM! 200 TICKETS BEFORE NOON!
DING!
201!
BEEP BEEP

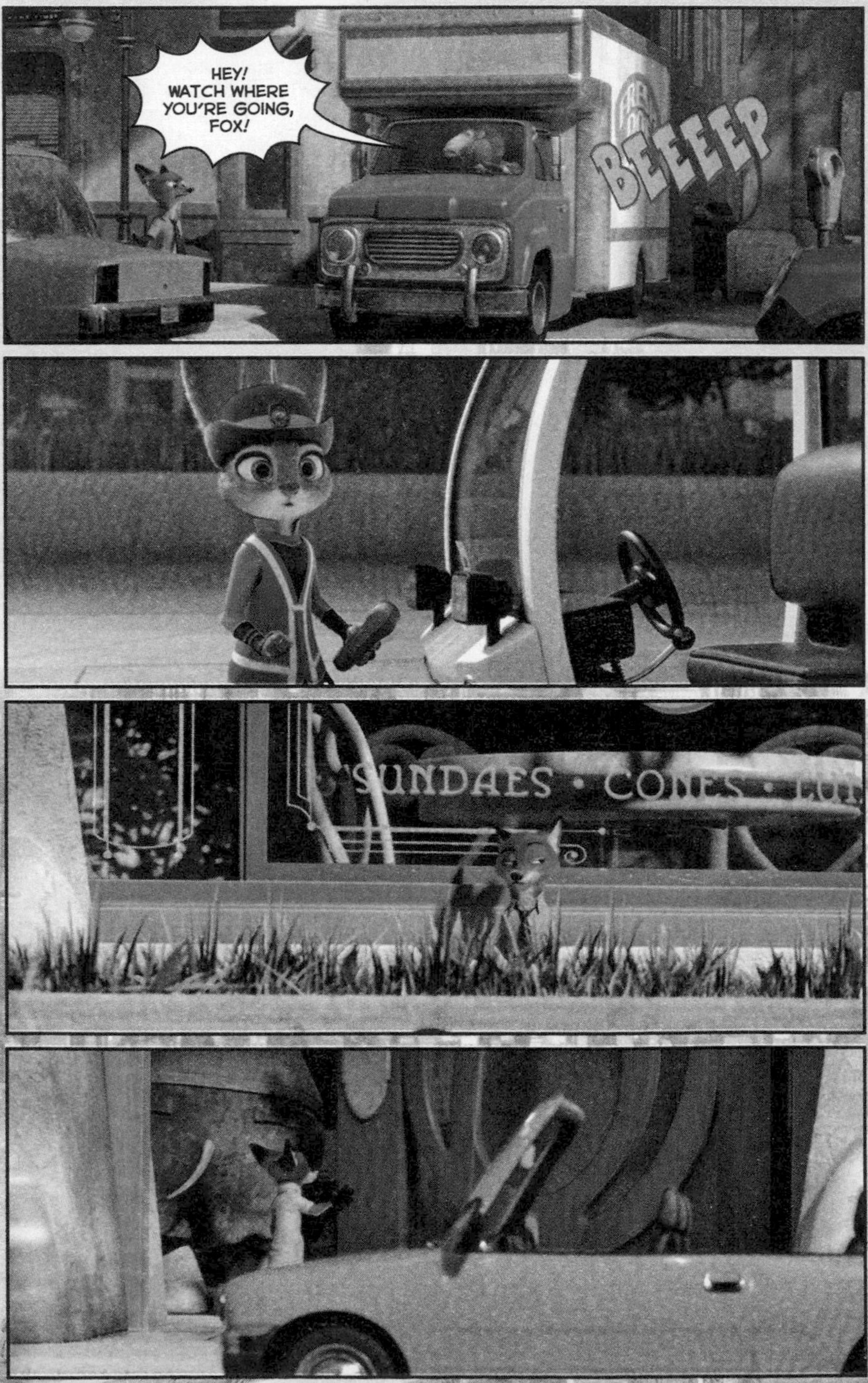
HEY! WATCH WHERE YOU'RE GOING, FOX!
BEEEEP
SUNDAES • CONES •

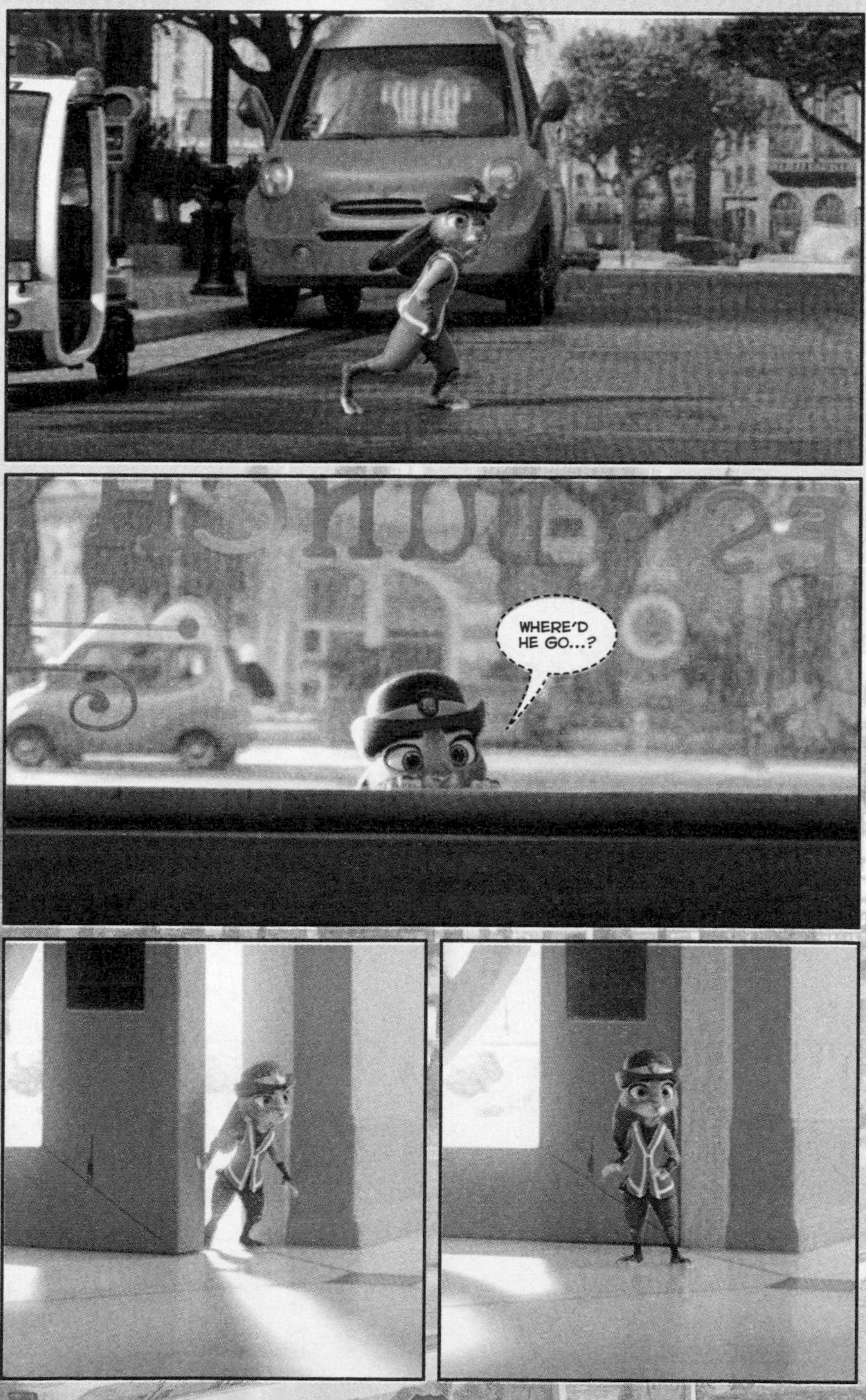
WHERE'D HE GO...?

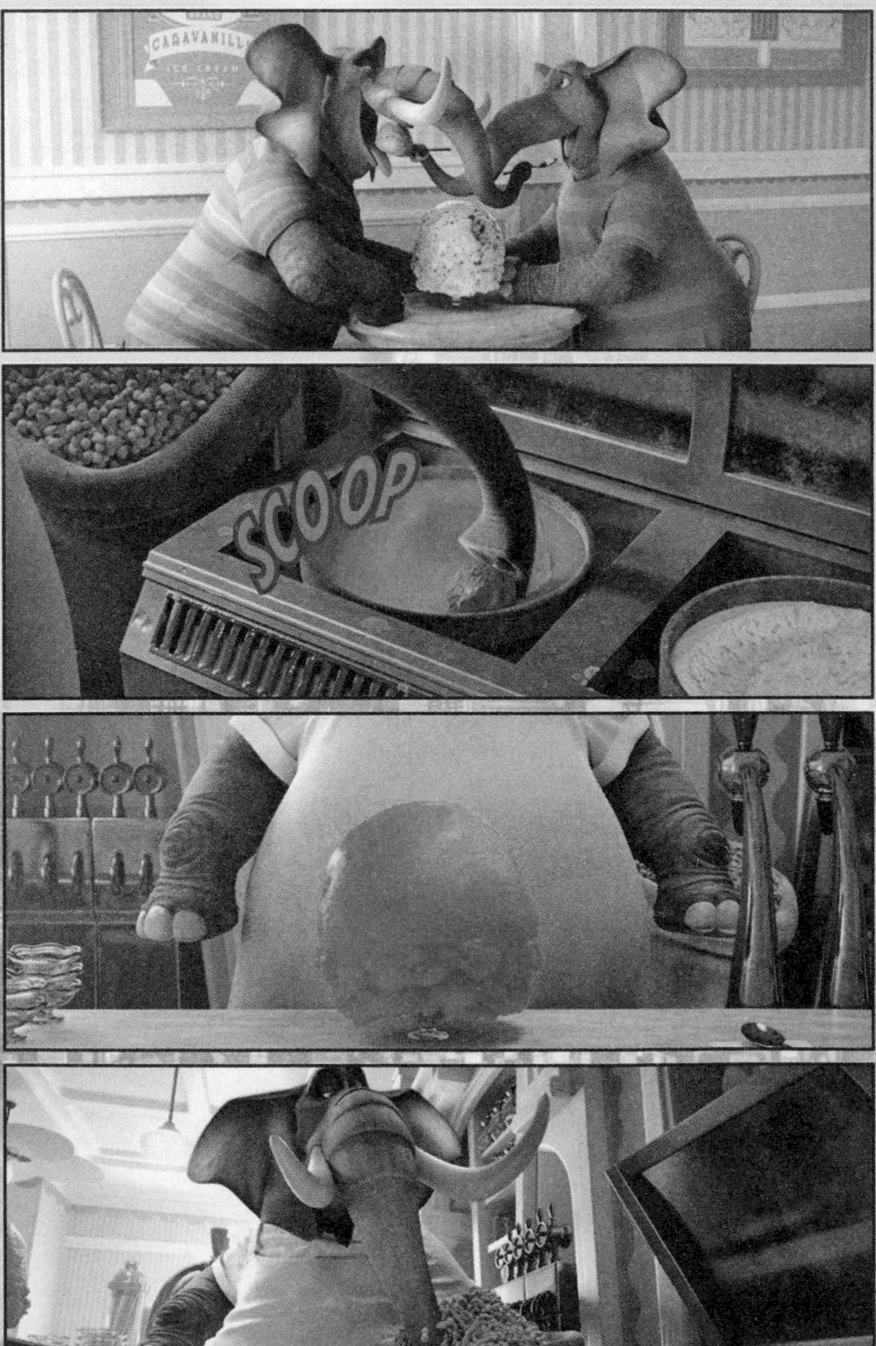
SCOOP

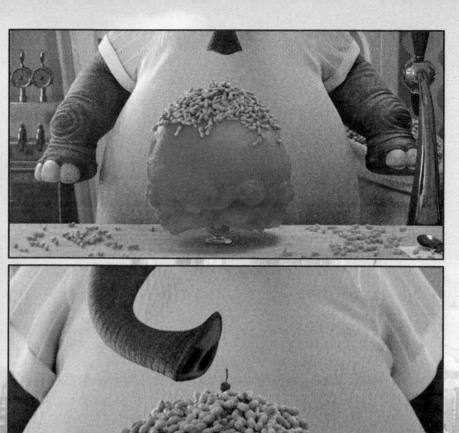

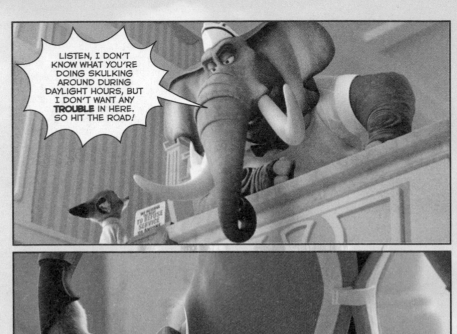

LISTEN, I DON'T KNOW WHAT YOU'RE DOING SKULKING AROUND DURING DAYLIGHT HOURS, BUT I DON'T WANT ANY **TROUBLE** IN HERE. SO HIT THE ROAD!

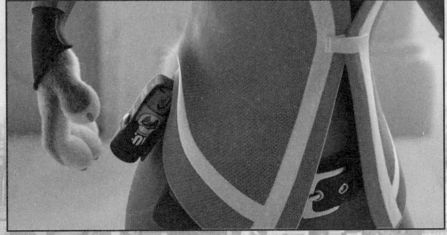

SNAP

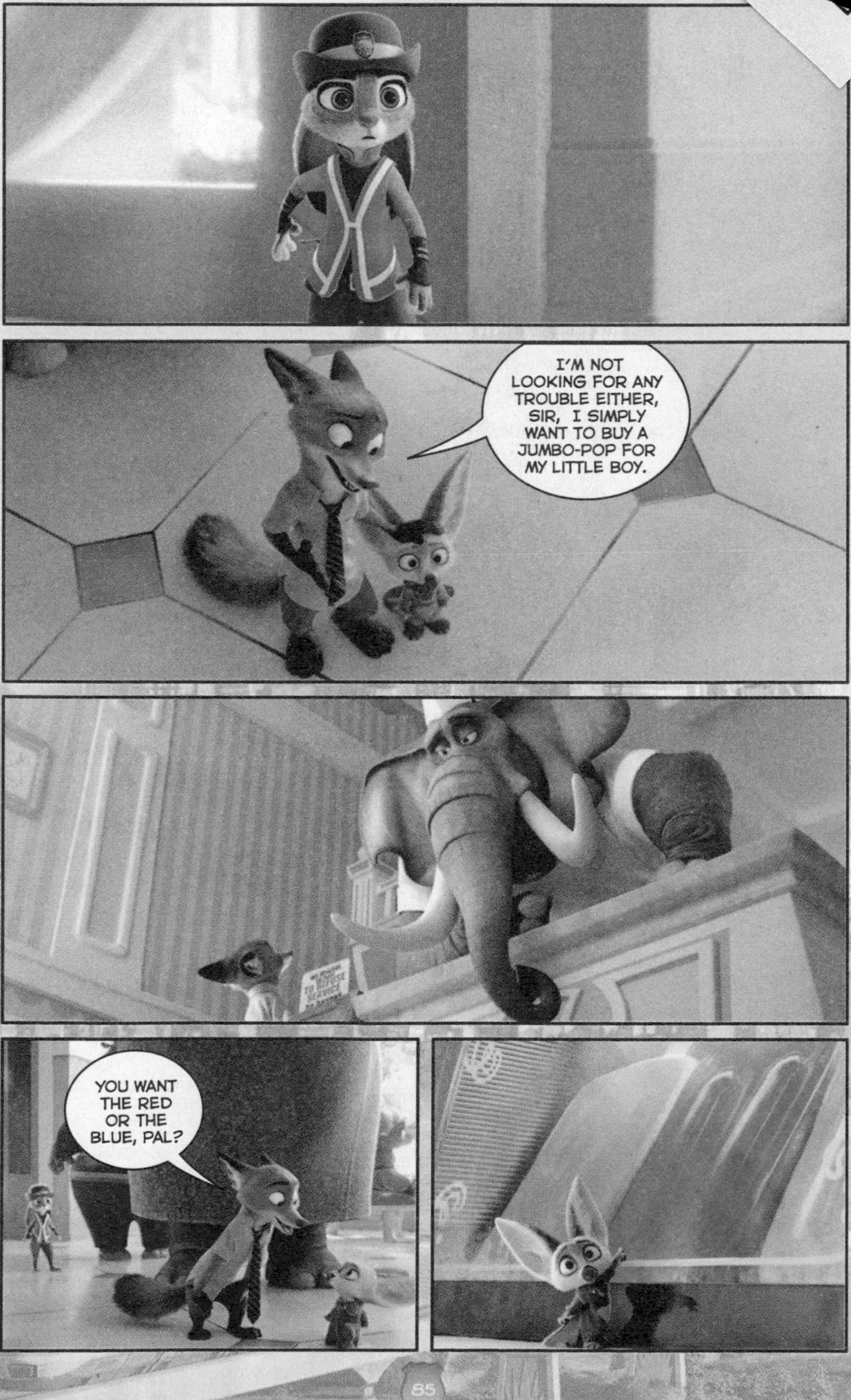
I'M NOT LOOKING FOR ANY TROUBLE EITHER, SIR, I SIMPLY WANT TO BUY A JUMBO-POP FOR MY LITTLE BOY.
YOU WANT THE RED OR THE BLUE, PAL?

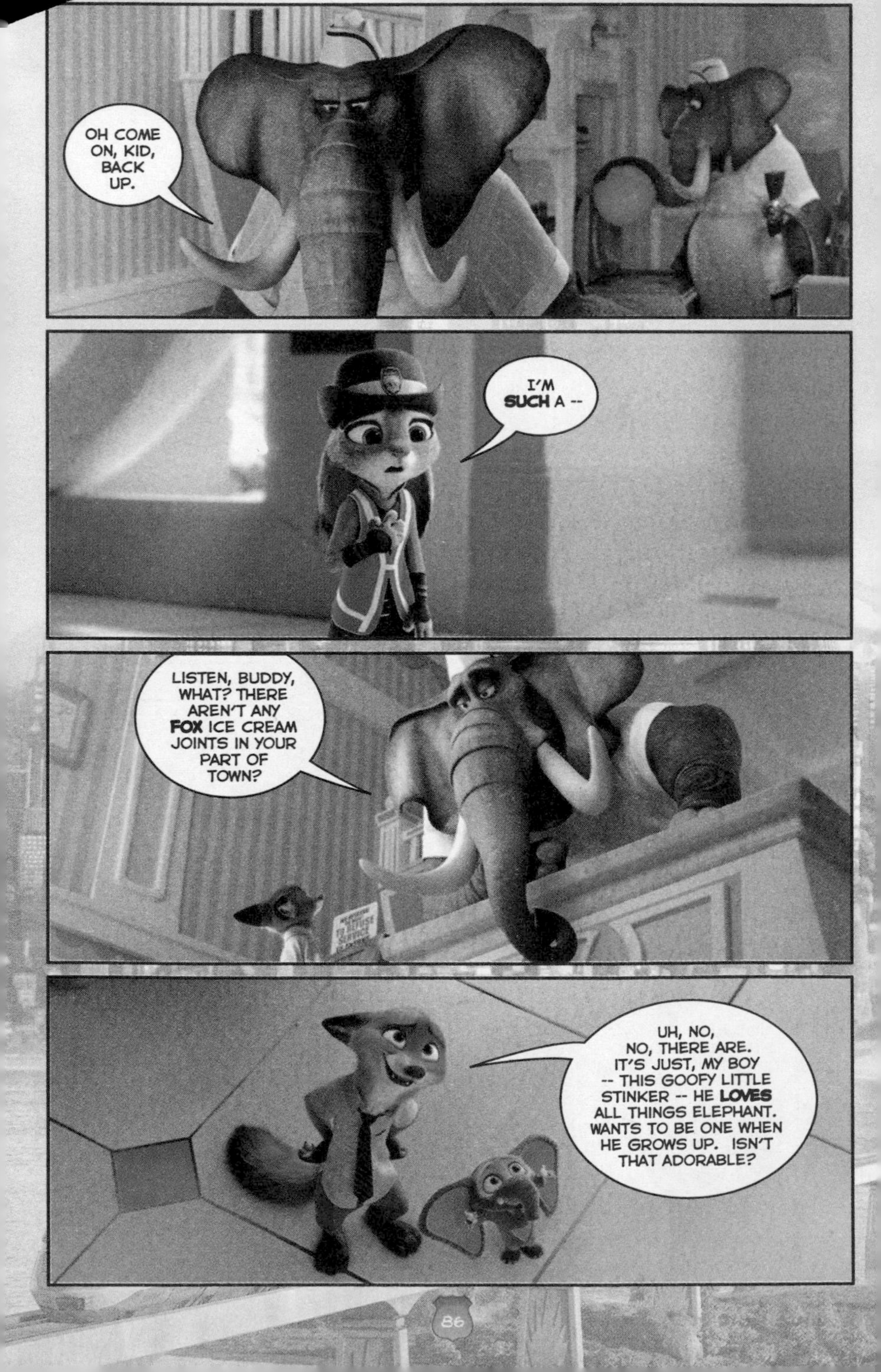
OH COME ON, KID, BACK UP.
I'M SUCH A --
LISTEN, BUDDY, WHAT? THERE AREN'T ANY FOX ICE CREAM JOINTS IN YOUR PART OF TOWN?
UH, NO, NO, THERE ARE. IT'S JUST, MY BOY -- THIS GOOFY LITTLE STINKER -- HE LOVES ALL THINGS ELEPHANT. WANTS TO BE ONE WHEN HE GROWS UP. ISN'T THAT ADORABLE?

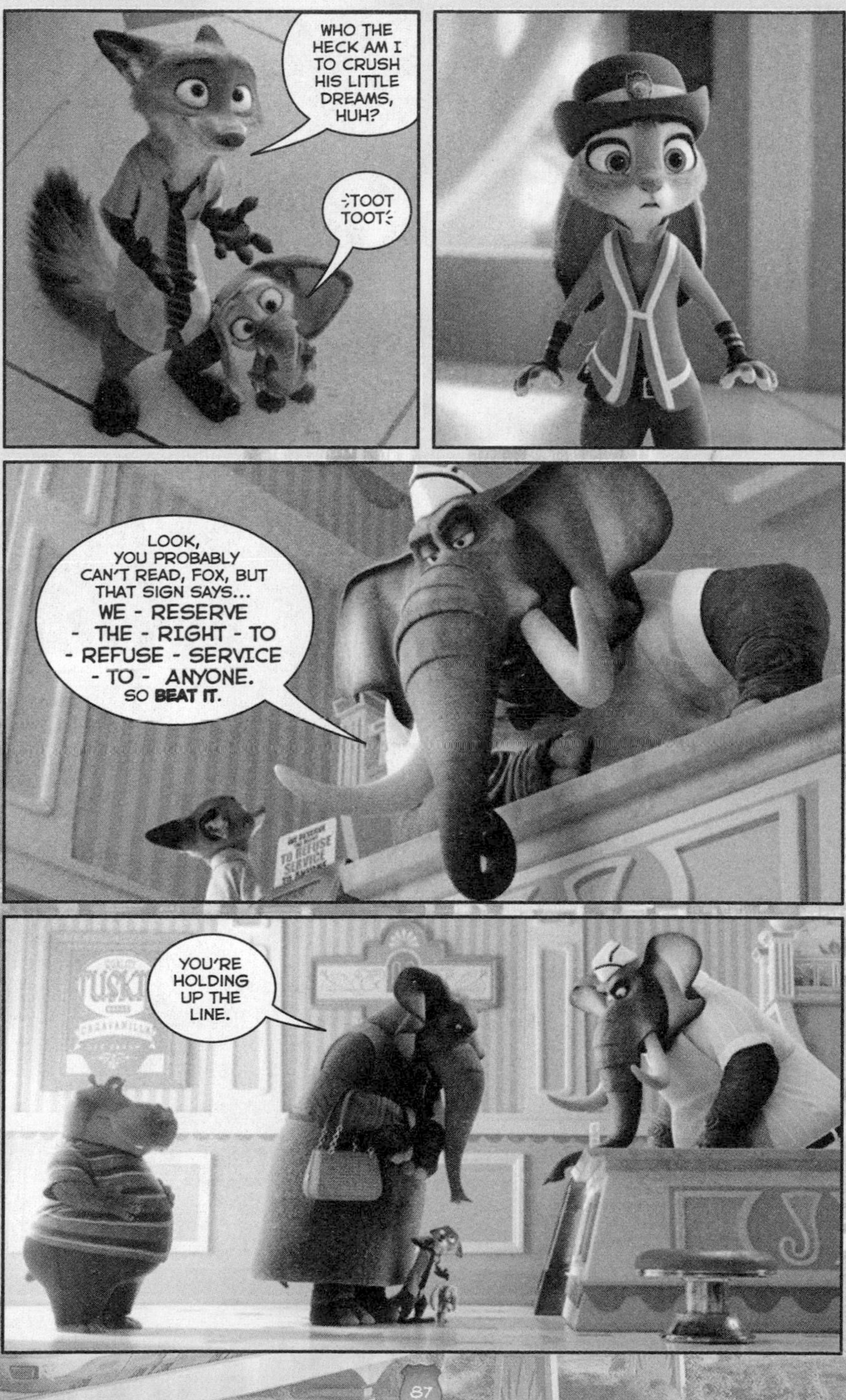
WHO THE HECK AM I TO CRUSH HIS LITTLE DREAMS, HUH?
TOOT TOOT
LOOK, YOU PROBABLY CAN'T READ, FOX, BUT THAT SIGN SAYS... WE - RESERVE - THE - RIGHT - TO - REFUSE - SERVICE - TO - ANYONE. SO BEAT IT.
YOU'RE HOLDING UP THE LINE.

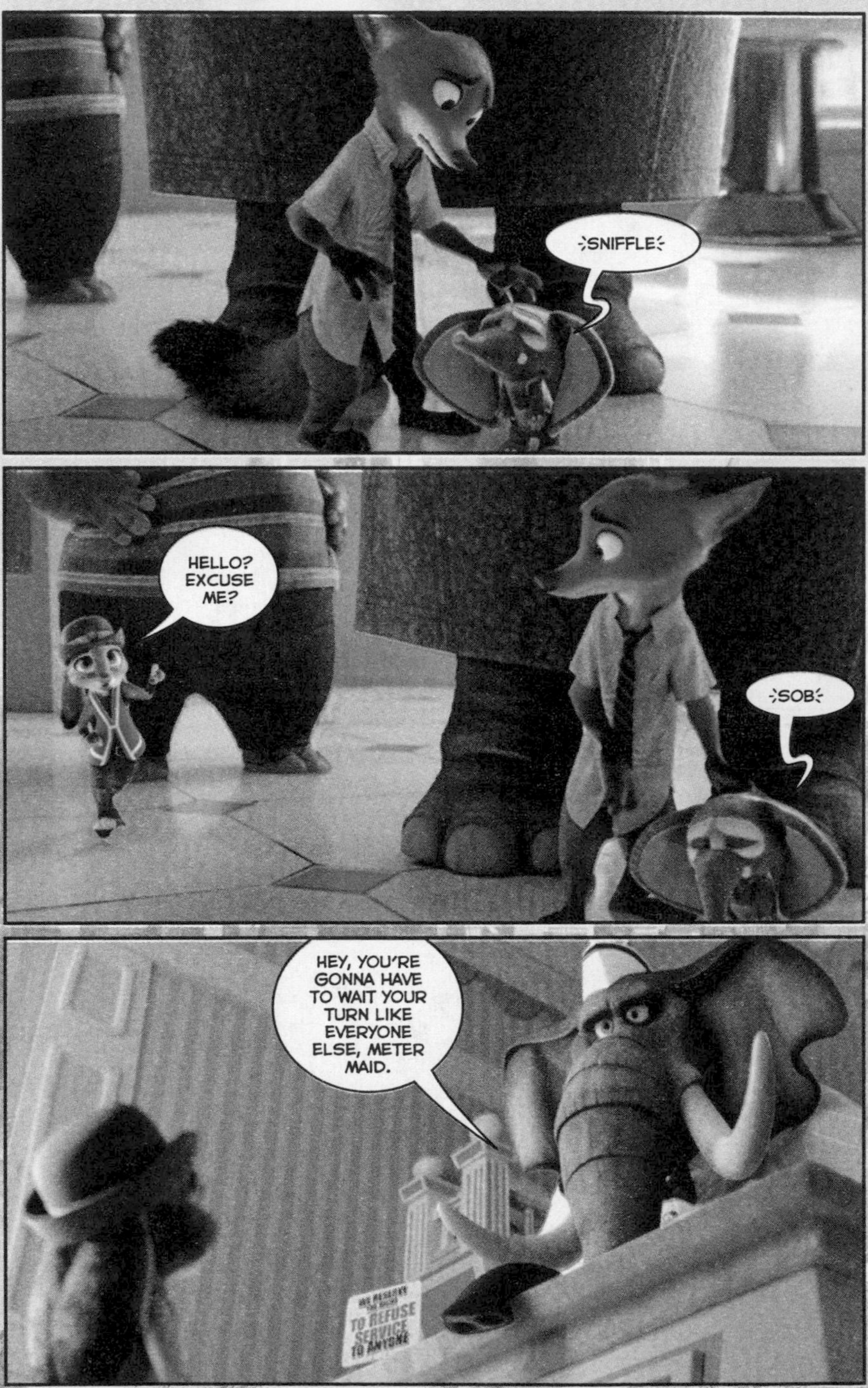

SNIFFLE
HELLO? EXCUSE ME?
SOB
HEY, YOU'RE GONNA HAVE TO WAIT YOUR TURN LIKE EVERYONE ELSE, METER MAID.
TO REFUSE SERVICE TO ANYONE

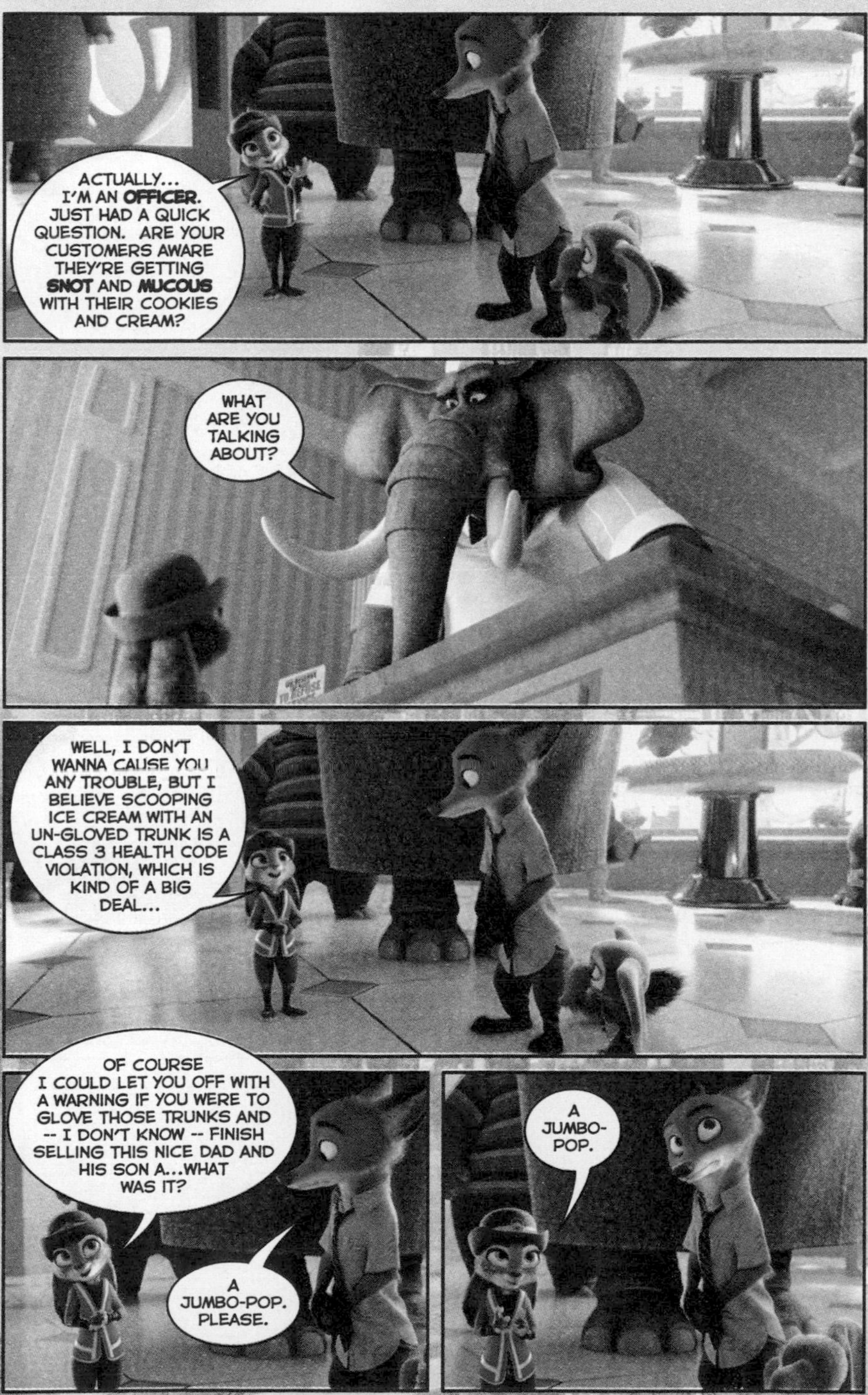
ACTUALLY...
I'M AN OFFICER. JUST HAD A QUICK QUESTION. ARE YOUR CUSTOMERS AWARE THEY'RE GETTING SNOT AND MUCOUS WITH THEIR COOKIES AND CREAM?
WHAT ARE YOU TALKING ABOUT?
WELL, I DON'T WANNA CAUSE YOU ANY TROUBLE, BUT I BELIEVE SCOOPING ICE CREAM WITH AN UN-GLOVED TRUNK IS A CLASS 3 HEALTH CODE VIOLATION, WHICH IS KIND OF A BIG DEAL...
OF COURSE I COULD LET YOU OFF WITH A WARNING IF YOU WERE TO GLOVE THOSE TRUNKS AND -- I DON'T KNOW -- FINISH SELLING THIS NICE DAD AND HIS SON A...WHAT WAS IT?
A JUMBO-POP. PLEASE.
A JUMBO-POP.

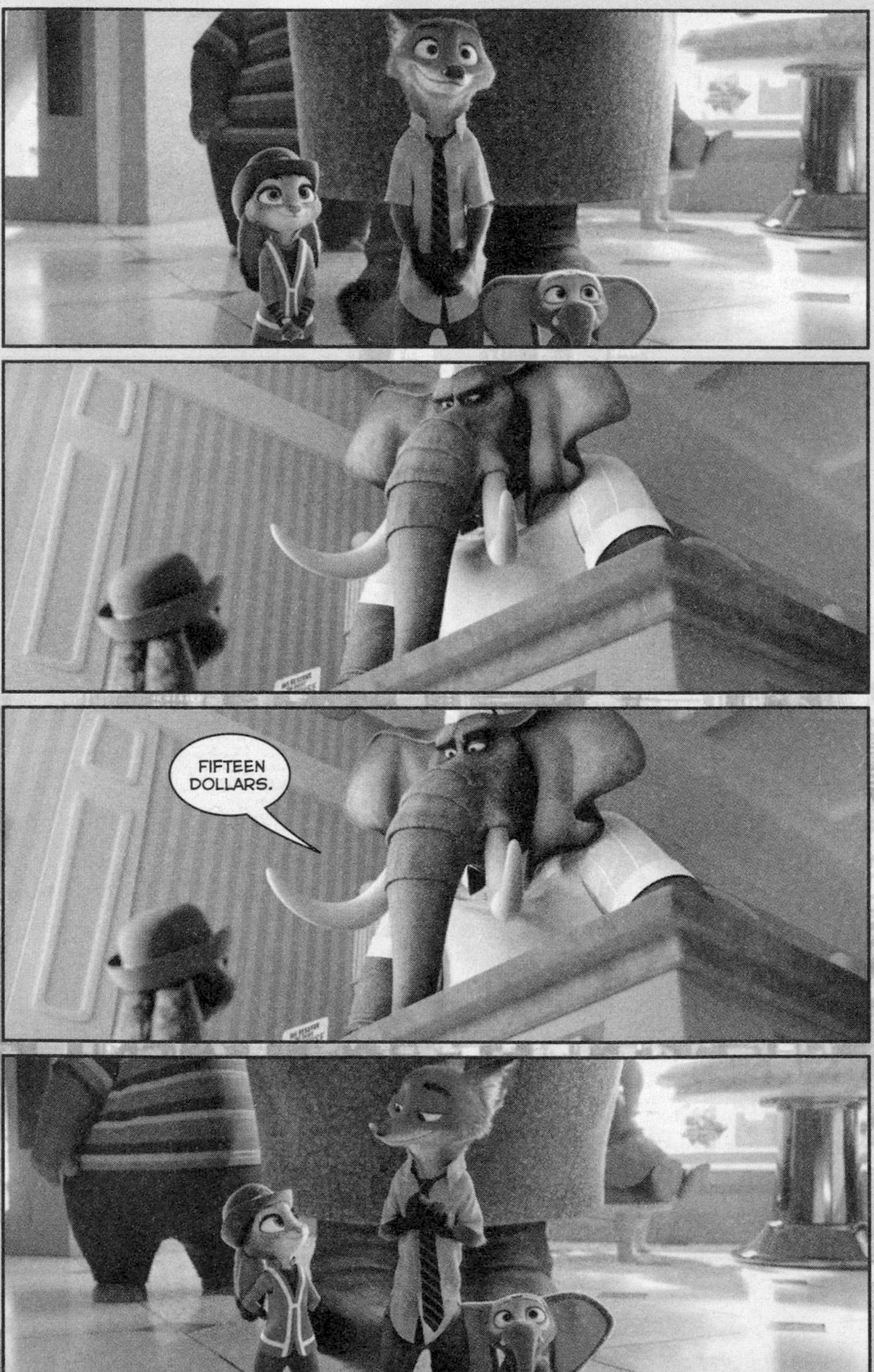
FIFTEEN DOLLARS.

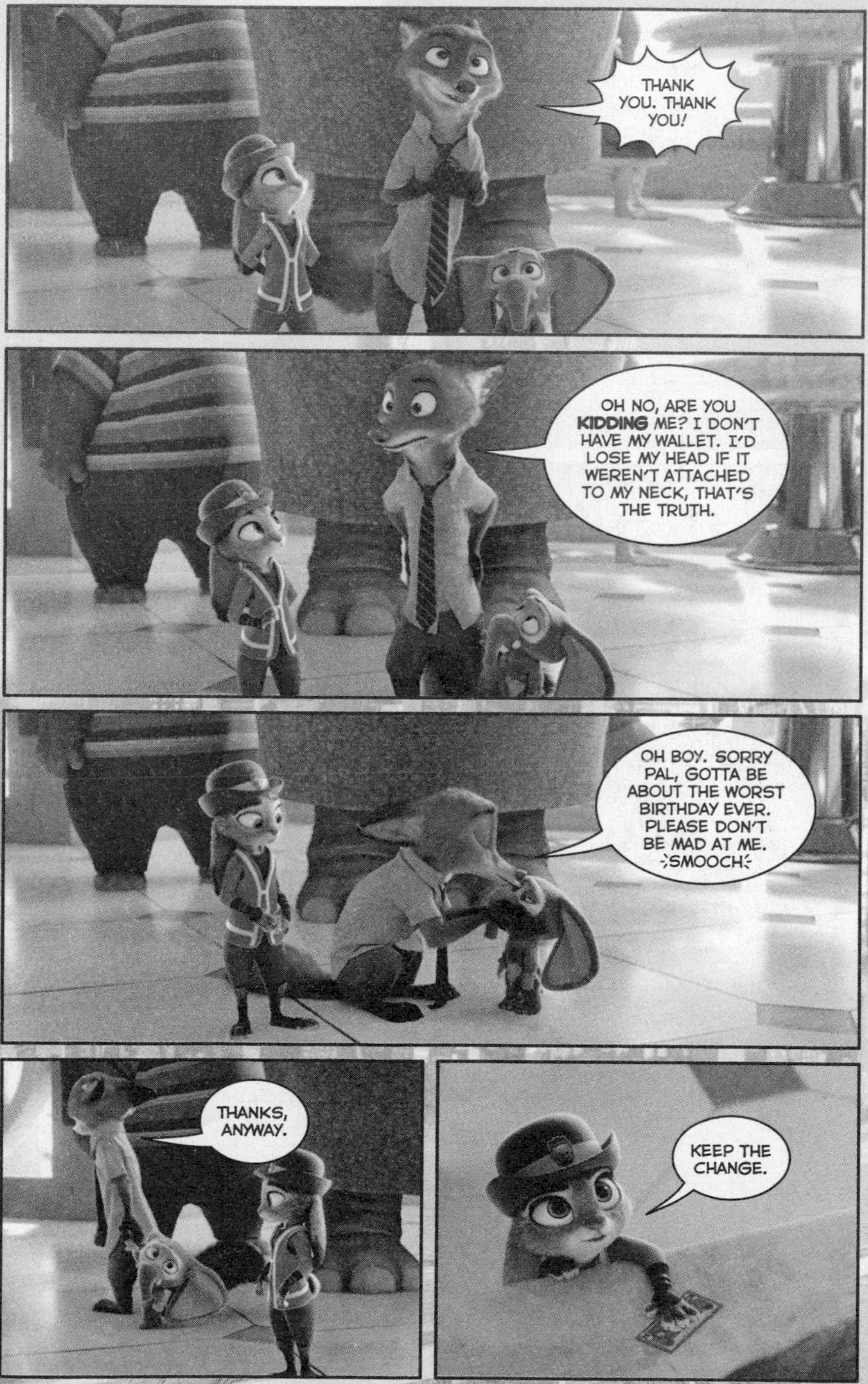
THANK YOU. THANK YOU!
OH NO, ARE YOU KIDDING ME? I DON'T HAVE MY WALLET. I'D LOSE MY HEAD IF IT WEREN'T ATTACHED TO MY NECK, THAT'S THE TRUTH.
OH BOY. SORRY PAL, GOTTA BE ABOUT THE WORST BIRTHDAY EVER. PLEASE DON'T BE MAD AT ME. SMOOCH
THANKS, ANYWAY.
KEEP THE CHANGE.

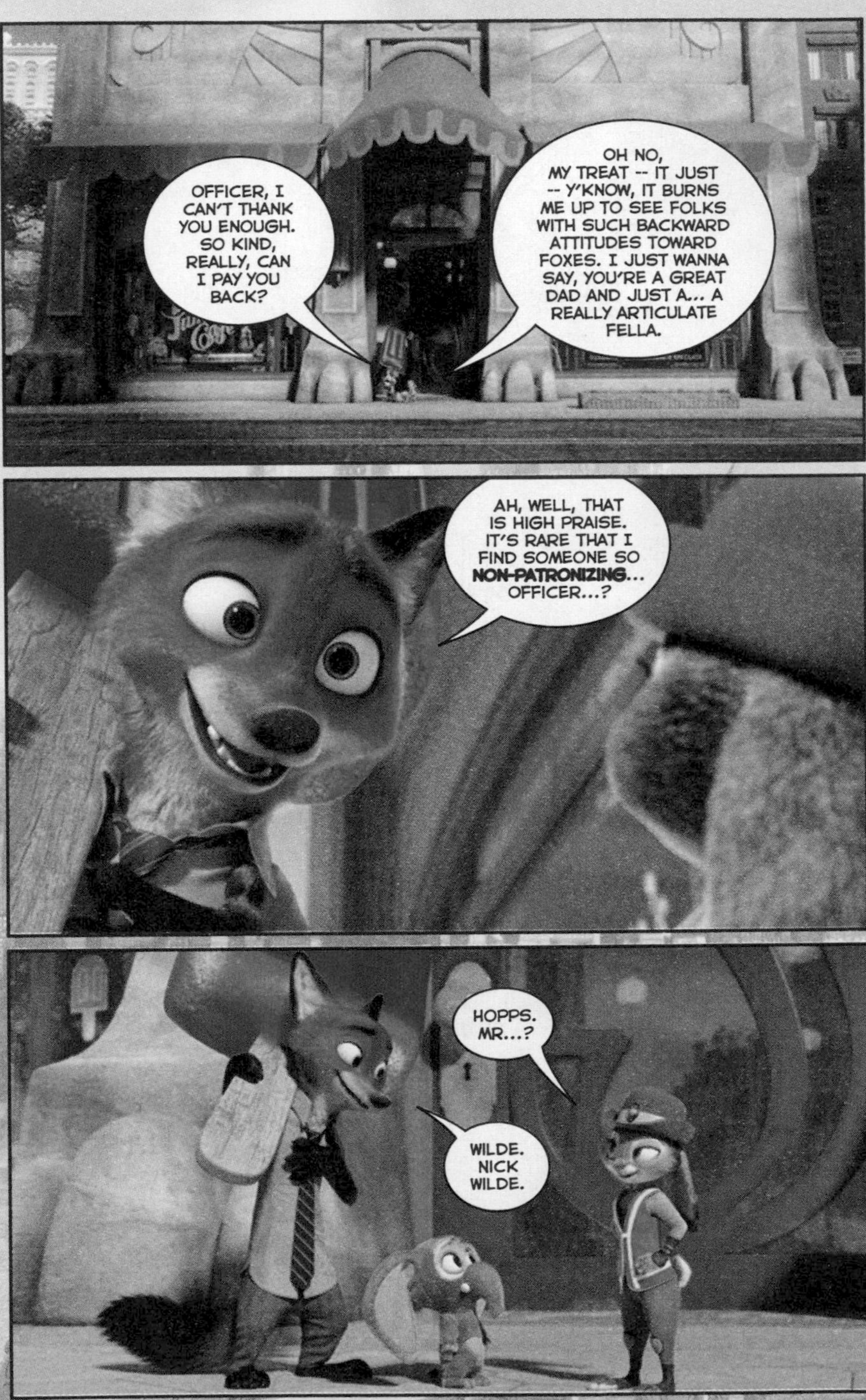
OFFICER, I CAN'T THANK YOU ENOUGH. SO KIND, REALLY, CAN I PAY YOU BACK?
OH NO, MY TREAT -- IT JUST -- Y'KNOW, IT BURNS ME UP TO SEE FOLKS WITH SUCH BACKWARD ATTITUDES TOWARD FOXES. I JUST WANNA SAY, YOU'RE A GREAT DAD AND JUST A... A REALLY ARTICULATE FELLA.
AH, WELL, THAT IS HIGH PRAISE. IT'S RARE THAT I FIND SOMEONE SO **NON-PATRONIZING**... OFFICER...?
HOPPS. MR...?
WILDE. NICK WILDE.

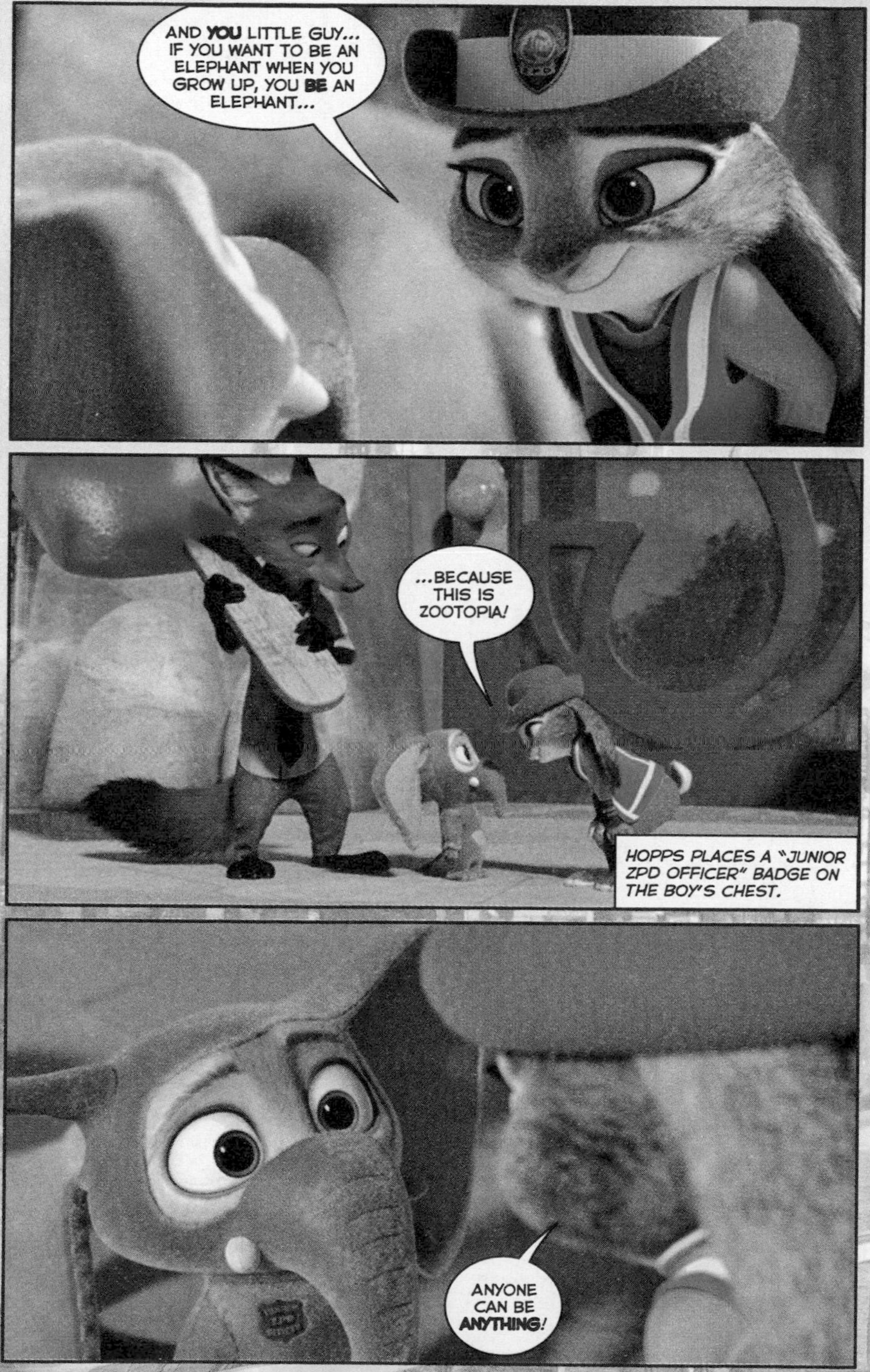
AND YOU LITTLE GUY... IF YOU WANT TO BE AN ELEPHANT WHEN YOU GROW UP, YOU BE AN ELEPHANT...
...BECAUSE THIS IS ZOOTOPIA!
HOPPS PLACES A "JUNIOR ZPD OFFICER" BADGE ON THE BOY'S CHEST.
ANYONE CAN BE ANYTHING!

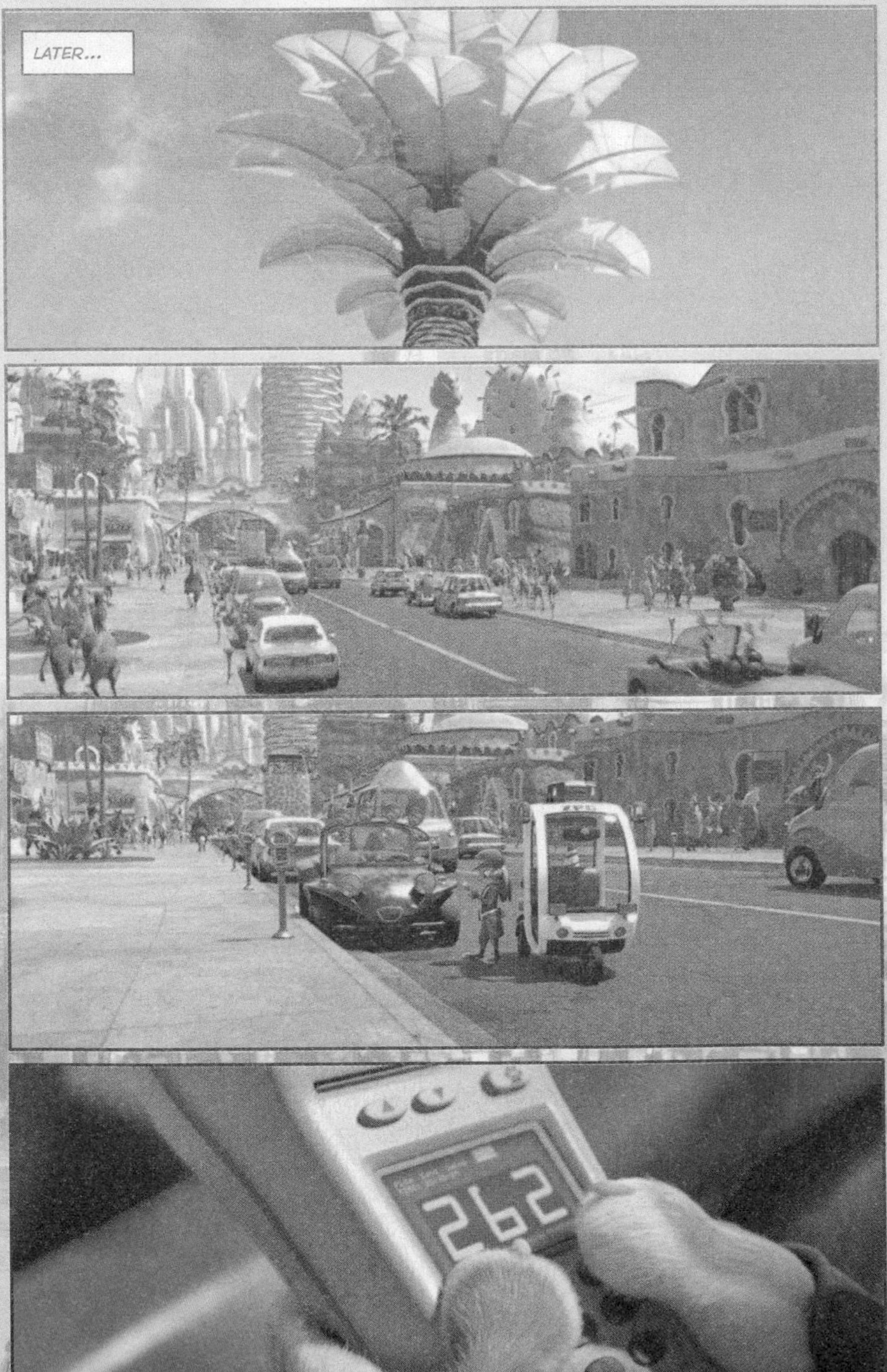
LATER...
262

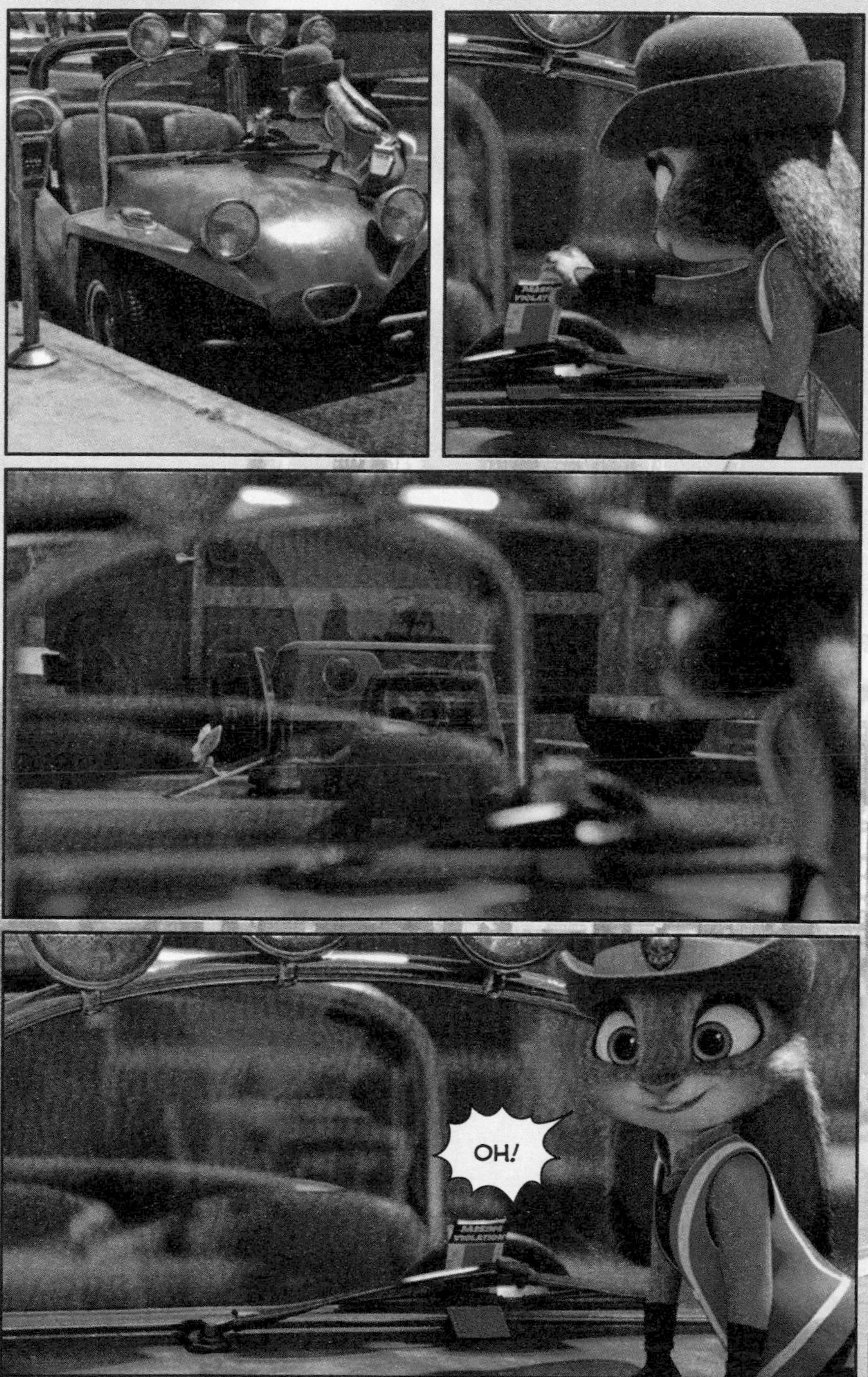
OH!

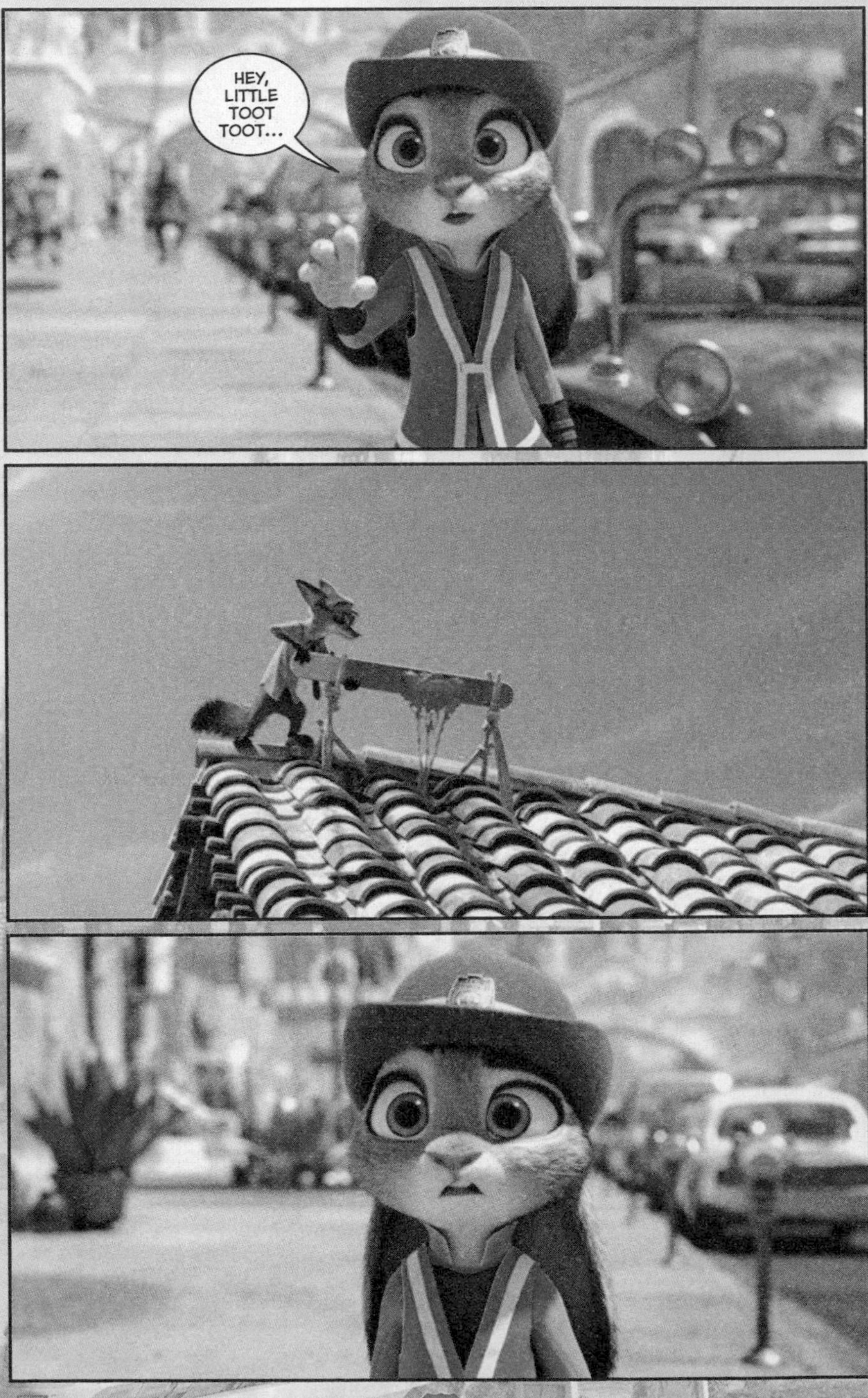
HEY, LITTLE TOOT TOOT...

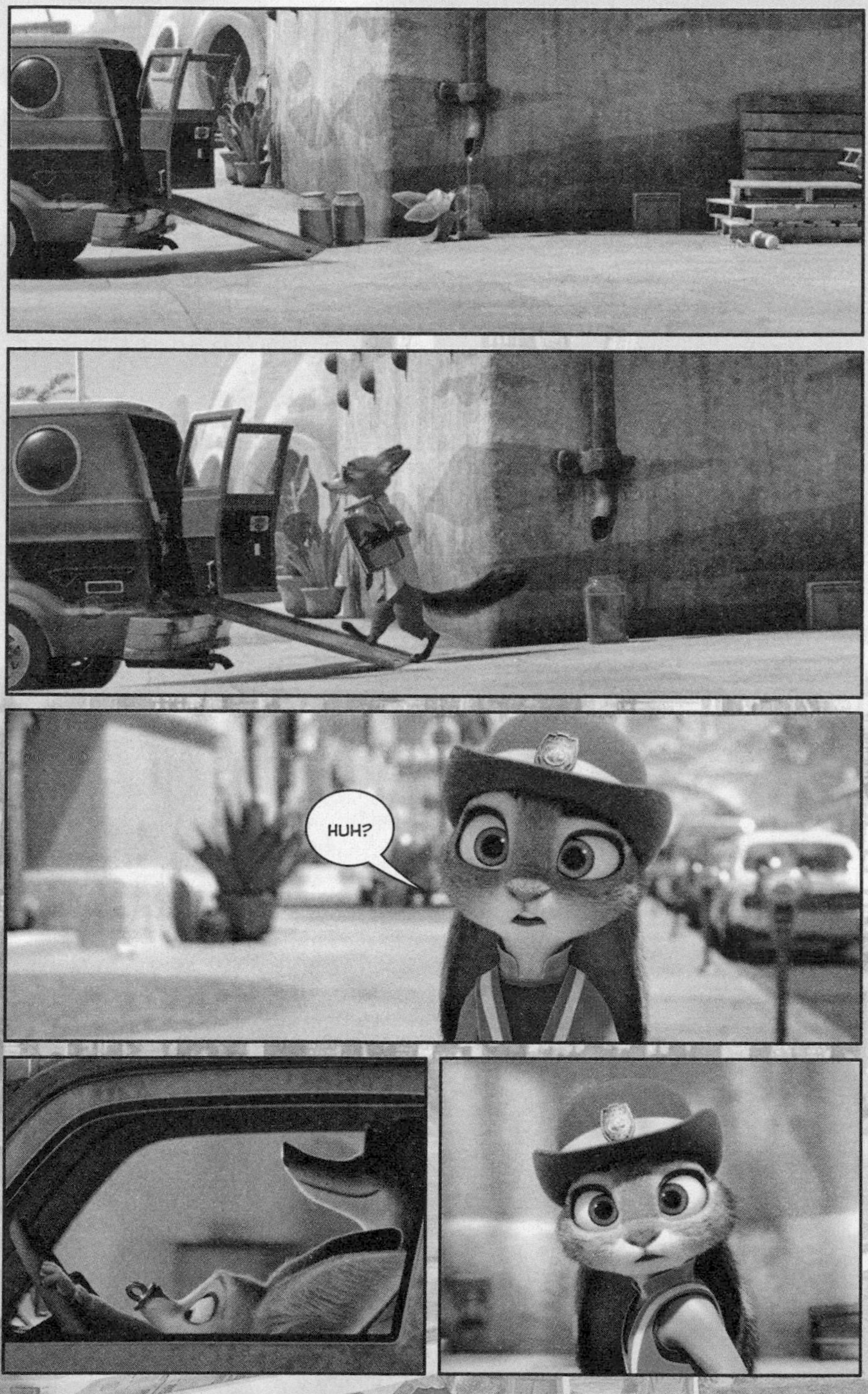
HUH?

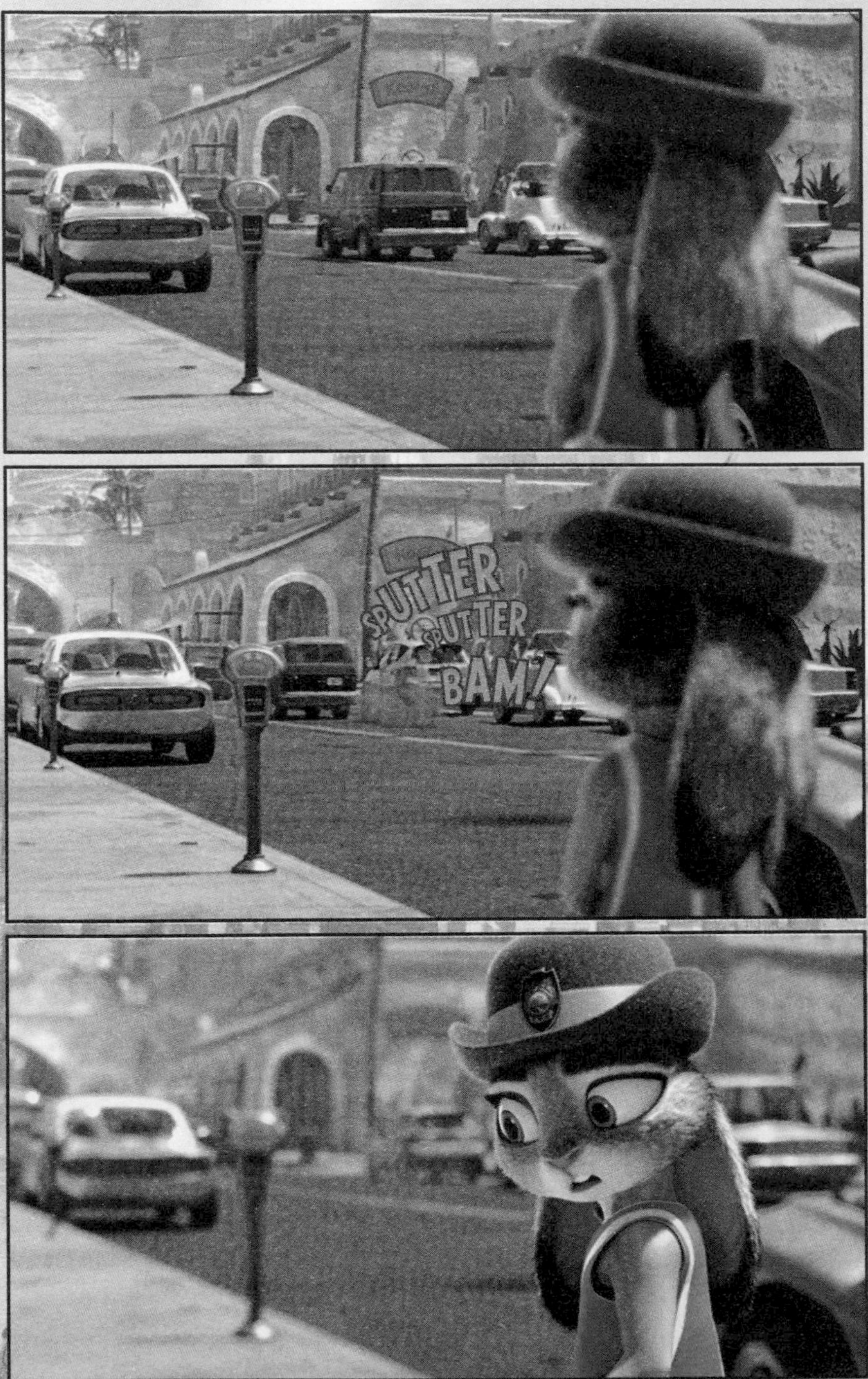
SPUTTER
SPUTTER
BAM!

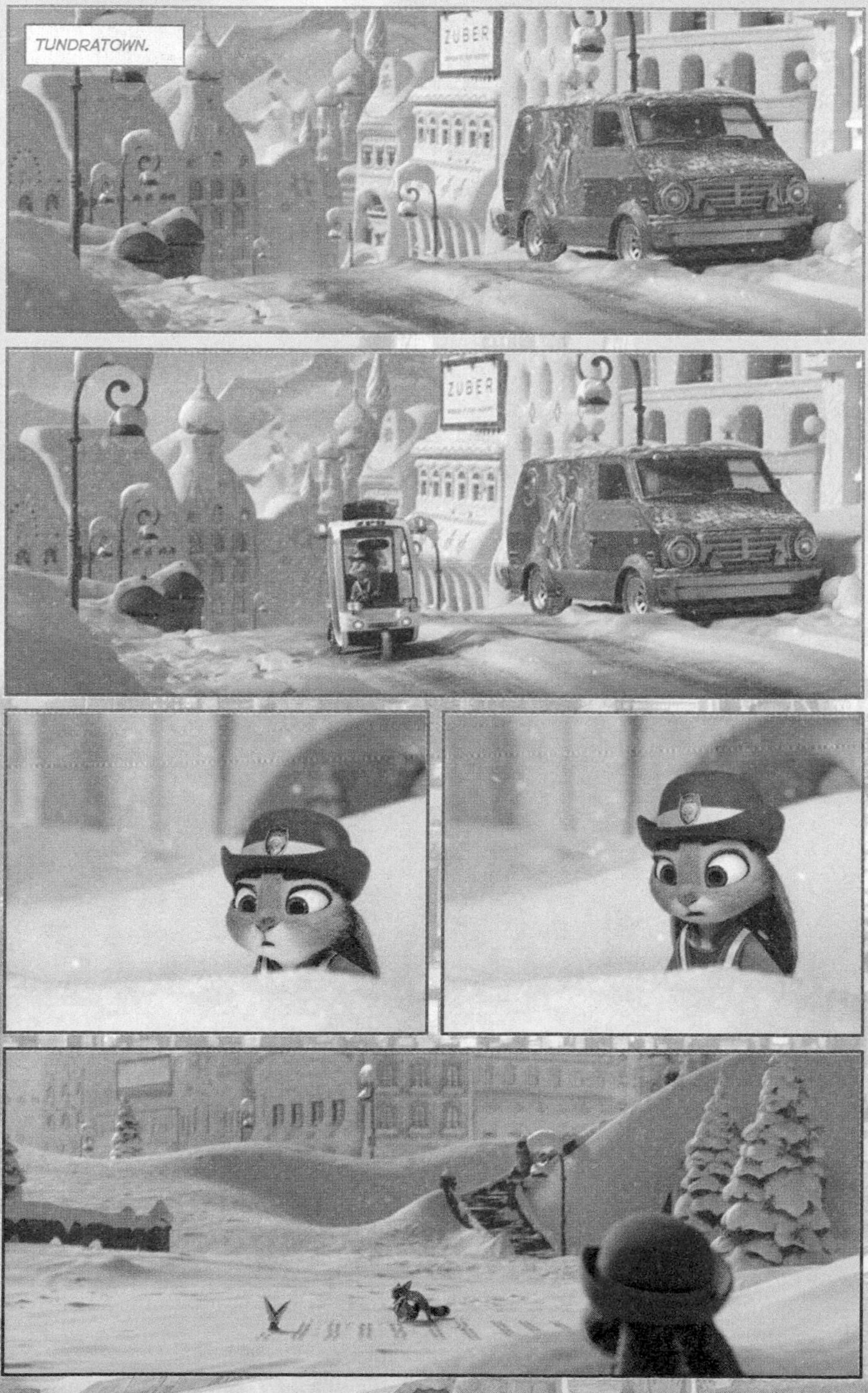
TUNDRATOWN.
ZUBER
ZUBER

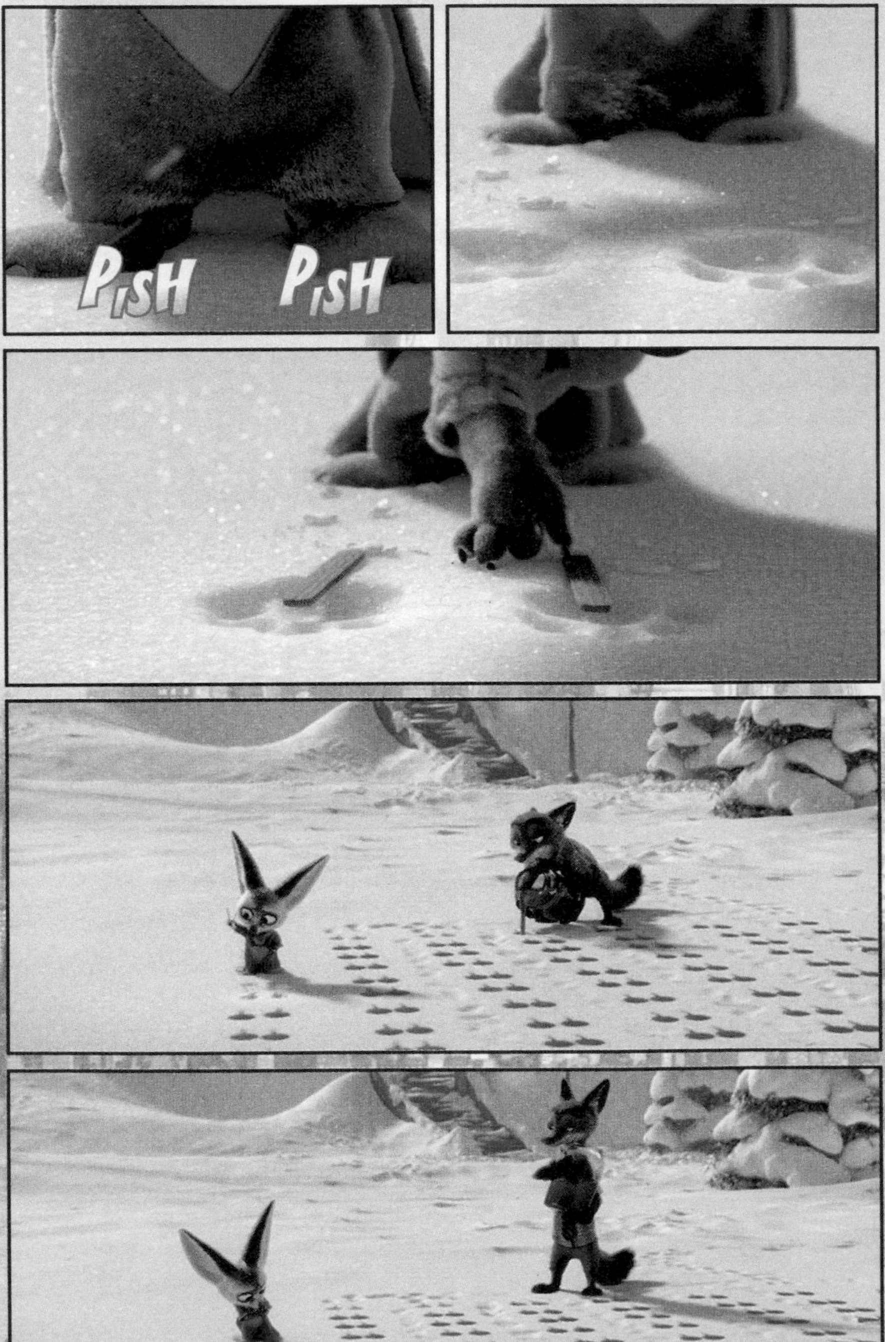
PISH
PISH

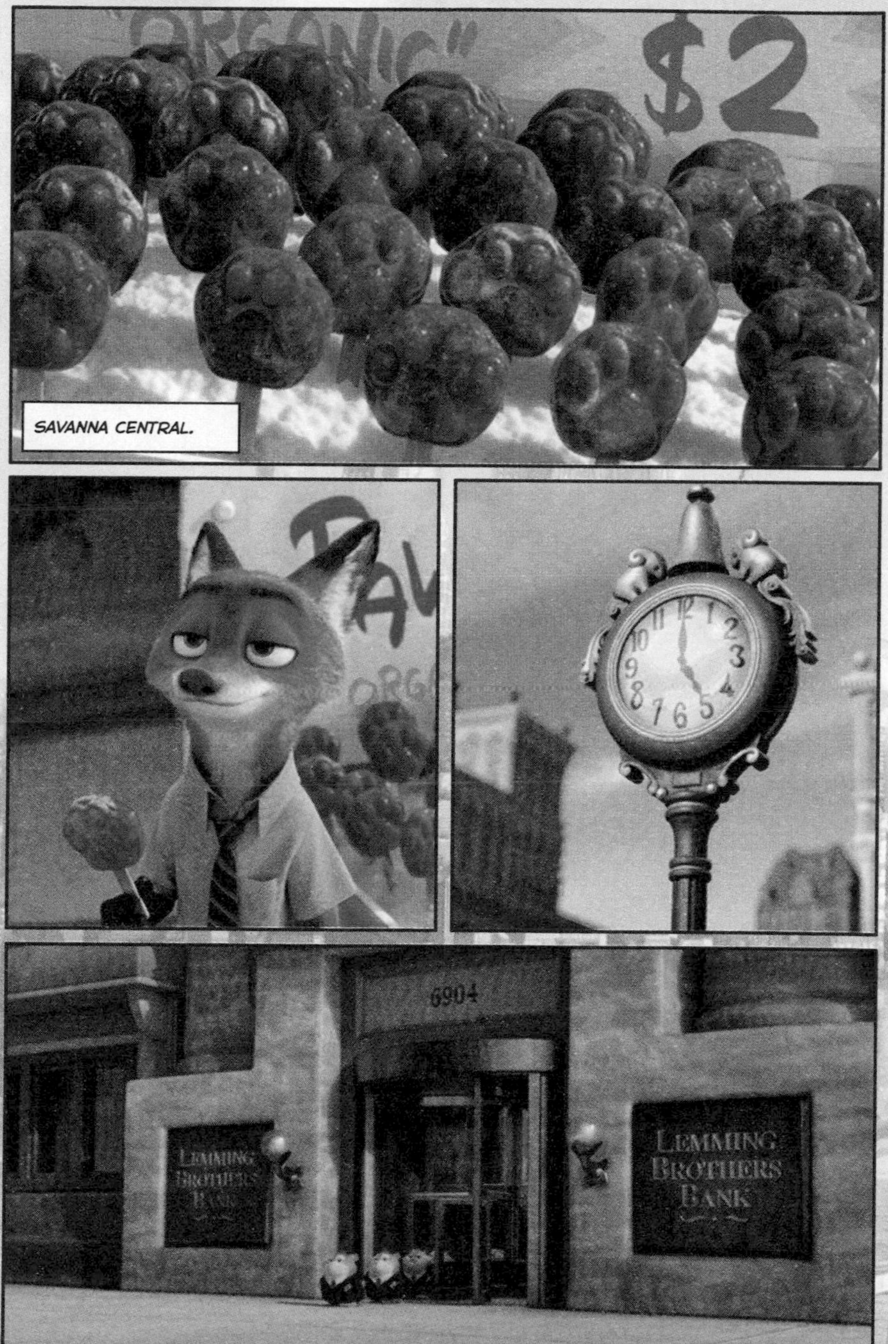
$2
SAVANNA CENTRAL.
LEMMING BROTHERS BANK
LEMMING BROTHERS BANK

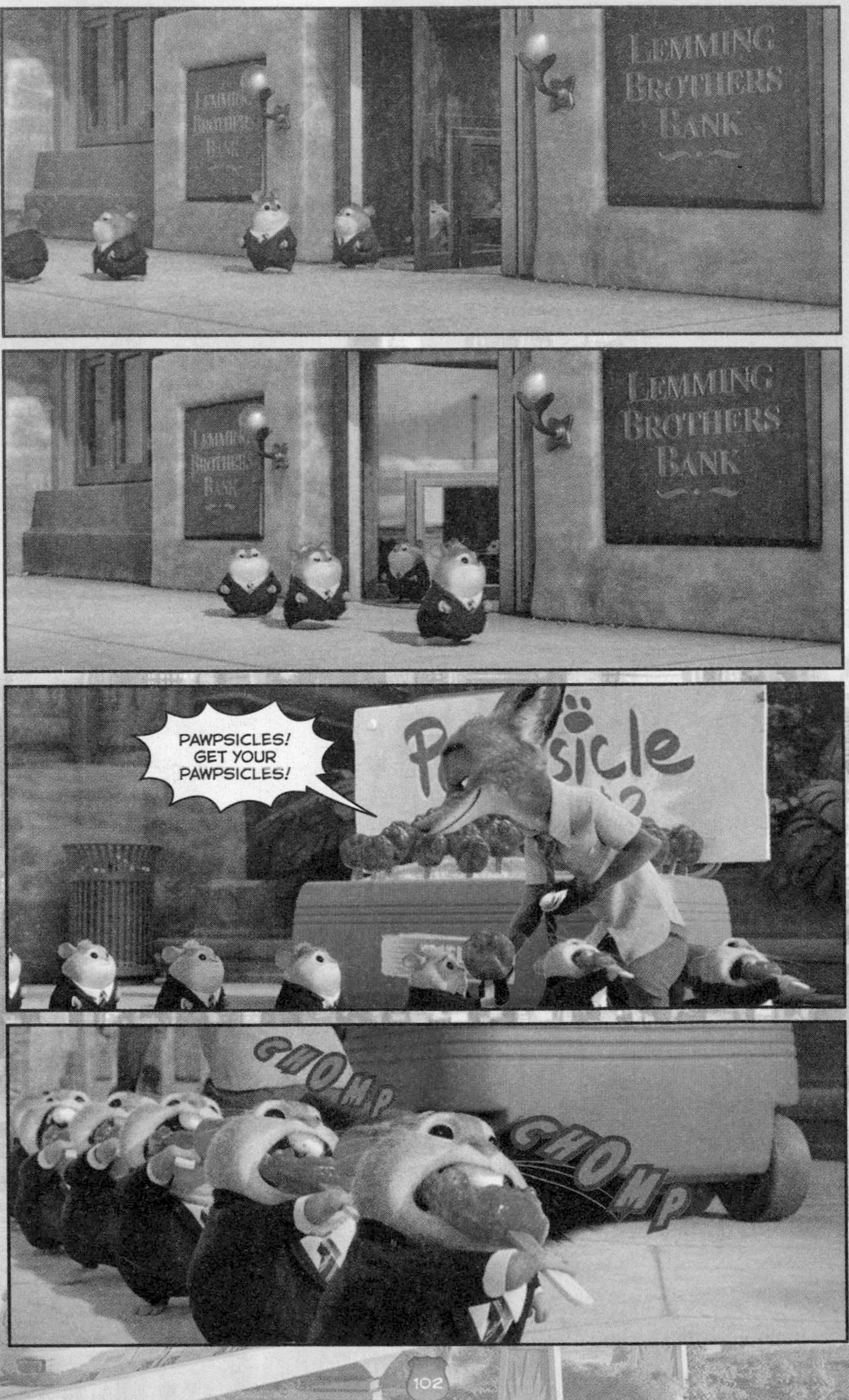
LEMMING BROTHERS BANK
LEMMING BROTHERS BANK
PAWPSICLES! GET YOUR PAWPSICLES!
CHOMP
CHOMP

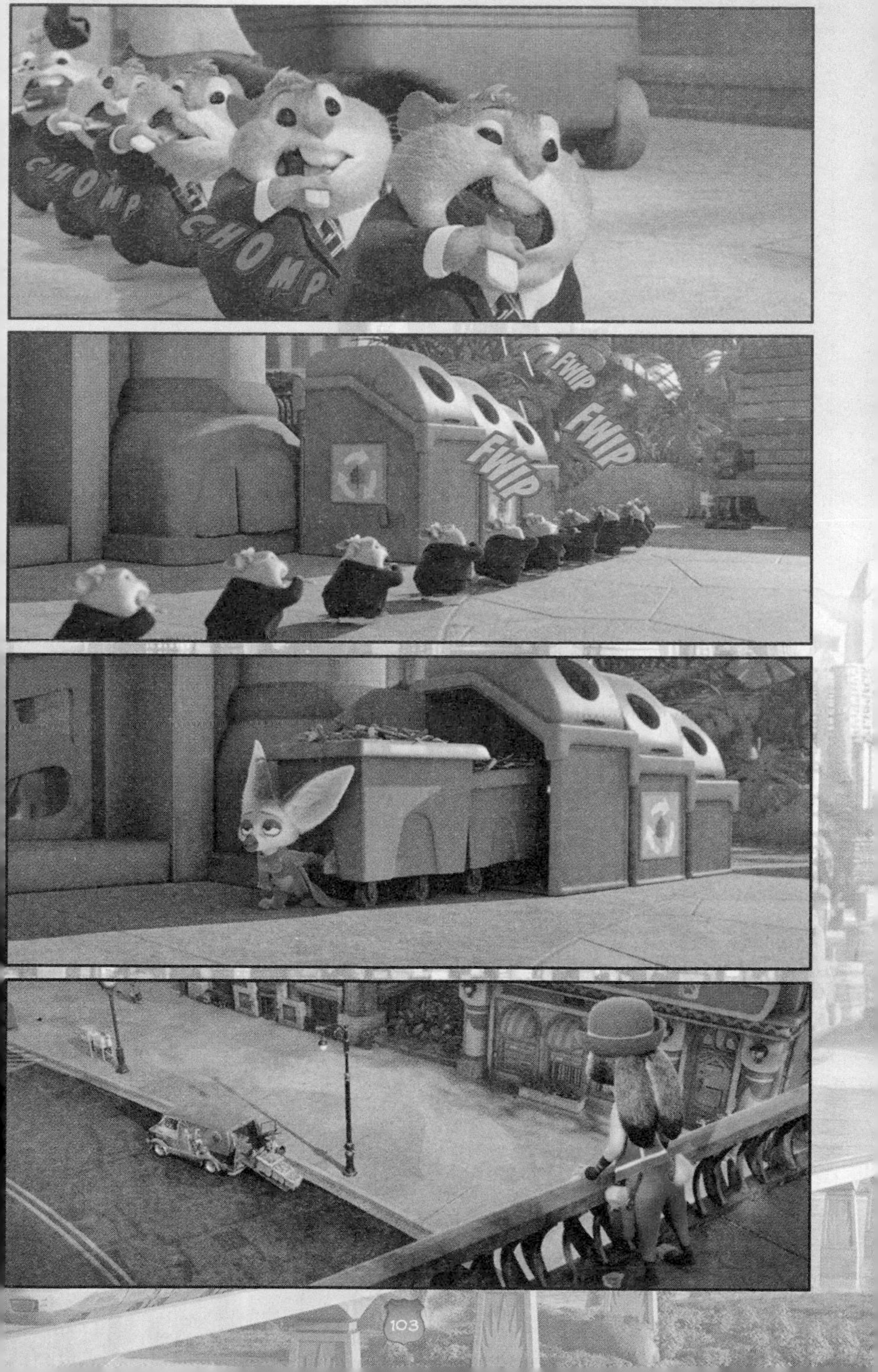
CHOMP
CHOMP
CHOMP
FWIP
FWIP
FWIP

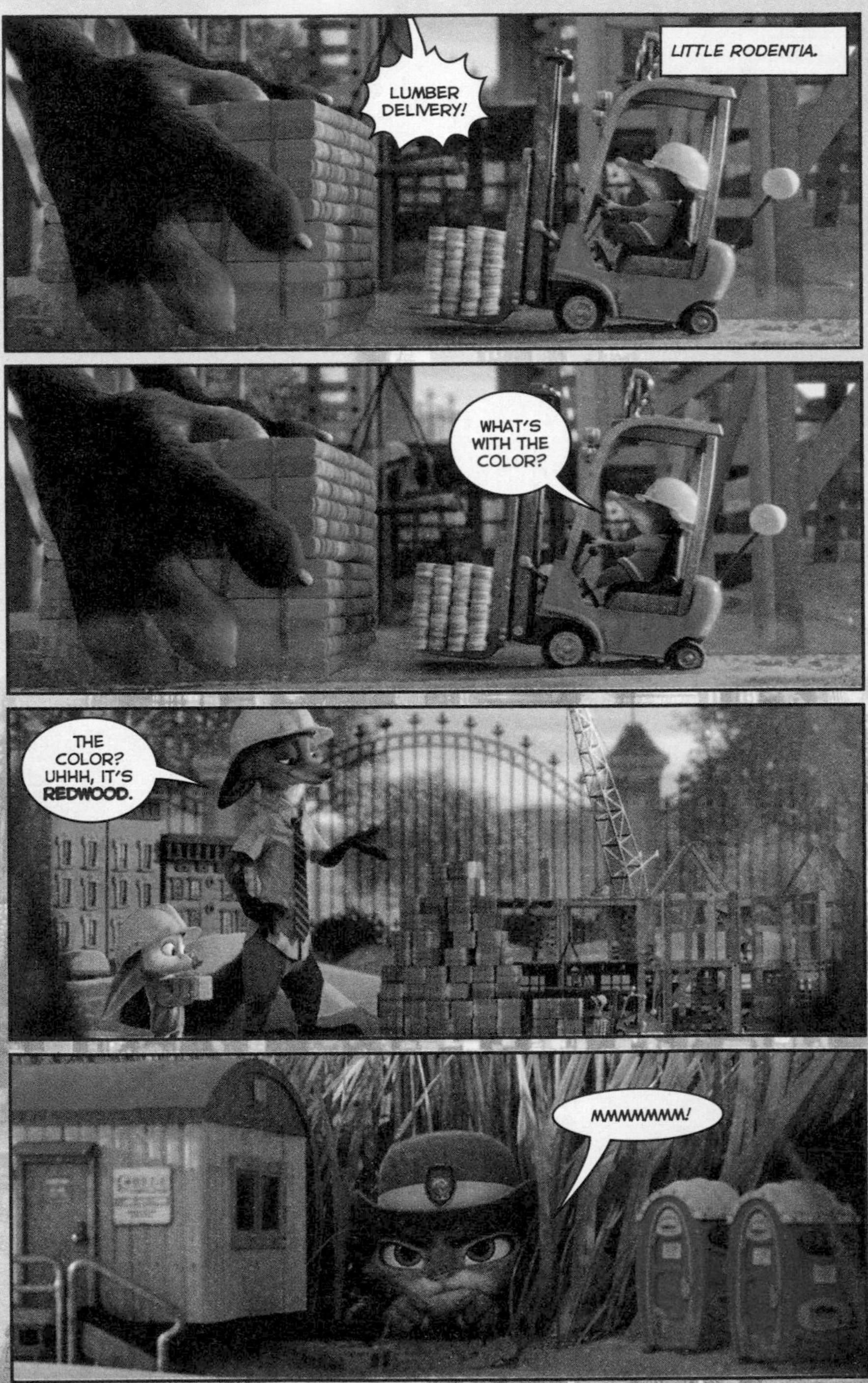
LITTLE RODENTIA.
LUMBER DELIVERY!
WHAT'S WITH THE COLOR?
THE COLOR? UHHH, IT'S **REDWOOD.**
MMMMMMMM!

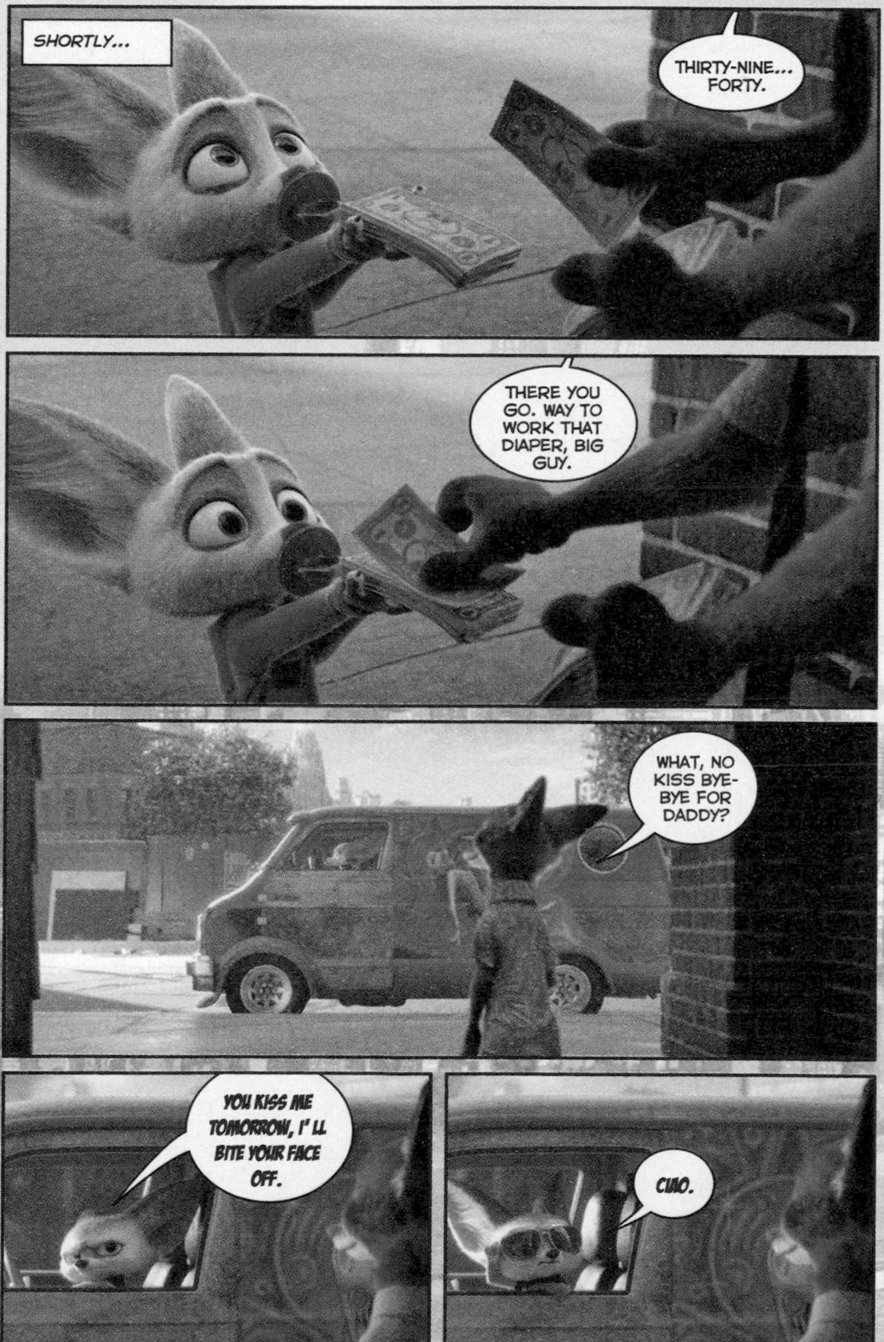
SHORTLY...
THIRTY-NINE... FORTY.
THERE YOU GO. WAY TO WORK THAT DIAPER, BIG GUY.
WHAT, NO KISS BYE-BYE FOR DADDY?
YOU KISS ME TOMORROW, I'LL BITE YOUR FACE OFF.
CIAO.

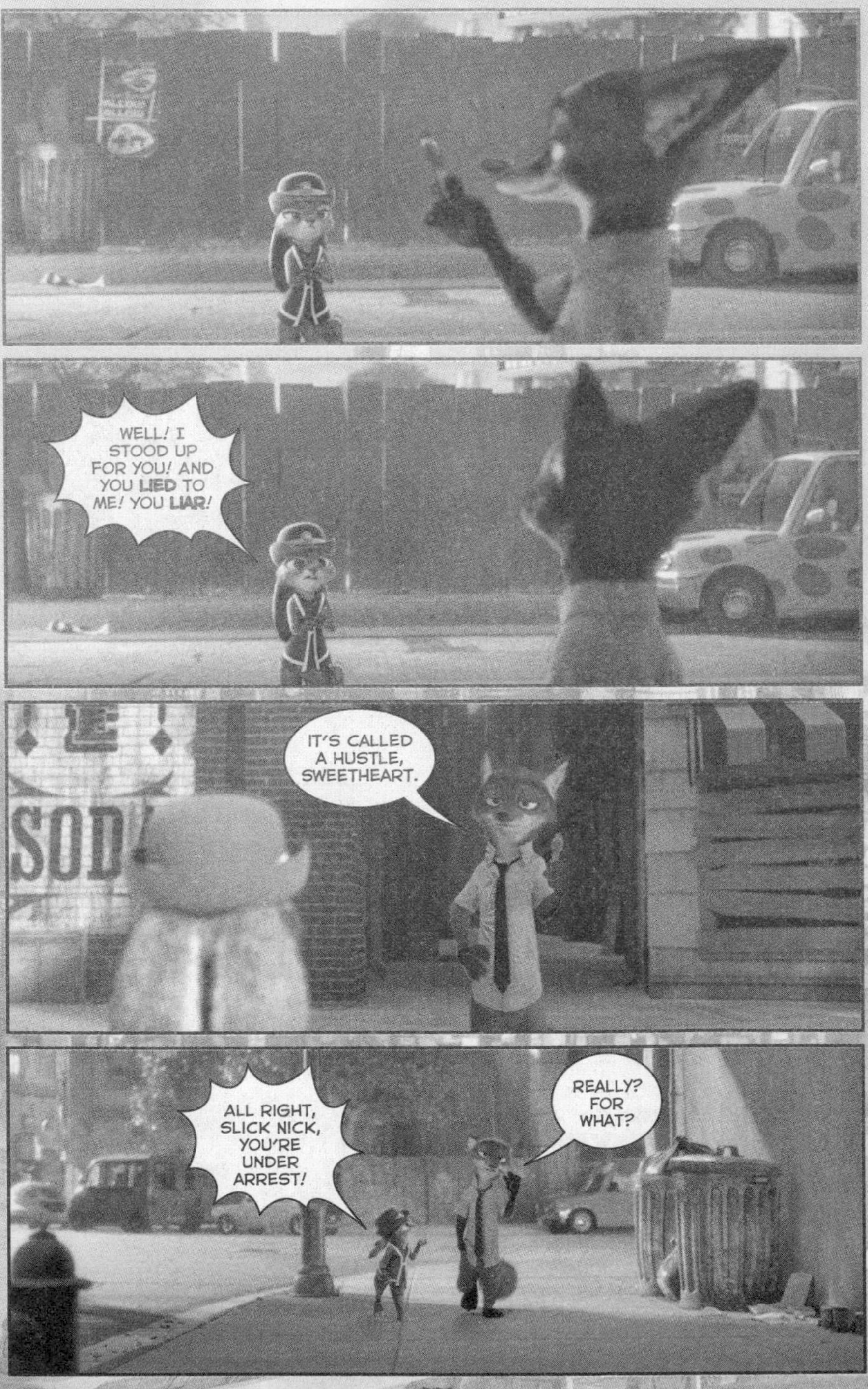
WELL! I STOOD UP FOR YOU! AND YOU LIED TO ME! YOU LIAR!
IT'S CALLED A HUSTLE, SWEETHEART.
ALL RIGHT, SLICK NICK, YOU'RE UNDER ARREST!
REALLY? FOR WHAT?

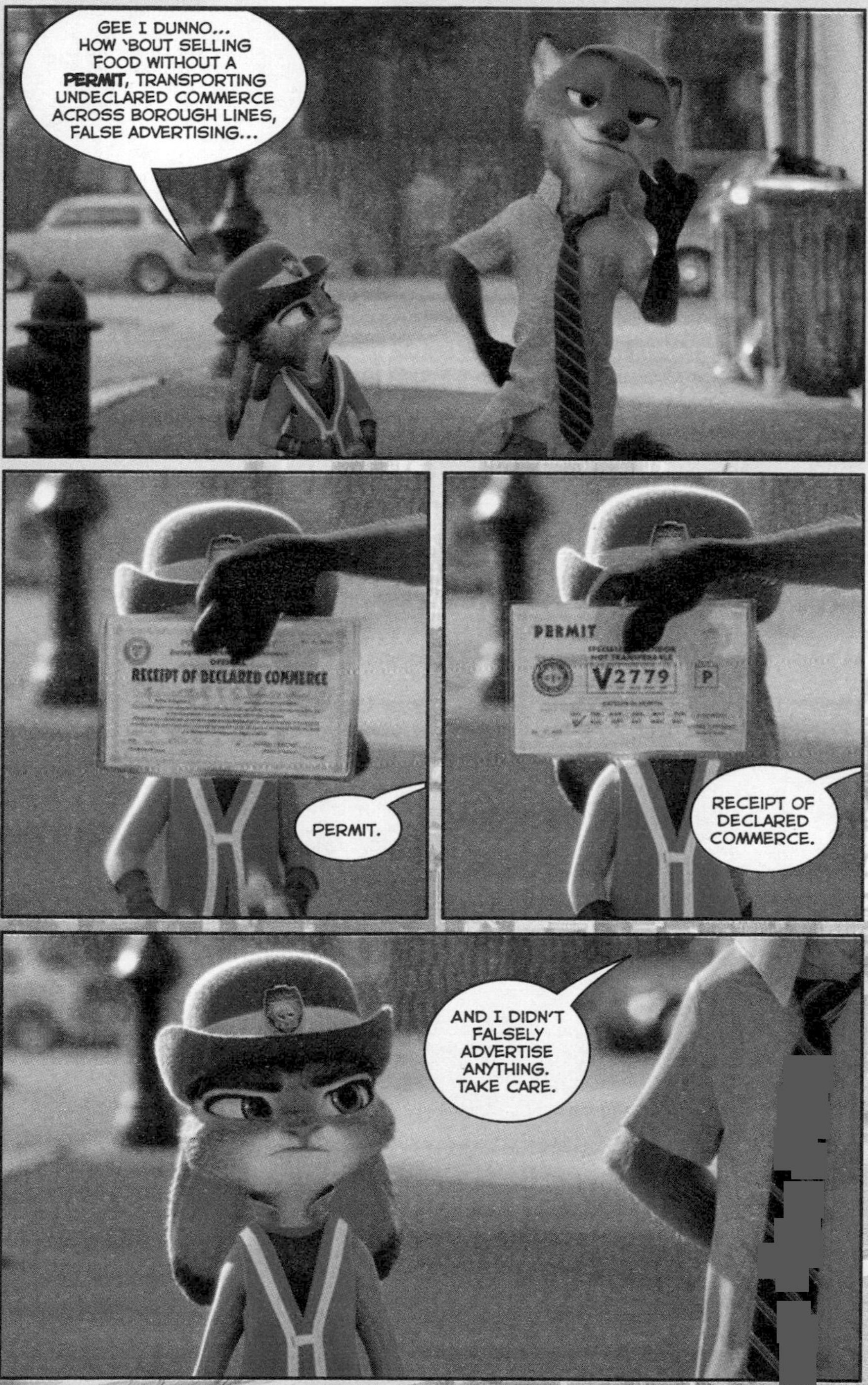
GEE I DUNNO... HOW 'BOUT SELLING FOOD WITHOUT A **PERMIT**, TRANSPORTING UNDECLARED COMMERCE ACROSS BOROUGH LINES, FALSE ADVERTISING...
RECEIPT OF DECLARED COMMERCE
PERMIT.
PERMIT
V2779
P
RECEIPT OF DECLARED COMMERCE.
AND I DIDN'T FALSELY ADVERTISE ANYTHING. TAKE CARE.

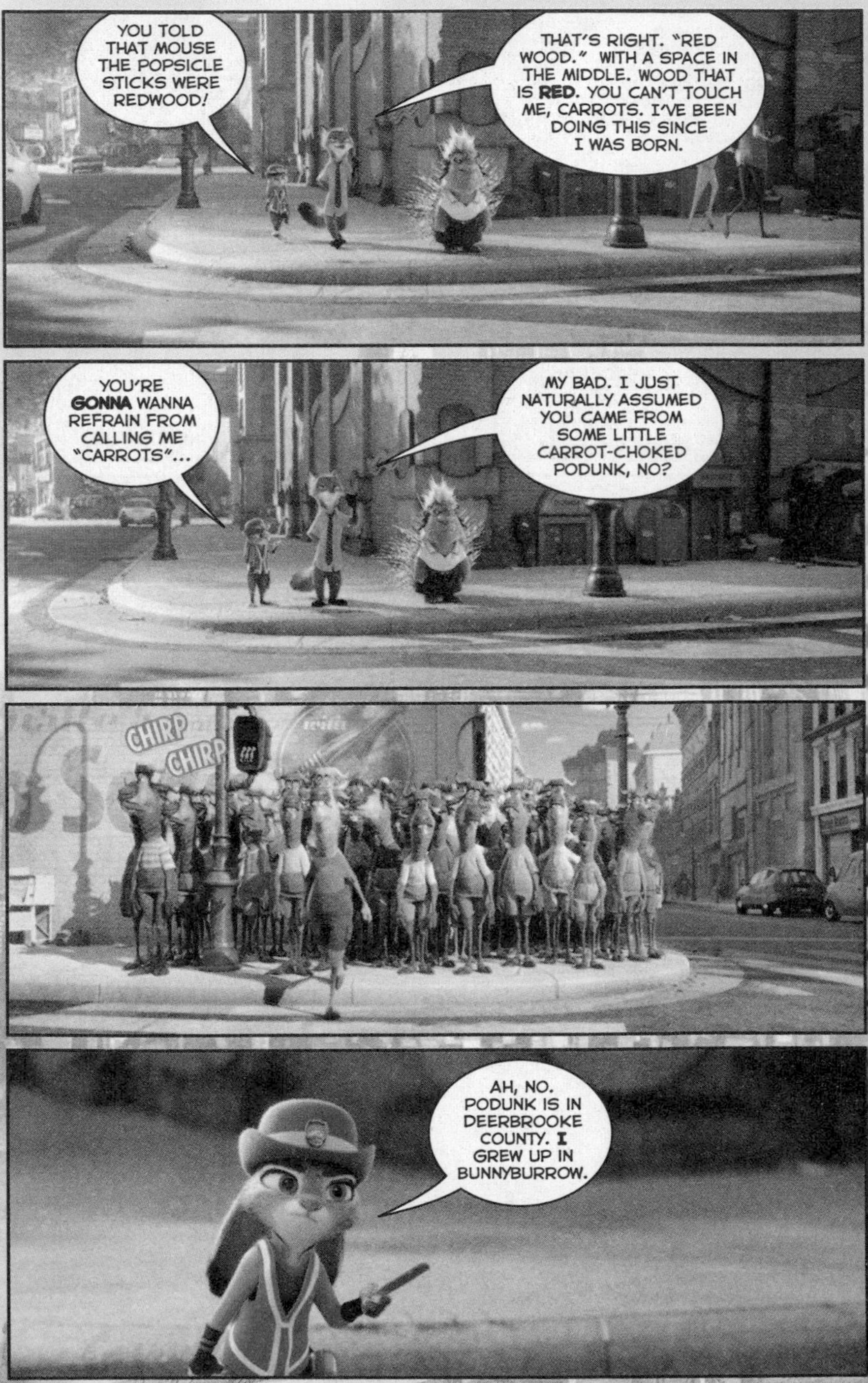
YOU TOLD THAT MOUSE THE POPSICLE STICKS WERE REDWOOD!
THAT'S RIGHT. "RED WOOD." WITH A SPACE IN THE MIDDLE. WOOD THAT IS **RED**. YOU CAN'T TOUCH ME, CARROTS. I'VE BEEN DOING THIS SINCE I WAS BORN.
YOU'RE **GONNA** WANNA REFRAIN FROM CALLING ME "CARROTS"...
MY BAD. I JUST NATURALLY ASSUMED YOU CAME FROM SOME LITTLE CARROT-CHOKED PODUNK, NO?
CHIRP
CHIRP
AH, NO. PODUNK IS IN DEERBROOKE COUNTY. **I** GREW UP IN BUNNYBURROW.

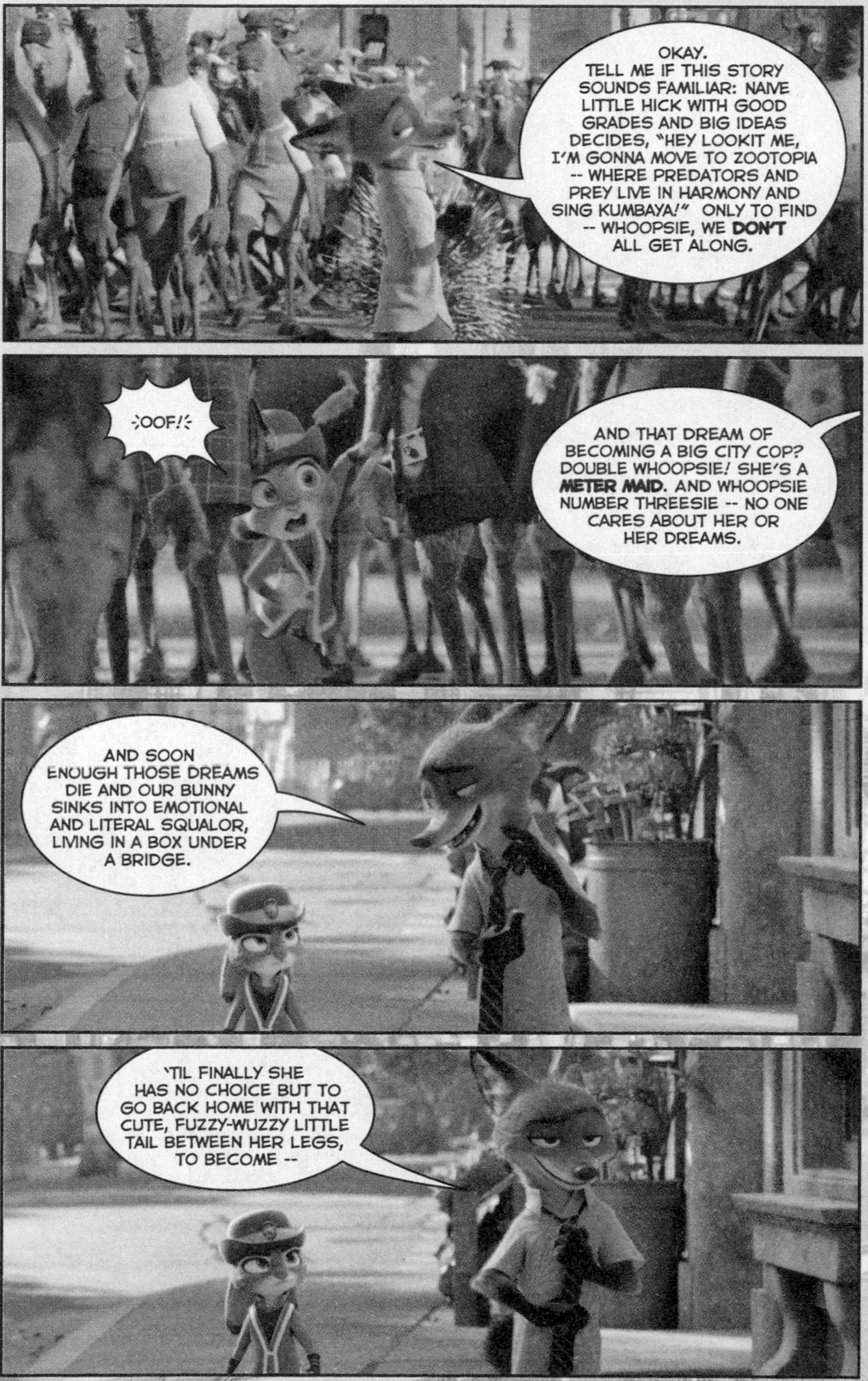
OKAY. TELL ME IF THIS STORY SOUNDS FAMILIAR: NAIVE LITTLE HICK WITH GOOD GRADES AND BIG IDEAS DECIDES, "HEY LOOKIT ME, I'M GONNA MOVE TO ZOOTOPIA -- WHERE PREDATORS AND PREY LIVE IN HARMONY AND SING KUMBAYA!" ONLY TO FIND -- WHOOPSIE, WE **DON'T** ALL GET ALONG.
OOF!
AND THAT DREAM OF BECOMING A BIG CITY COP? DOUBLE WHOOPSIE! SHE'S A **METER MAID**. AND WHOOPSIE NUMBER THREESIE -- NO ONE CARES ABOUT HER OR HER DREAMS.
AND SOON ENOUGH THOSE DREAMS DIE AND OUR BUNNY SINKS INTO EMOTIONAL AND LITERAL SQUALOR, LIVING IN A BOX UNDER A BRIDGE.
'TIL FINALLY SHE HAS NO CHOICE BUT TO GO BACK HOME WITH THAT CUTE, FUZZY-WUZZY LITTLE TAIL BETWEEN HER LEGS, TO BECOME --

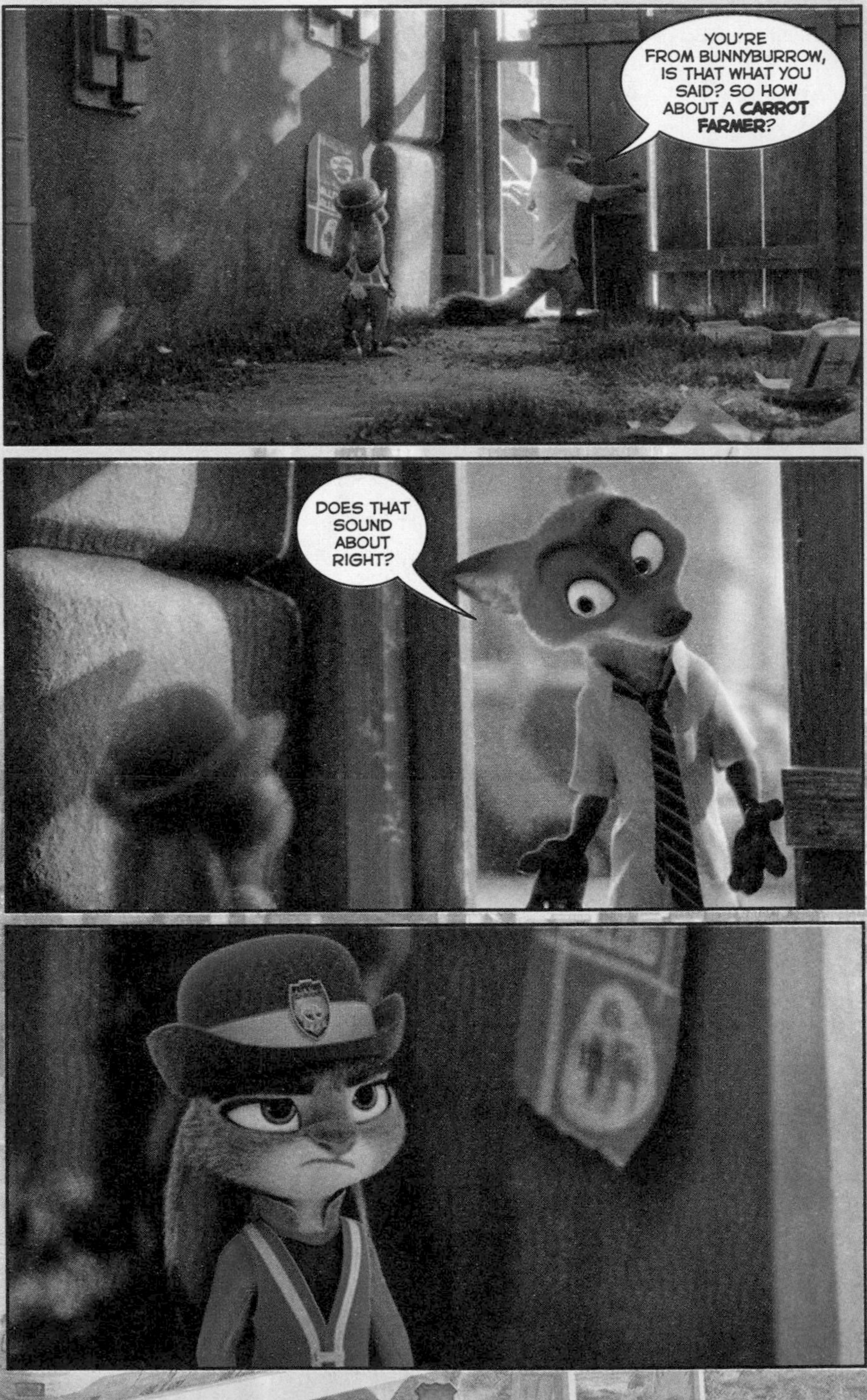
YOU'RE FROM BUNNYBURROW, IS THAT WHAT YOU SAID? SO HOW ABOUT A **CARROT FARMER**?
DOES THAT SOUND ABOUT RIGHT?

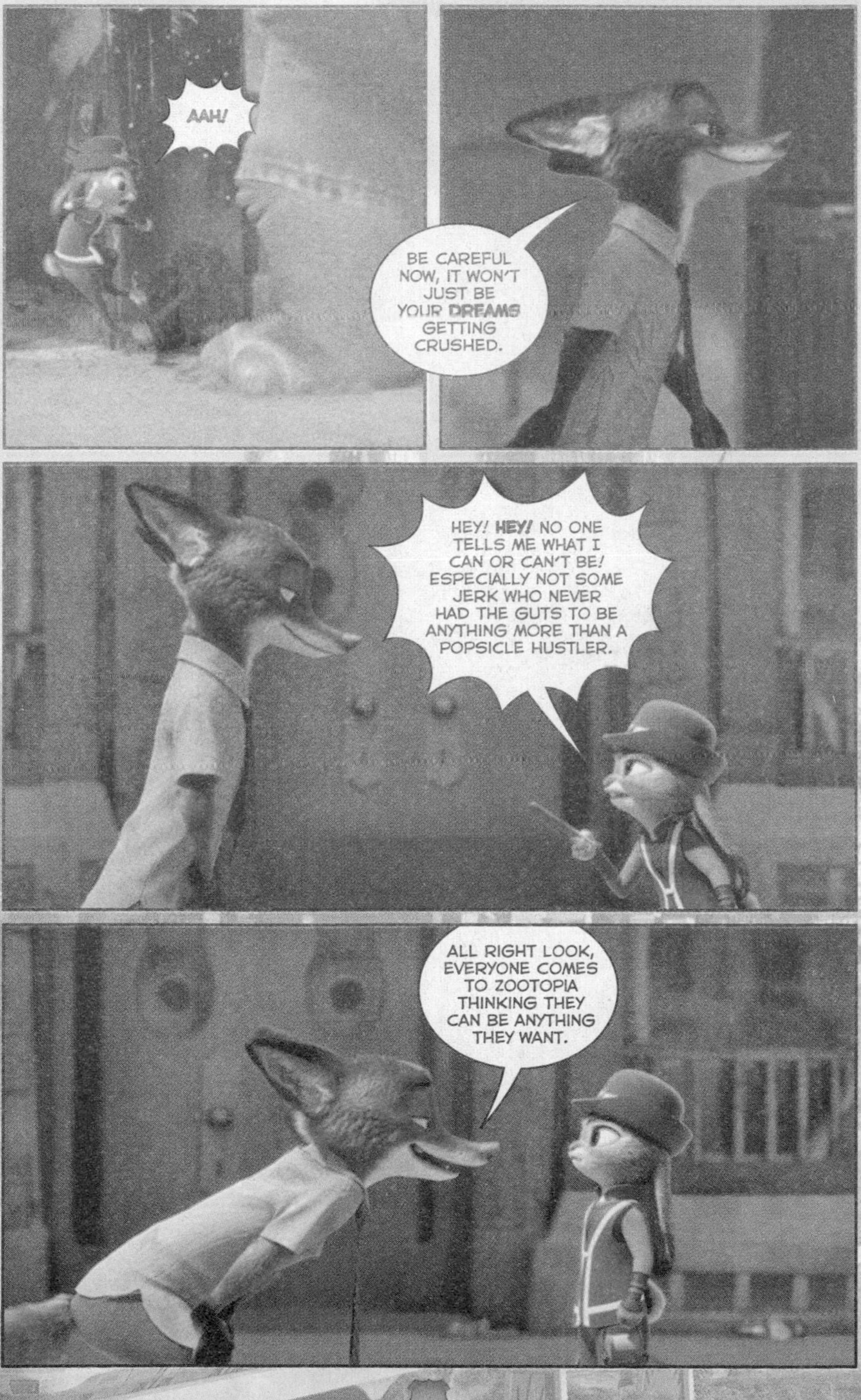
AAH!
BE CAREFUL NOW, IT WON'T JUST BE YOUR DREAMS GETTING CRUSHED.
HEY! HEY! NO ONE TELLS ME WHAT I CAN OR CAN'T BE! ESPECIALLY NOT SOME JERK WHO NEVER HAD THE GUTS TO BE ANYTHING MORE THAN A POPSICLE HUSTLER.
ALL RIGHT LOOK, EVERYONE COMES TO ZOOTOPIA THINKING THEY CAN BE ANYTHING THEY WANT.

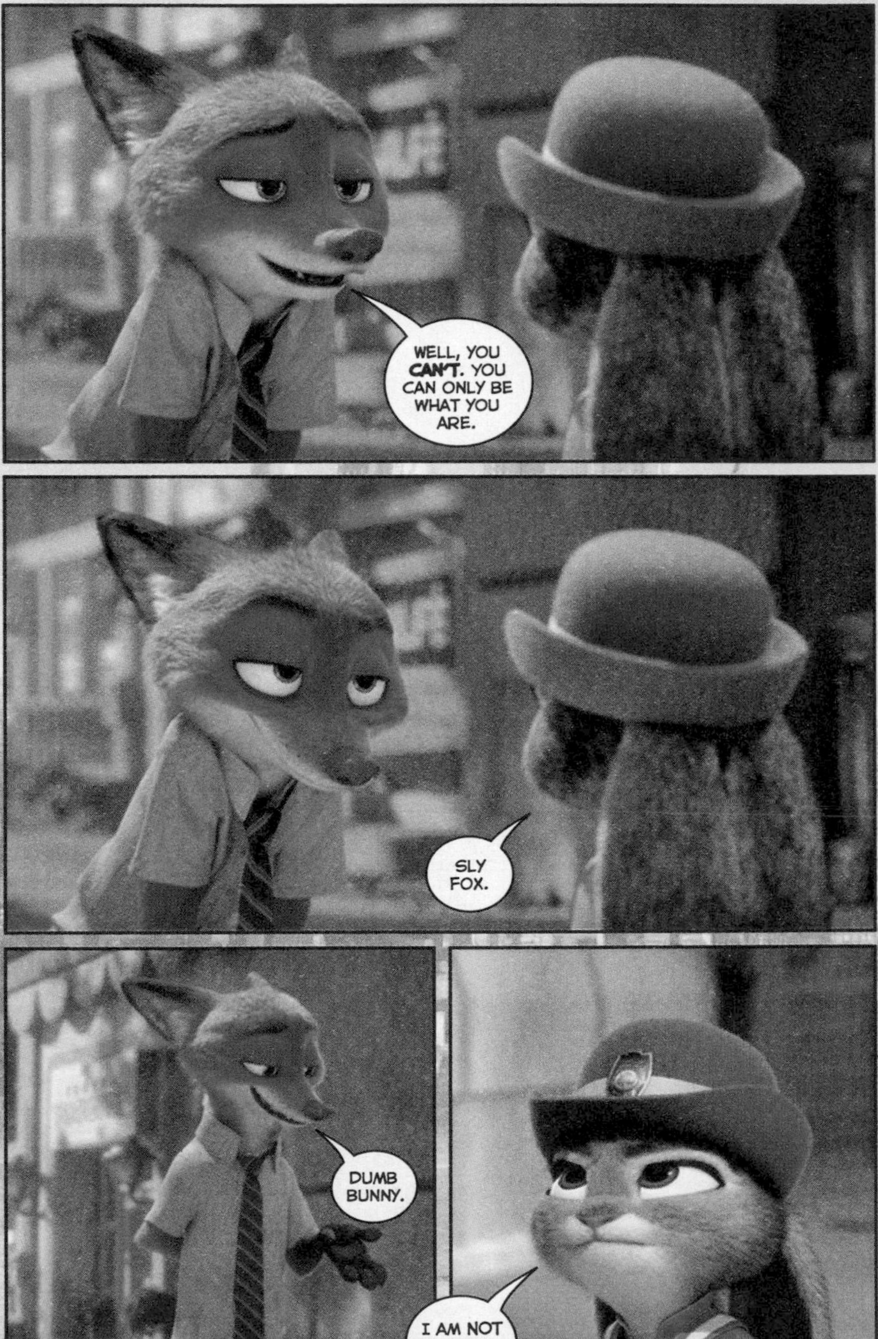
WELL, YOU **CAN'T**. YOU CAN ONLY BE WHAT YOU ARE.
SLY FOX.
DUMB BUNNY.
I AM NOT A DUMB BUNNY!

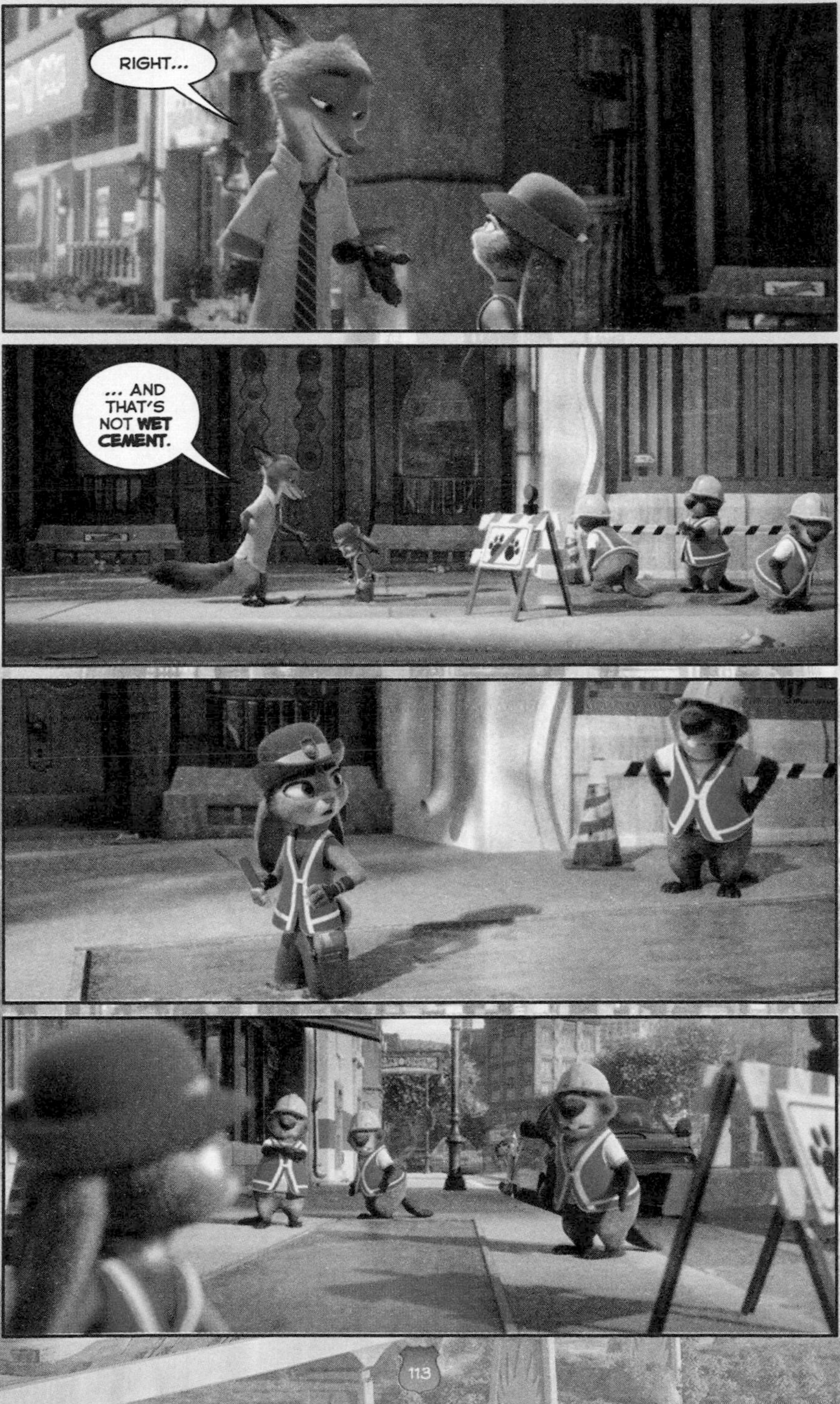
RIGHT...
... AND THAT'S NOT **WET CEMENT**.

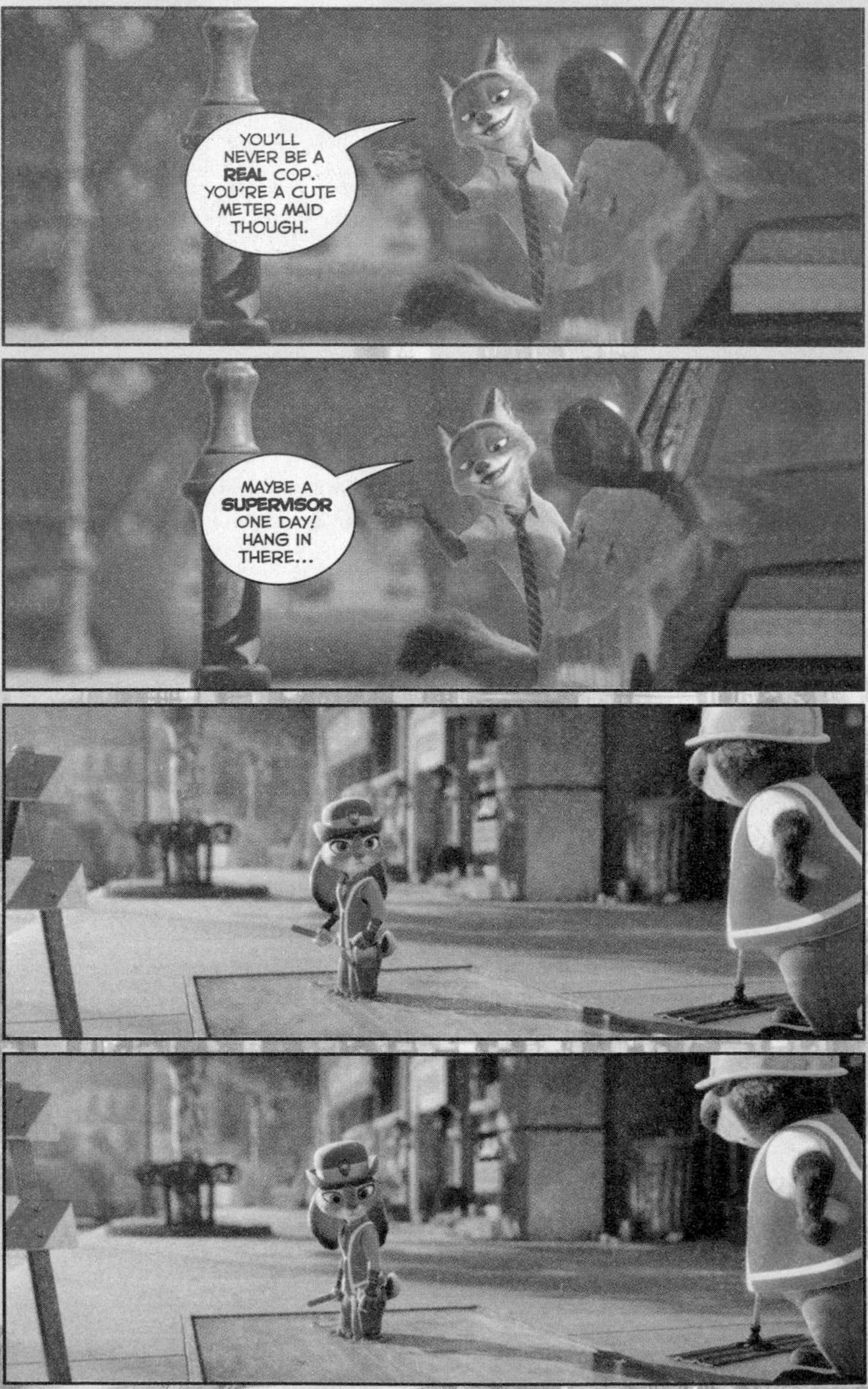
YOU'LL NEVER BE A REAL COP. YOU'RE A CUTE METER MAID THOUGH.
MAYBE A SUPERVISOR ONE DAY! HANG IN THERE...

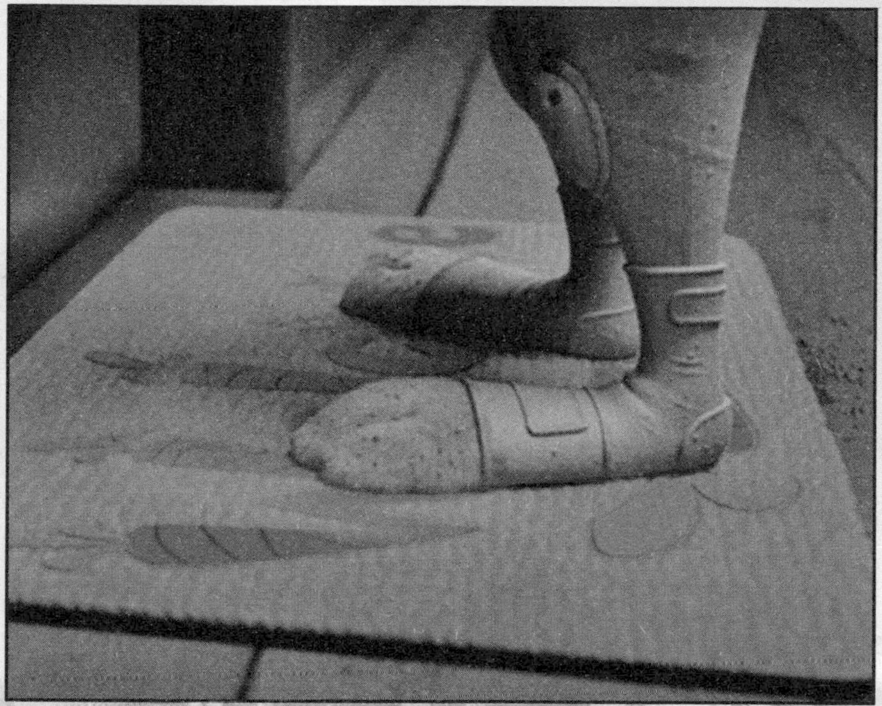

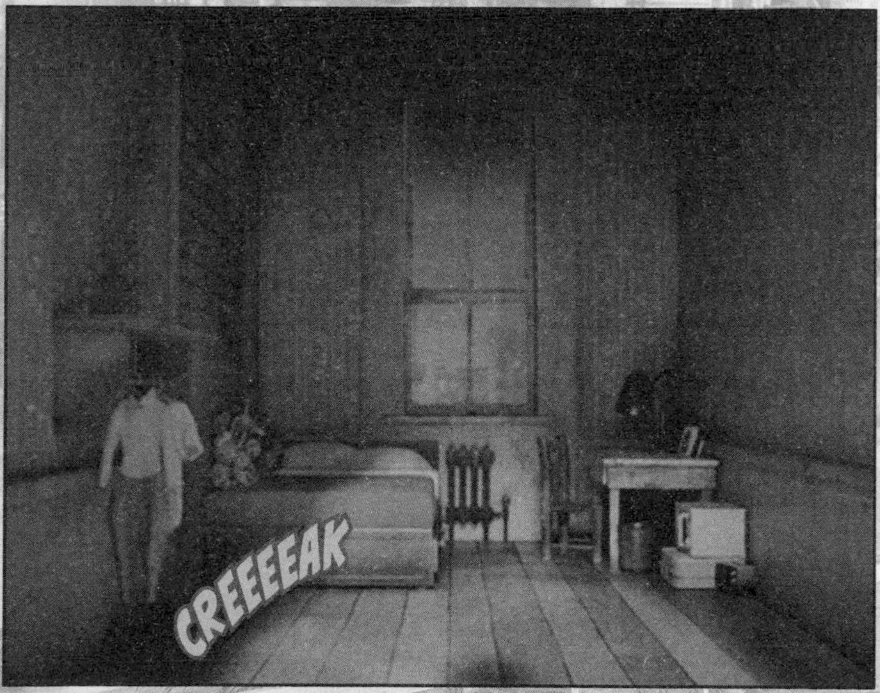
CREEEEAK

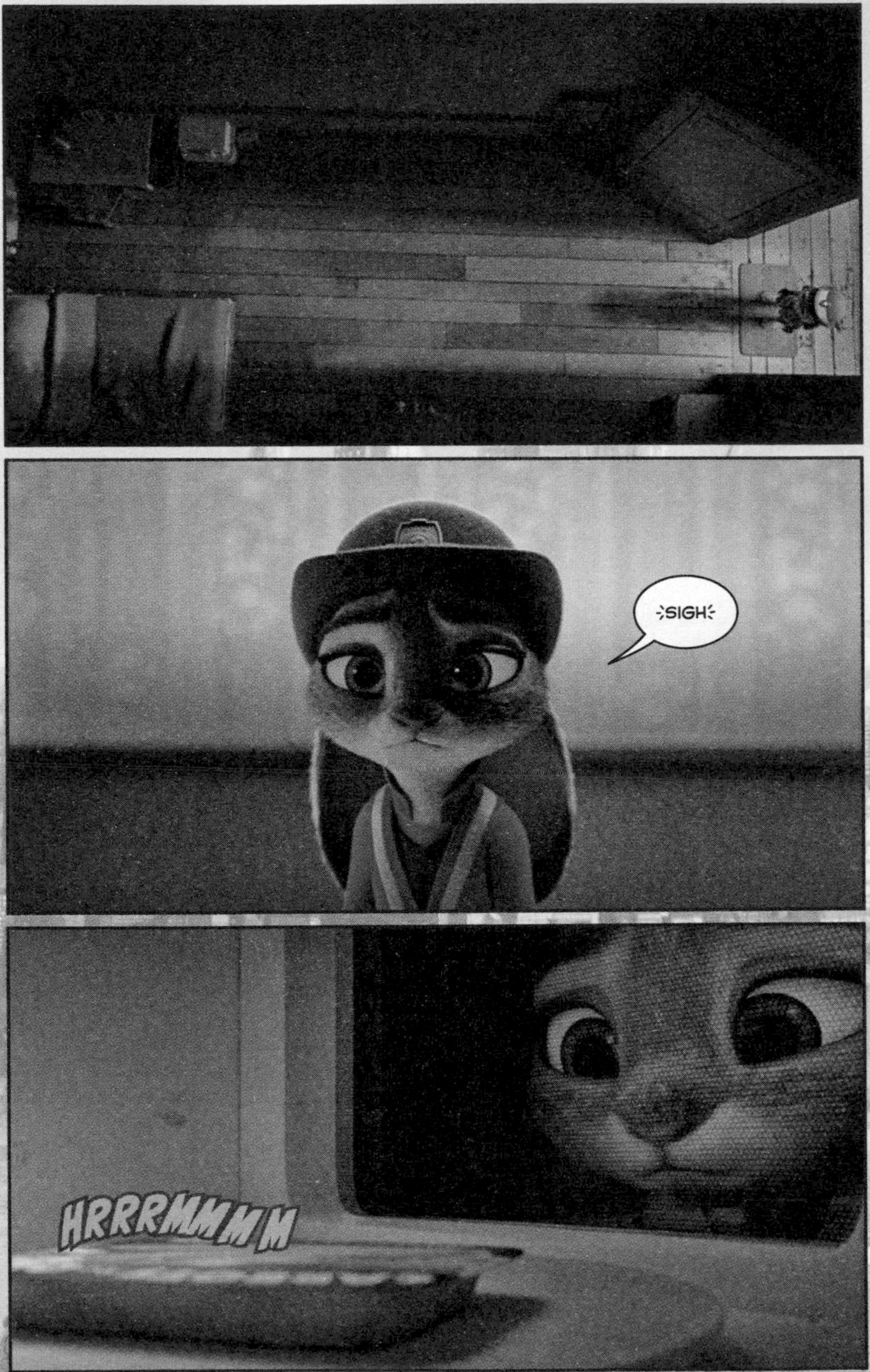
SIGH
HRRRMMMMM

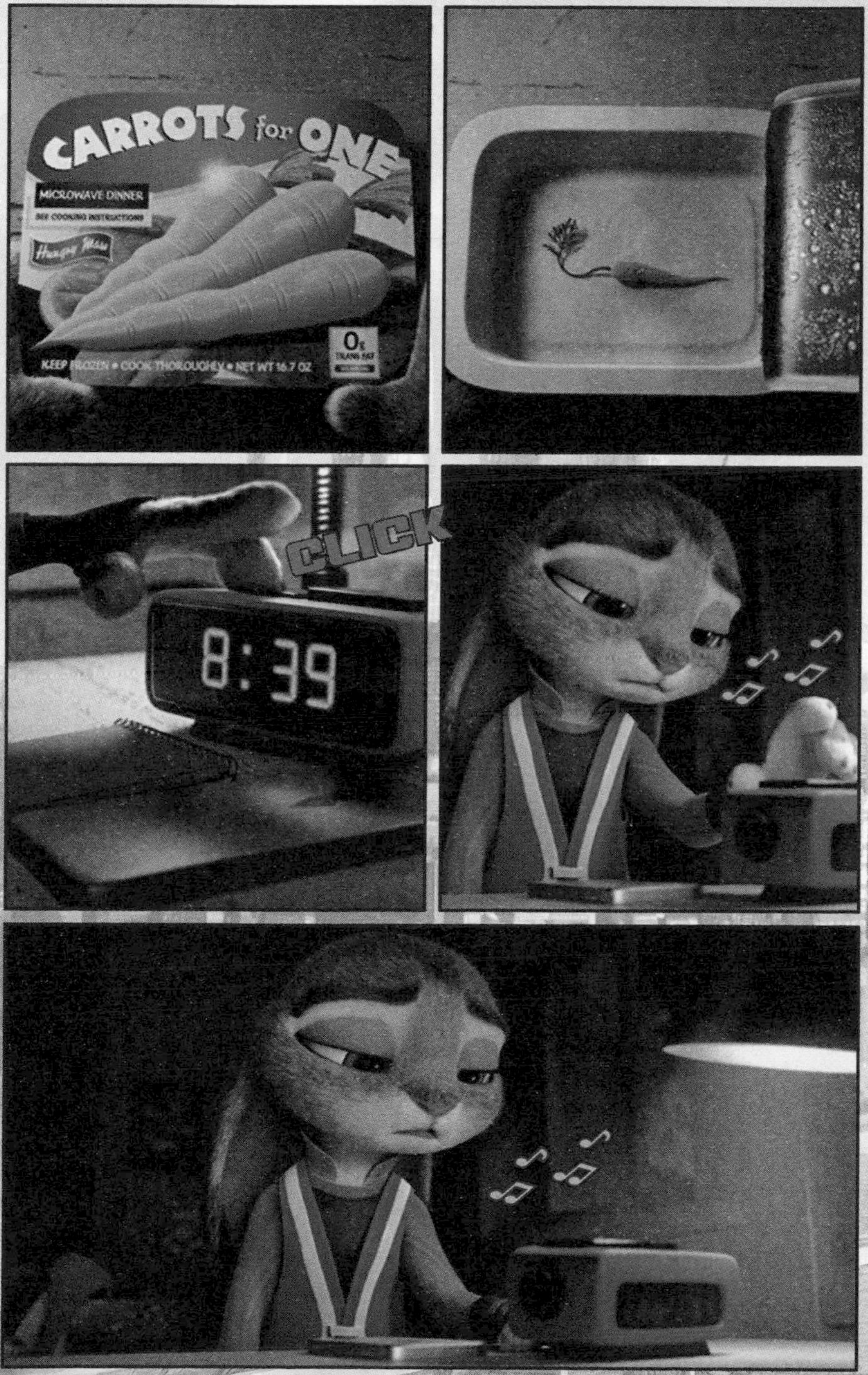
CARROTS for ONE
MICROWAVE DINNER
SEE COOKING INSTRUCTIONS
0g TRANS FAT
8:39
CLICK

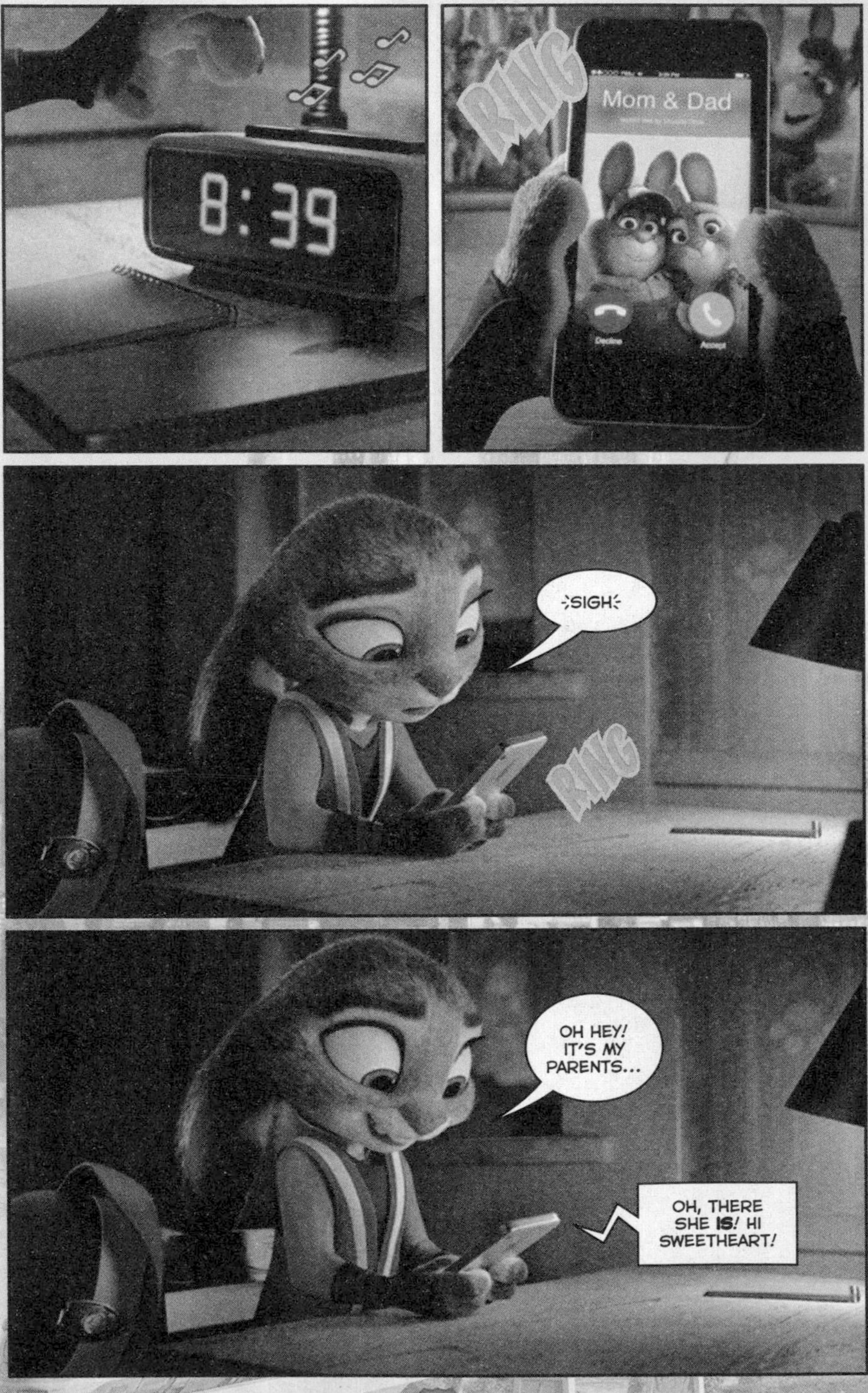
8:39
RING
Mom & Dad
SIGH
RING
OH HEY! IT'S MY PARENTS...
OH, THERE SHE **IS**! HI SWEETHEART!

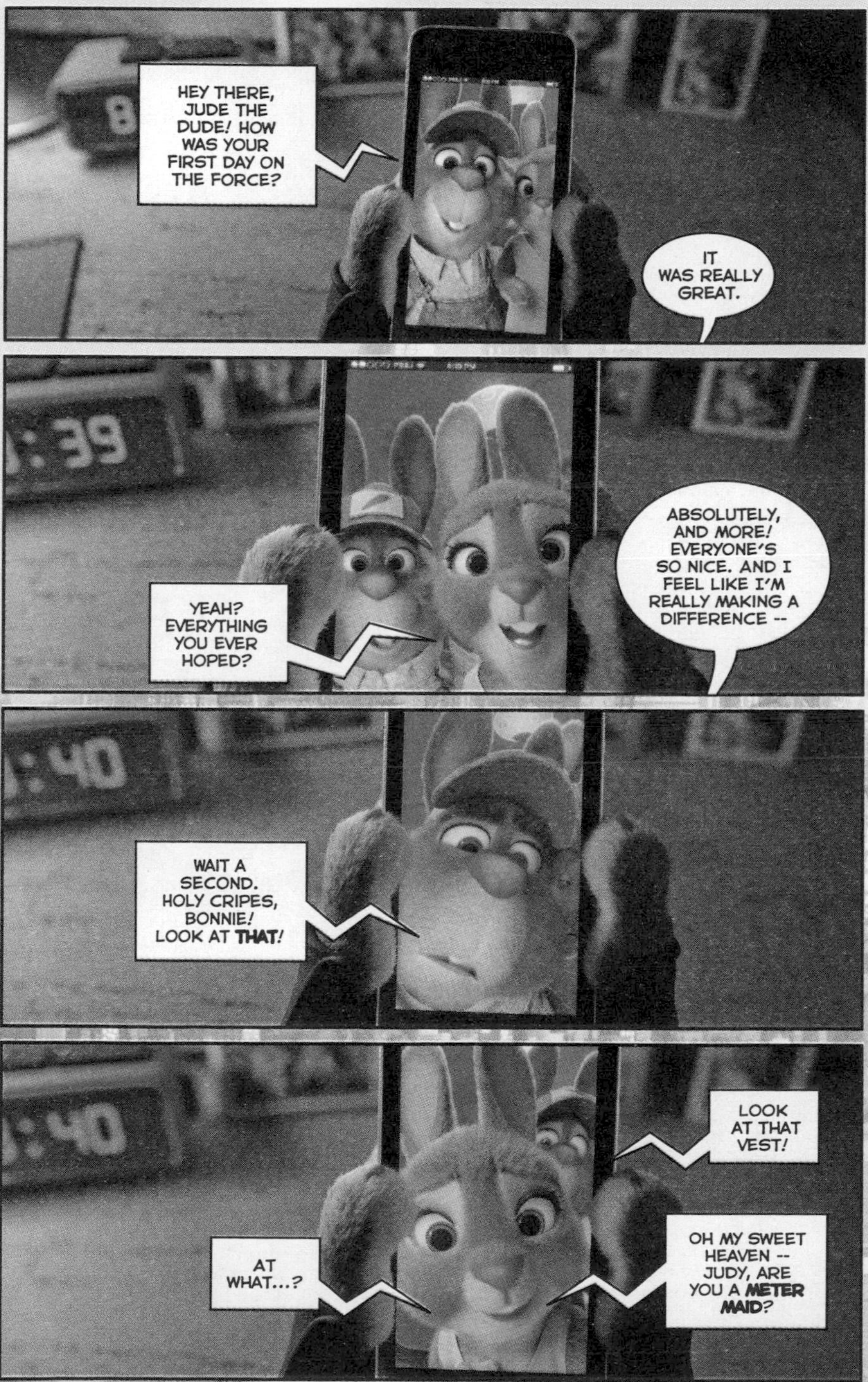
HEY THERE, JUDE THE DUDE! HOW WAS YOUR FIRST DAY ON THE FORCE?
IT WAS REALLY GREAT.
YEAH? EVERYTHING YOU EVER HOPED?
ABSOLUTELY, AND MORE! EVERYONE'S SO NICE. AND I FEEL LIKE I'M REALLY MAKING A DIFFERENCE --
WAIT A SECOND. HOLY CRIPES, BONNIE! LOOK AT **THAT**!
LOOK AT THAT VEST!
AT WHAT...?
OH MY SWEET HEAVEN -- JUDY, ARE YOU A **METER MAID**?

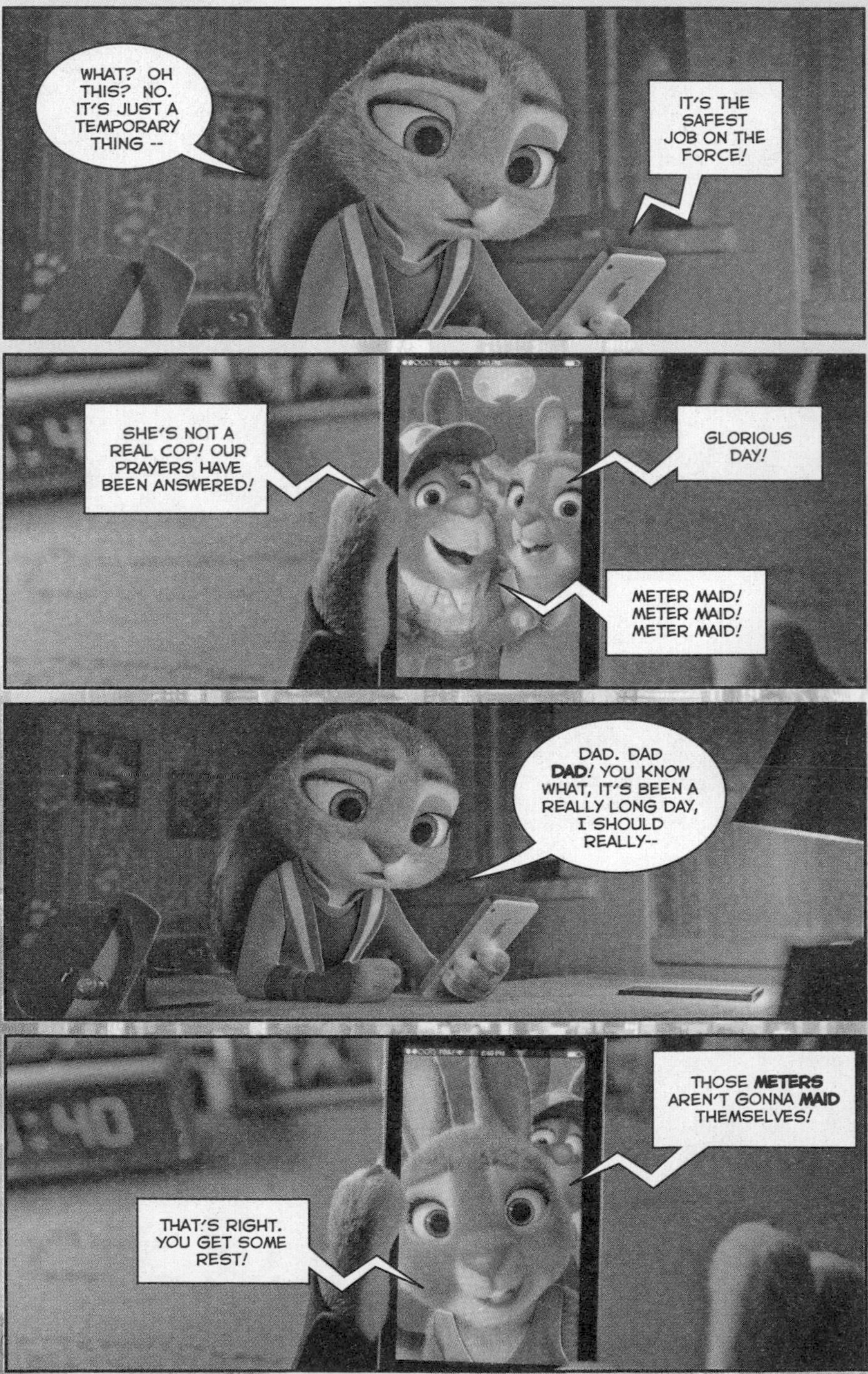
WHAT? OH THIS? NO. IT'S JUST A TEMPORARY THING --
IT'S THE SAFEST JOB ON THE FORCE!
SHE'S NOT A REAL COP! OUR PRAYERS HAVE BEEN ANSWERED!
GLORIOUS DAY!
METER MAID! METER MAID! METER MAID!
DAD. DAD **DAD**! YOU KNOW WHAT, IT'S BEEN A REALLY LONG DAY, I SHOULD REALLY--
THOSE **METERS** AREN'T GONNA **MAID** THEMSELVES!
THAT'S RIGHT. YOU GET SOME REST!

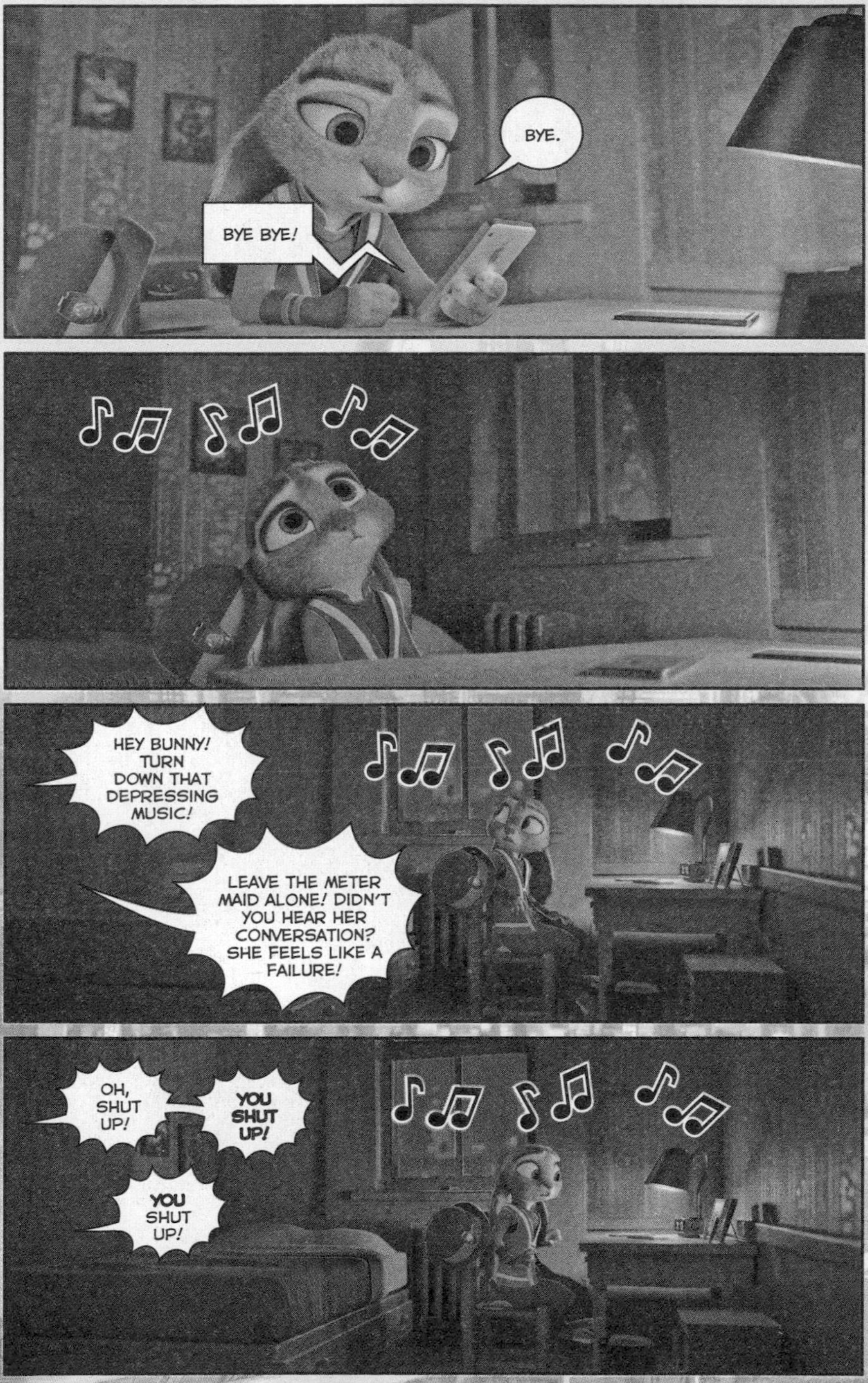
BYE.
BYE BYE!
HEY BUNNY! TURN DOWN THAT DEPRESSING MUSIC!
LEAVE THE METER MAID ALONE! DIDN'T YOU HEAR HER CONVERSATION? SHE FEELS LIKE A FAILURE!
OH, SHUT UP!
YOU SHUT UP!
YOU SHUT UP!

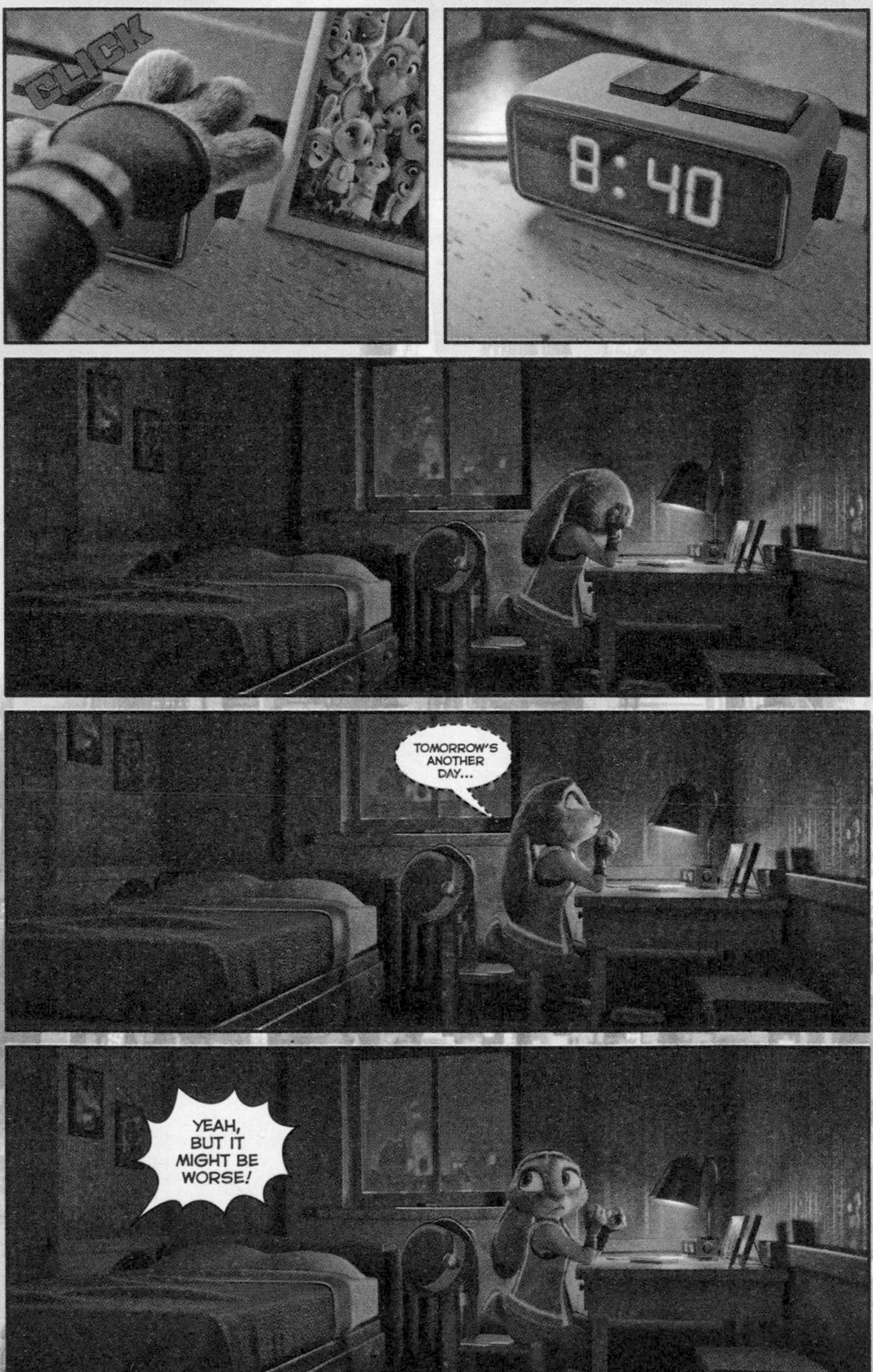
CLICK
8:40
TOMORROW'S ANOTHER DAY...
YEAH, BUT IT MIGHT BE WORSE!

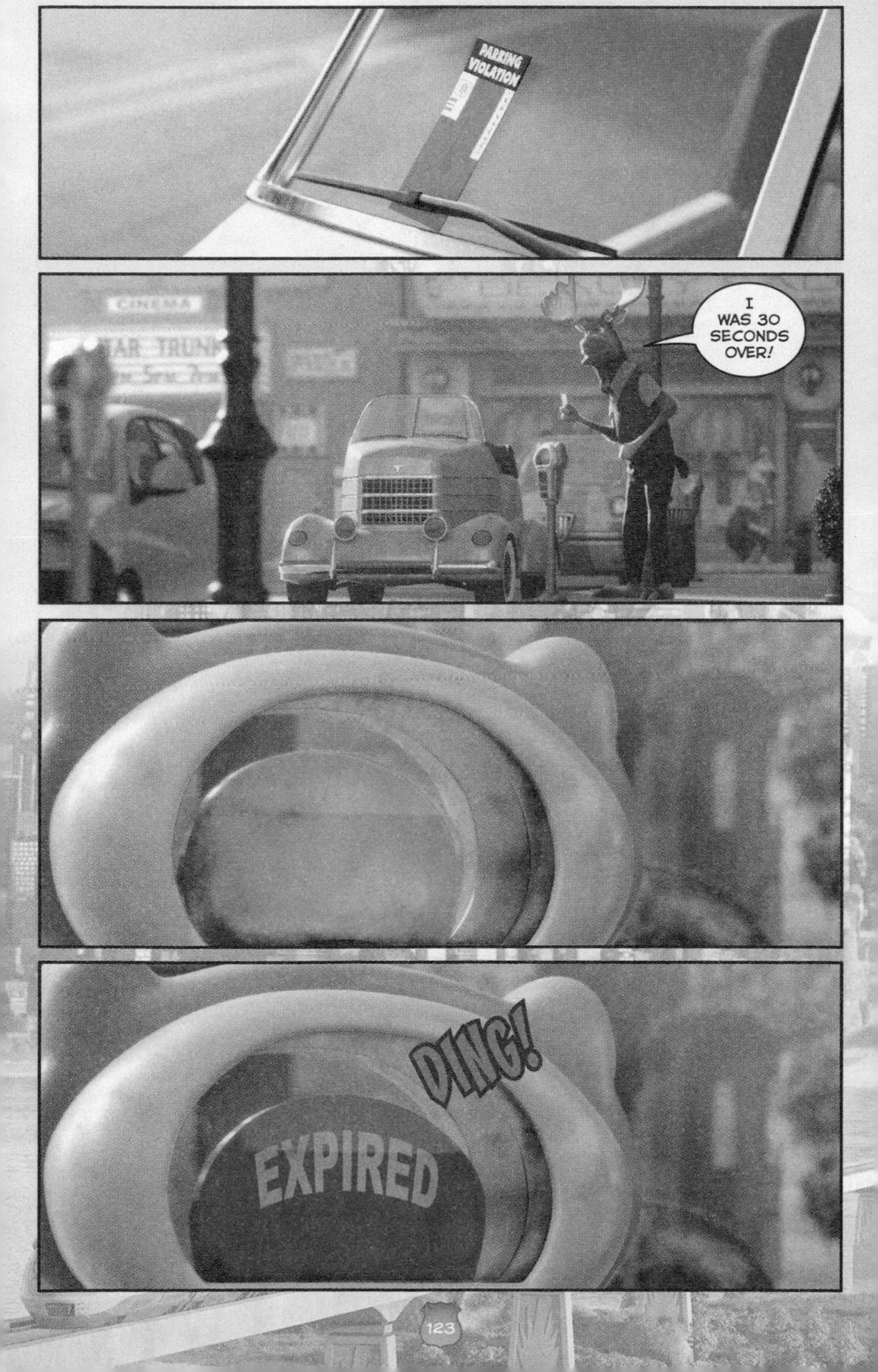
PARKING VIOLATION
CINEMA
I WAS 30 SECONDS OVER!
DING!
EXPIRED

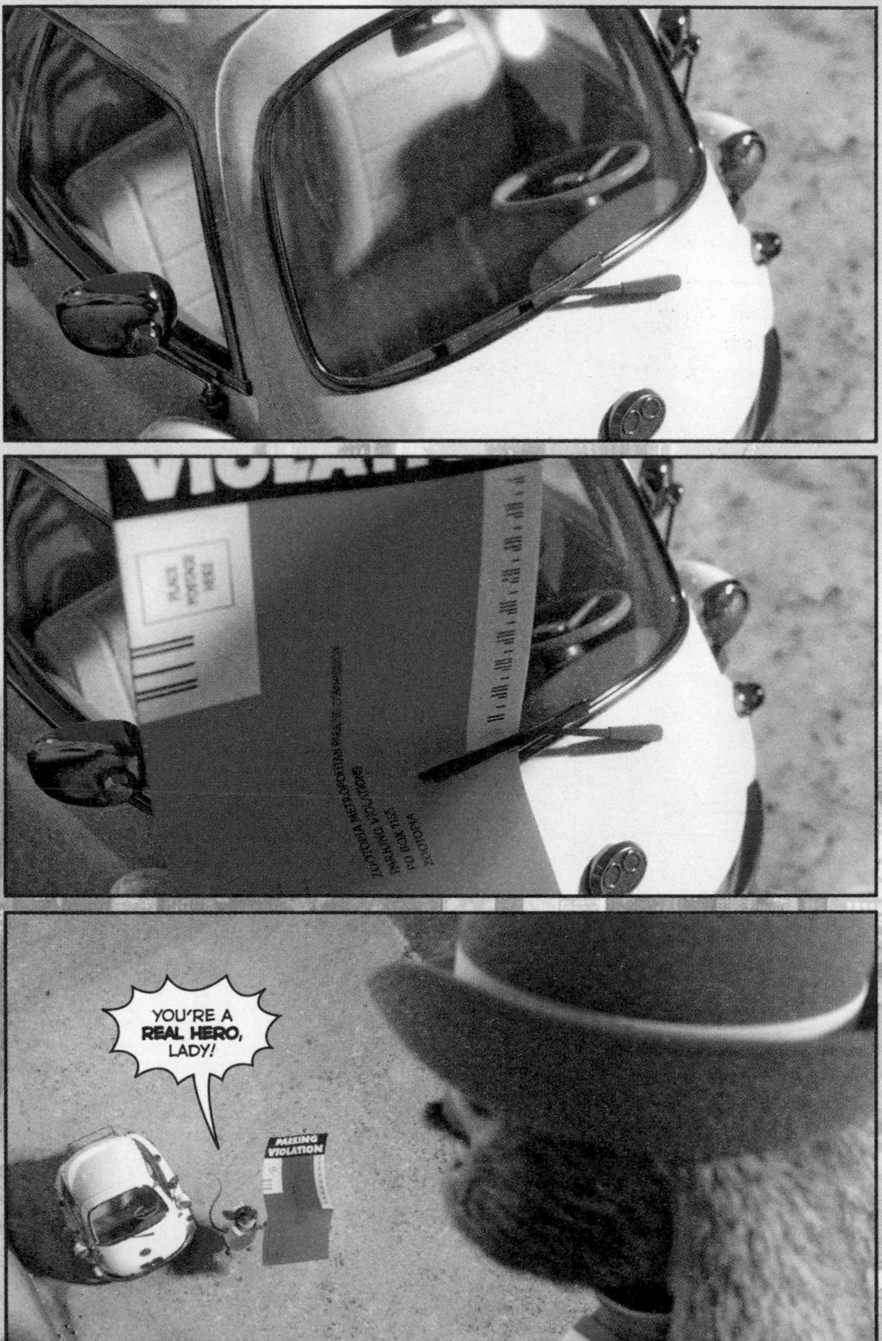
YOU'RE A REAL HERO, LADY!
PARKING VIOLATION

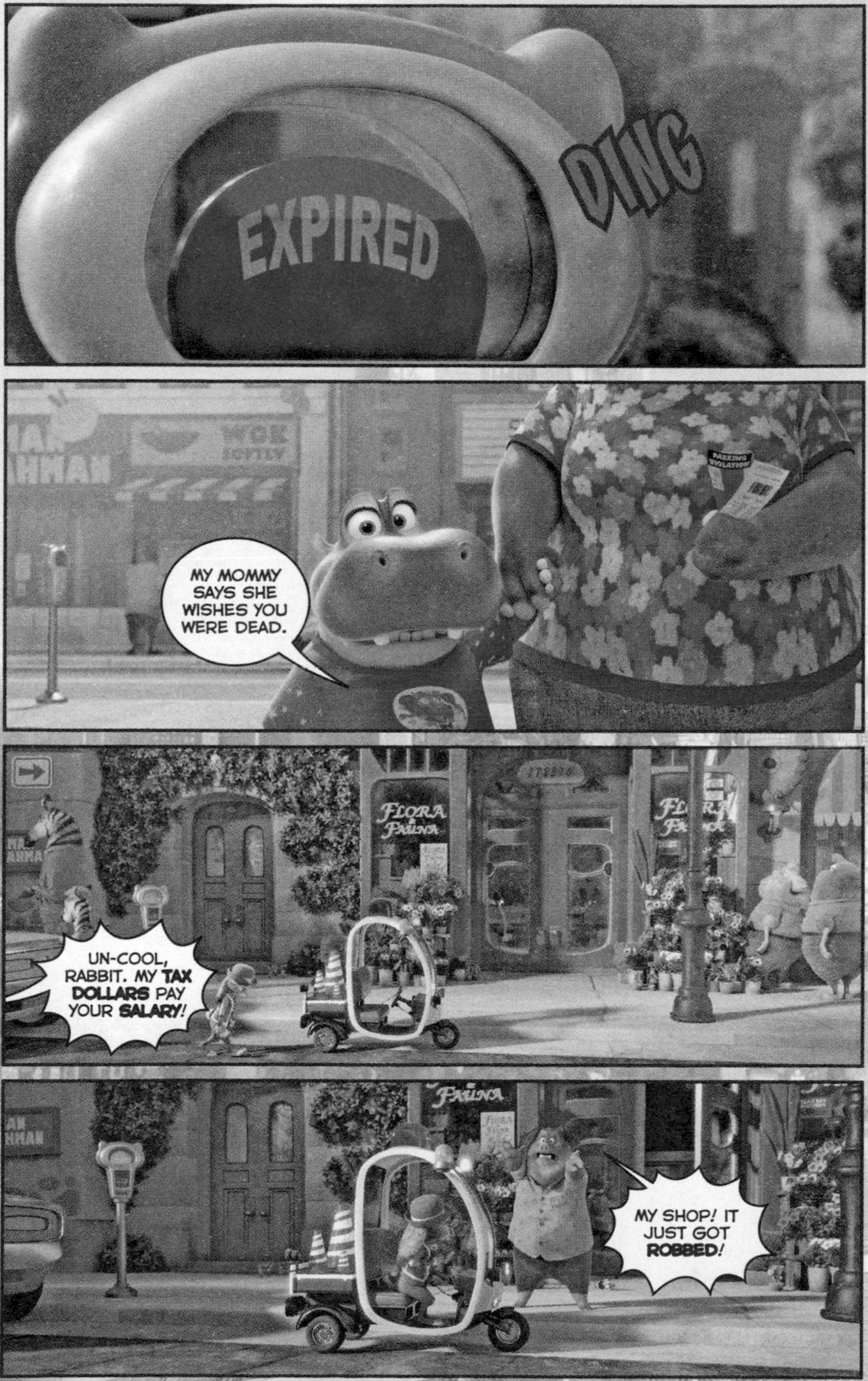
EXPIRED
DING
MY MOMMY SAYS SHE WISHES YOU WERE DEAD.
FLORA & FAUNA
UN-COOL, RABBIT. MY TAX DOLLARS PAY YOUR SALARY!
MY SHOP! IT JUST GOT ROBBED!

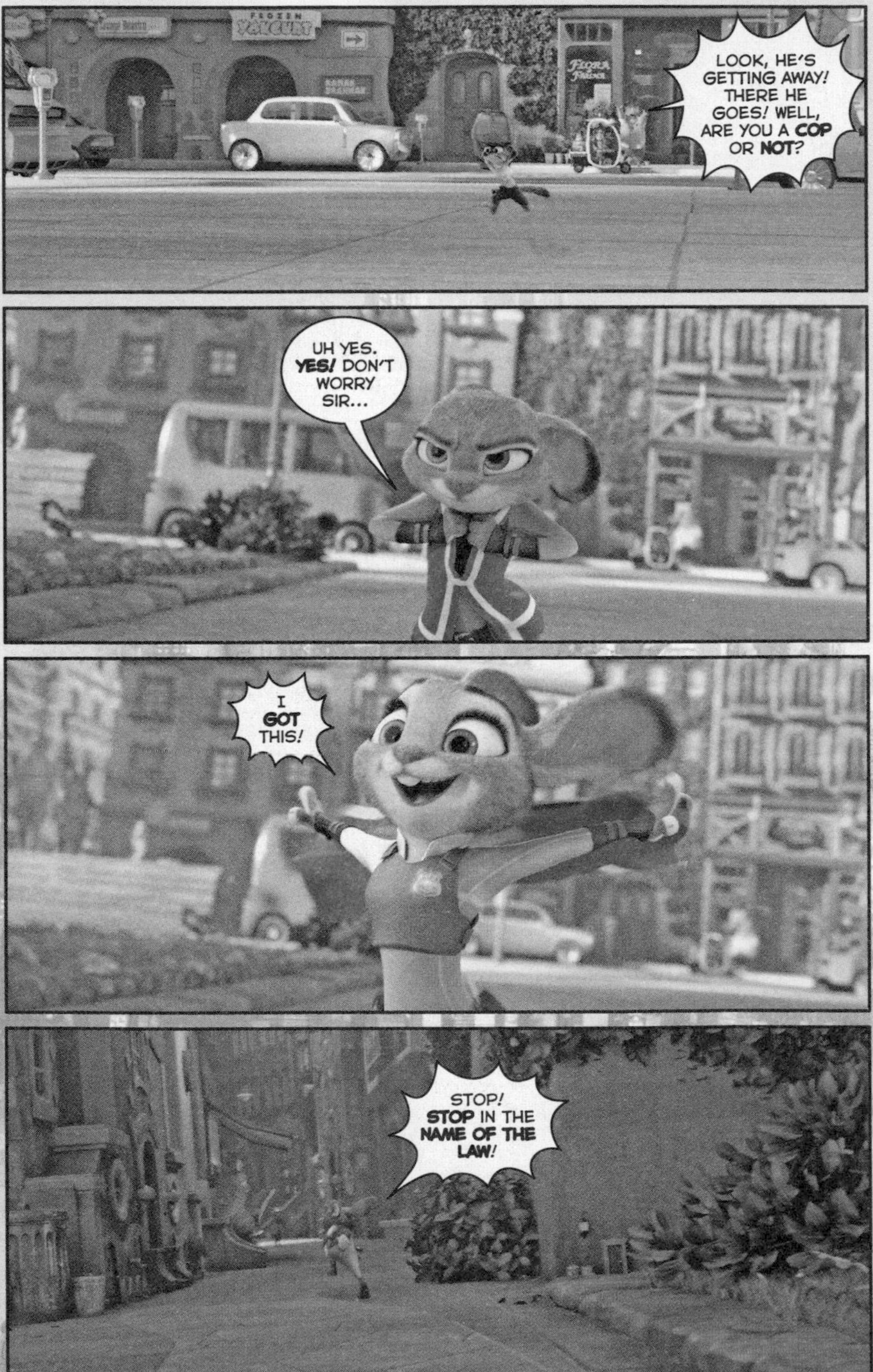
LOOK, HE'S GETTING AWAY! THERE HE GOES! WELL, ARE YOU A COP OR NOT?
UH YES. YES! DON'T WORRY SIR...
I GOT THIS!
STOP! STOP IN THE NAME OF THE LAW!

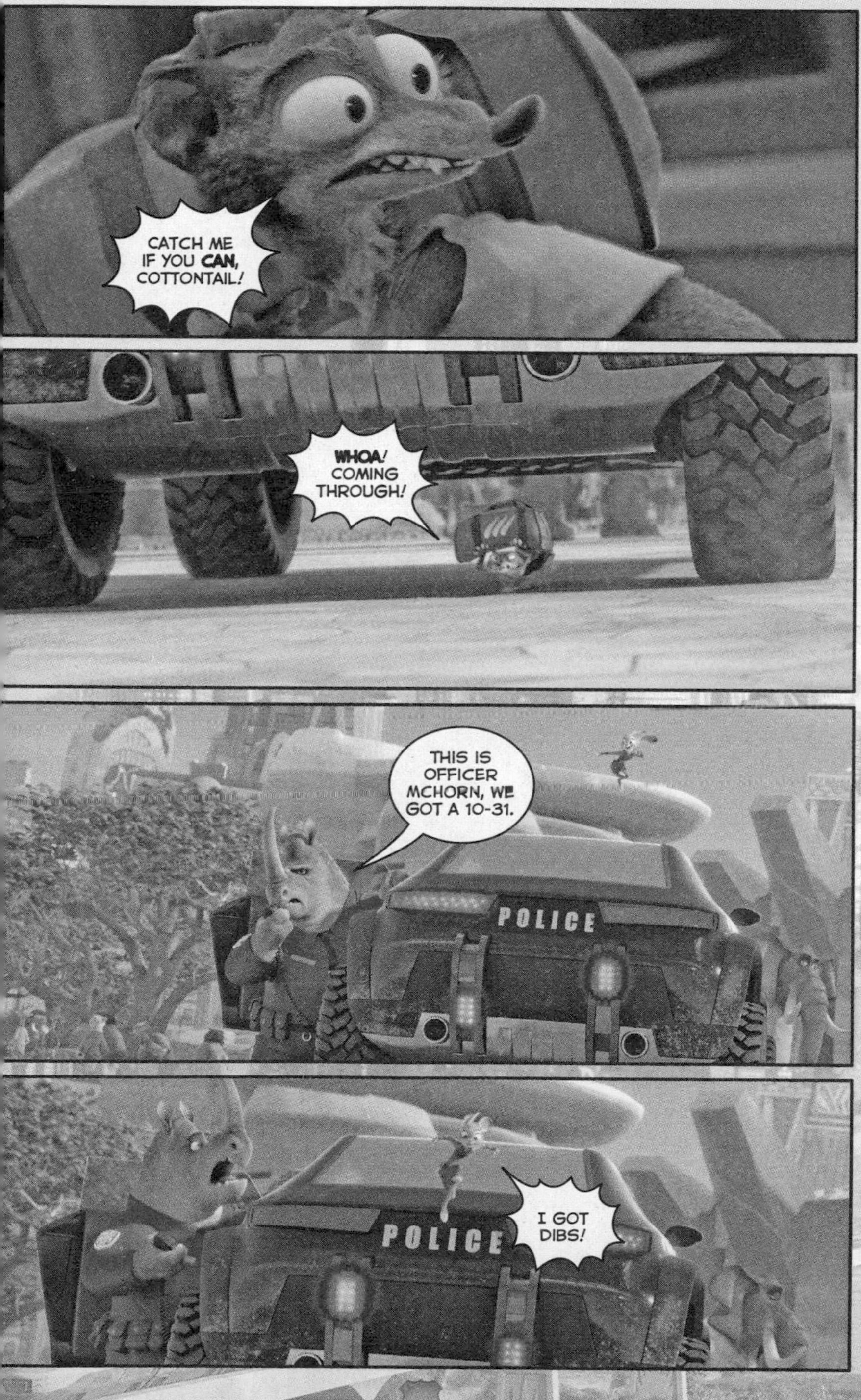
CATCH ME IF YOU **CAN**, COTTONTAIL!
WHOA! COMING THROUGH!
THIS IS OFFICER MCHORN, WE GOT A 10-31.
POLICE
POLICE
I GOT DIBS!

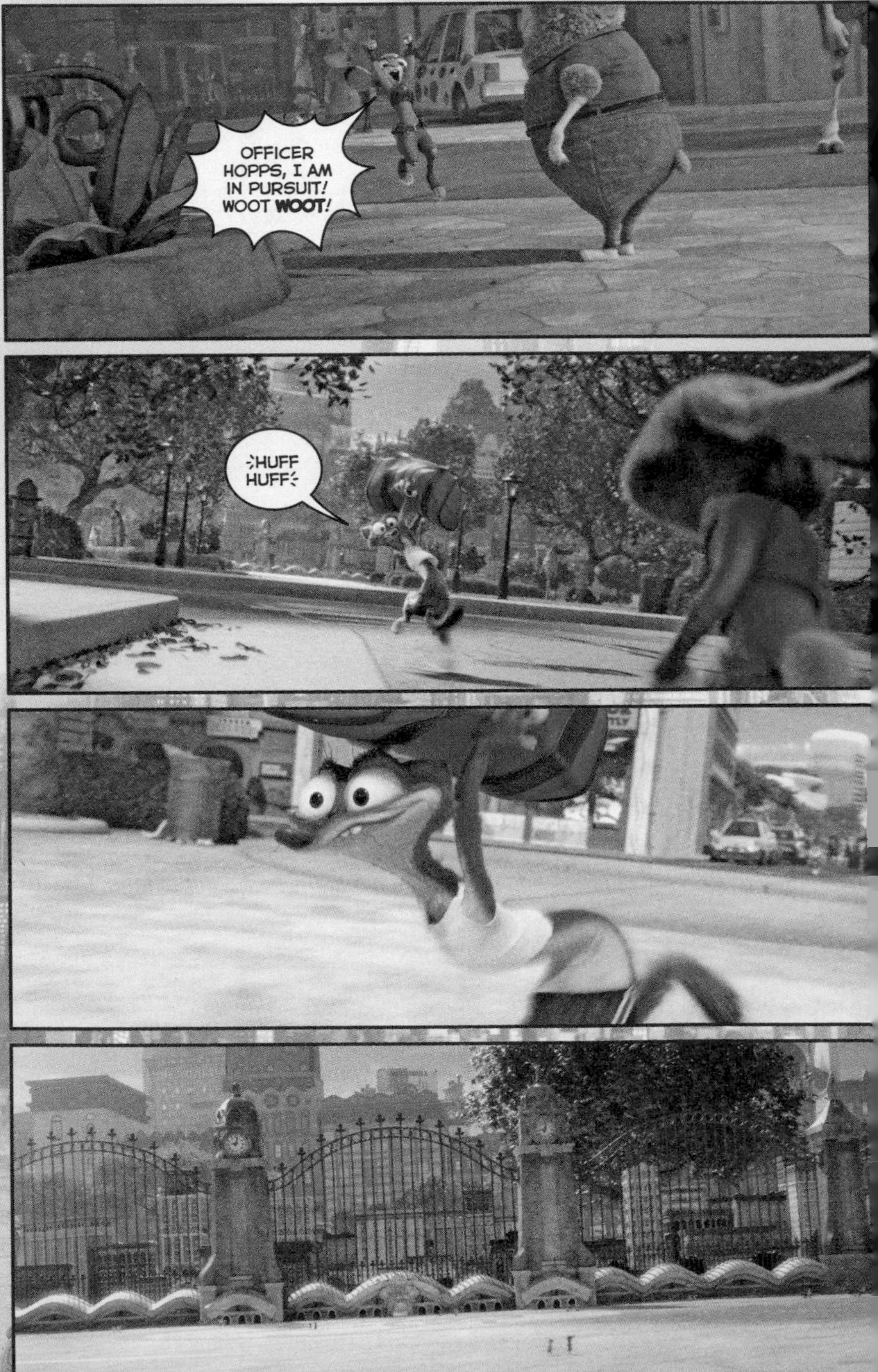
OFFICER HOPPS, I AM IN PURSUIT! WOOT **WOOT**!
HUFF HUFF

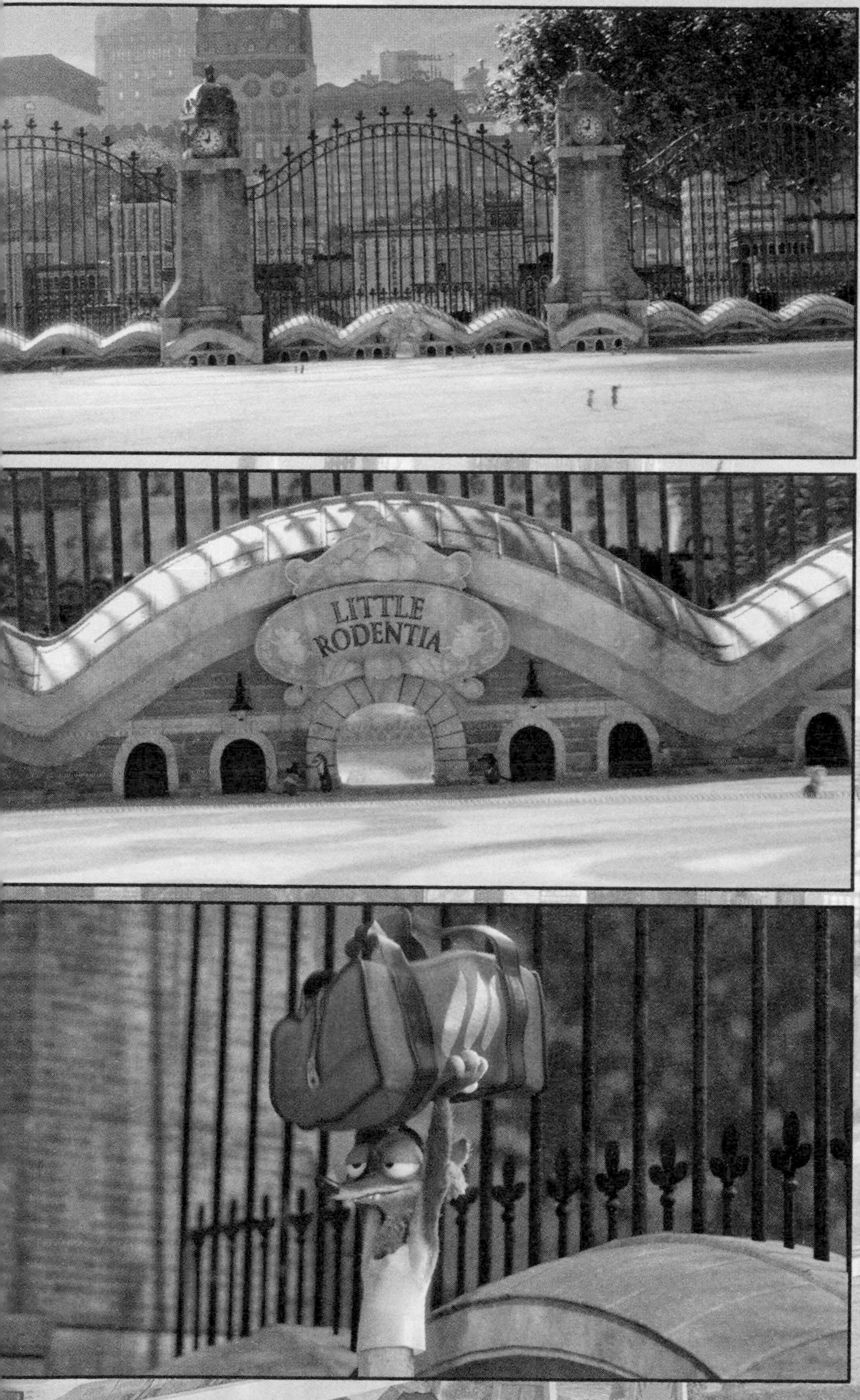
LITTLE RODENTIA

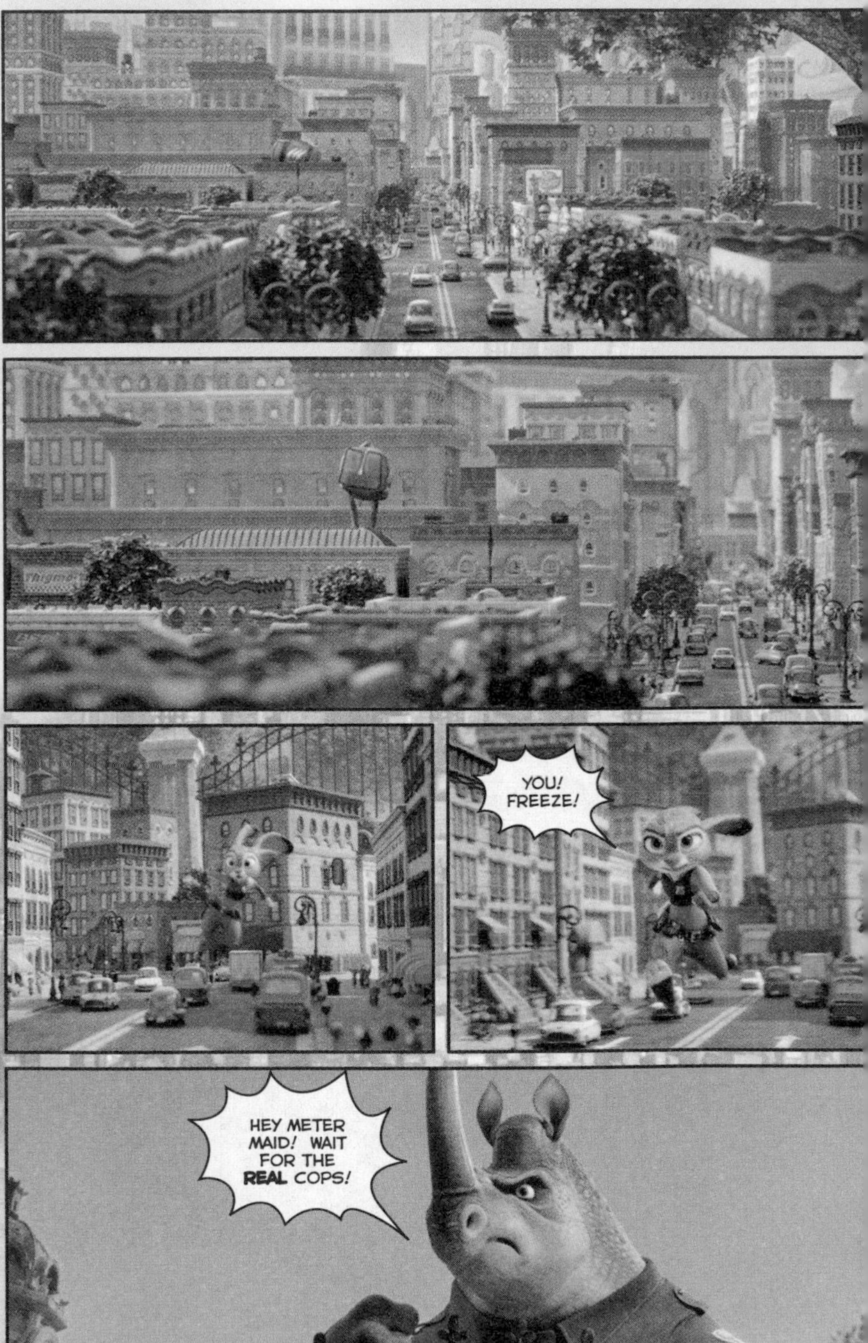
YOU! FREEZE!
HEY METER MAID! WAIT FOR THE REAL COPS!

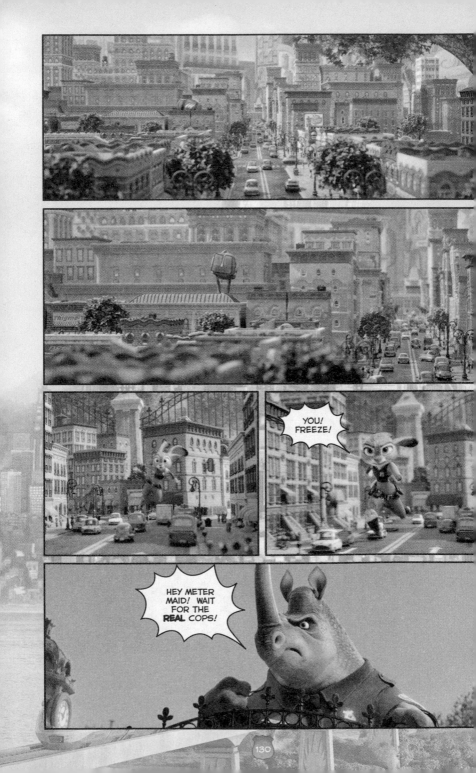

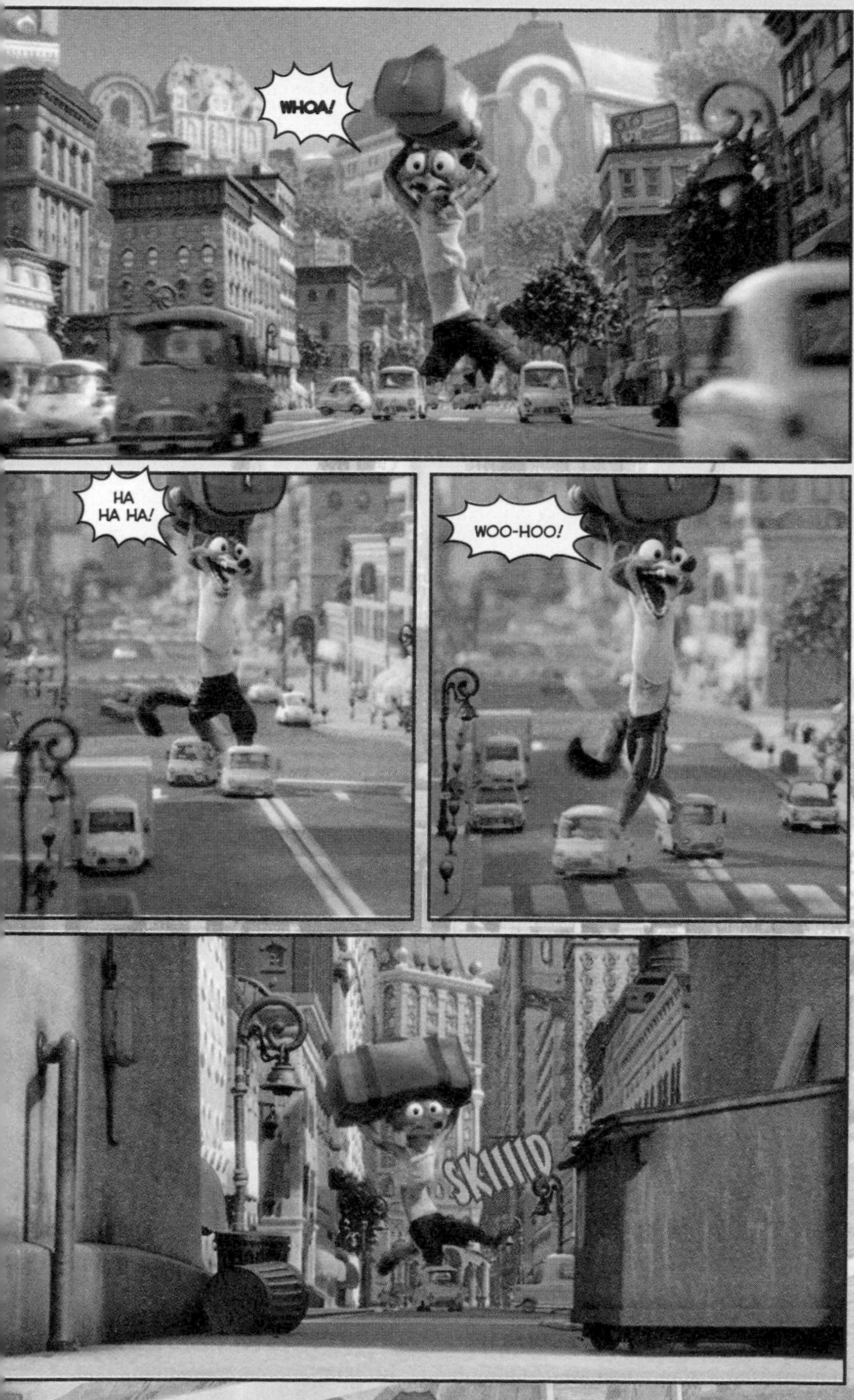
WHOA!
HA HA HA!
WOO-HOO!
SKIIIID

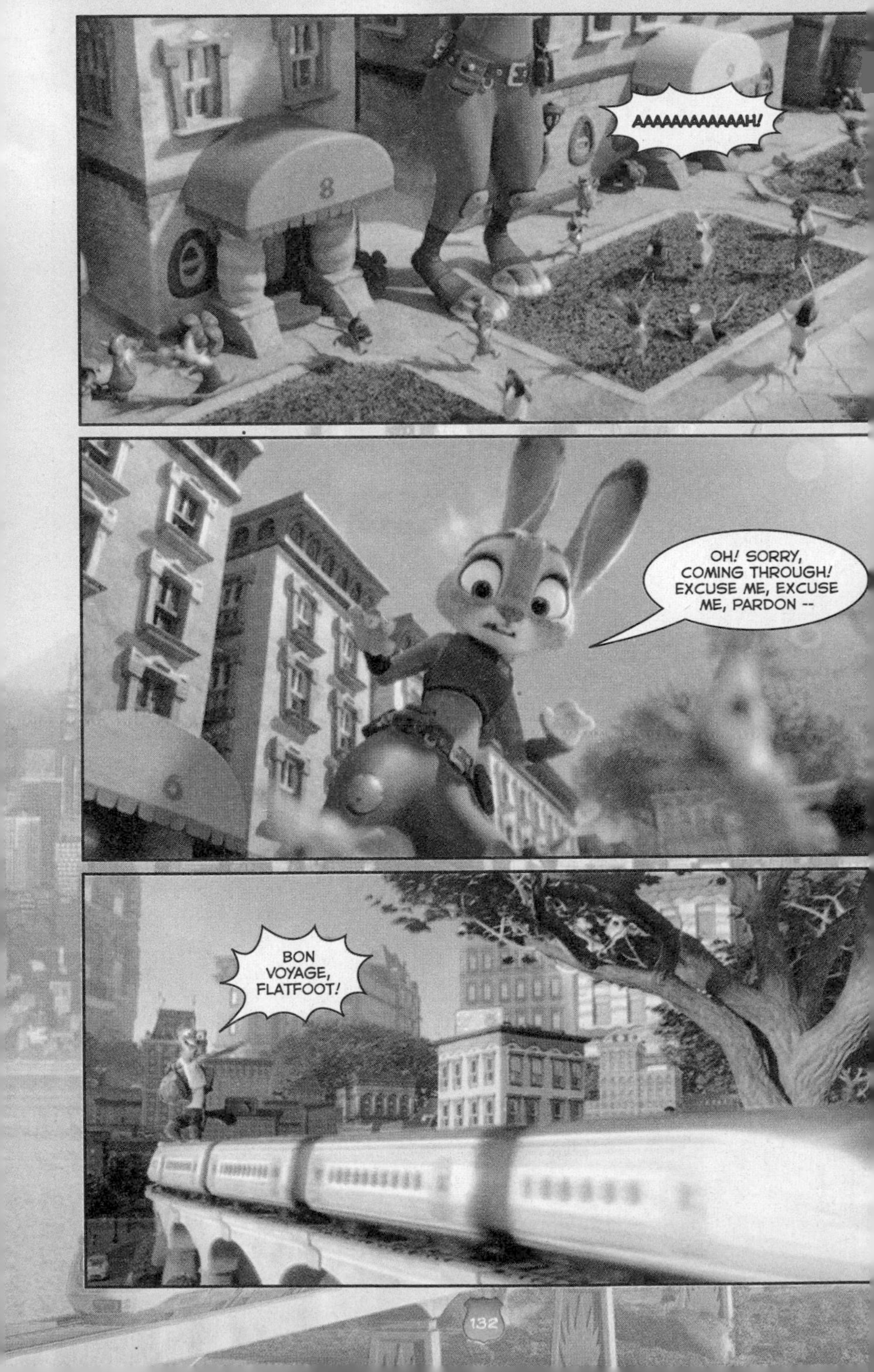
AAAAAAAAAAAAAH!
OH! SORRY, COMING THROUGH! EXCUSE ME, EXCUSE ME, PARDON --
BON VOYAGE, FLATFOOT!

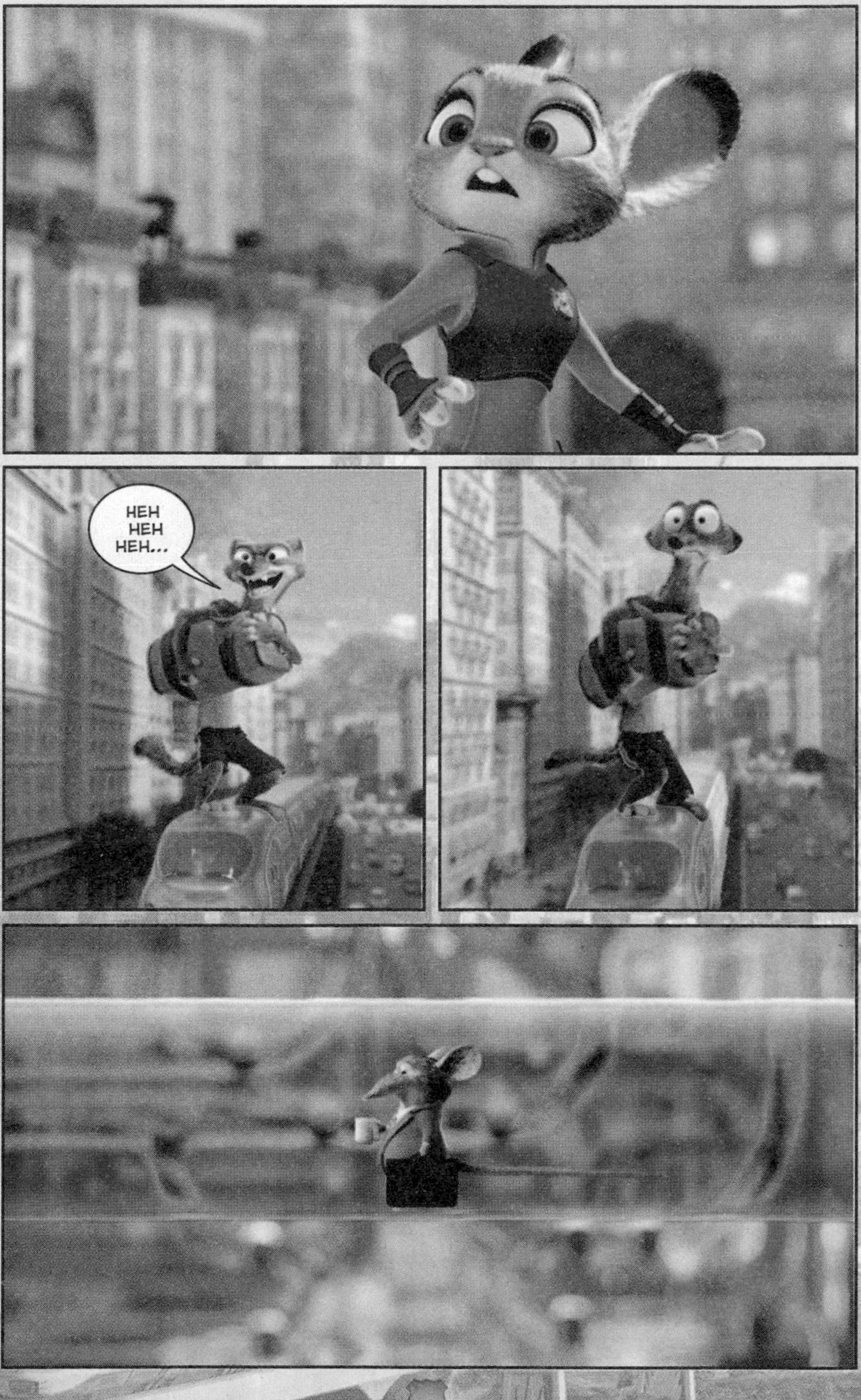
HEH
HEH
HEH...

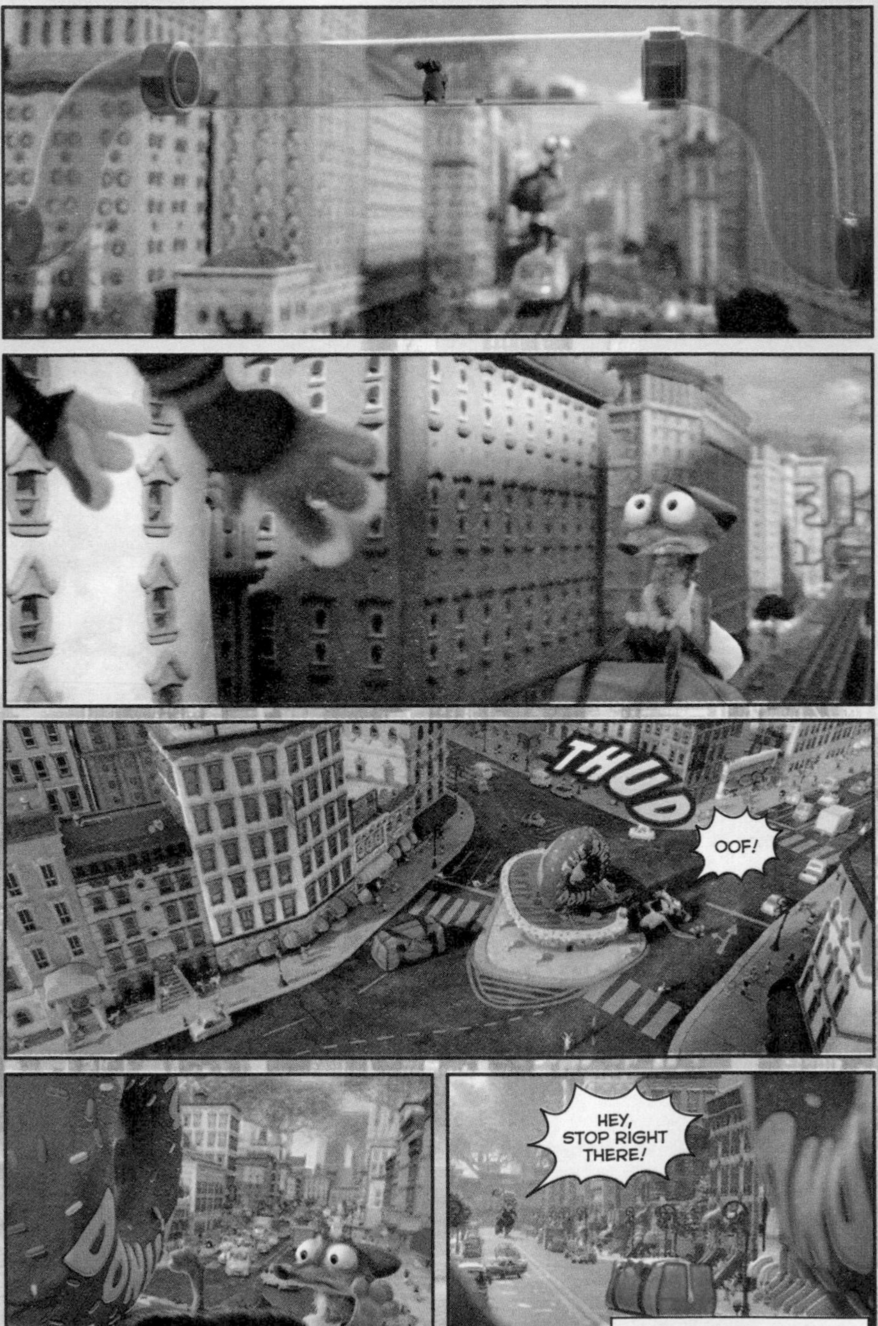
THUD
OOF!
HEY, STOP RIGHT THERE!
SEEING OFFICER HOPPS CHARGE, THE WEASEL KICKS THE DONUT FREE...

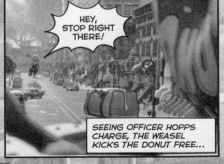

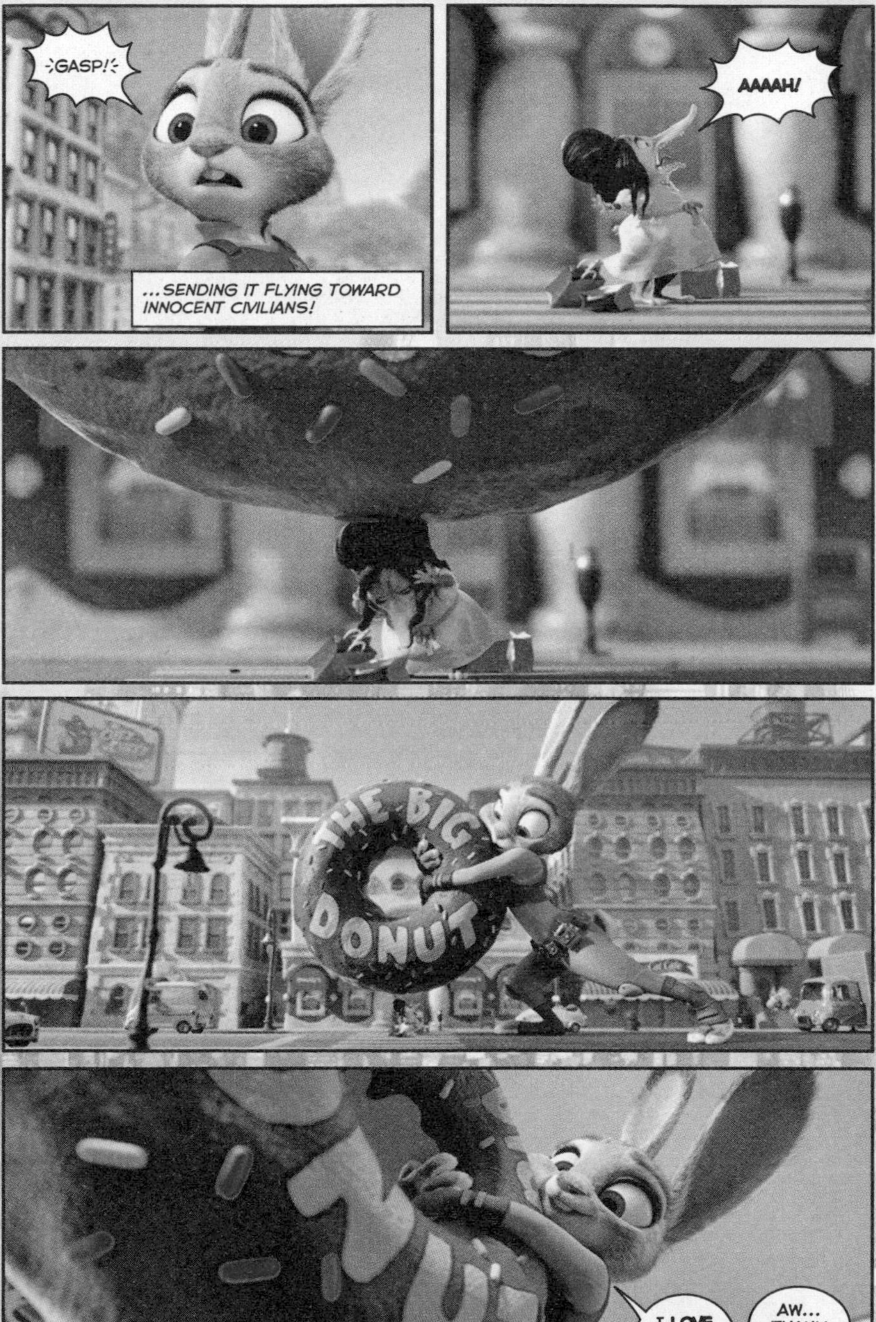
GASP!
...SENDING IT FLYING TOWARD INNOCENT CIVILIANS!
AAAAH!
THE BIG DONUT
I LOVE YOUR HAIR.
AW... THANK YOU.

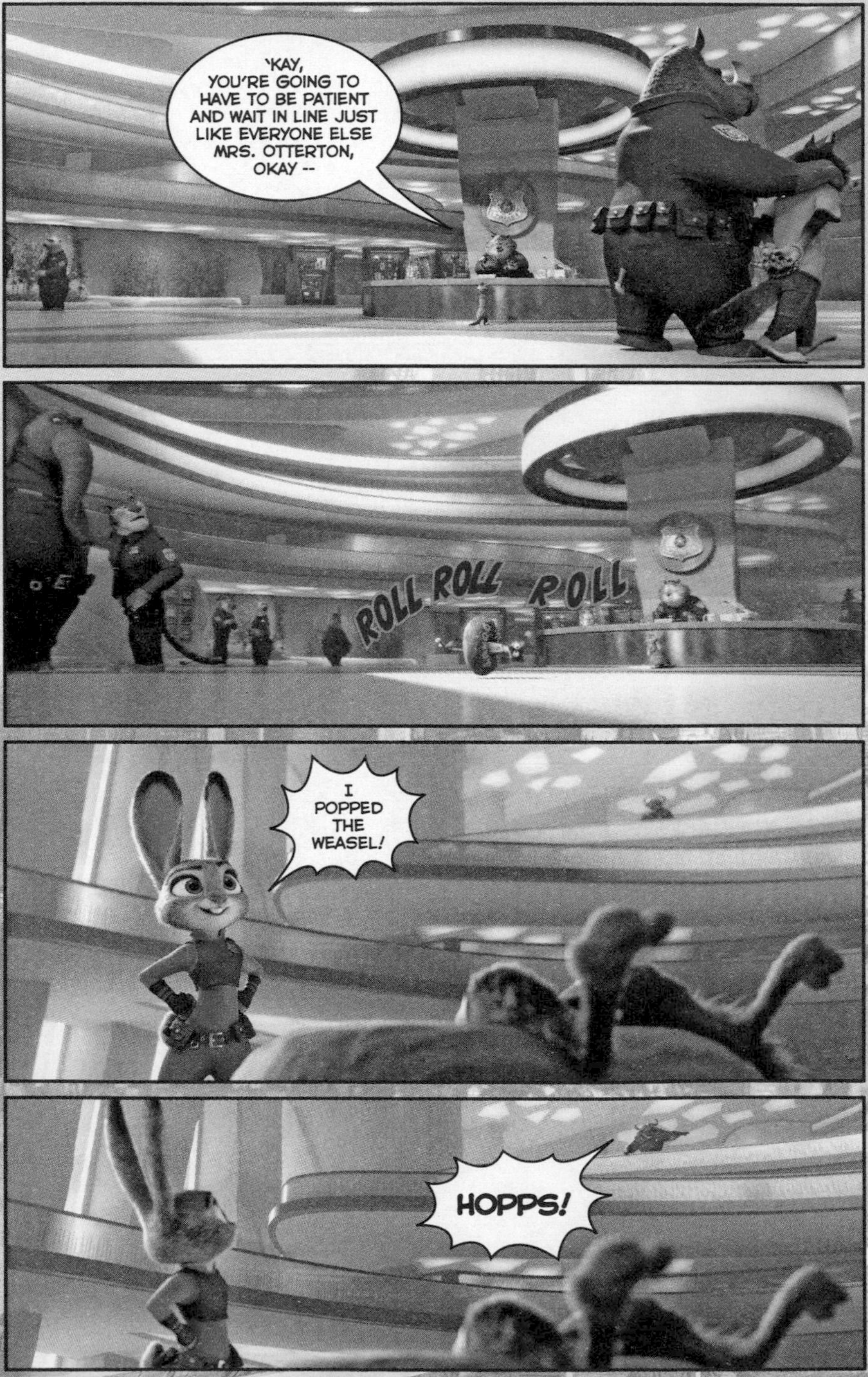
'KAY, YOU'RE GOING TO HAVE TO BE PATIENT AND WAIT IN LINE JUST LIKE EVERYONE ELSE MRS. OTTERTON, OKAY --
ROLL ROLL ROLL
I POPPED THE WEASEL!
HOPPS!

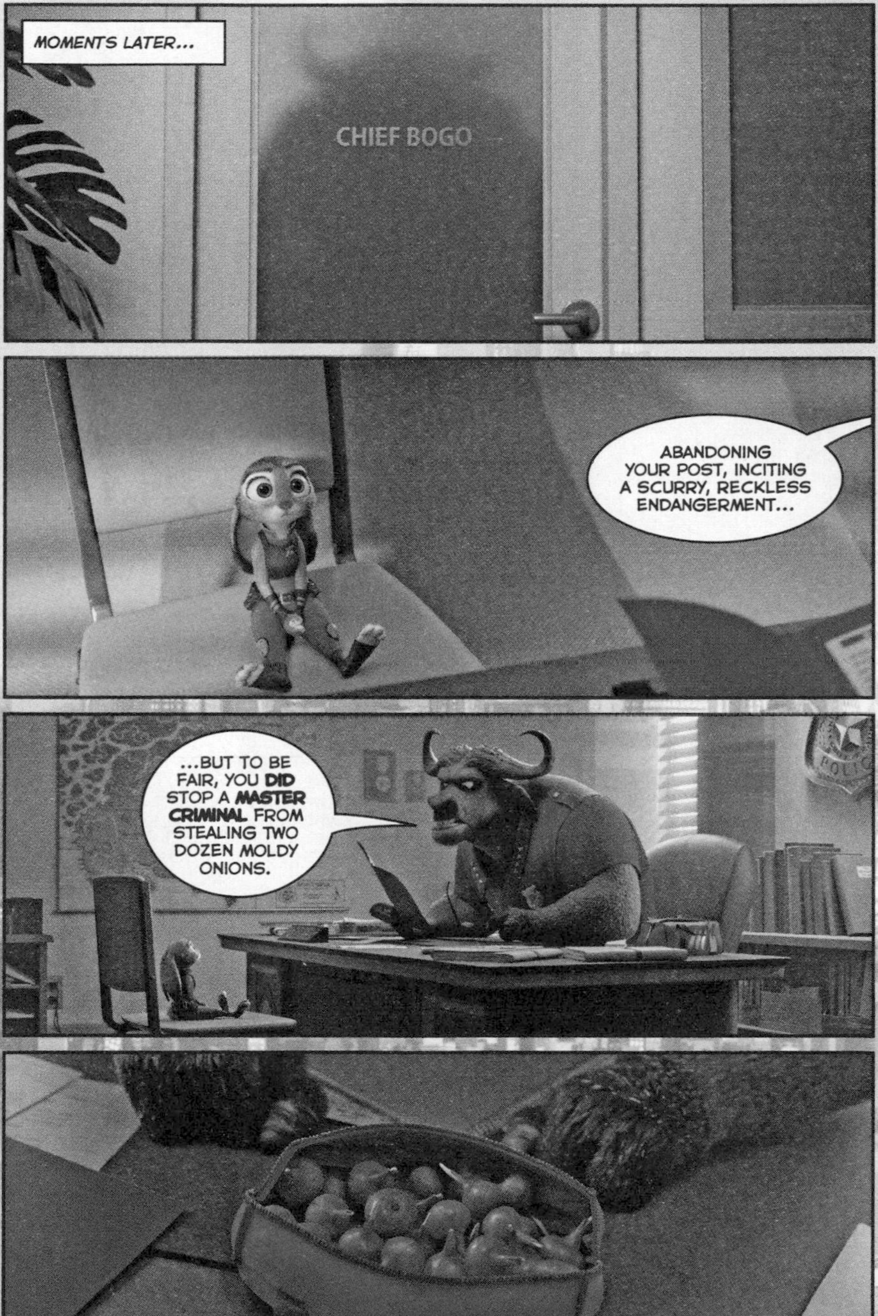
MOMENTS LATER...
CHIEF BOGO
ABANDONING YOUR POST, INCITING A SCURRY, RECKLESS ENDANGERMENT...
...BUT TO BE FAIR, YOU DID STOP A MASTER CRIMINAL FROM STEALING TWO DOZEN MOLDY ONIONS.

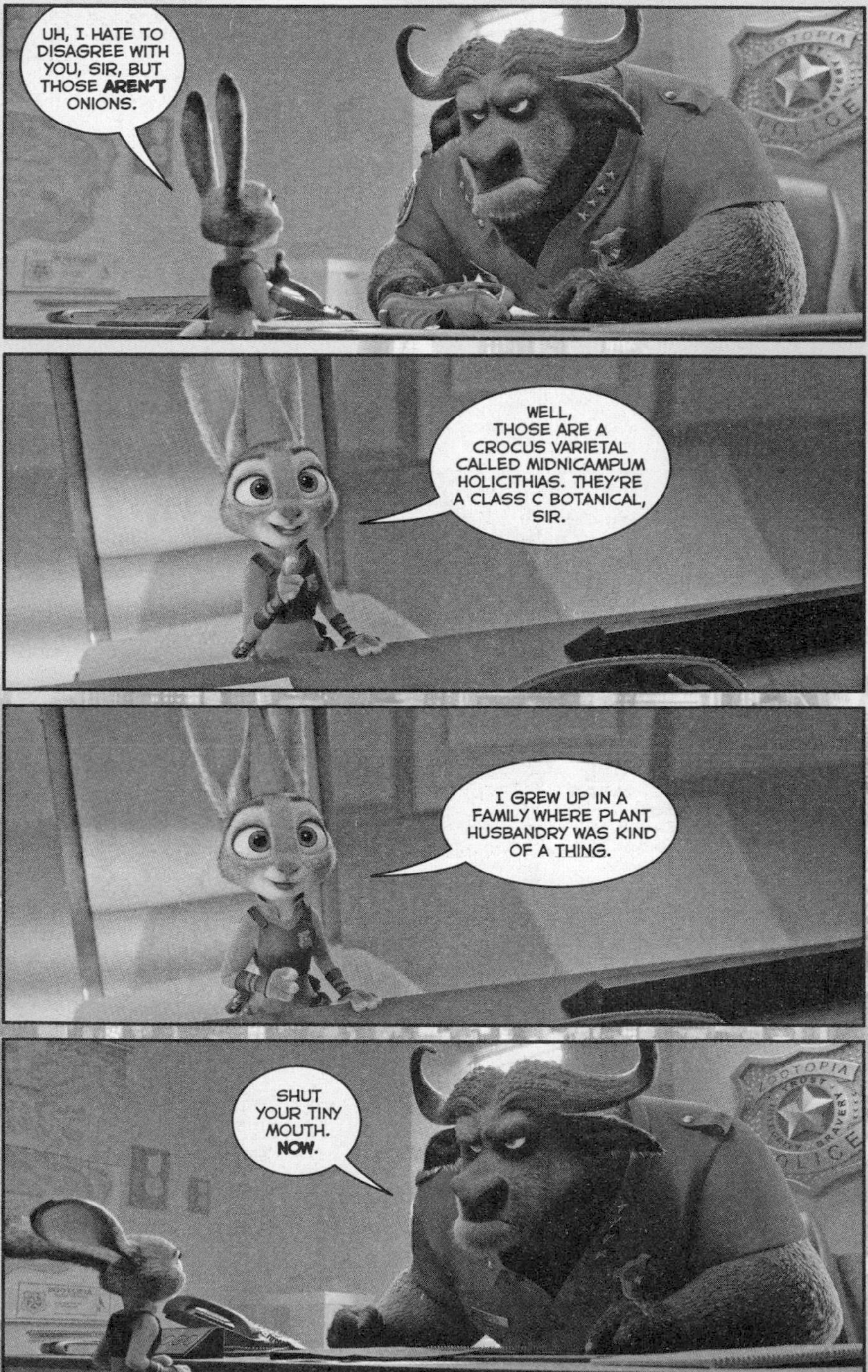
UH, I HATE TO DISAGREE WITH YOU, SIR, BUT THOSE **AREN'T** ONIONS.
WELL, THOSE ARE A CROCUS VARIETAL CALLED MIDNICAMPUM HOLICITHIAS. THEY'RE A CLASS C BOTANICAL, SIR.
I GREW UP IN A FAMILY WHERE PLANT HUSBANDRY WAS KIND OF A THING.
SHUT YOUR TINY MOUTH. **NOW**.

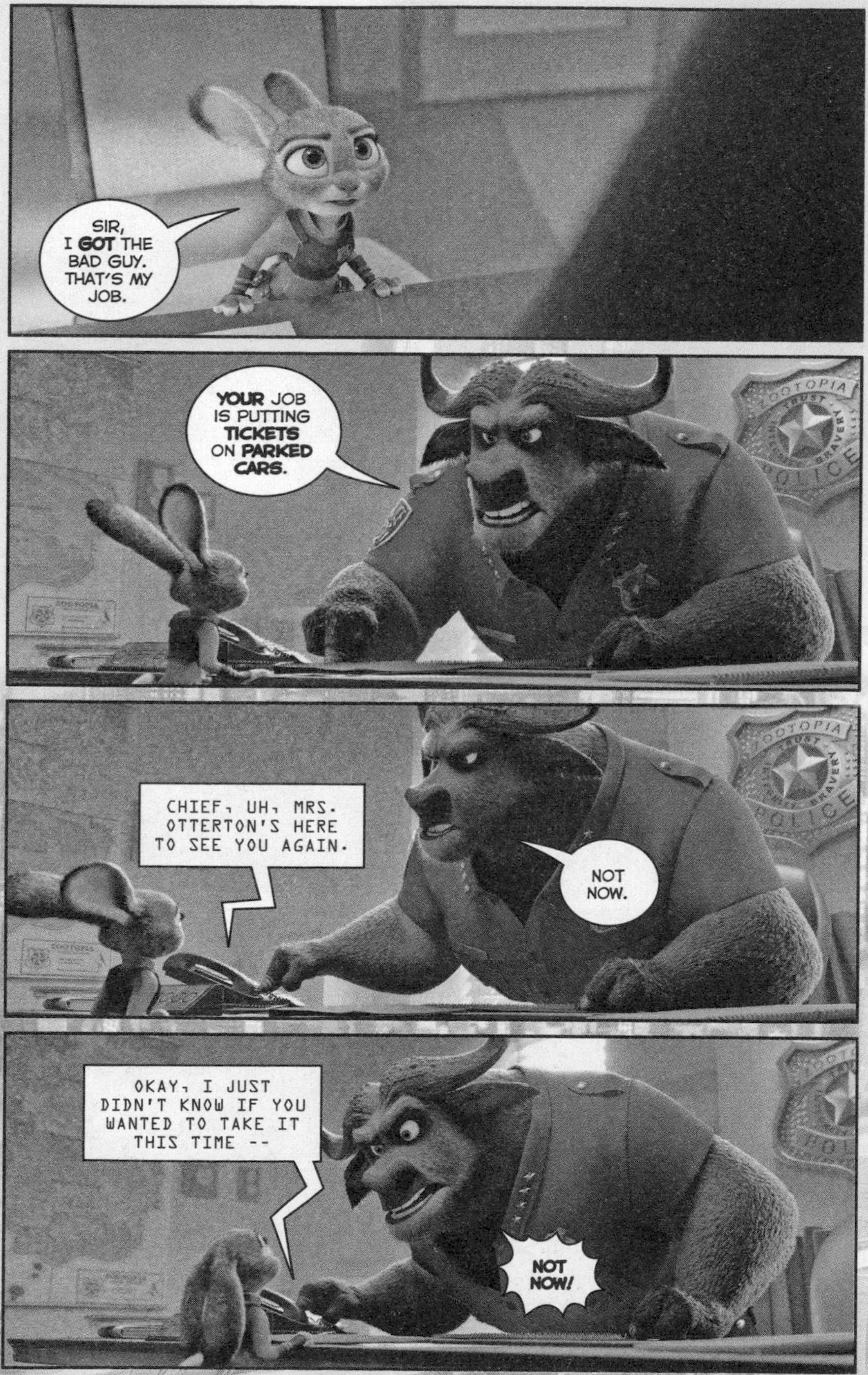
SIR, I **GOT** THE BAD GUY. THAT'S MY JOB.
YOUR JOB IS PUTTING **TICKETS** ON **PARKED CARS.**
CHIEF, UH, MRS. OTTERTON'S HERE TO SEE YOU AGAIN.
NOT NOW.
OKAY, I JUST DIDN'T KNOW IF YOU WANTED TO TAKE IT THIS TIME --
NOT NOW!

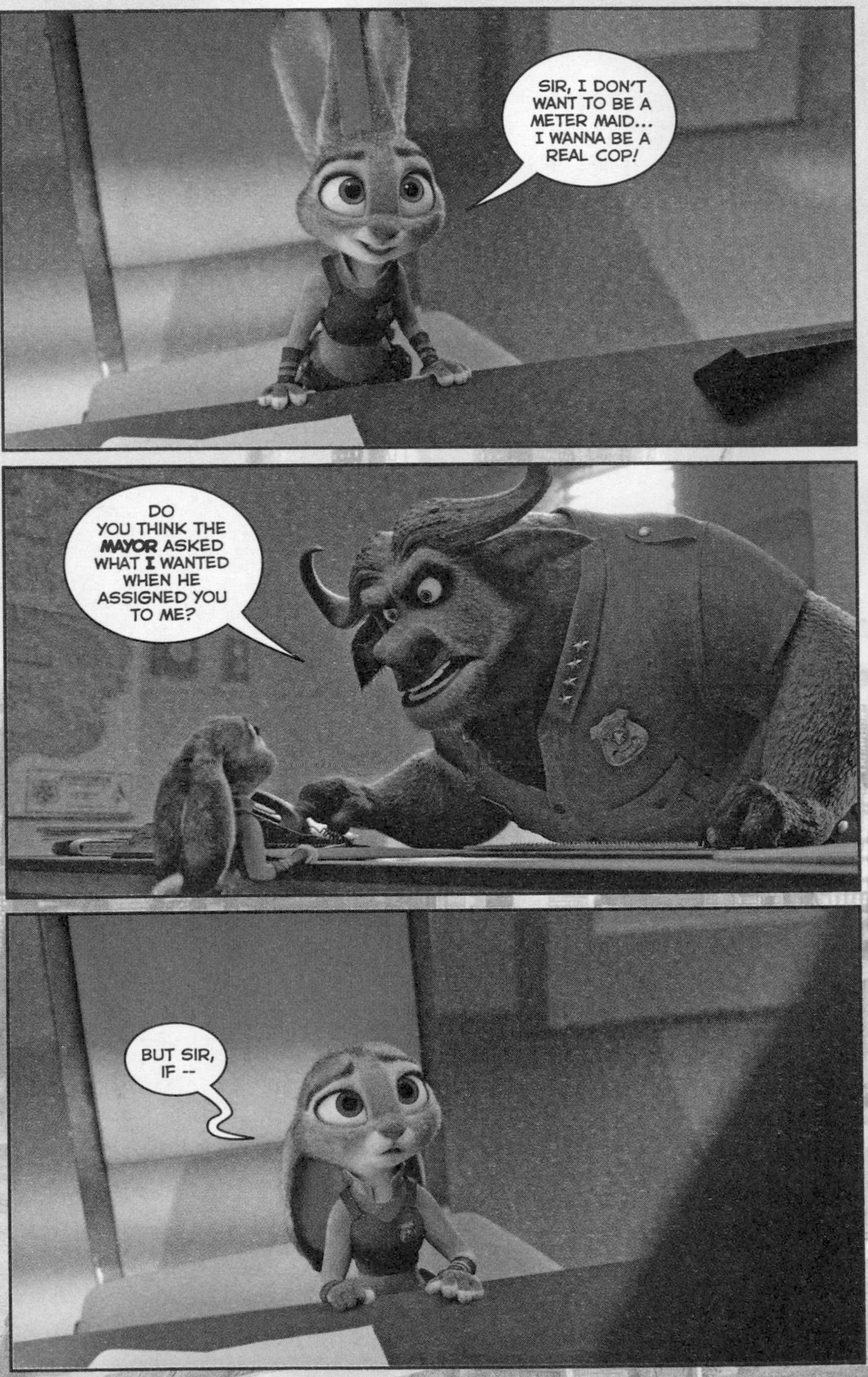
SIR, I DON'T WANT TO BE A METER MAID... I WANNA BE A REAL COP!
DO YOU THINK THE MAYOR ASKED WHAT I WANTED WHEN HE ASSIGNED YOU TO ME?
BUT SIR, IF --

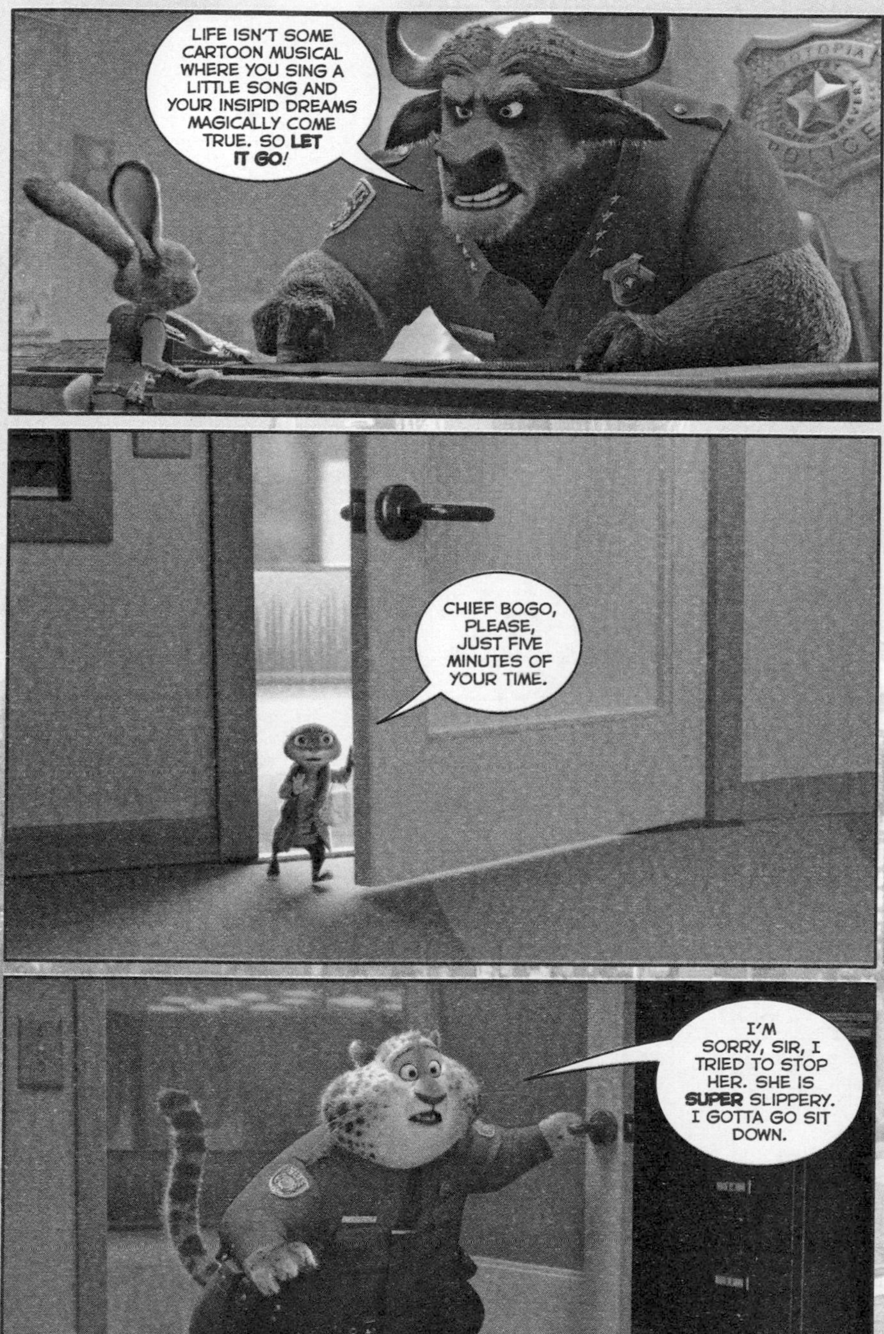
LIFE ISN'T SOME CARTOON MUSICAL WHERE YOU SING A LITTLE SONG AND YOUR INSIPID DREAMS MAGICALLY COME TRUE. SO **LET IT GO**!
CHIEF BOGO, PLEASE, JUST FIVE MINUTES OF YOUR TIME.
I'M SORRY, SIR, I TRIED TO STOP HER. SHE IS **SUPER** SLIPPERY. I GOTTA GO SIT DOWN.

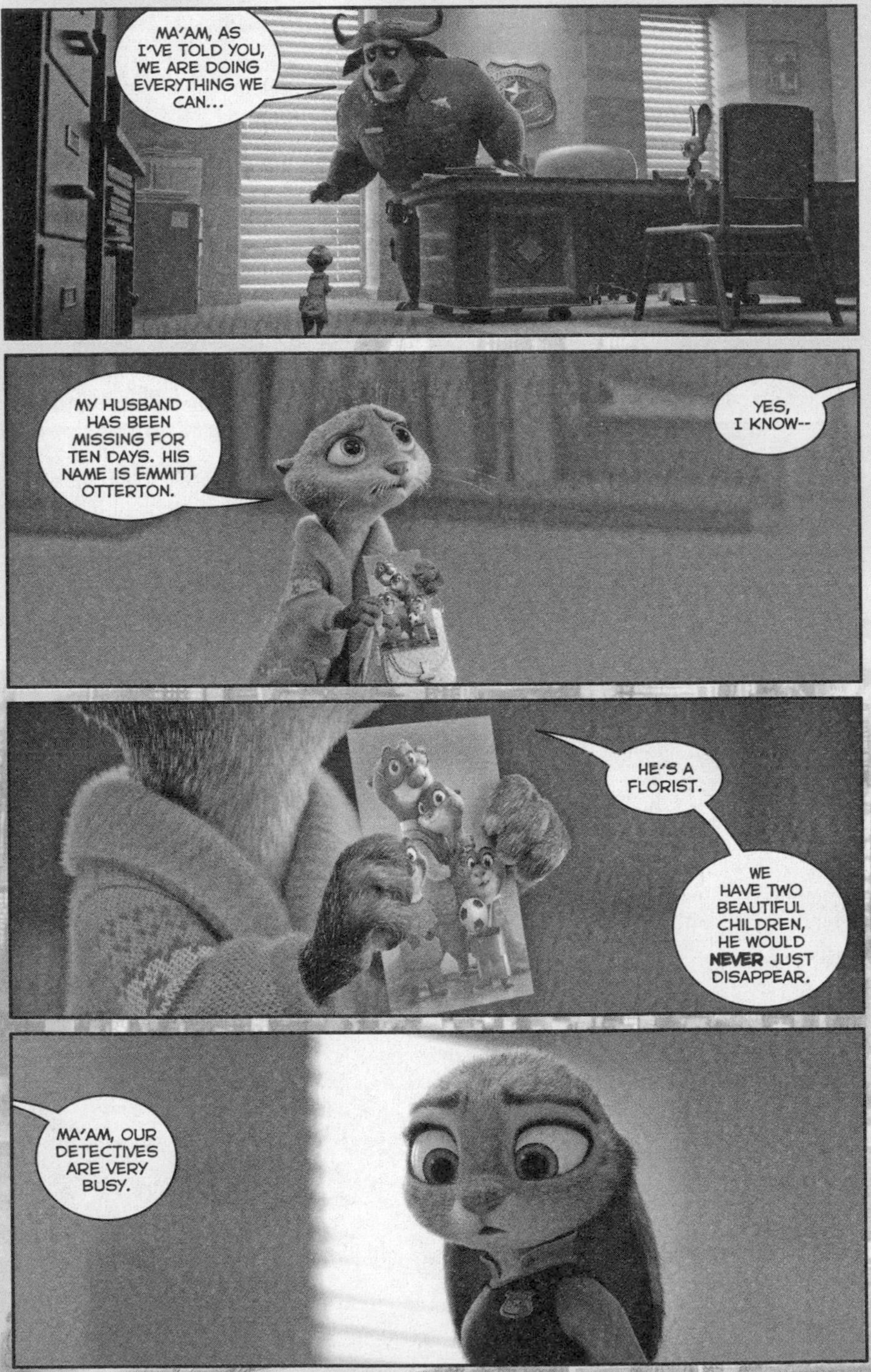
MA'AM, AS I'VE TOLD YOU, WE ARE DOING EVERYTHING WE CAN...
MY HUSBAND HAS BEEN MISSING FOR TEN DAYS. HIS NAME IS EMMITT OTTERTON.
YES, I KNOW--
HE'S A FLORIST.
WE HAVE TWO BEAUTIFUL CHILDREN, HE WOULD **NEVER** JUST DISAPPEAR.
MA'AM, OUR DETECTIVES ARE VERY BUSY.

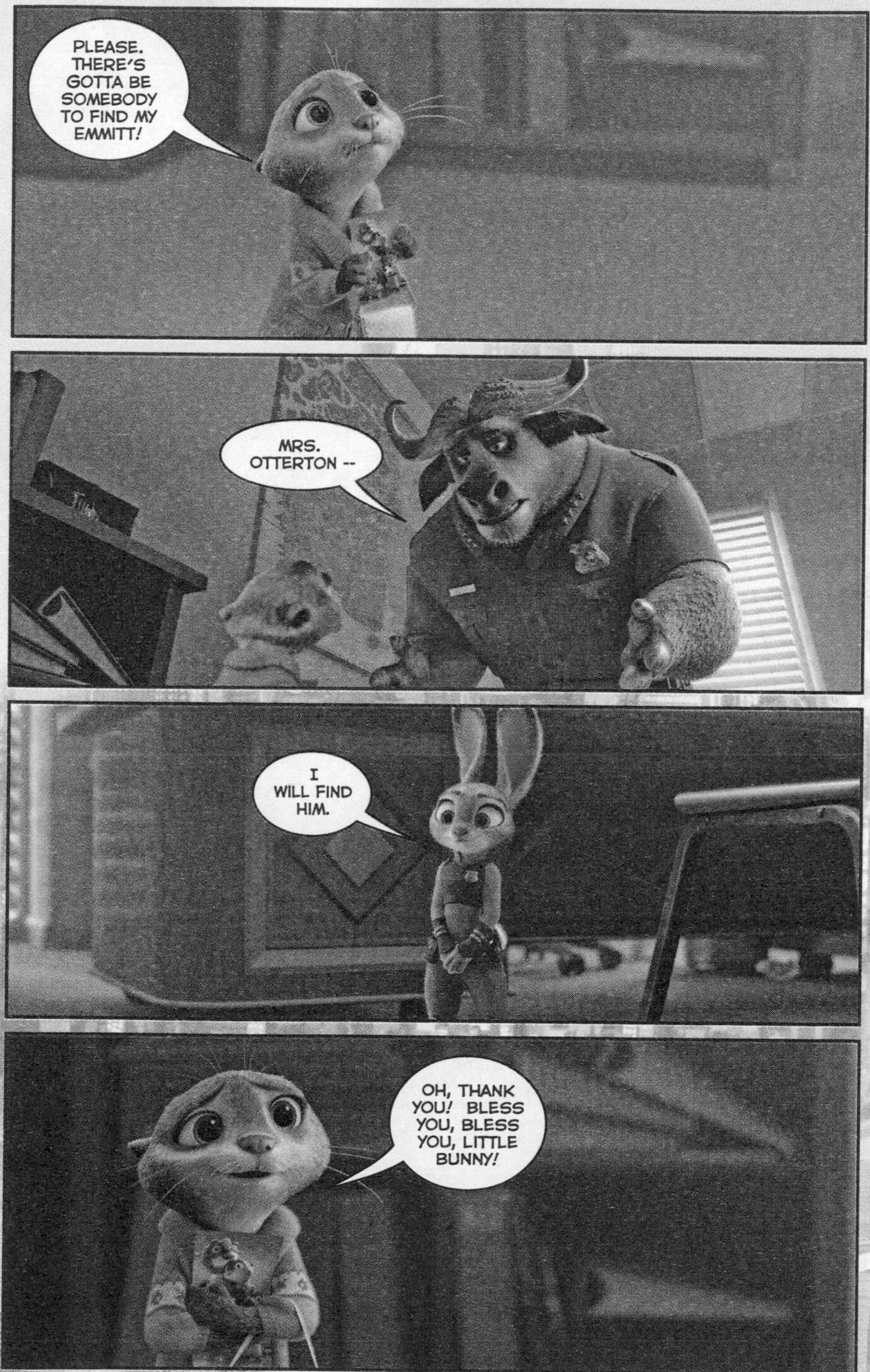
PLEASE. THERE'S GOTTA BE SOMEBODY TO FIND MY EMMITT!
MRS. OTTERTON --
I WILL FIND HIM.
OH, THANK YOU! BLESS YOU, BLESS YOU, LITTLE BUNNY!

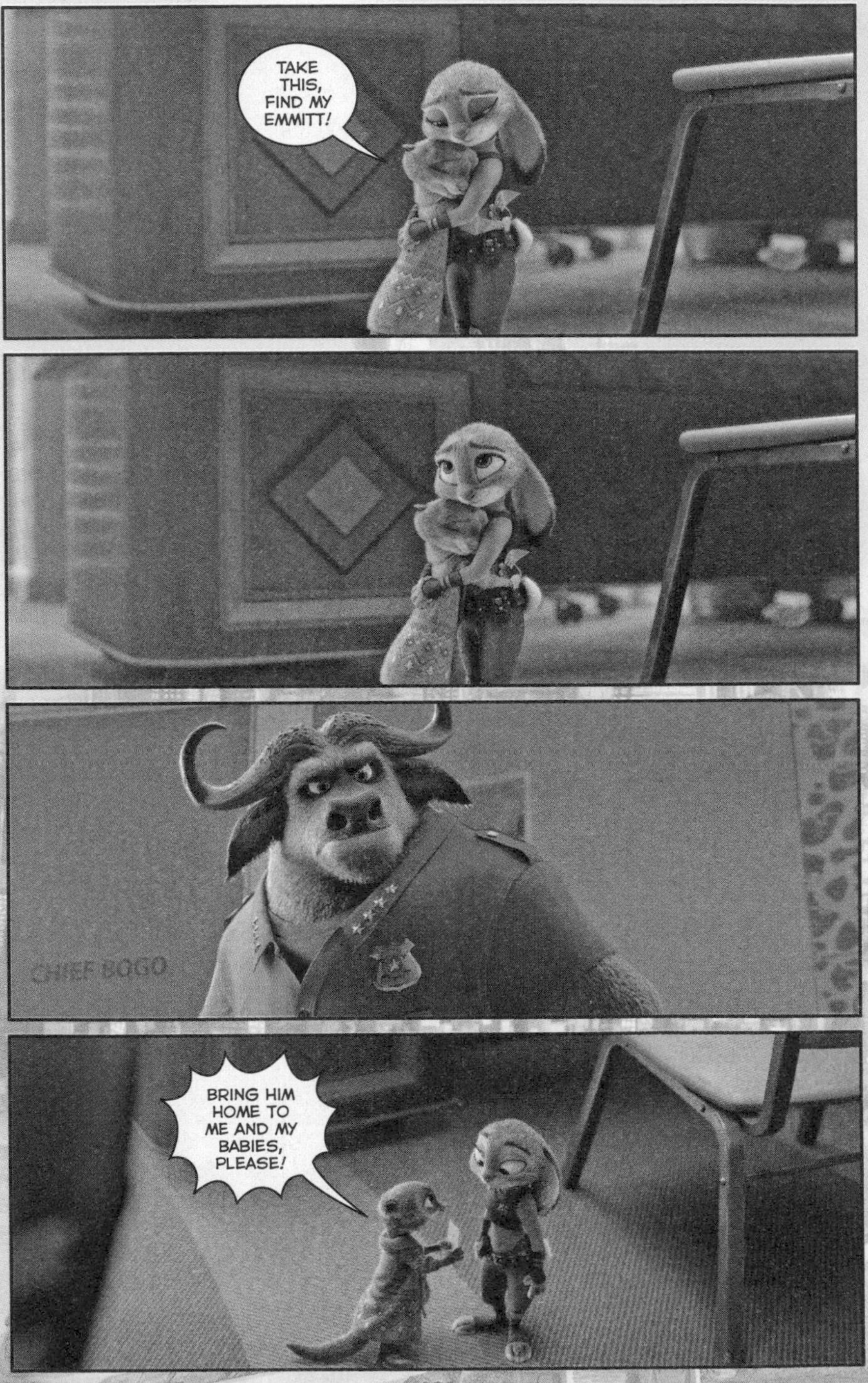
TAKE THIS, FIND MY EMMITT!
CHIEF BOGO
BRING HIM HOME TO ME AND MY BABIES, PLEASE!

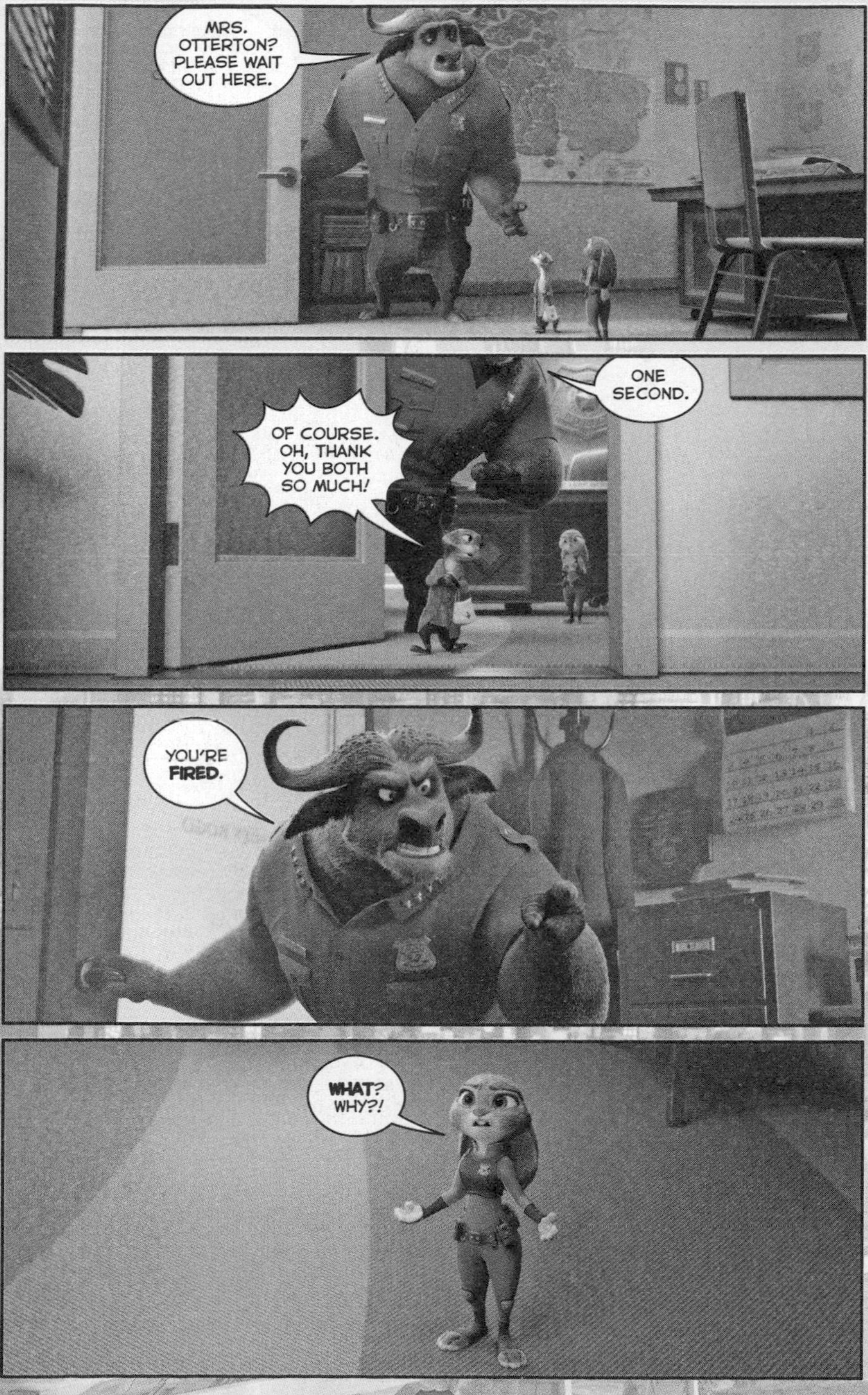
MRS. OTTERTON? PLEASE WAIT OUT HERE.
ONE SECOND.
OF COURSE. OH, THANK YOU BOTH SO MUCH!
YOU'RE **FIRED**.
WHAT? WHY?!

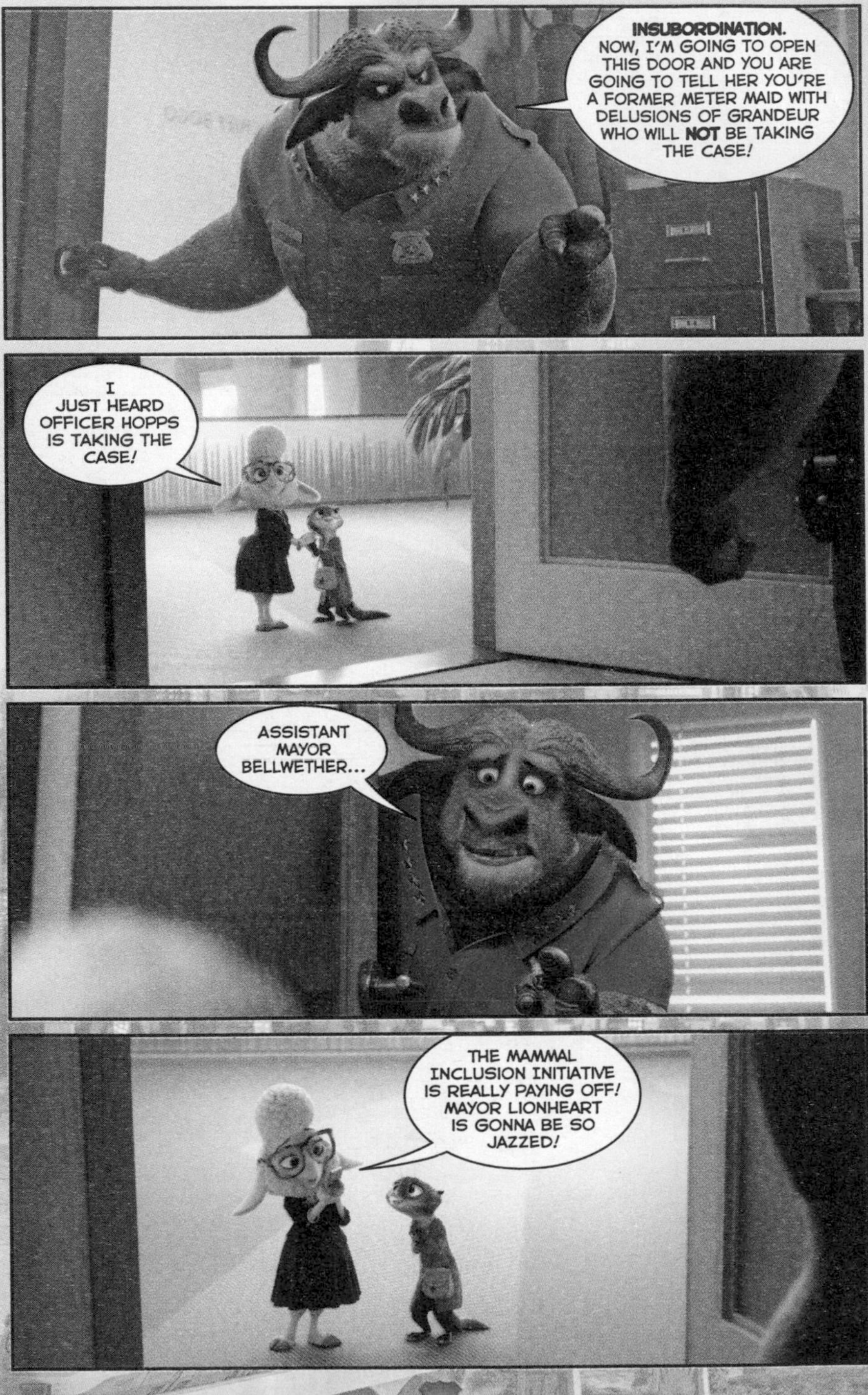
INSUBORDINATION. NOW, I'M GOING TO OPEN THIS DOOR AND YOU ARE GOING TO TELL HER YOU'RE A FORMER METER MAID WITH DELUSIONS OF GRANDEUR WHO WILL NOT BE TAKING THE CASE!
I JUST HEARD OFFICER HOPPS IS TAKING THE CASE!
ASSISTANT MAYOR BELLWETHER...
THE MAMMAL INCLUSION INITIATIVE IS REALLY PAYING OFF! MAYOR LIONHEART IS GONNA BE SO JAZZED!

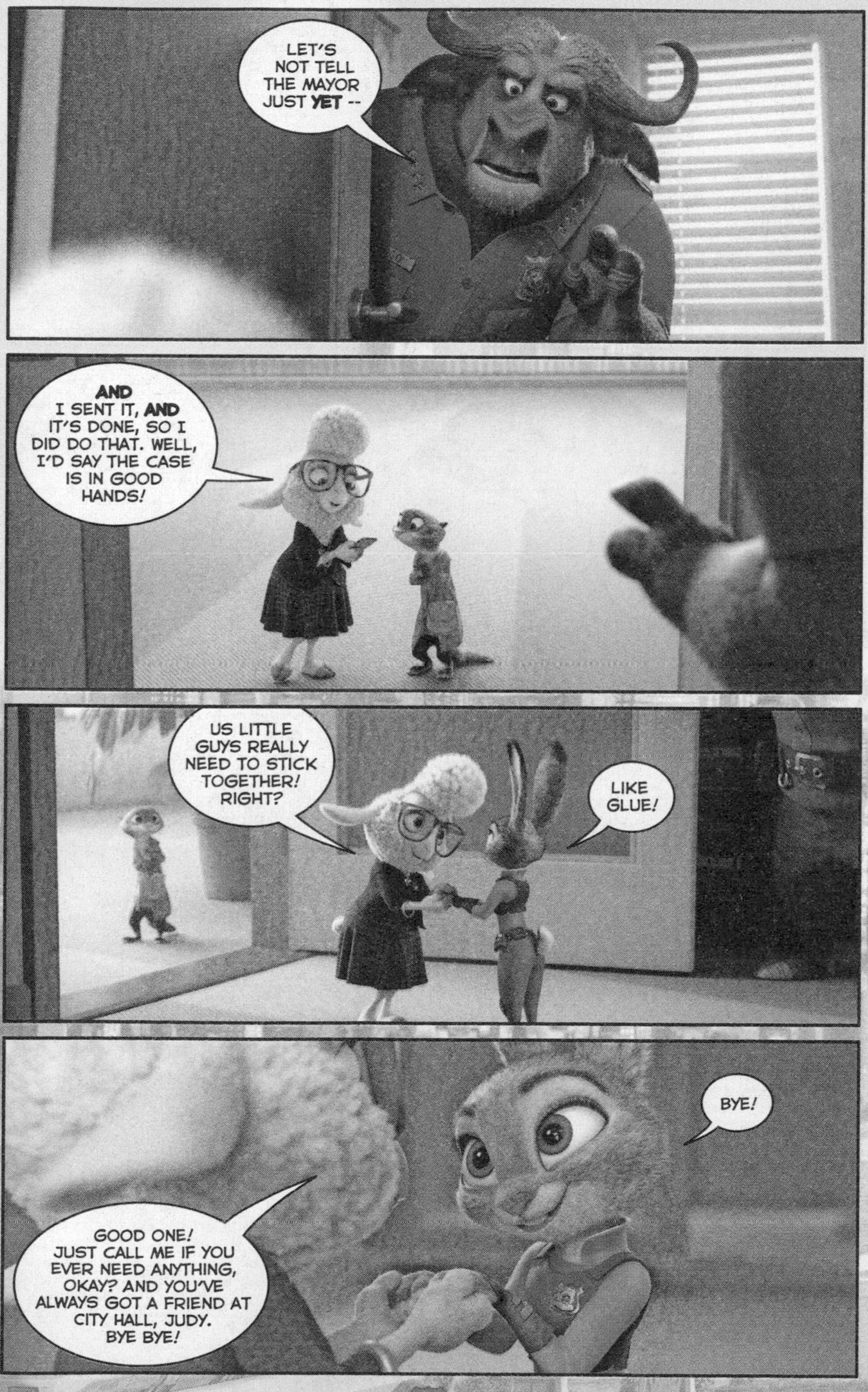
LET'S NOT TELL THE MAYOR JUST YET --
AND I SENT IT, AND IT'S DONE, SO I DID DO THAT. WELL, I'D SAY THE CASE IS IN GOOD HANDS!
US LITTLE GUYS REALLY NEED TO STICK TOGETHER! RIGHT?
LIKE GLUE!
BYE!
GOOD ONE! JUST CALL ME IF YOU EVER NEED ANYTHING, OKAY? AND YOU'VE ALWAYS GOT A FRIEND AT CITY HALL, JUDY. BYE BYE!

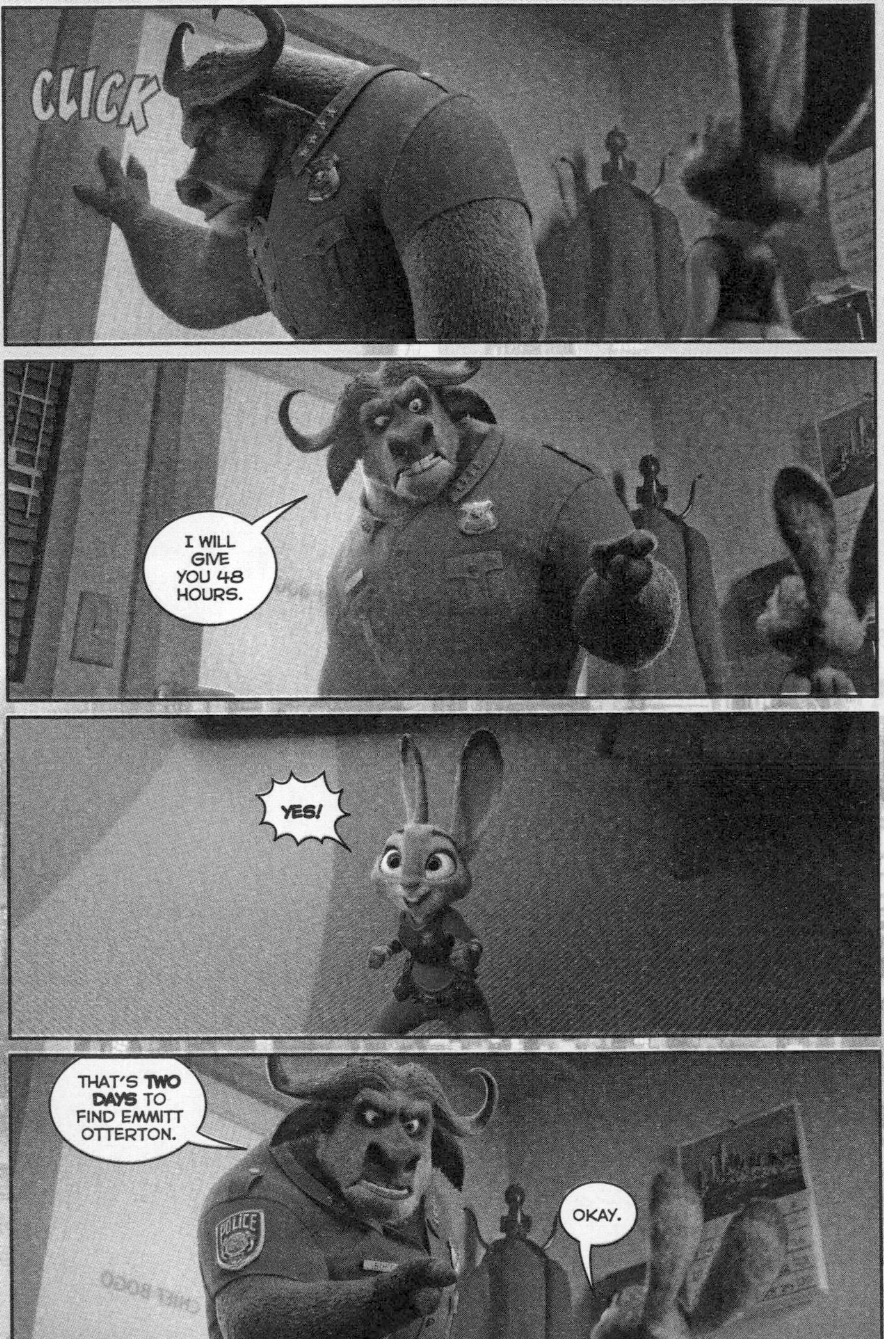
CLICK
I WILL GIVE YOU 48 HOURS.
YES!
THAT'S **TWO DAYS** TO FIND EMMITT OTTERTON.
OKAY.

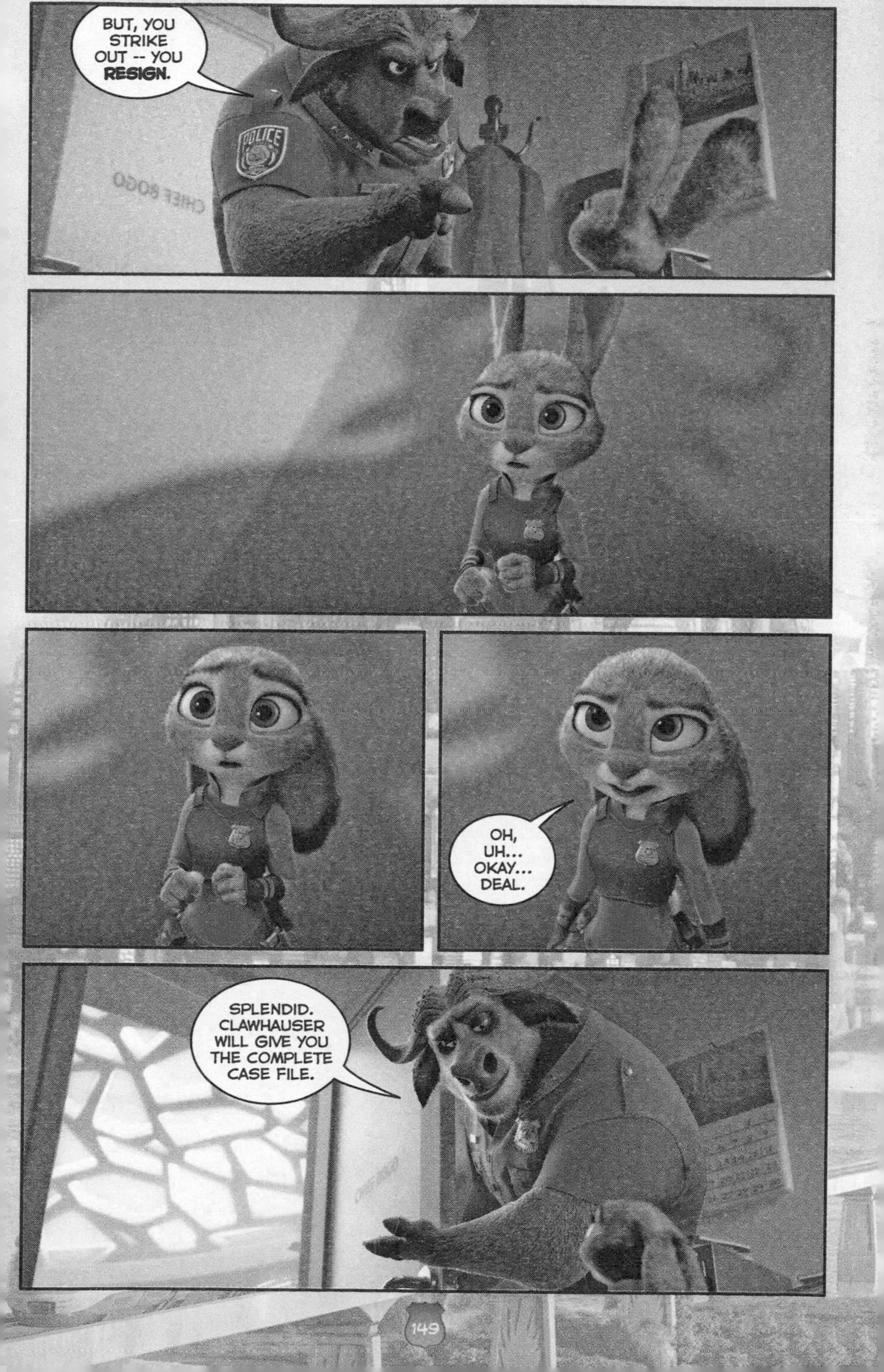
BUT, YOU STRIKE OUT -- YOU **RESIGN.**
OH, UH... OKAY... DEAL.
SPLENDID. CLAWHAUSER WILL GIVE YOU THE COMPLETE CASE FILE.

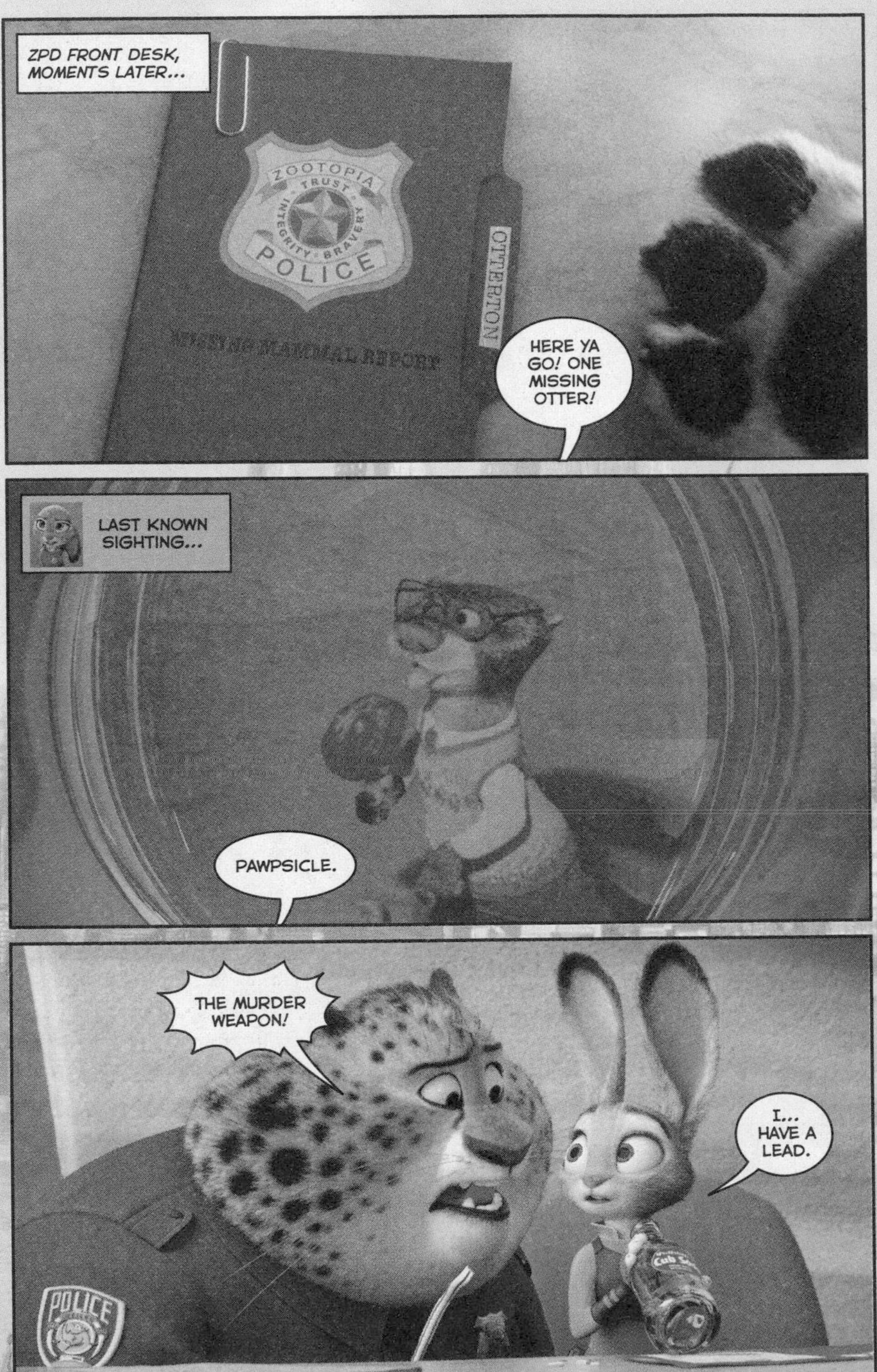
ZPD FRONT DESK, MOMENTS LATER...
ZOOTOPIA TRUST INTEGRITY BRAVERY POLICE
MISSING MAMMAL REPORT
OTTERTON
HERE YA GO! ONE MISSING OTTER!
LAST KNOWN SIGHTING...
PAWPSICLE.
THE MURDER WEAPON!
I... HAVE A LEAD.
POLICE

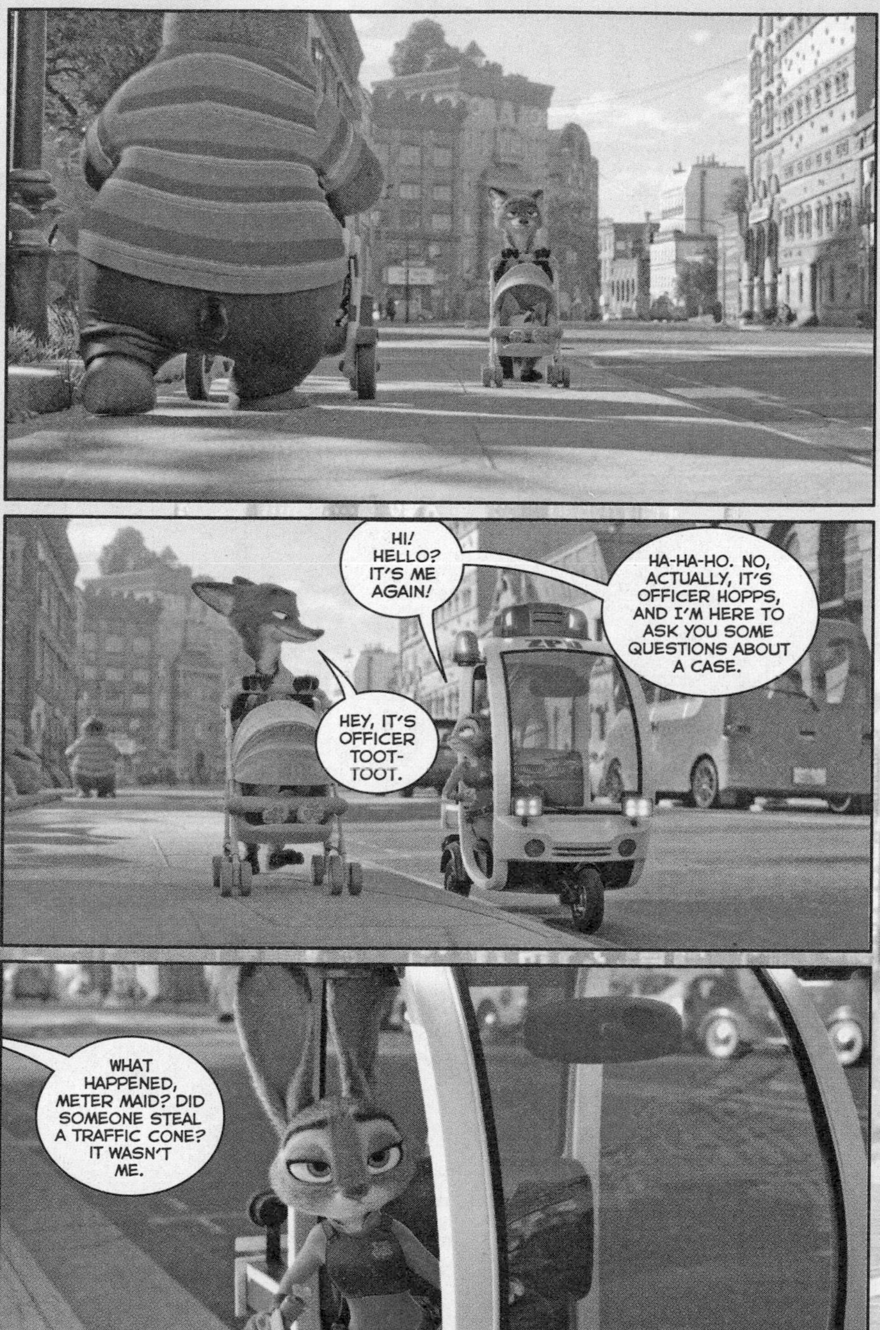
HI! HELLO? IT'S ME AGAIN!
HEY, IT'S OFFICER TOOT-TOOT.
HA-HA-HO. NO, ACTUALLY, IT'S OFFICER HOPPS, AND I'M HERE TO ASK YOU SOME QUESTIONS ABOUT A CASE.
WHAT HAPPENED, METER MAID? DID SOMEONE STEAL A TRAFFIC CONE? IT WASN'T ME.

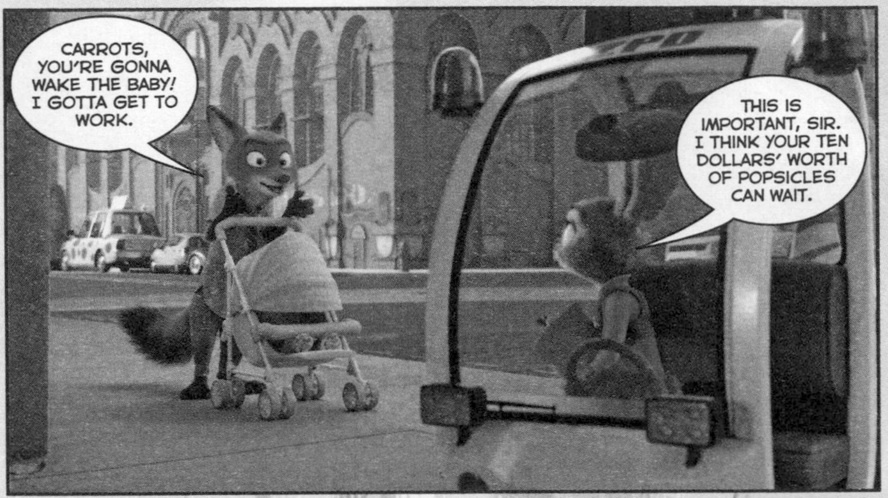
CARROTS, YOU'RE GONNA WAKE THE BABY! I GOTTA GET TO WORK.
THIS IS IMPORTANT, SIR. I THINK YOUR TEN DOLLARS' WORTH OF POPSICLES CAN WAIT.

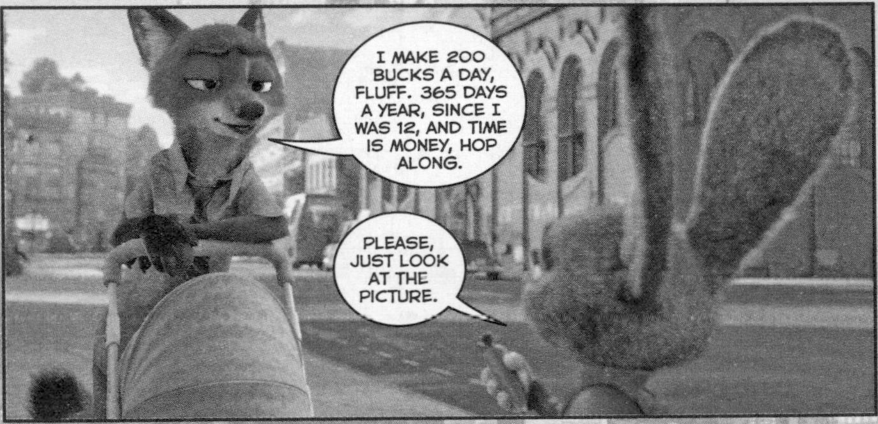
I MAKE 200 BUCKS A DAY, FLUFF. 365 DAYS A YEAR, SINCE I WAS 12, AND TIME IS MONEY, HOP ALONG.
PLEASE, JUST LOOK AT THE PICTURE.

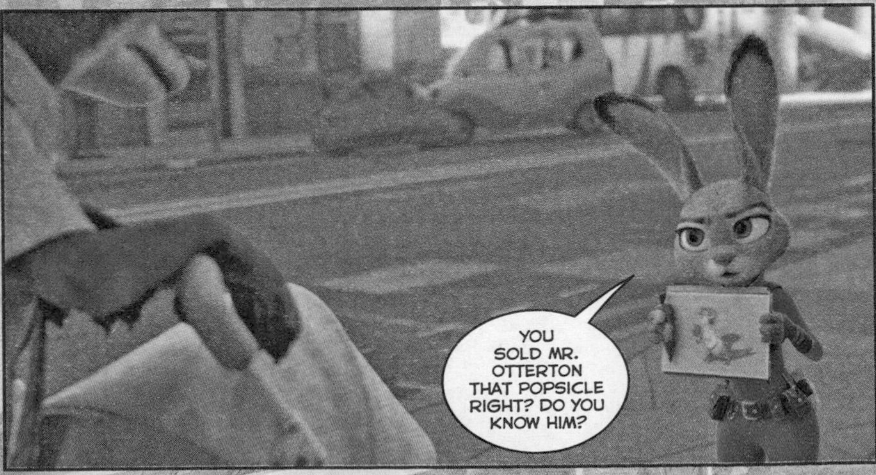
YOU SOLD MR. OTTERTON THAT POPSICLE RIGHT? DO YOU KNOW HIM?

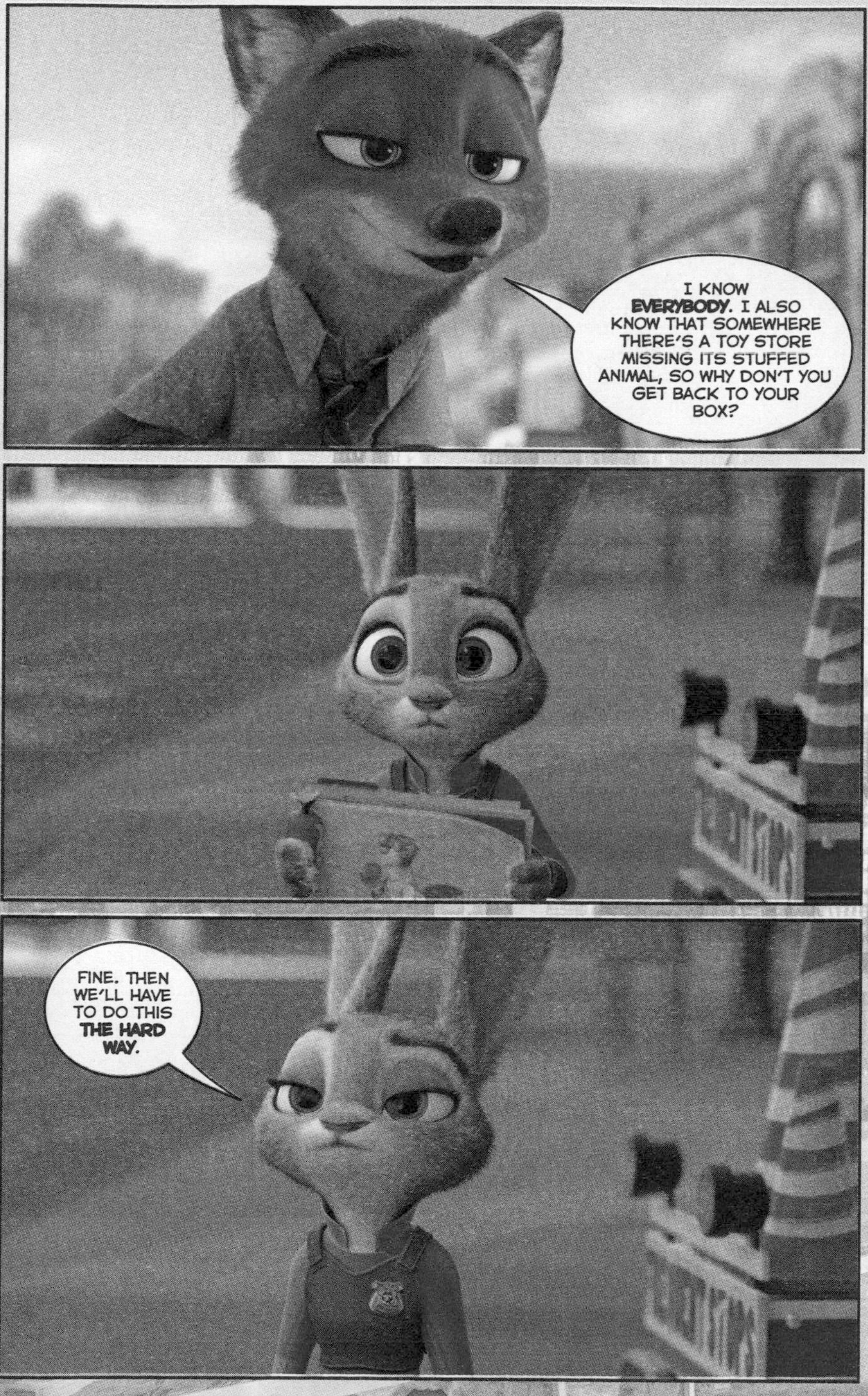
I KNOW EVERYBODY. I ALSO KNOW THAT SOMEWHERE THERE'S A TOY STORE MISSING ITS STUFFED ANIMAL, SO WHY DON'T YOU GET BACK TO YOUR BOX?
FINE. THEN WE'LL HAVE TO DO THIS THE HARD WAY.

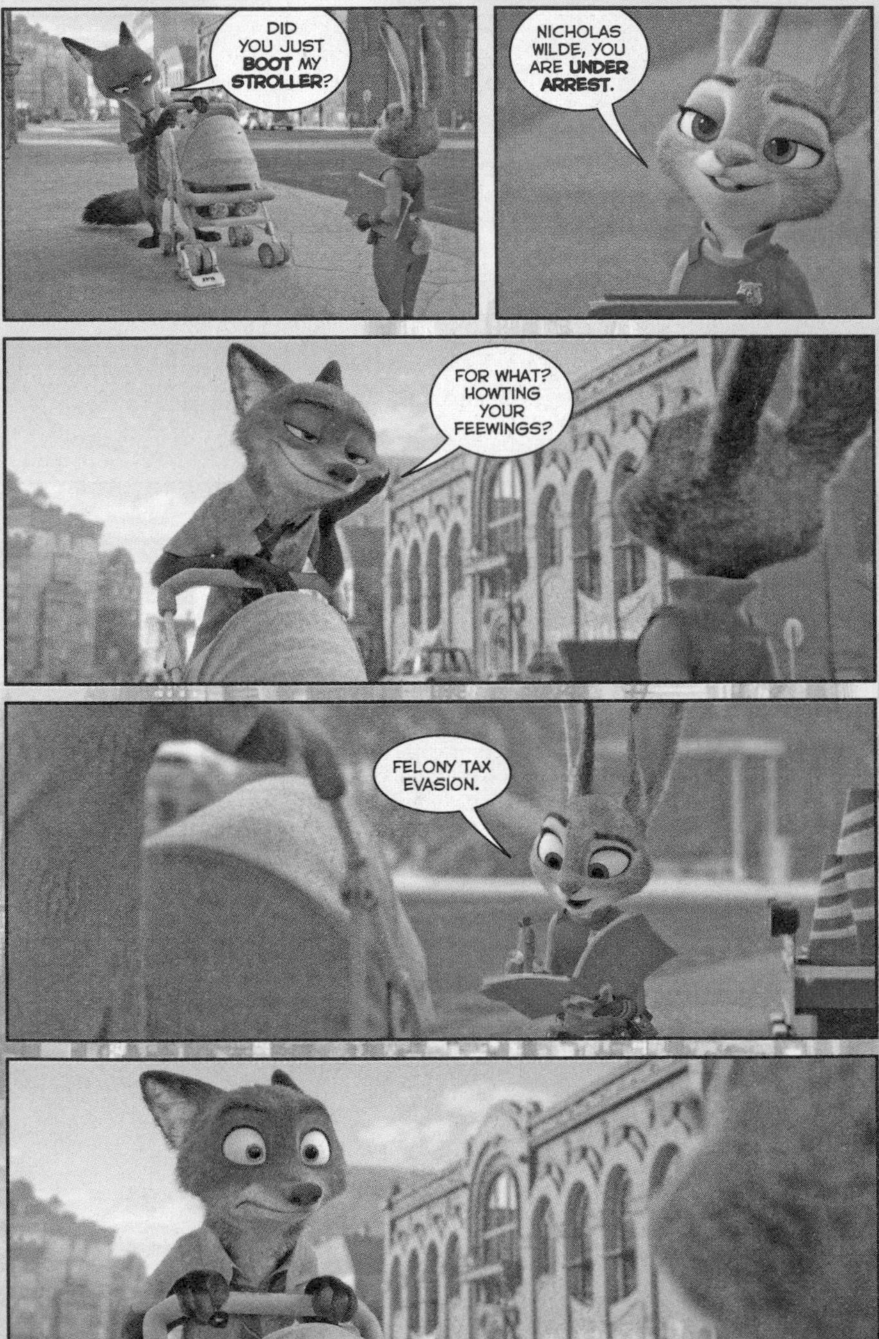

DID YOU JUST BOOT MY STROLLER?
NICHOLAS WILDE, YOU ARE UNDER ARREST.
FOR WHAT? HOWTING YOUR FEEWINGS?
FELONY TAX EVASION.

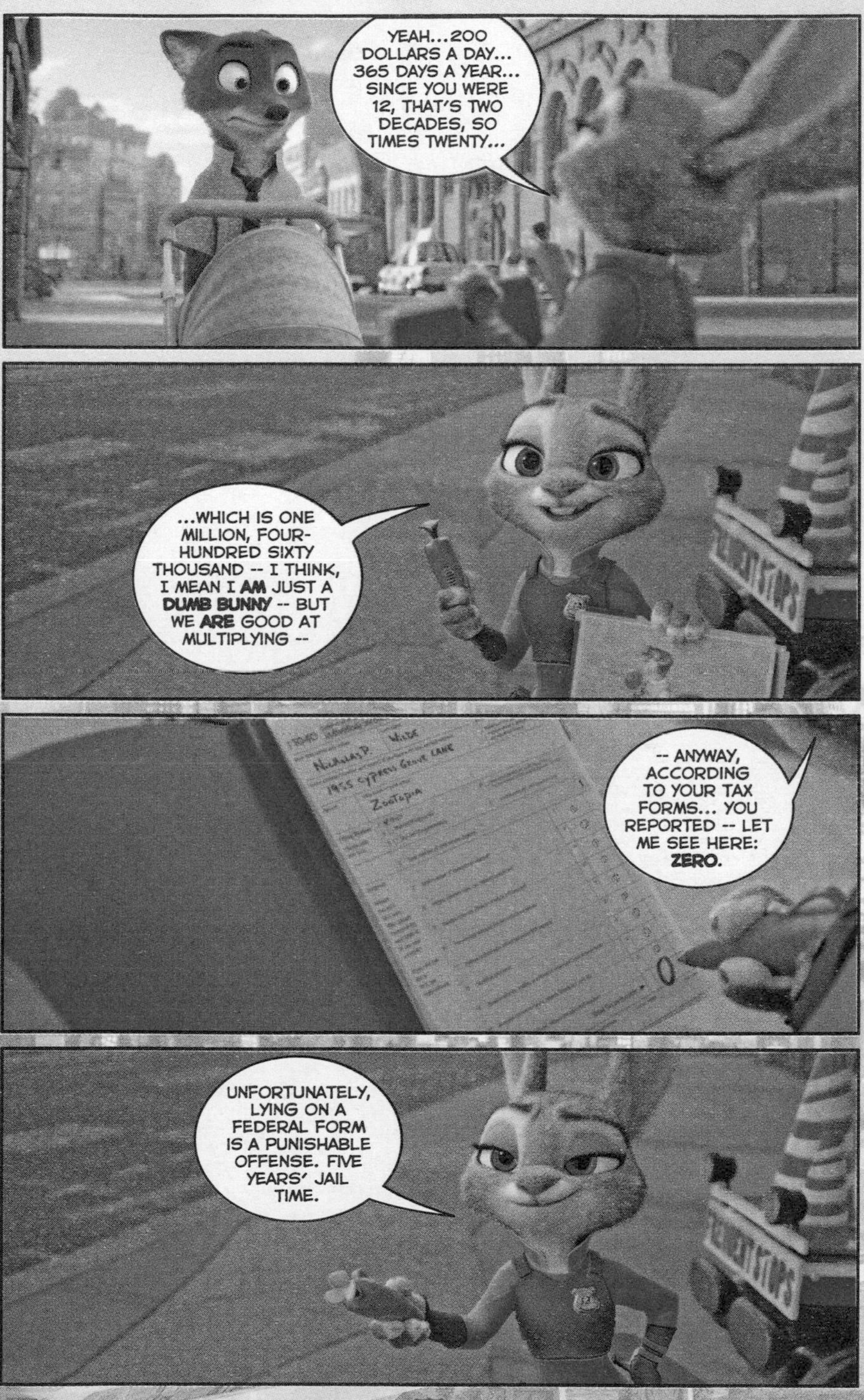
YEAH... 200 DOLLARS A DAY... 365 DAYS A YEAR... SINCE YOU WERE 12, THAT'S TWO DECADES, SO TIMES TWENTY...
...WHICH IS ONE MILLION, FOUR-HUNDRED SIXTY THOUSAND -- I THINK, I MEAN I **AM** JUST A **DUMB BUNNY** -- BUT WE **ARE** GOOD AT MULTIPLYING --
-- ANYWAY, ACCORDING TO YOUR TAX FORMS... YOU REPORTED -- LET ME SEE HERE: **ZERO**.
UNFORTUNATELY, LYING ON A FEDERAL FORM IS A PUNISHABLE OFFENSE. FIVE YEARS' JAIL TIME.

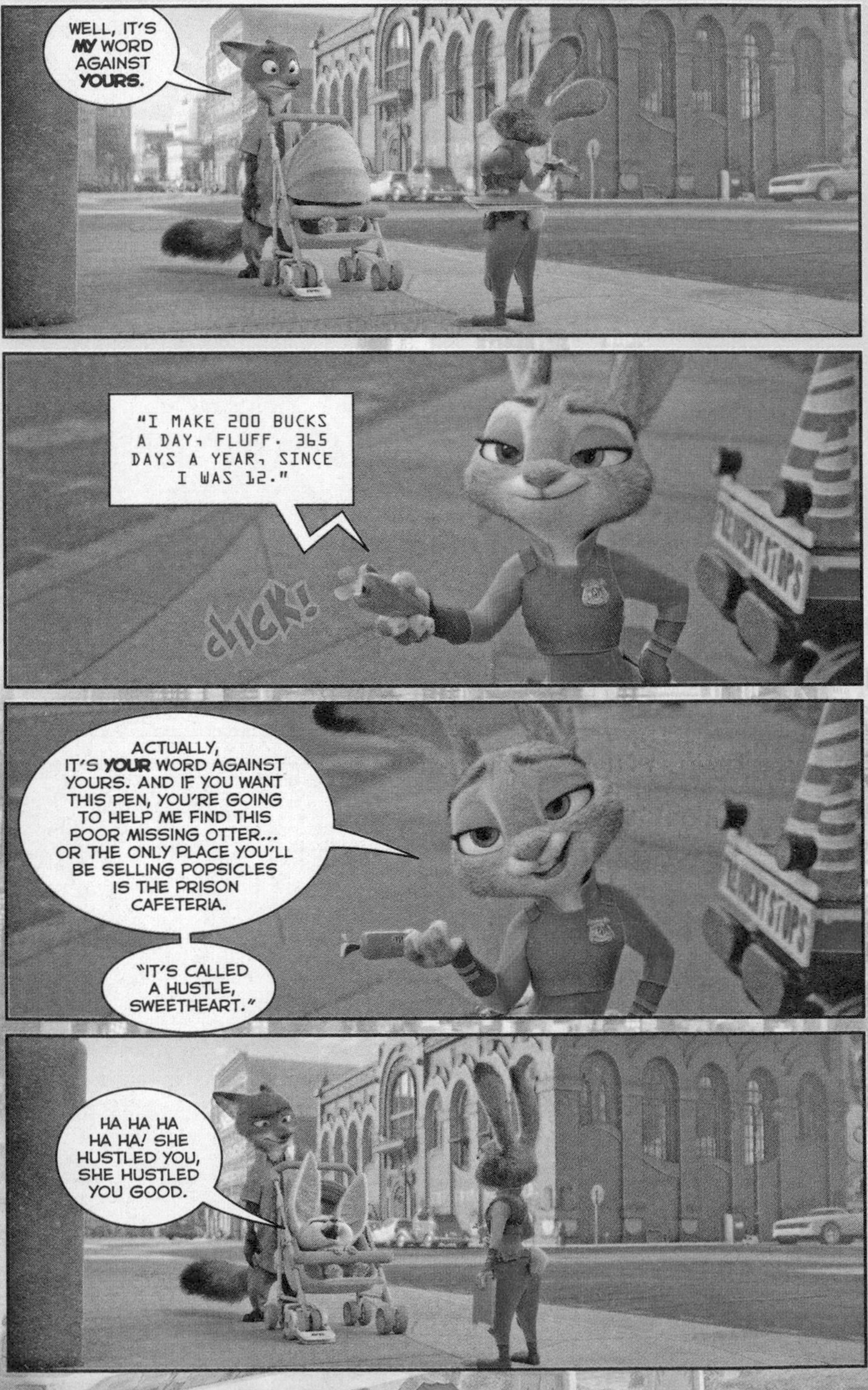
WELL, IT'S **MY** WORD AGAINST **YOURS.**
"I MAKE 200 BUCKS A DAY, FLUFF. 365 DAYS A YEAR, SINCE I WAS 12."
CLICK!
ACTUALLY, IT'S **YOUR** WORD AGAINST YOURS. AND IF YOU WANT THIS PEN, YOU'RE GOING TO HELP ME FIND THIS POOR MISSING OTTER... OR THE ONLY PLACE YOU'LL BE SELLING POPSICLES IS THE PRISON CAFETERIA.
"IT'S CALLED A HUSTLE, SWEETHEART."
HA HA HA HA HA! SHE HUSTLED YOU, SHE HUSTLED YOU GOOD.

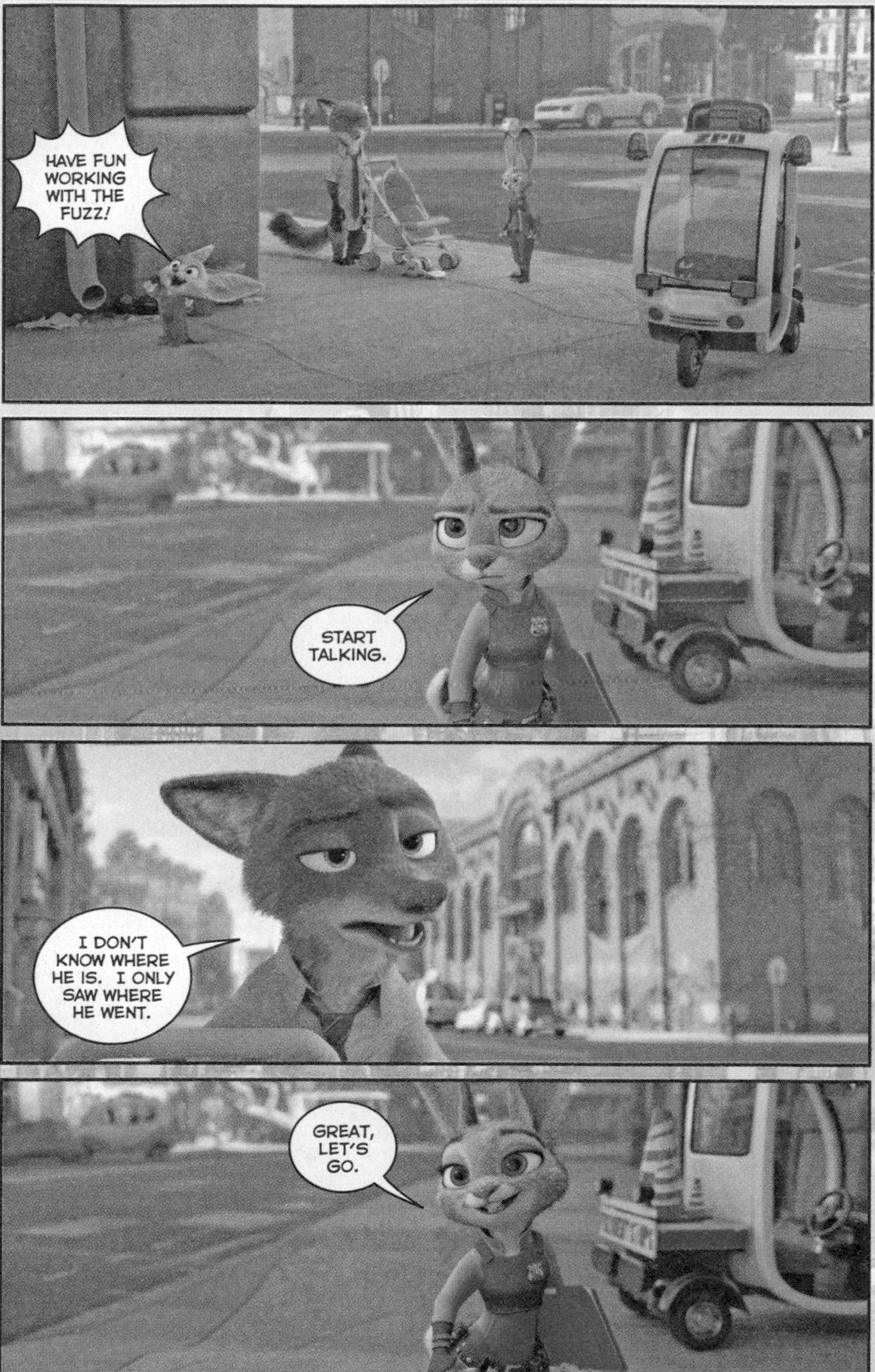
HAVE FUN WORKING WITH THE FUZZ!
ZPD
START TALKING.
I DON'T KNOW WHERE HE IS. I ONLY SAW WHERE HE WENT.
GREAT, LET'S GO.

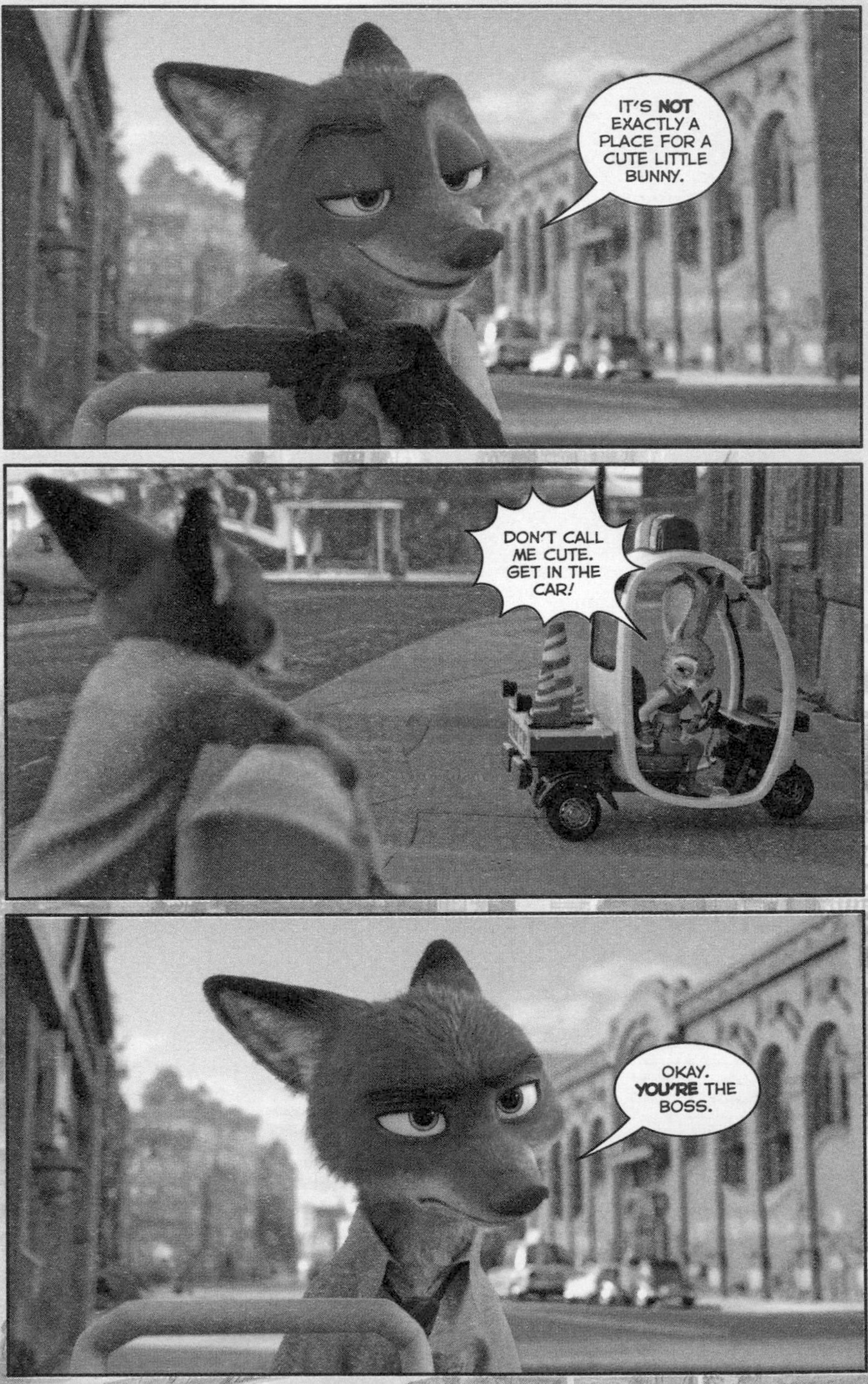
IT'S **NOT** EXACTLY A PLACE FOR A CUTE LITTLE BUNNY.
DON'T CALL ME CUTE. GET IN THE CAR!
OKAY. **YOU'RE** THE BOSS.

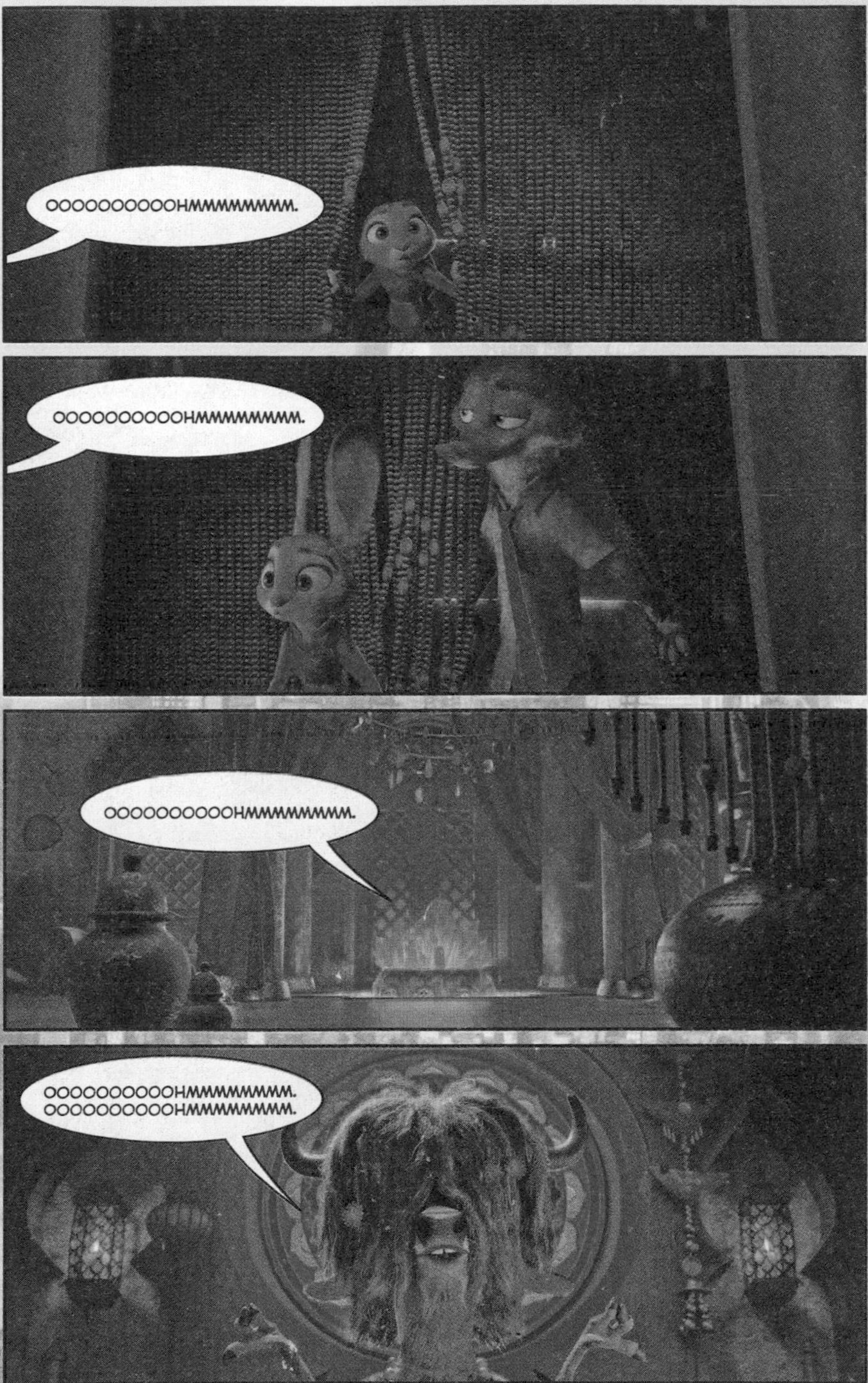
OOOOOOOOOOHMMMMMMMM.
OOOOOOOOOOHMMMMMMMM.
OOOOOOOOOOHMMMMMMMM.
OOOOOOOOOOHMMMMMMMM.
OOOOOOOOOOHMMMMMMMM.

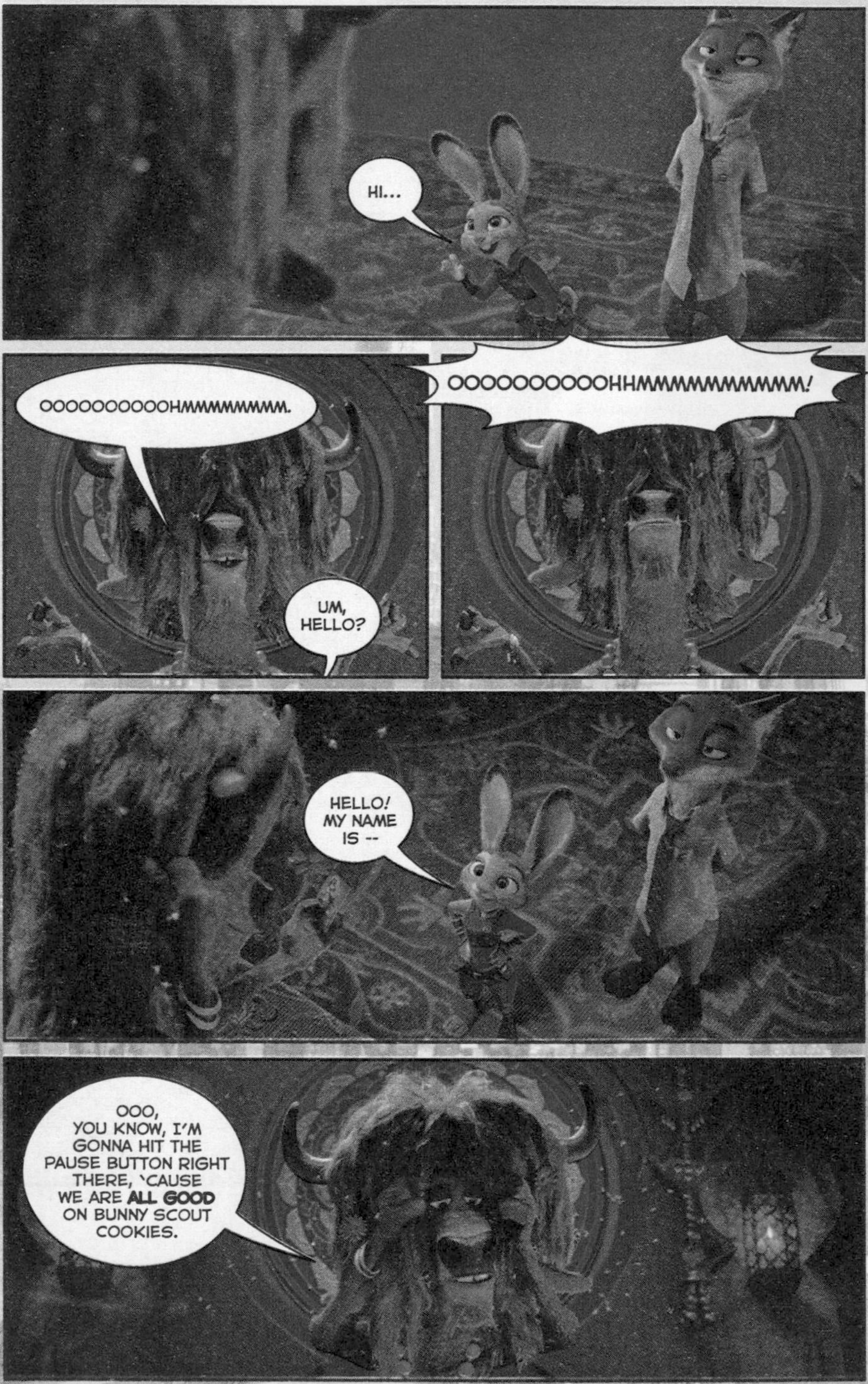
HI...
OOOOOOOOOOHMMMMMMMM.
UM, HELLO?
OOOOOOOOOOHHMMMMMMMMMMM!
HELLO! MY NAME IS --
OOO, YOU KNOW, I'M GONNA HIT THE PAUSE BUTTON RIGHT THERE, 'CAUSE WE ARE ALL GOOD ON BUNNY SCOUT COOKIES.

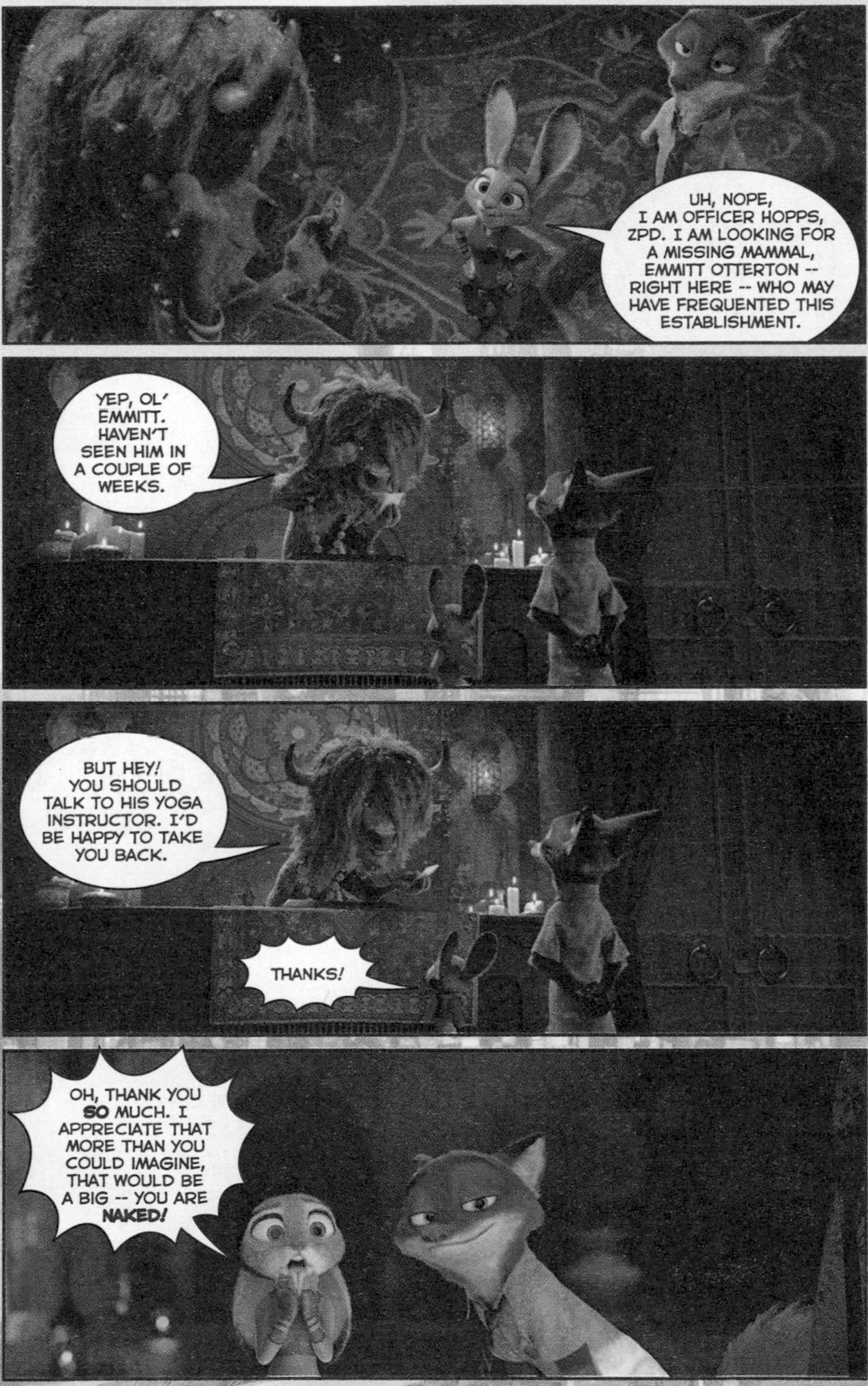
UH, NOPE, I AM OFFICER HOPPS, ZPD. I AM LOOKING FOR A MISSING MAMMAL, EMMITT OTTERTON -- RIGHT HERE -- WHO MAY HAVE FREQUENTED THIS ESTABLISHMENT.
YEP, OL' EMMITT. HAVEN'T SEEN HIM IN A COUPLE OF WEEKS.
BUT HEY! YOU SHOULD TALK TO HIS YOGA INSTRUCTOR. I'D BE HAPPY TO TAKE YOU BACK.
THANKS!
OH, THANK YOU **SO** MUCH. I APPRECIATE THAT MORE THAN YOU COULD IMAGINE, THAT WOULD BE A BIG -- YOU ARE **NAKED!**

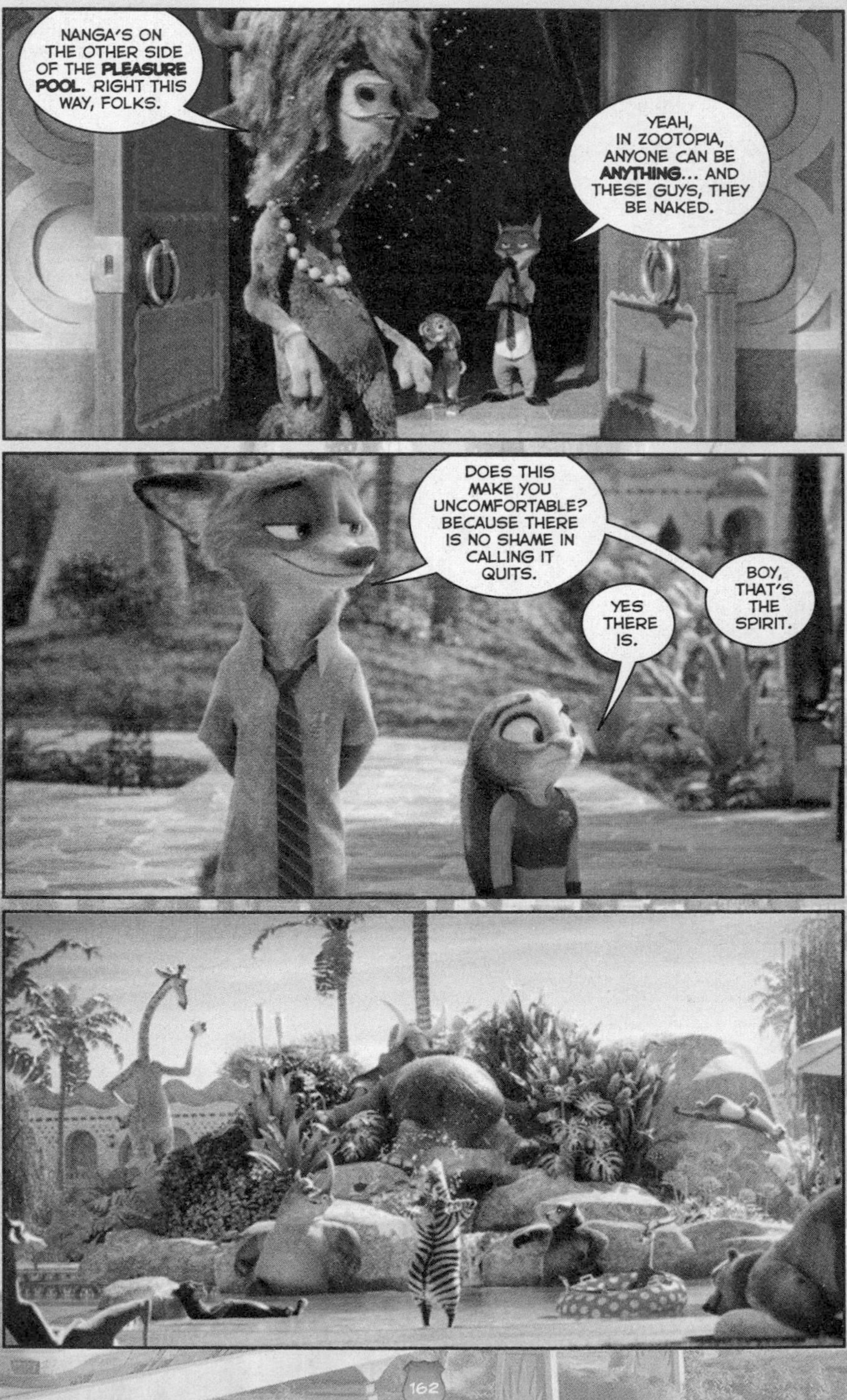
NANGA'S ON THE OTHER SIDE OF THE **PLEASURE POOL.** RIGHT THIS WAY, FOLKS.
YEAH, IN ZOOTOPIA, ANYONE CAN BE **ANYTHING**... AND THESE GUYS, THEY BE NAKED.
DOES THIS MAKE YOU UNCOMFORTABLE? BECAUSE THERE IS NO SHAME IN CALLING IT QUITS.
YES THERE IS.
BOY, THAT'S THE SPIRIT.

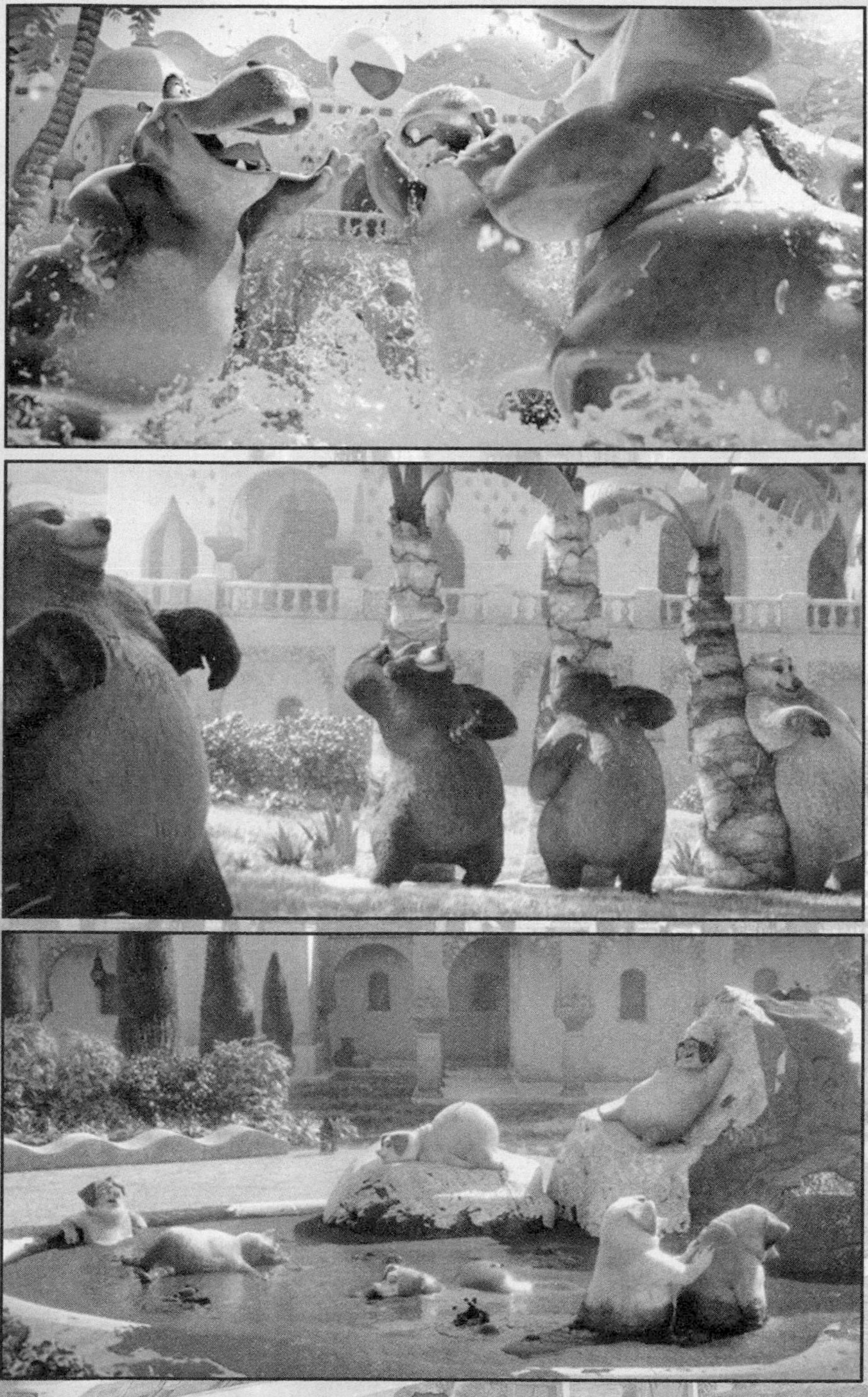

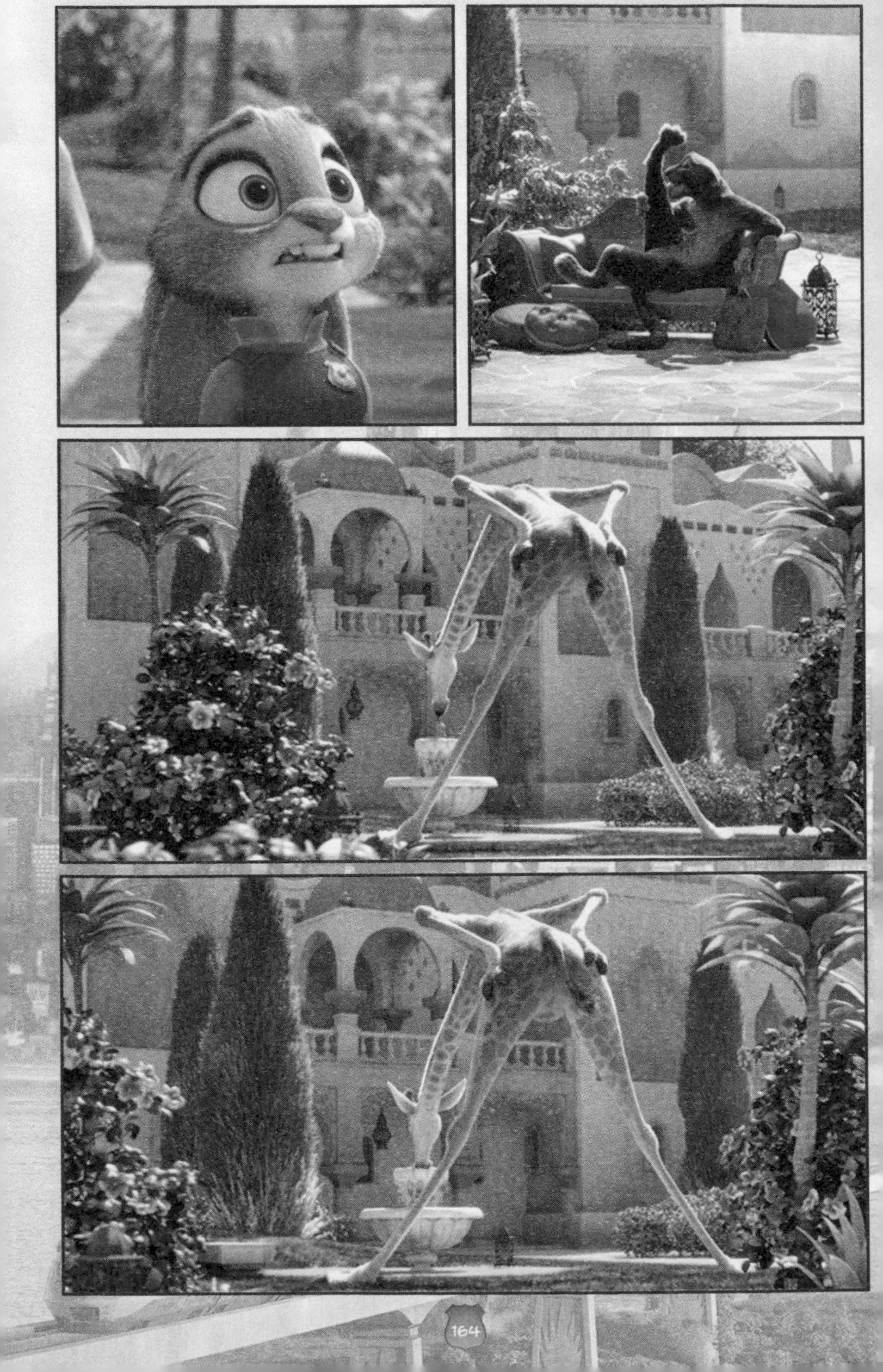

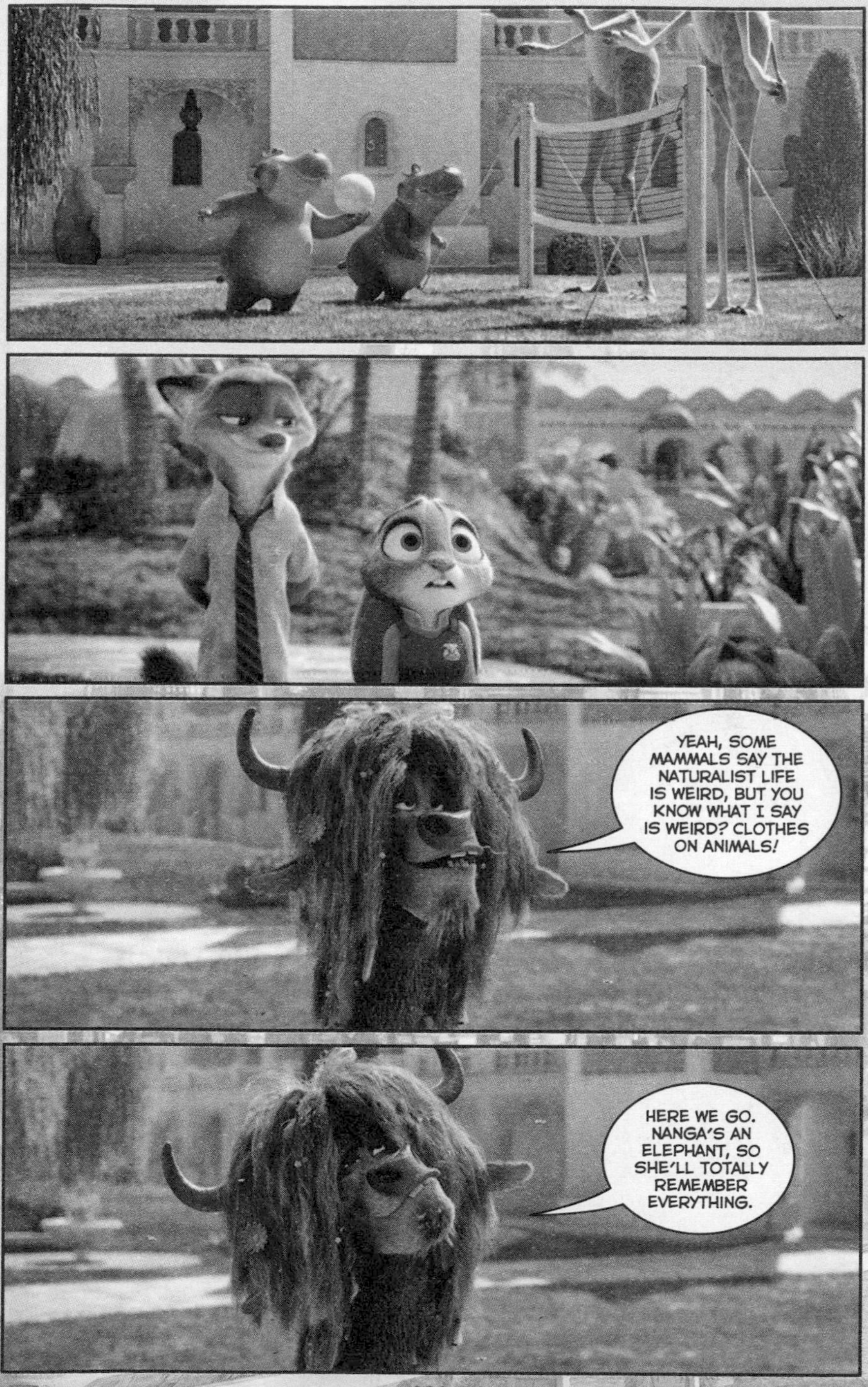
YEAH, SOME MAMMALS SAY THE NATURALIST LIFE IS WEIRD, BUT YOU KNOW WHAT I SAY IS WEIRD? CLOTHES ON ANIMALS!
HERE WE GO. NANGA'S AN ELEPHANT, SO SHE'LL TOTALLY REMEMBER EVERYTHING.

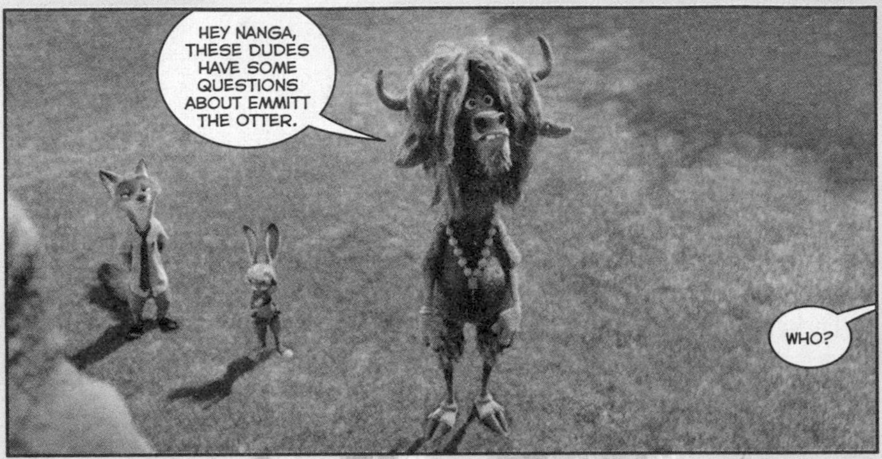
HEY NANGA, THESE DUDES HAVE SOME QUESTIONS ABOUT EMMITT THE OTTER.
WHO?

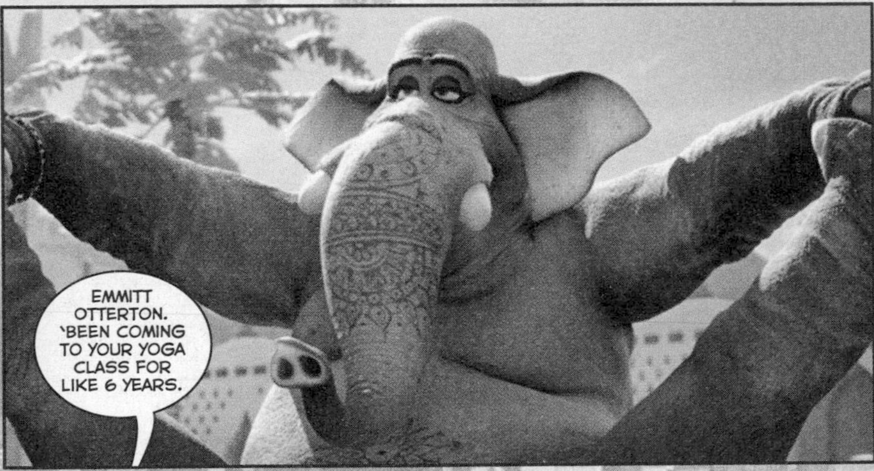
EMMITT OTTERTON. 'BEEN COMING TO YOUR YOGA CLASS FOR LIKE 6 YEARS.

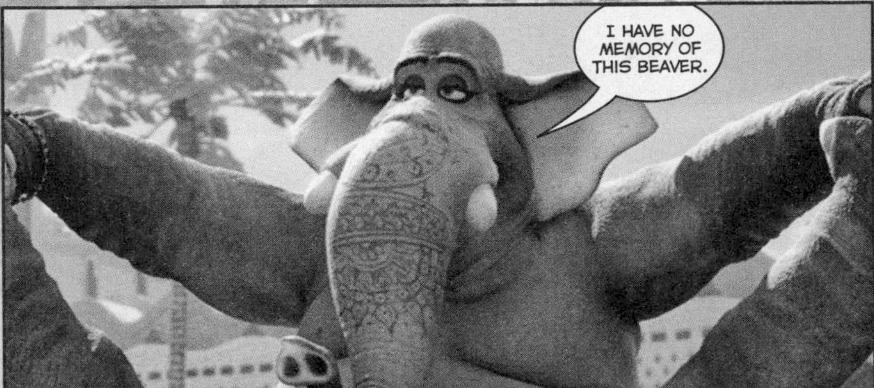
I HAVE NO MEMORY OF THIS BEAVER.

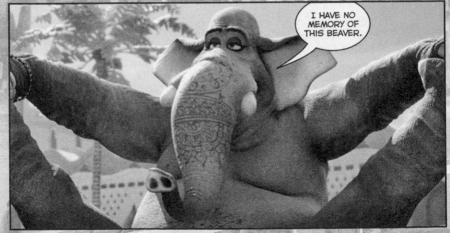

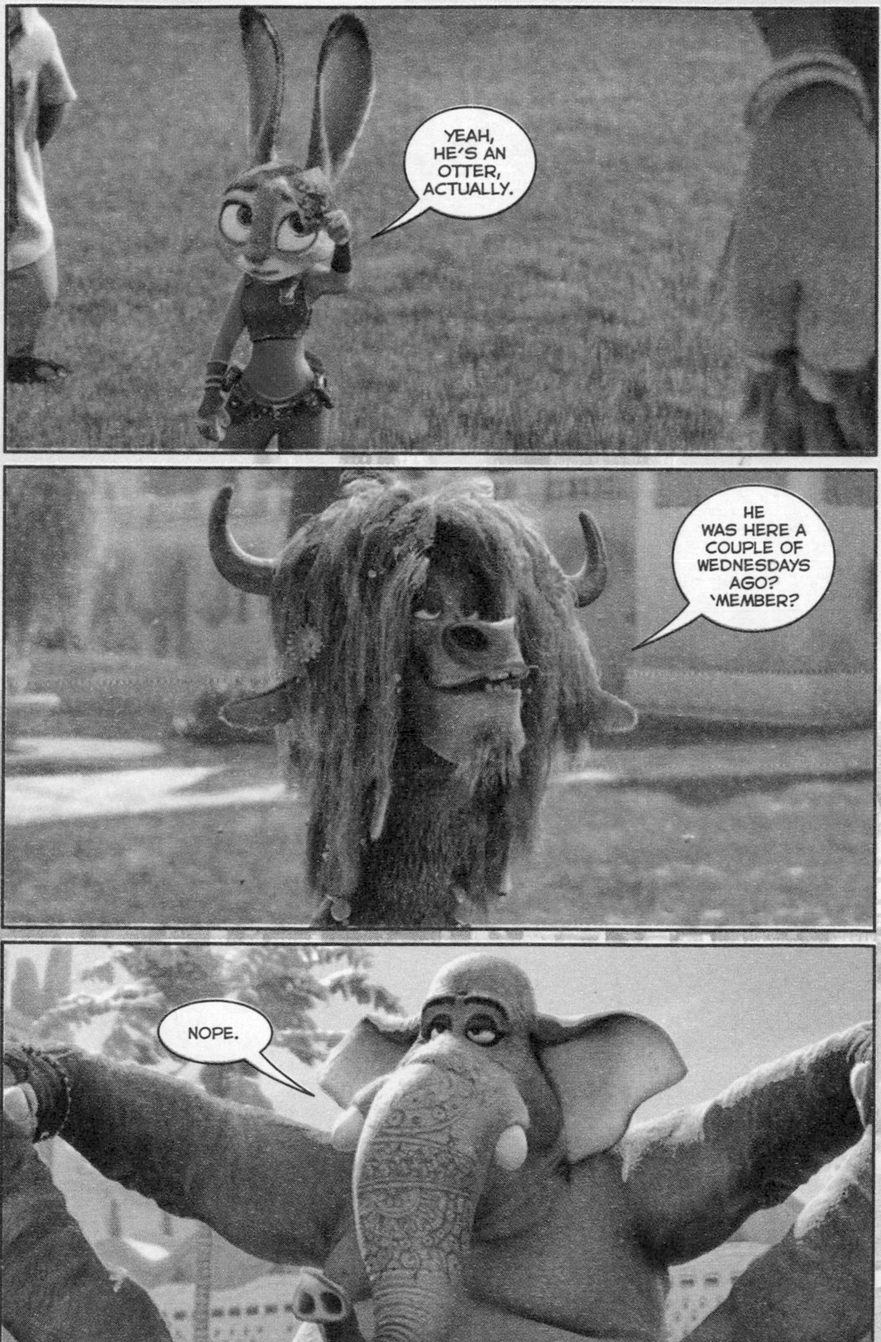
YEAH, HE'S AN OTTER, ACTUALLY.
HE WAS HERE A COUPLE OF WEDNESDAYS AGO? 'MEMBER?
NOPE.

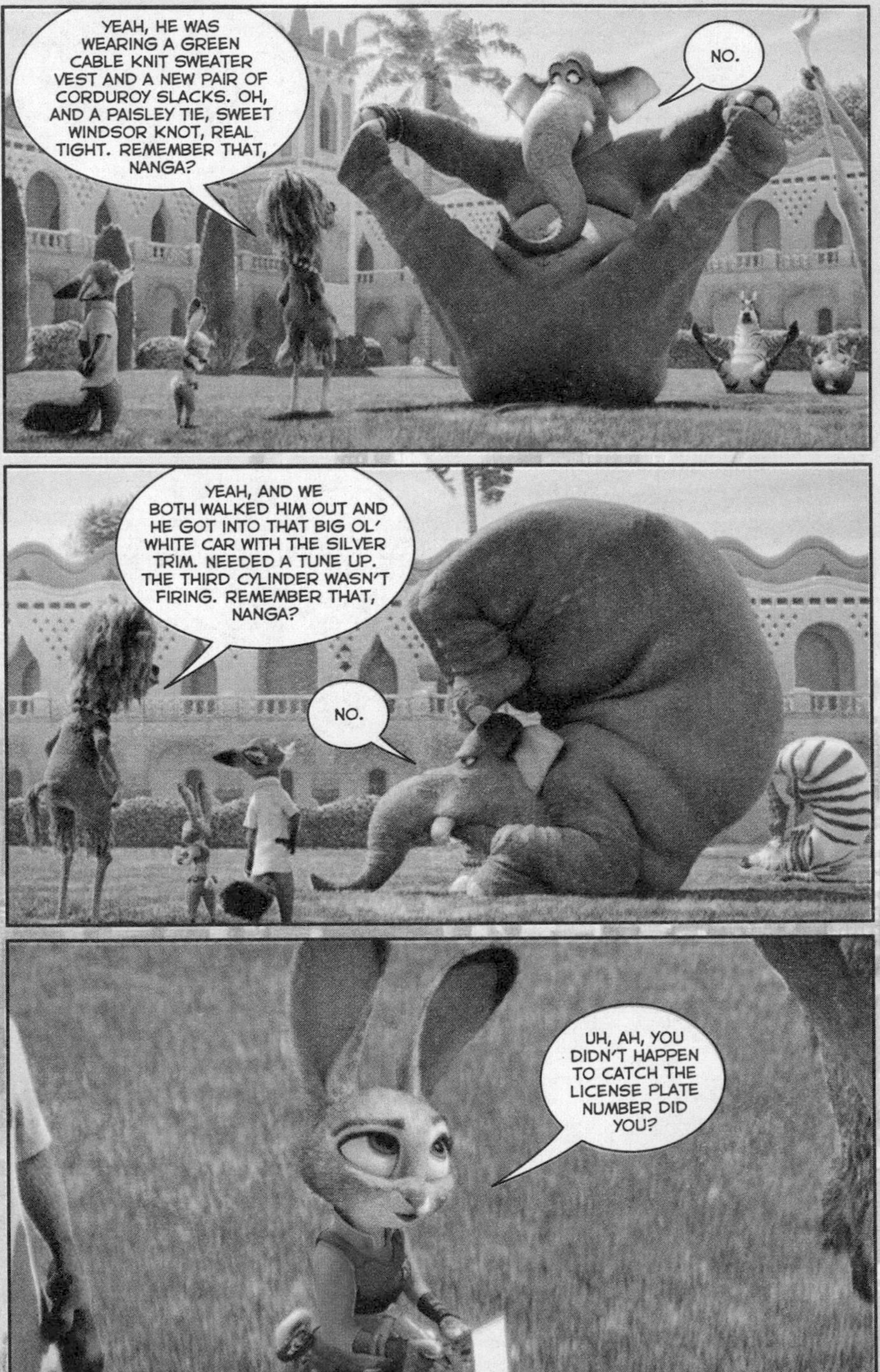
YEAH, HE WAS WEARING A GREEN CABLE KNIT SWEATER VEST AND A NEW PAIR OF CORDUROY SLACKS. OH, AND A PAISLEY TIE, SWEET WINDSOR KNOT, REAL TIGHT. REMEMBER THAT, NANGA?
NO.
YEAH, AND WE BOTH WALKED HIM OUT AND HE GOT INTO THAT BIG OL' WHITE CAR WITH THE SILVER TRIM. NEEDED A TUNE UP. THE THIRD CYLINDER WASN'T FIRING. REMEMBER THAT, NANGA?
NO.
UH, AH, YOU DIDN'T HAPPEN TO CATCH THE LICENSE PLATE NUMBER DID YOU?

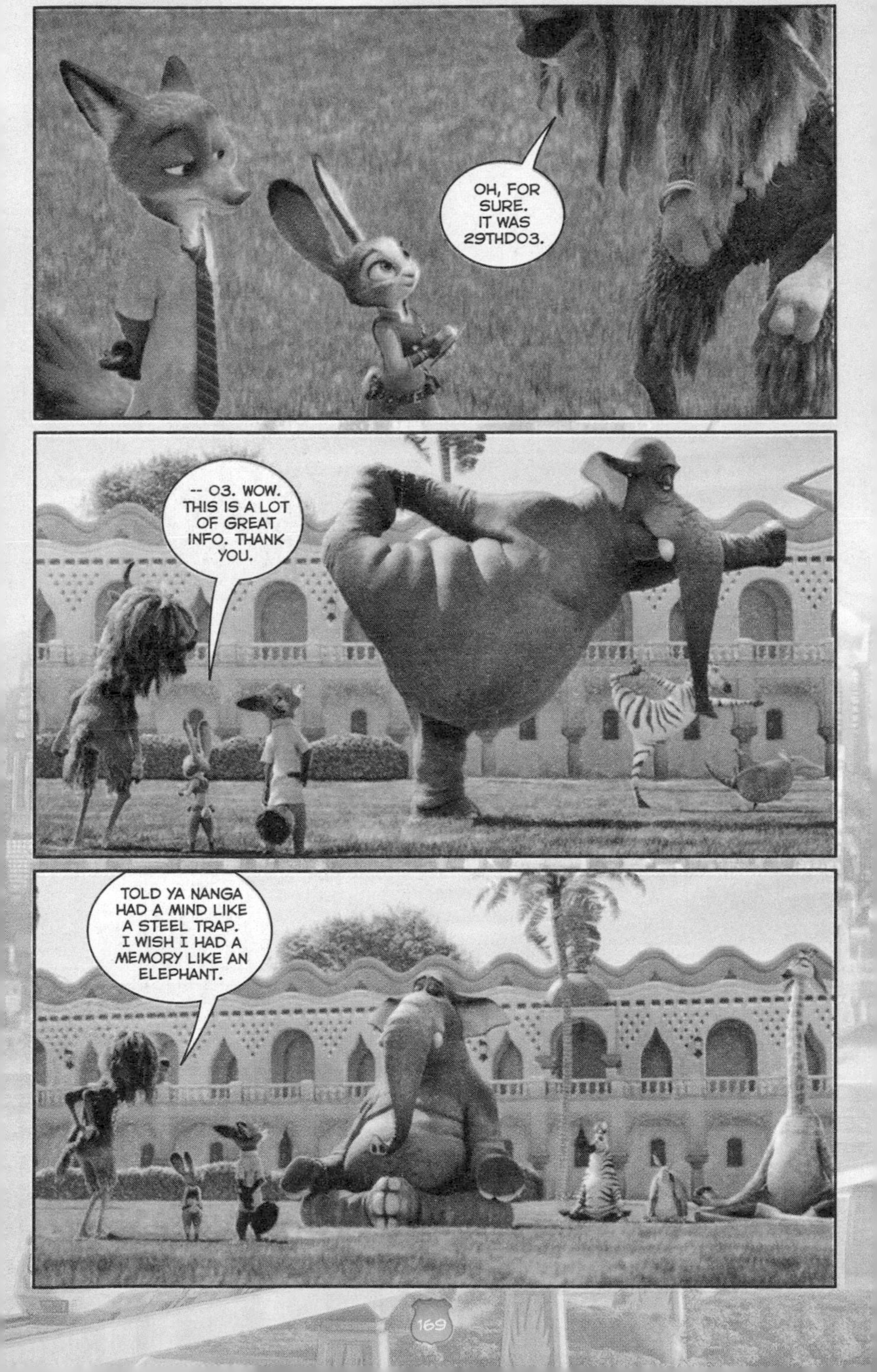
OH, FOR SURE. IT WAS 29THD03.
-- 03. WOW. THIS IS A LOT OF GREAT INFO. THANK YOU.
TOLD YA NANGA HAD A MIND LIKE A STEEL TRAP. I WISH I HAD A MEMORY LIKE AN ELEPHANT.

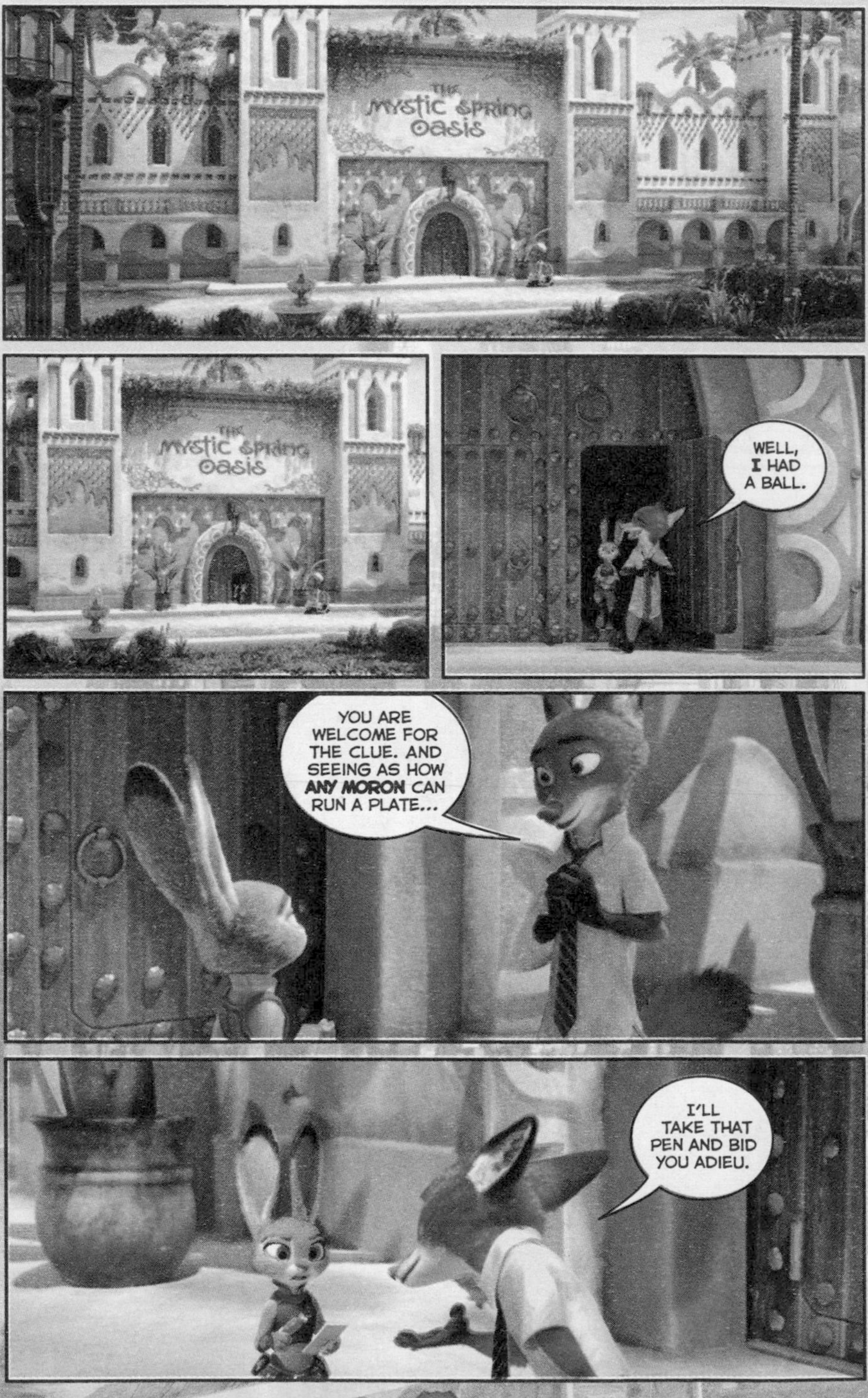
THE MYSTIC SPRING OASIS
THE MYSTIC SPRING OASIS
WELL, I HAD A BALL.
YOU ARE WELCOME FOR THE CLUE. AND SEEING AS HOW **ANY MORON** CAN RUN A PLATE...
I'LL TAKE THAT PEN AND BID YOU ADIEU.

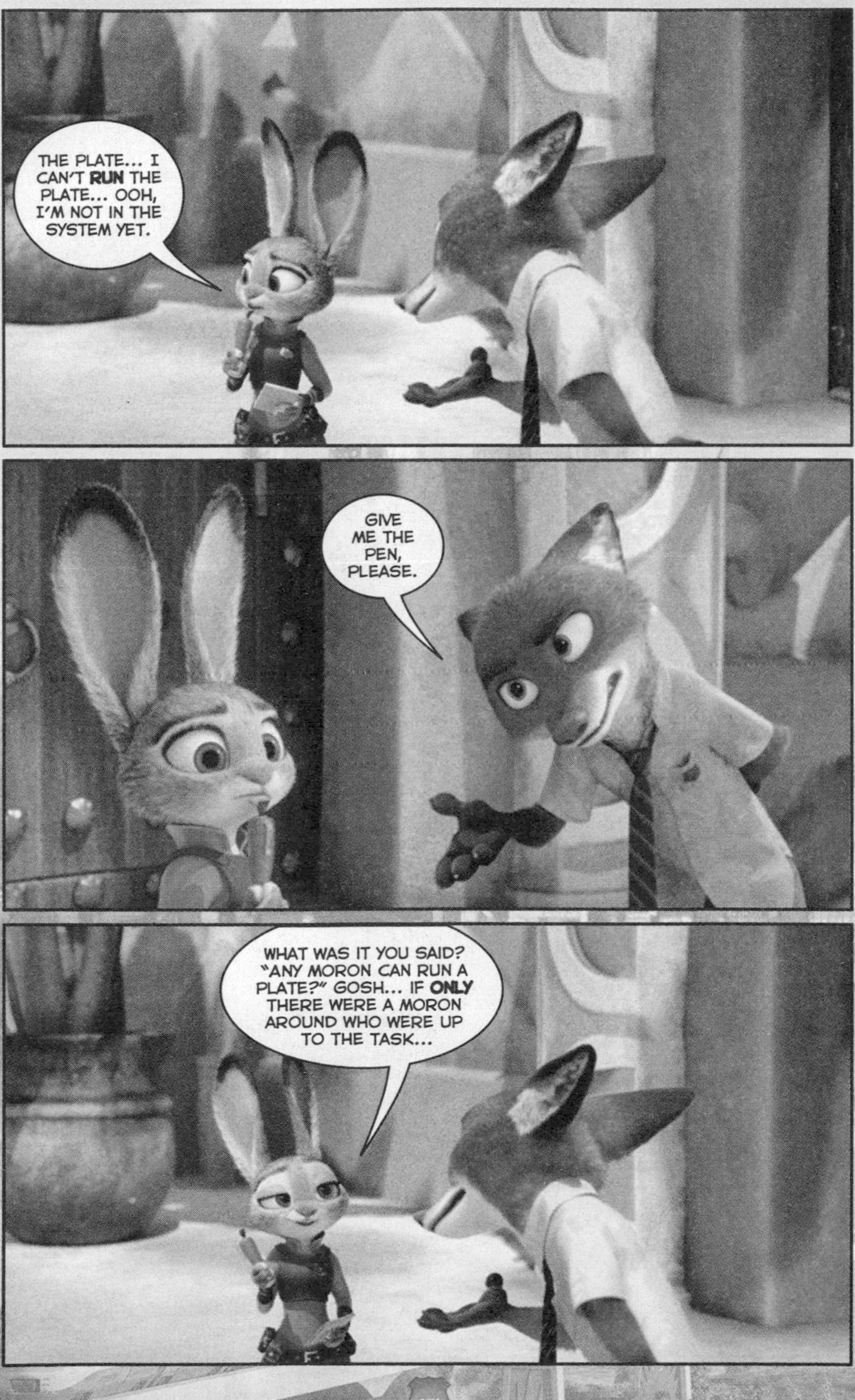
THE PLATE... I CAN'T **RUN** THE PLATE... OOH, I'M NOT IN THE SYSTEM YET.
GIVE ME THE PEN, PLEASE.
WHAT WAS IT YOU SAID? "ANY MORON CAN RUN A PLATE?" GOSH... IF **ONLY** THERE WERE A MORON AROUND WHO WERE UP TO THE TASK...

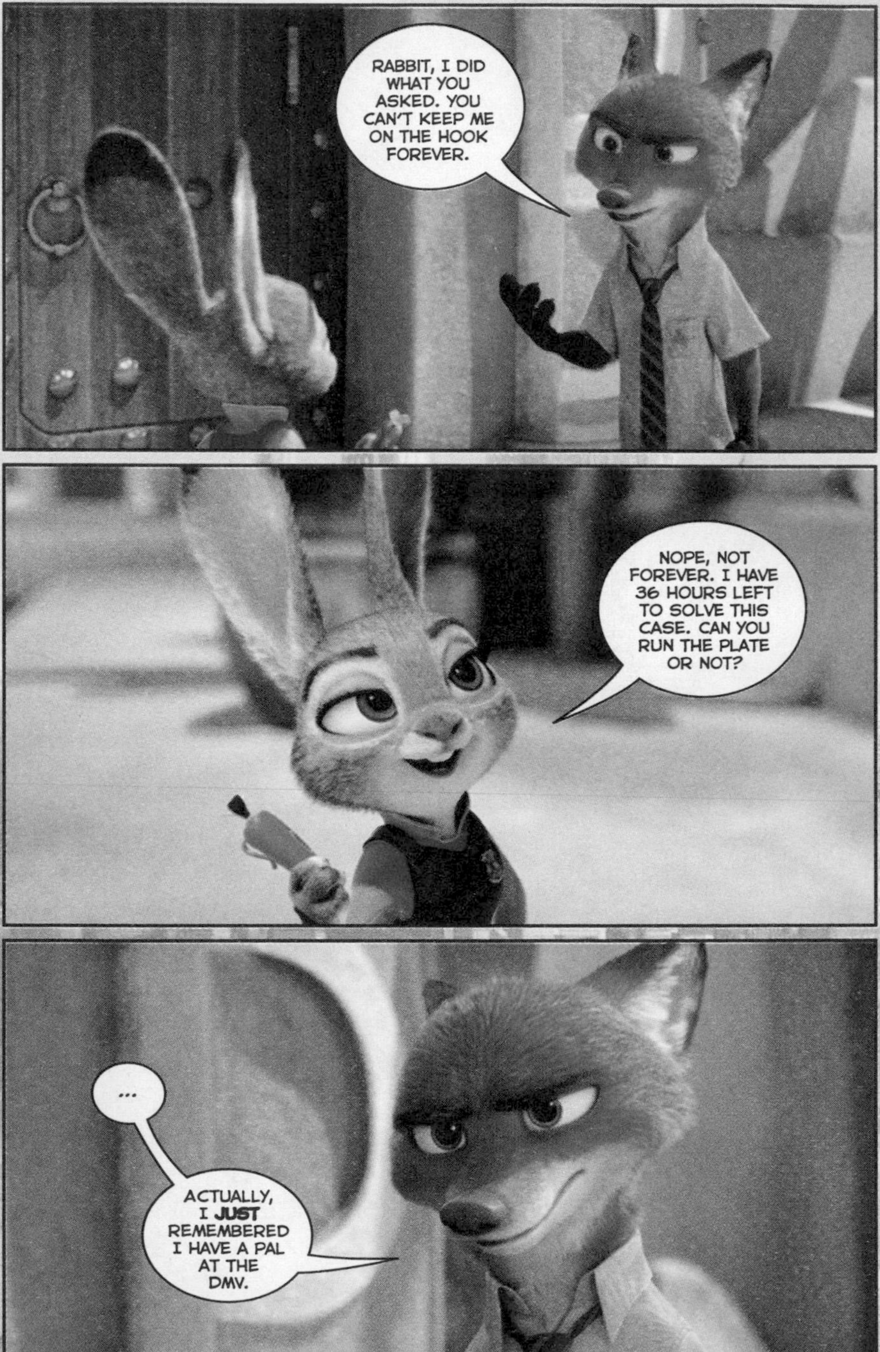
RABBIT, I DID WHAT YOU ASKED. YOU CAN'T KEEP ME ON THE HOOK FOREVER.
NOPE, NOT FOREVER. I HAVE 36 HOURS LEFT TO SOLVE THIS CASE. CAN YOU RUN THE PLATE OR NOT?
...
ACTUALLY, I **JUST** REMEMBERED I HAVE A PAL AT THE DMV.

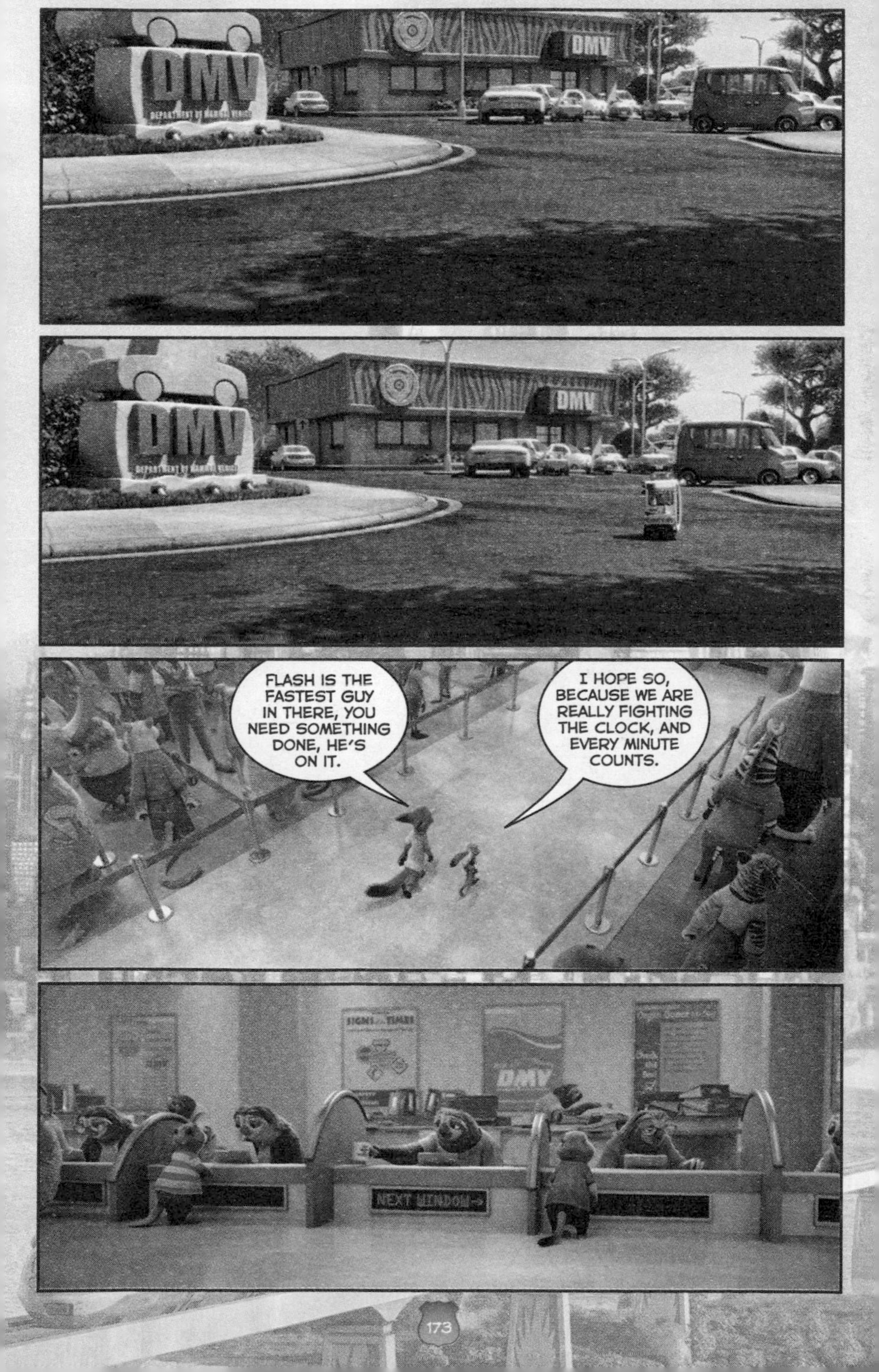
DMV
DMV
FLASH IS THE FASTEST GUY IN THERE, YOU NEED SOMETHING DONE, HE'S ON IT.
I HOPE SO, BECAUSE WE ARE REALLY FIGHTING THE CLOCK, AND EVERY MINUTE COUNTS.
NEXT WINDOW→

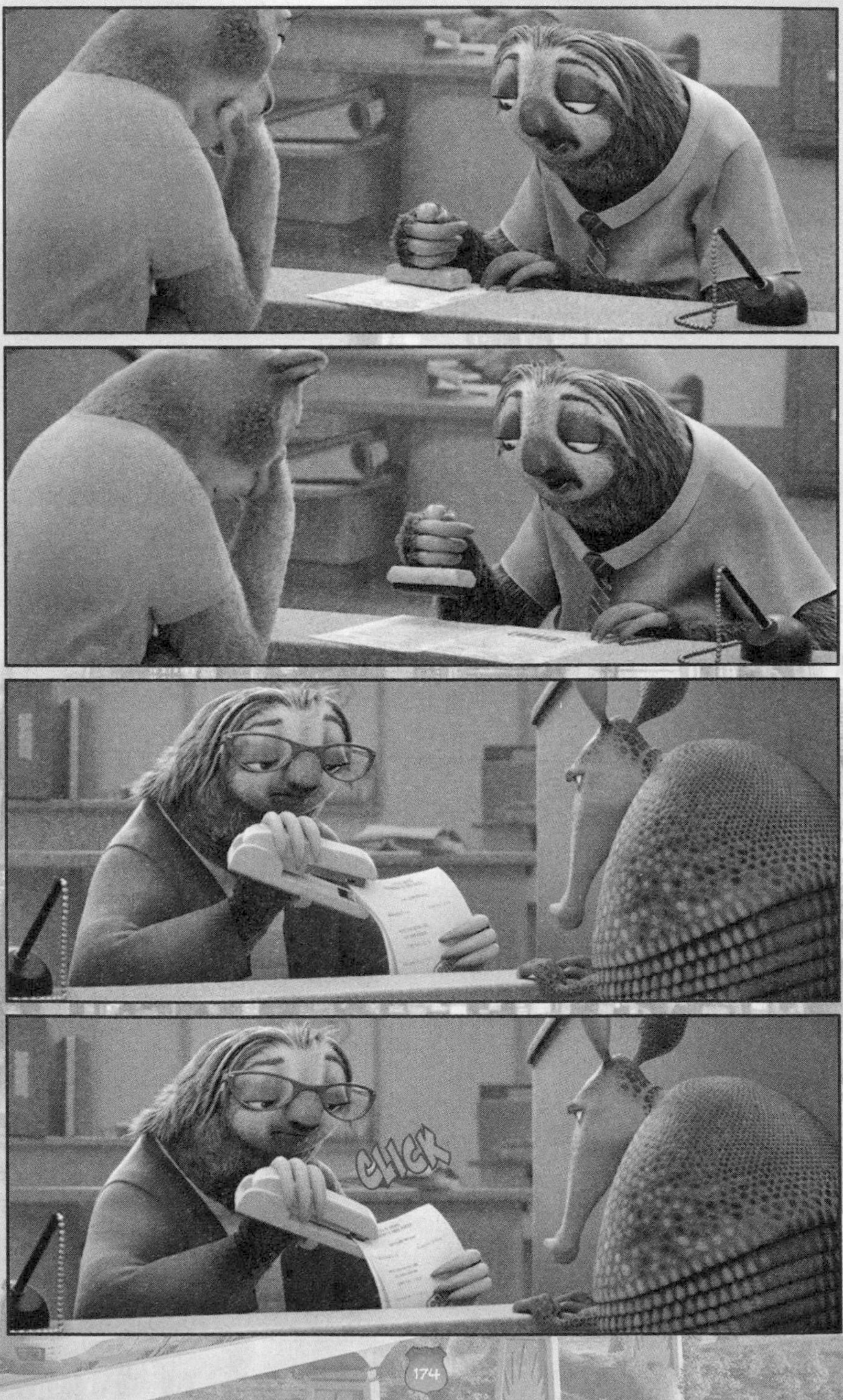
CLICK

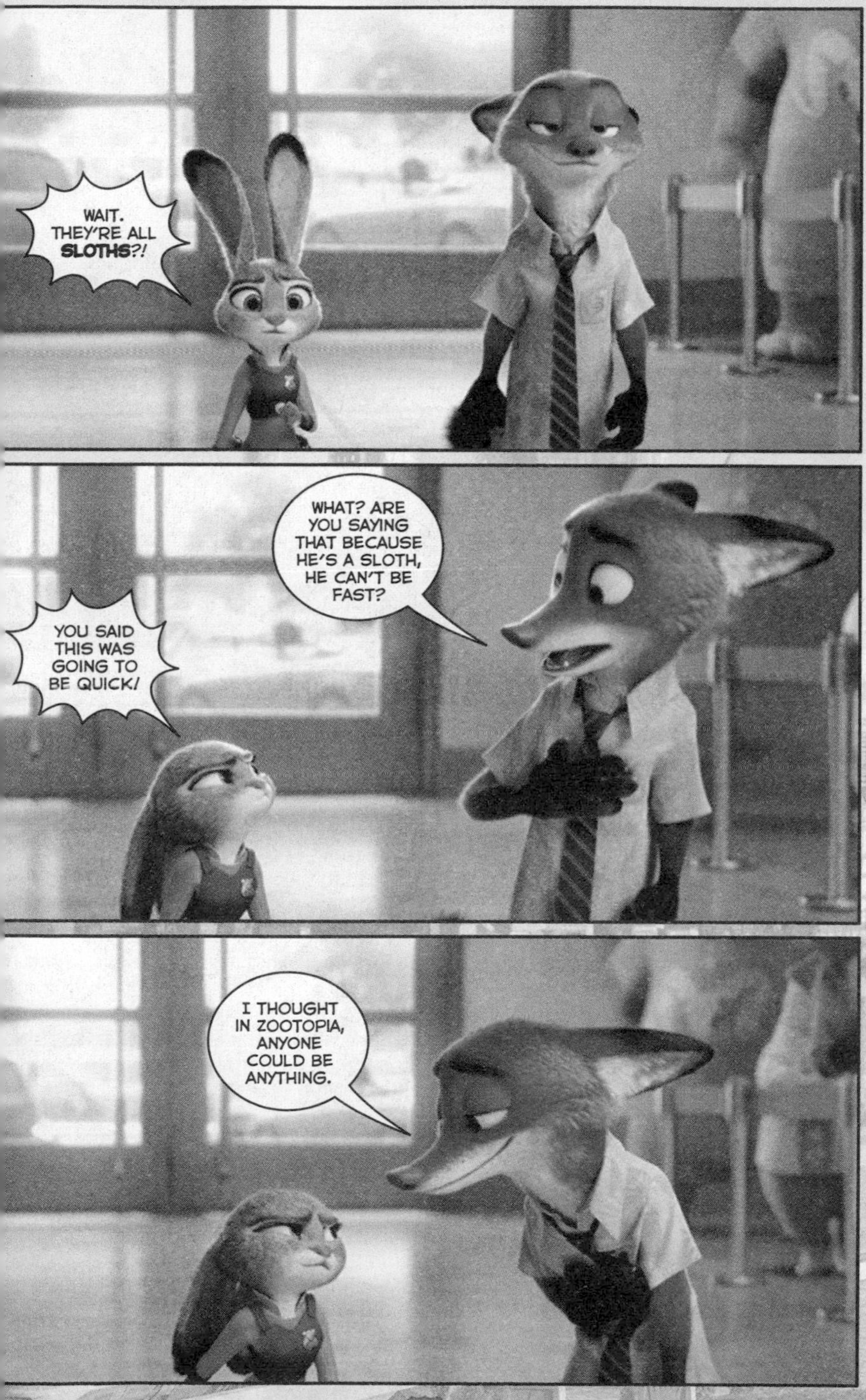
WAIT. THEY'RE ALL SLOTHS?!
YOU SAID THIS WAS GOING TO BE QUICK!
WHAT? ARE YOU SAYING THAT BECAUSE HE'S A SLOTH, HE CAN'T BE FAST?
I THOUGHT IN ZOOTOPIA, ANYONE COULD BE ANYTHING.

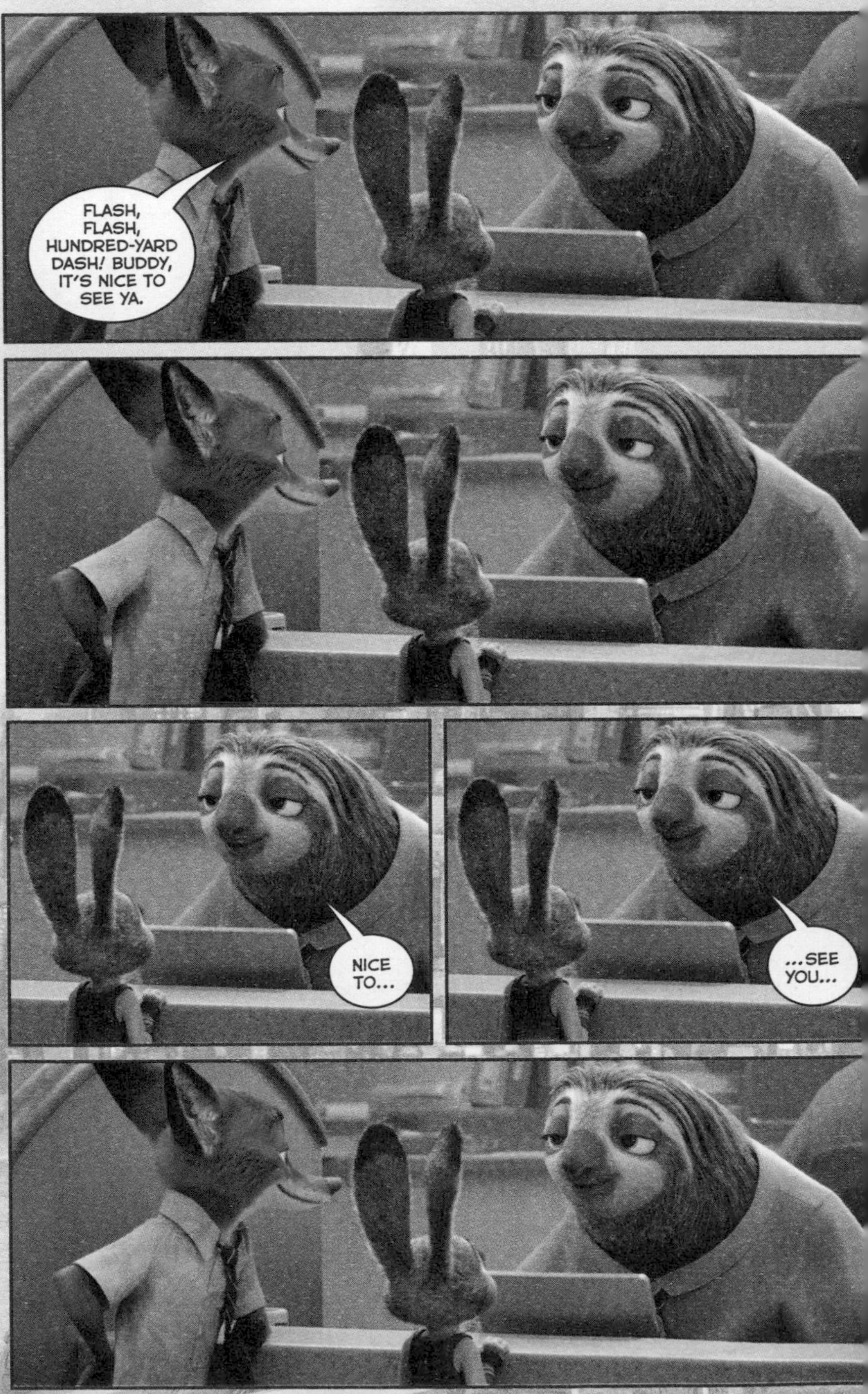
FLASH, FLASH, HUNDRED-YARD DASH! BUDDY, IT'S NICE TO SEE YA.
NICE TO...
...SEE YOU...

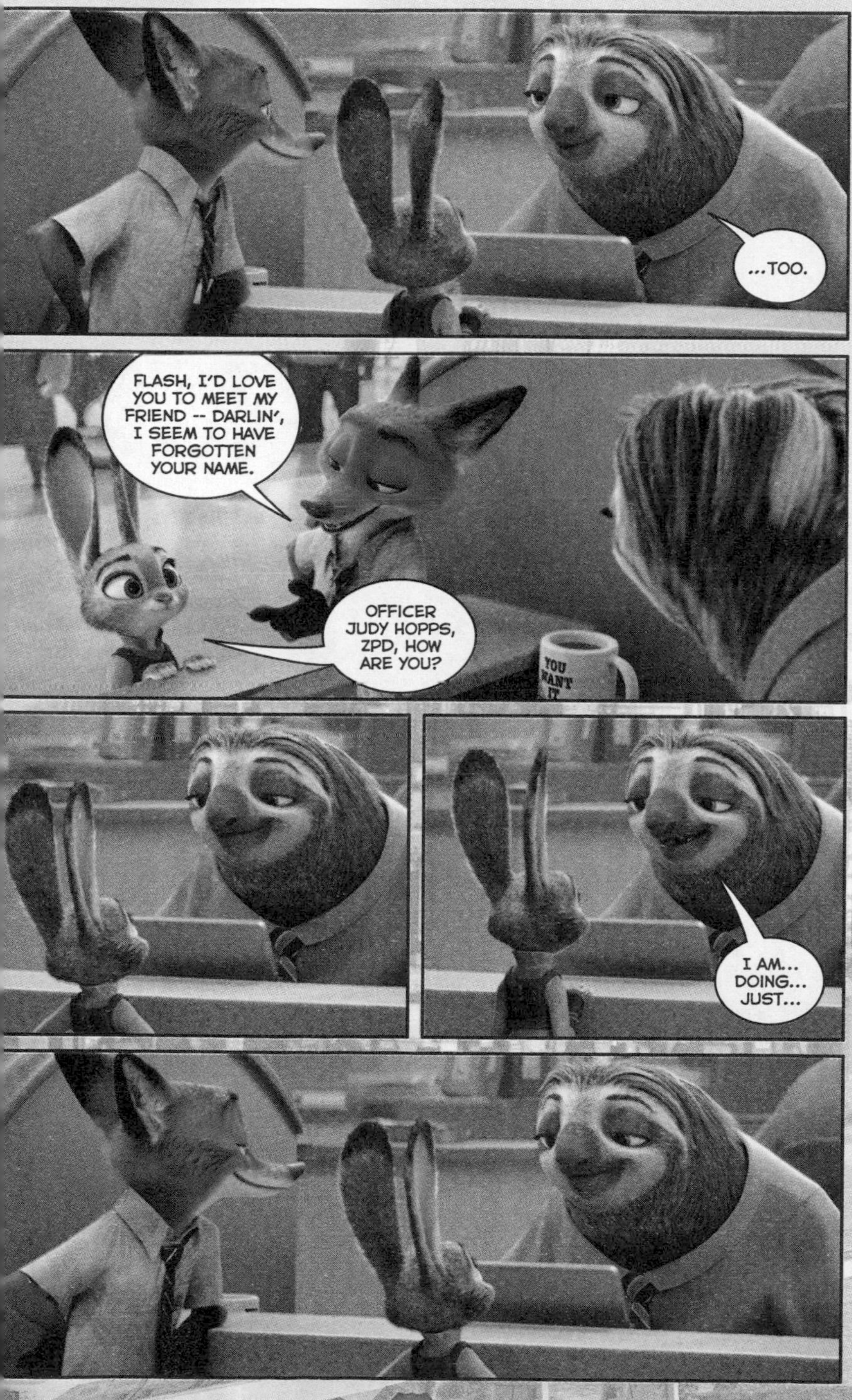
...TOO.
FLASH, I'D LOVE YOU TO MEET MY FRIEND -- DARLIN', I SEEM TO HAVE FORGOTTEN YOUR NAME.
OFFICER JUDY HOPPS, ZPD, HOW ARE YOU?
YOU WANT IT
I AM... DOING... JUST...

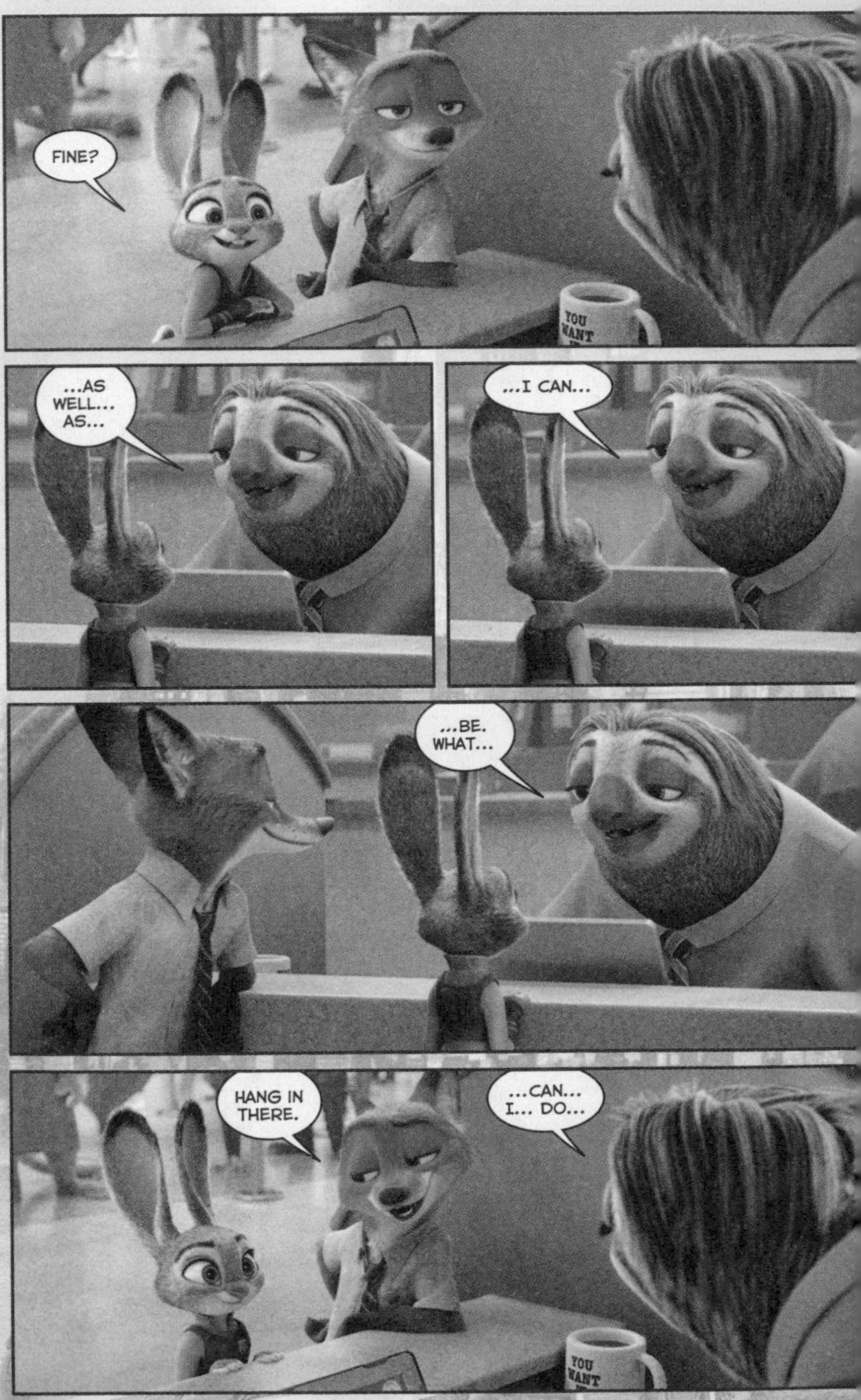
FINE?
YOU WANT
...AS WELL... AS...
...I CAN...
...BE. WHAT...
HANG IN THERE.
...CAN... I... DO...
YOU WANT

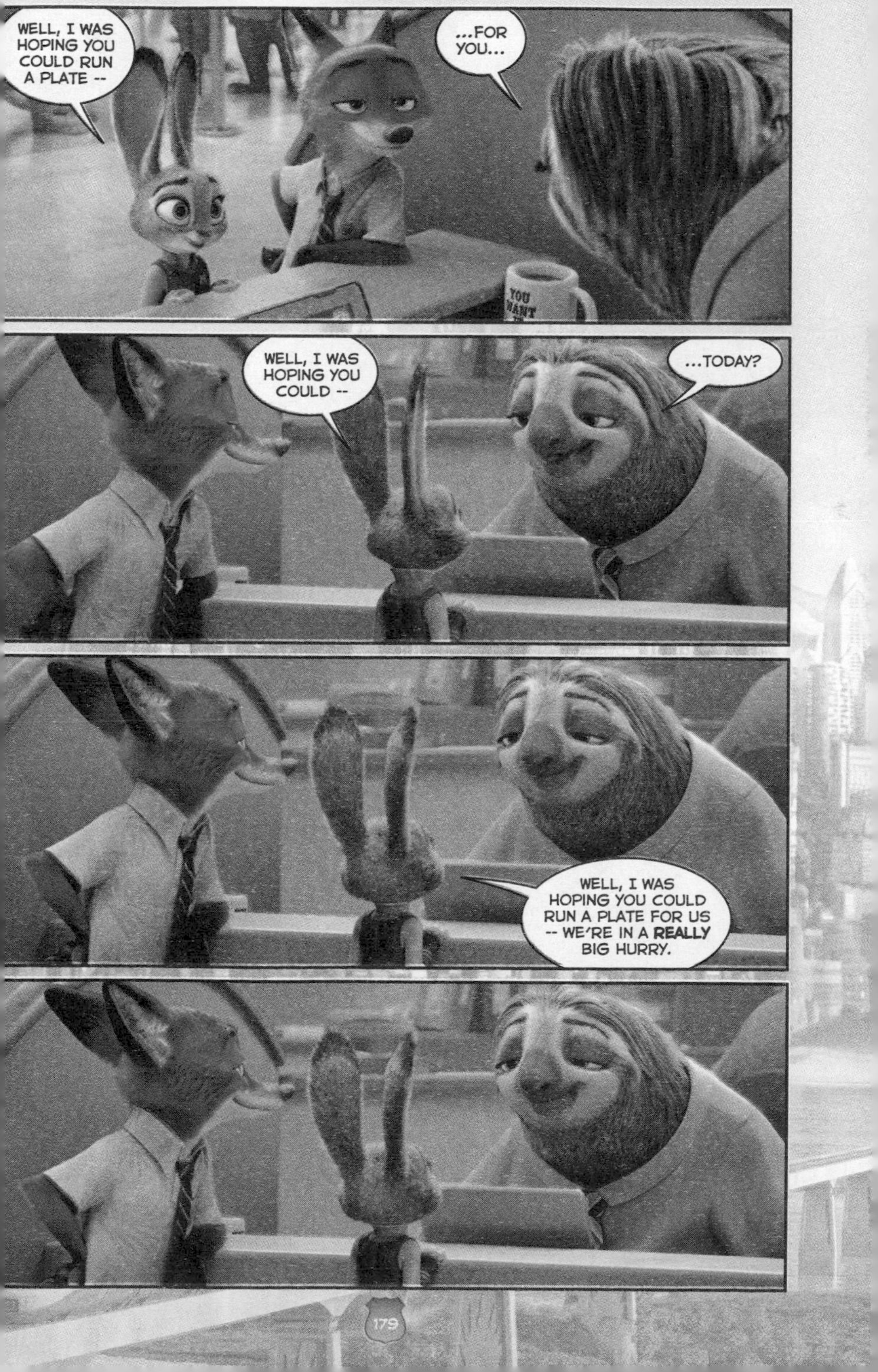
WELL, I WAS HOPING YOU COULD RUN A PLATE --
...FOR YOU...
WELL, I WAS HOPING YOU COULD --
...TODAY?
WELL, I WAS HOPING YOU COULD RUN A PLATE FOR US -- WE'RE IN A **REALLY** BIG HURRY.

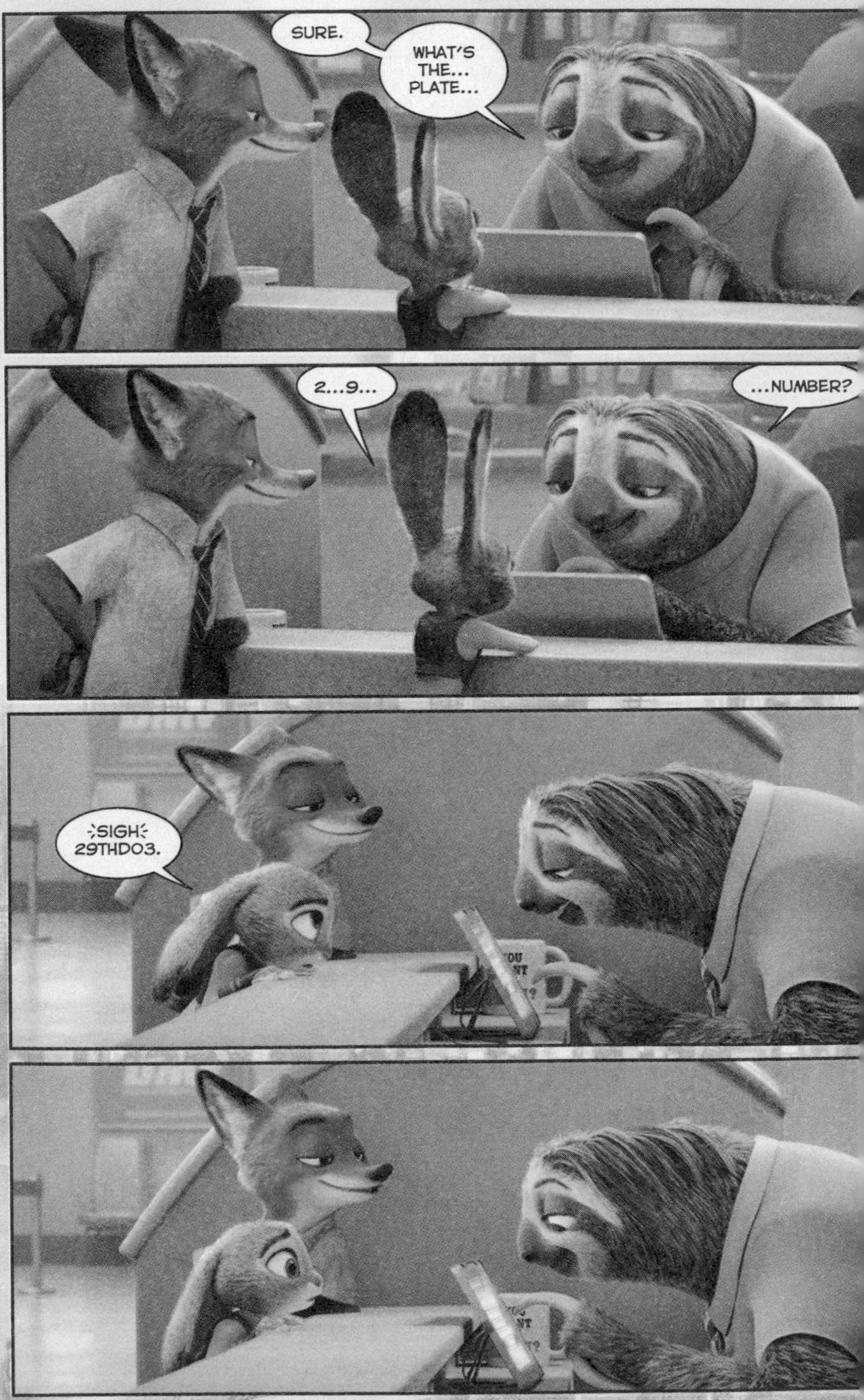
SURE.
WHAT'S THE... PLATE...
2...9...
...NUMBER?
SIGH 29THD03.

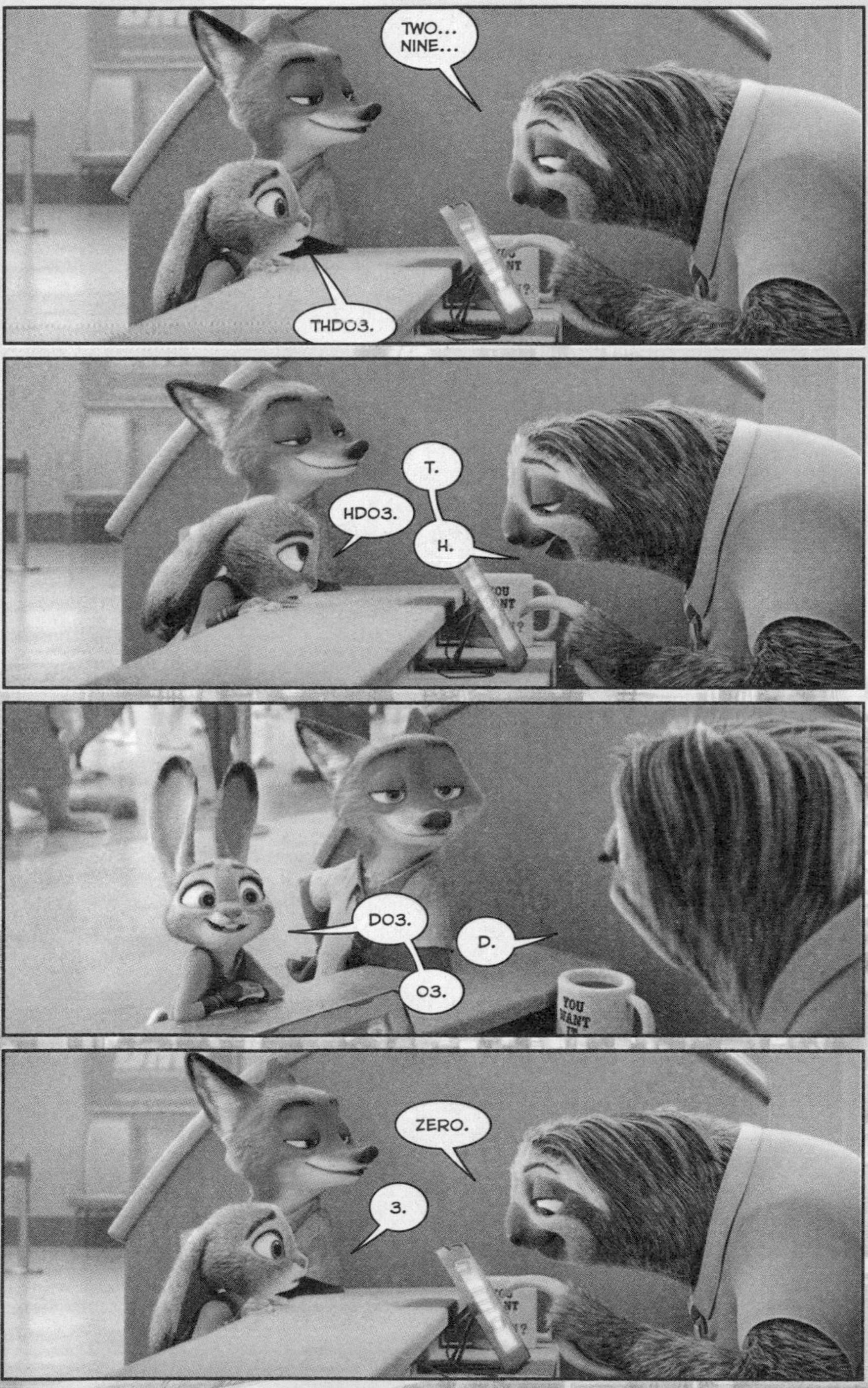
TWO...
NINE...
THDO3.
T.
HDO3.
H.
DO3.
D.
O3.
ZERO.
3.

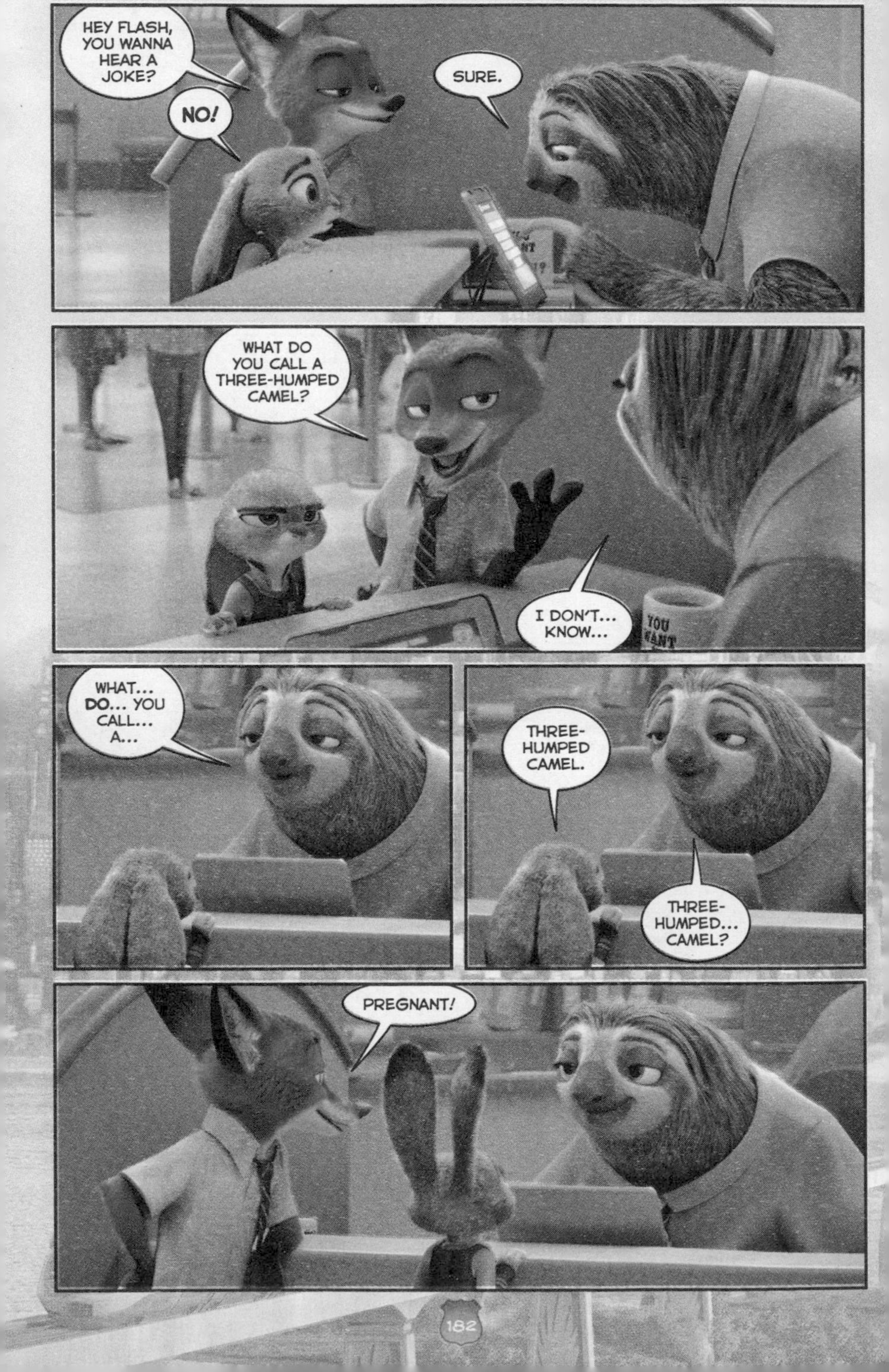
HEY FLASH, YOU WANNA HEAR A JOKE?
NO!
SURE.
WHAT DO YOU CALL A THREE-HUMPED CAMEL?
I DON'T... KNOW...
WHAT... DO... YOU CALL... A...
THREE-HUMPED CAMEL.
THREE-HUMPED... CAMEL?
PREGNANT!

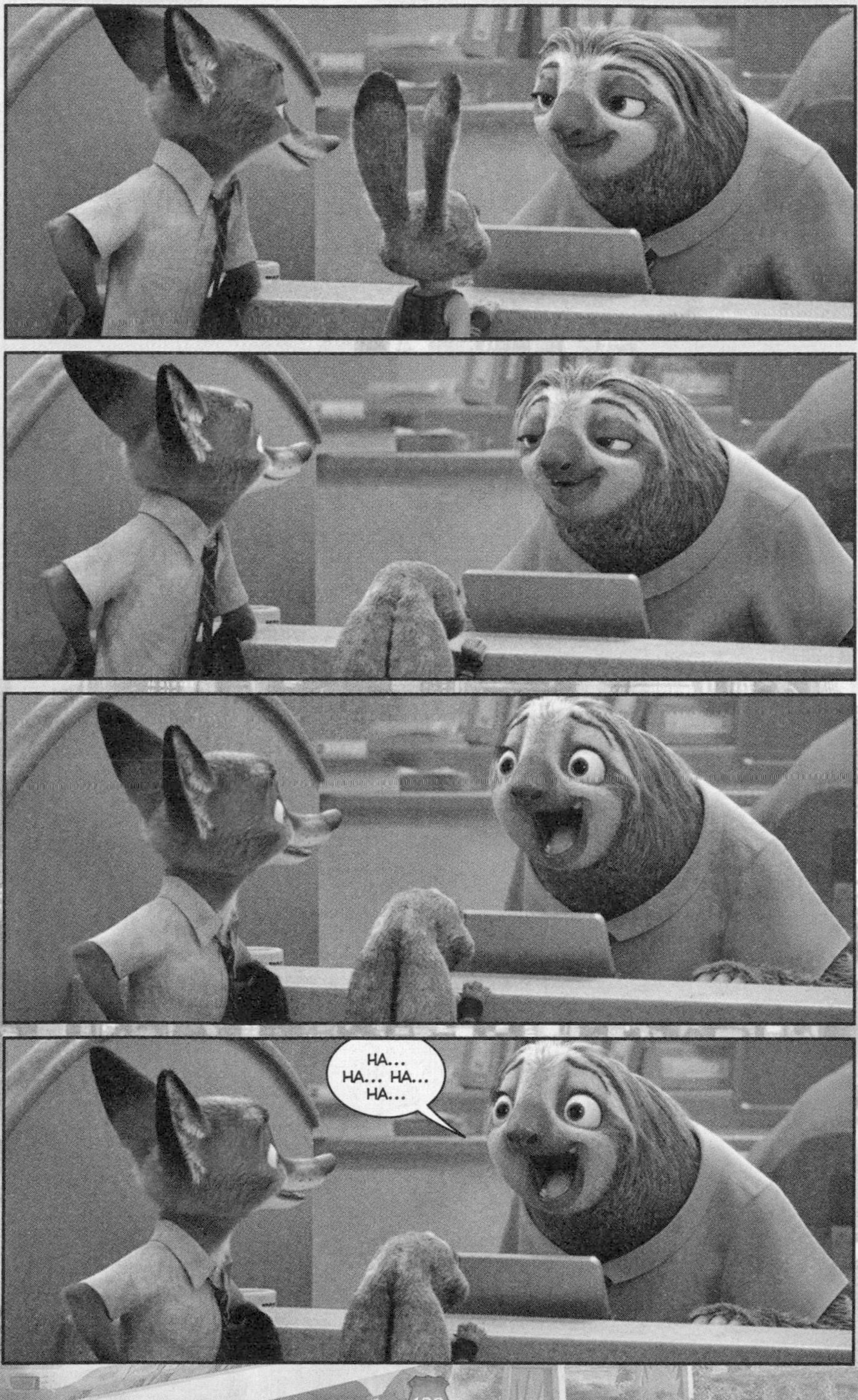
HA...
HA... HA...
HA...

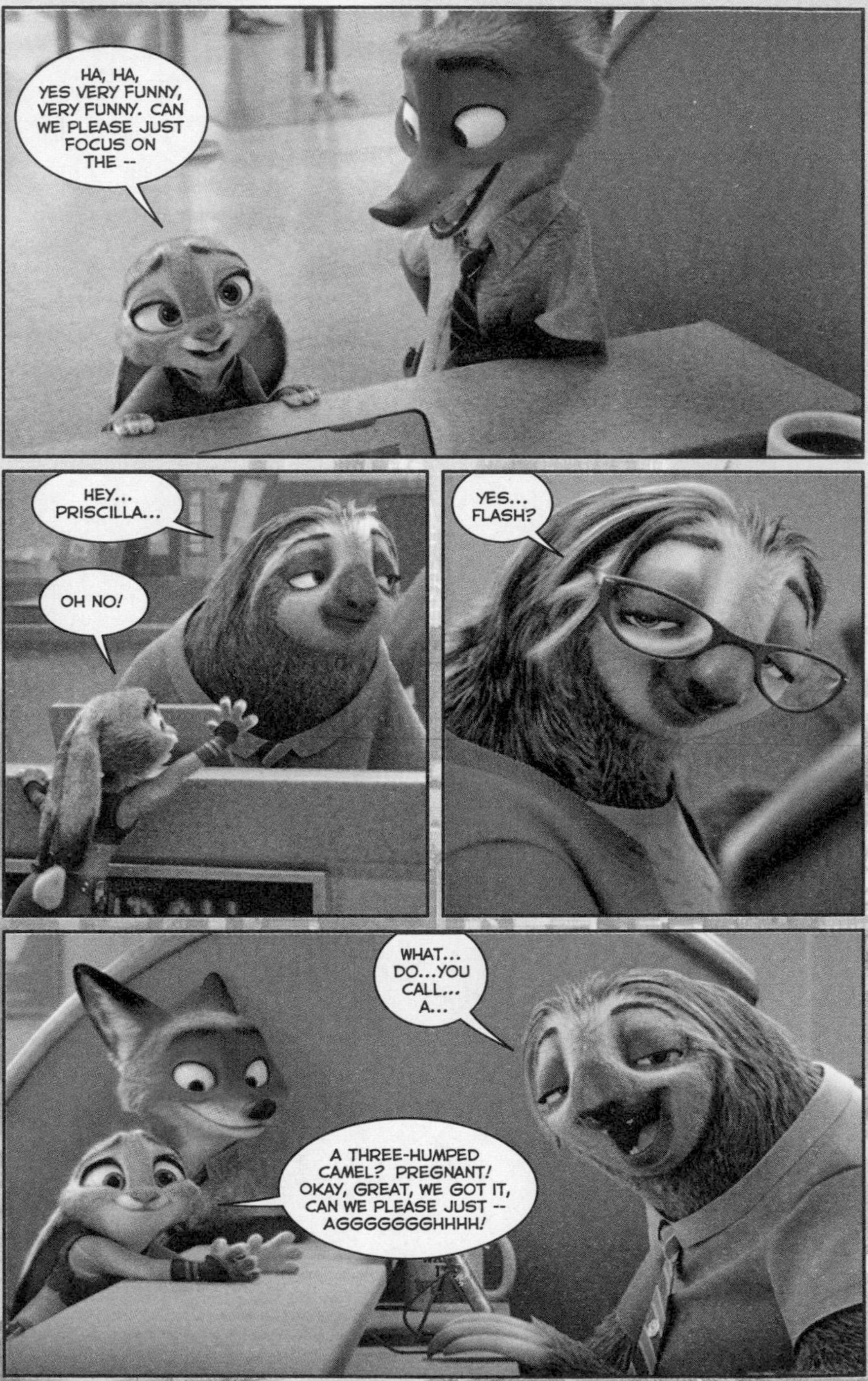
HA, HA, YES VERY FUNNY, VERY FUNNY. CAN WE PLEASE JUST FOCUS ON THE --
HEY... PRISCILLA...
OH NO!
YES... FLASH?
WHAT... DO...YOU CALL... A...
A THREE-HUMPED CAMEL? PREGNANT! OKAY, GREAT, WE GOT IT, CAN WE PLEASE JUST -- AGGGGGGGHHHH!

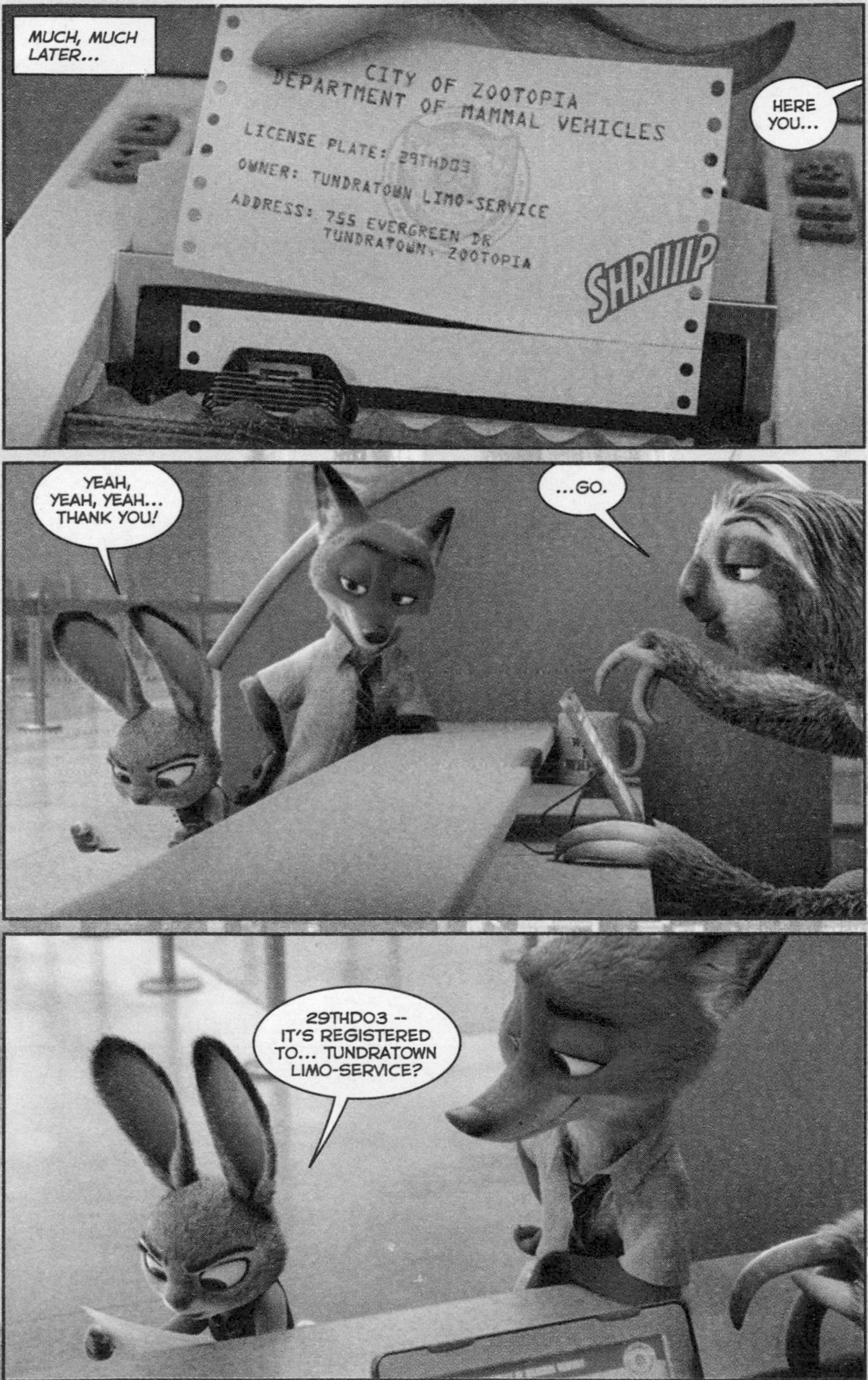
MUCH, MUCH LATER...
CITY OF ZOOTOPIA
DEPARTMENT OF MAMMAL VEHICLES
LICENSE PLATE: 29THD03
OWNER: TUNDRATOWN LIMO-SERVICE
ADDRESS: 755 EVERGREEN DR
TUNDRATOWN, ZOOTOPIA
HERE YOU...
SHRIIIIP
YEAH, YEAH, YEAH... THANK YOU!
...GO.
29THD03 -- IT'S REGISTERED TO... TUNDRATOWN LIMO-SERVICE?

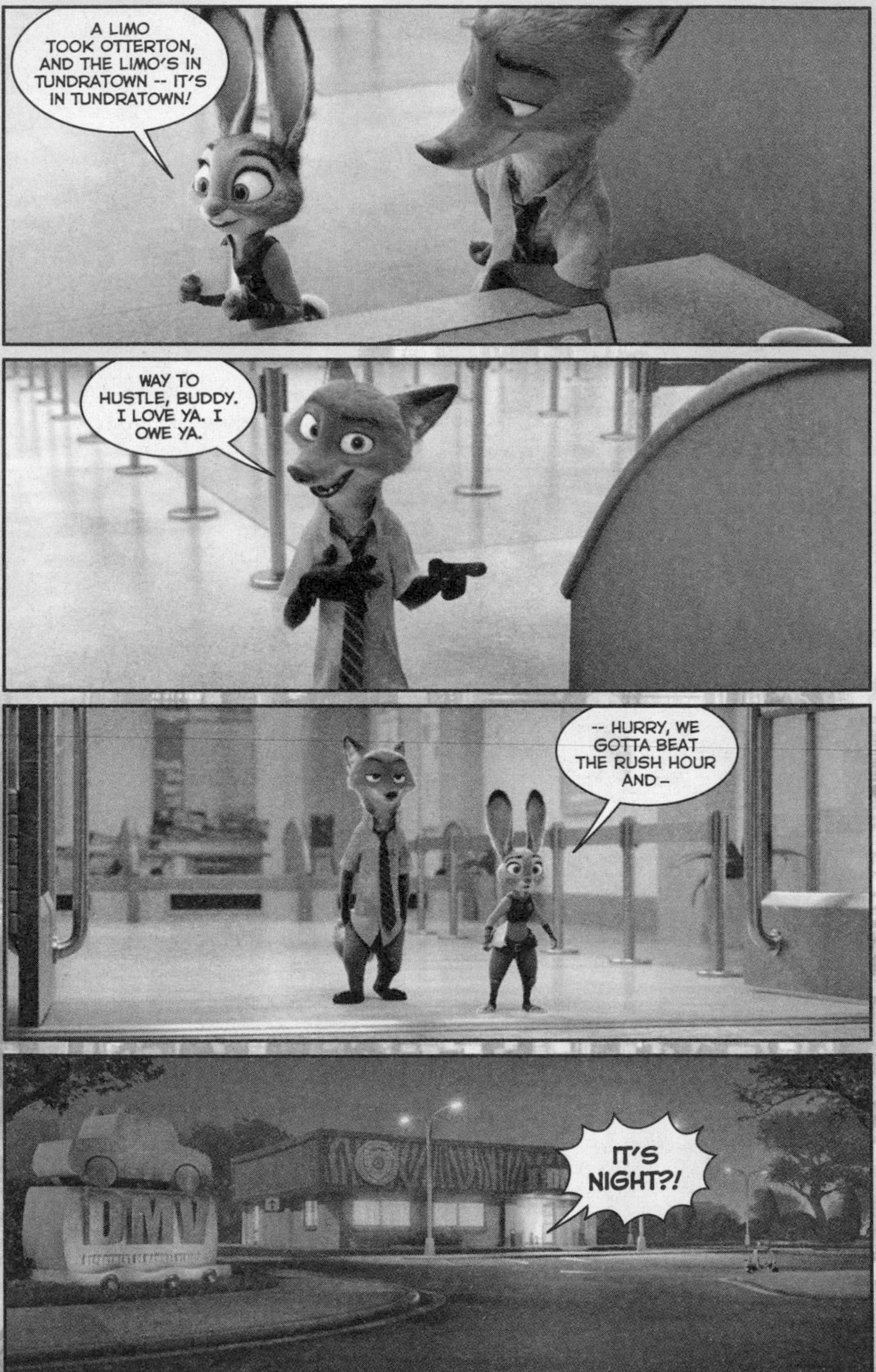
A LIMO TOOK OTTERTON, AND THE LIMO'S IN TUNDRATOWN -- IT'S IN TUNDRATOWN!
WAY TO HUSTLE, BUDDY. I LOVE YA. I OWE YA.
-- HURRY, WE GOTTA BEAT THE RUSH HOUR AND –
IT'S NIGHT?!
DMV

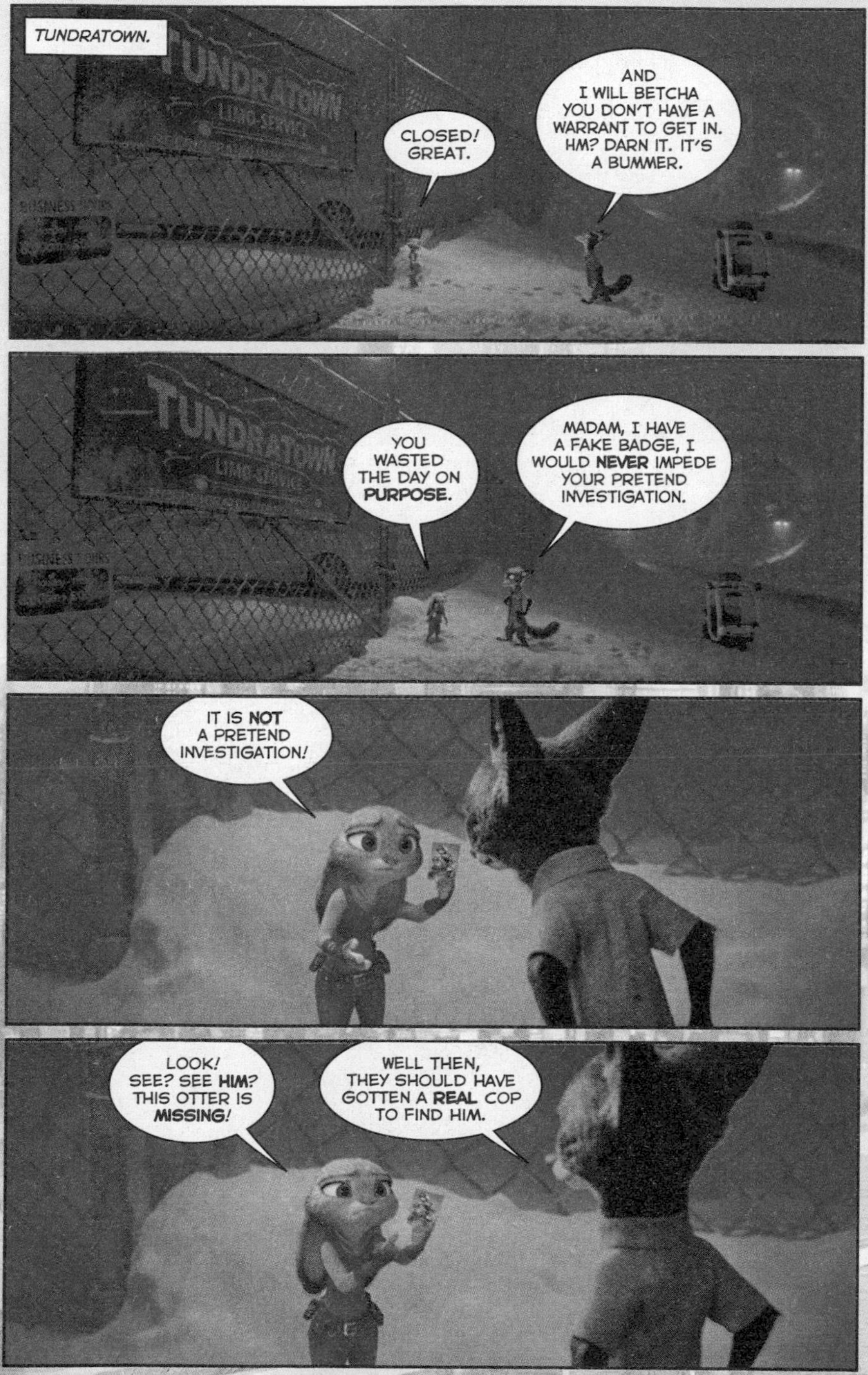
TUNDRATOWN.
TUNDRATOWN LIMO SERVICE
CLOSED! GREAT.
AND I WILL BETCHA YOU DON'T HAVE A WARRANT TO GET IN. HM? DARN IT. IT'S A BUMMER.
YOU WASTED THE DAY ON **PURPOSE.**
MADAM, I HAVE A FAKE BADGE, I WOULD **NEVER** IMPEDE YOUR PRETEND INVESTIGATION.
IT IS **NOT** A PRETEND INVESTIGATION!
LOOK! SEE? SEE **HIM**? THIS OTTER IS **MISSING**!
WELL THEN, THEY SHOULD HAVE GOTTEN A **REAL** COP TO FIND HIM.

NICK AND HOPPS
ENTER THE LIMO
YARD...

29THD03...
THIS IS IT.

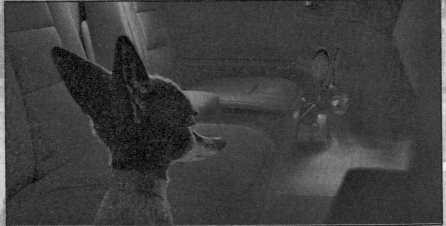

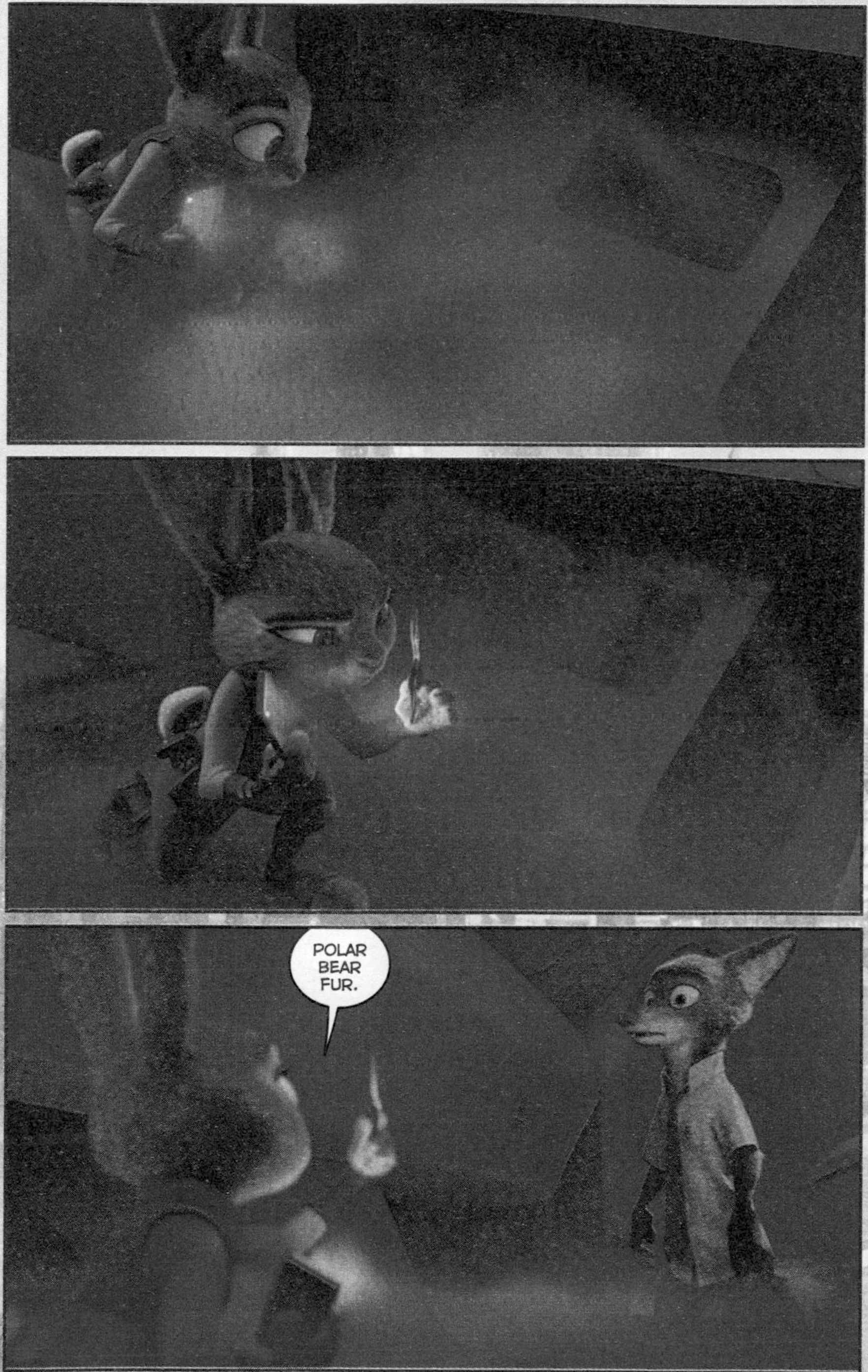
POLAR BEAR FUR.

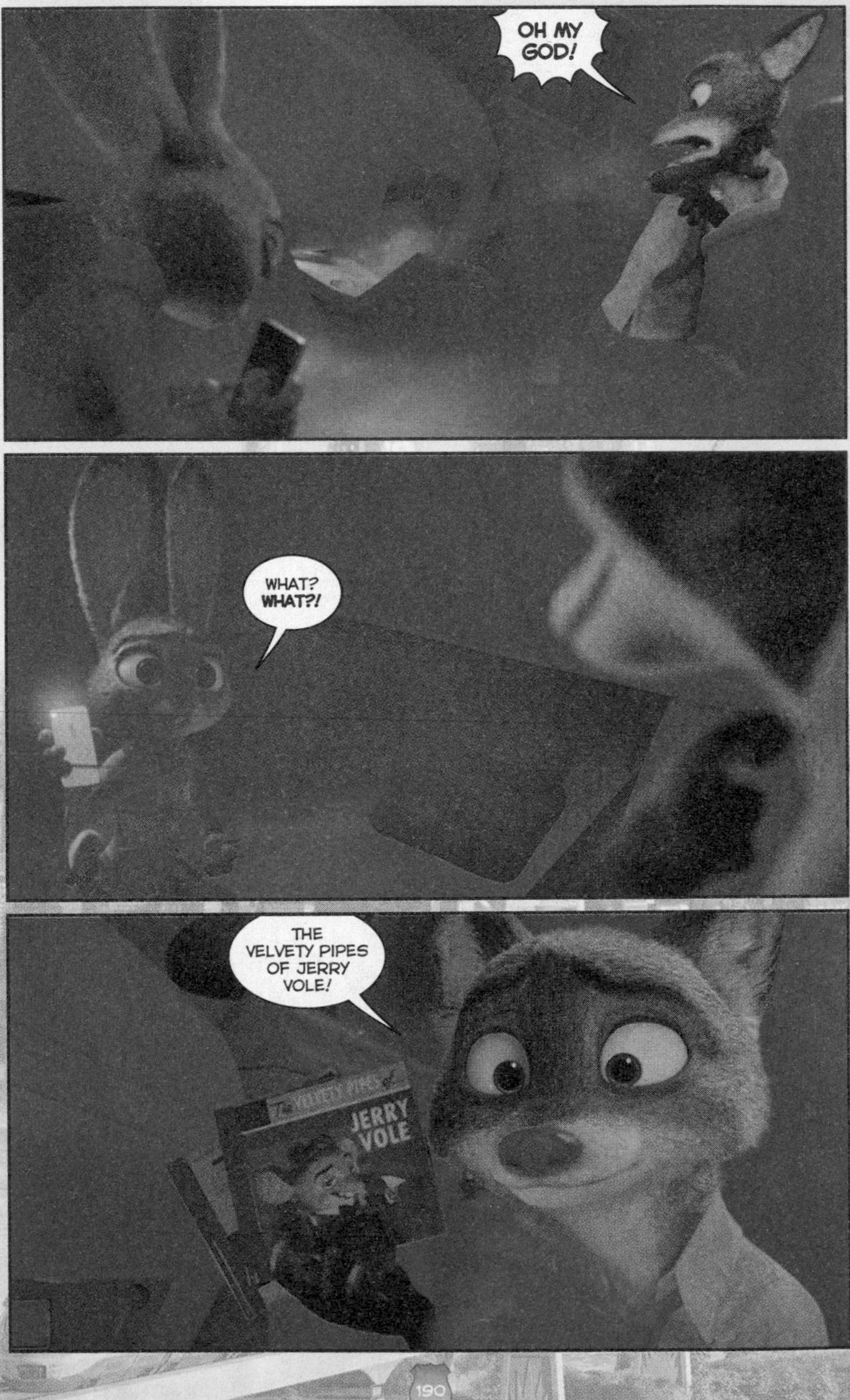
OH MY GOD!
WHAT? WHAT?!
THE VELVETY PIPES OF JERRY VOLE!
JERRY VOLE

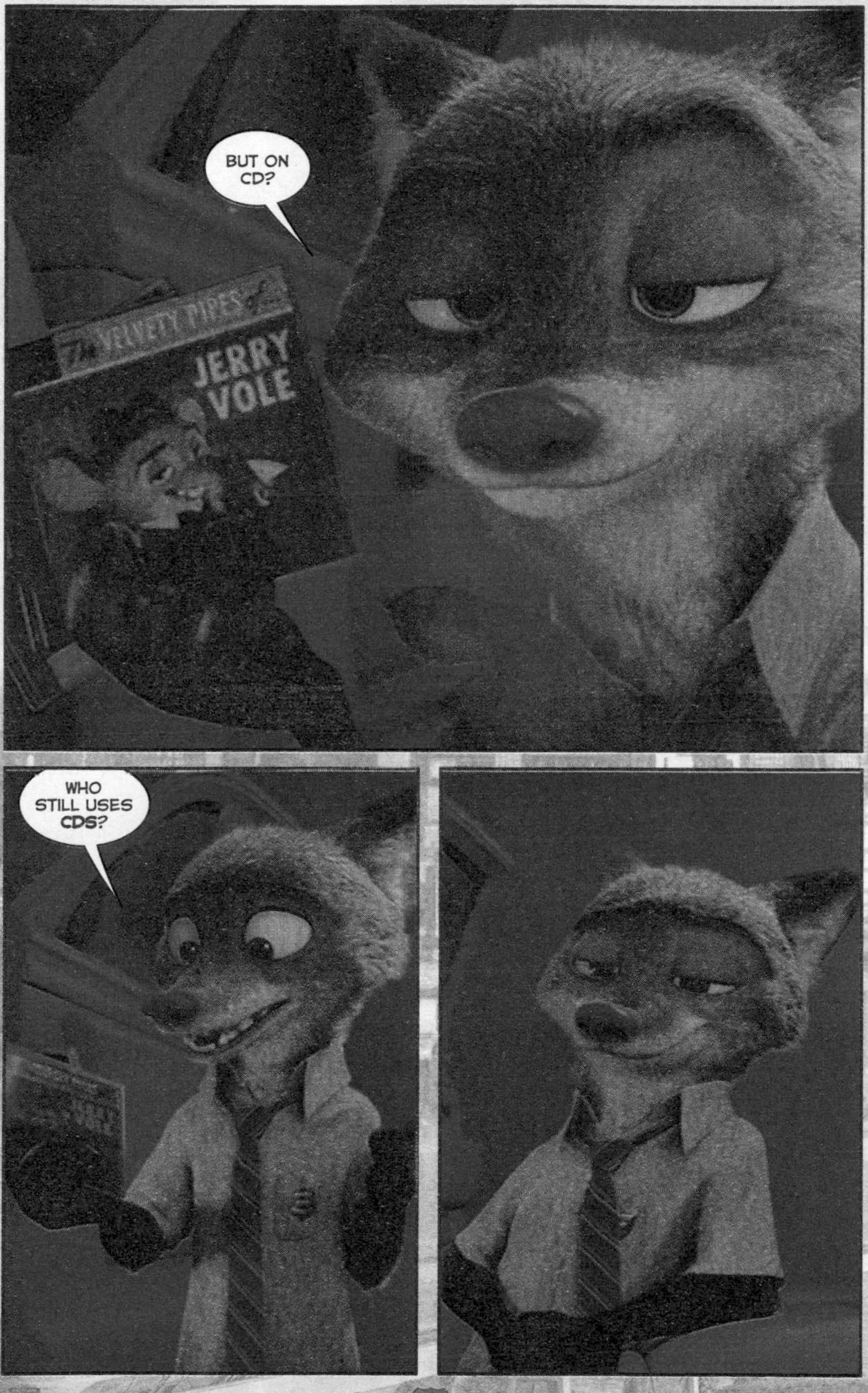
BUT ON CD?
VELVETY PIPES
JERRY VOLE
WHO STILL USES **CDS**?

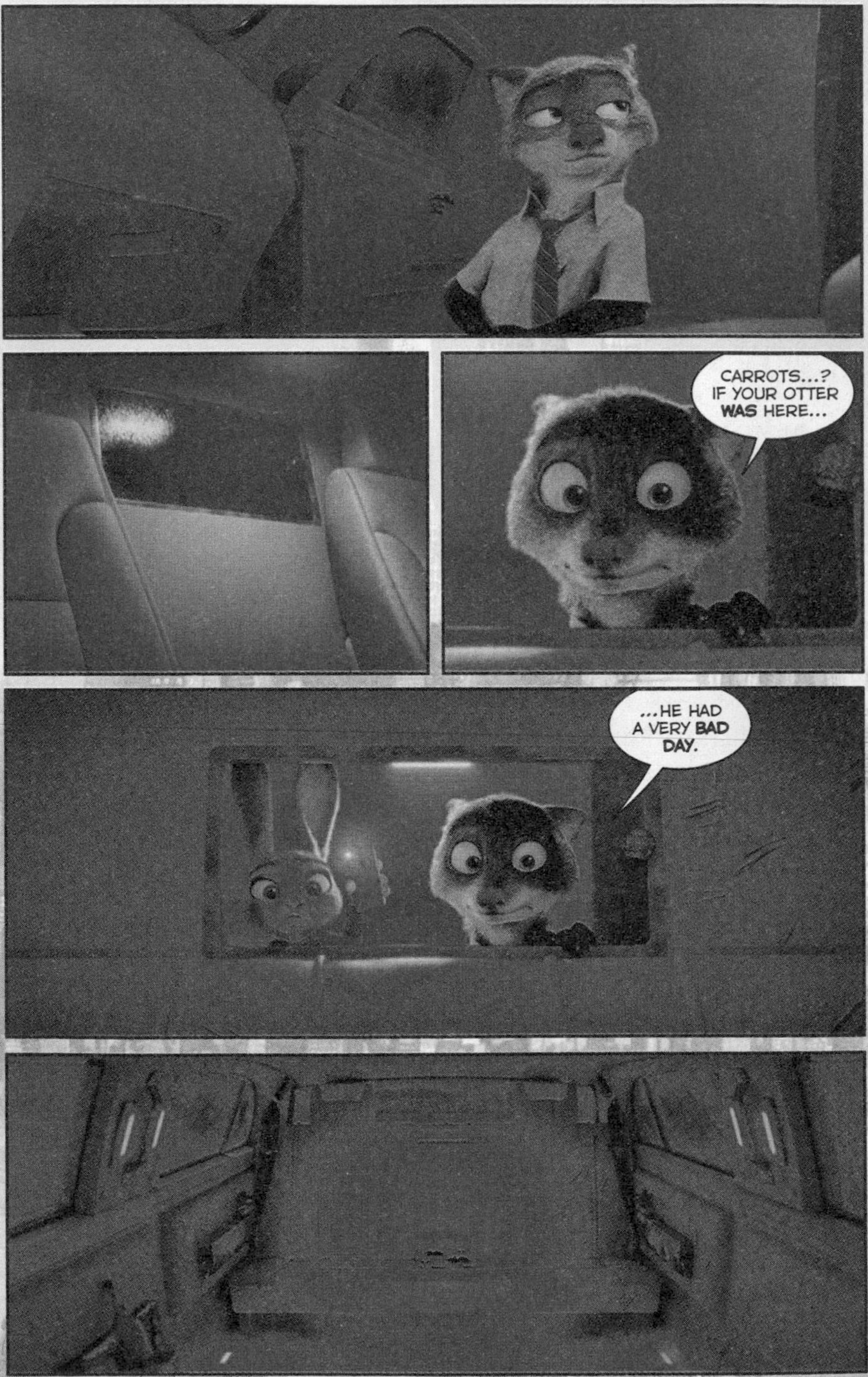
CARROTS...? IF YOUR OTTER WAS HERE...
...HE HAD A VERY BAD DAY.

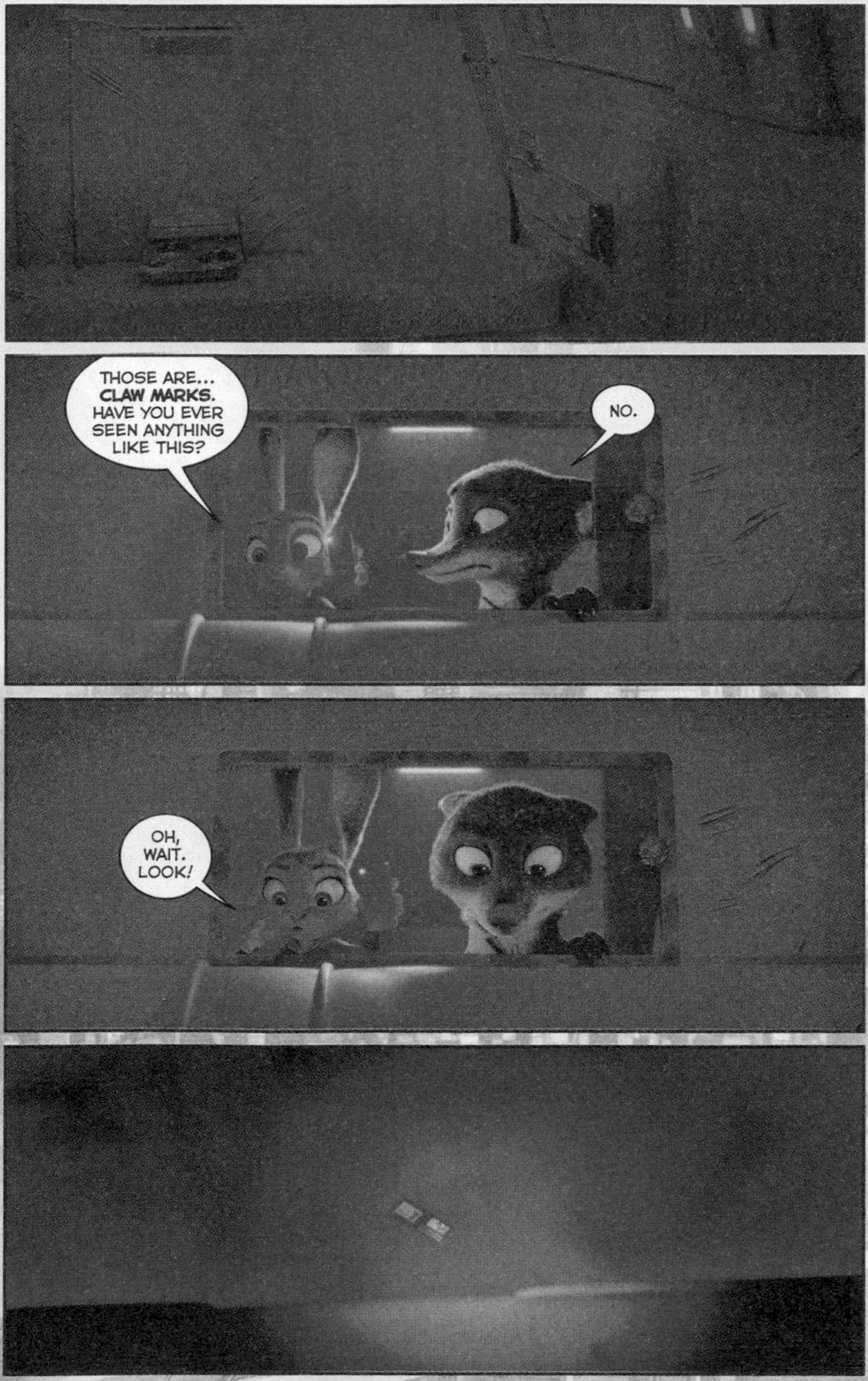
THOSE ARE... **CLAW MARKS.** HAVE YOU EVER SEEN ANYTHING LIKE THIS?
NO.
OH, WAIT. LOOK!

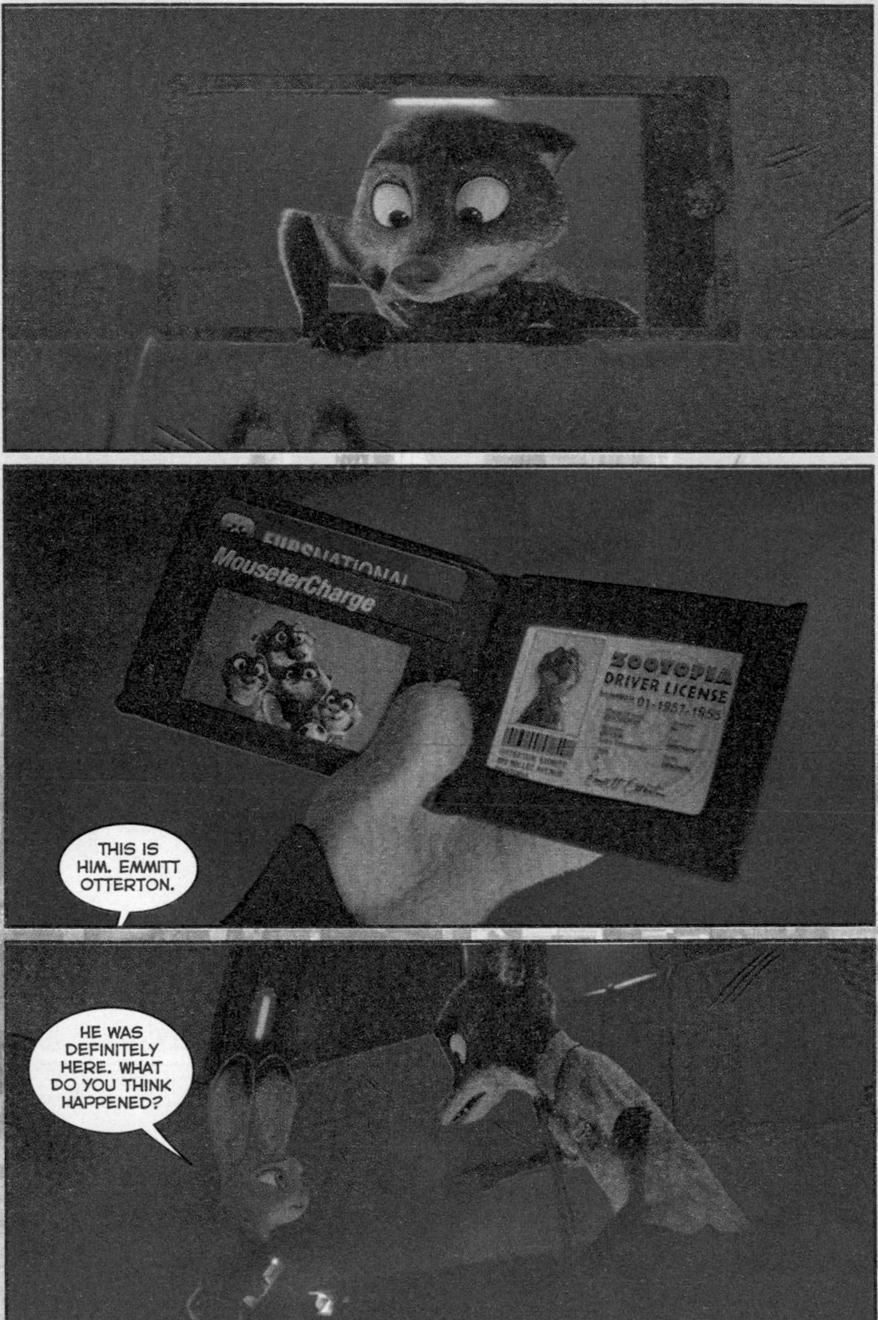
MouseterCharge
ZOOTOPIA
DRIVER LICENSE
THIS IS HIM. EMMITT OTTERTON.
HE WAS DEFINITELY HERE. WHAT DO YOU THINK HAPPENED?

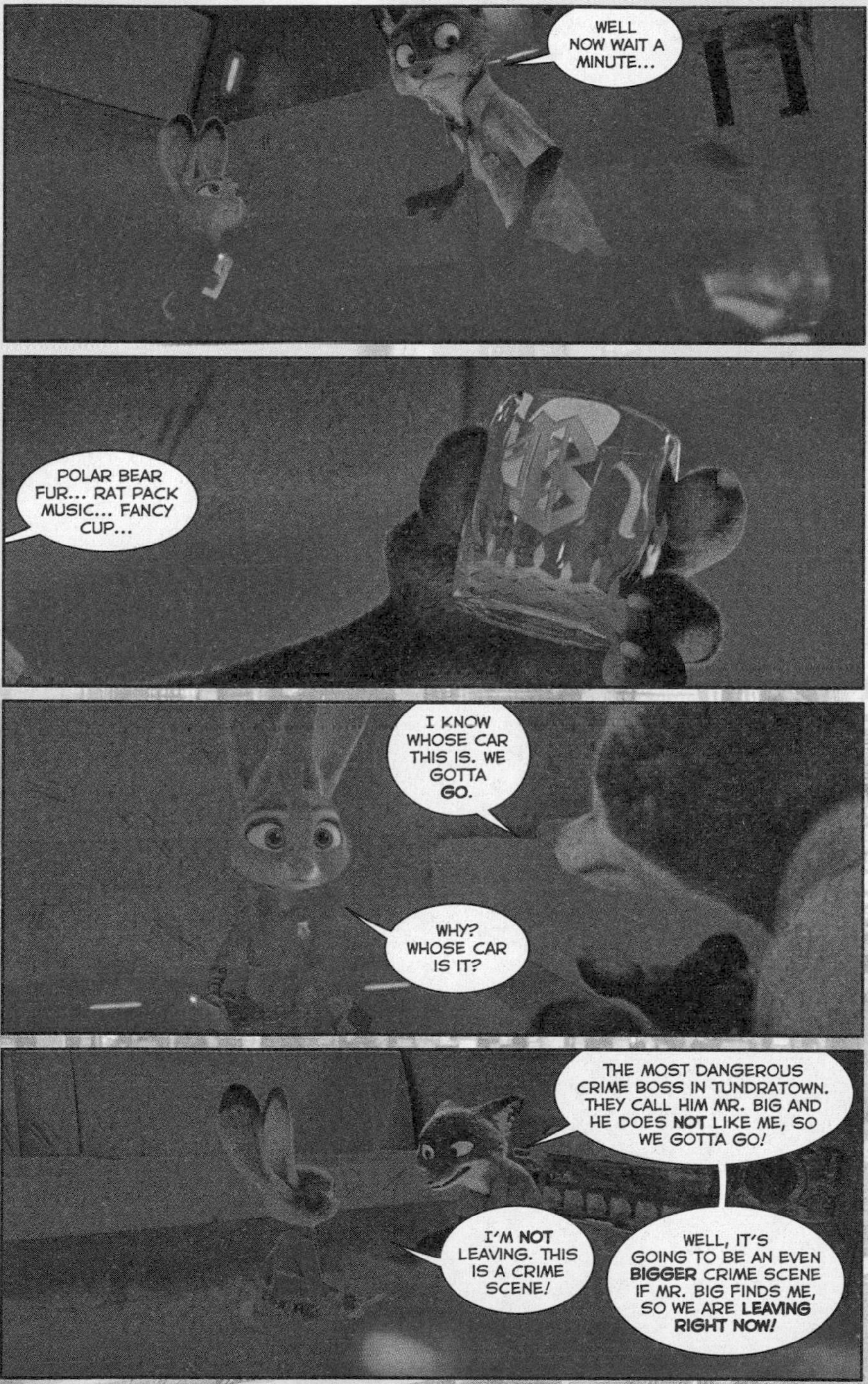
WELL NOW WAIT A MINUTE...
POLAR BEAR FUR... RAT PACK MUSIC... FANCY CUP...
I KNOW WHOSE CAR THIS IS. WE GOTTA **GO.**
WHY? WHOSE CAR IS IT?
THE MOST DANGEROUS CRIME BOSS IN TUNDRATOWN. THEY CALL HIM MR. BIG AND HE DOES **NOT** LIKE ME, SO WE GOTTA GO!
I'M **NOT** LEAVING. THIS IS A CRIME SCENE!
WELL, IT'S GOING TO BE AN EVEN **BIGGER** CRIME SCENE IF MR. BIG FINDS ME, SO WE ARE **LEAVING RIGHT NOW!**

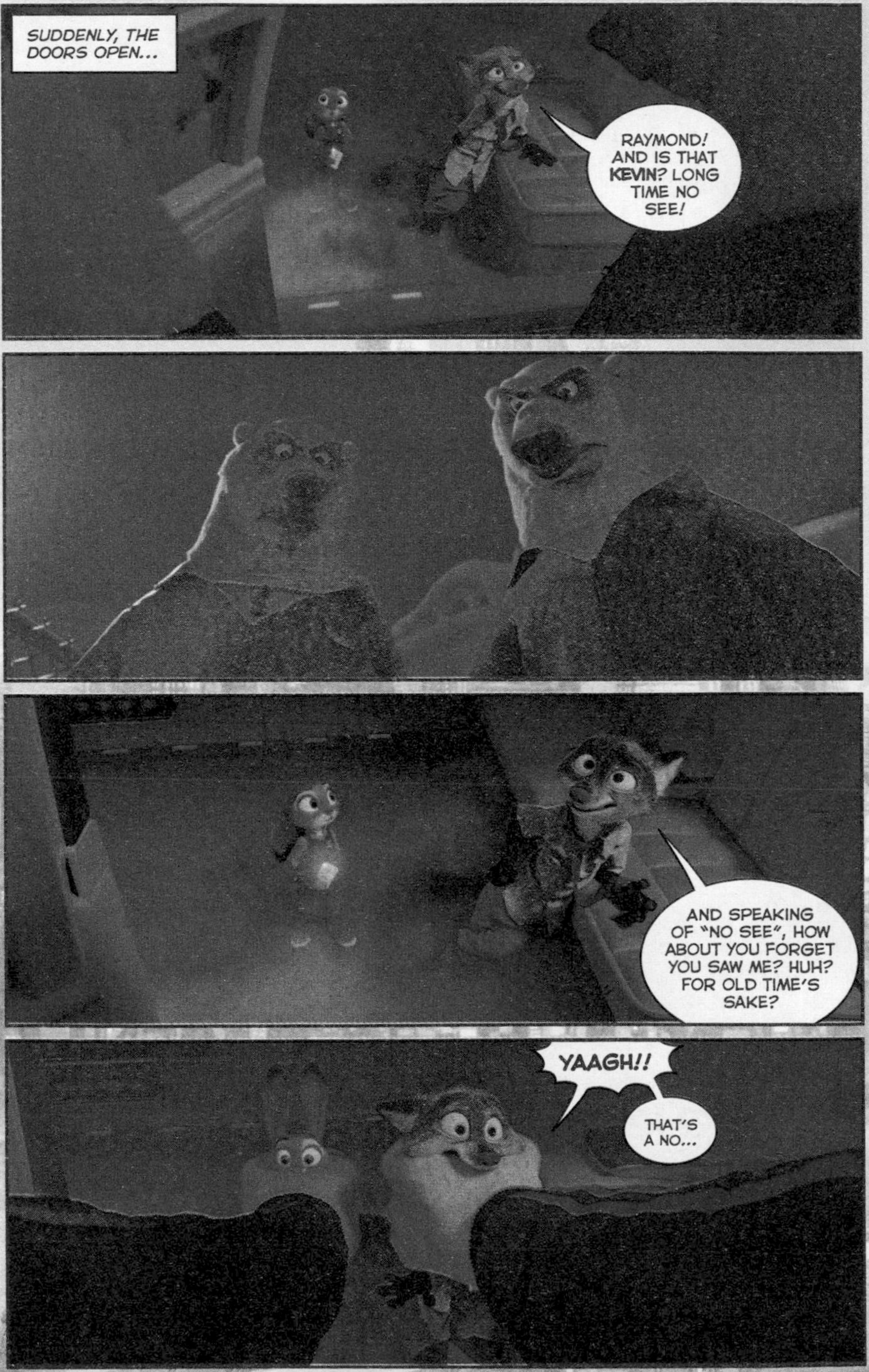
SUDDENLY, THE DOORS OPEN...
RAYMOND! AND IS THAT KEVIN? LONG TIME NO SEE!
AND SPEAKING OF "NO SEE", HOW ABOUT YOU FORGET YOU SAW ME? HUH? FOR OLD TIME'S SAKE?
YAAGH!!
THAT'S A NO...

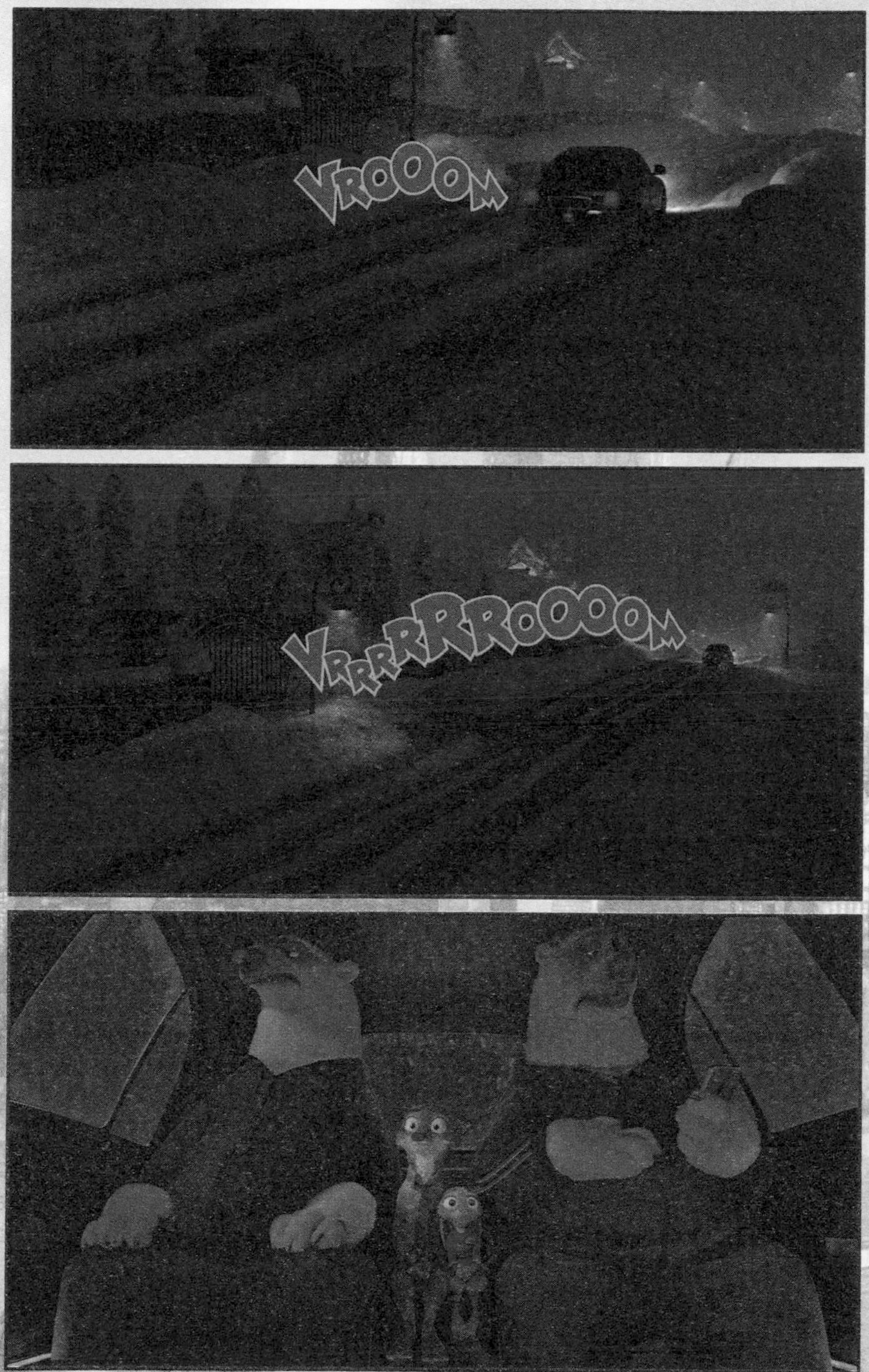
VROOOOM
VRRRRRROOOOOM

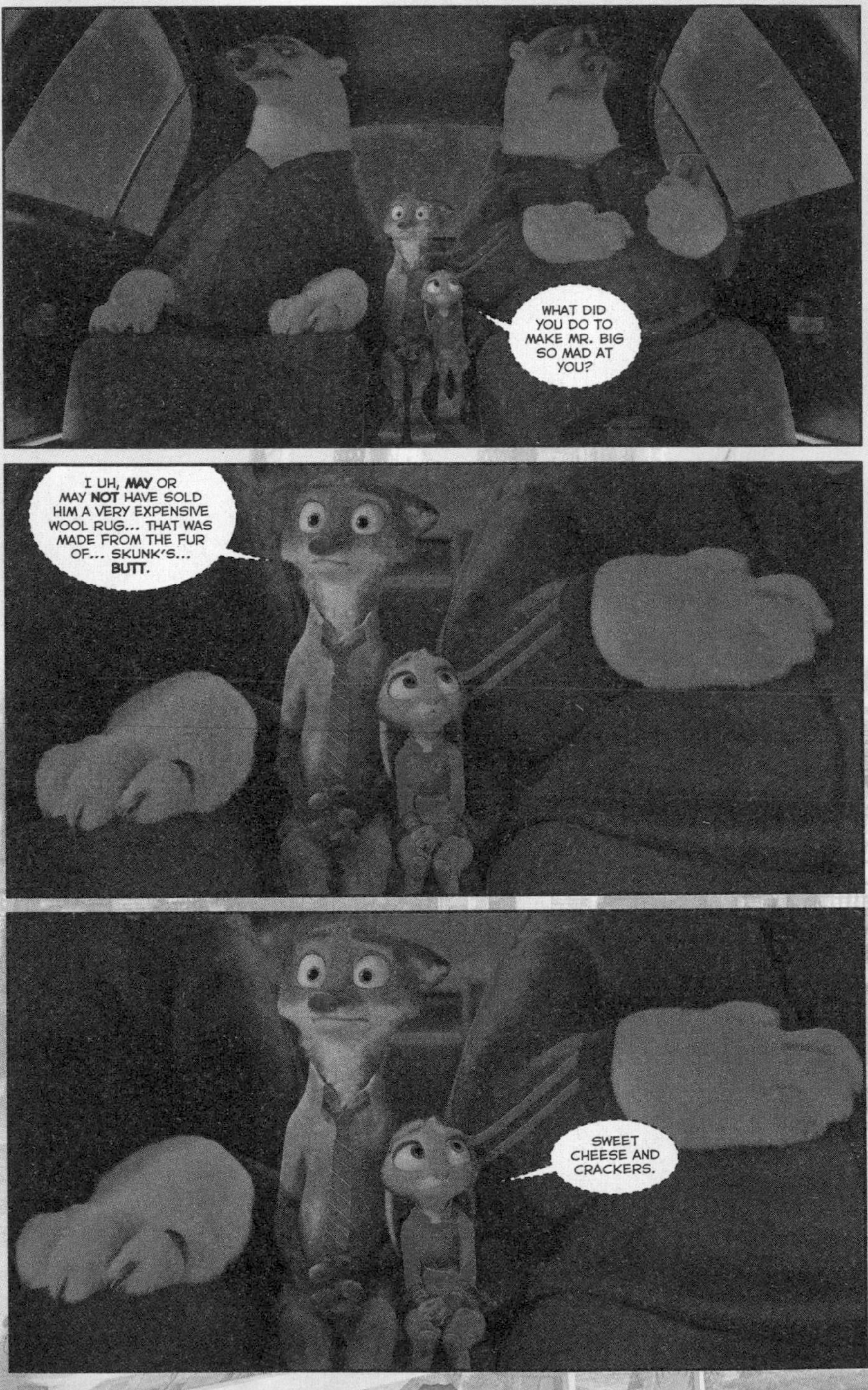
WHAT DID YOU DO TO MAKE MR. BIG SO MAD AT YOU?
I UH, **MAY** OR MAY **NOT** HAVE SOLD HIM A VERY EXPENSIVE WOOL RUG... THAT WAS MADE FROM THE FUR OF... SKUNK'S... **BUTT.**
SWEET CHEESE AND CRACKERS.

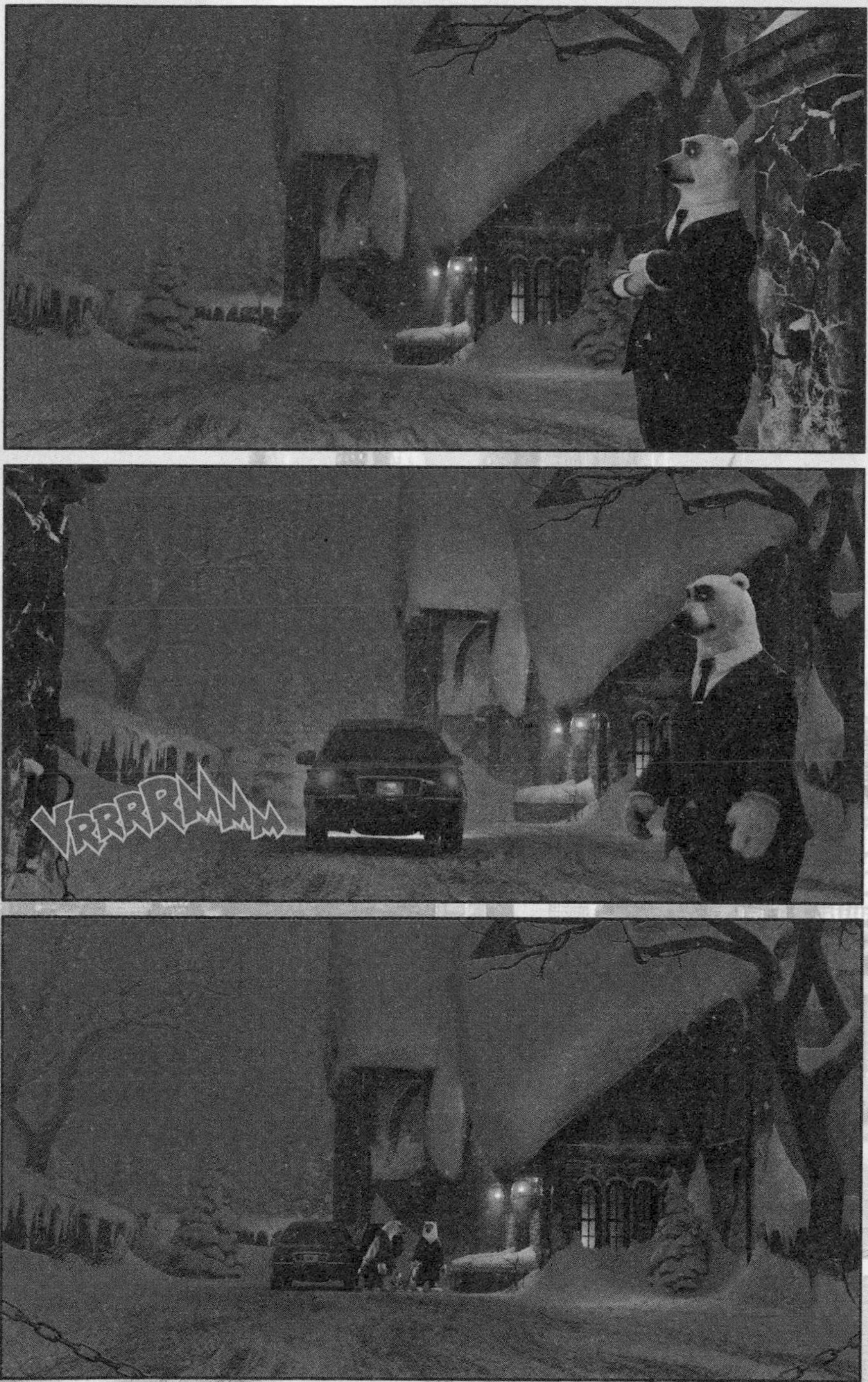
VRRRMMM

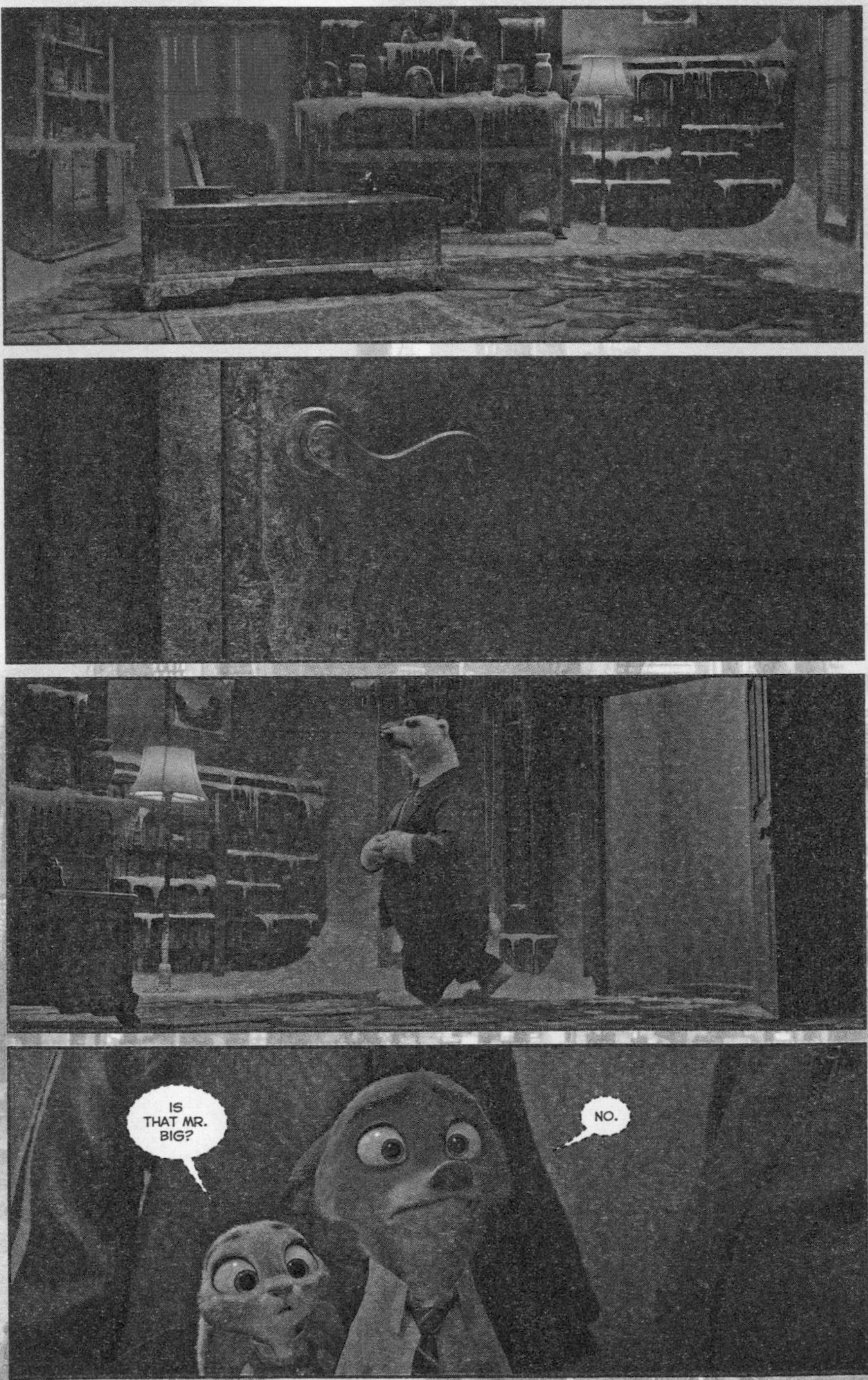
IS THAT MR. BIG?
NO.

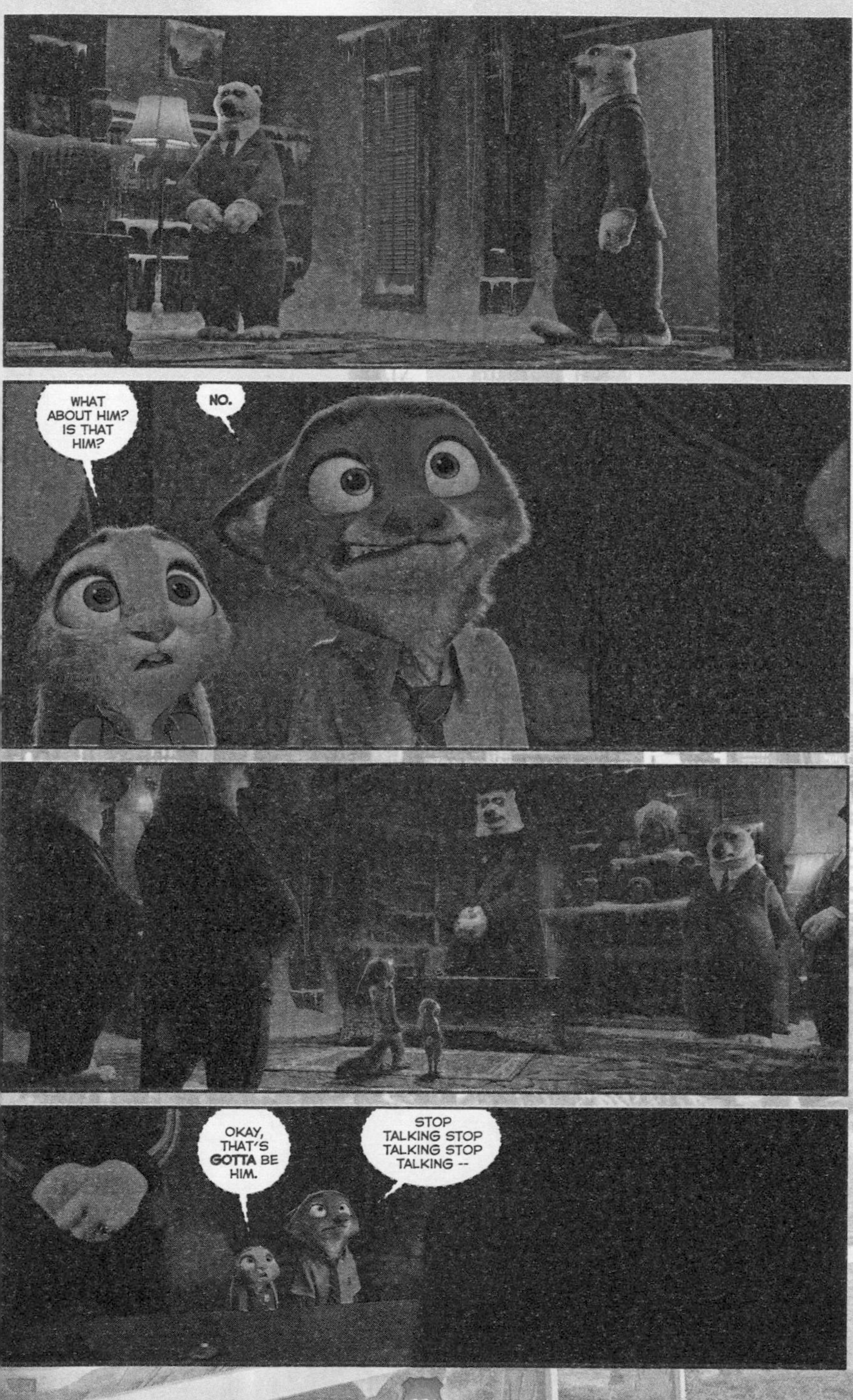
WHAT ABOUT HIM? IS THAT HIM?
NO.
OKAY, THAT'S GOTTA BE HIM.
STOP TALKING STOP TALKING STOP TALKING --

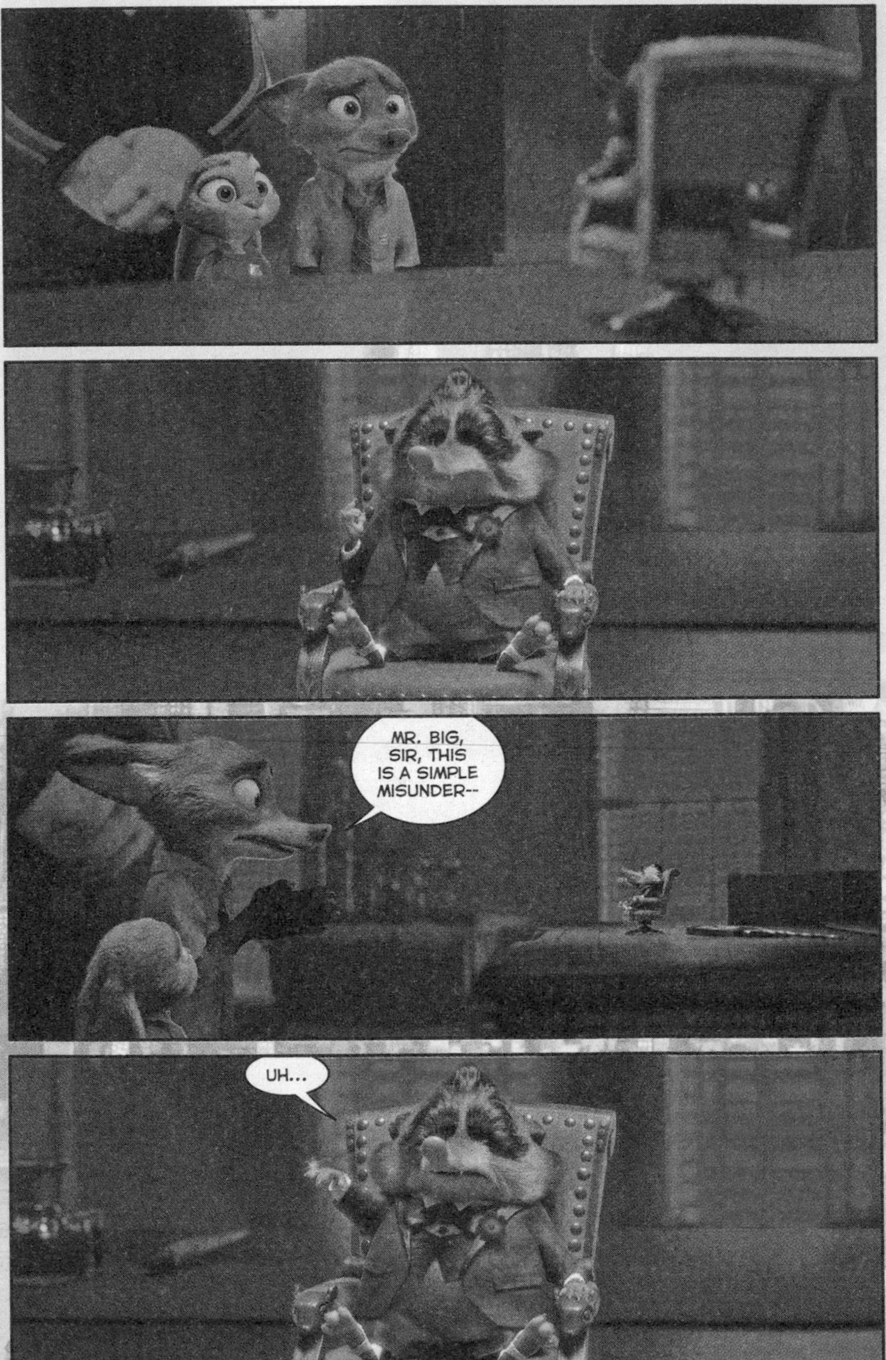
MR. BIG, SIR, THIS IS A SIMPLE MISUNDER--
UH...

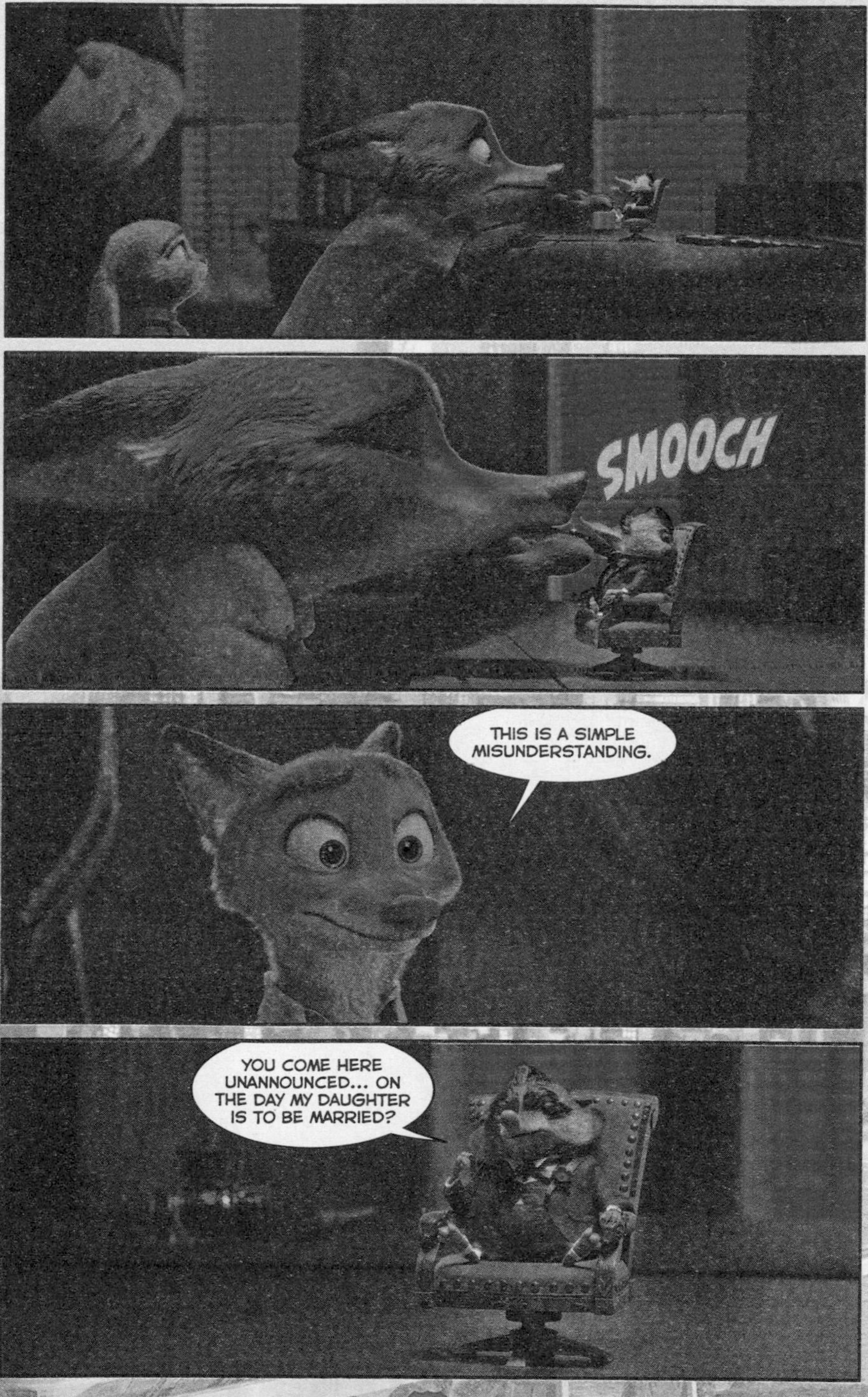
SMOOCH
THIS IS A SIMPLE MISUNDERSTANDING.
YOU COME HERE UNANNOUNCED... ON THE DAY MY DAUGHTER IS TO BE MARRIED?

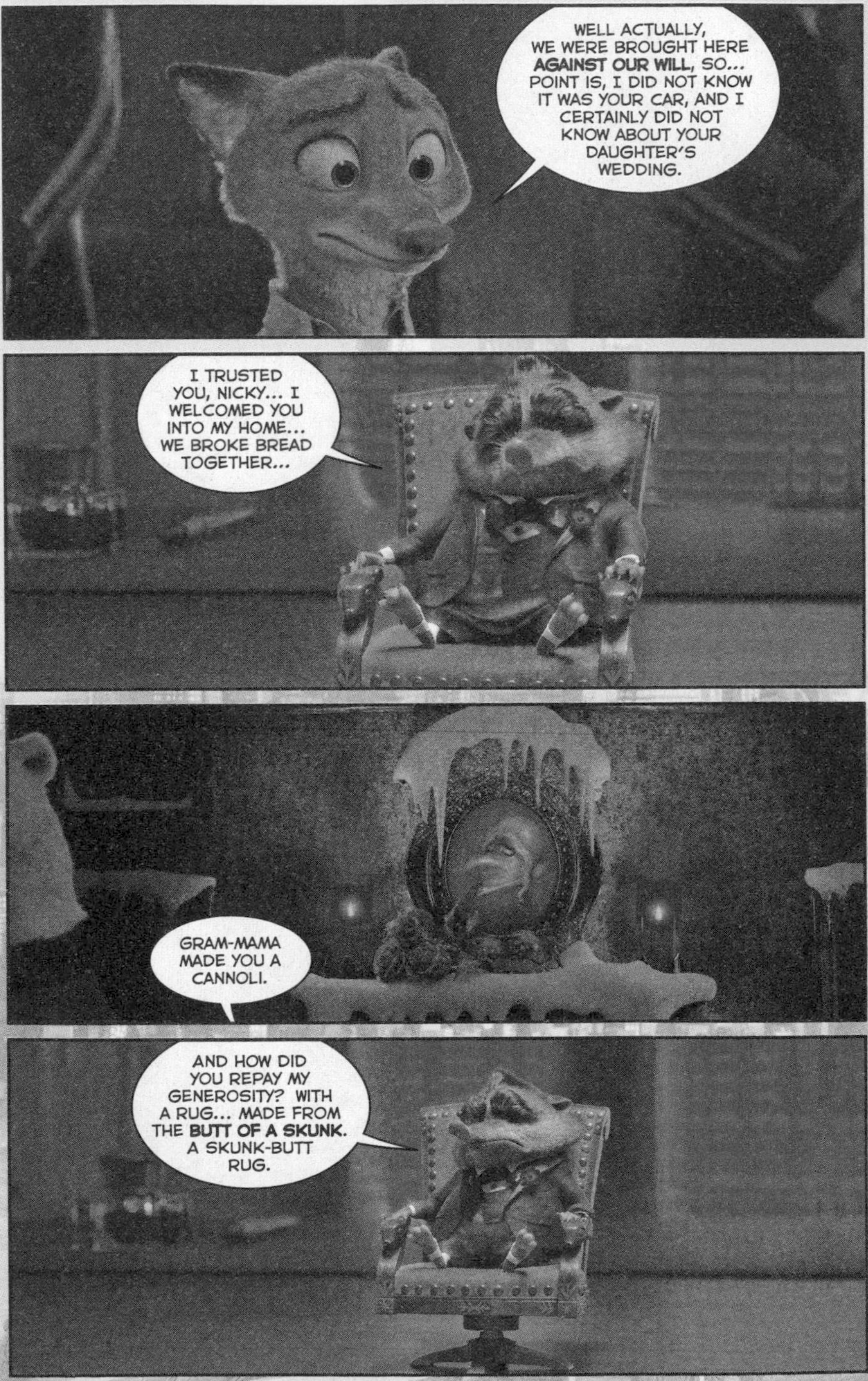
WELL ACTUALLY, WE WERE BROUGHT HERE **AGAINST OUR WILL**, SO... POINT IS, I DID NOT KNOW IT WAS YOUR CAR, AND I CERTAINLY DID NOT KNOW ABOUT YOUR DAUGHTER'S WEDDING.
I TRUSTED YOU, NICKY... I WELCOMED YOU INTO MY HOME... WE BROKE BREAD TOGETHER...
GRAM-MAMA MADE YOU A CANNOLI.
AND HOW DID YOU REPAY MY GENEROSITY? WITH A RUG... MADE FROM THE **BUTT OF A SKUNK**. A SKUNK-BUTT RUG.

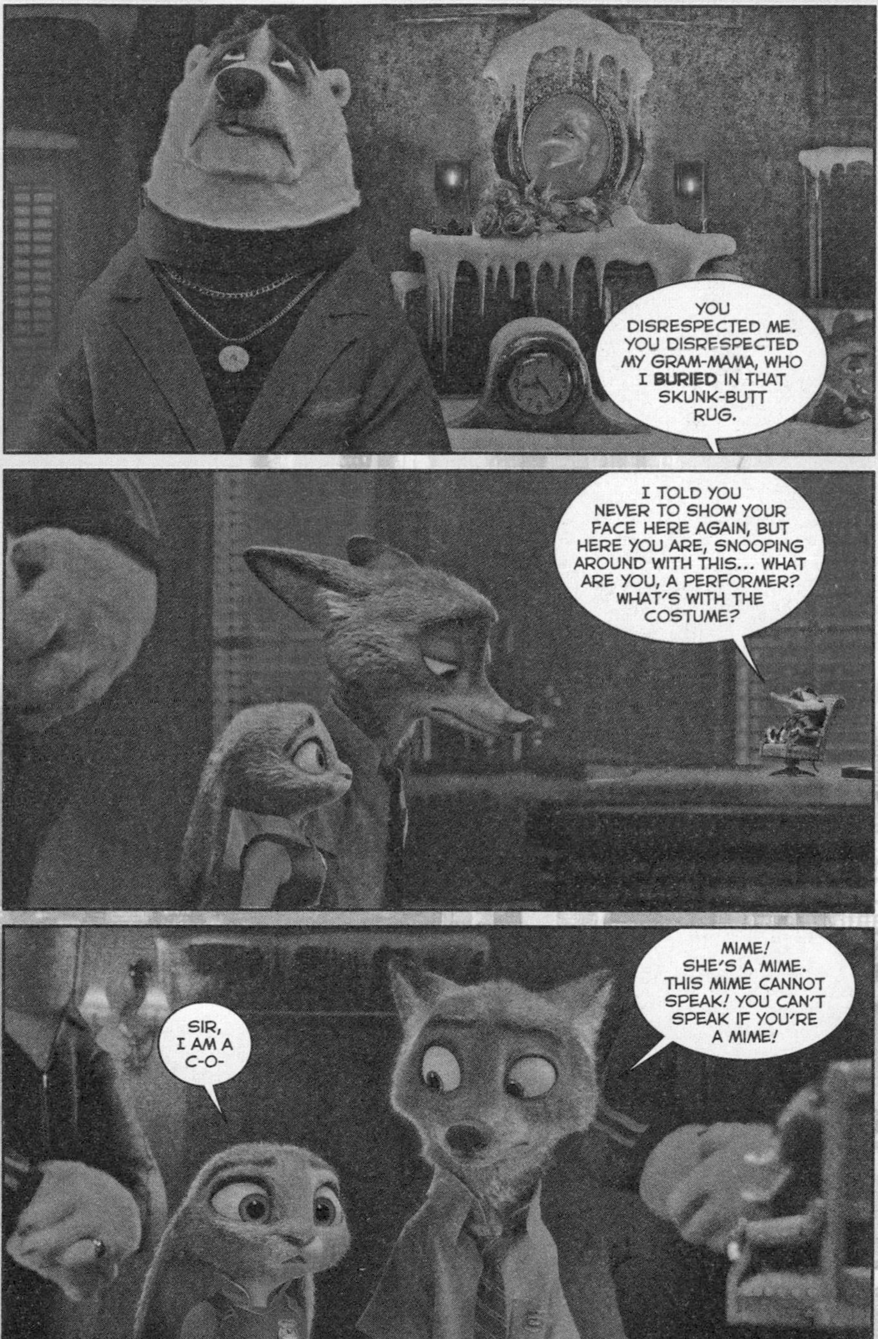
YOU DISRESPECTED ME. YOU DISRESPECTED MY GRAM-MAMA, WHO I **BURIED** IN THAT SKUNK-BUTT RUG.
I TOLD YOU NEVER TO SHOW YOUR FACE HERE AGAIN, BUT HERE YOU ARE, SNOOPING AROUND WITH THIS... WHAT ARE YOU, A PERFORMER? WHAT'S WITH THE COSTUME?
SIR, I AM A C-O-
MIME! SHE'S A MIME. THIS MIME CANNOT SPEAK! YOU CAN'T SPEAK IF YOU'RE A MIME!

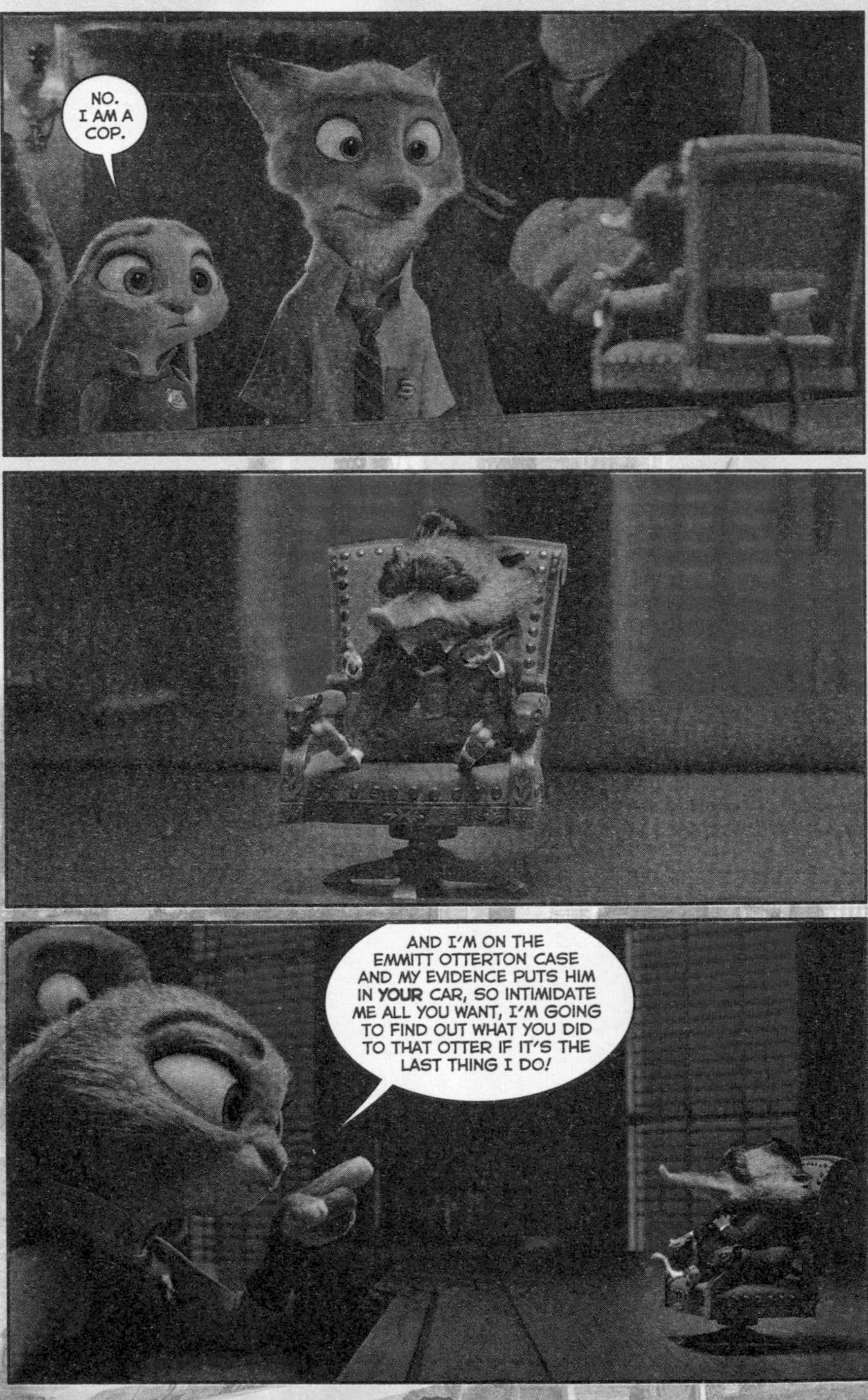
NO. I AM A COP.
AND I'M ON THE EMMITT OTTERTON CASE AND MY EVIDENCE PUTS HIM IN **YOUR** CAR, SO INTIMIDATE ME ALL YOU WANT, I'M GOING TO FIND OUT WHAT YOU DID TO THAT OTTER IF IT'S THE LAST THING I DO!

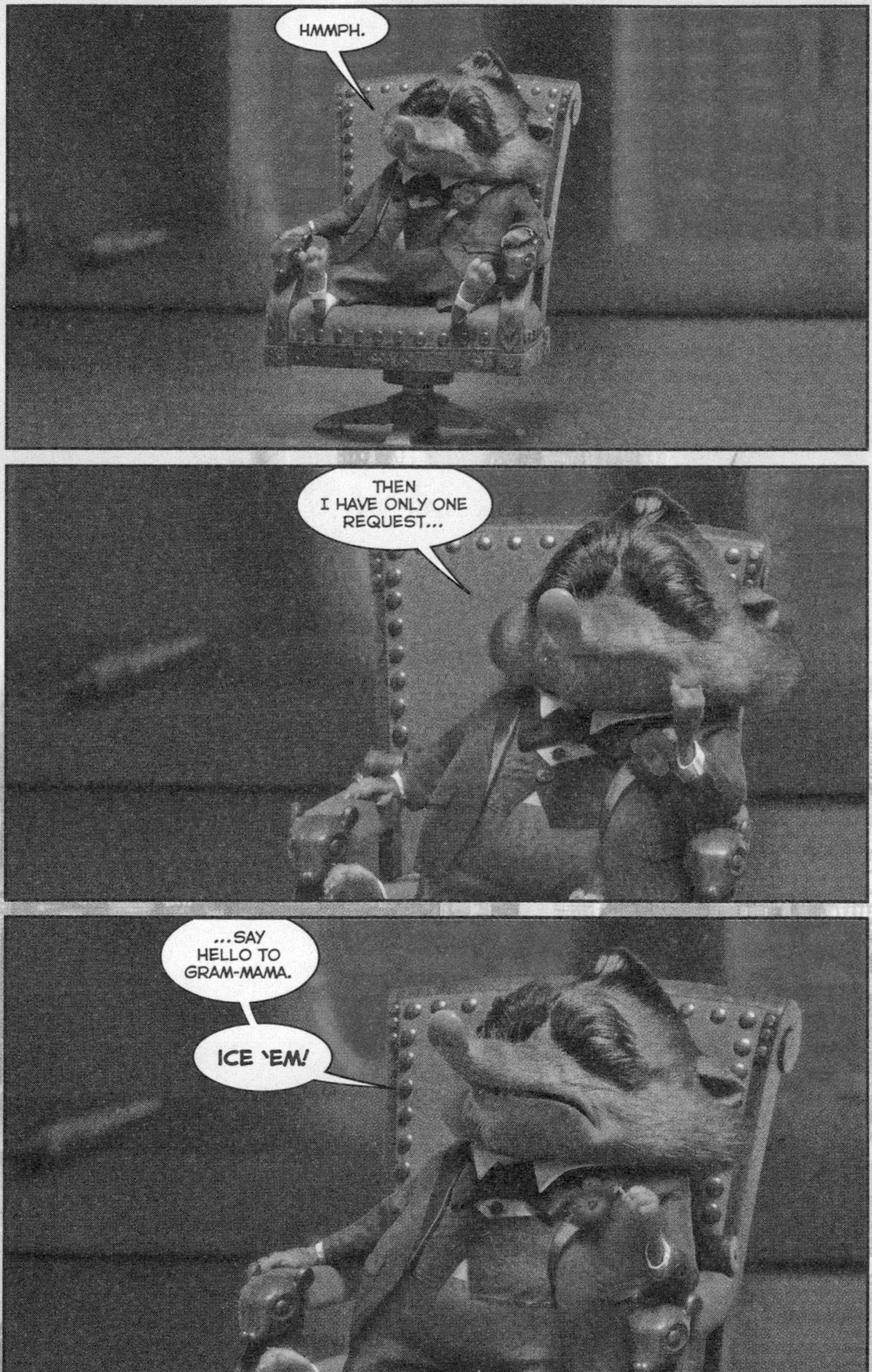
HMMPH.
THEN I HAVE ONLY ONE REQUEST...
...SAY HELLO TO GRAM-MAMA.
ICE 'EM!

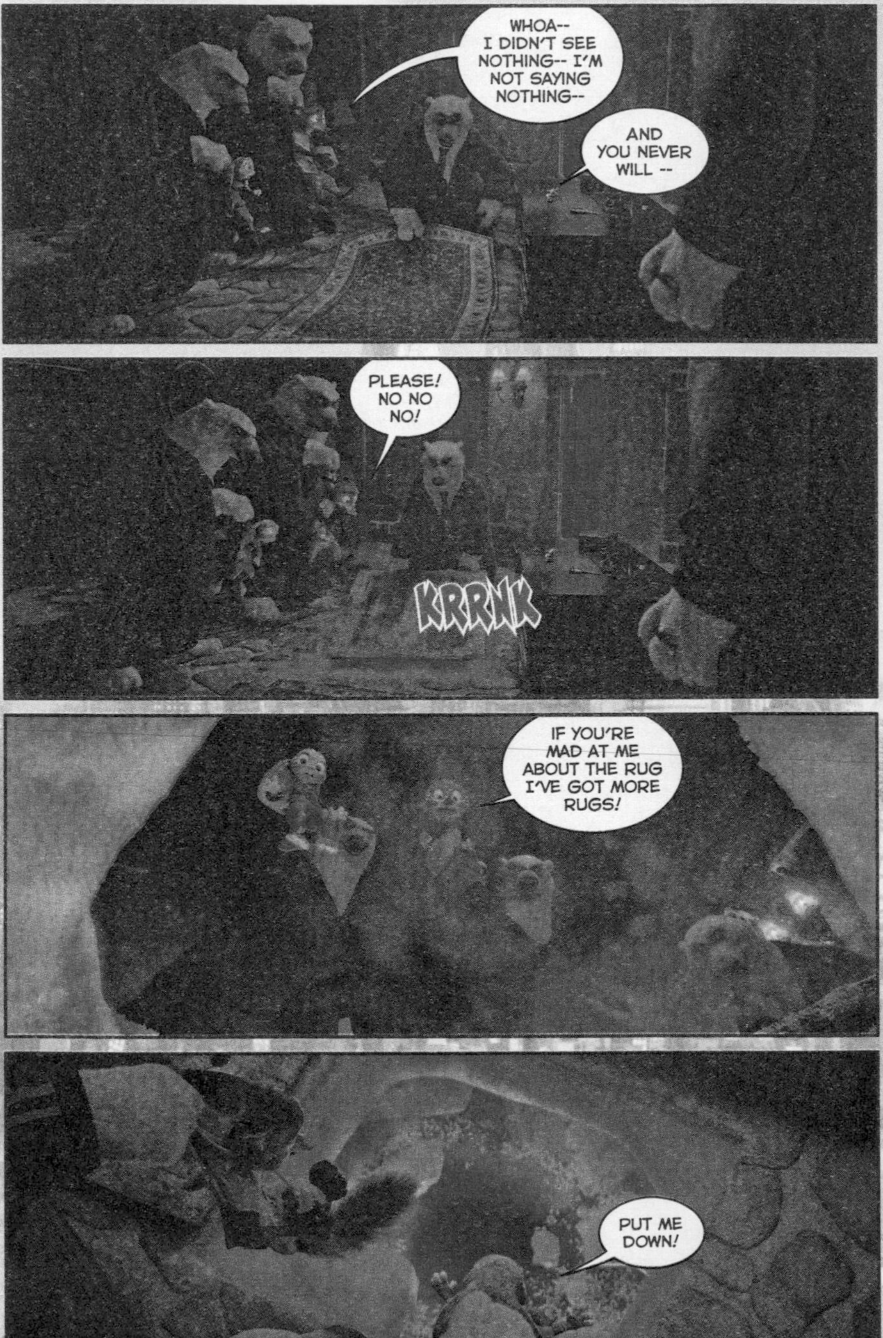
WHOA-- I DIDN'T SEE NOTHING-- I'M NOT SAYING NOTHING--
AND YOU NEVER WILL --
PLEASE! NO NO NO!
KRRNK
IF YOU'RE MAD AT ME ABOUT THE RUG I'VE GOT MORE RUGS!
PUT ME DOWN!

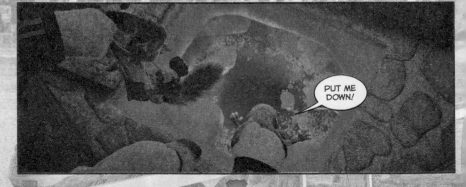

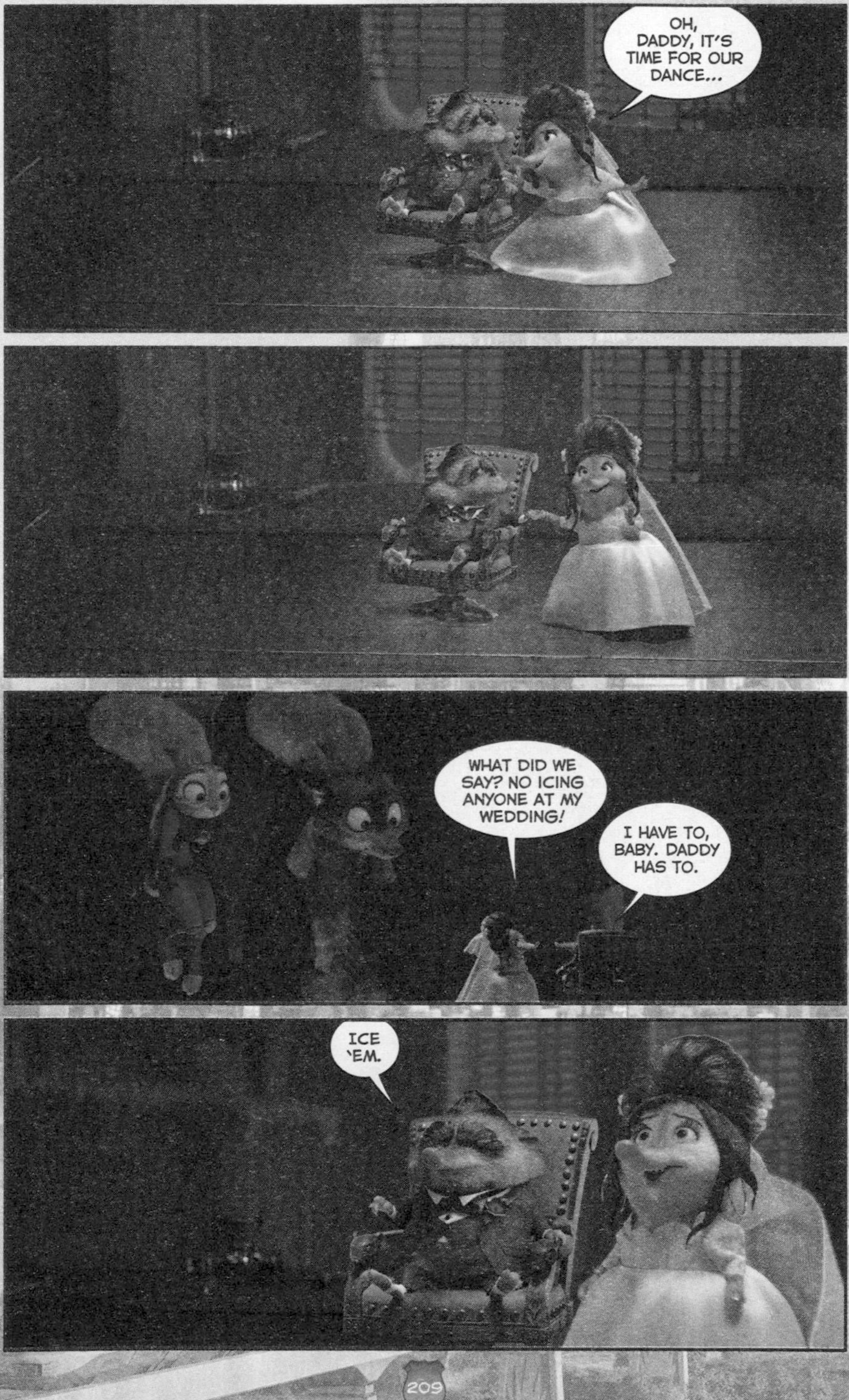
OH, DADDY, IT'S TIME FOR OUR DANCE...
WHAT DID WE SAY? NO ICING ANYONE AT MY WEDDING!
I HAVE TO, BABY. DADDY HAS TO.
ICE 'EM.

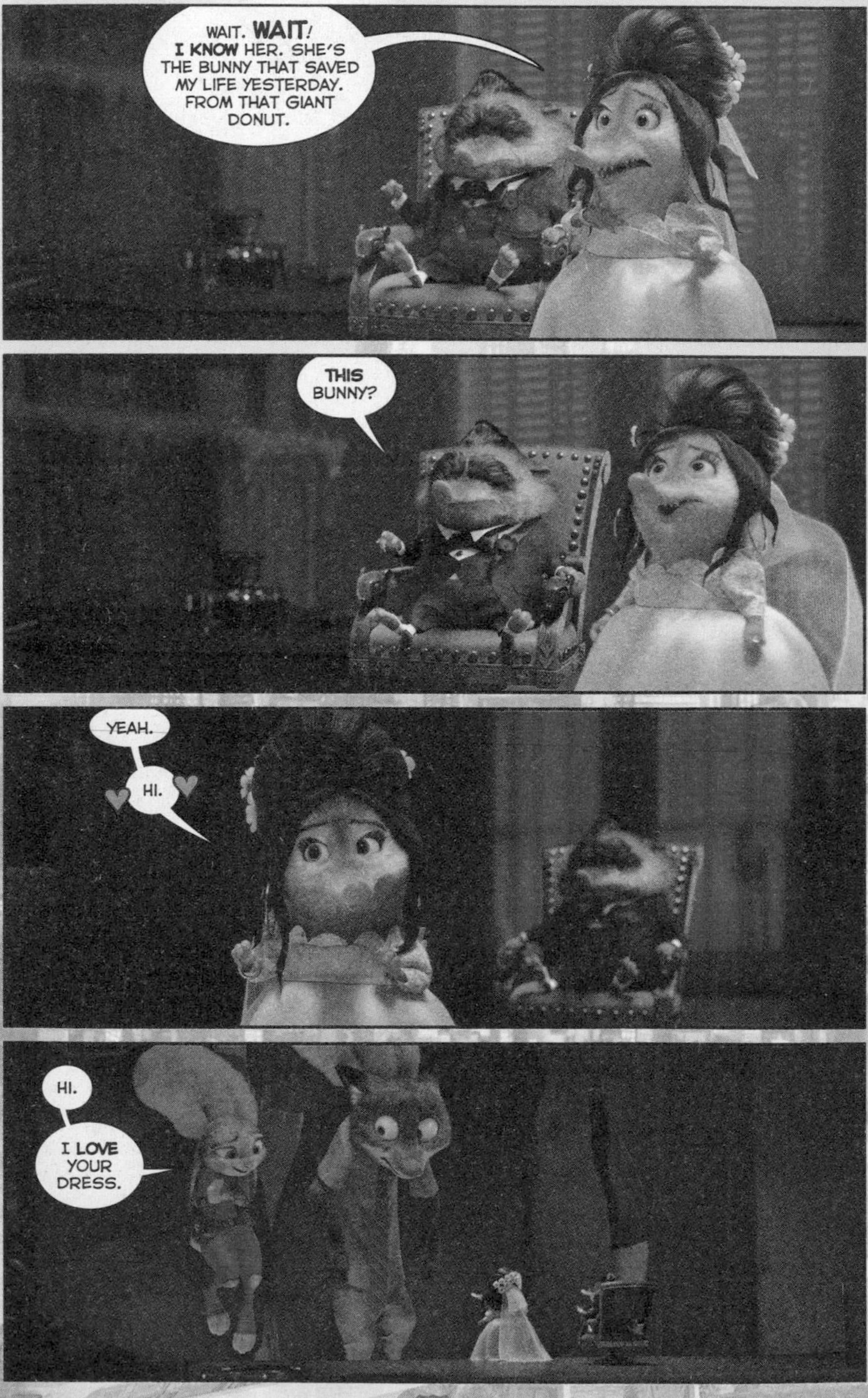

WAIT. **WAIT**! **I KNOW** HER. SHE'S THE BUNNY THAT SAVED MY LIFE YESTERDAY. FROM THAT GIANT DONUT.
THIS BUNNY?
YEAH.
HI.
HI.
I **LOVE** YOUR DRESS.

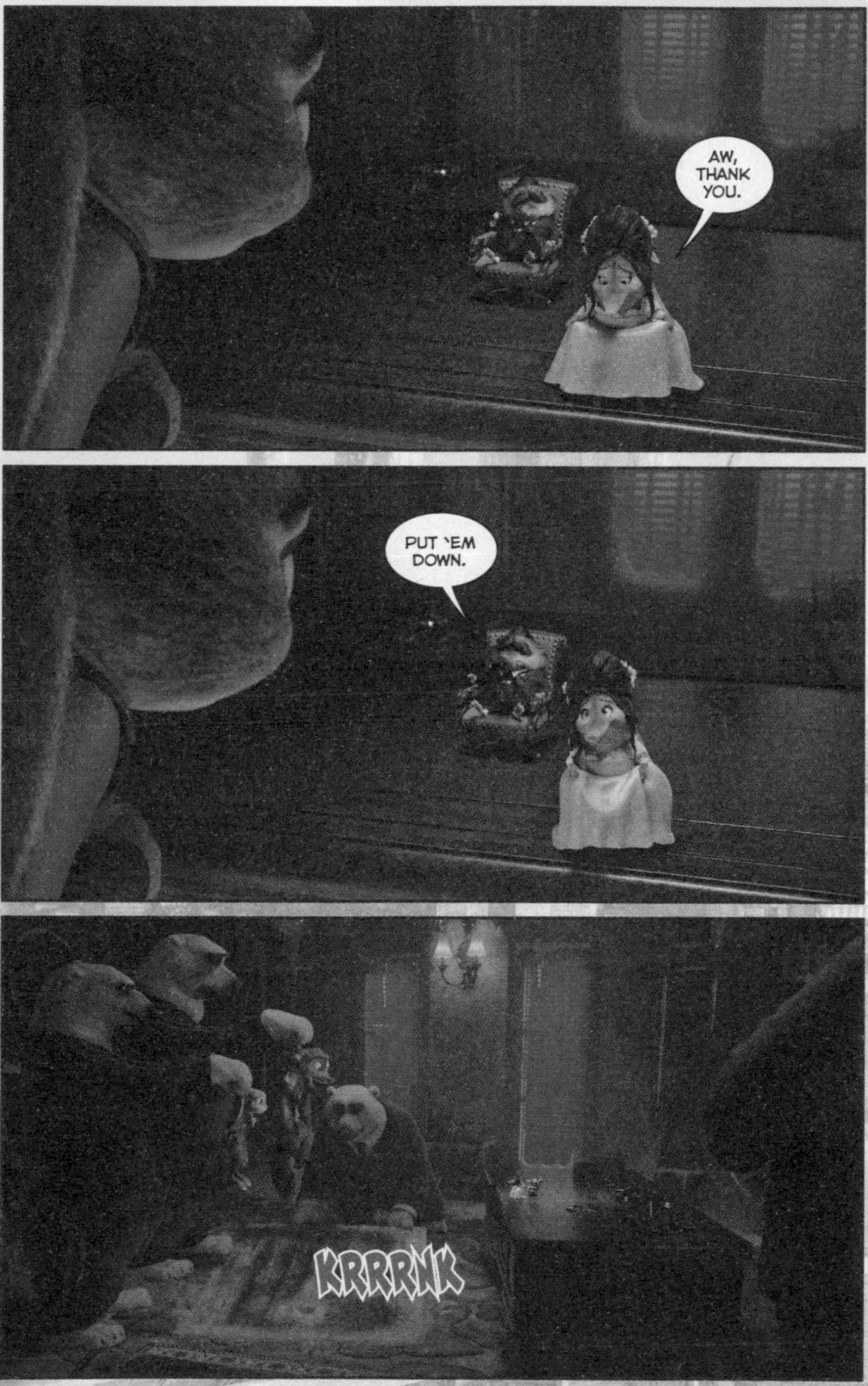
AW, THANK YOU.
PUT 'EM DOWN.
KRRRNK

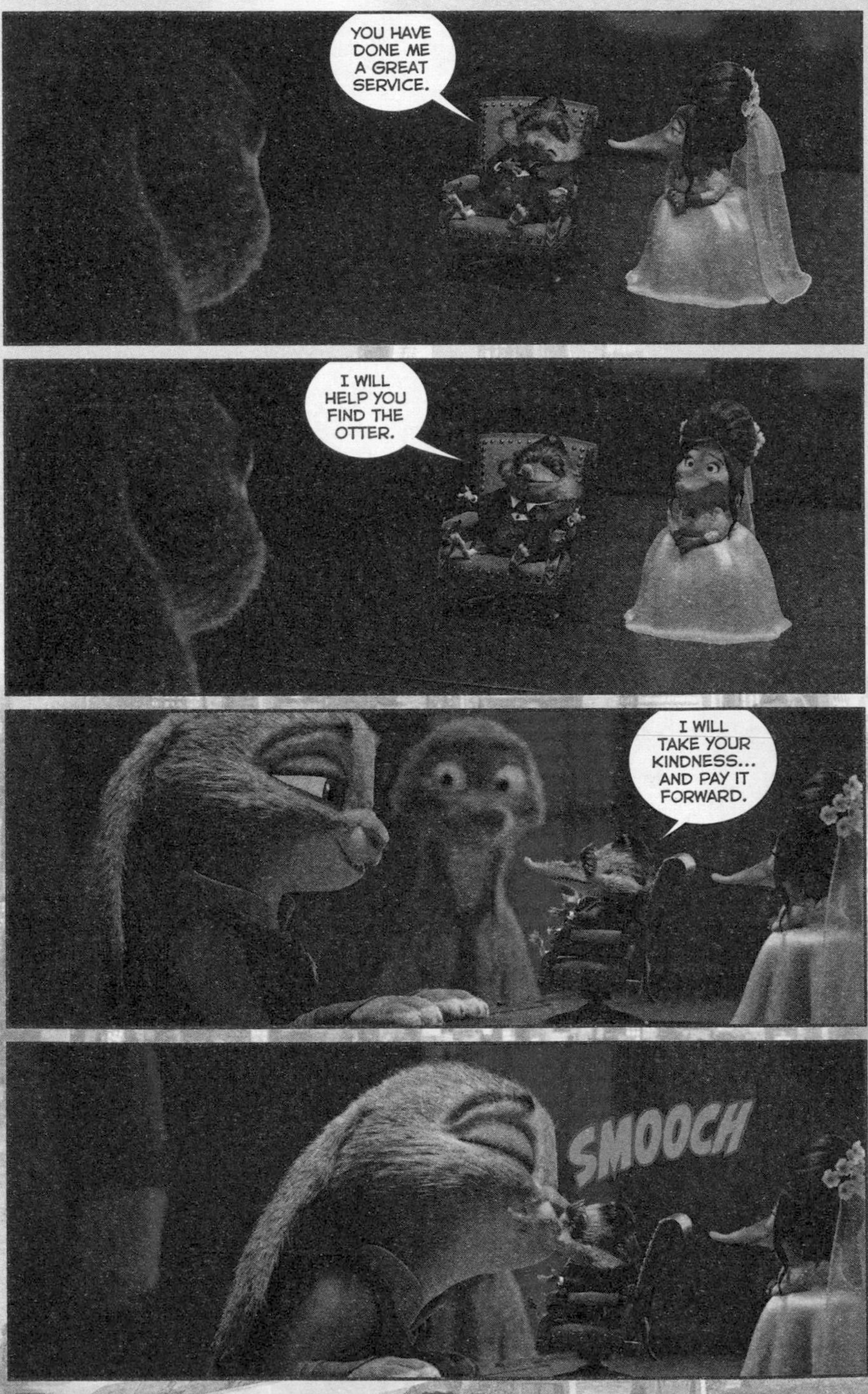
YOU HAVE DONE ME A GREAT SERVICE.
I WILL HELP YOU FIND THE OTTER.
I WILL TAKE YOUR KINDNESS... AND PAY IT FORWARD.
SMOOCH

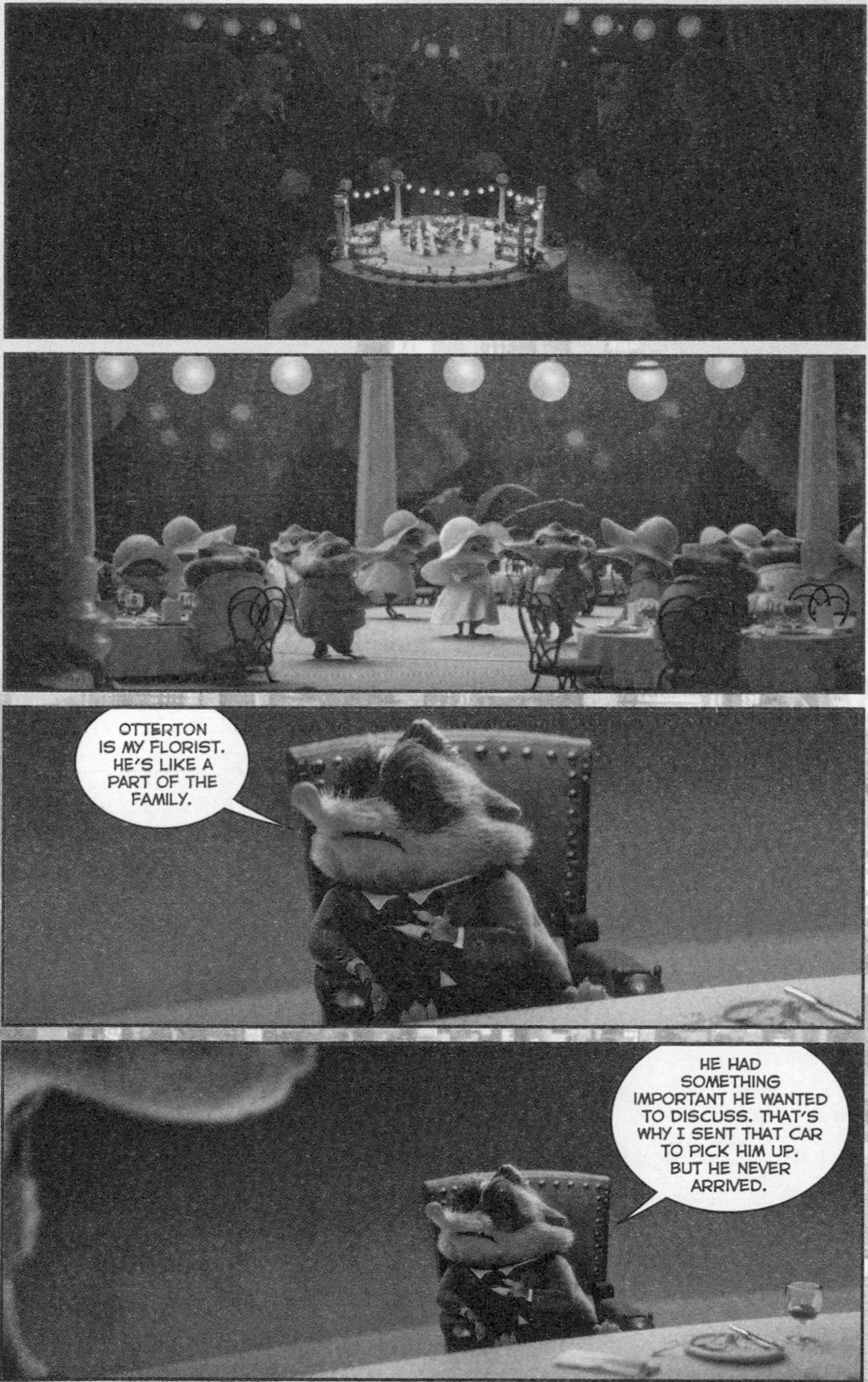
OTTERTON IS MY FLORIST. HE'S LIKE A PART OF THE FAMILY.
HE HAD SOMETHING IMPORTANT HE WANTED TO DISCUSS. THAT'S WHY I SENT THAT CAR TO PICK HIM UP. BUT HE NEVER ARRIVED.

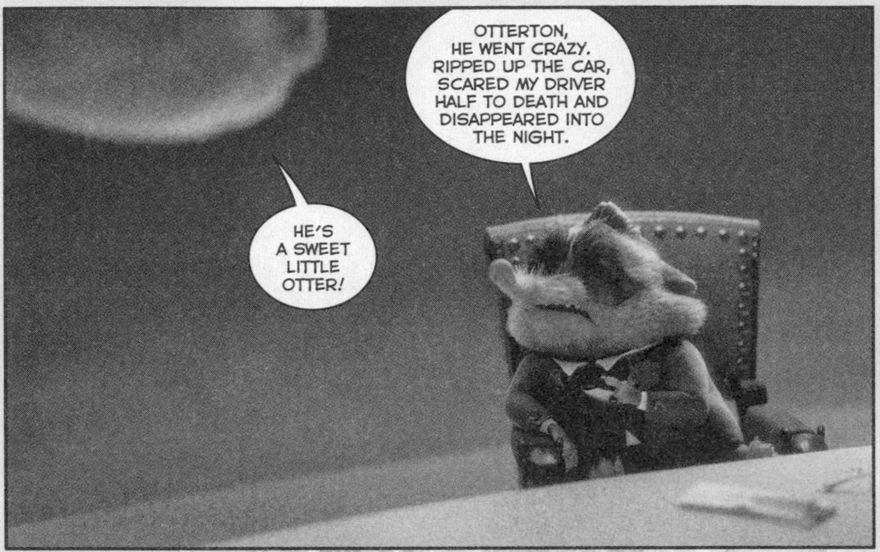
OTTERTON, HE WENT CRAZY. RIPPED UP THE CAR, SCARED MY DRIVER HALF TO DEATH AND DISAPPEARED INTO THE NIGHT.
HE'S A SWEET LITTLE OTTER!

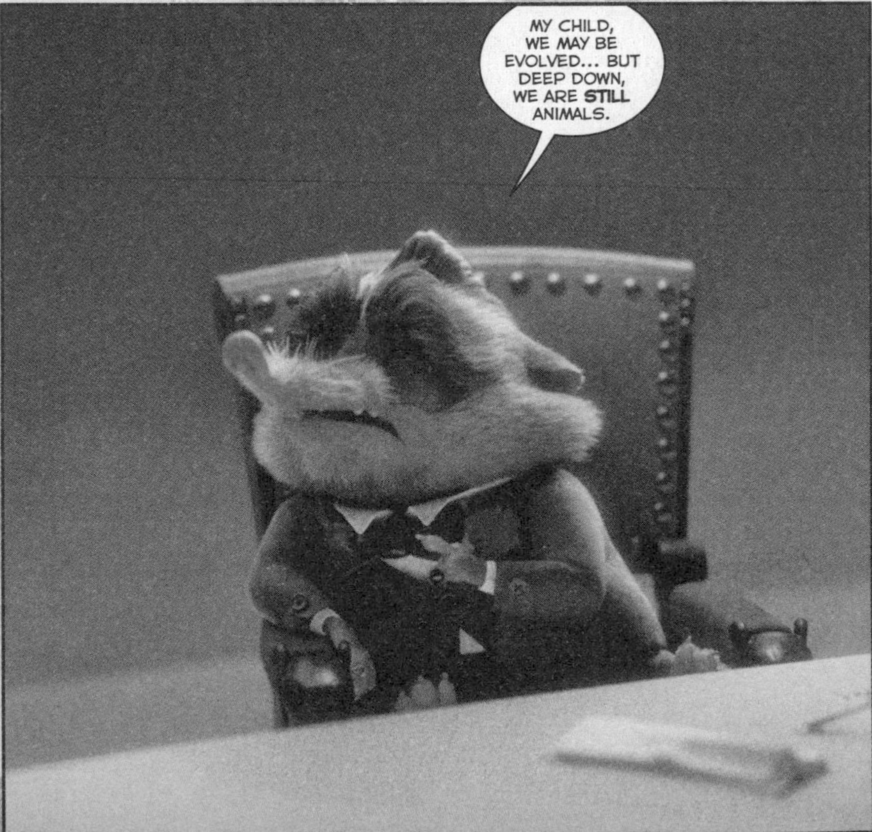
MY CHILD, WE MAY BE EVOLVED... BUT DEEP DOWN, WE ARE **STILL** ANIMALS.

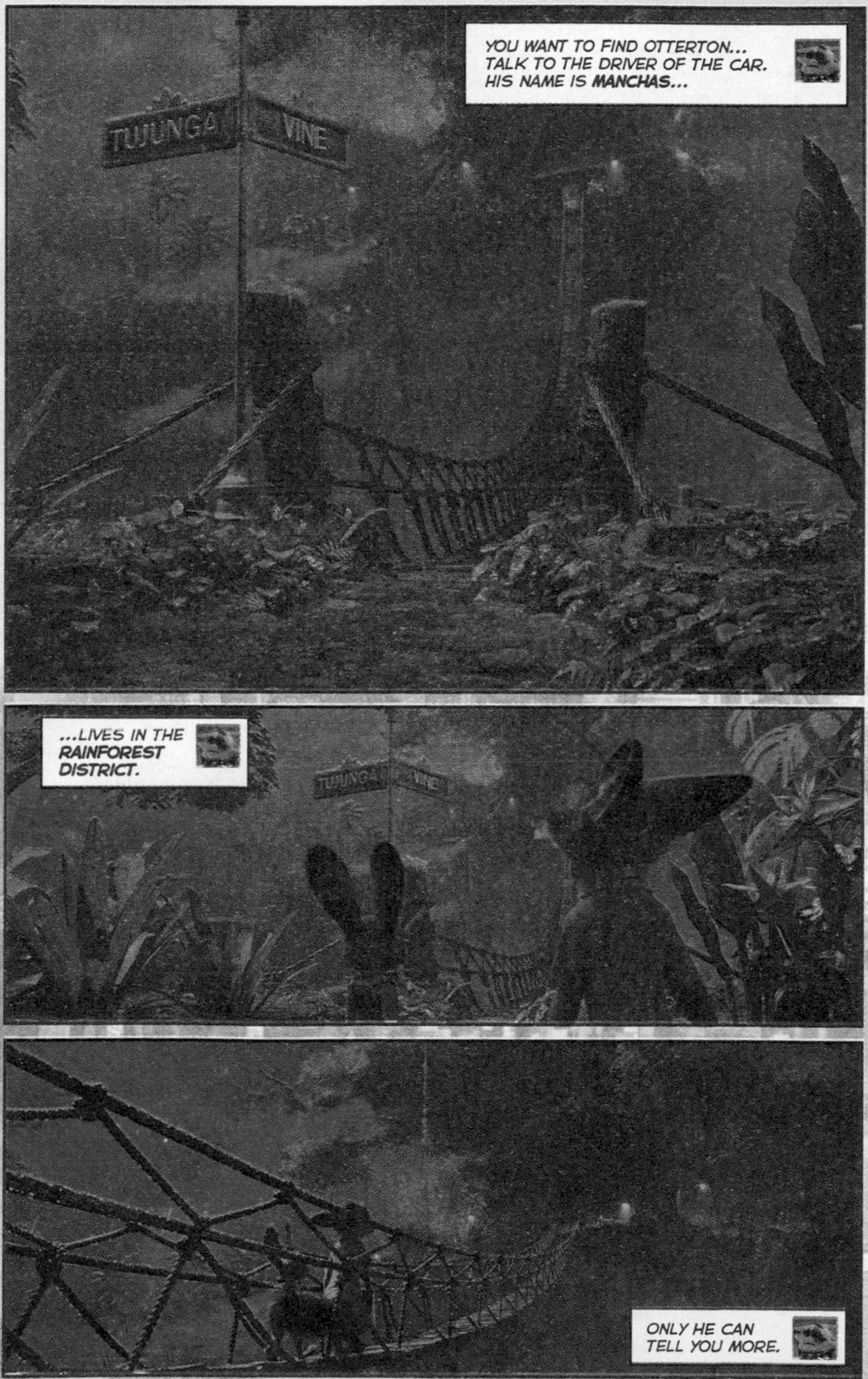
TUJUNGA
VINE
YOU WANT TO FIND OTTERTON... TALK TO THE DRIVER OF THE CAR. HIS NAME IS MANCHAS...
...LIVES IN THE RAINFOREST DISTRICT.
TUJUNGA
VINE
ONLY HE CAN TELL YOU MORE.

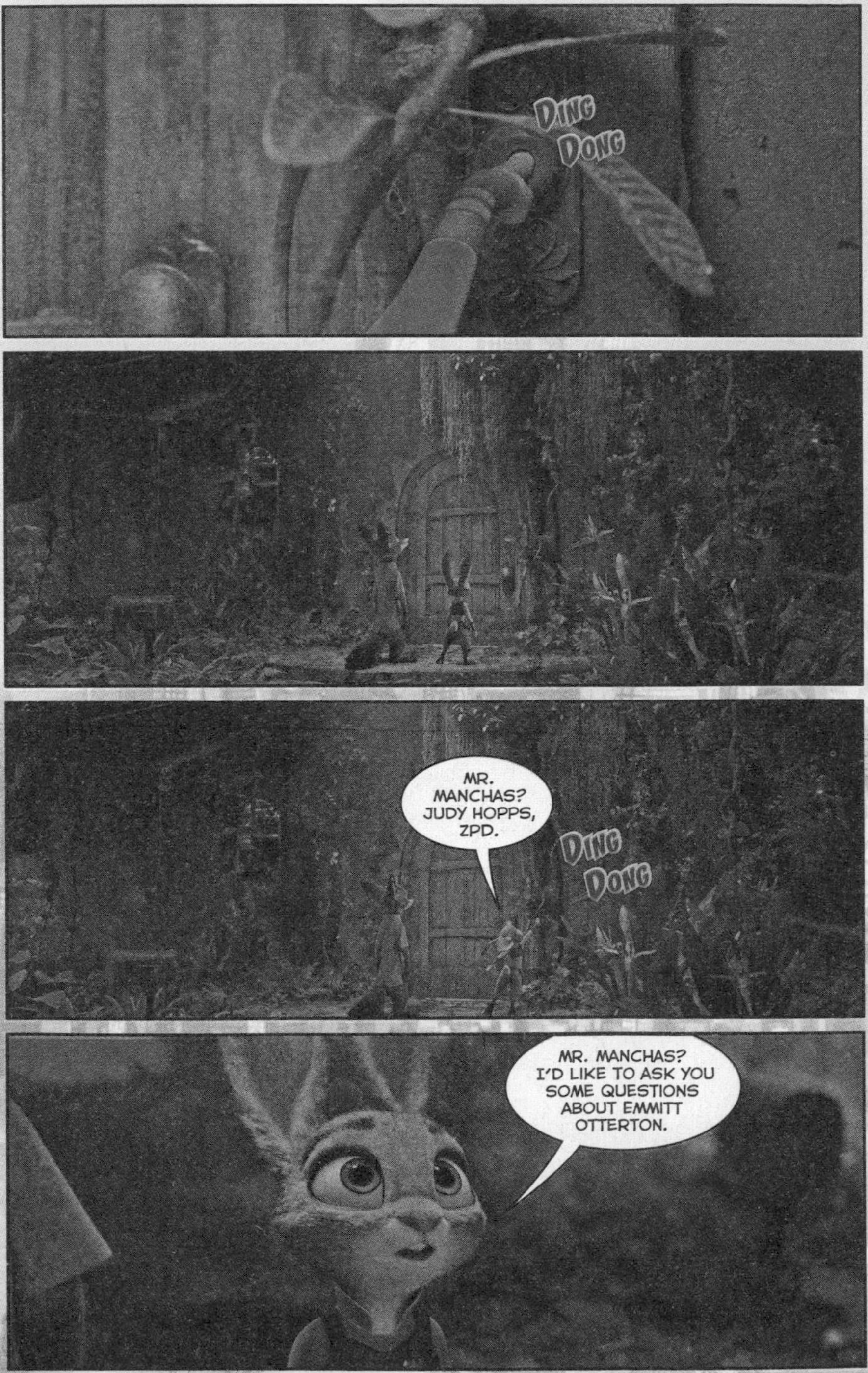
DING
DONG
MR. MANCHAS? JUDY HOPPS, ZPD.
DING
DONG
MR. MANCHAS? I'D LIKE TO ASK YOU SOME QUESTIONS ABOUT EMMITT OTTERTON.

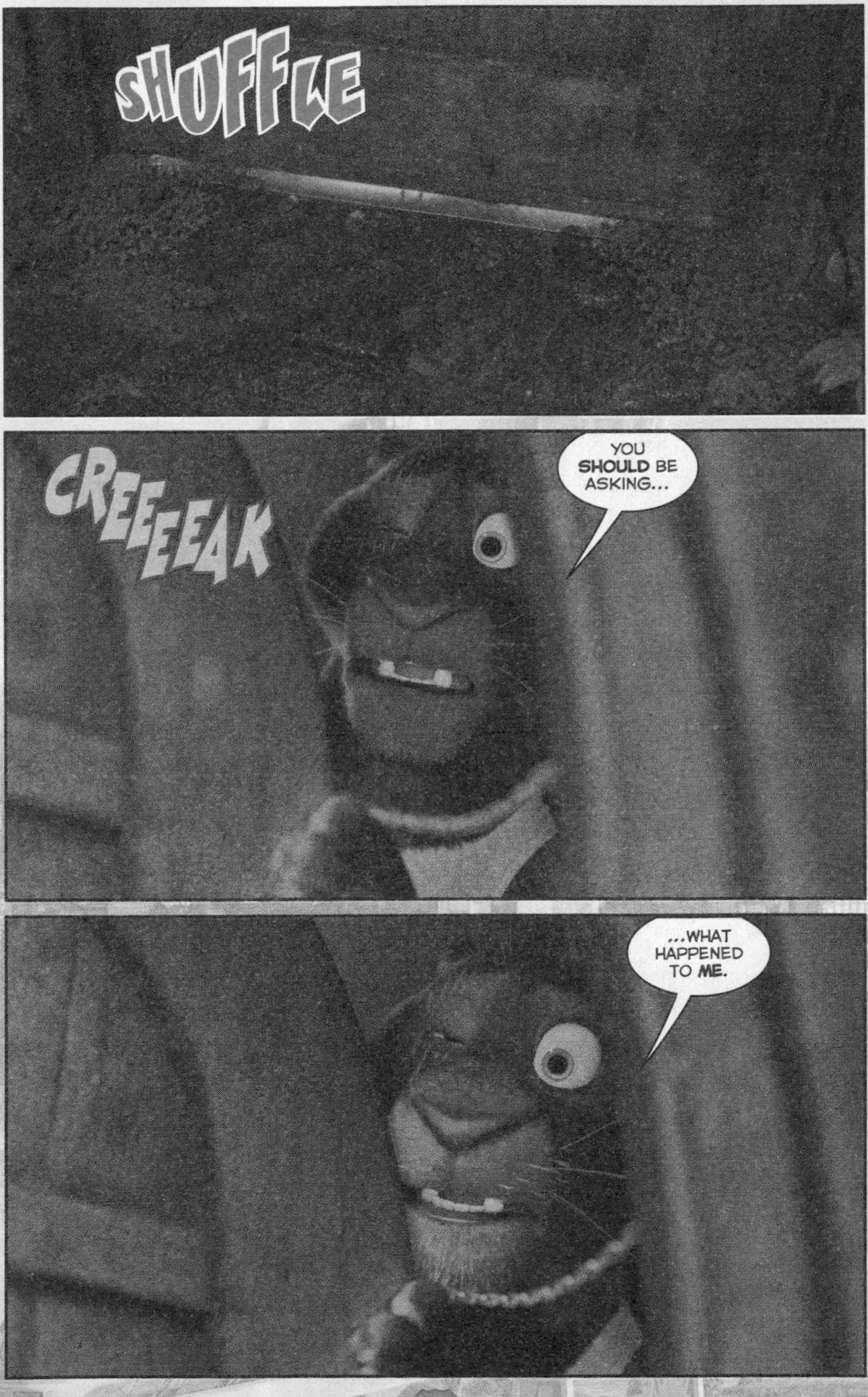
SHUFFLE
CREEEEAK
YOU SHOULD BE ASKING...
...WHAT HAPPENED TO ME.

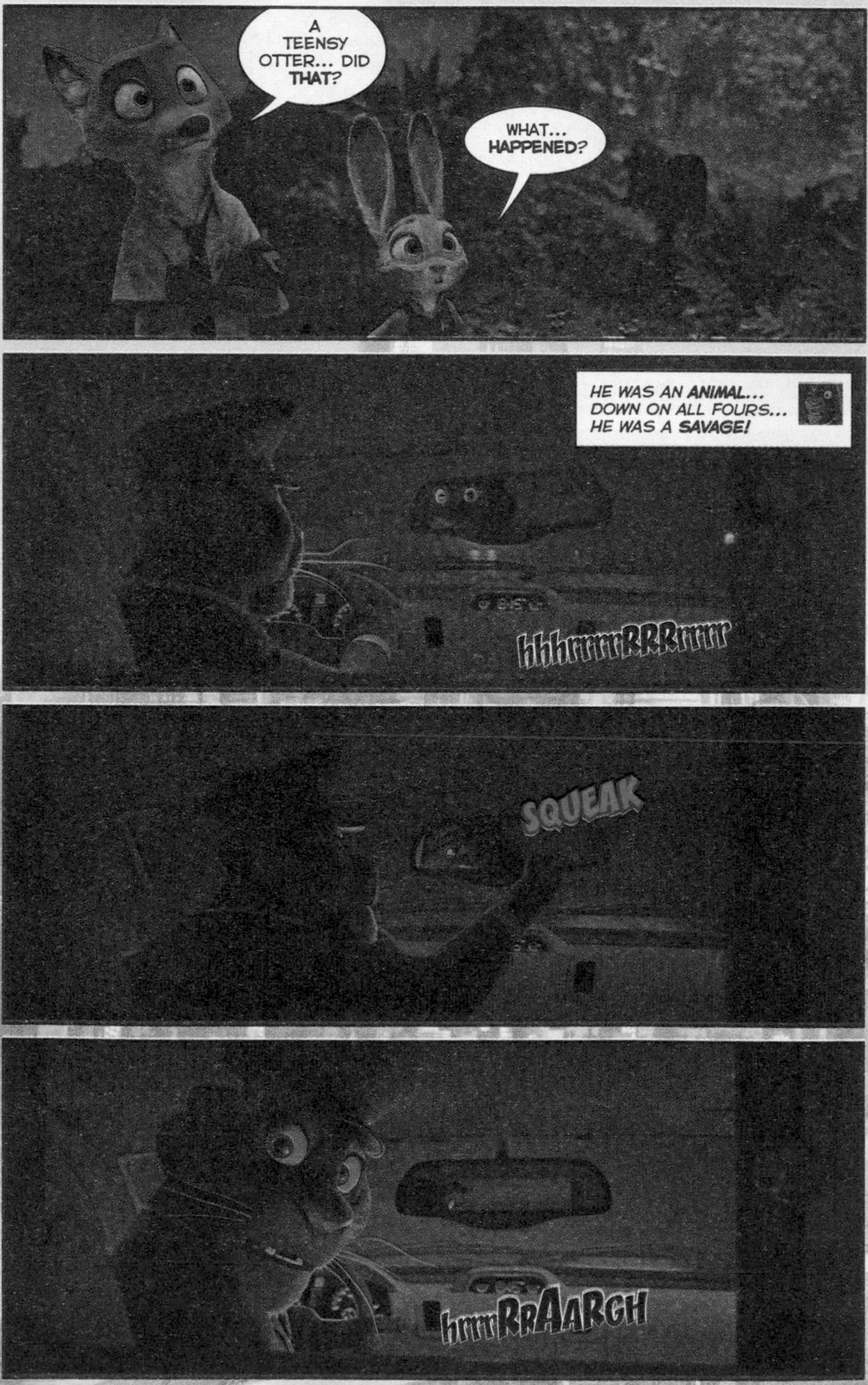
A TEENSY OTTER... DID THAT?
WHAT... HAPPENED?
HE WAS AN ANIMAL... DOWN ON ALL FOURS... HE WAS A SAVAGE!
hhhrrrrrRRRrrrrr
SQUEAK
hrrrRRAARGH

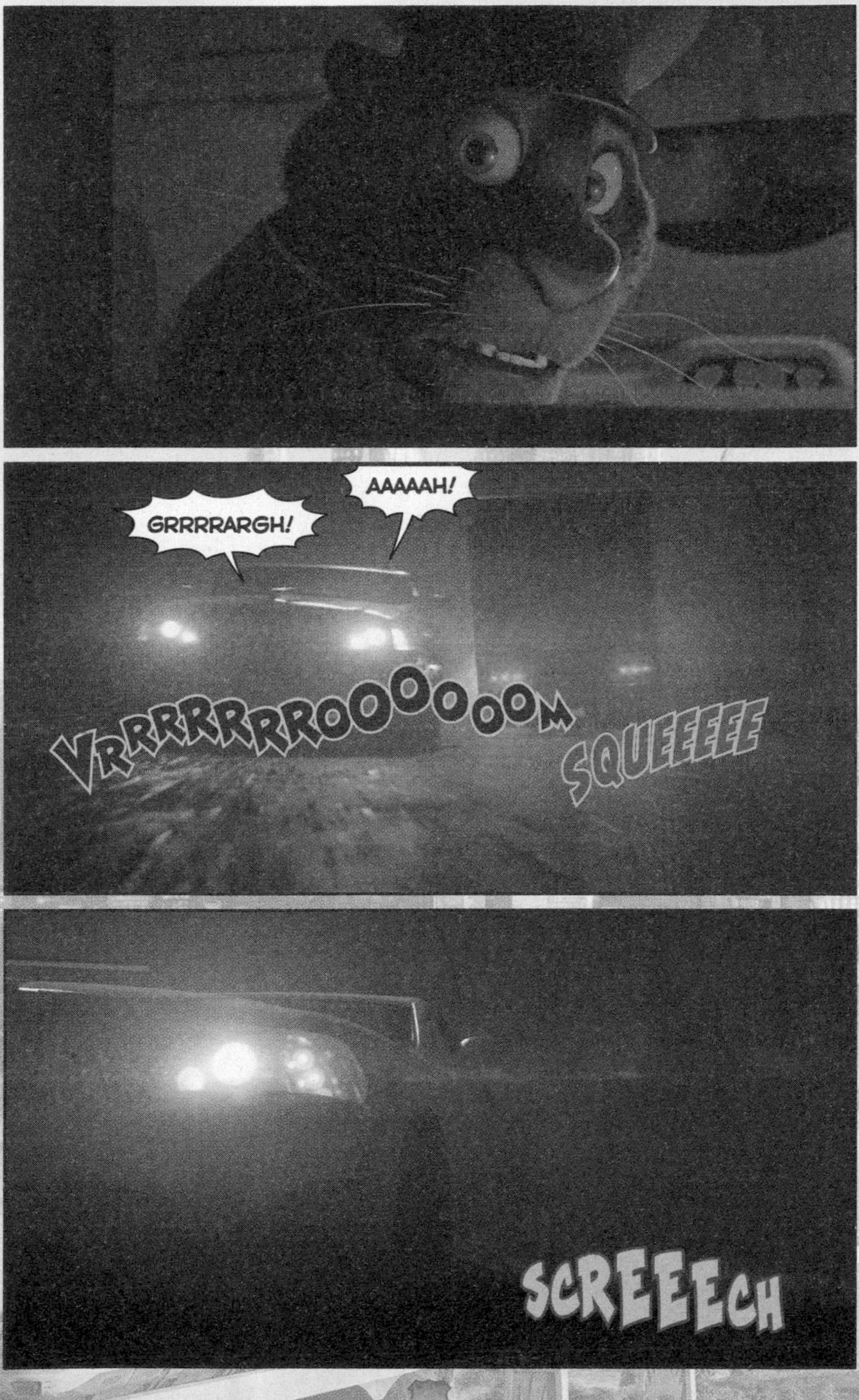

GRRRRARGH!
AAAAAH!
VRRRRRRROOOOOOOM
SQUEEEEE
SCREEECH

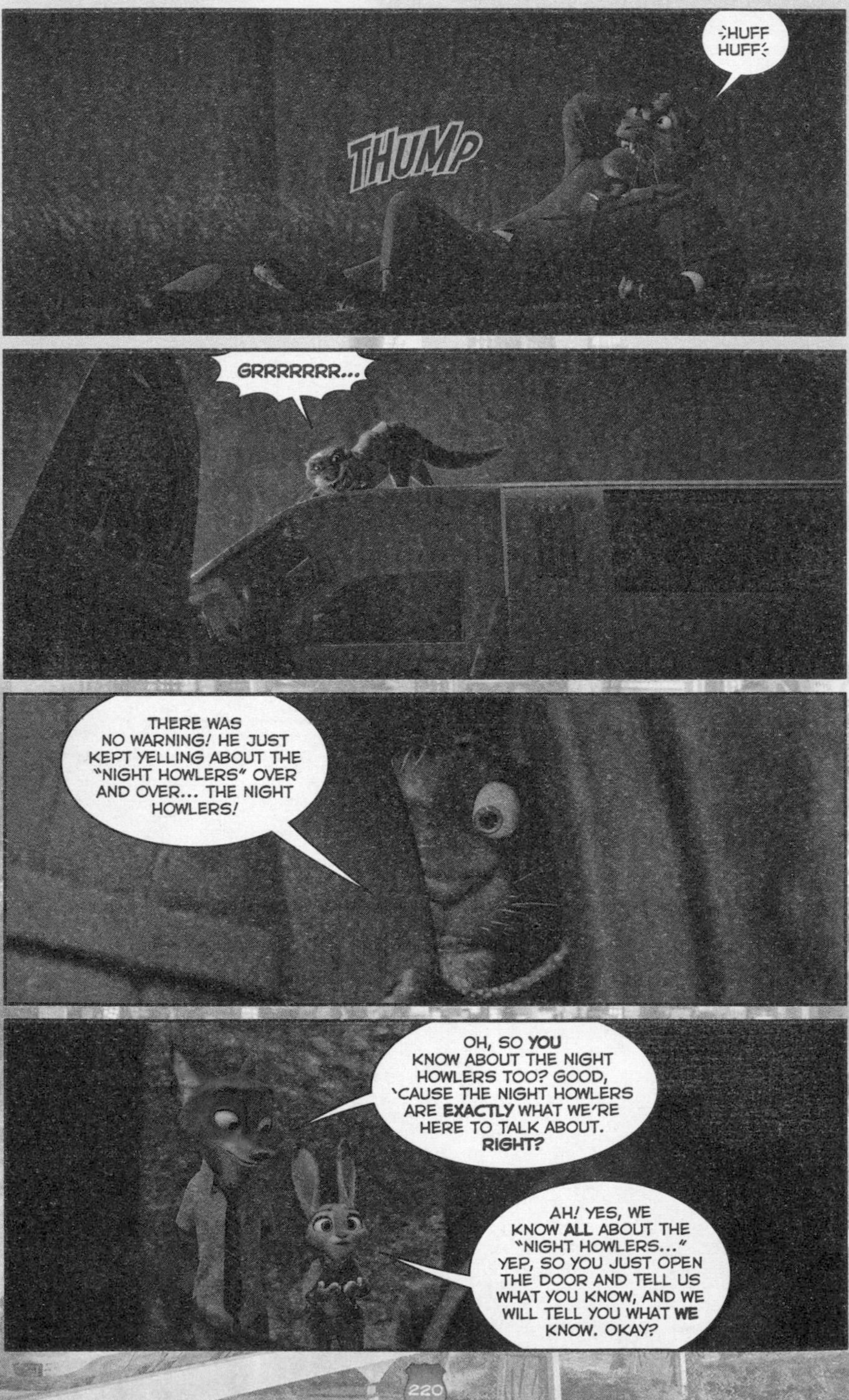

HUFF HUFF
THUMP
GRRRRRRR...
THERE WAS NO WARNING! HE JUST KEPT YELLING ABOUT THE "NIGHT HOWLERS" OVER AND OVER... THE NIGHT HOWLERS!
OH, SO YOU KNOW ABOUT THE NIGHT HOWLERS TOO? GOOD, 'CAUSE THE NIGHT HOWLERS ARE EXACTLY WHAT WE'RE HERE TO TALK ABOUT. RIGHT?
AH! YES, WE KNOW ALL ABOUT THE "NIGHT HOWLERS..." YEP, SO YOU JUST OPEN THE DOOR AND TELL US WHAT YOU KNOW, AND WE WILL TELL YOU WHAT WE KNOW. OKAY?

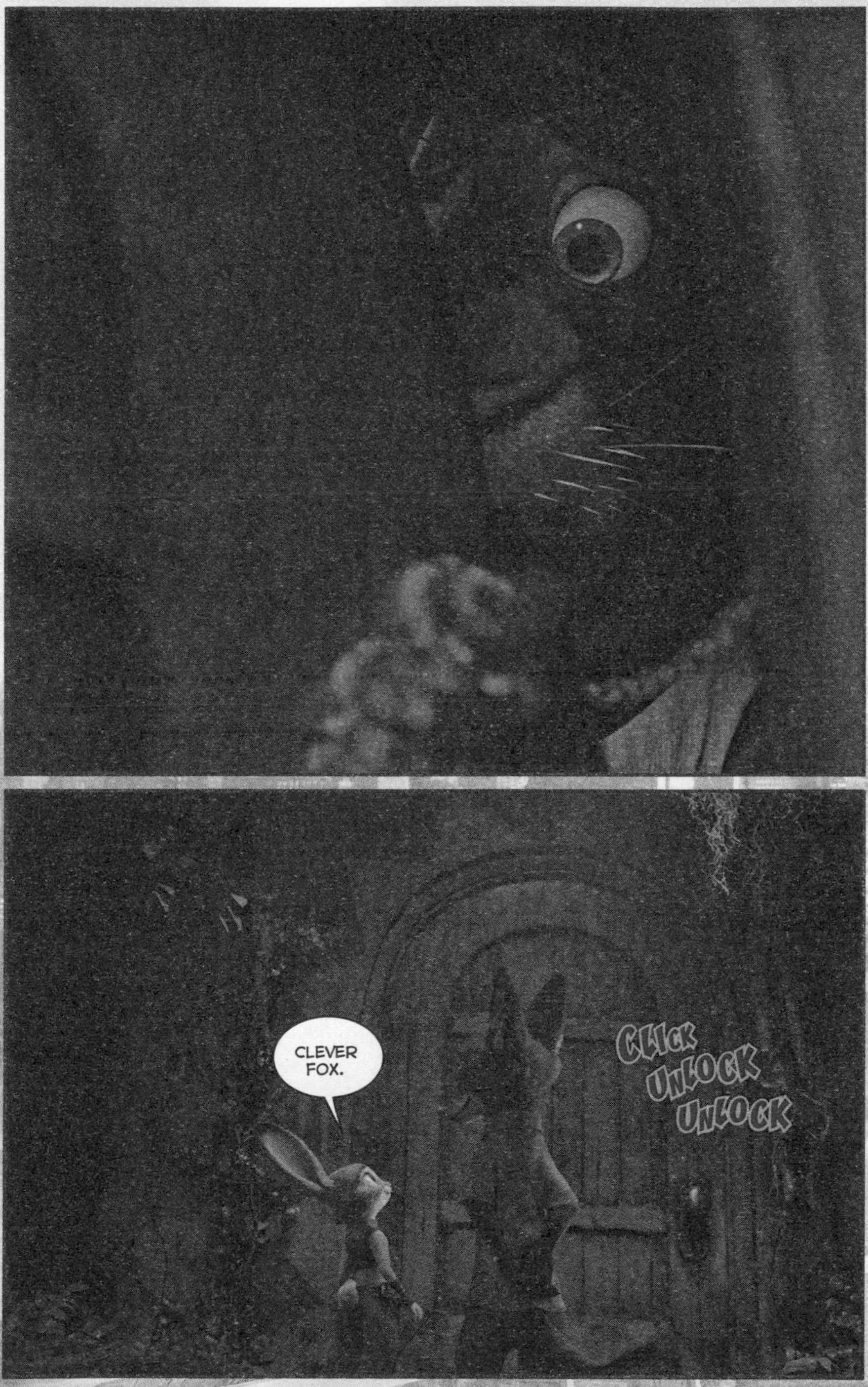
CLEVER FOX.
CLICK
UNLOCK
UNLOCK

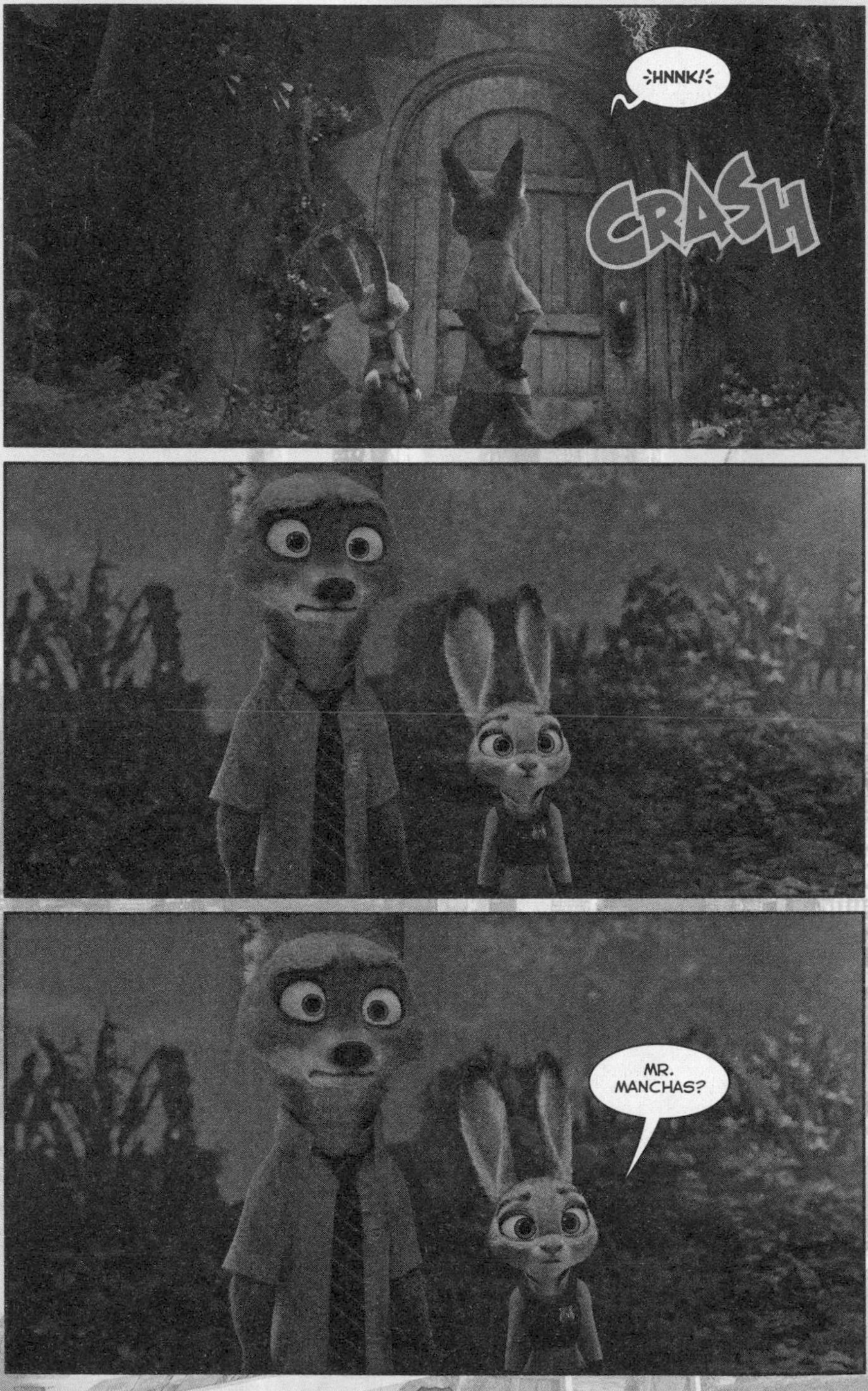
HNNK!
CRASH
MR. MANCHAS?

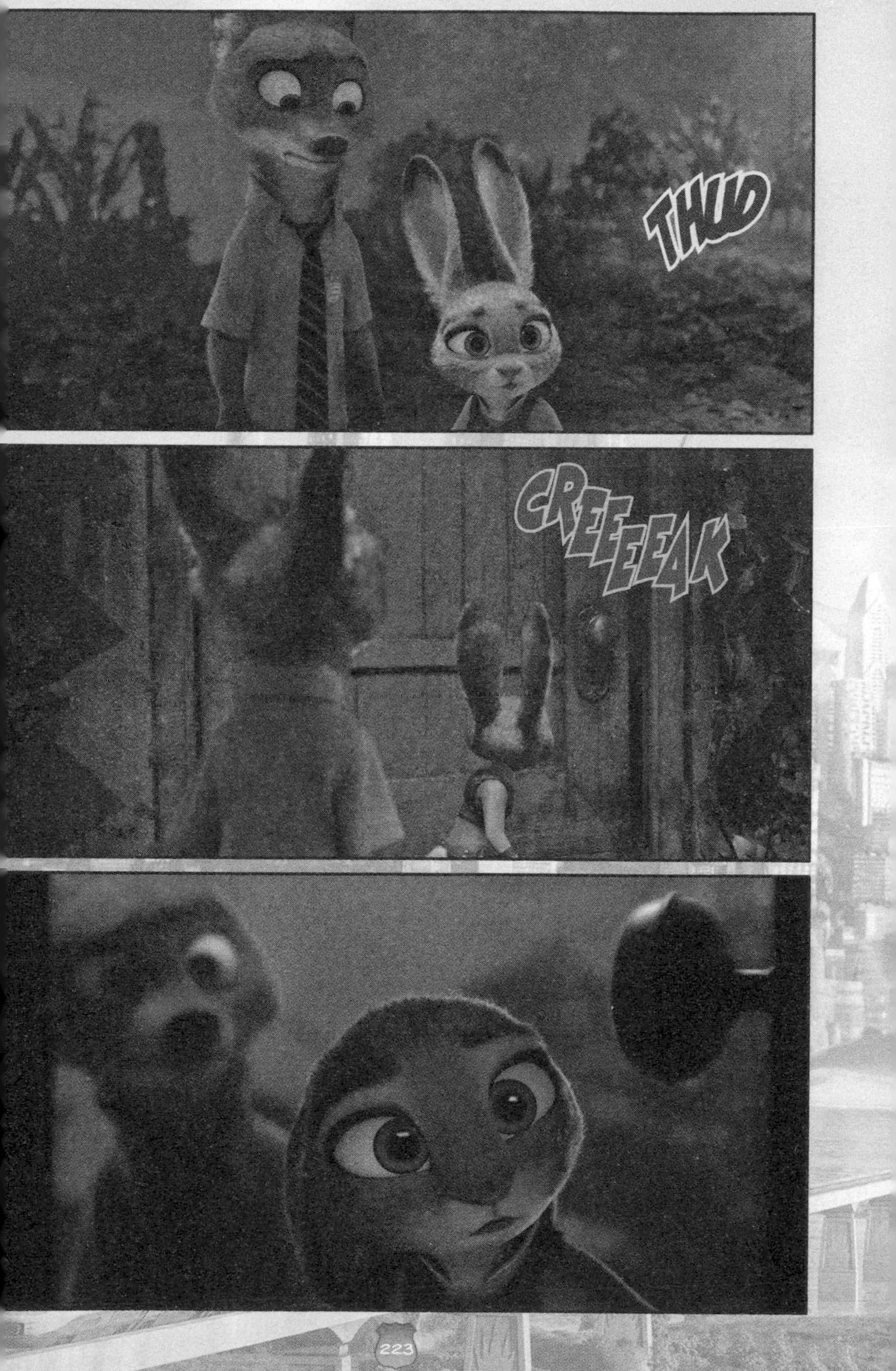
THUD
CREEEEAK

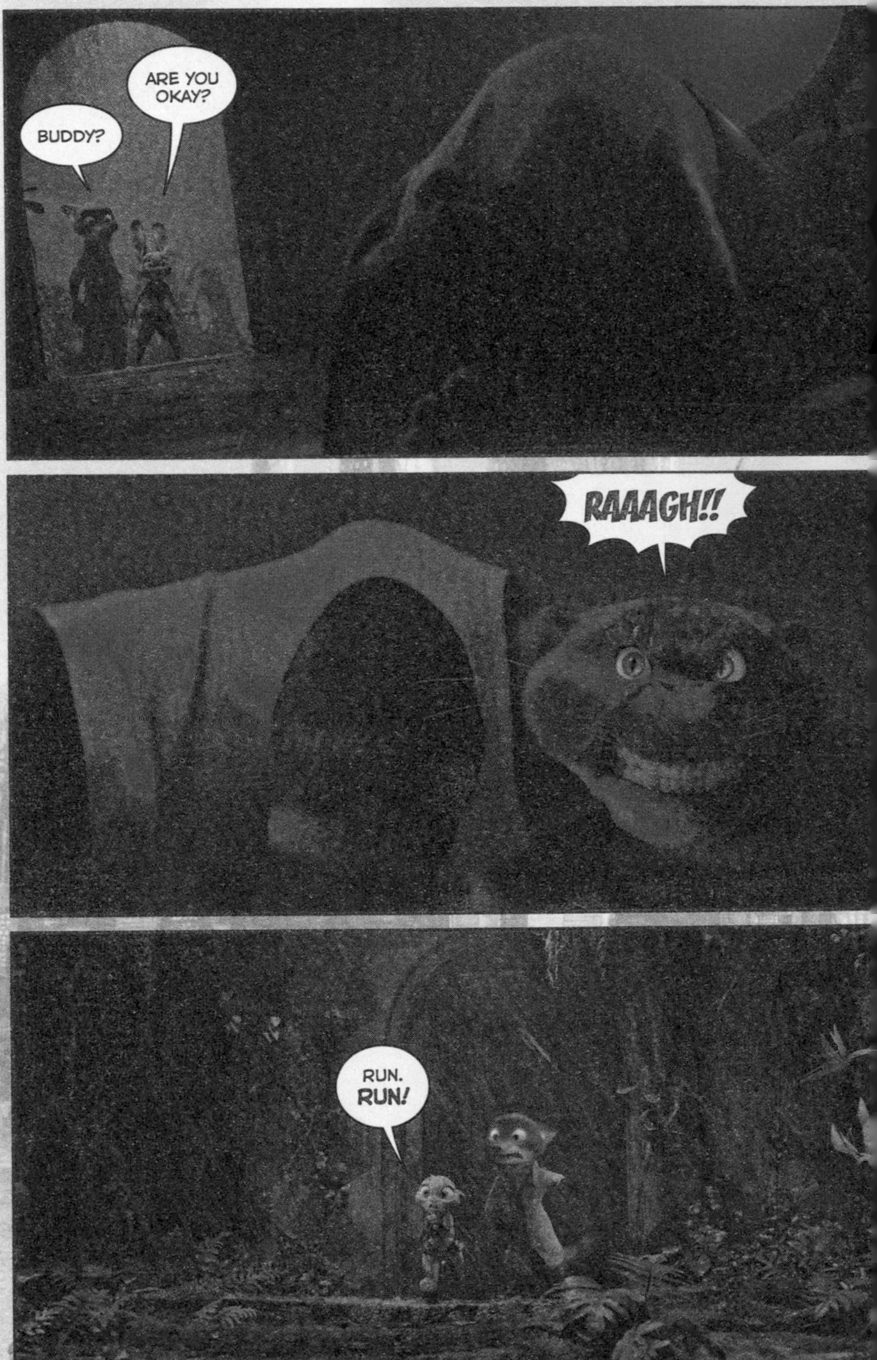
BUDDY?
ARE YOU OKAY?
RAAAGH!!
RUN. RUN!

hhhrrrRRRrrrrr...

WHAT IS WRONG WITH HIM?!

I DON'T KNOW!

RAAARGH!

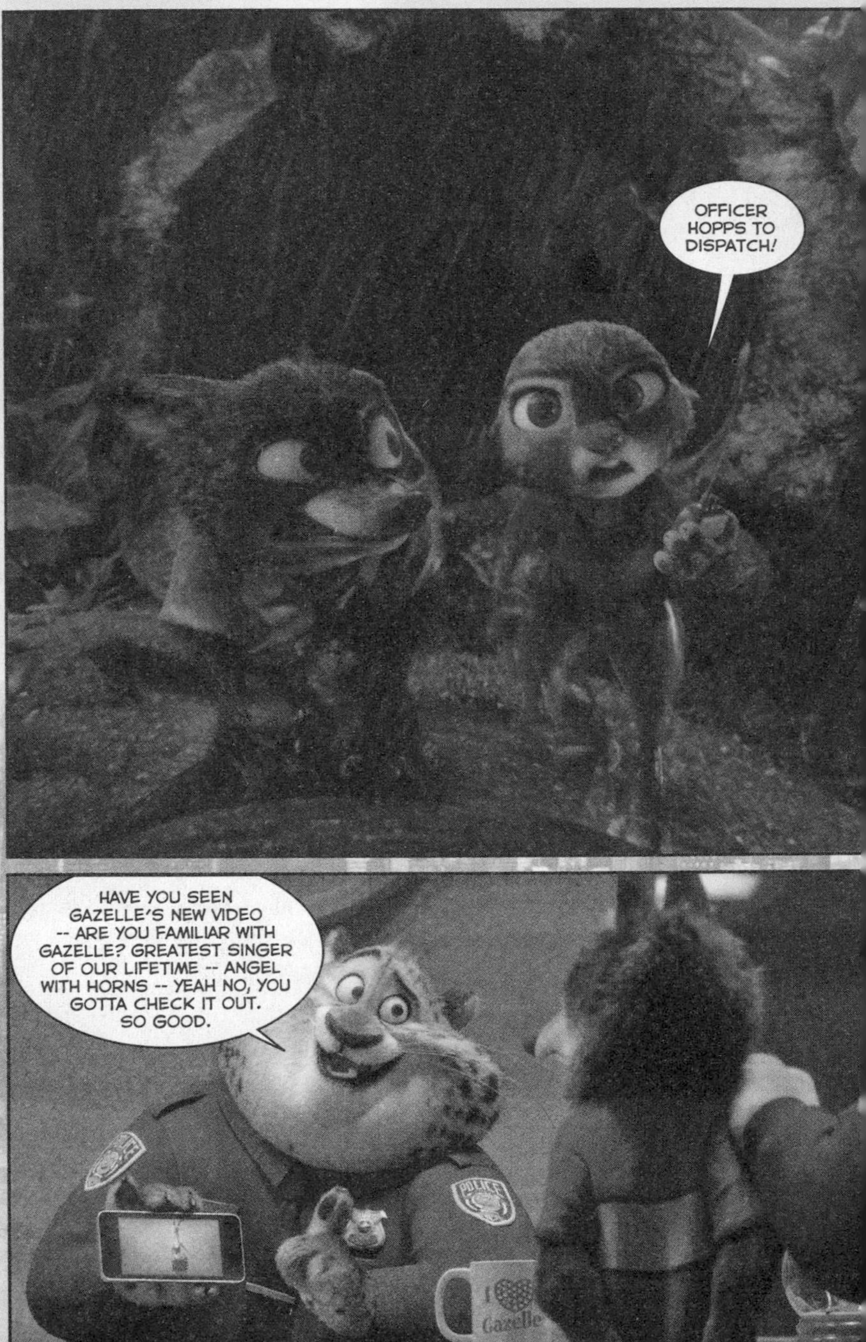
OFFICER HOPPS TO DISPATCH!
HAVE YOU SEEN GAZELLE'S NEW VIDEO -- ARE YOU FAMILIAR WITH GAZELLE? GREATEST SINGER OF OUR LIFETIME -- ANGEL WITH HORNS -- YEAH NO, YOU GOTTA CHECK IT OUT. SO GOOD.

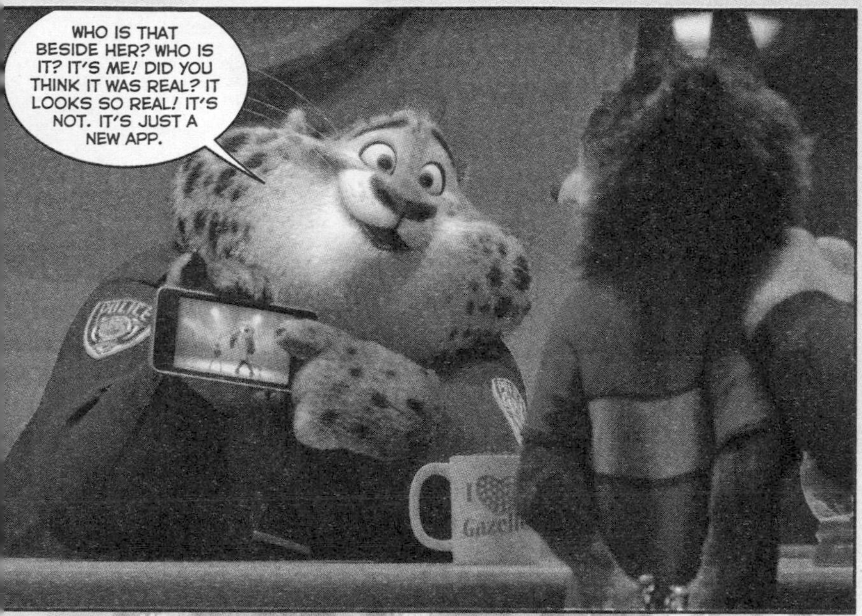
WHO IS THAT BESIDE HER? WHO IS IT? IT'S ME! DID YOU THINK IT WAS REAL? IT LOOKS SO REAL! IT'S NOT. IT'S JUST A NEW APP.
I ♥ Gazelle

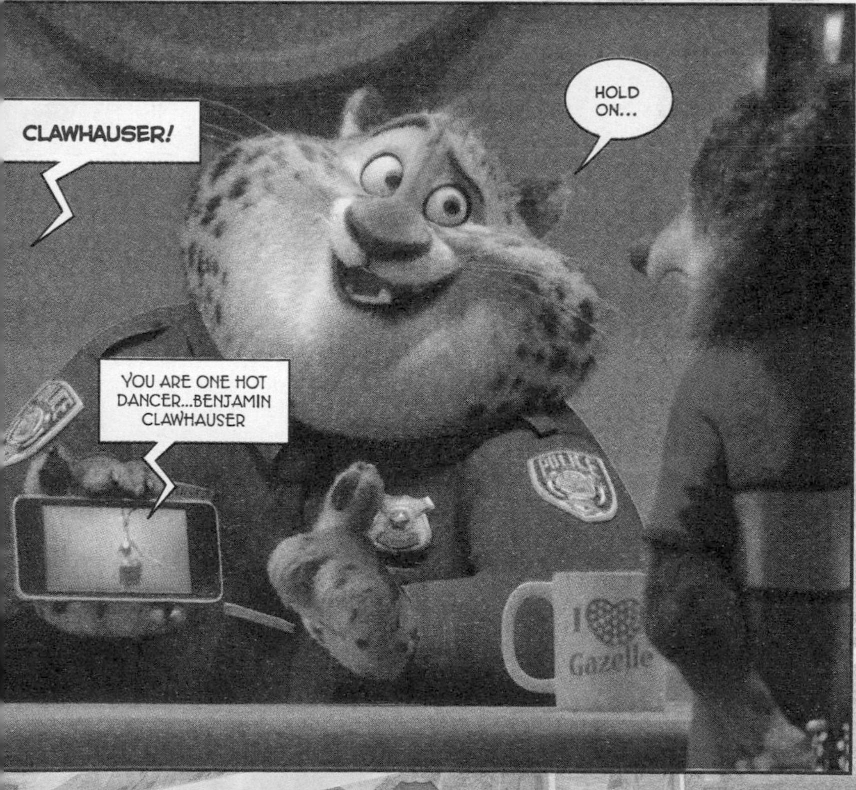
CLAWHAUSER!
HOLD ON...
YOU ARE ONE HOT DANCER...BENJAMIN CLAWHAUSER
POLICE
I ♥ Gazelle

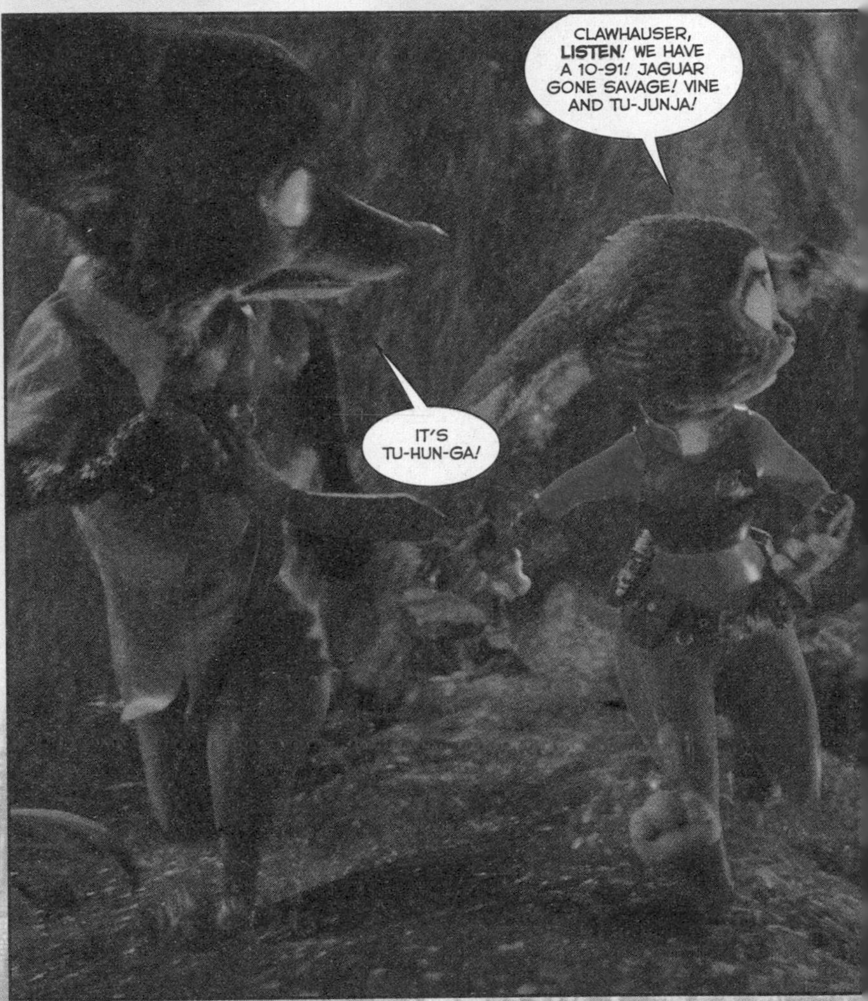
CLAWHAUSER, **LISTEN!** WE HAVE A 10-91! JAGUAR GONE SAVAGE! VINE AND TU-JUNJA!
IT'S TU-HUN-GA!

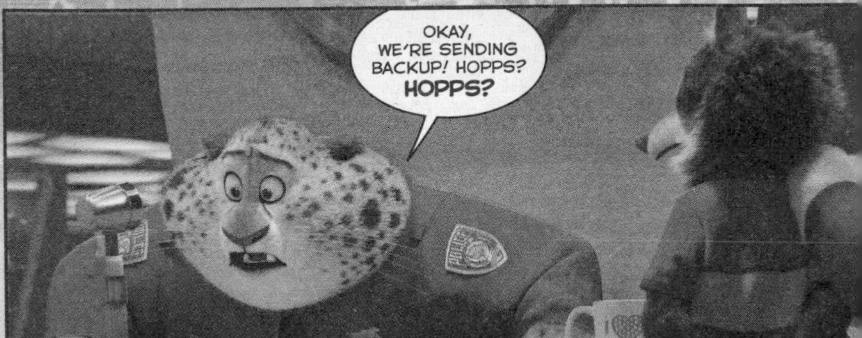
OKAY, WE'RE SENDING BACKUP! HOPPS? **HOPPS?**

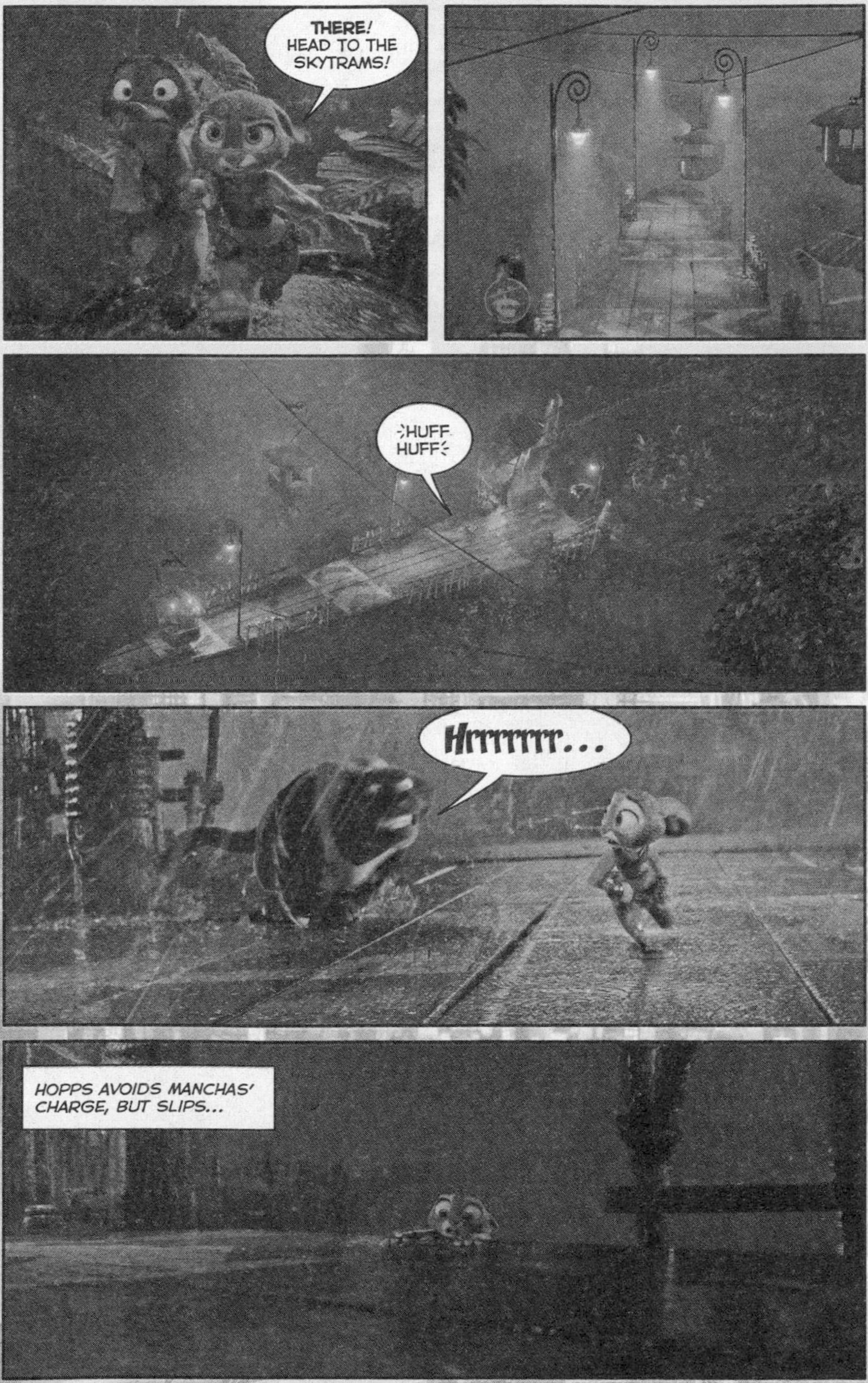
THERE! HEAD TO THE SKYTRAMS!
HUFF HUFF
Hrrrrrrr...
HOPPS AVOIDS MANCHAS' CHARGE, BUT SLIPS...

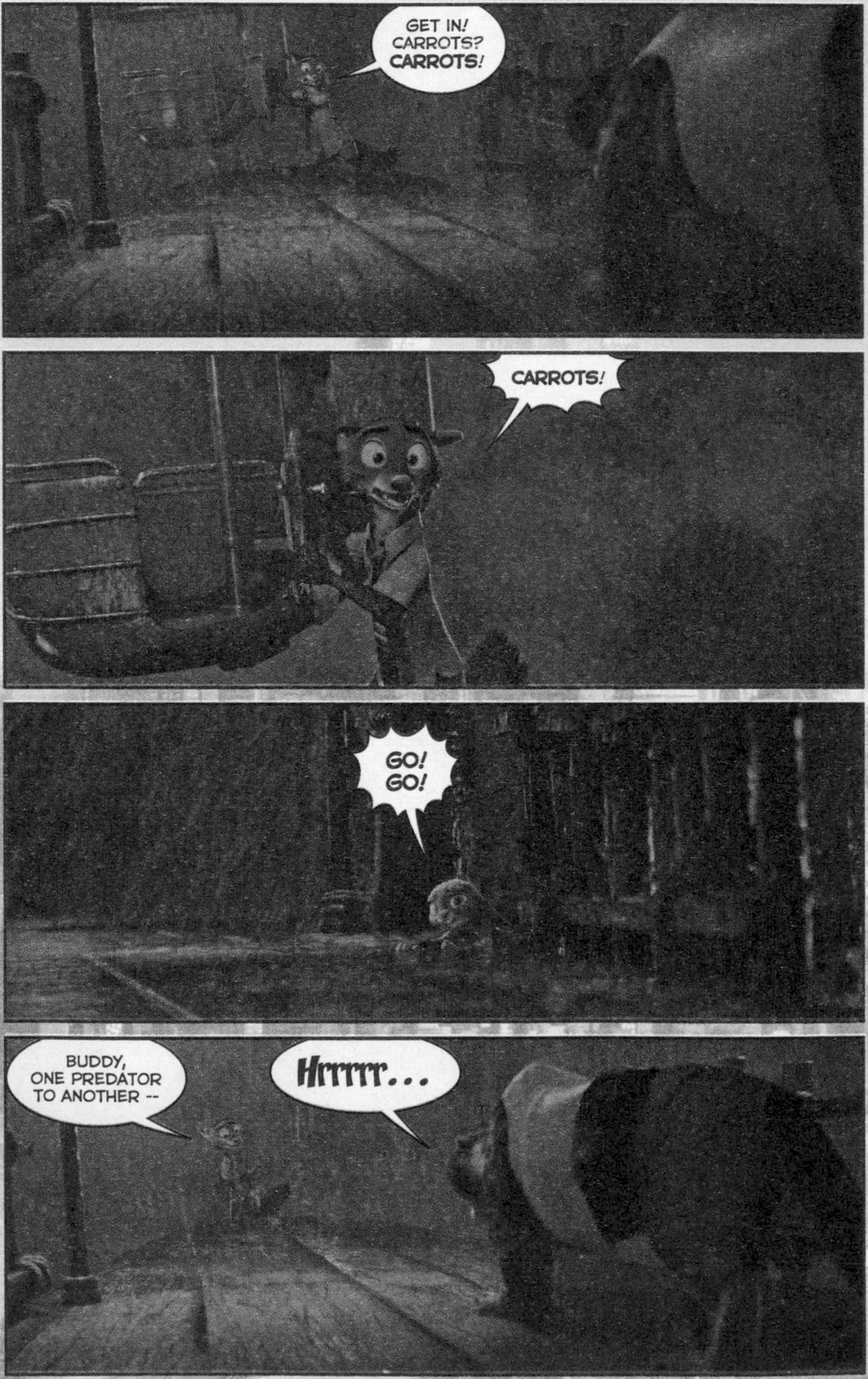
GET IN! CARROTS? CARROTS!
CARROTS!
GO! GO!
BUDDY, ONE PREDATOR TO ANOTHER --
Hrrrrr...

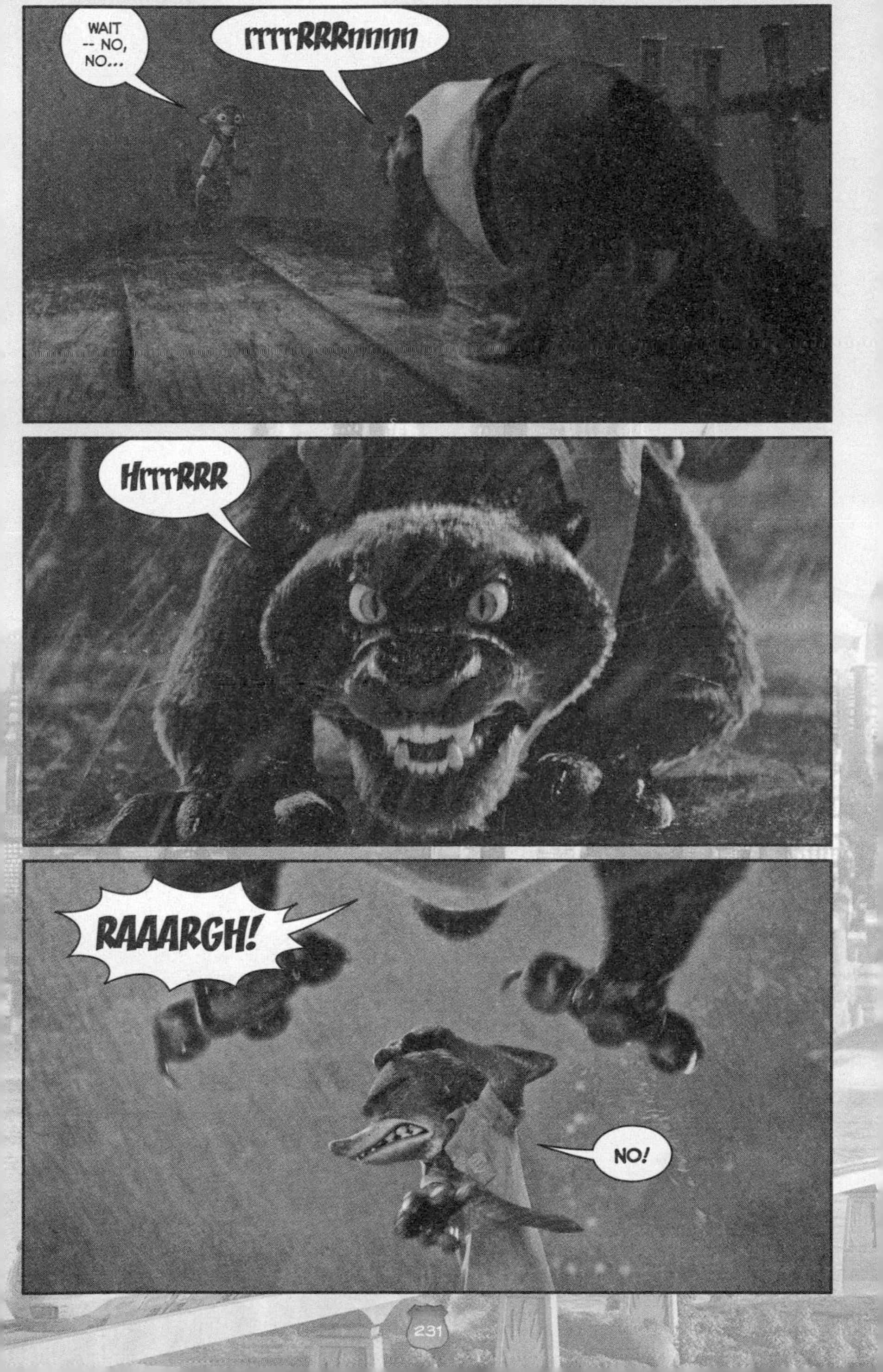
WAIT -- NO, NO...
rrrrRRRnnnn
HrrrRRR
RAAARGH!
NO!

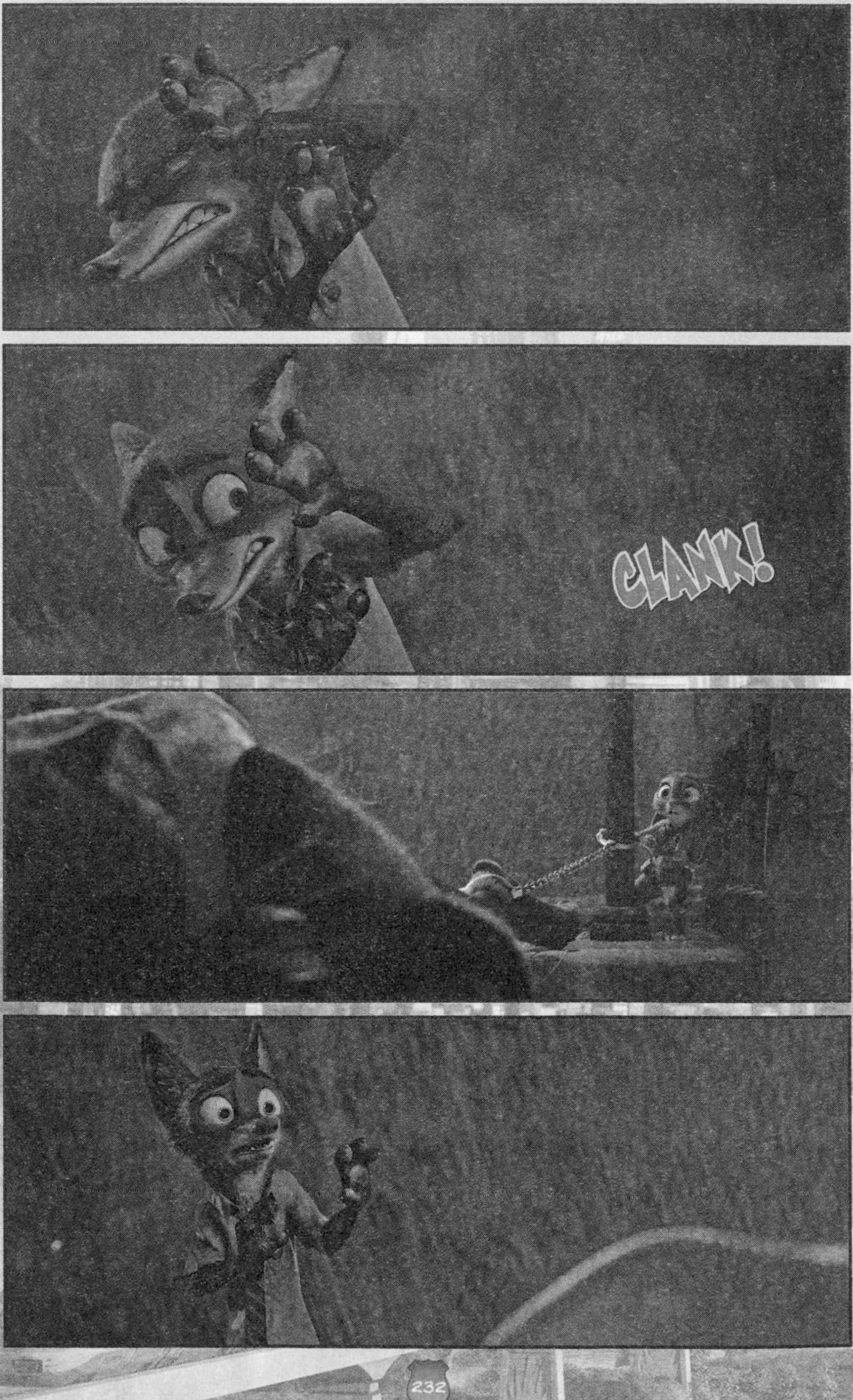
CLANK!

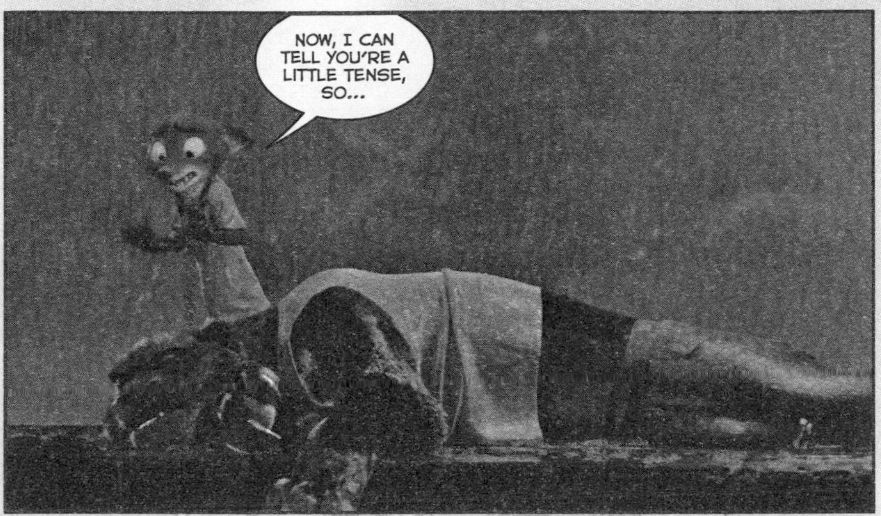
NOW, I CAN TELL YOU'RE A LITTLE TENSE, SO...

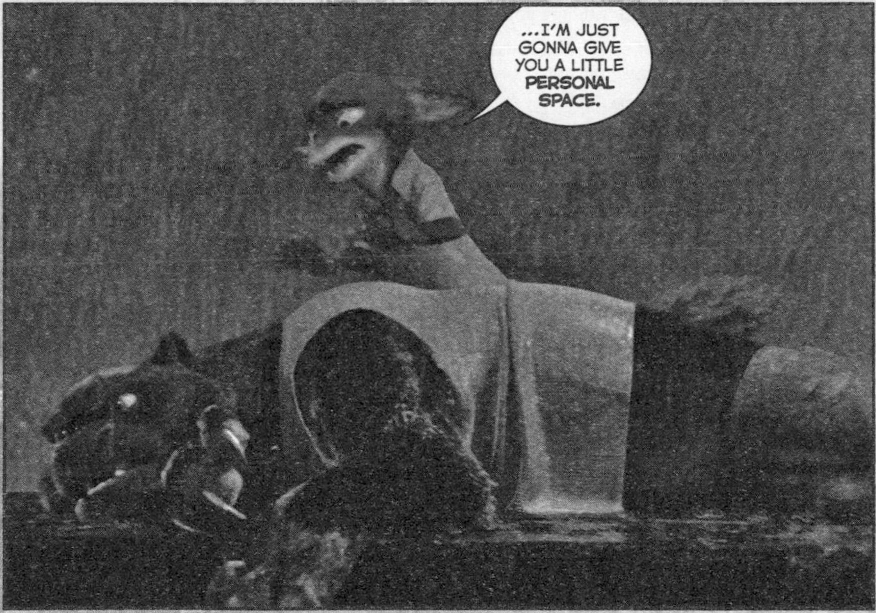
...I'M JUST GONNA GIVE YOU A LITTLE **PERSONAL SPACE.**

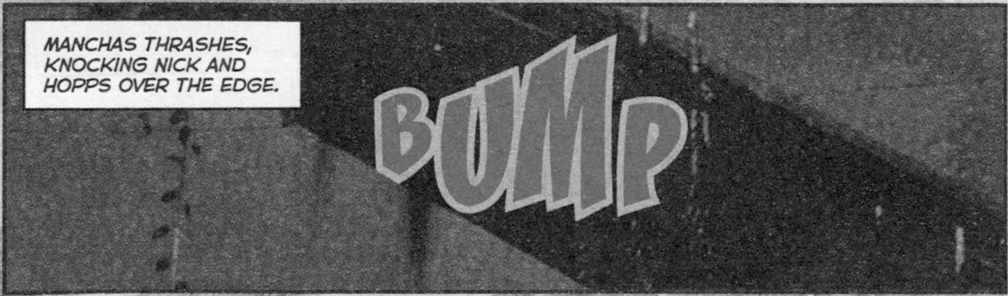
MANCHAS THRASHES, KNOCKING NICK AND HOPPS OVER THE EDGE.
BUMP

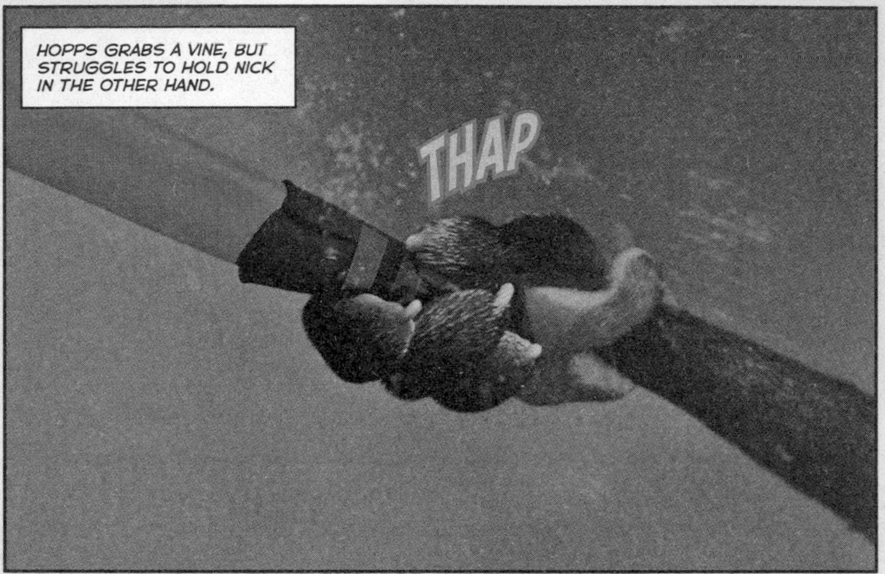
HOPPS GRABS A VINE, BUT STRUGGLES TO HOLD NICK IN THE OTHER HAND.
THAP

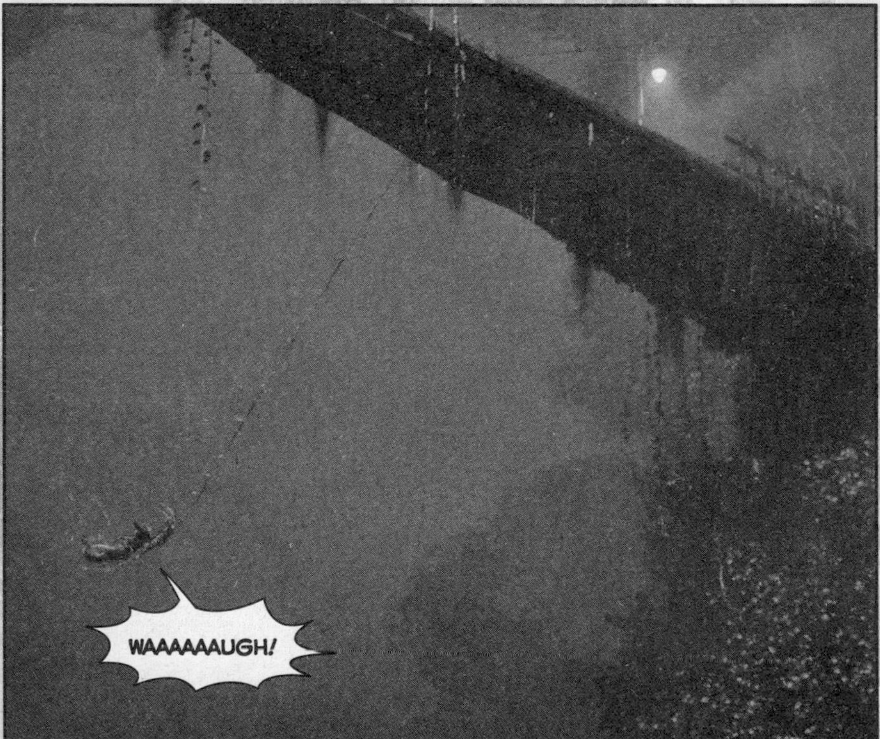
WAAAAAAUGH!

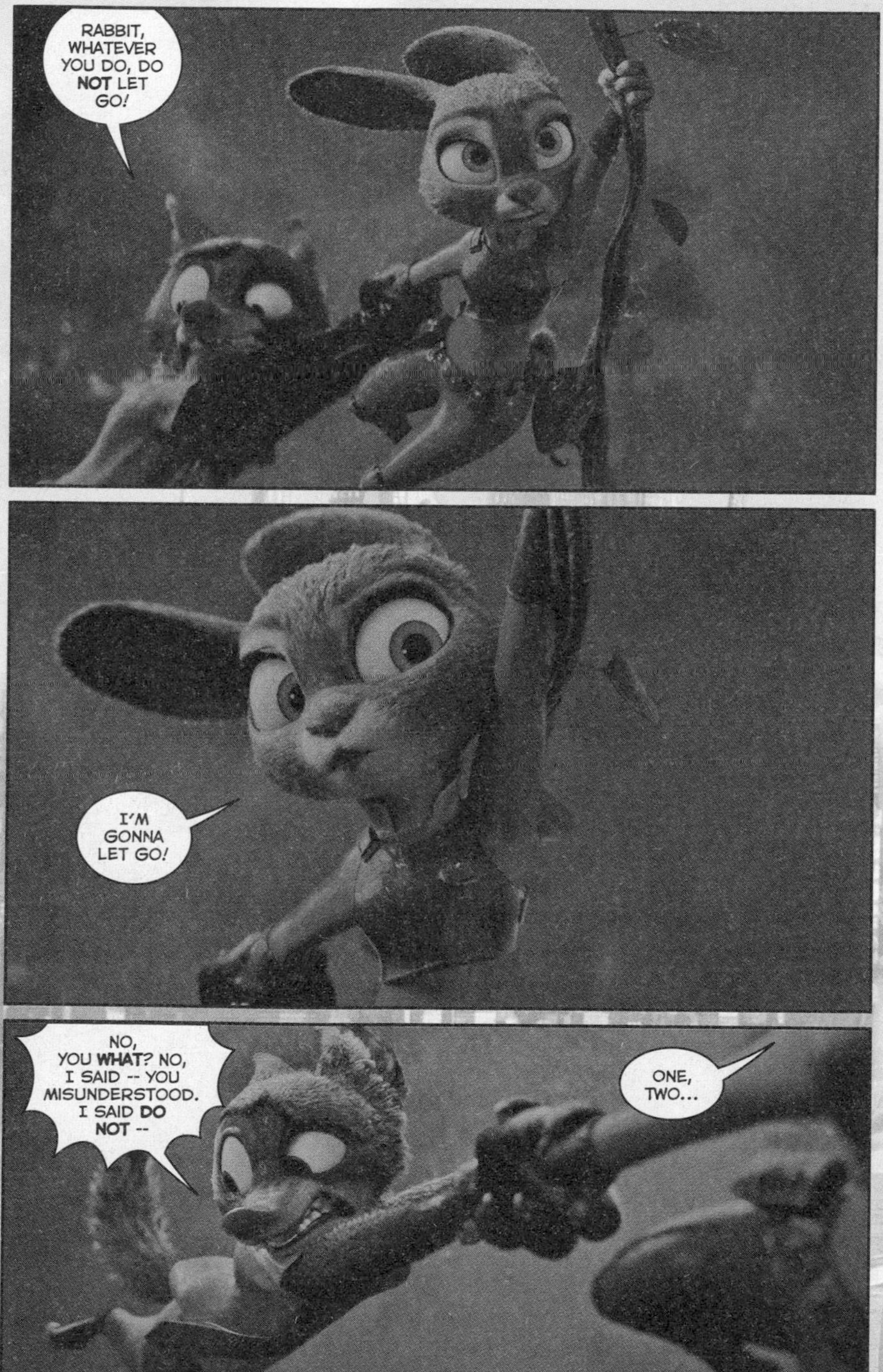
RABBIT, WHATEVER YOU DO, DO **NOT** LET GO!
I'M GONNA LET GO!
NO, YOU **WHAT**? NO, I SAID -- YOU MISUNDERSTOOD. I SAID **DO NOT** --
ONE, TWO...

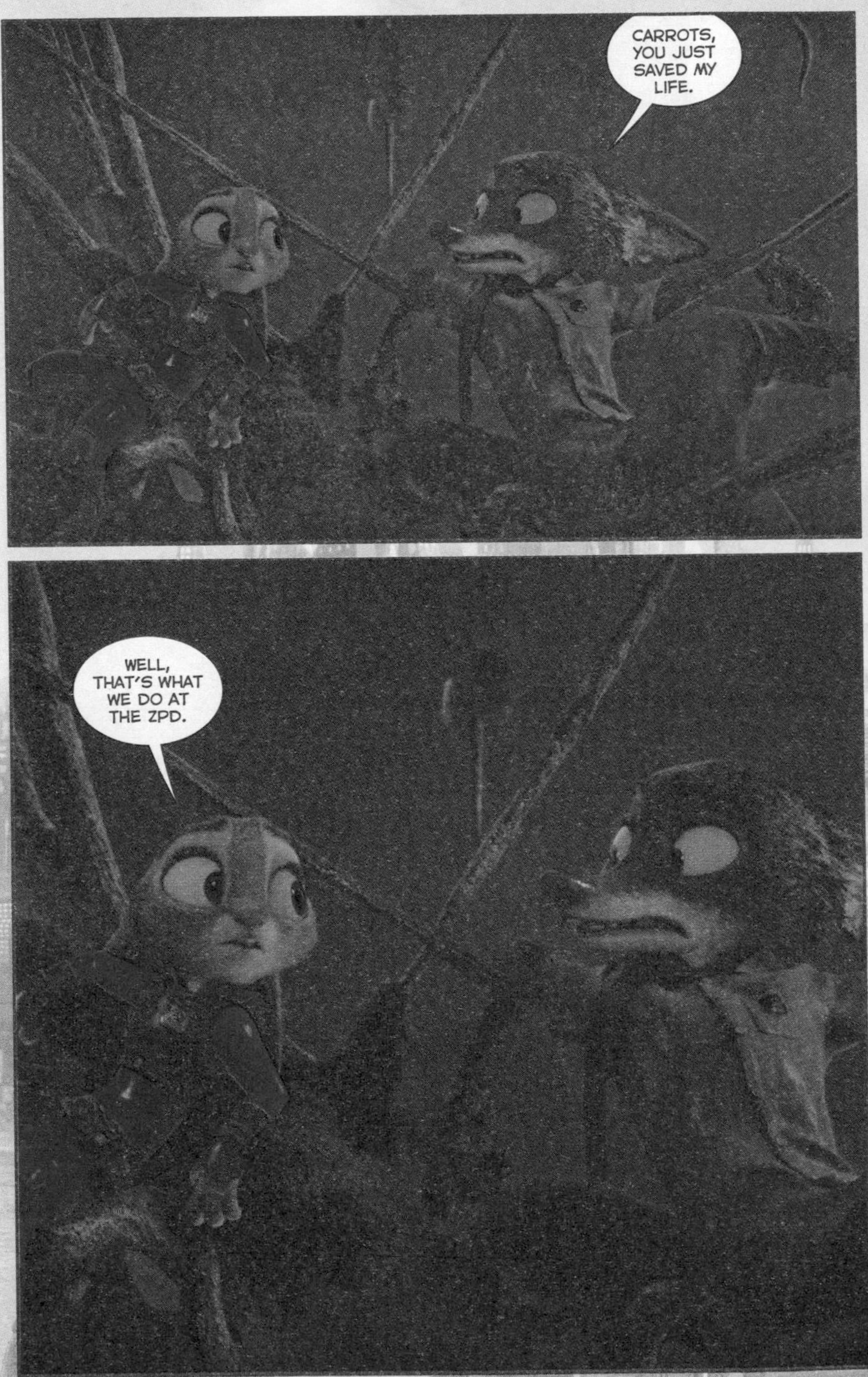
CARROTS, YOU JUST SAVED MY LIFE.
WELL, THAT'S WHAT WE DO AT THE ZPD.

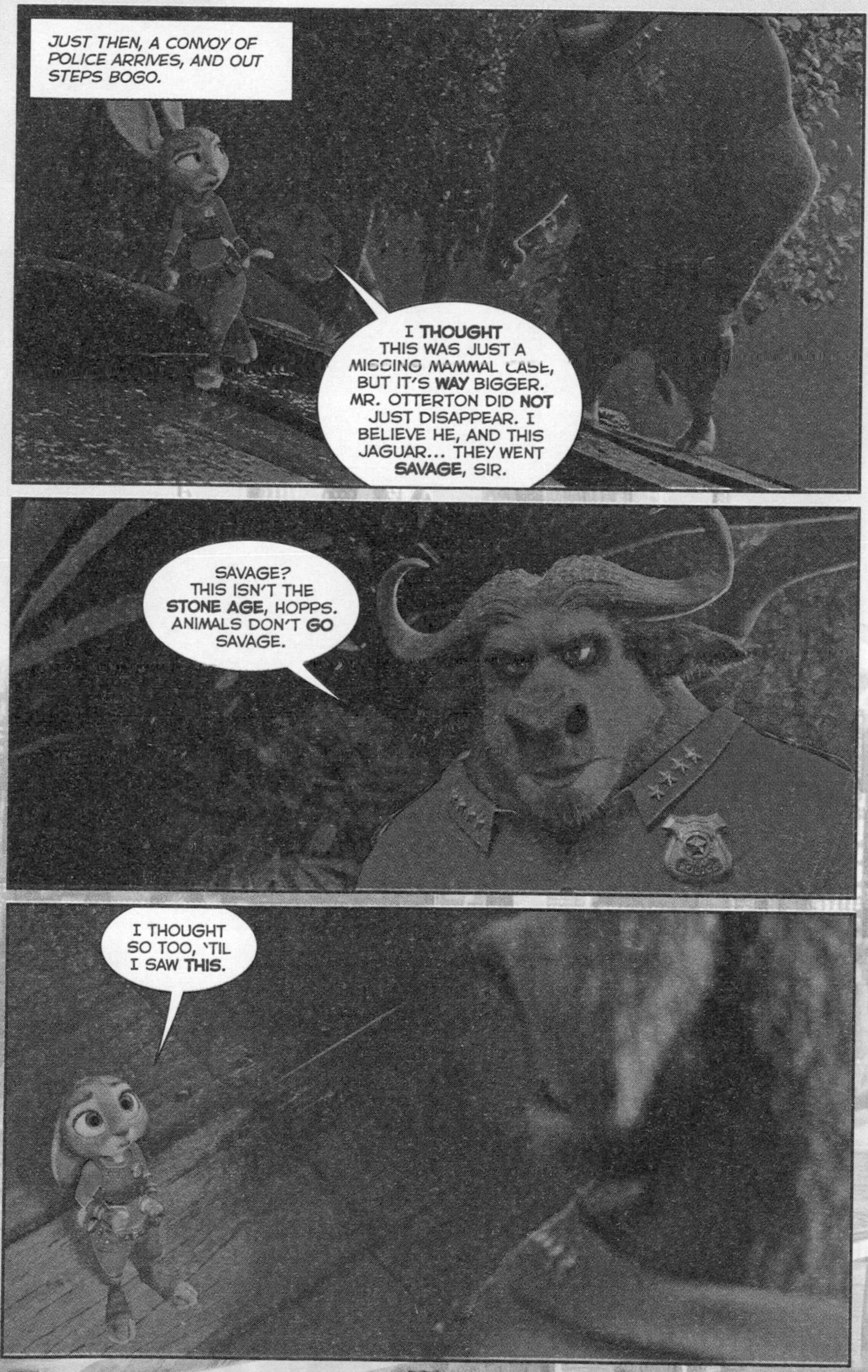
JUST THEN, A CONVOY OF POLICE ARRIVES, AND OUT STEPS BOGO.
I THOUGHT THIS WAS JUST A MISSING MAMMAL CASE, BUT IT'S WAY BIGGER. MR. OTTERTON DID NOT JUST DISAPPEAR. I BELIEVE HE, AND THIS JAGUAR... THEY WENT SAVAGE, SIR.
SAVAGE? THIS ISN'T THE STONE AGE, HOPPS. ANIMALS DON'T GO SAVAGE.
I THOUGHT SO TOO, 'TIL I SAW THIS.

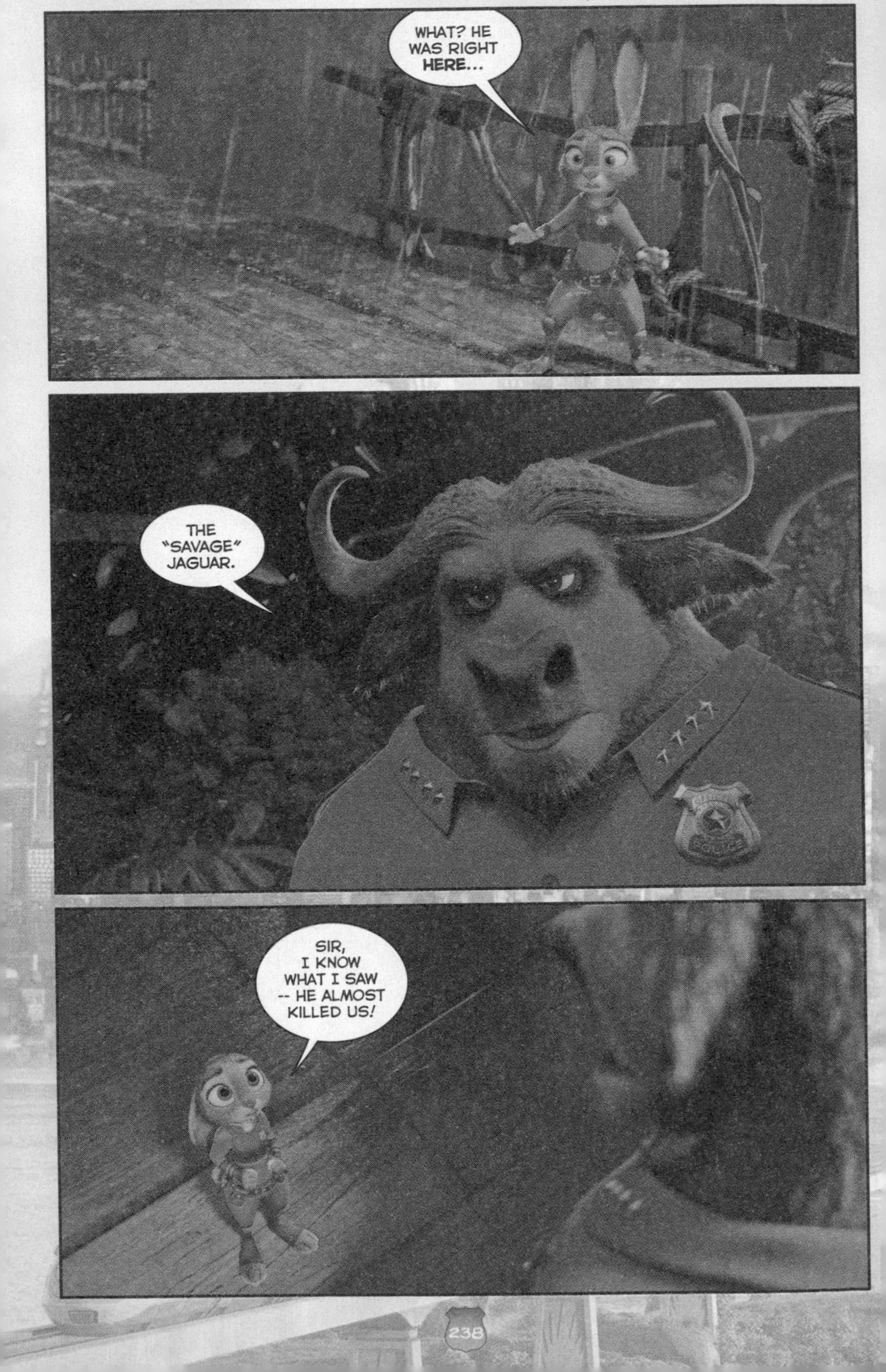
WHAT? HE WAS RIGHT HERE...
THE "SAVAGE" JAGUAR.
SIR, I KNOW WHAT I SAW -- HE ALMOST KILLED US!

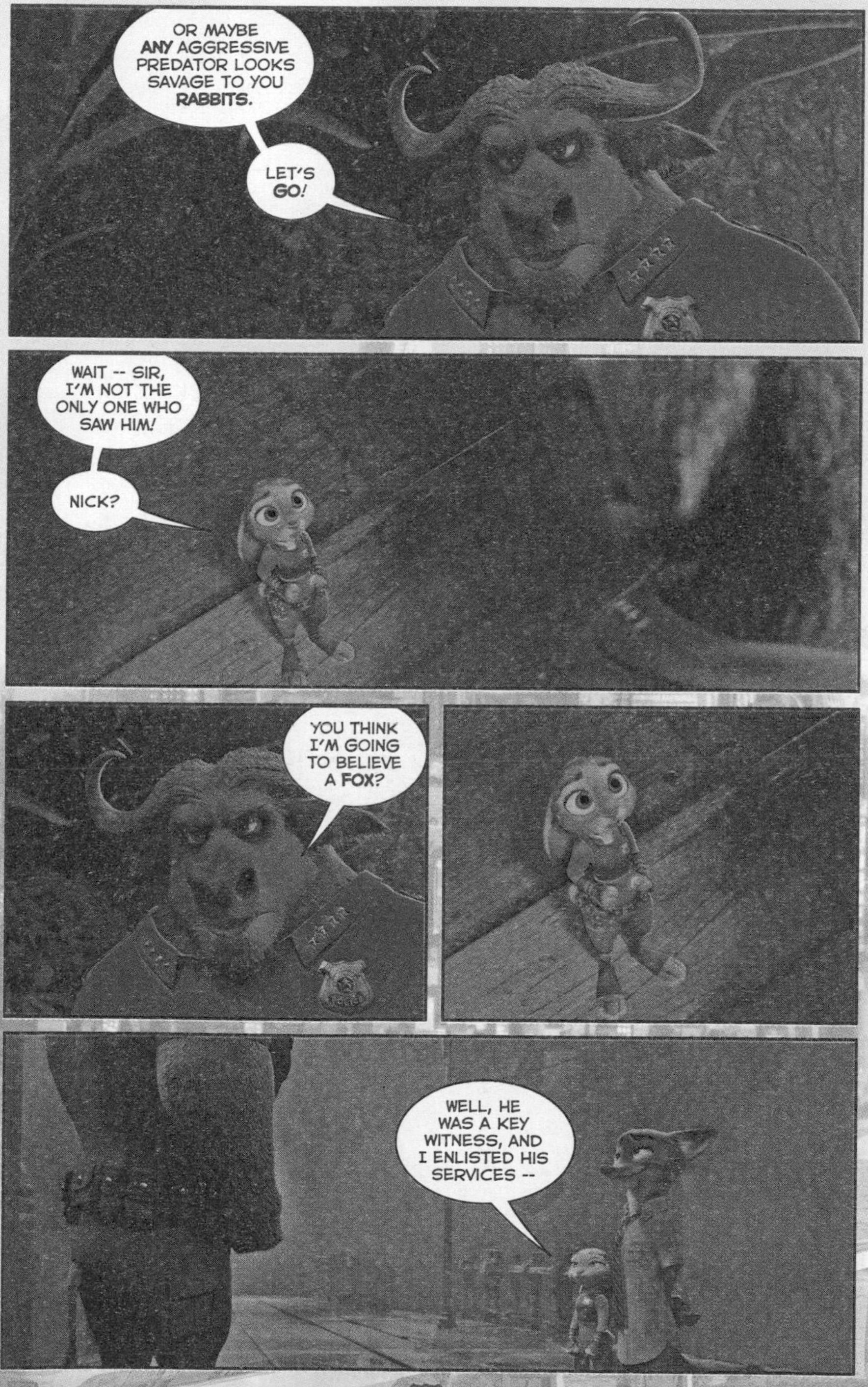
OR MAYBE ANY AGGRESSIVE PREDATOR LOOKS SAVAGE TO YOU RABBITS.
LET'S GO!
WAIT -- SIR, I'M NOT THE ONLY ONE WHO SAW HIM!
NICK?
YOU THINK I'M GOING TO BELIEVE A FOX?
WELL, HE WAS A KEY WITNESS, AND I ENLISTED HIS SERVICES --

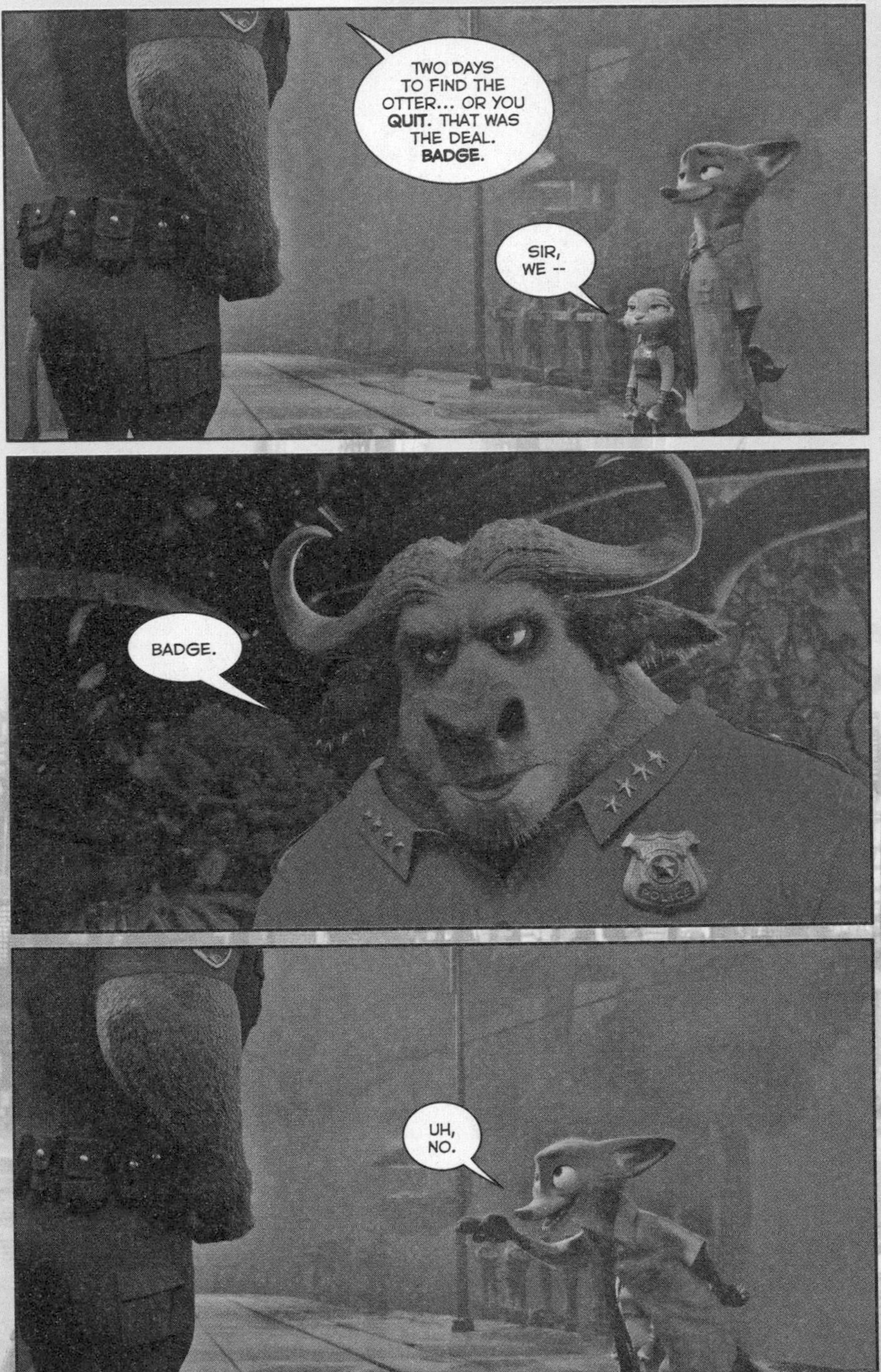
TWO DAYS TO FIND THE OTTER... OR YOU **QUIT**. THAT WAS THE DEAL. **BADGE.**
SIR, WE --
BADGE.
UH, NO.

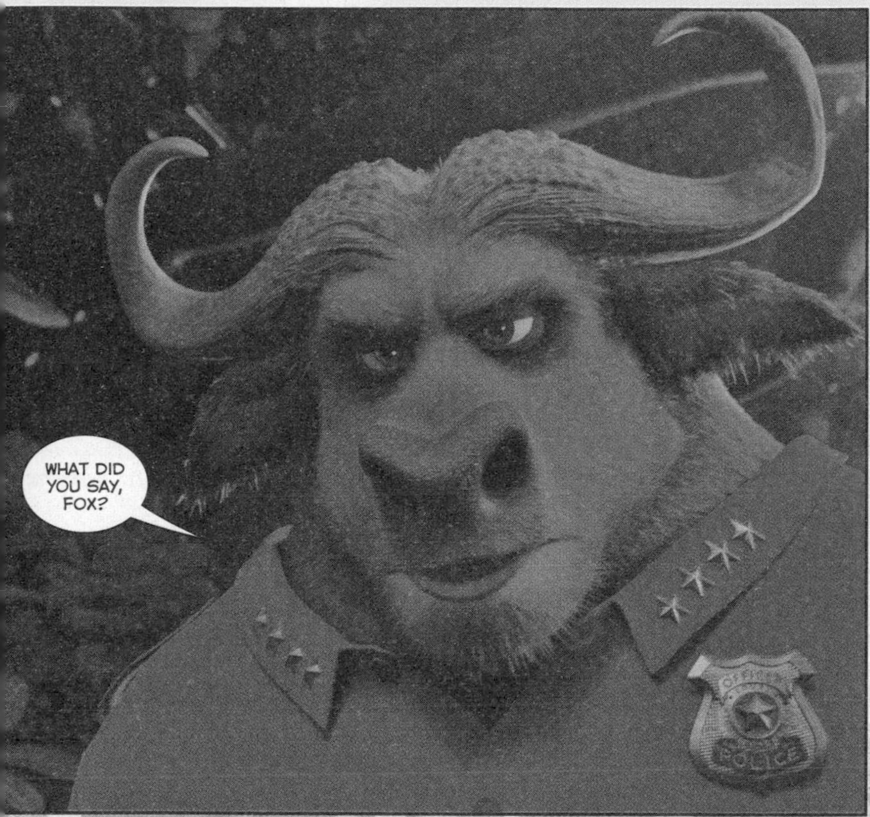
WHAT DID YOU SAY, FOX?

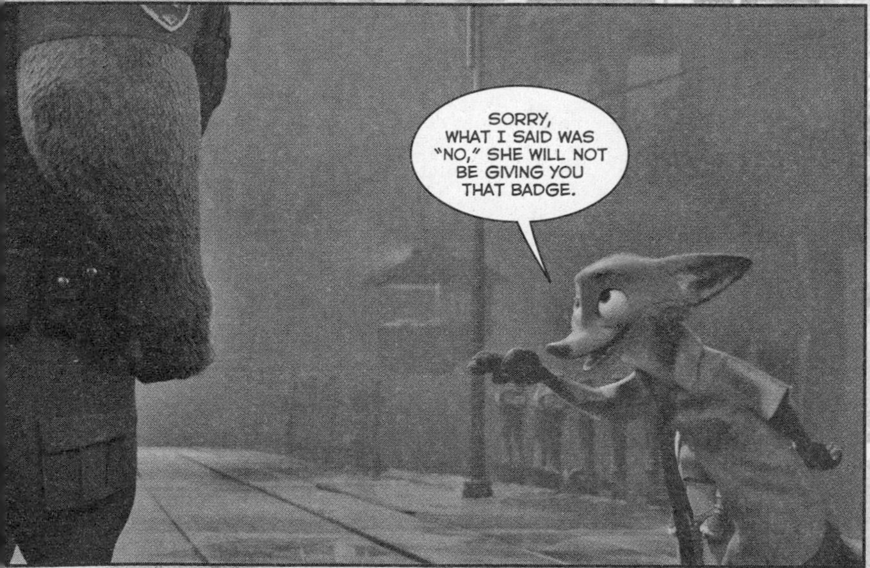
SORRY, WHAT I SAID WAS "NO," SHE WILL NOT BE GIVING YOU THAT BADGE.

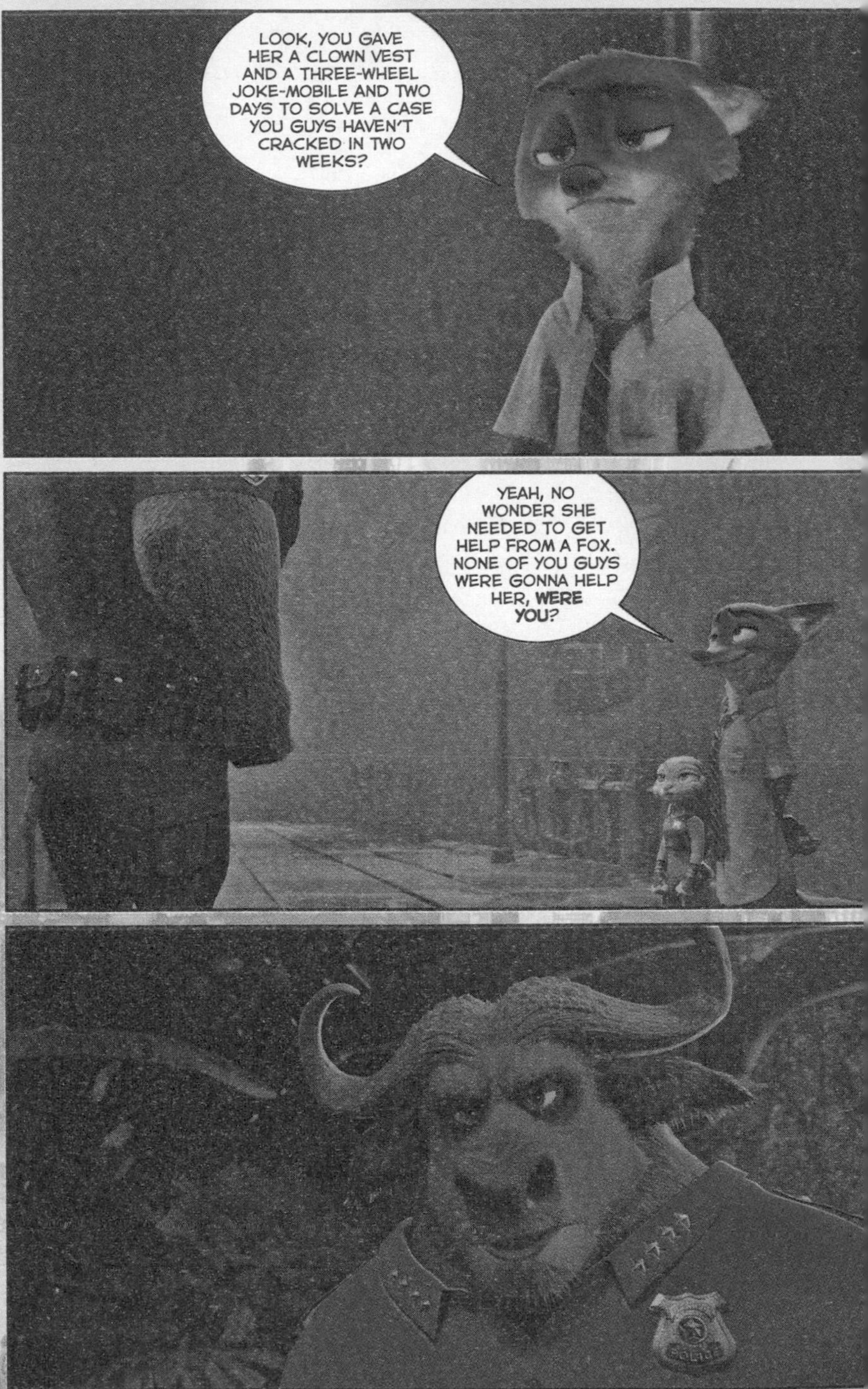
LOOK, YOU GAVE HER A CLOWN VEST AND A THREE-WHEEL JOKE-MOBILE AND TWO DAYS TO SOLVE A CASE YOU GUYS HAVEN'T CRACKED IN TWO WEEKS?
YEAH, NO WONDER SHE NEEDED TO GET HELP FROM A FOX. NONE OF YOU GUYS WERE GONNA HELP HER, **WERE YOU**?

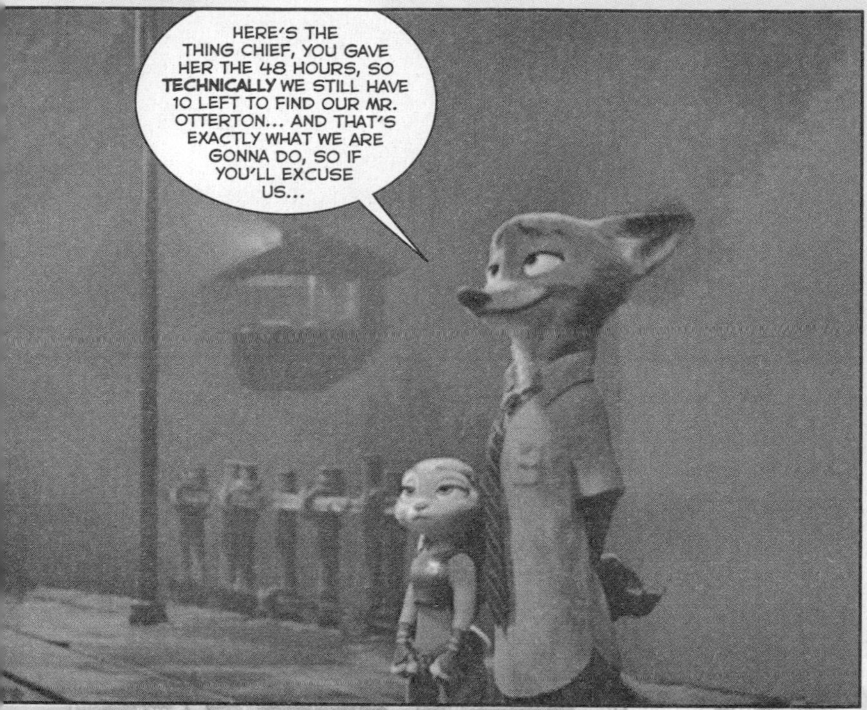
HERE'S THE THING CHIEF, YOU GAVE HER THE 48 HOURS, SO **TECHNICALLY** WE STILL HAVE 10 LEFT TO FIND OUR MR. OTTERTON... AND THAT'S EXACTLY WHAT WE ARE GONNA DO, SO IF YOU'LL EXCUSE US...

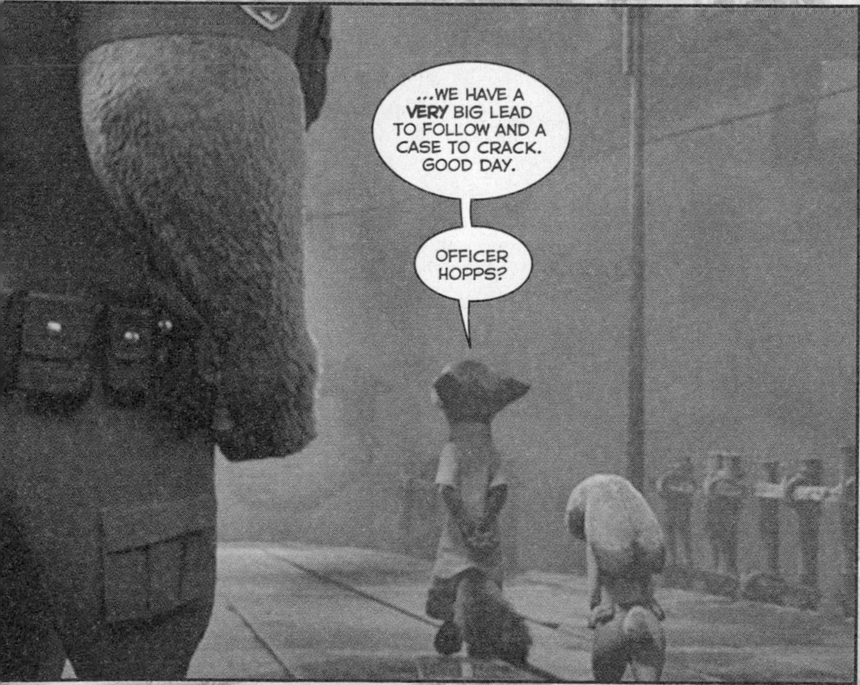
...WE HAVE A **VERY** BIG LEAD TO FOLLOW AND A CASE TO CRACK. GOOD DAY.
OFFICER HOPPS?

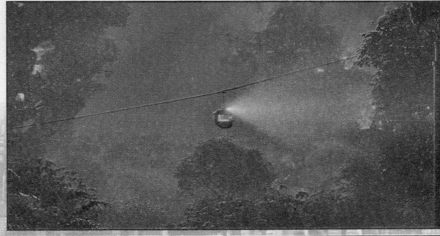

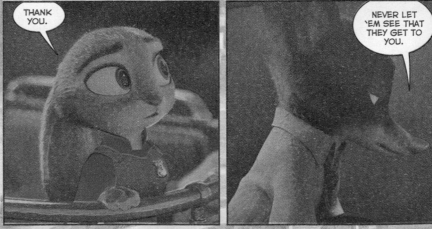

THANK YOU.

NEVER LET 'EM SEE THAT THEY GET TO YOU.

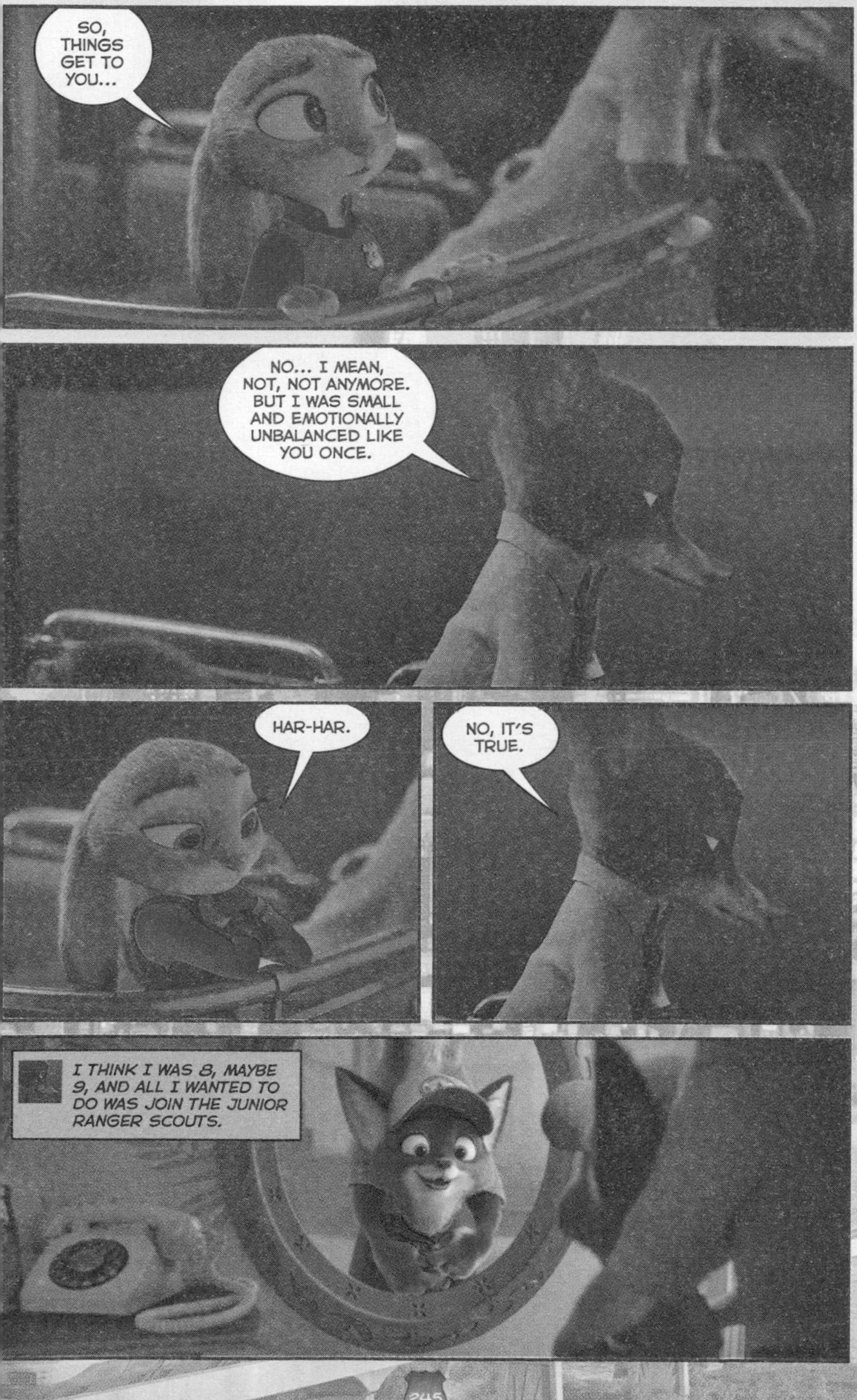
SO, THINGS GET TO YOU...
NO... I MEAN, NOT, NOT ANYMORE. BUT I WAS SMALL AND EMOTIONALLY UNBALANCED LIKE YOU ONCE.
HAR-HAR.
NO, IT'S TRUE.
I THINK I WAS 8, MAYBE 9, AND ALL I WANTED TO DO WAS JOIN THE JUNIOR RANGER SCOUTS.

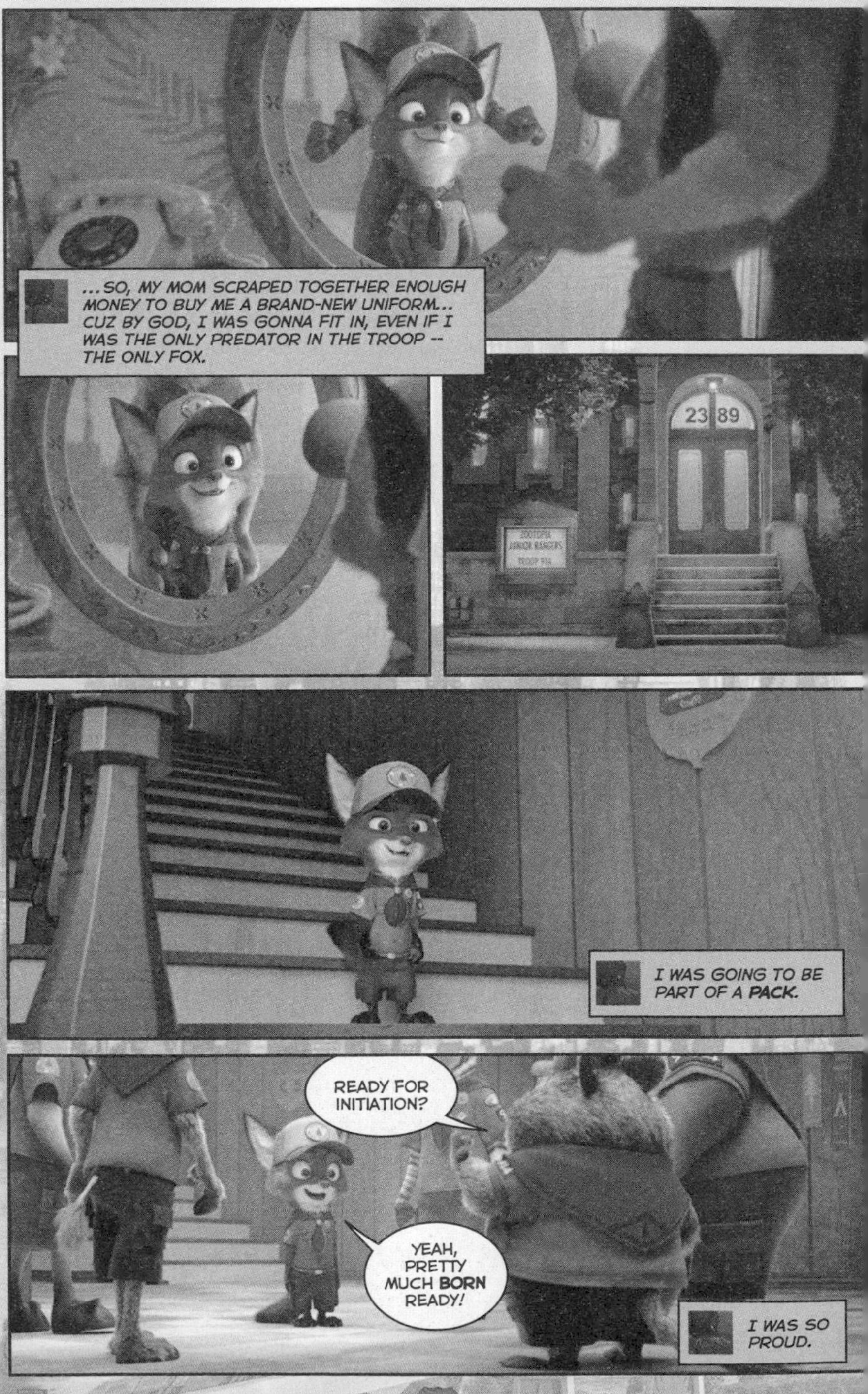
...SO, MY MOM SCRAPED TOGETHER ENOUGH MONEY TO BUY ME A BRAND-NEW UNIFORM... CUZ BY GOD, I WAS GONNA FIT IN, EVEN IF I WAS THE ONLY PREDATOR IN THE TROOP -- THE ONLY FOX.
2389
ZOOTOPIA JUNIOR RANGERS
I WAS GOING TO BE PART OF A **PACK.**
READY FOR INITIATION?
YEAH, PRETTY MUCH **BORN** READY!
I WAS SO PROUD.

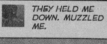
THEY HELD ME DOWN. MUZZLED ME.

‡HUFF HUFF‡

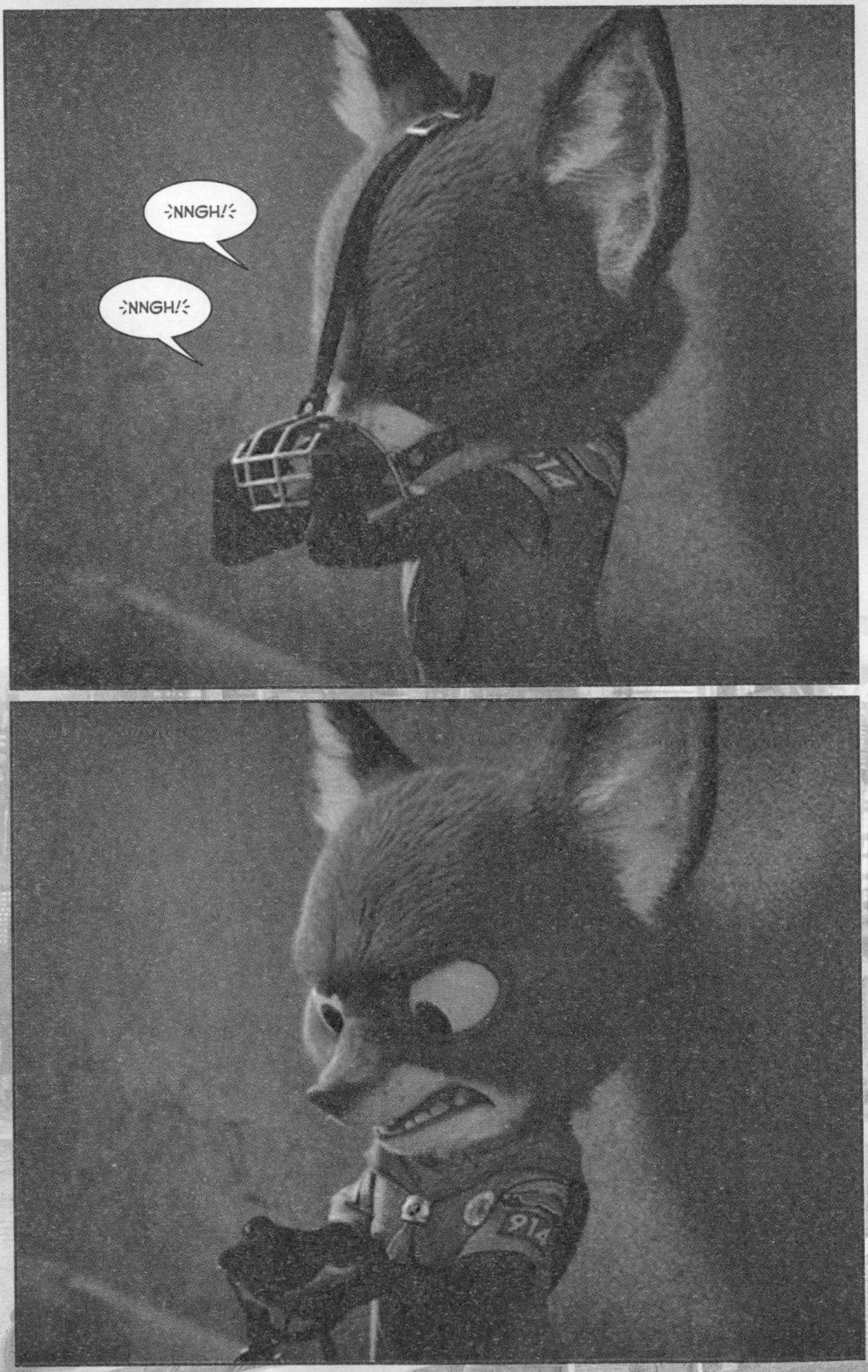
NNGH!
NNGH!

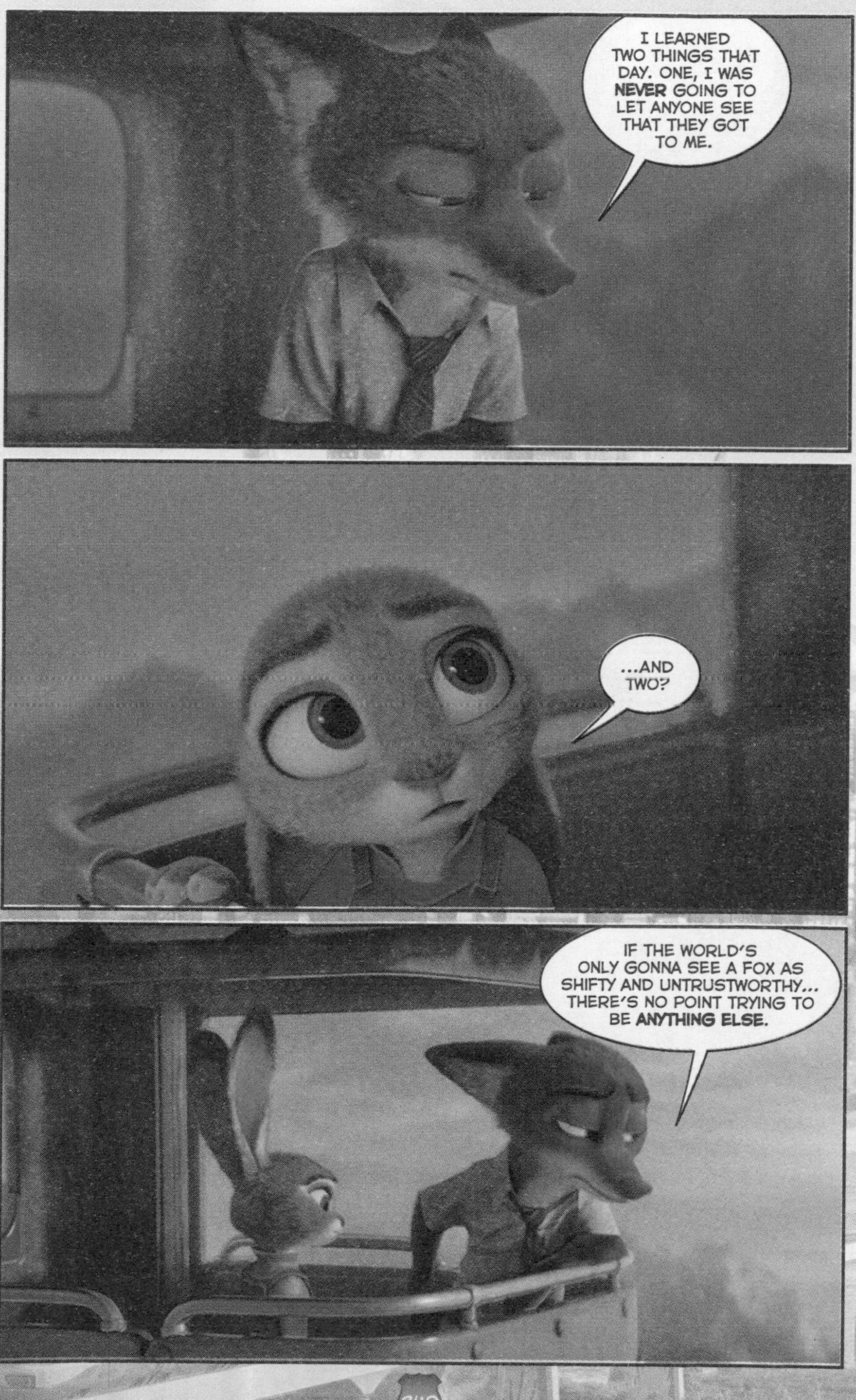
I LEARNED TWO THINGS THAT DAY. ONE, I WAS **NEVER** GOING TO LET ANYONE SEE THAT THEY GOT TO ME.
...AND TWO?
IF THE WORLD'S ONLY GONNA SEE A FOX AS SHIFTY AND UNTRUSTWORTHY... THERE'S NO POINT TRYING TO BE **ANYTHING ELSE**.

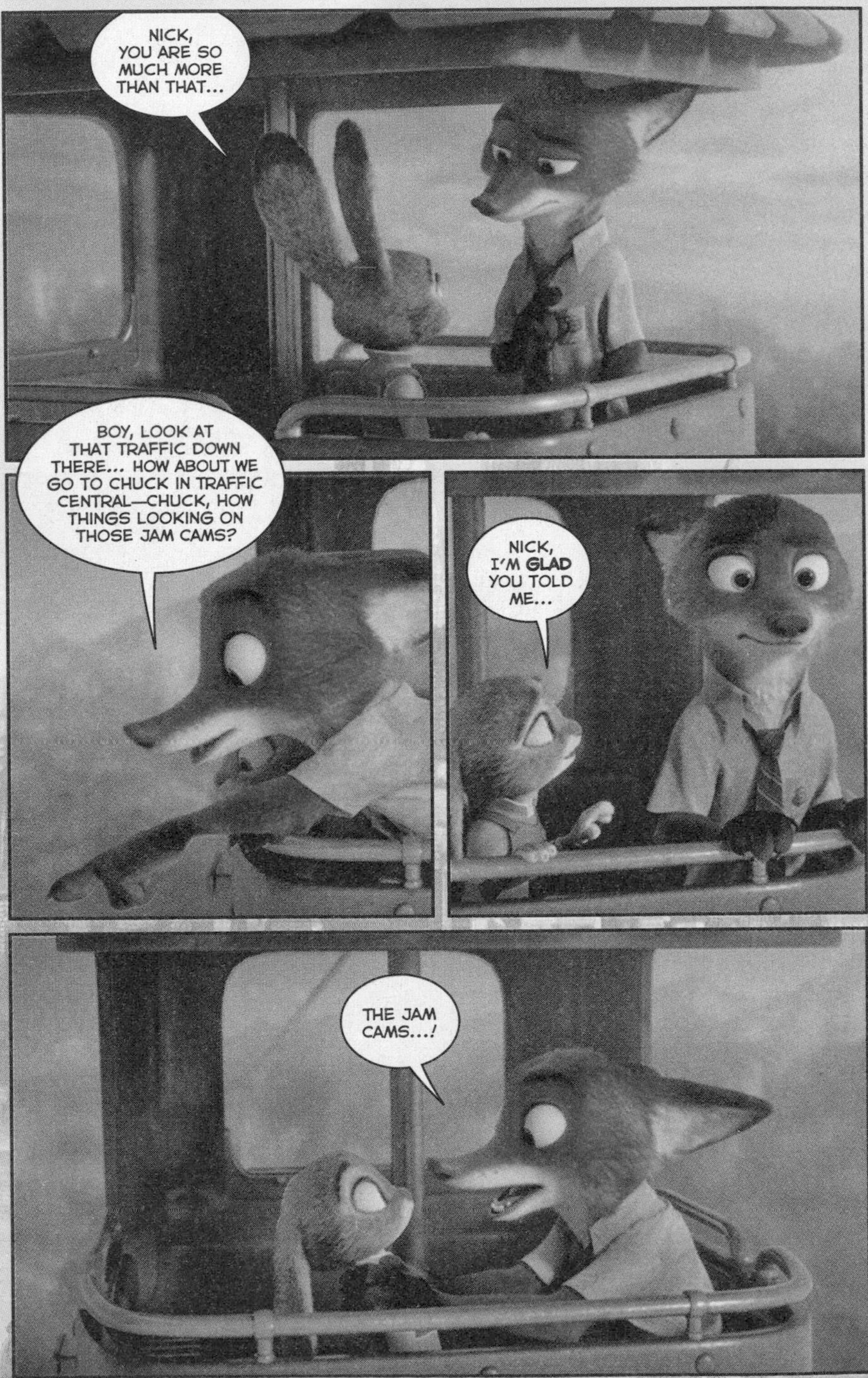
NICK, YOU ARE SO MUCH MORE THAN THAT...
BOY, LOOK AT THAT TRAFFIC DOWN THERE... HOW ABOUT WE GO TO CHUCK IN TRAFFIC CENTRAL—CHUCK, HOW THINGS LOOKING ON THOSE JAM CAMS?
NICK, I'M GLAD YOU TOLD ME...
THE JAM CAMS...!

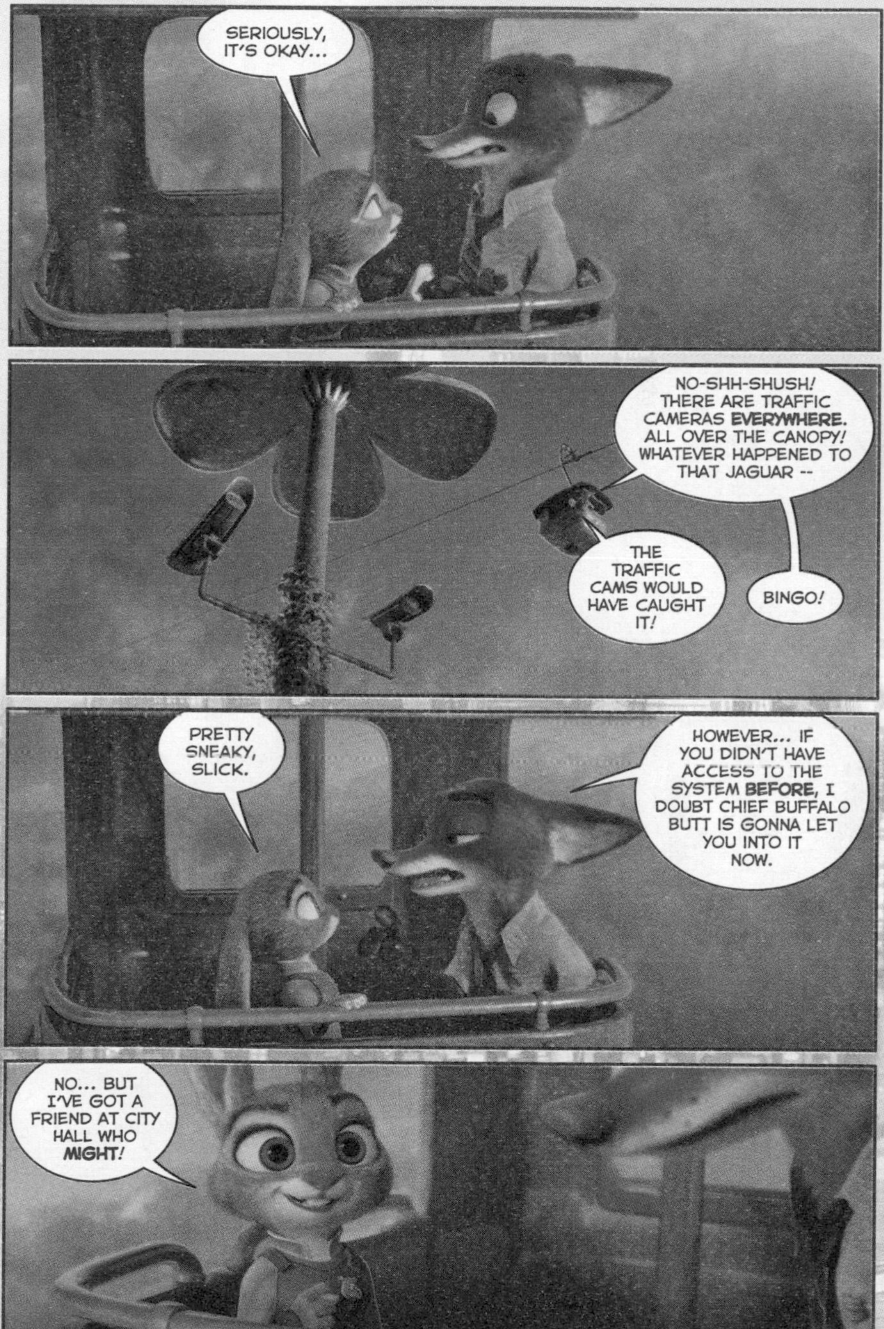
SERIOUSLY, IT'S OKAY...
NO-SHH-SHUSH! THERE ARE TRAFFIC CAMERAS **EVERYWHERE.** ALL OVER THE CANOPY! WHATEVER HAPPENED TO THAT JAGUAR --
THE TRAFFIC CAMS WOULD HAVE CAUGHT IT!
BINGO!
PRETTY SNEAKY, SLICK.
HOWEVER... IF YOU DIDN'T HAVE ACCESS TO THE SYSTEM **BEFORE,** I DOUBT CHIEF BUFFALO BUTT IS GONNA LET YOU INTO IT NOW.
NO... BUT I'VE GOT A FRIEND AT CITY HALL WHO **MIGHT**!

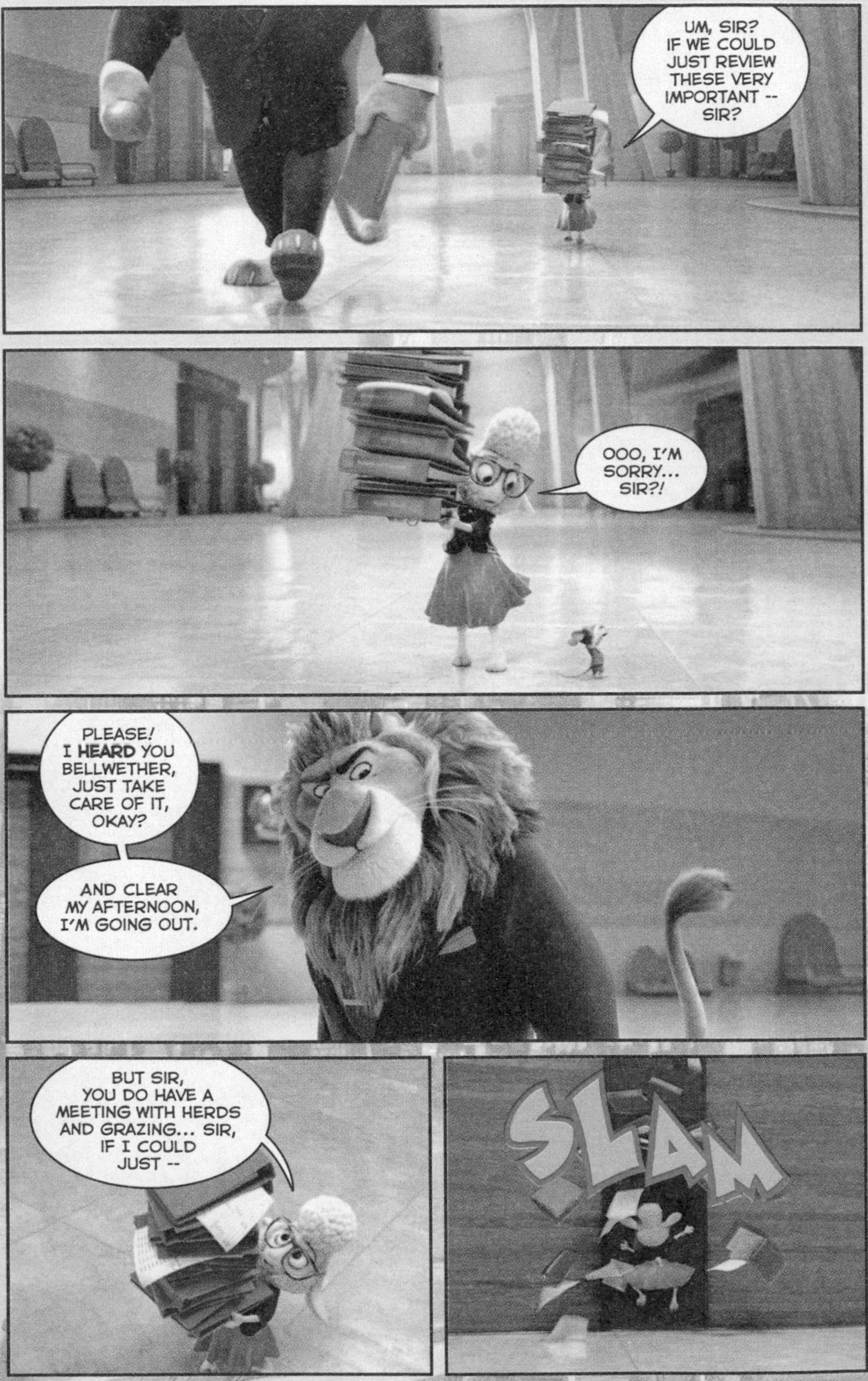
UM, SIR? IF WE COULD JUST REVIEW THESE VERY IMPORTANT -- SIR?
OOO, I'M SORRY... SIR?!
PLEASE! I **HEARD** YOU BELLWETHER, JUST TAKE CARE OF IT, OKAY?
AND CLEAR MY AFTERNOON, I'M GOING OUT.
BUT SIR, YOU DO HAVE A MEETING WITH HERDS AND GRAZING... SIR, IF I COULD JUST --
SLAM

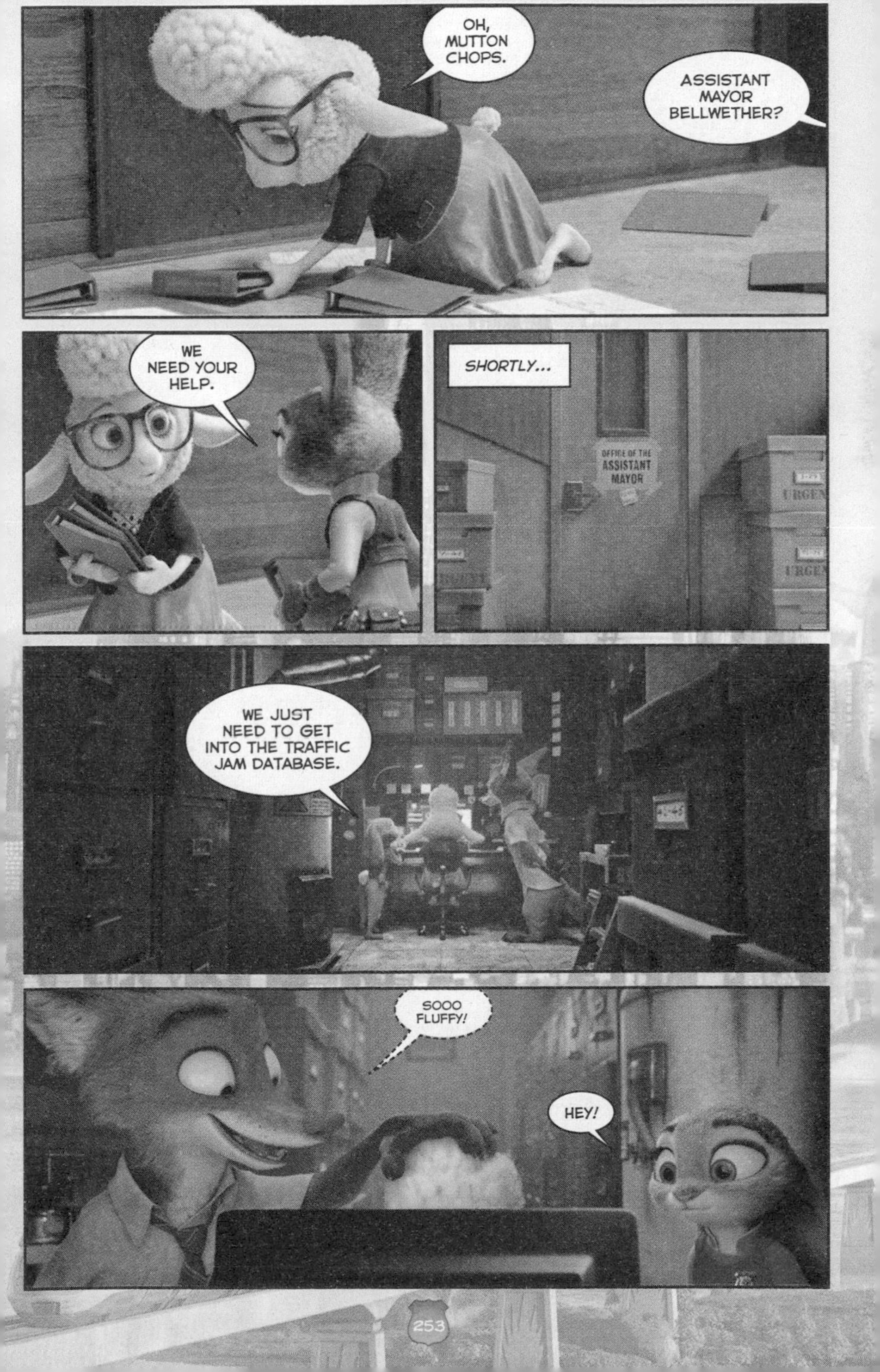
OH, MUTTON CHOPS.
ASSISTANT MAYOR BELLWETHER?
WE NEED YOUR HELP.
SHORTLY...
OFFICE OF THE ASSISTANT MAYOR
WE JUST NEED TO GET INTO THE TRAFFIC JAM DATABASE.
SOOO FLUFFY!
HEY!

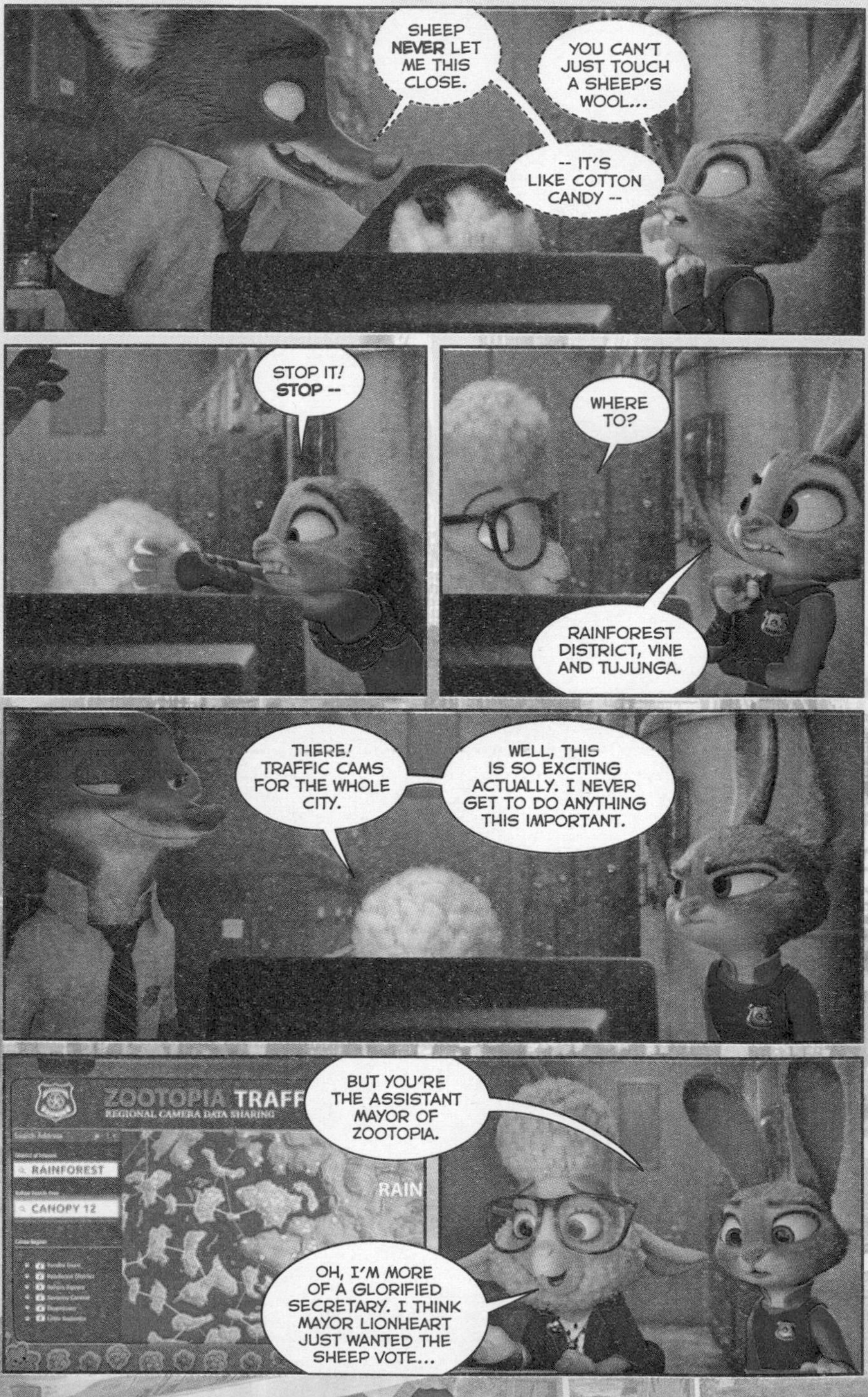
SHEEP NEVER LET ME THIS CLOSE.
YOU CAN'T JUST TOUCH A SHEEP'S WOOL...
-- IT'S LIKE COTTON CANDY --
STOP IT! STOP --
WHERE TO?
RAINFOREST DISTRICT, VINE AND TUJUNGA.
THERE! TRAFFIC CAMS FOR THE WHOLE CITY.
WELL, THIS IS SO EXCITING ACTUALLY. I NEVER GET TO DO ANYTHING THIS IMPORTANT.
ZOOTOPIA TRAFF
REGIONAL CAMERA DATA SHARING
RAINFOREST
CANOPY 12
RAIN
BUT YOU'RE THE ASSISTANT MAYOR OF ZOOTOPIA.
OH, I'M MORE OF A GLORIFIED SECRETARY. I THINK MAYOR LIONHEART JUST WANTED THE SHEEP VOTE...

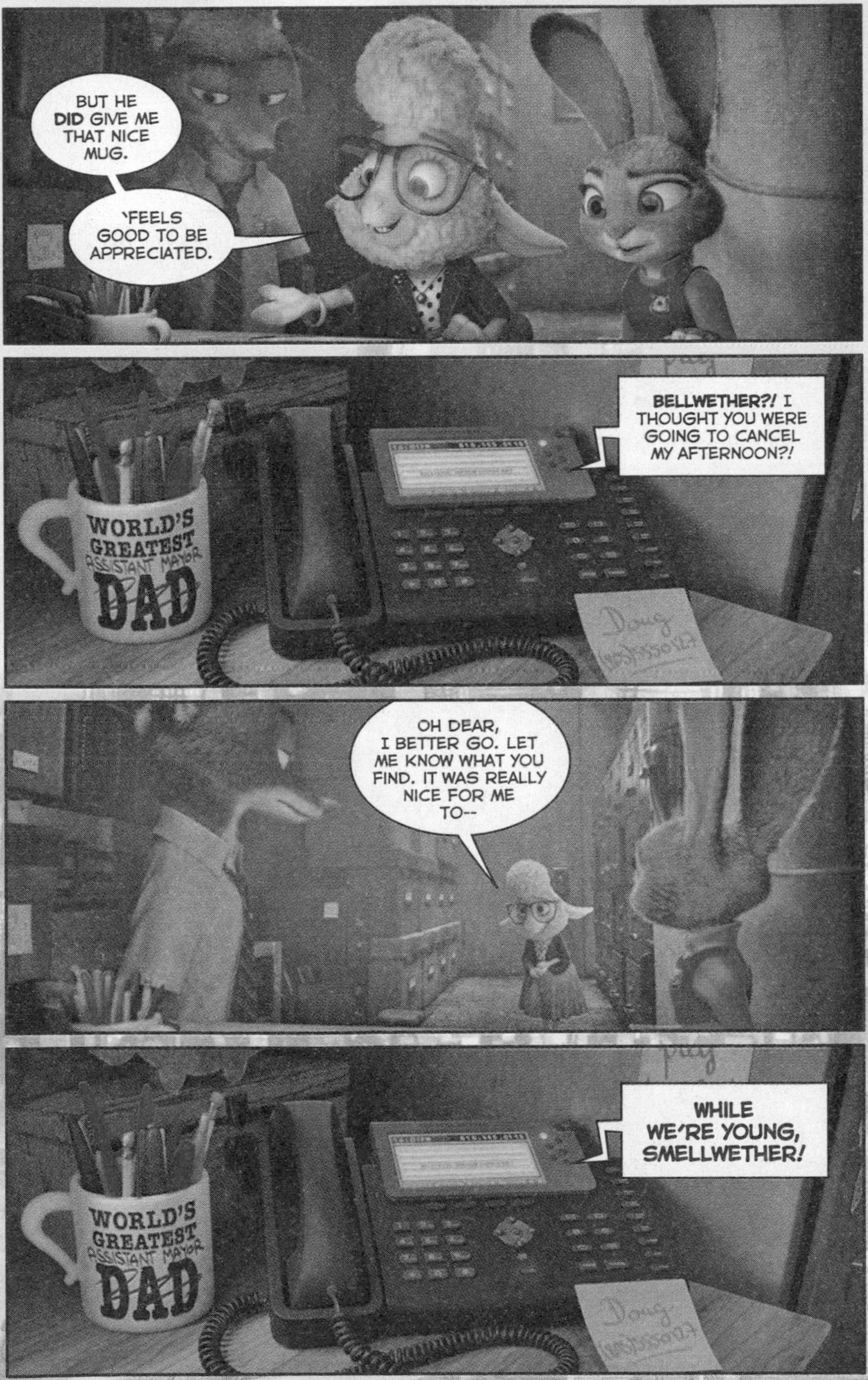
BUT HE DID GIVE ME THAT NICE MUG.
'FEELS GOOD TO BE APPRECIATED.
BELLWETHER?! I THOUGHT YOU WERE GOING TO CANCEL MY AFTERNOON?!
WORLD'S GREATEST ASSISTANT MAYOR DAD
OH DEAR, I BETTER GO. LET ME KNOW WHAT YOU FIND. IT WAS REALLY NICE FOR ME TO--
WHILE WE'RE YOUNG, SMELLWETHER!
WORLD'S GREATEST ASSISTANT MAYOR DAD

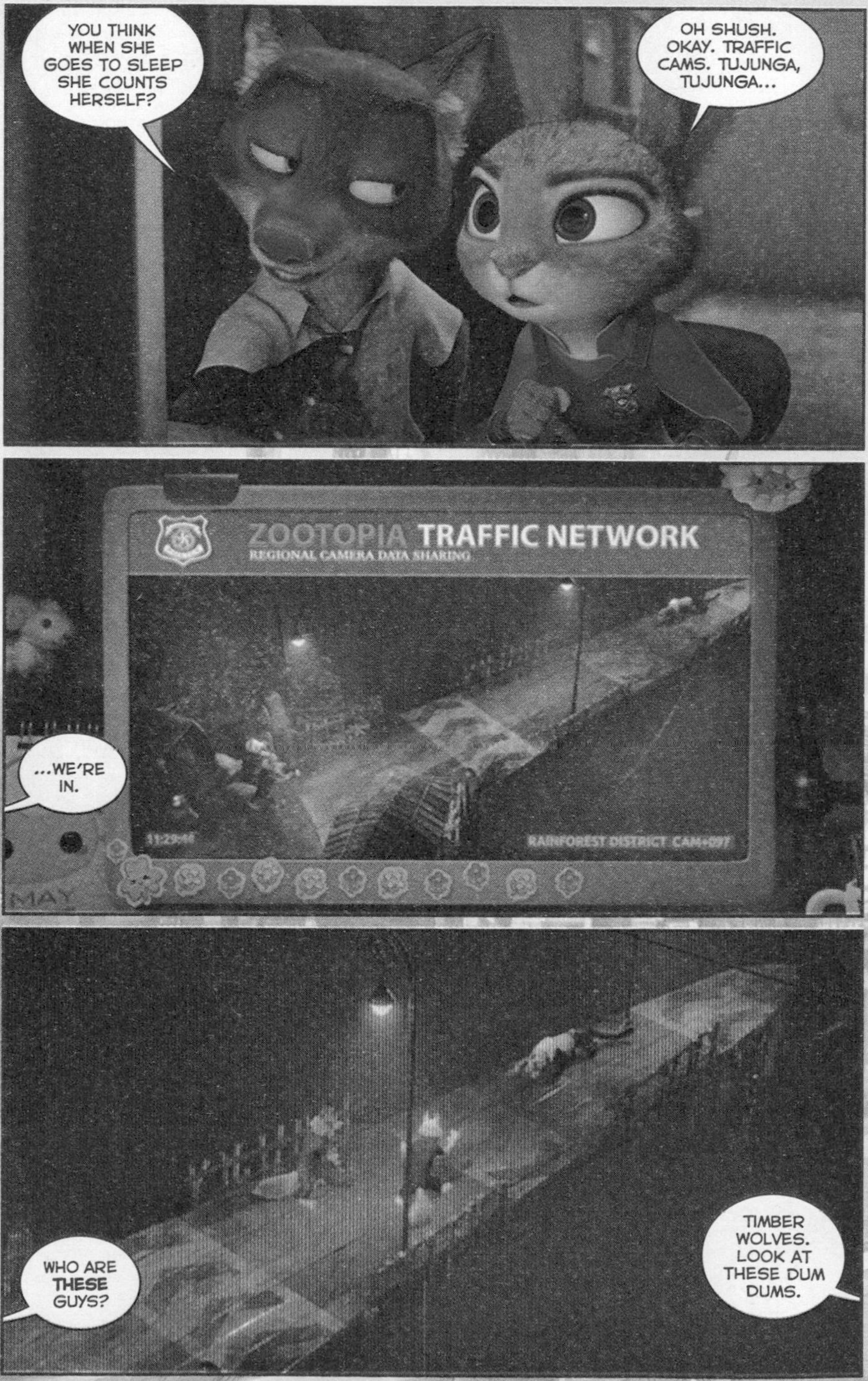
YOU THINK WHEN SHE GOES TO SLEEP SHE COUNTS HERSELF?
OH SHUSH. OKAY. TRAFFIC CAMS. TUJUNGA, TUJUNGA...
ZOOTOPIA TRAFFIC NETWORK
REGIONAL CAMERA DATA SHARING
...WE'RE IN.
WHO ARE **THESE** GUYS?
TIMBER WOLVES. LOOK AT THESE DUM DUMS.

BETCHA A NICKEL ONE OF 'EM'S GONNA HOWL.
OOOOOOOOO!
THERE IT IS. WHAT IS **WITH** WOLVES AND HOWLING?
HOWLERS. **NIGHT HOWLERS!**
THAT'S WHAT MANCHAS WAS AFRAID OF... **WOLVES!** THE WOLVES ARE THE NIGHT HOWLERS! IF THEY TOOK MANCHAS...
I BET THEY TOOK OTTERTON TOO!

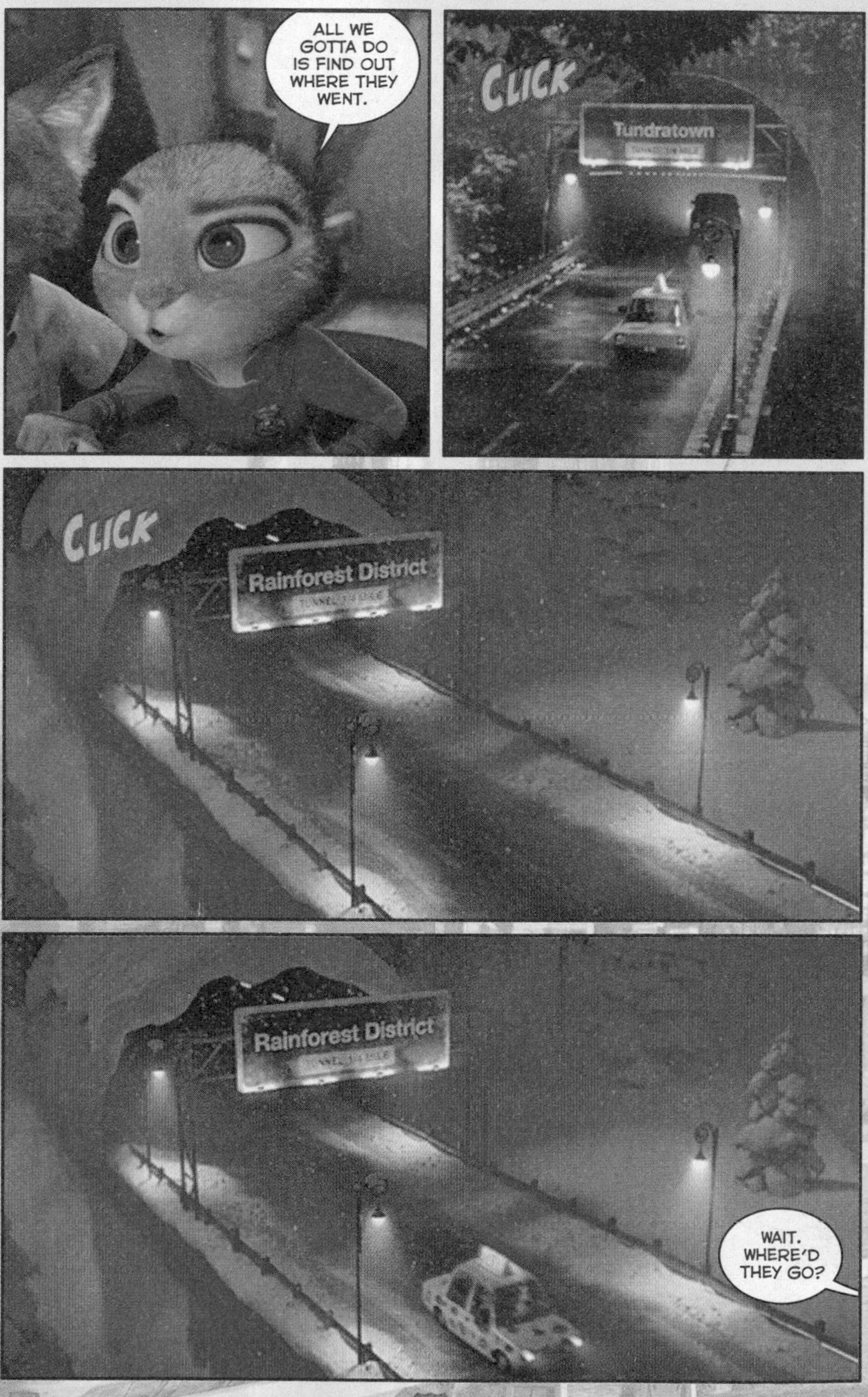
ALL WE GOTTA DO IS FIND OUT WHERE THEY WENT.
CLICK
Tundratown
CLICK
Rainforest District
Rainforest District
WAIT. WHERE'D THEY GO?

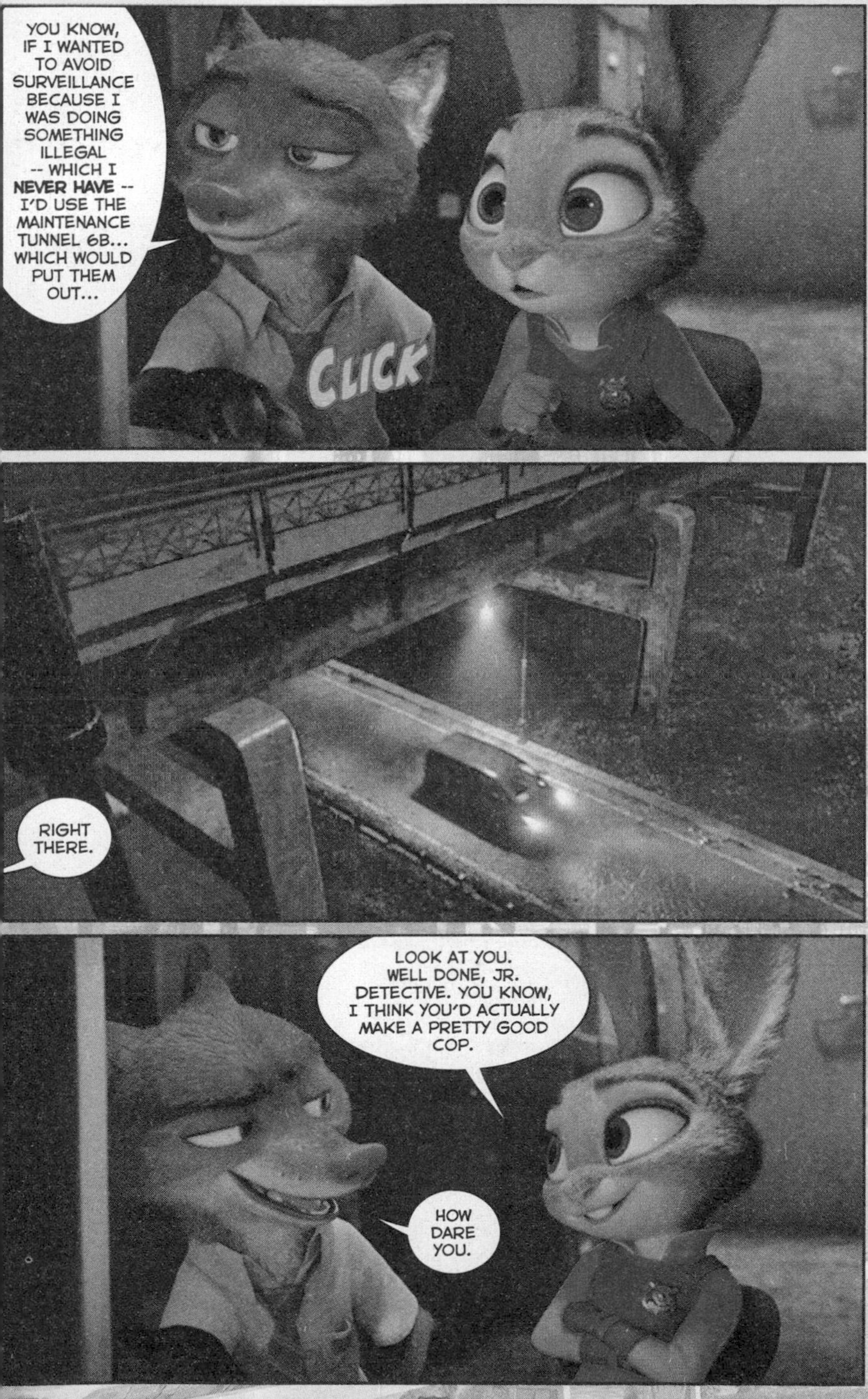
YOU KNOW, IF I WANTED TO AVOID SURVEILLANCE BECAUSE I WAS DOING SOMETHING ILLEGAL -- WHICH I NEVER HAVE -- I'D USE THE MAINTENANCE TUNNEL 6B... WHICH WOULD PUT THEM OUT...
CLICK
RIGHT THERE.
LOOK AT YOU. WELL DONE, JR. DETECTIVE. YOU KNOW, I THINK YOU'D ACTUALLY MAKE A PRETTY GOOD COP.
HOW DARE YOU.

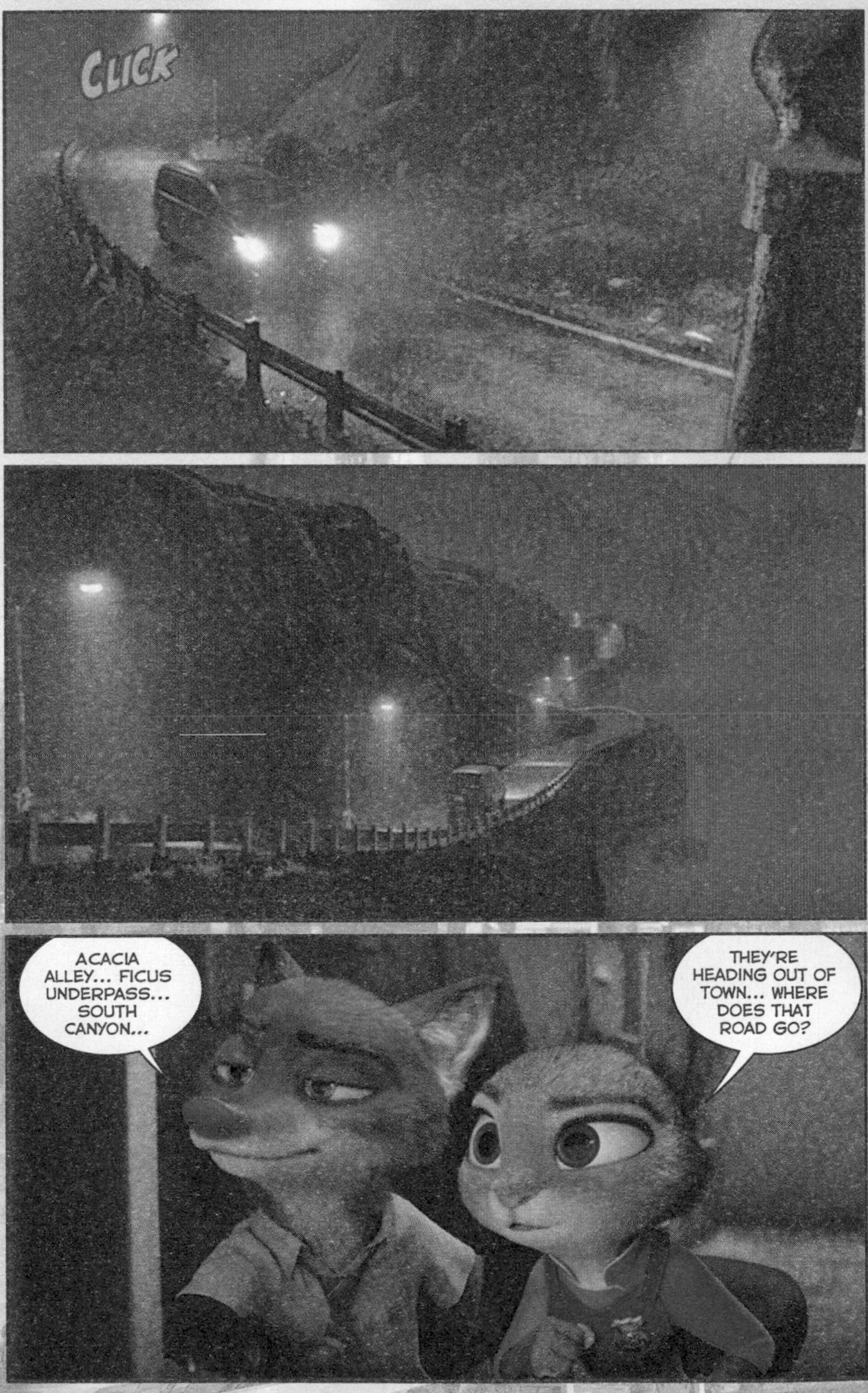
CLICK
ACACIA ALLEY... FICUS UNDERPASS... SOUTH CANYON...
THEY'RE HEADING OUT OF TOWN... WHERE DOES THAT ROAD GO?

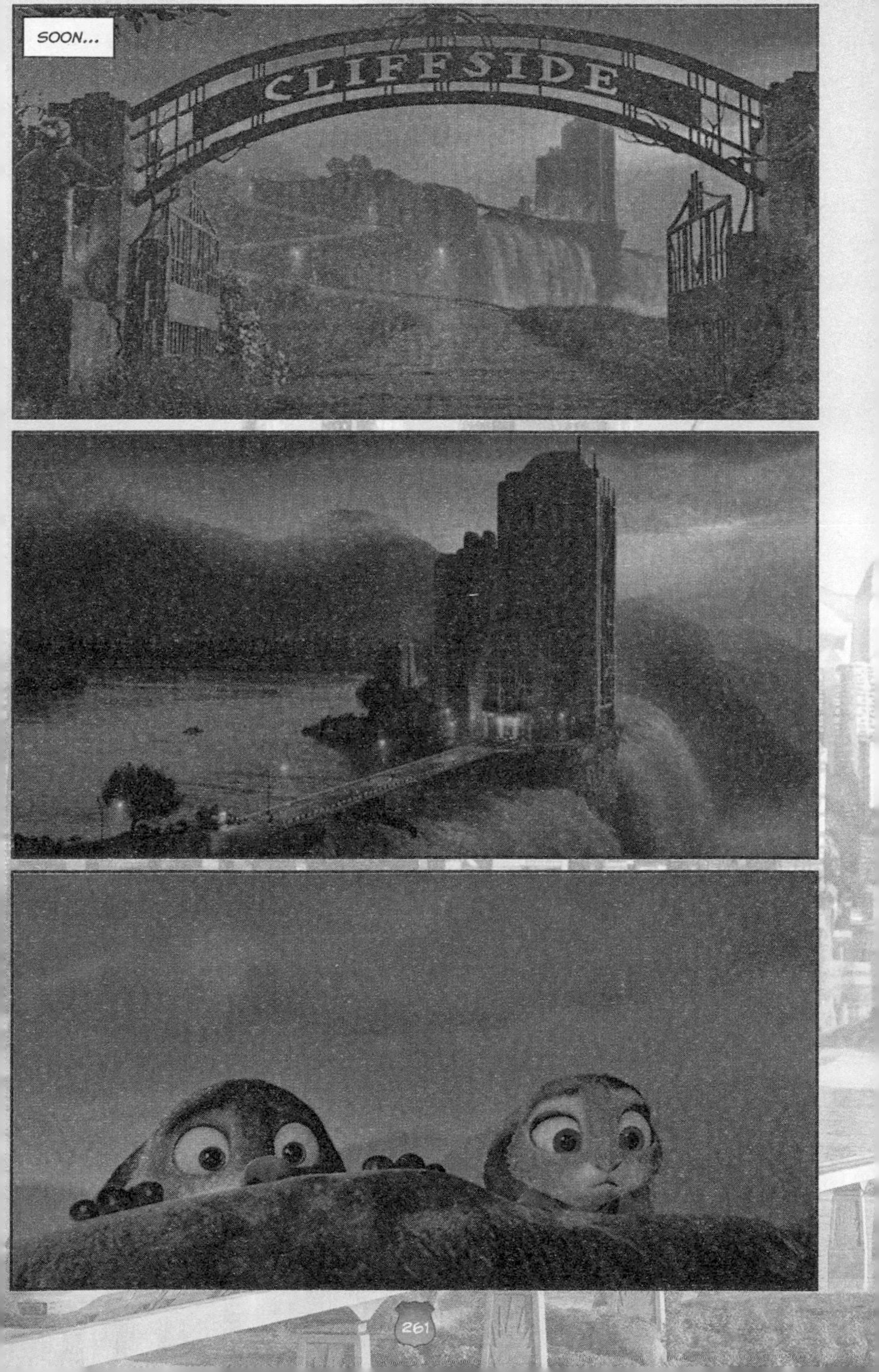
SOON...
CLIFFSIDE

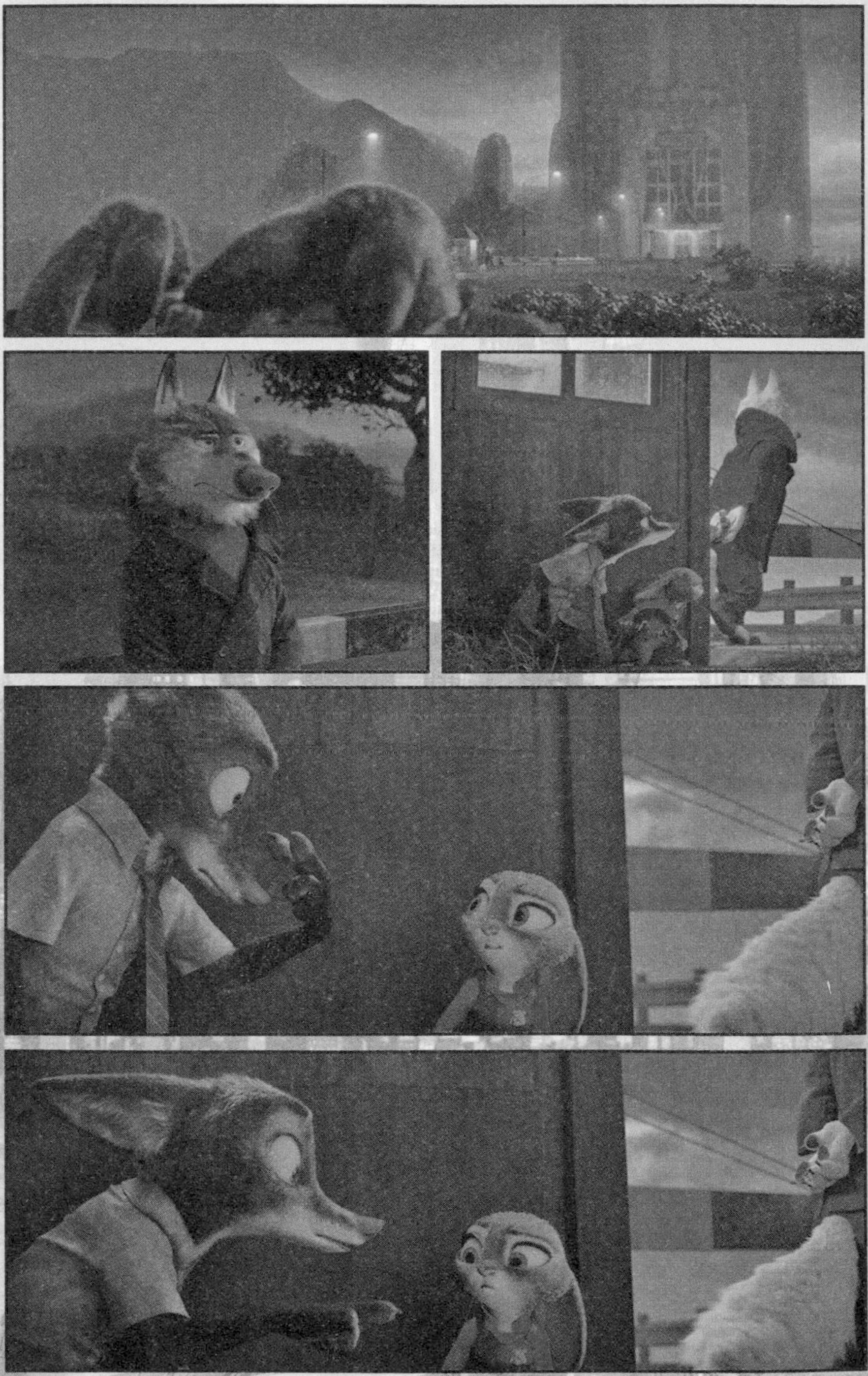

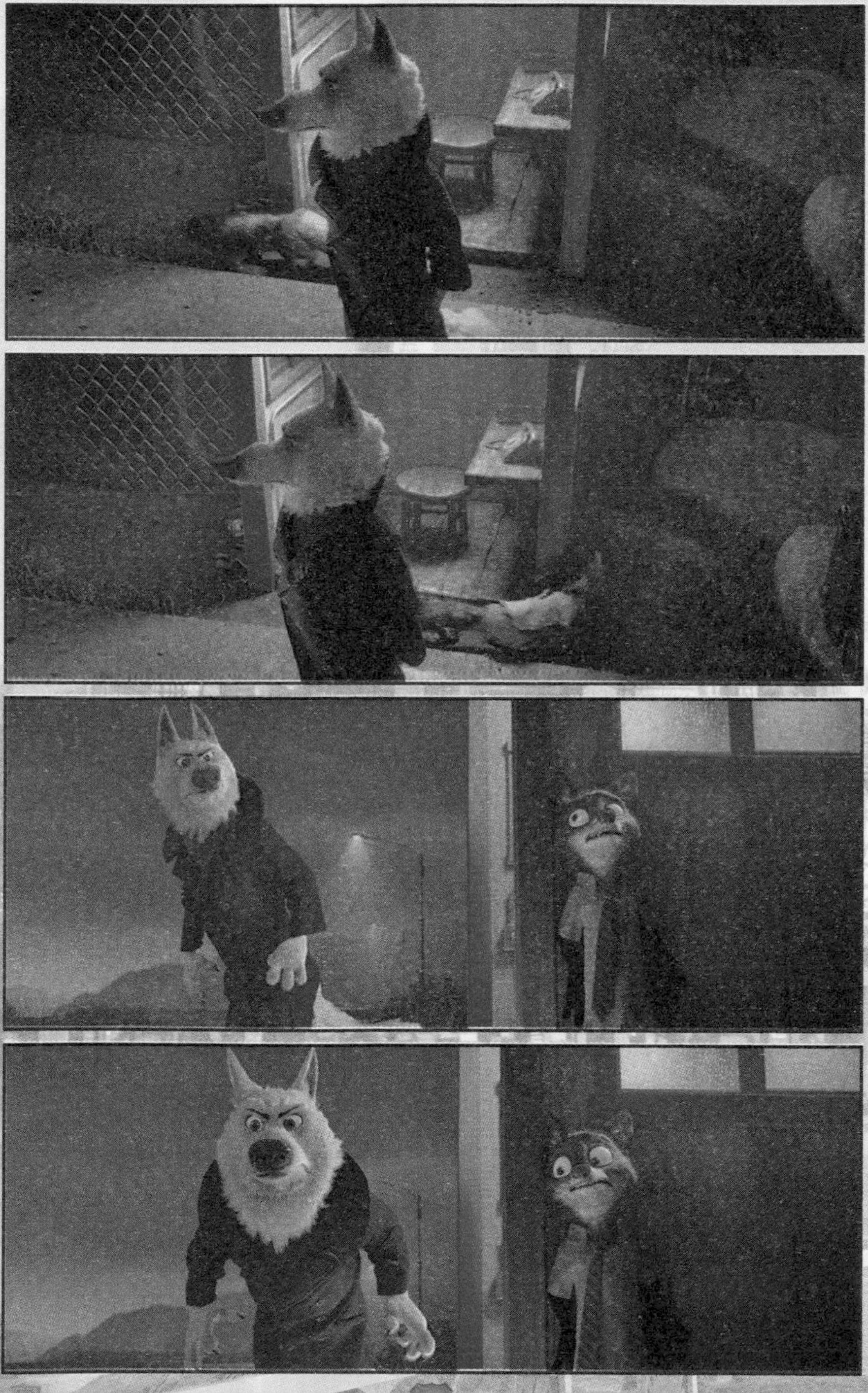

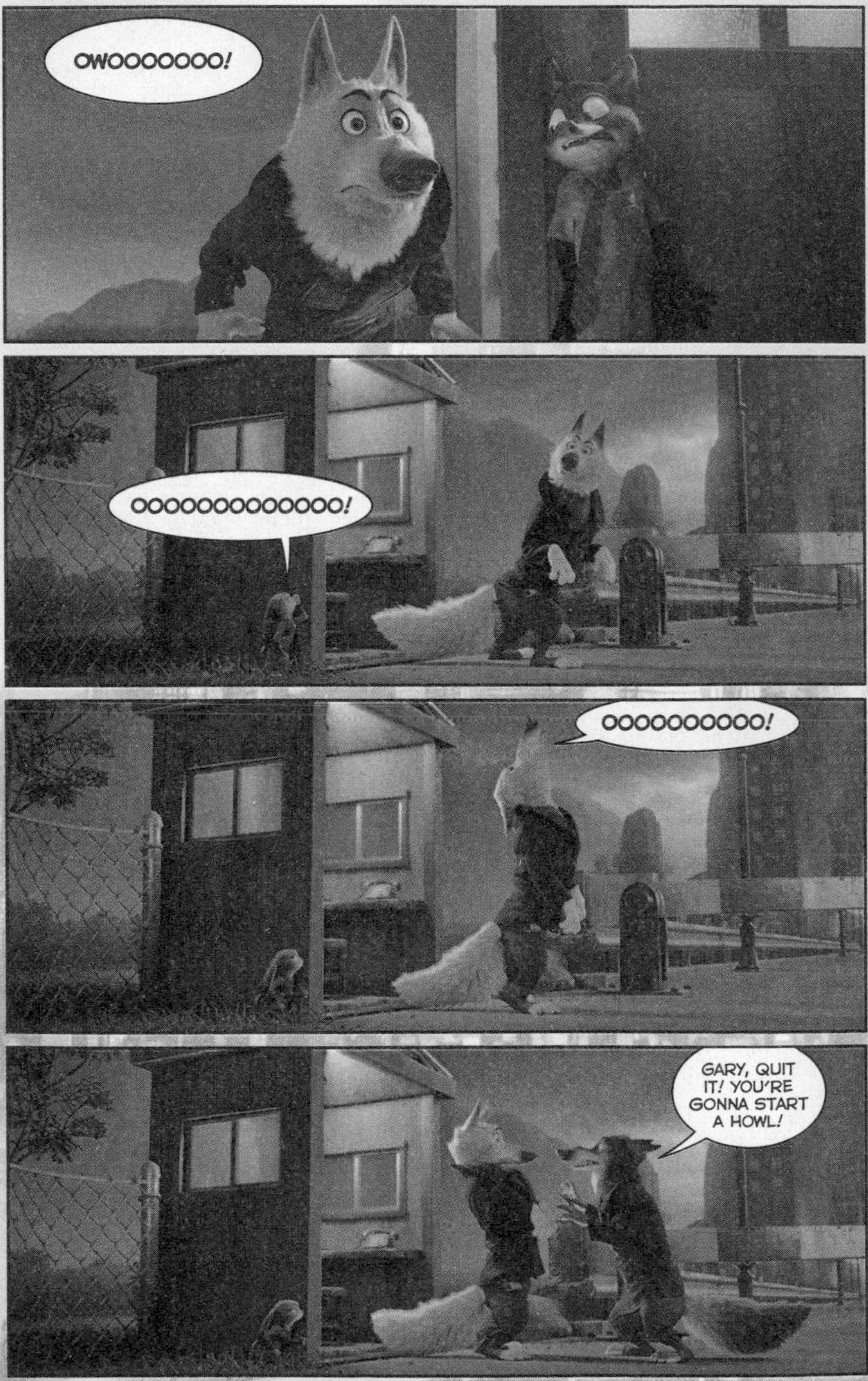
OWOOOOOOO!
OOOOOOOOOOOOOO!
OOOOOOOOOOO!
GARY, QUIT IT! YOU'RE GONNA START A HOWL!

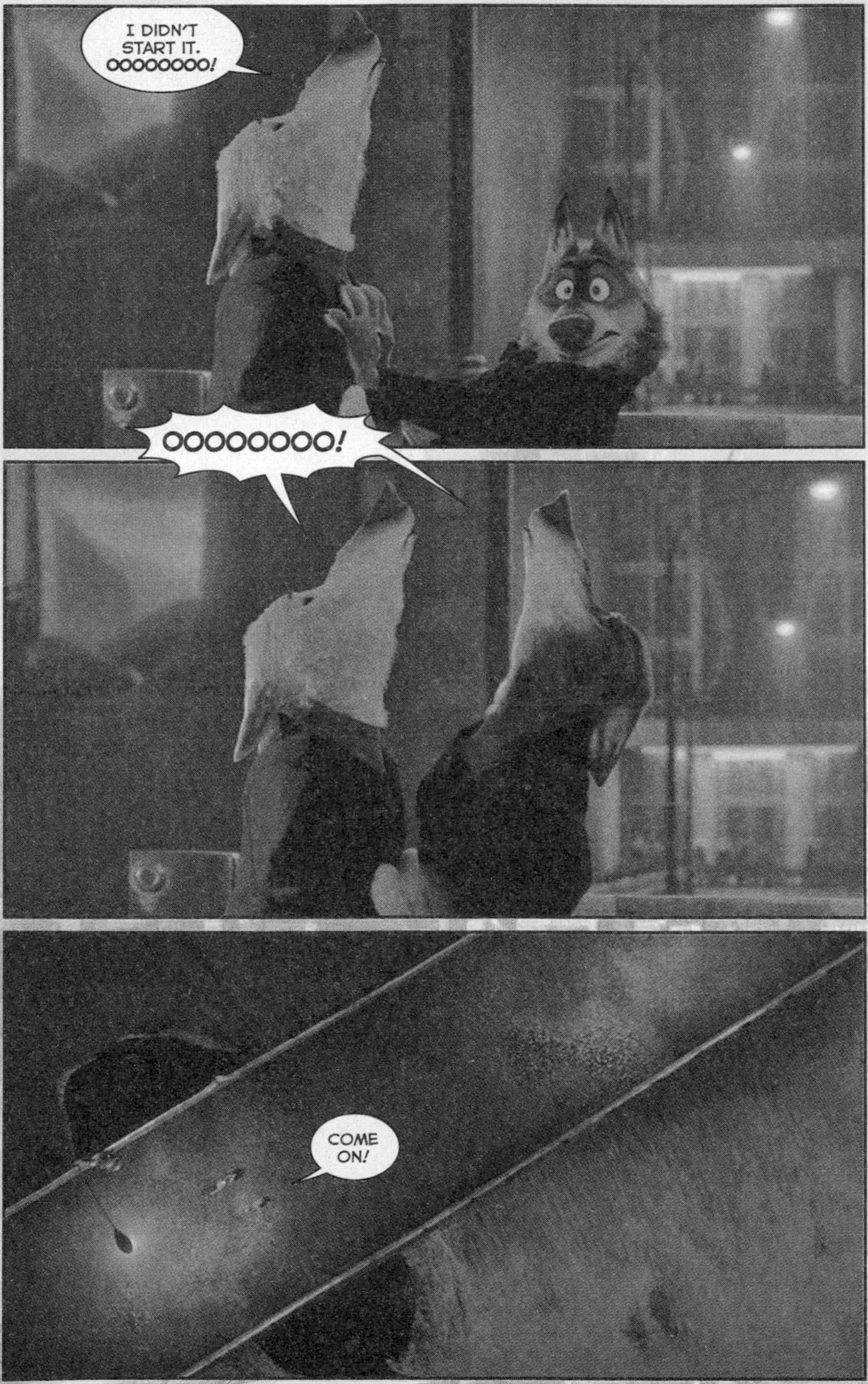
I DIDN'T START IT. OOOOOOOO!
OOOOOOOO!
COME ON!

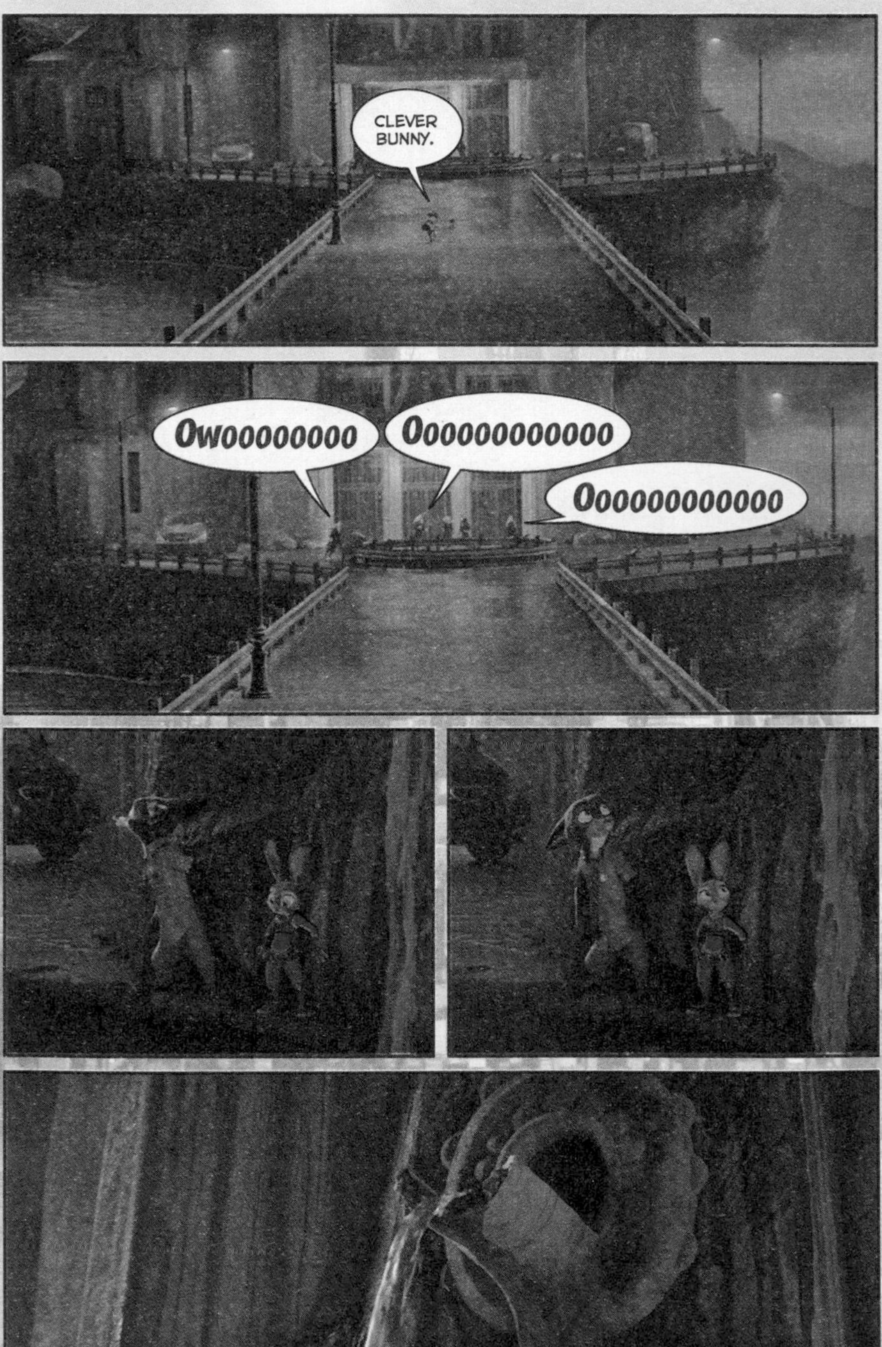
CLEVER BUNNY.
Owoooooooo
Oooooooooooo
Oooooooooooo

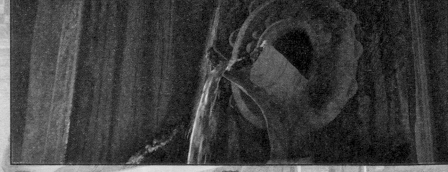

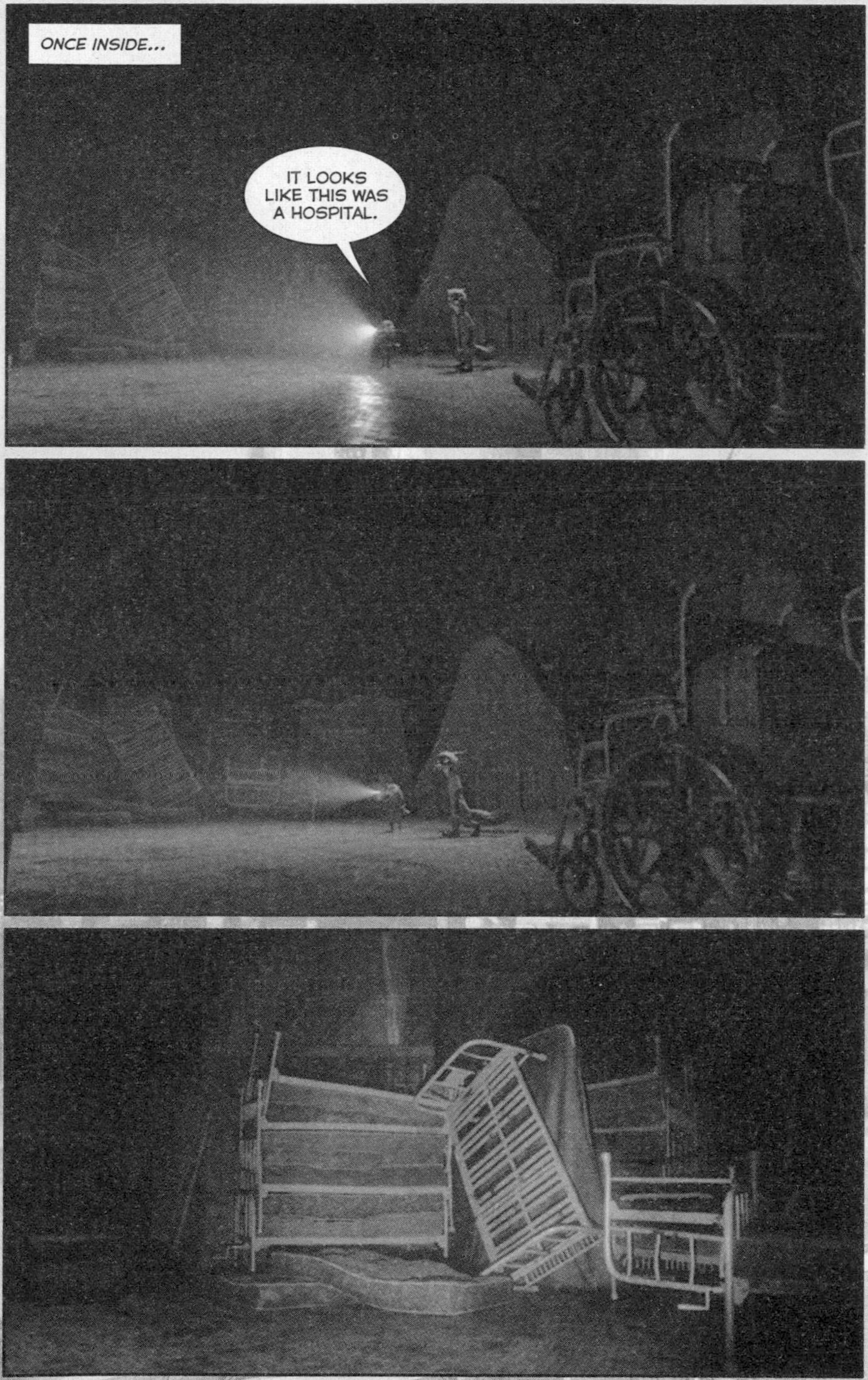
ONCE INSIDE...
IT LOOKS LIKE THIS WAS A HOSPITAL.

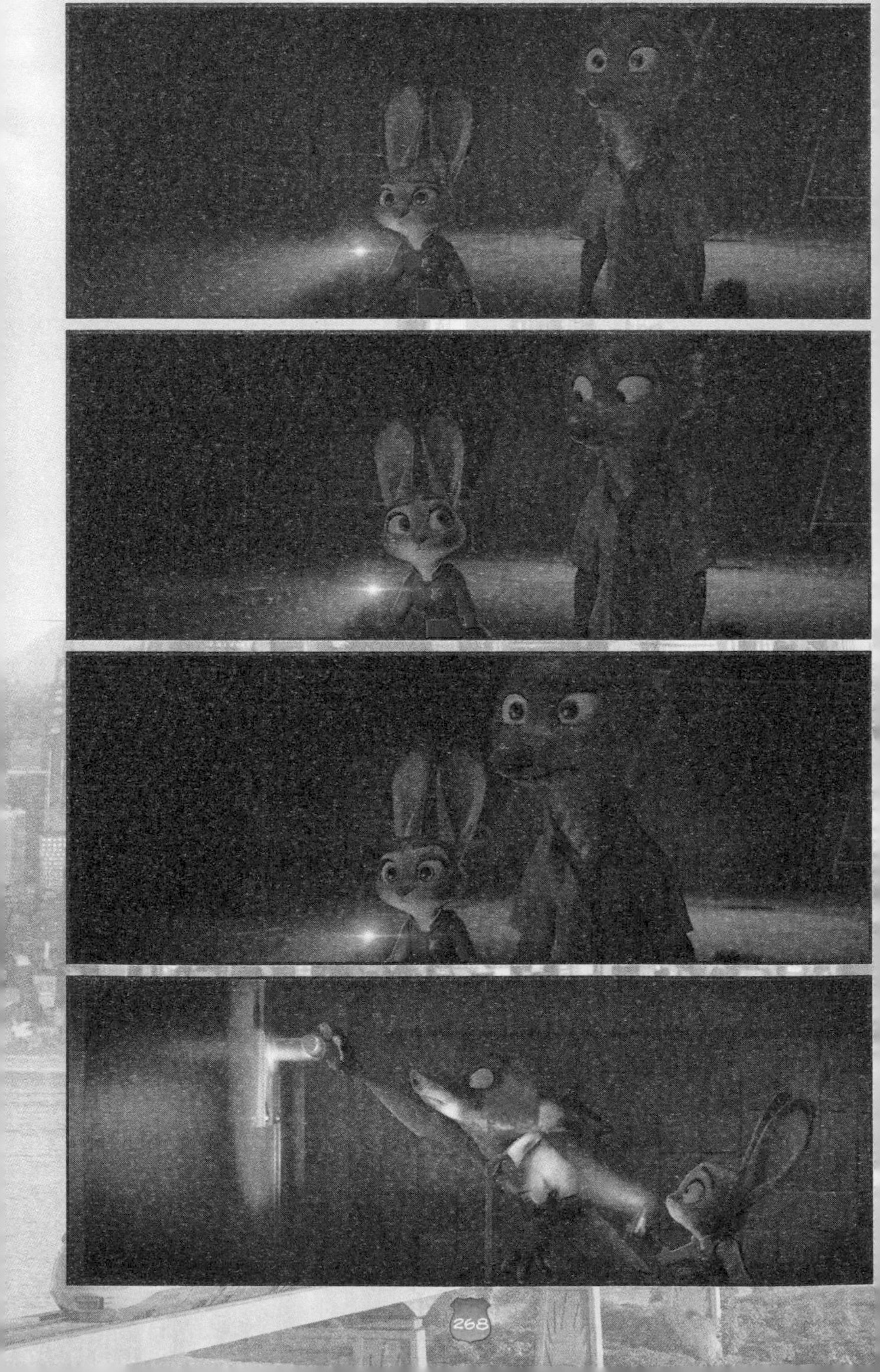

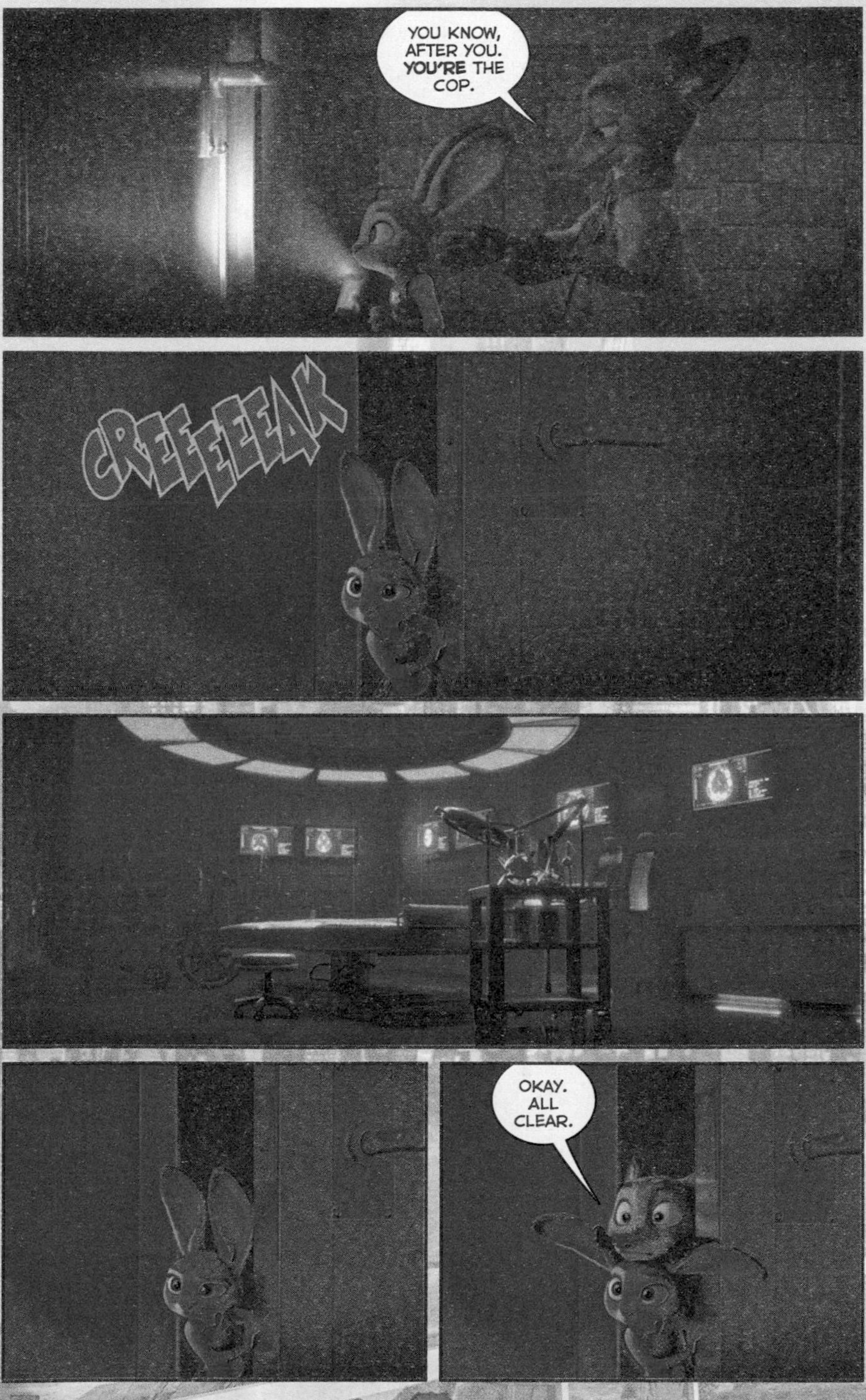
YOU KNOW, AFTER YOU. **YOU'RE** THE COP.
CREEEEEAK
OKAY. ALL CLEAR.

ALL THIS EQUIPMENT IS **BRAND** NEW...

CARROTS...?

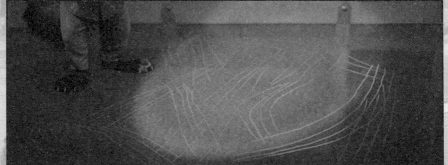

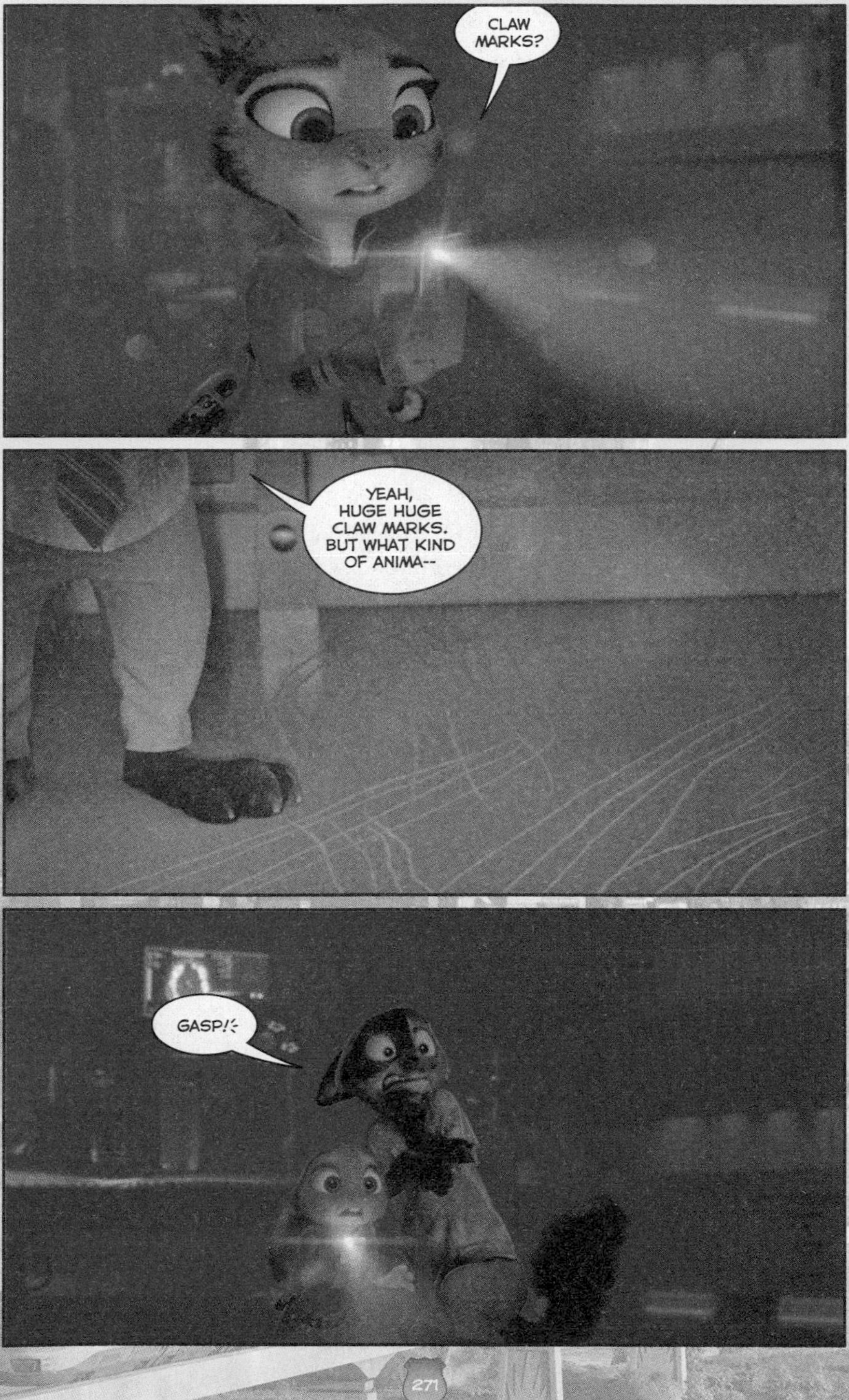
CLAW MARKS?
YEAH, HUGE HUGE CLAW MARKS. BUT WHAT KIND OF ANIMA--
GASP!

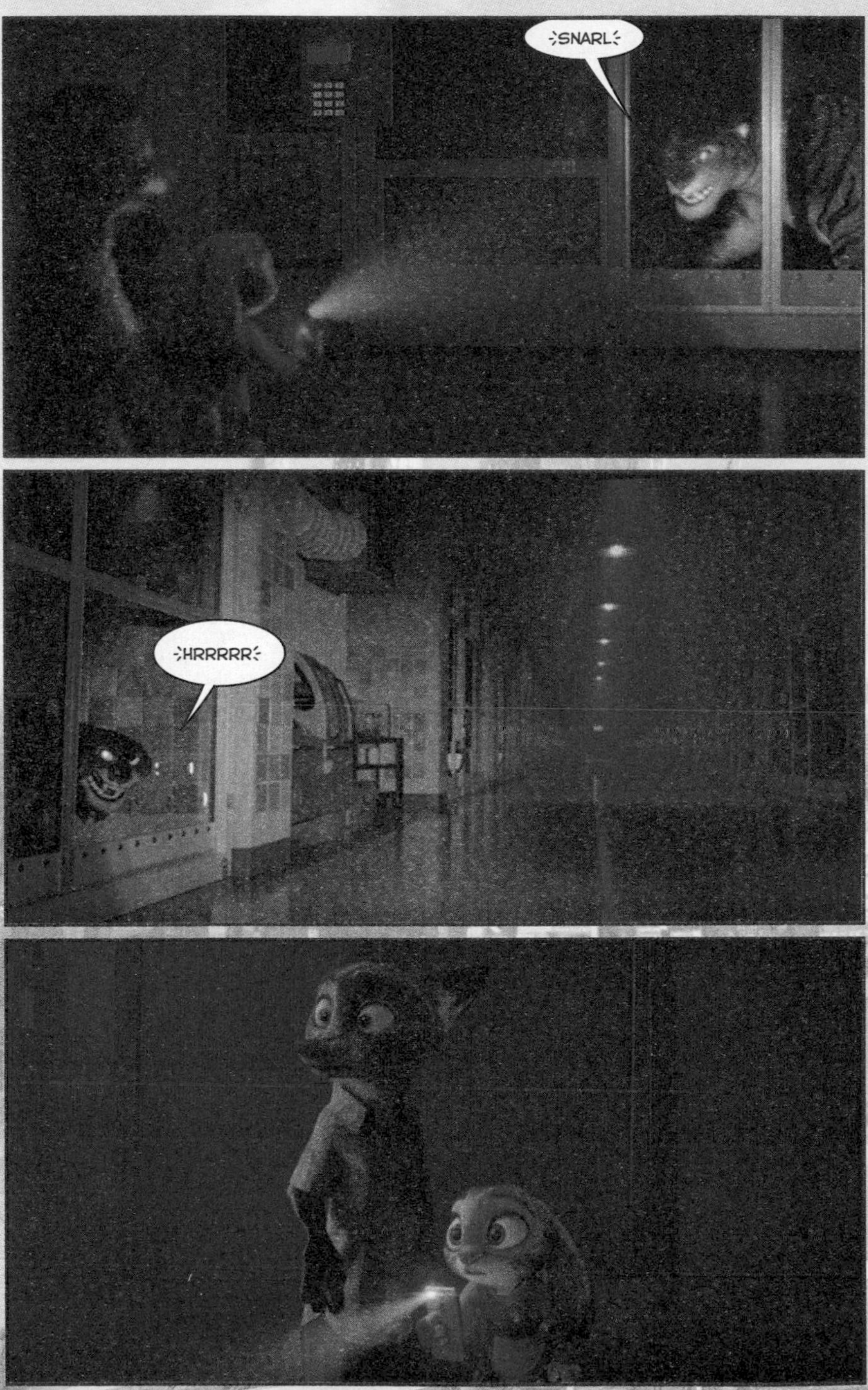
SNARL
HRRRRR

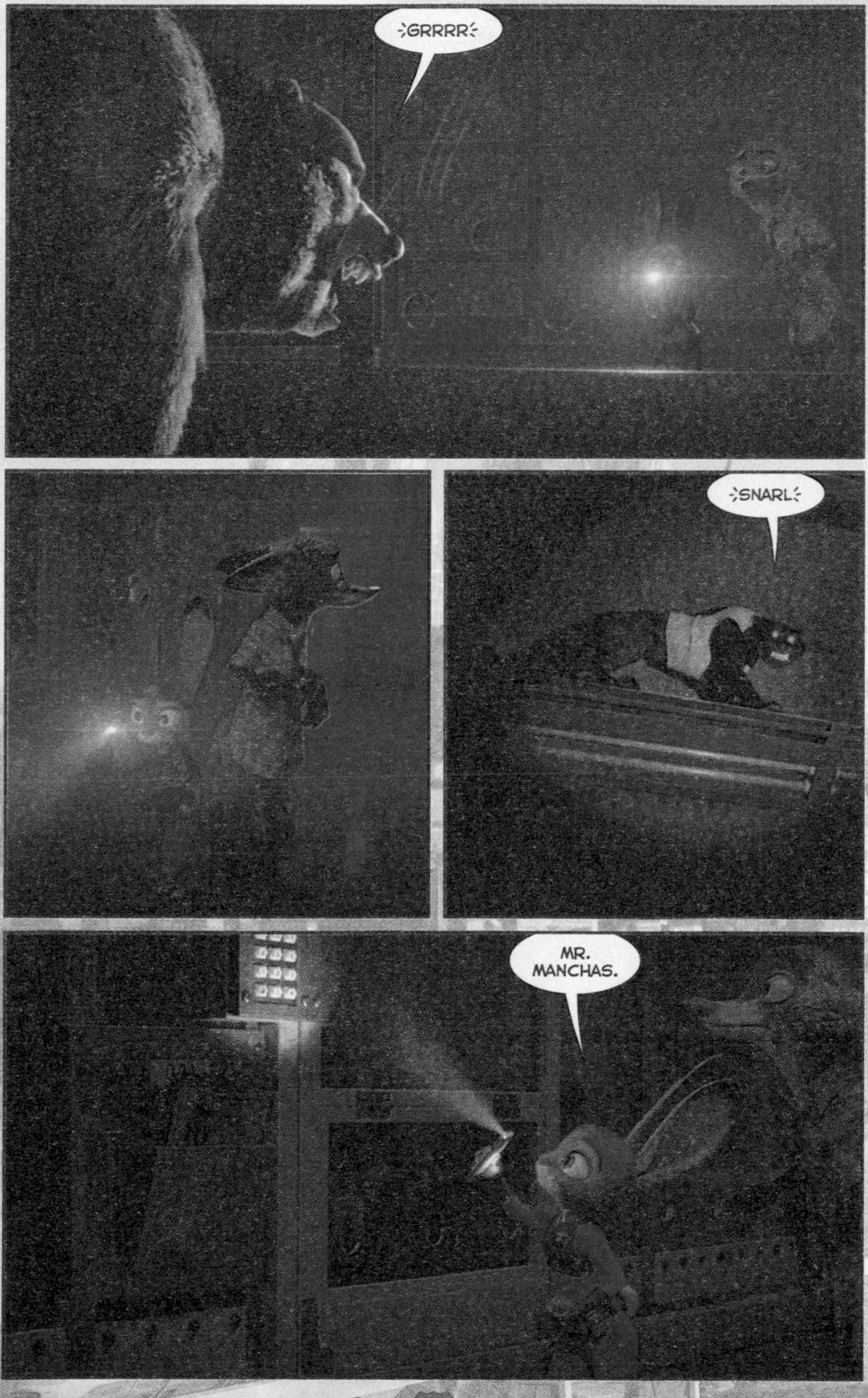
GRRRR
SNARL
MR. MANCHAS.

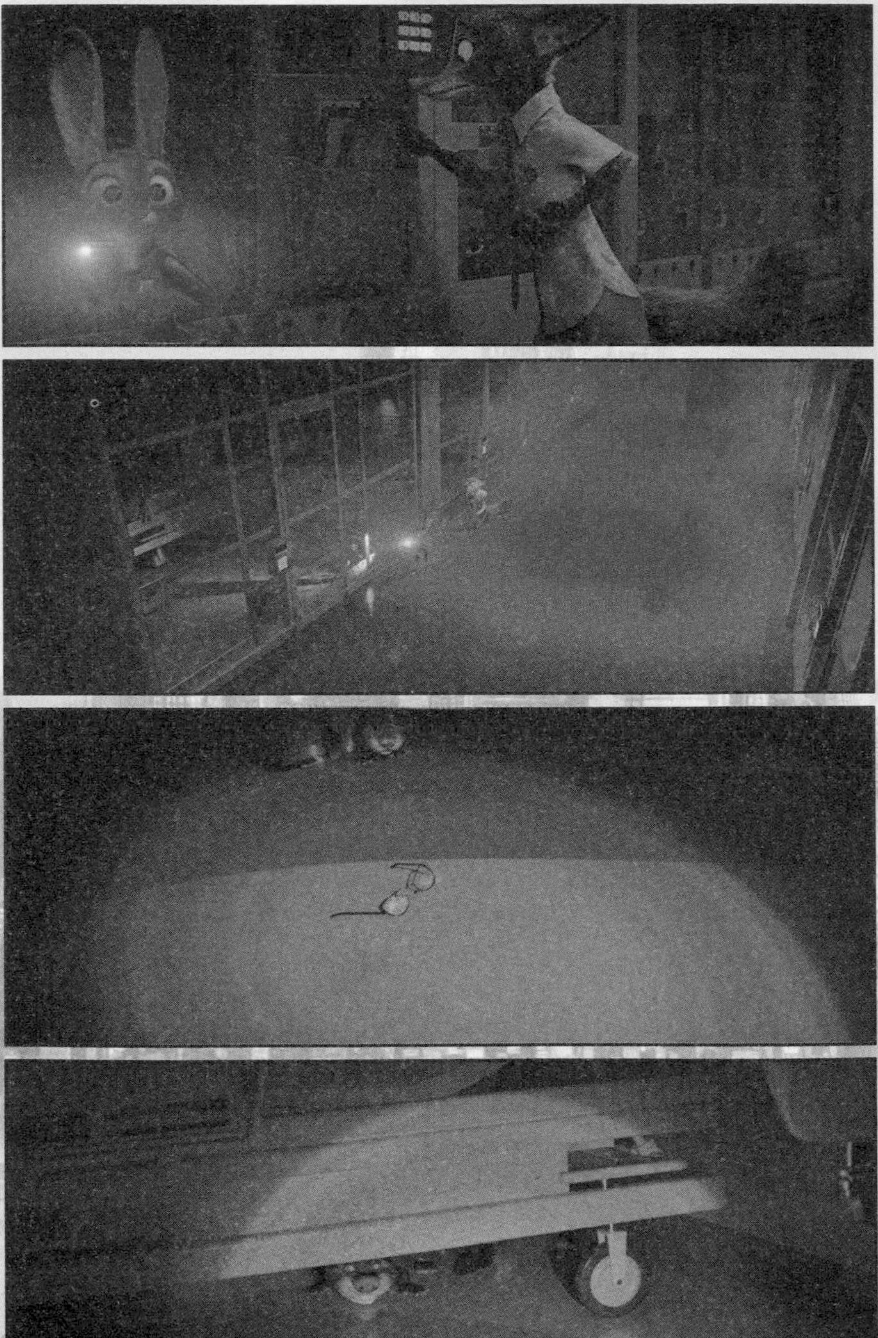

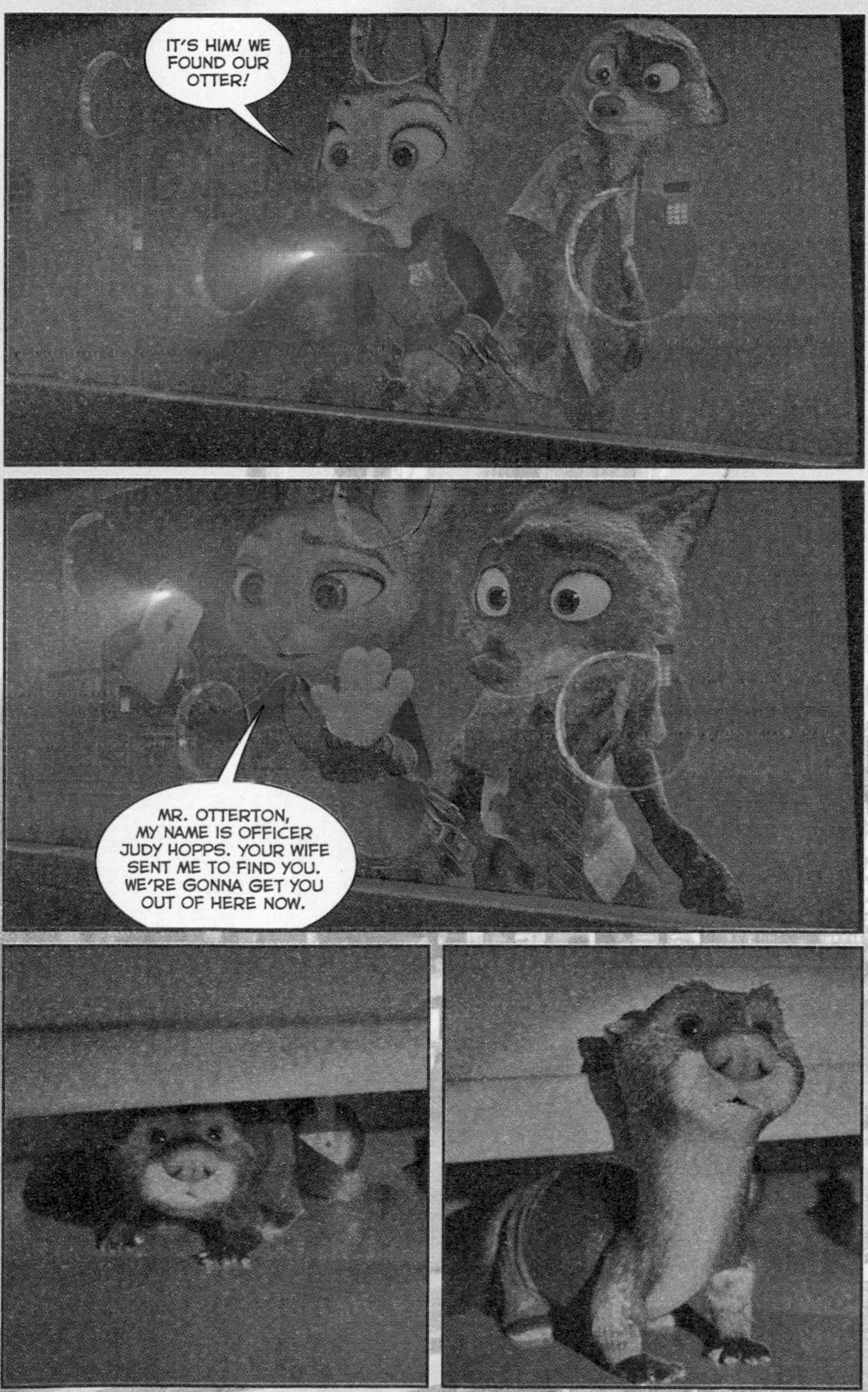
IT'S HIM! WE FOUND OUR OTTER!
MR. OTTERTON, MY NAME IS OFFICER JUDY HOPPS. YOUR WIFE SENT ME TO FIND YOU. WE'RE GONNA GET YOU OUT OF HERE NOW.

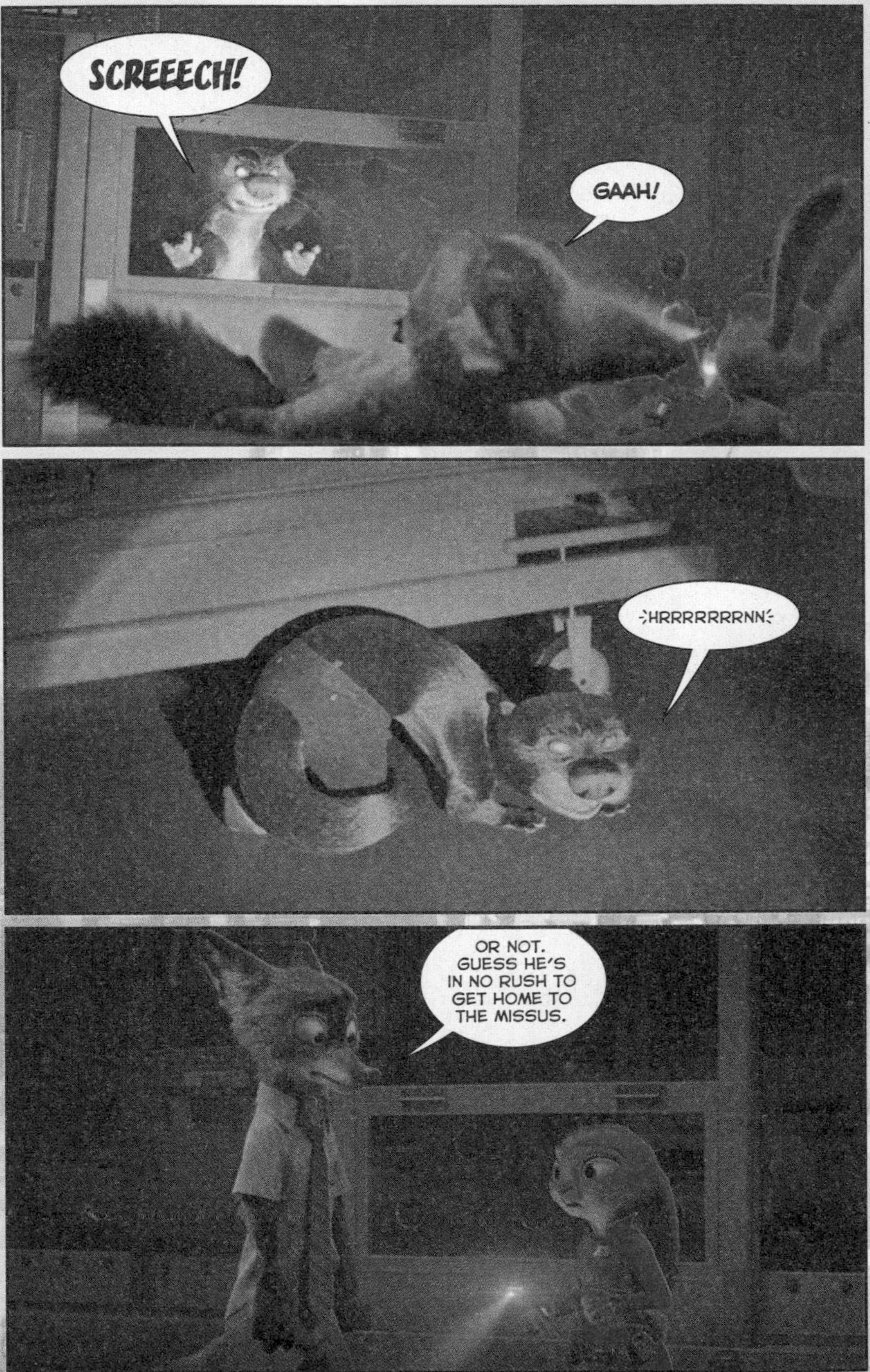
SCREEECH!
GAAH!
HRRRRRRRNN
OR NOT. GUESS HE'S IN NO RUSH TO GET HOME TO THE MISSUS.

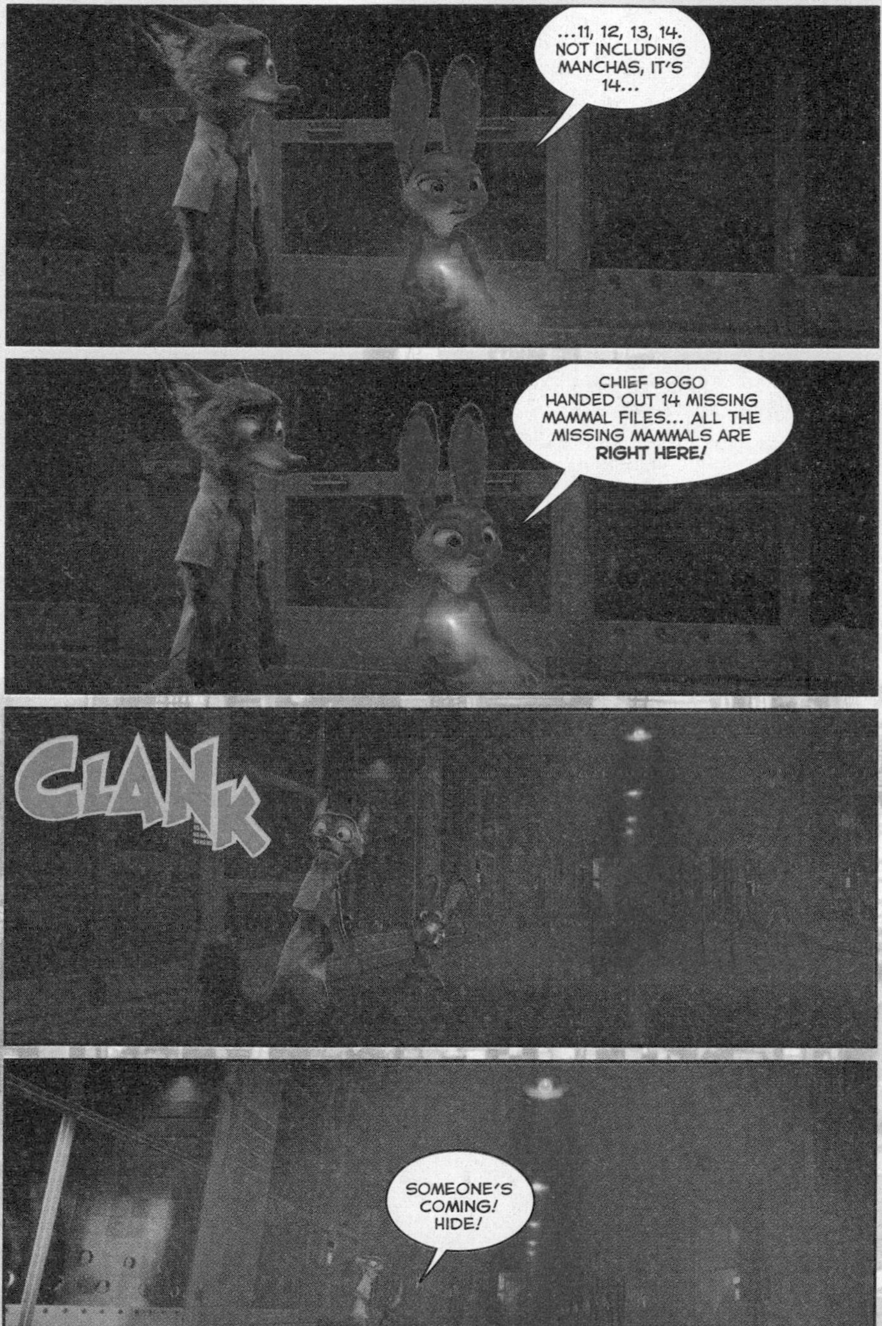
...11, 12, 13, 14. NOT INCLUDING MANCHAS, IT'S 14...
CHIEF BOGO HANDED OUT 14 MISSING MAMMAL FILES... ALL THE MISSING MAMMALS ARE **RIGHT HERE!**
CLANK
SOMEONE'S COMING! HIDE!

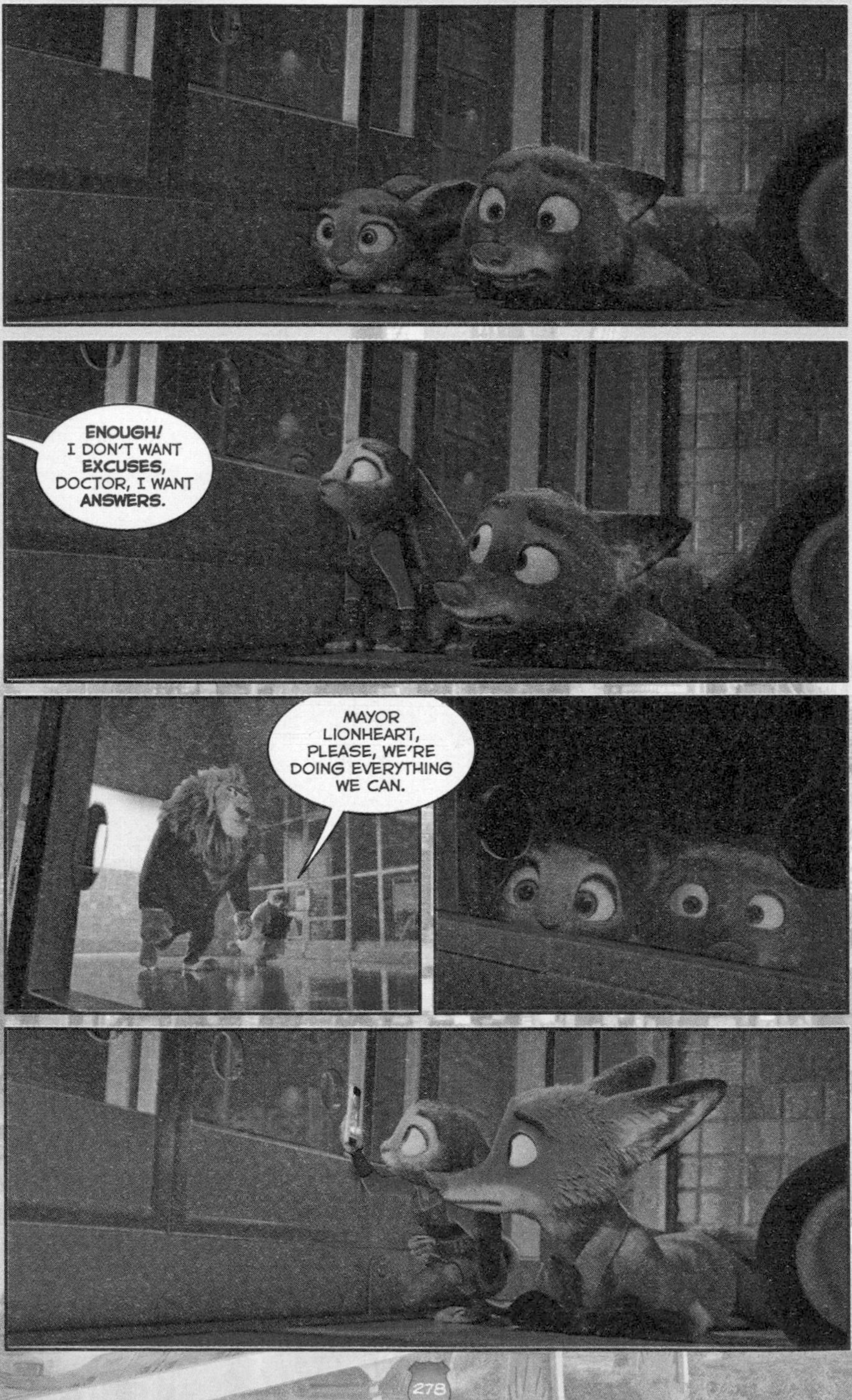
ENOUGH! I DON'T WANT EXCUSES, DOCTOR, I WANT ANSWERS.
MAYOR LIONHEART, PLEASE, WE'RE DOING EVERYTHING WE CAN.

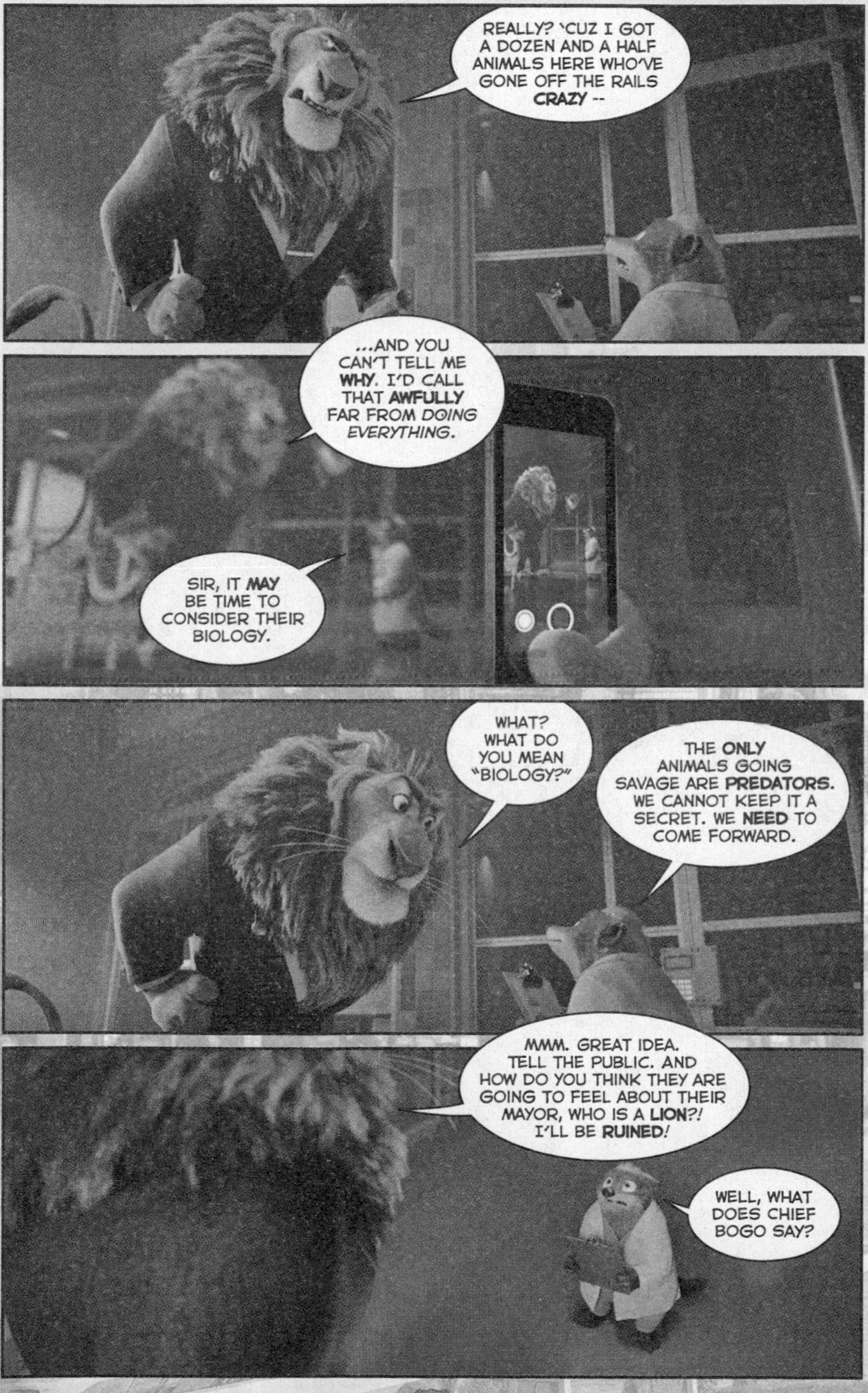
REALLY? 'CUZ I GOT A DOZEN AND A HALF ANIMALS HERE WHO'VE GONE OFF THE RAILS **CRAZY** --
...AND YOU CAN'T TELL ME **WHY**. I'D CALL THAT **AWFULLY** FAR FROM *DOING EVERYTHING*.
SIR, IT **MAY** BE TIME TO CONSIDER THEIR BIOLOGY.
WHAT? WHAT DO YOU MEAN "BIOLOGY?"
THE **ONLY** ANIMALS GOING SAVAGE ARE **PREDATORS**. WE CANNOT KEEP IT A SECRET. WE **NEED** TO COME FORWARD.
MMM. GREAT IDEA. TELL THE PUBLIC. AND HOW DO YOU THINK THEY ARE GOING TO FEEL ABOUT THEIR MAYOR, WHO IS A **LION**?! I'LL BE **RUINED**!
WELL, WHAT DOES CHIEF BOGO SAY?

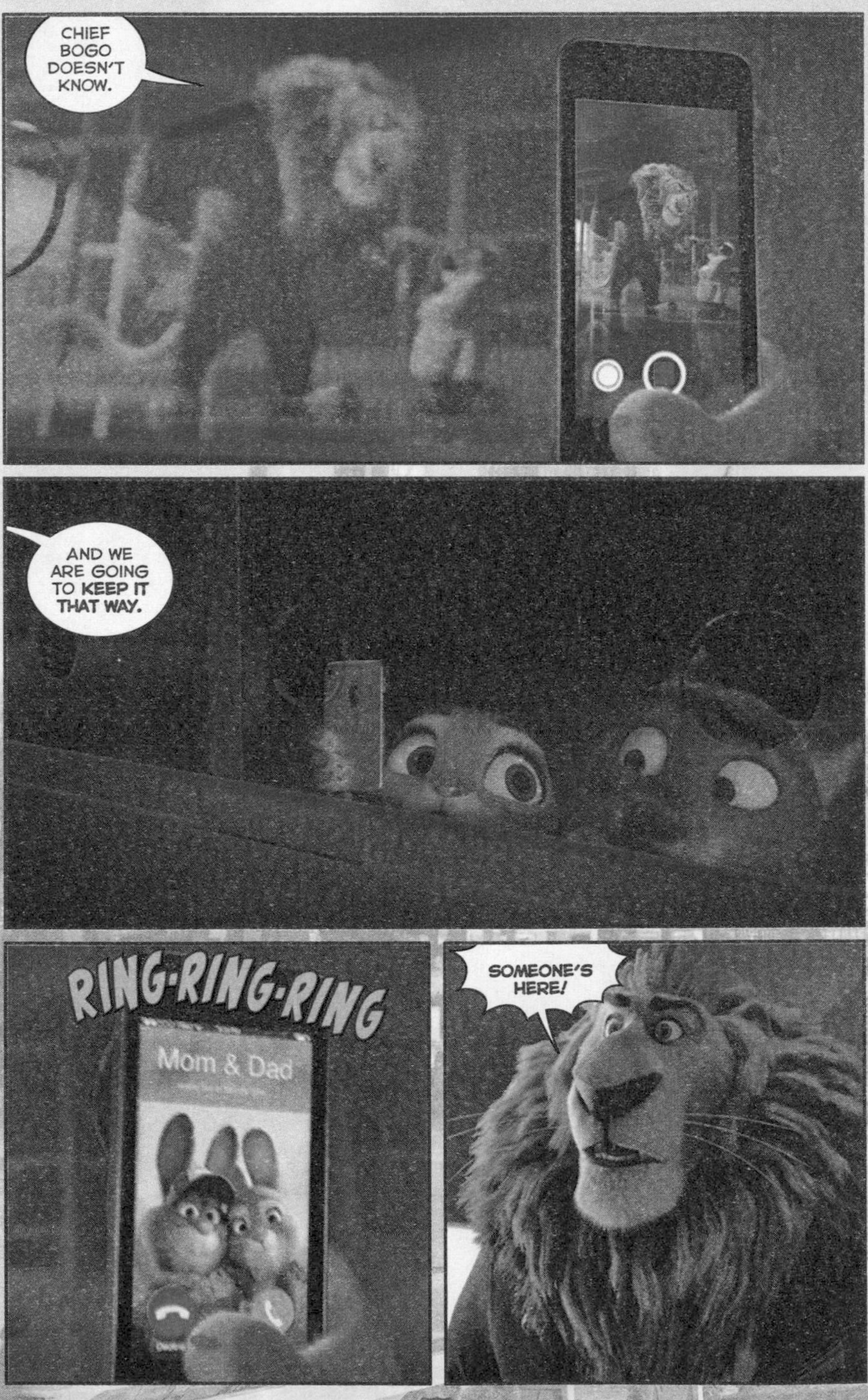
CHIEF BOGO DOESN'T KNOW.
AND WE ARE GOING TO KEEP IT THAT WAY.
RING-RING-RING
Mom & Dad
SOMEONE'S HERE!

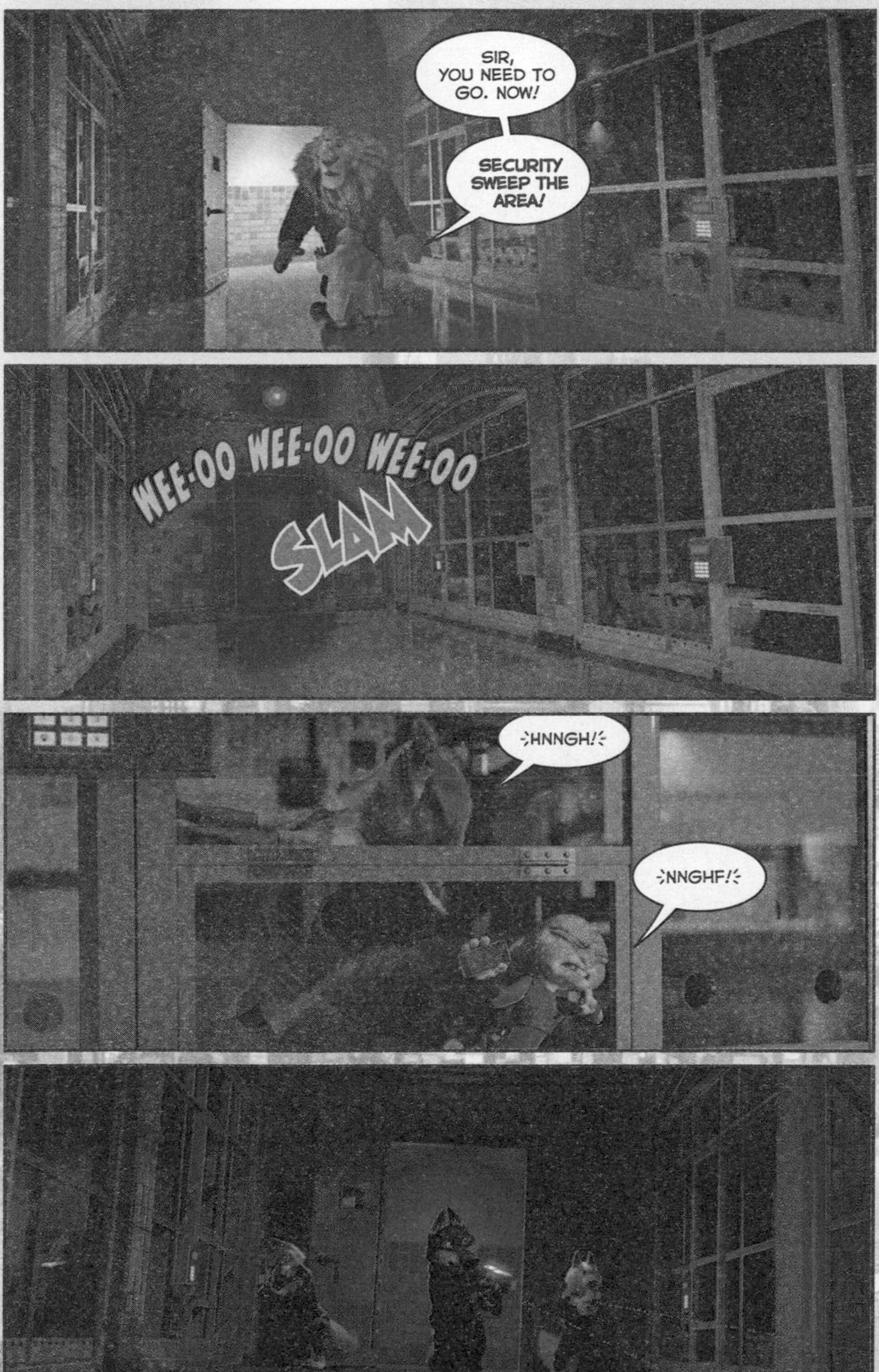
SIR, YOU NEED TO GO. NOW!
SECURITY SWEEP THE AREA!
WEE-OO WEE-OO WEE-OO
SLAM
HNNGH!
NNGHF!

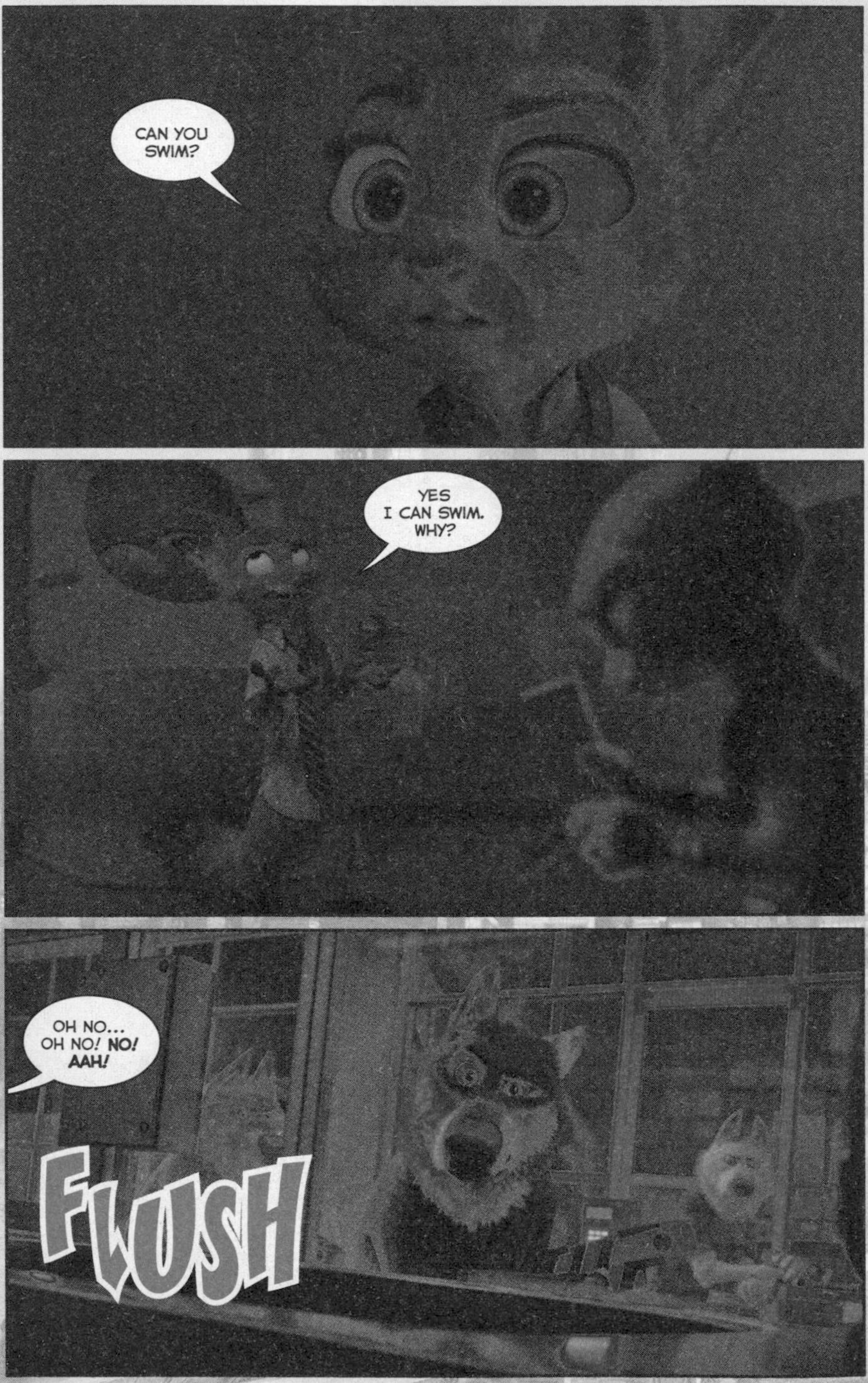
CAN YOU SWIM?
YES I CAN SWIM. WHY?
OH NO... OH NO! NO! AAH!
FLUSH

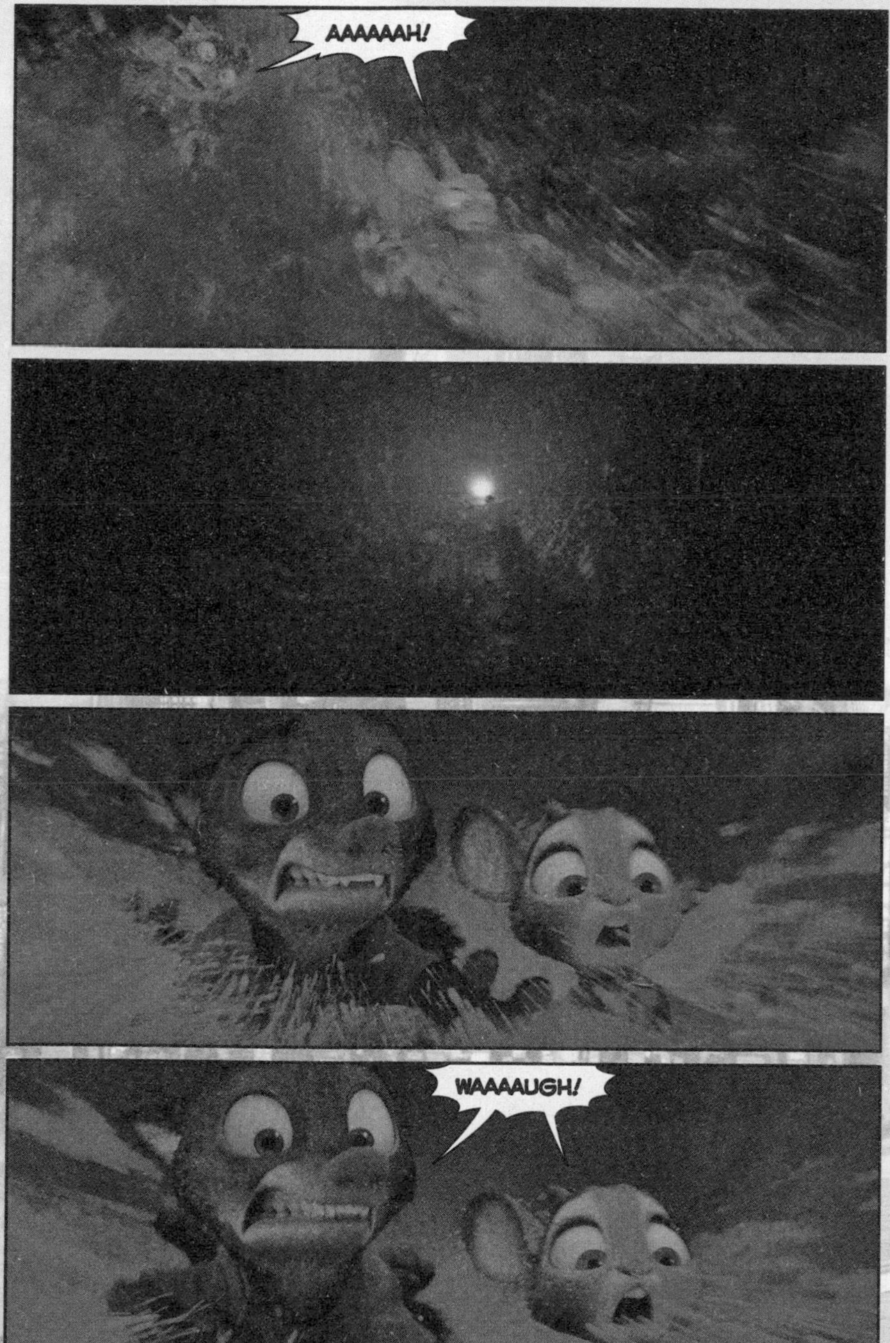
AAAAAAH!
WAAAAUGH!

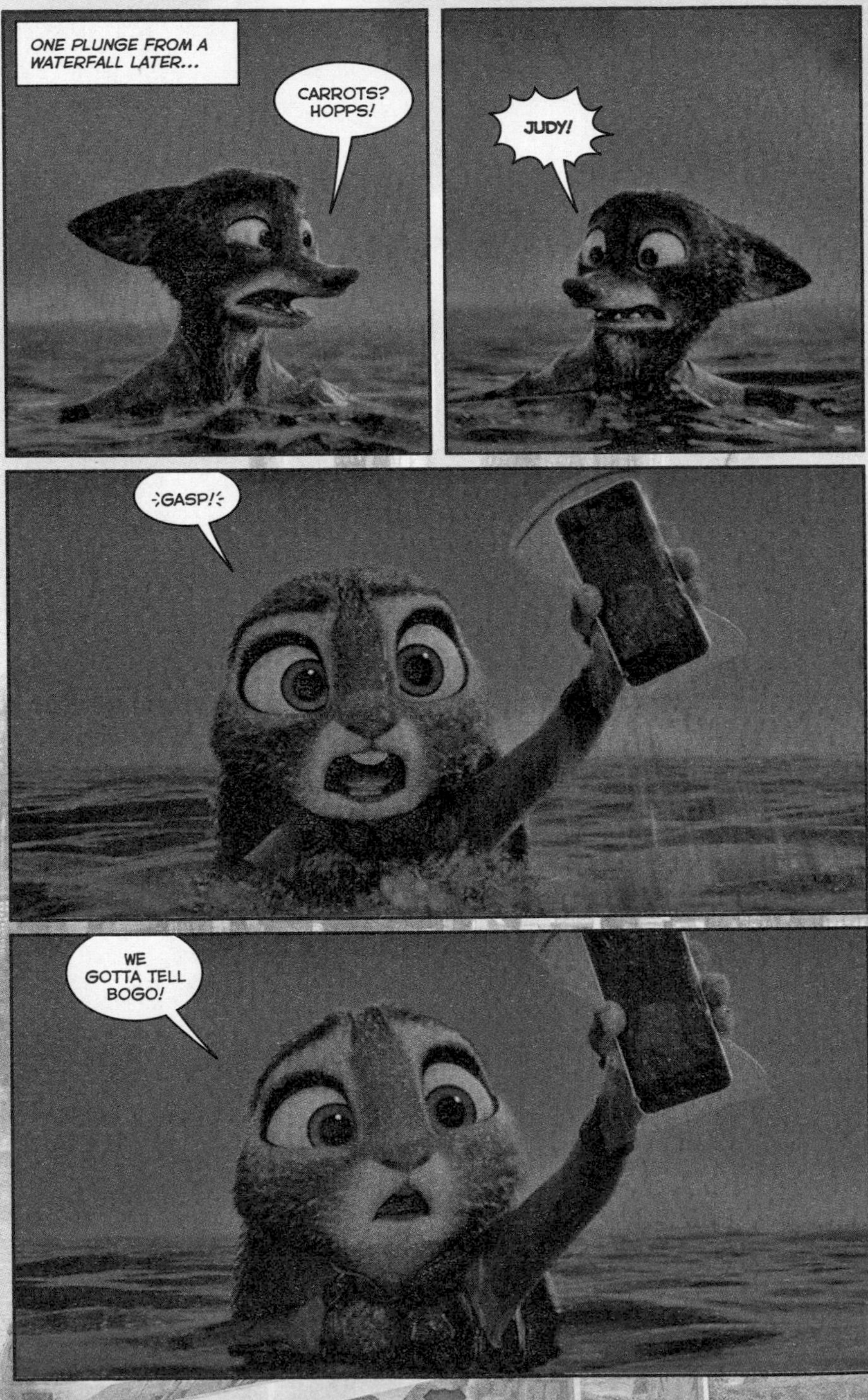
ONE PLUNGE FROM A WATERFALL LATER...
CARROTS? HOPPS!
JUDY!
GASP!
WE GOTTA TELL BOGO!

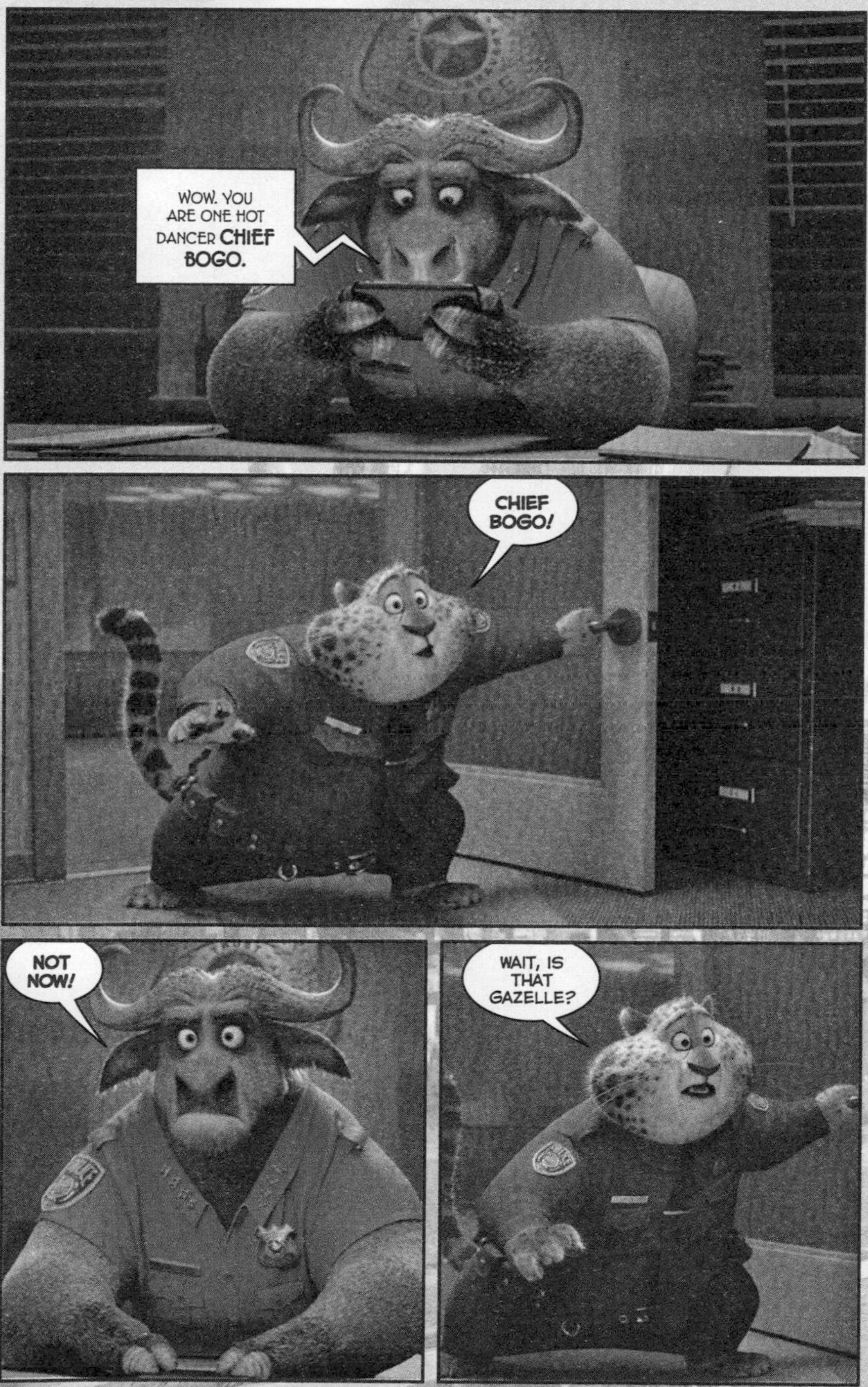
WOW. YOU ARE ONE HOT DANCER CHIEF BOGO.
CHIEF BOGO!
NOT NOW!
WAIT, IS THAT GAZELLE?

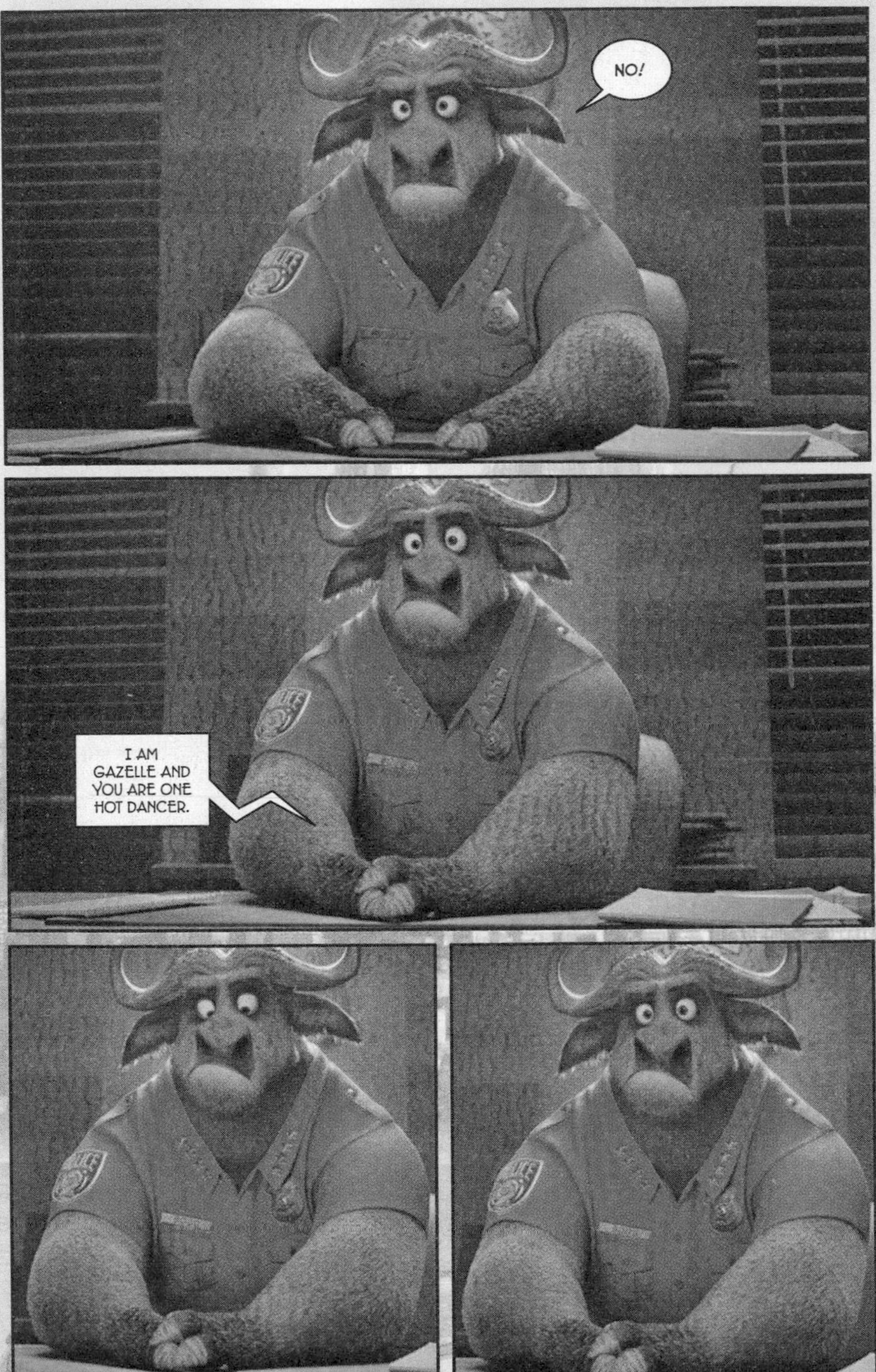
NO!
I AM GAZELLE AND YOU ARE ONE HOT DANCER.

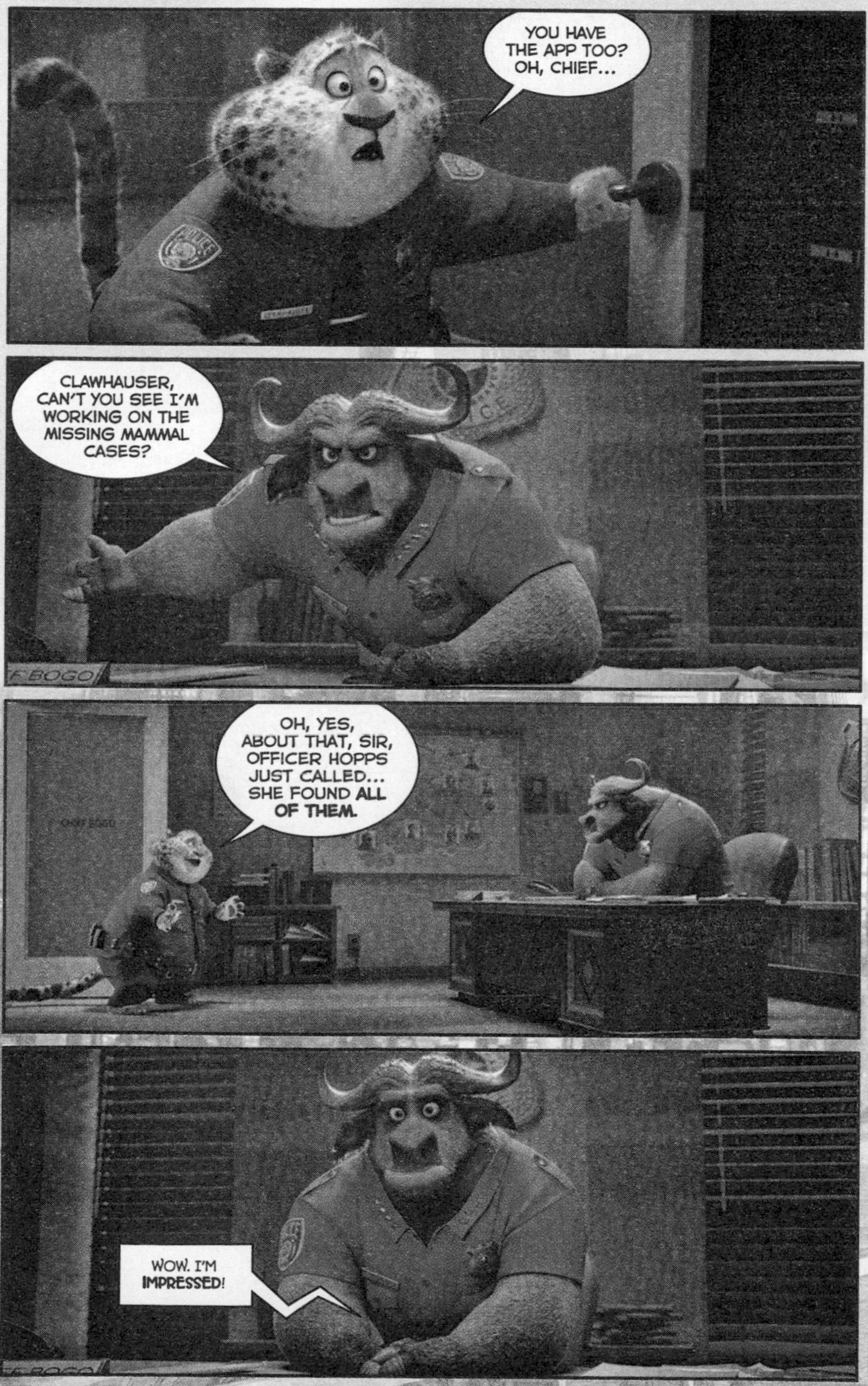
YOU HAVE THE APP TOO? OH, CHIEF...
CLAWHAUSER, CAN'T YOU SEE I'M WORKING ON THE MISSING MAMMAL CASES?
F. BOGO
OH, YES, ABOUT THAT, SIR, OFFICER HOPPS JUST CALLED... SHE FOUND **ALL OF THEM.**
WOW. I'M **IMPRESSED!**

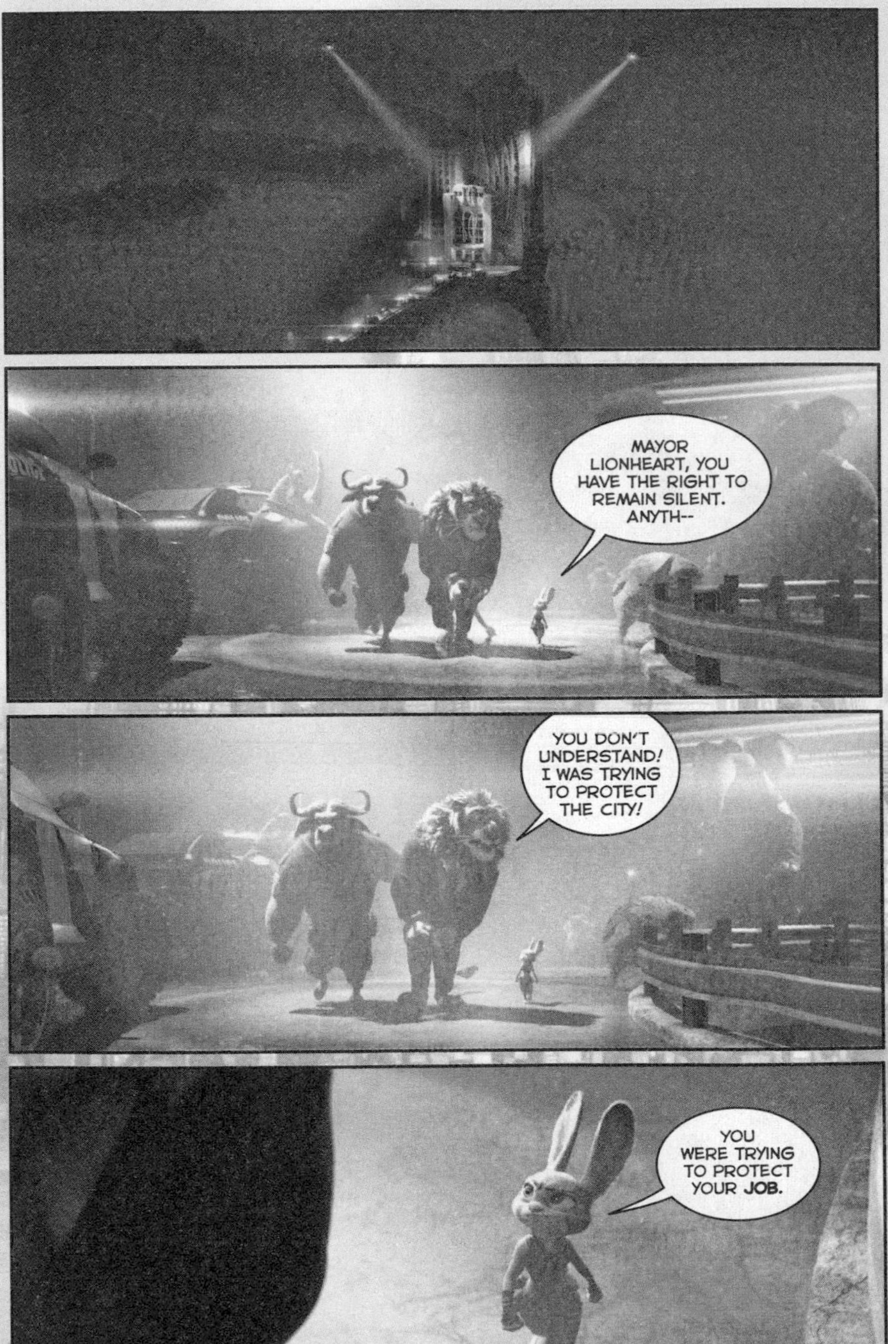
MAYOR LIONHEART, YOU HAVE THE RIGHT TO REMAIN SILENT. ANYTH--
YOU DON'T UNDERSTAND! I WAS TRYING TO PROTECT THE CITY!
YOU WERE TRYING TO PROTECT YOUR **JOB**.

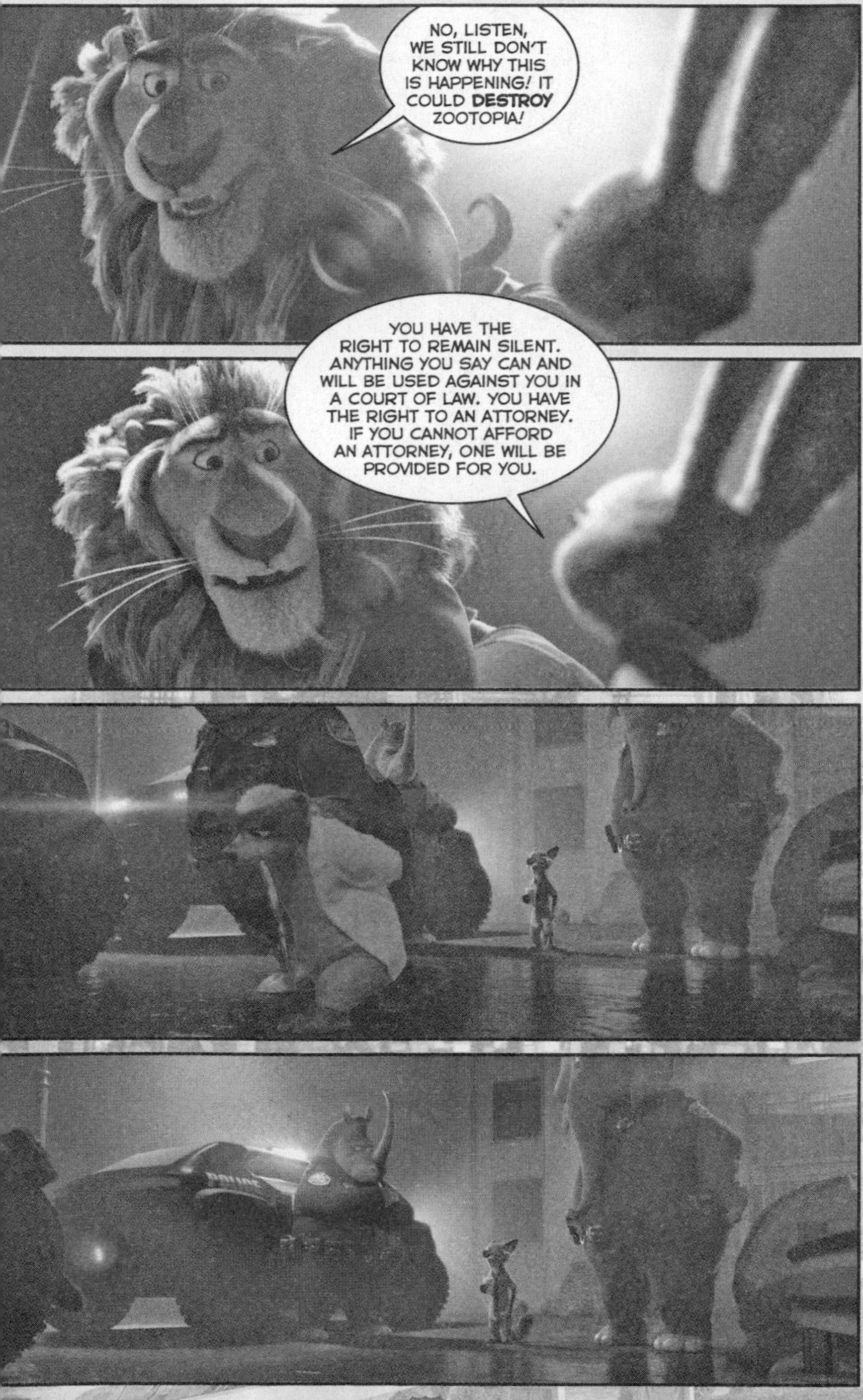
NO, LISTEN, WE STILL DON'T KNOW WHY THIS IS HAPPENING! IT COULD **DESTROY** ZOOTOPIA!
YOU HAVE THE RIGHT TO REMAIN SILENT. ANYTHING YOU SAY CAN AND WILL BE USED AGAINST YOU IN A COURT OF LAW. YOU HAVE THE RIGHT TO AN ATTORNEY. IF YOU CANNOT AFFORD AN ATTORNEY, ONE WILL BE PROVIDED FOR YOU.

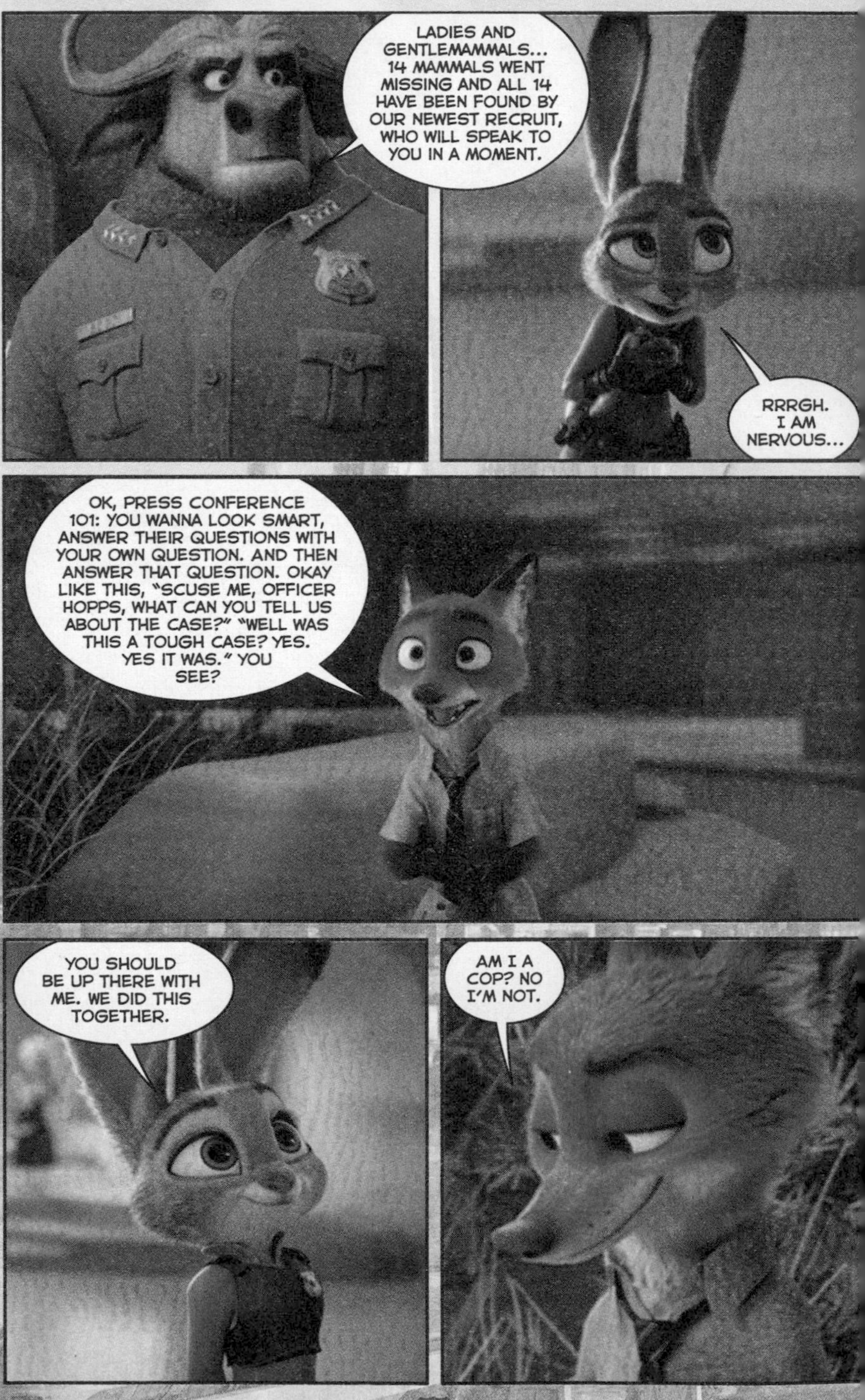
LADIES AND GENTLEMAMMALS... 14 MAMMALS WENT MISSING AND ALL 14 HAVE BEEN FOUND BY OUR NEWEST RECRUIT, WHO WILL SPEAK TO YOU IN A MOMENT.
RRRGH. I AM NERVOUS...
OK, PRESS CONFERENCE 101: YOU WANNA LOOK SMART, ANSWER THEIR QUESTIONS WITH YOUR OWN QUESTION. AND THEN ANSWER THAT QUESTION. OKAY LIKE THIS, "SCUSE ME, OFFICER HOPPS, WHAT CAN YOU TELL US ABOUT THE CASE?" "WELL WAS THIS A TOUGH CASE? YES. YES IT WAS." YOU SEE?
YOU SHOULD BE UP THERE WITH ME. WE DID THIS TOGETHER.
AM I A COP? NO I'M NOT.

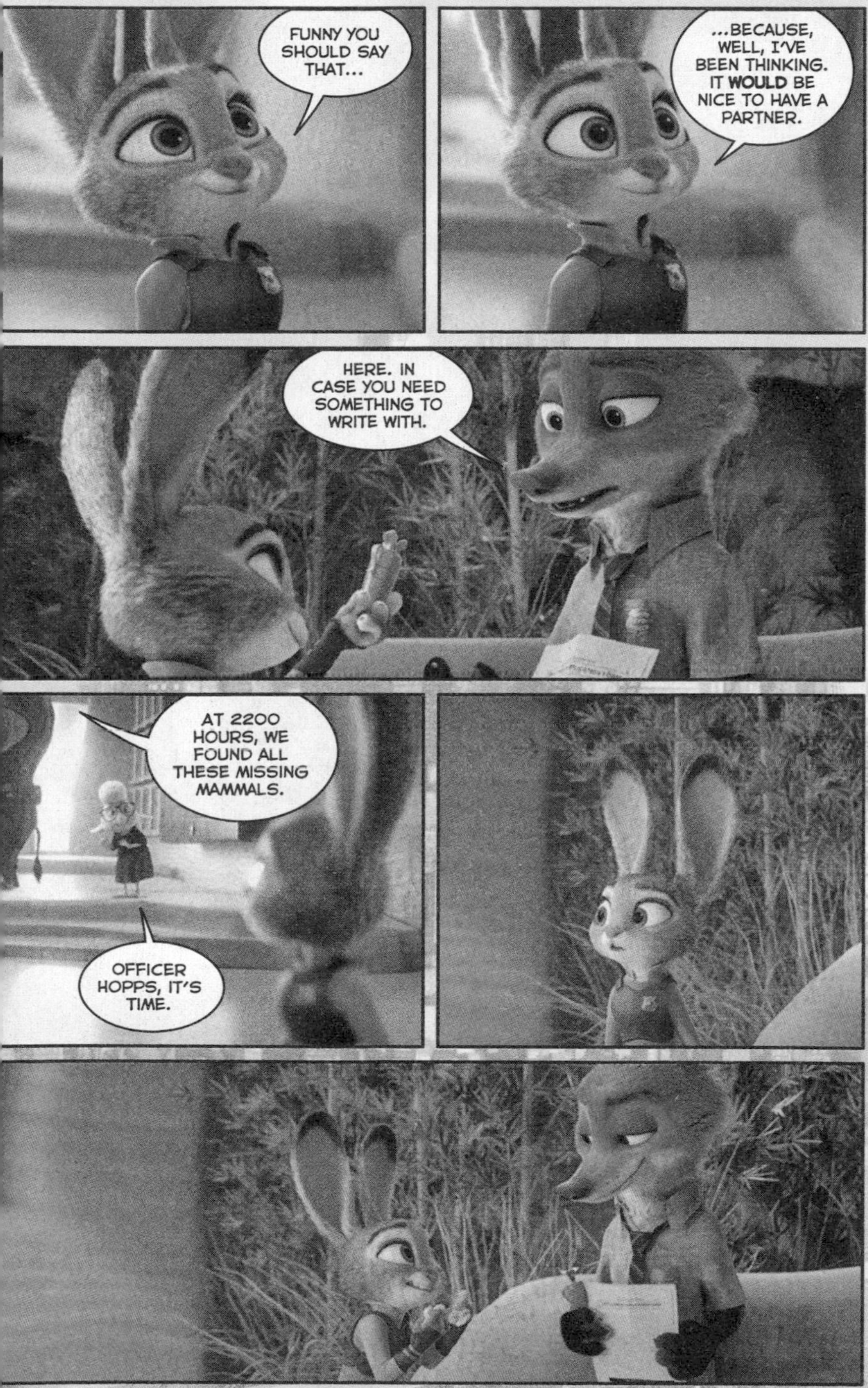
FUNNY YOU SHOULD SAY THAT...
...BECAUSE, WELL, I'VE BEEN THINKING. IT WOULD BE NICE TO HAVE A PARTNER.
HERE. IN CASE YOU NEED SOMETHING TO WRITE WITH.
AT 2200 HOURS, WE FOUND ALL THESE MISSING MAMMALS.
OFFICER HOPPS, IT'S TIME.

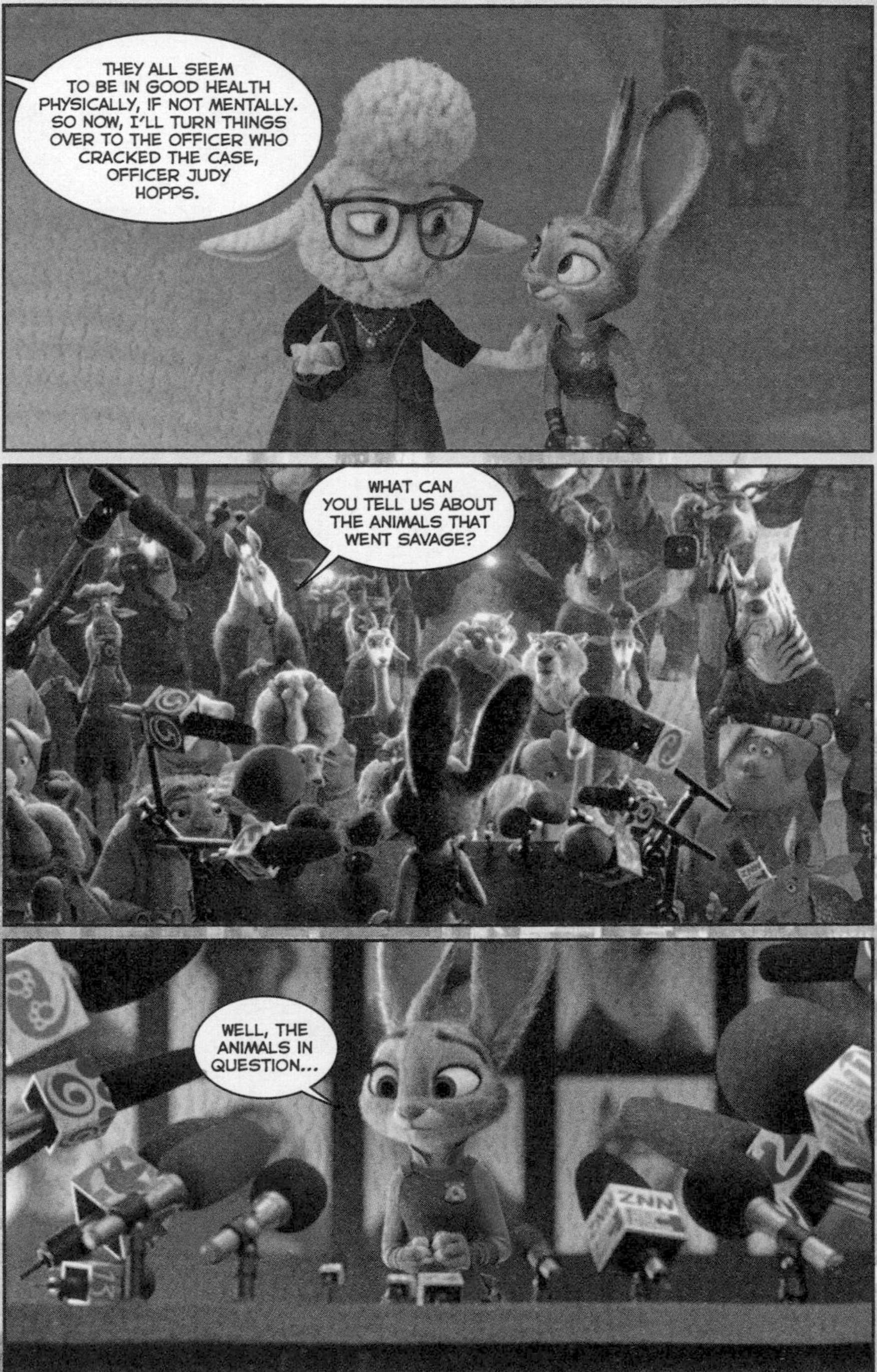
THEY ALL SEEM TO BE IN GOOD HEALTH PHYSICALLY, IF NOT MENTALLY. SO NOW, I'LL TURN THINGS OVER TO THE OFFICER WHO CRACKED THE CASE, OFFICER JUDY HOPPS.
WHAT CAN YOU TELL US ABOUT THE ANIMALS THAT WENT SAVAGE?
WELL, THE ANIMALS IN QUESTION...
ZNN

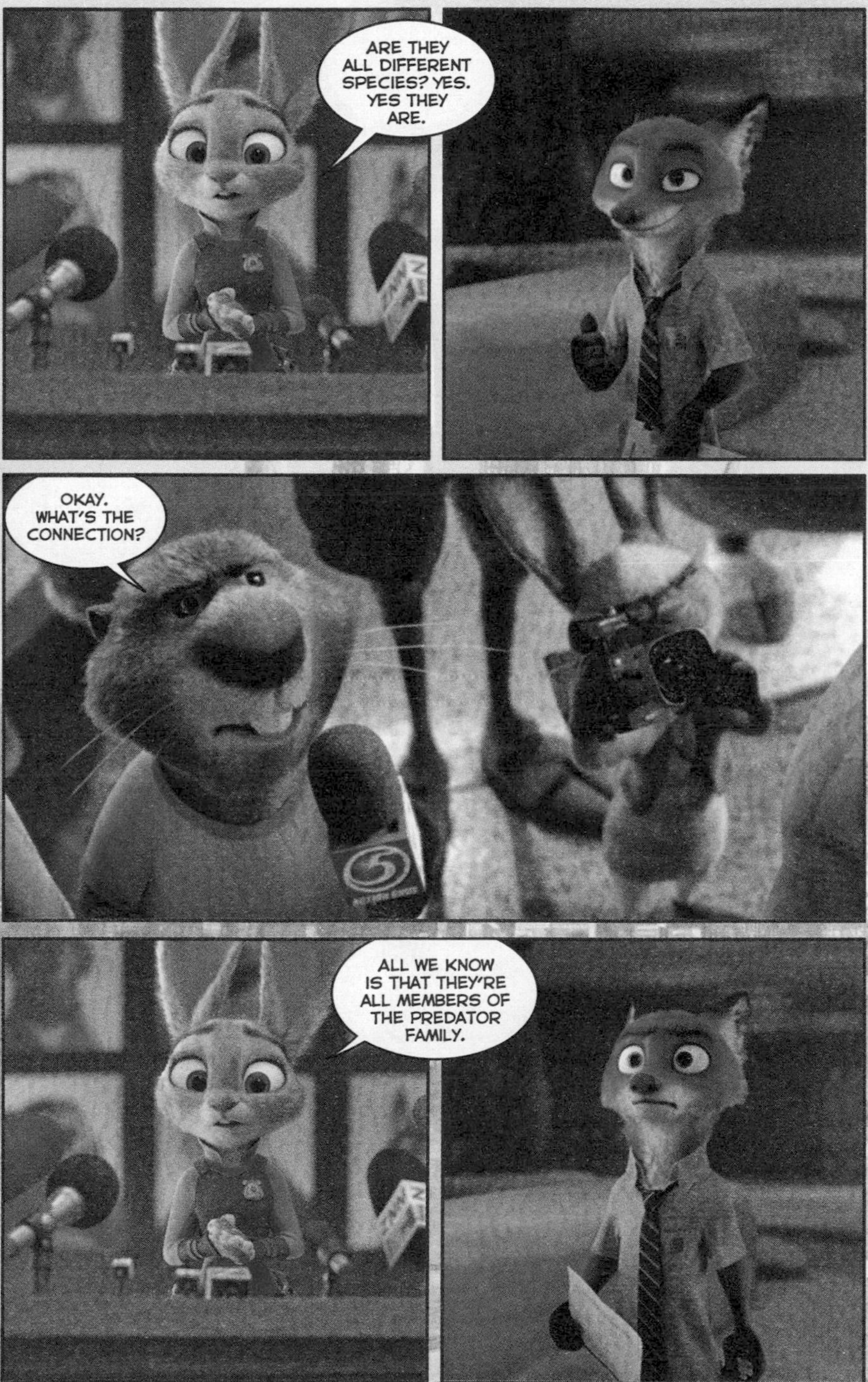
ARE THEY ALL DIFFERENT SPECIES? YES. YES THEY ARE.
OKAY. WHAT'S THE CONNECTION?
ALL WE KNOW IS THAT THEY'RE ALL MEMBERS OF THE PREDATOR FAMILY.

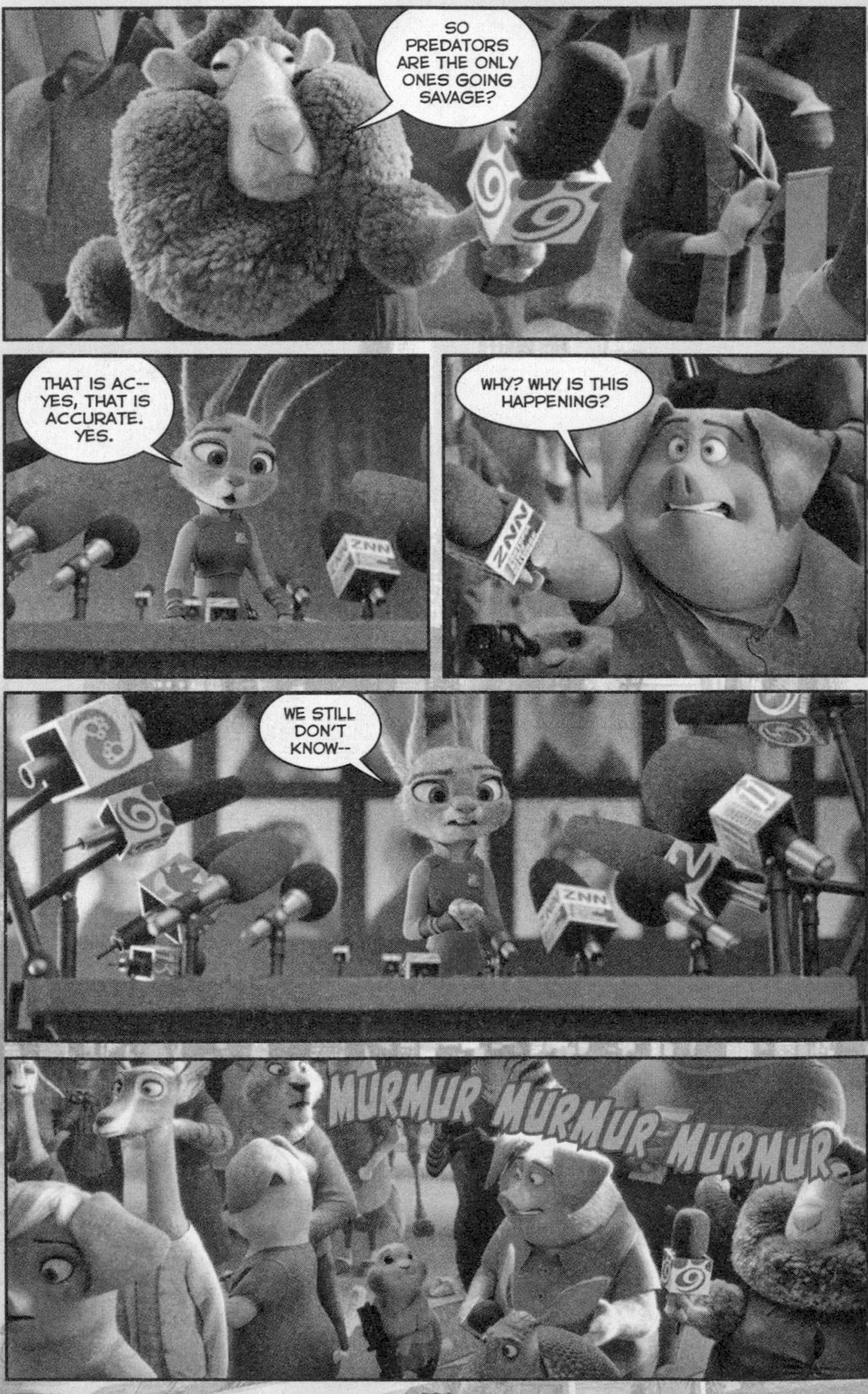
SO PREDATORS ARE THE ONLY ONES GOING SAVAGE?
THAT IS AC-- YES, THAT IS ACCURATE. YES.
WHY? WHY IS THIS HAPPENING?
WE STILL DON'T KNOW--
MURMUR MURMUR MURMUR

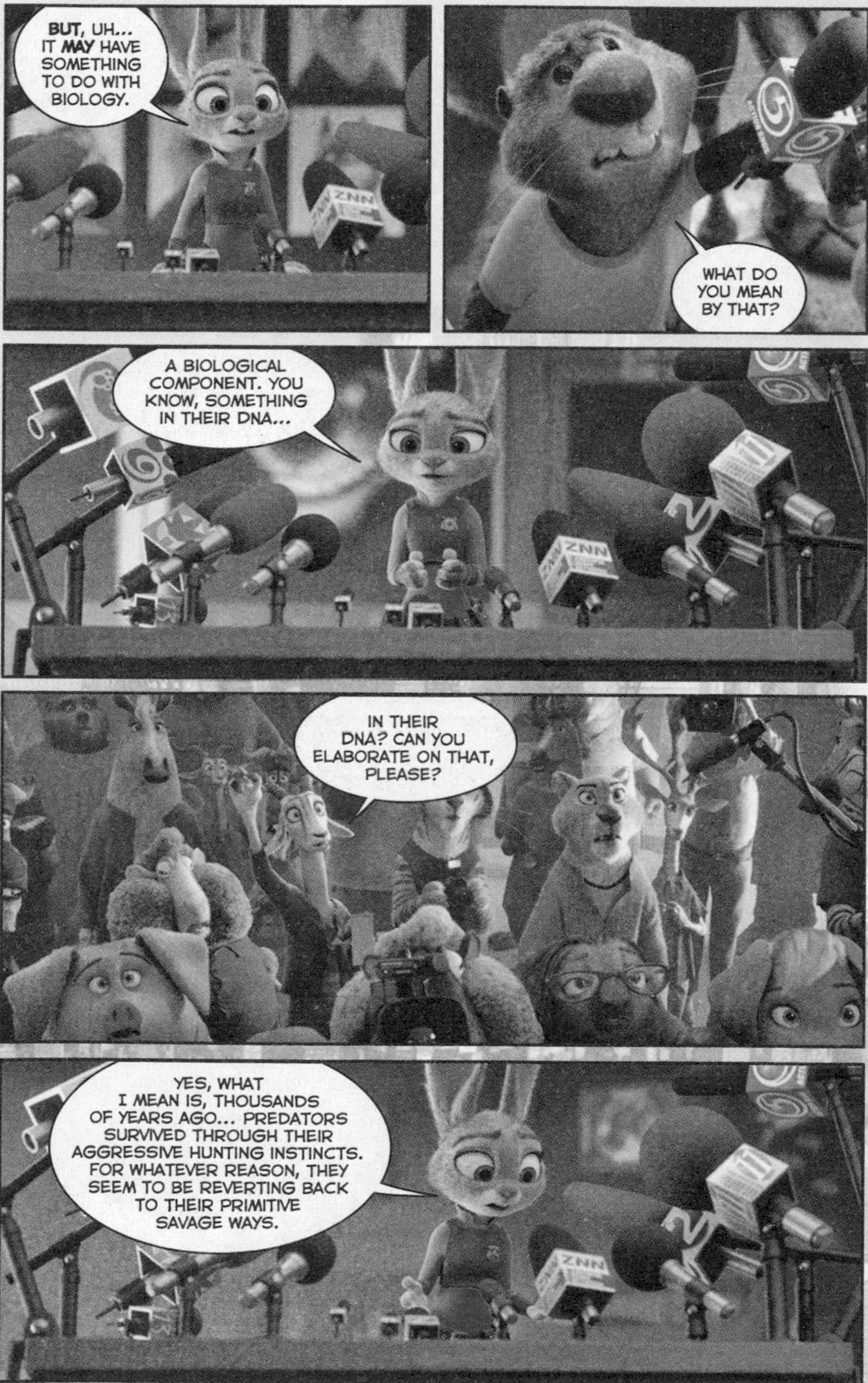
BUT, UH... IT MAY HAVE SOMETHING TO DO WITH BIOLOGY.
WHAT DO YOU MEAN BY THAT?
A BIOLOGICAL COMPONENT. YOU KNOW, SOMETHING IN THEIR DNA...
IN THEIR DNA? CAN YOU ELABORATE ON THAT, PLEASE?
YES, WHAT I MEAN IS, THOUSANDS OF YEARS AGO... PREDATORS SURVIVED THROUGH THEIR AGGRESSIVE HUNTING INSTINCTS. FOR WHATEVER REASON, THEY SEEM TO BE REVERTING BACK TO THEIR PRIMITIVE SAVAGE WAYS.

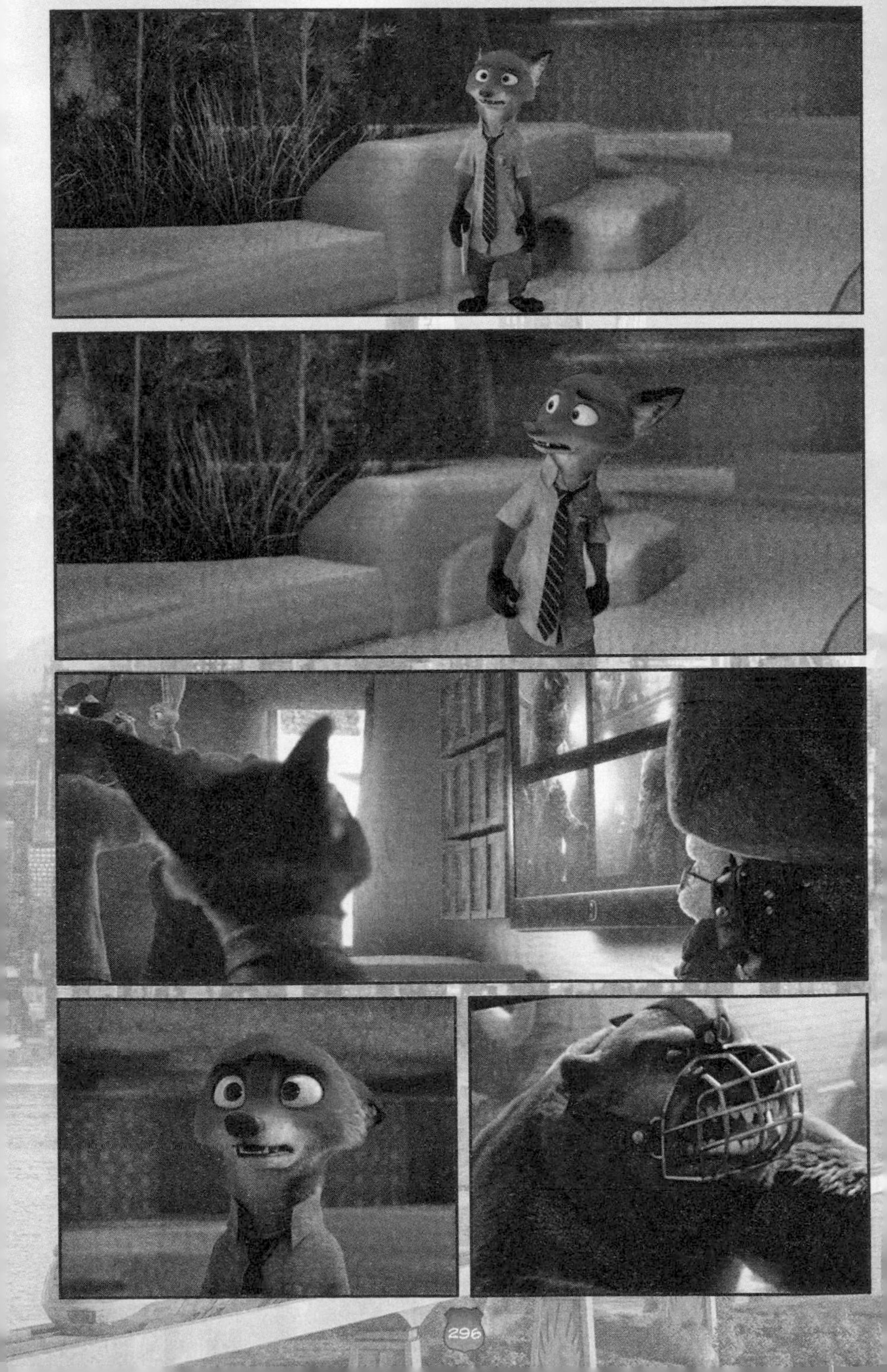

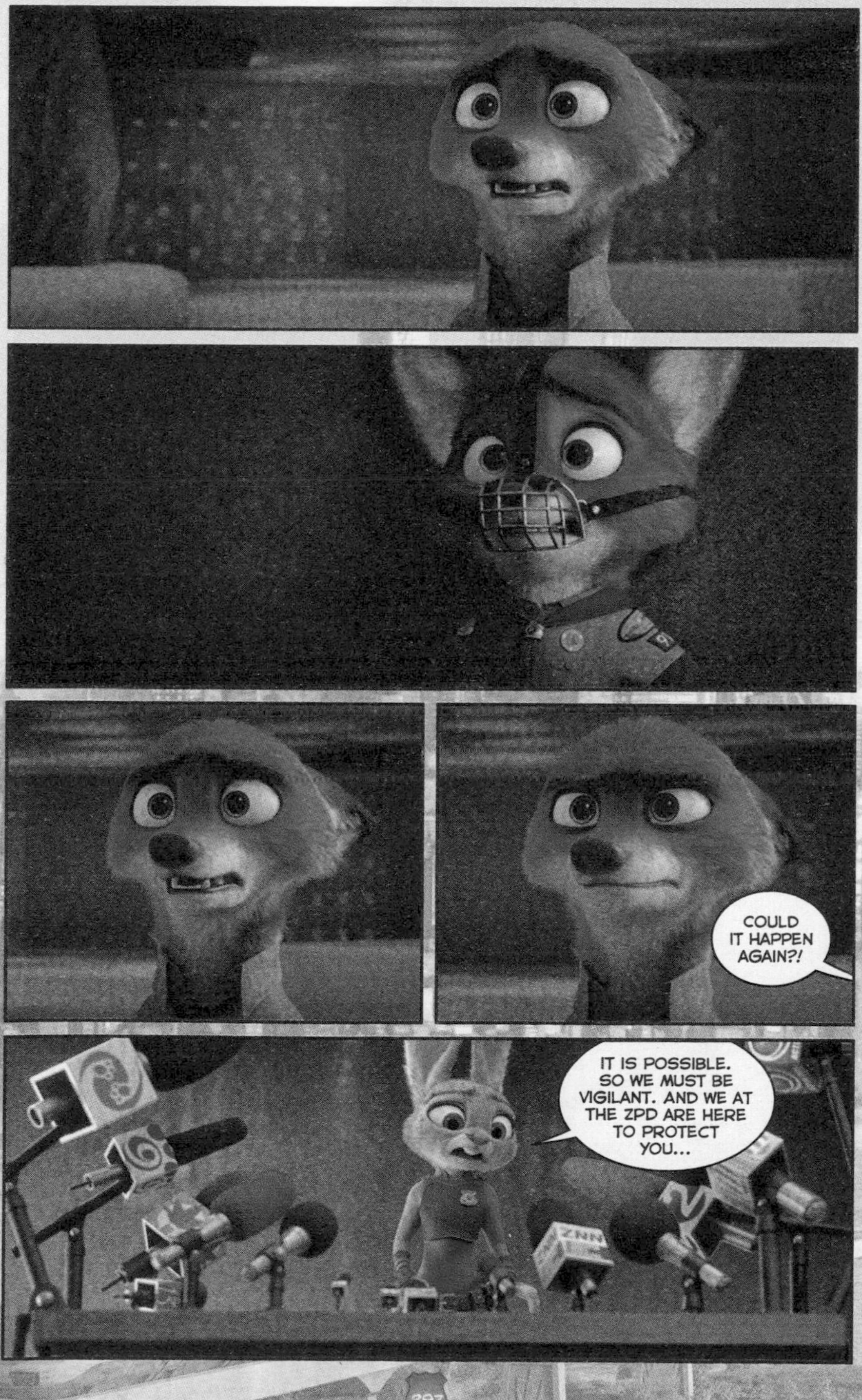
COULD IT HAPPEN AGAIN?!
IT IS POSSIBLE. SO WE MUST BE VIGILANT. AND WE AT THE ZPD ARE HERE TO PROTECT YOU...

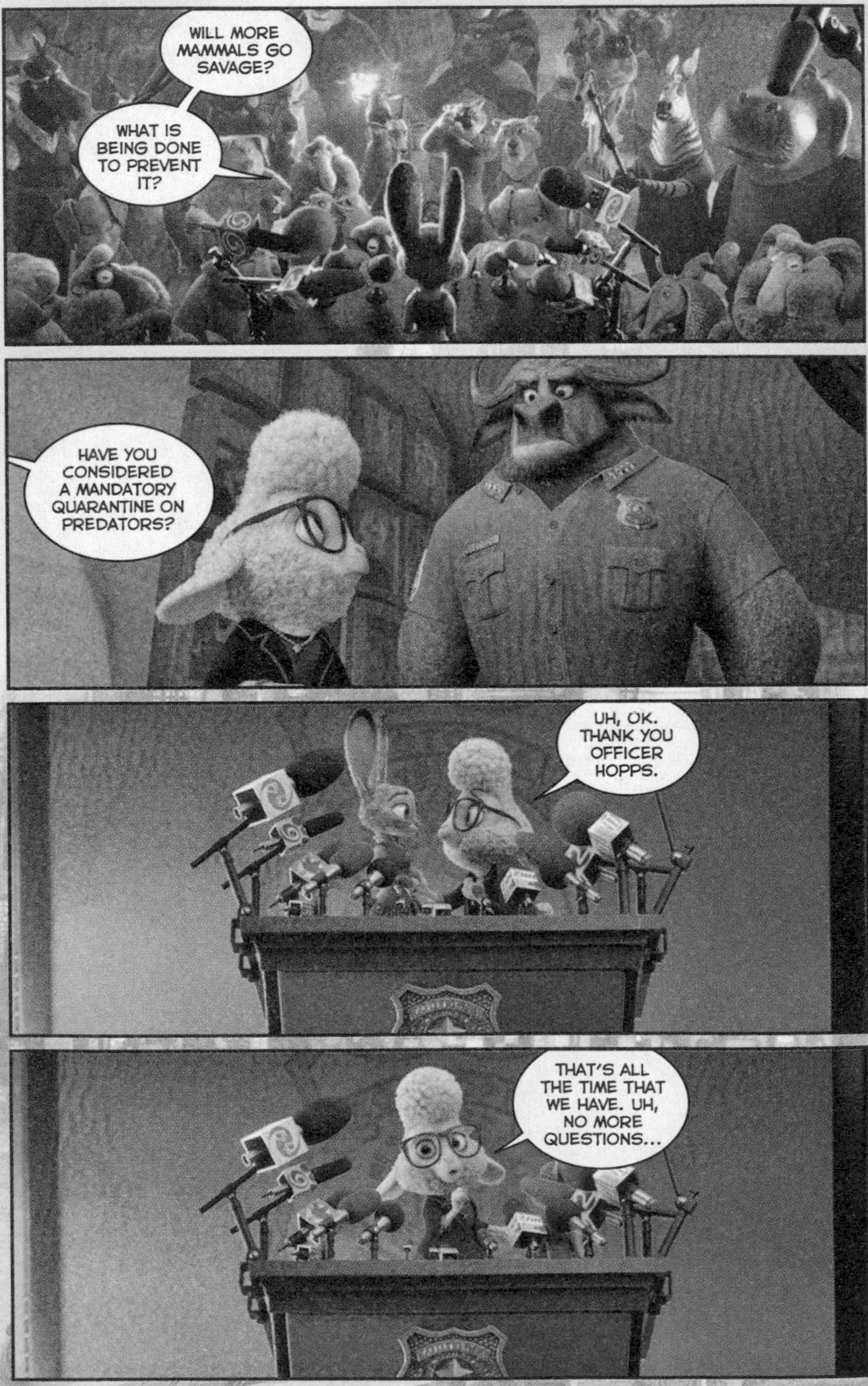
WILL MORE MAMMALS GO SAVAGE?
WHAT IS BEING DONE TO PREVENT IT?
HAVE YOU CONSIDERED A MANDATORY QUARANTINE ON PREDATORS?
UH, OK. THANK YOU OFFICER HOPPS.
THAT'S ALL THE TIME THAT WE HAVE. UH, NO MORE QUESTIONS...

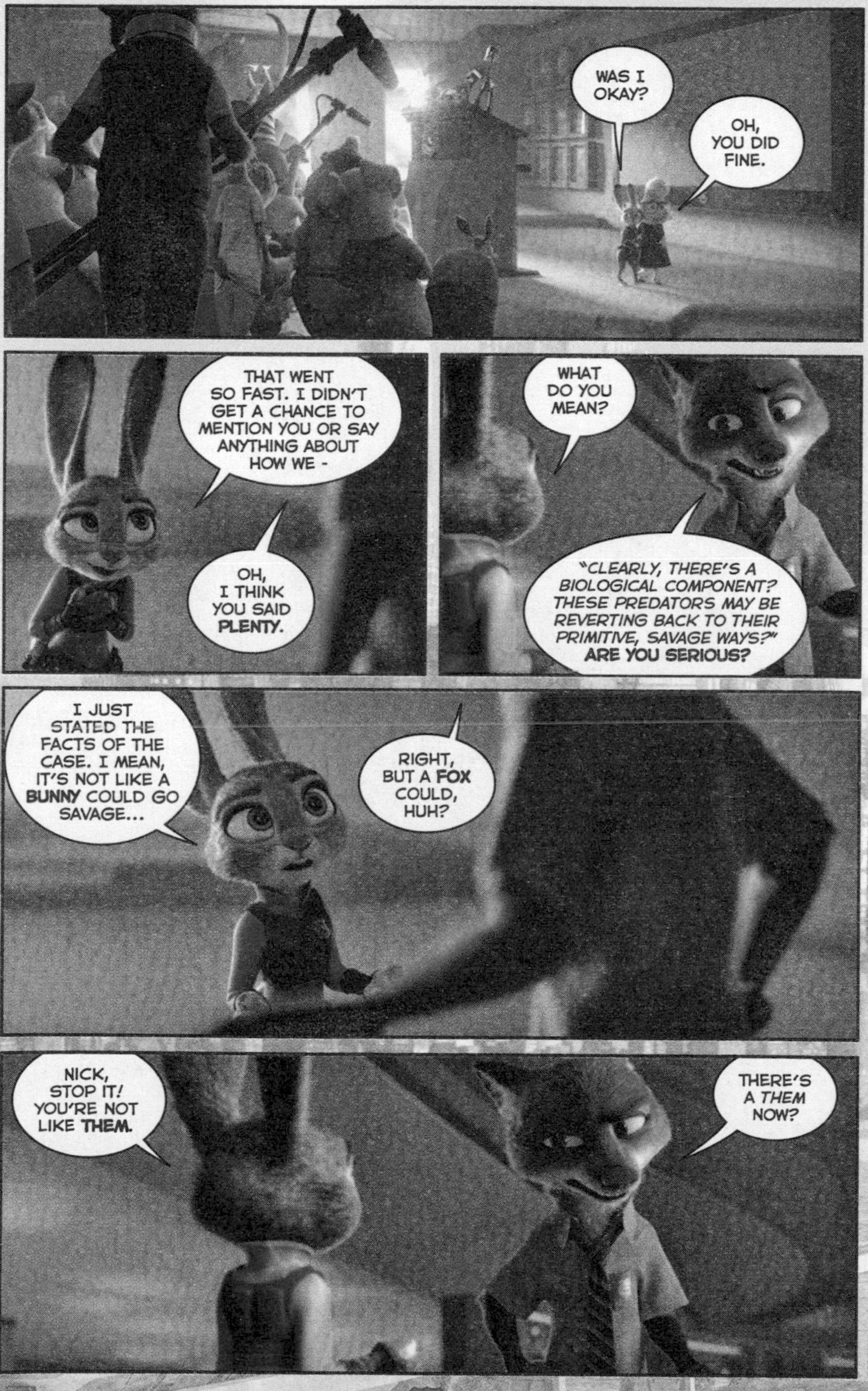
WAS I OKAY?
OH, YOU DID FINE.
THAT WENT SO FAST. I DIDN'T GET A CHANCE TO MENTION YOU OR SAY ANYTHING ABOUT HOW WE -
OH, I THINK YOU SAID **PLENTY**.
WHAT DO YOU MEAN?
"CLEARLY, THERE'S A BIOLOGICAL COMPONENT? THESE PREDATORS MAY BE REVERTING BACK TO THEIR PRIMITIVE, SAVAGE WAYS?" **ARE YOU SERIOUS?**
I JUST STATED THE FACTS OF THE CASE. I MEAN, IT'S NOT LIKE A **BUNNY** COULD GO SAVAGE...
RIGHT, BUT A **FOX** COULD, HUH?
NICK, STOP IT! YOU'RE NOT LIKE **THEM**.
THERE'S A *THEM* NOW?

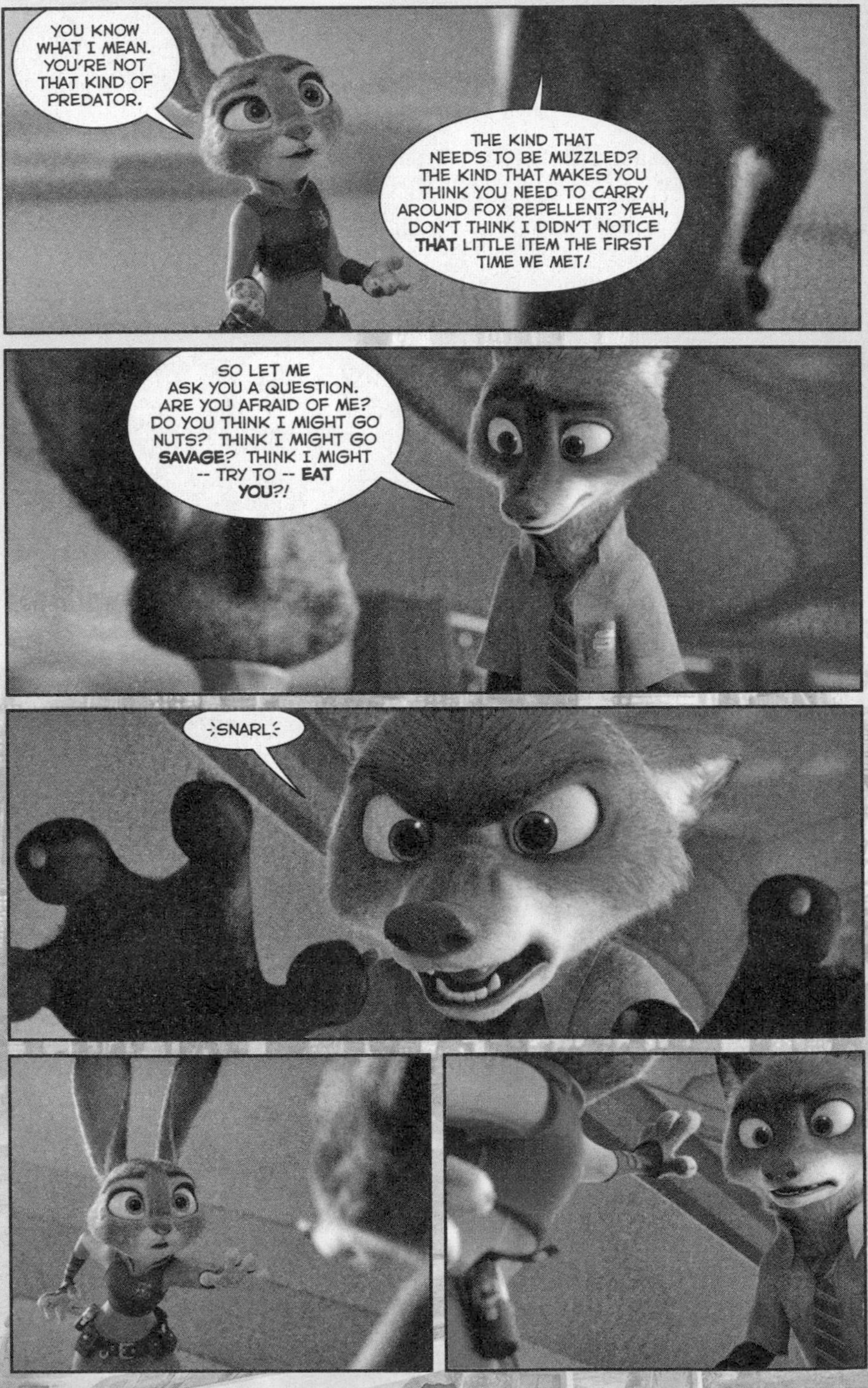
YOU KNOW WHAT I MEAN. YOU'RE NOT THAT KIND OF PREDATOR.
THE KIND THAT NEEDS TO BE MUZZLED? THE KIND THAT MAKES YOU THINK YOU NEED TO CARRY AROUND FOX REPELLENT? YEAH, DON'T THINK I DIDN'T NOTICE **THAT** LITTLE ITEM THE FIRST TIME WE MET!
SO LET ME ASK YOU A QUESTION. ARE YOU AFRAID OF ME? DO YOU THINK I MIGHT GO NUTS? THINK I MIGHT GO **SAVAGE**? THINK I MIGHT -- TRY TO -- **EAT YOU**?!
SNARL

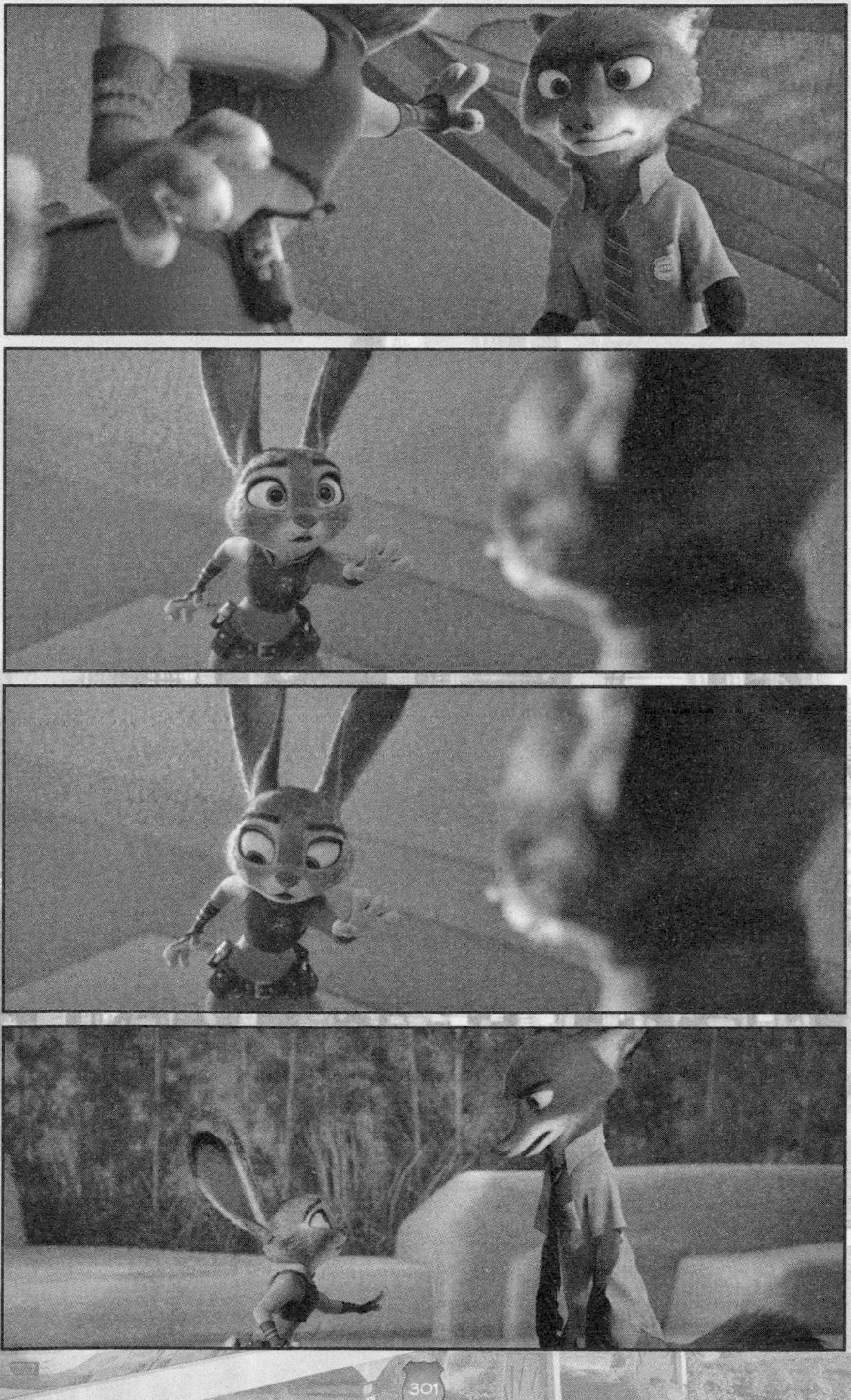

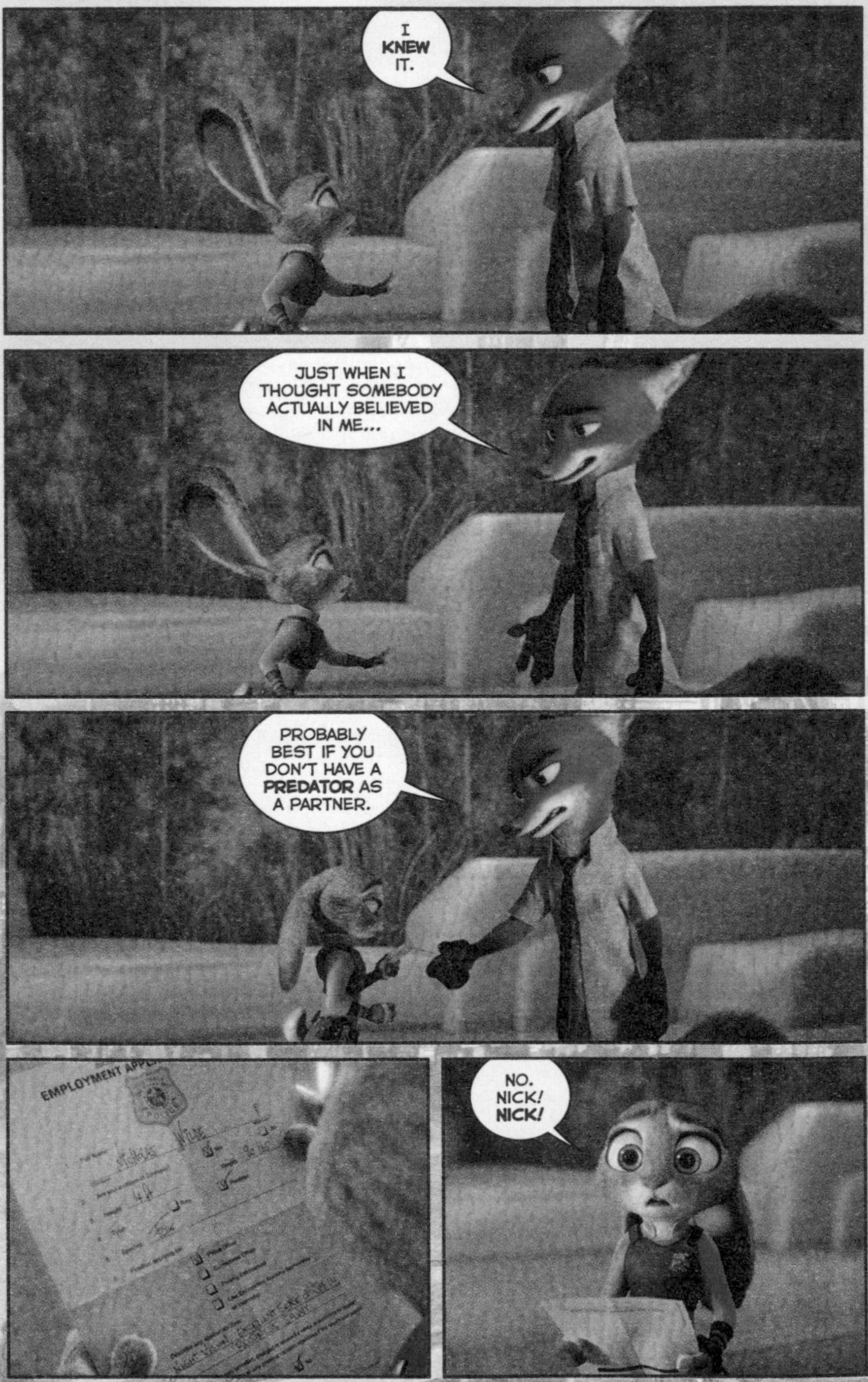
I KNEW IT.
JUST WHEN I THOUGHT SOMEBODY ACTUALLY BELIEVED IN ME...
PROBABLY BEST IF YOU DON'T HAVE A **PREDATOR** AS A PARTNER.
EMPLOYMENT APPL
NO. NICK! **NICK!**

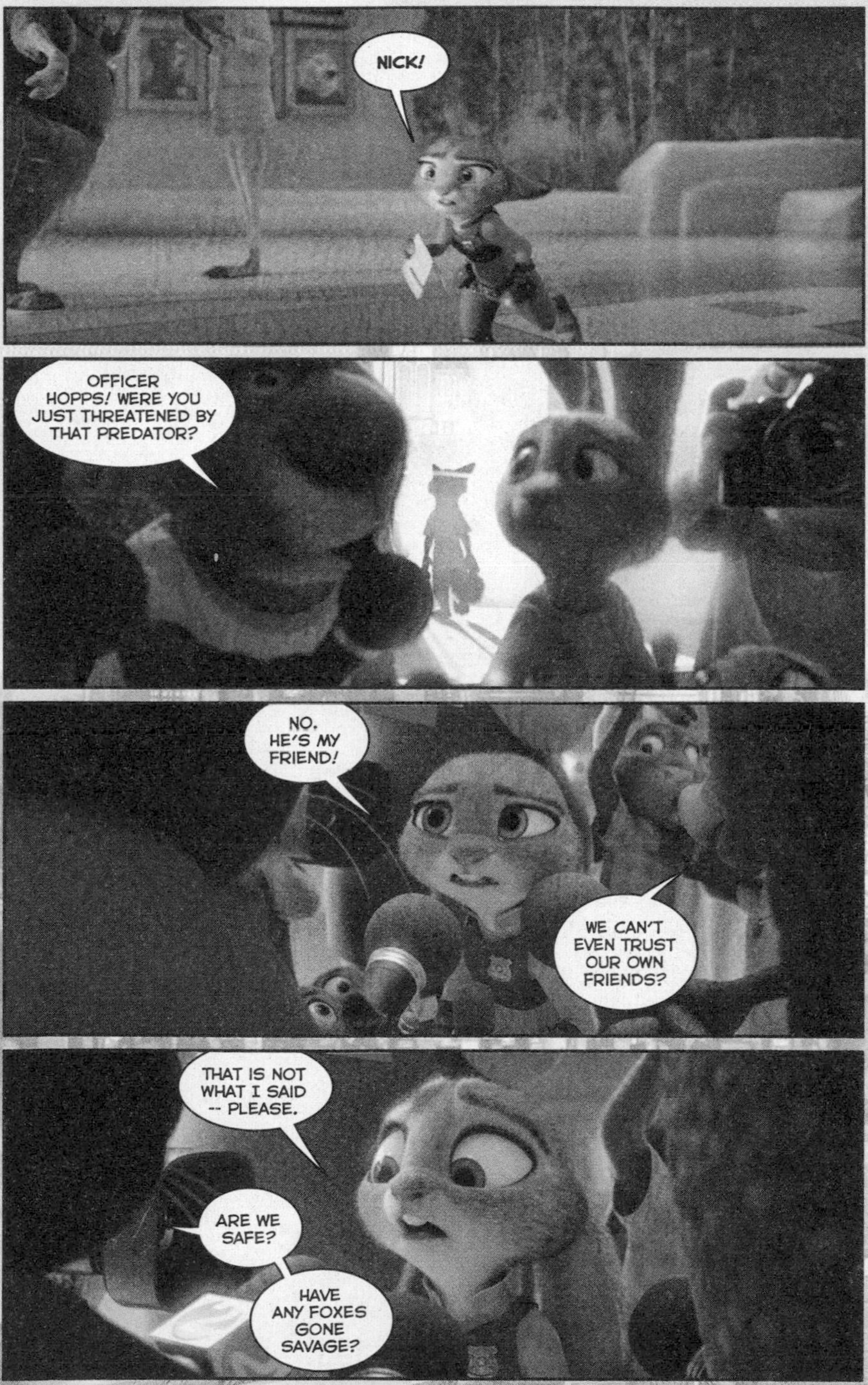
NICK!
OFFICER HOPPS! WERE YOU JUST THREATENED BY THAT PREDATOR?
NO. HE'S MY FRIEND!
WE CAN'T EVEN TRUST OUR OWN FRIENDS?
THAT IS NOT WHAT I SAID -- PLEASE.
ARE WE SAFE?
HAVE ANY FOXES GONE SAVAGE?

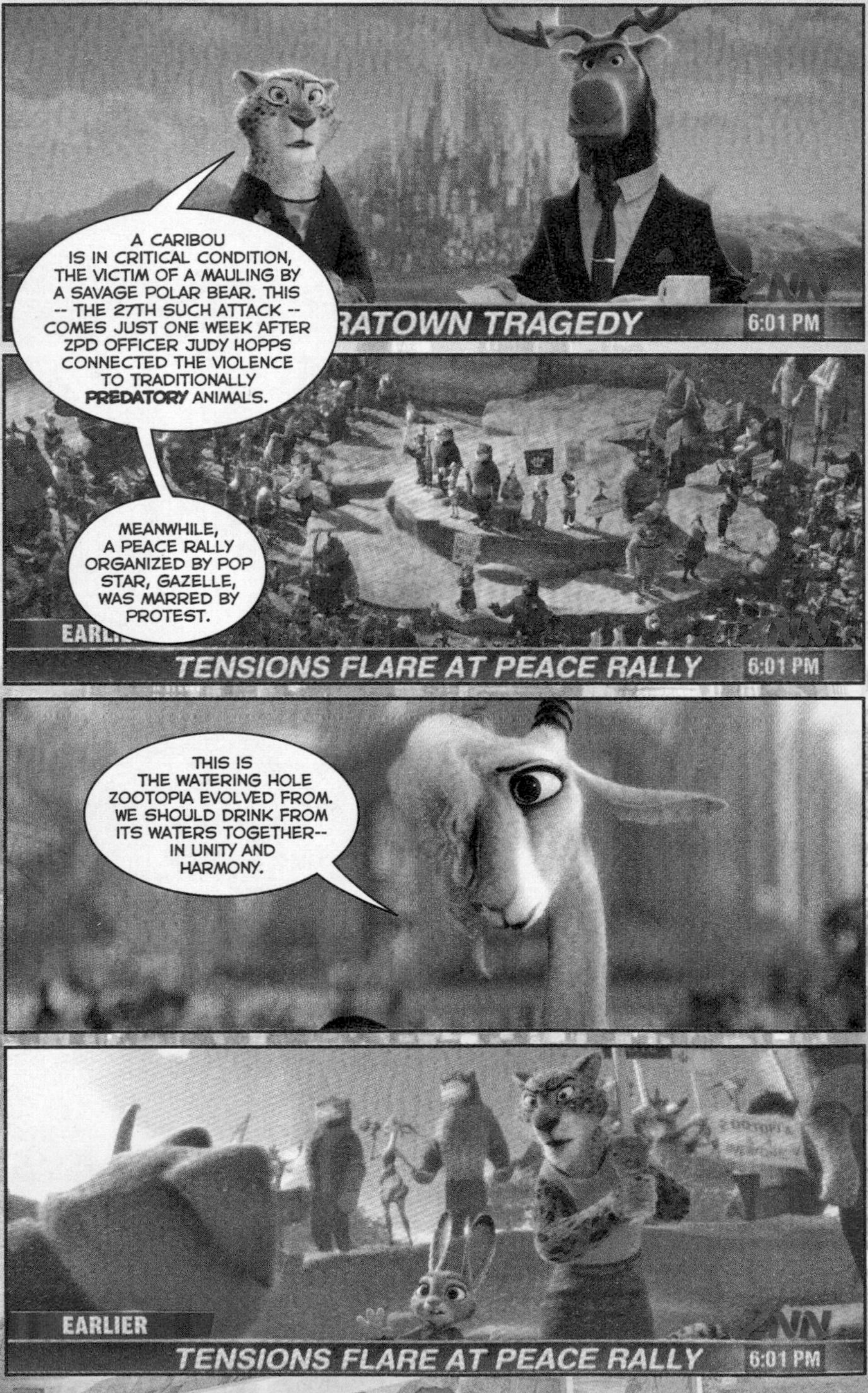
A CARIBOU IS IN CRITICAL CONDITION, THE VICTIM OF A MAULING BY A SAVAGE POLAR BEAR. THIS -- THE 27TH SUCH ATTACK -- COMES JUST ONE WEEK AFTER ZPD OFFICER JUDY HOPPS CONNECTED THE VIOLENCE TO TRADITIONALLY **PREDATORY** ANIMALS.
RATOWN TRAGEDY
6:01 PM
MEANWHILE, A PEACE RALLY ORGANIZED BY POP STAR, GAZELLE, WAS MARRED BY PROTEST.
TENSIONS FLARE AT PEACE RALLY
6:01 PM
THIS IS THE WATERING HOLE ZOOTOPIA EVOLVED FROM. WE SHOULD DRINK FROM ITS WATERS TOGETHER-- IN UNITY AND HARMONY.
EARLIER
TENSIONS FLARE AT PEACE RALLY
6:01 PM

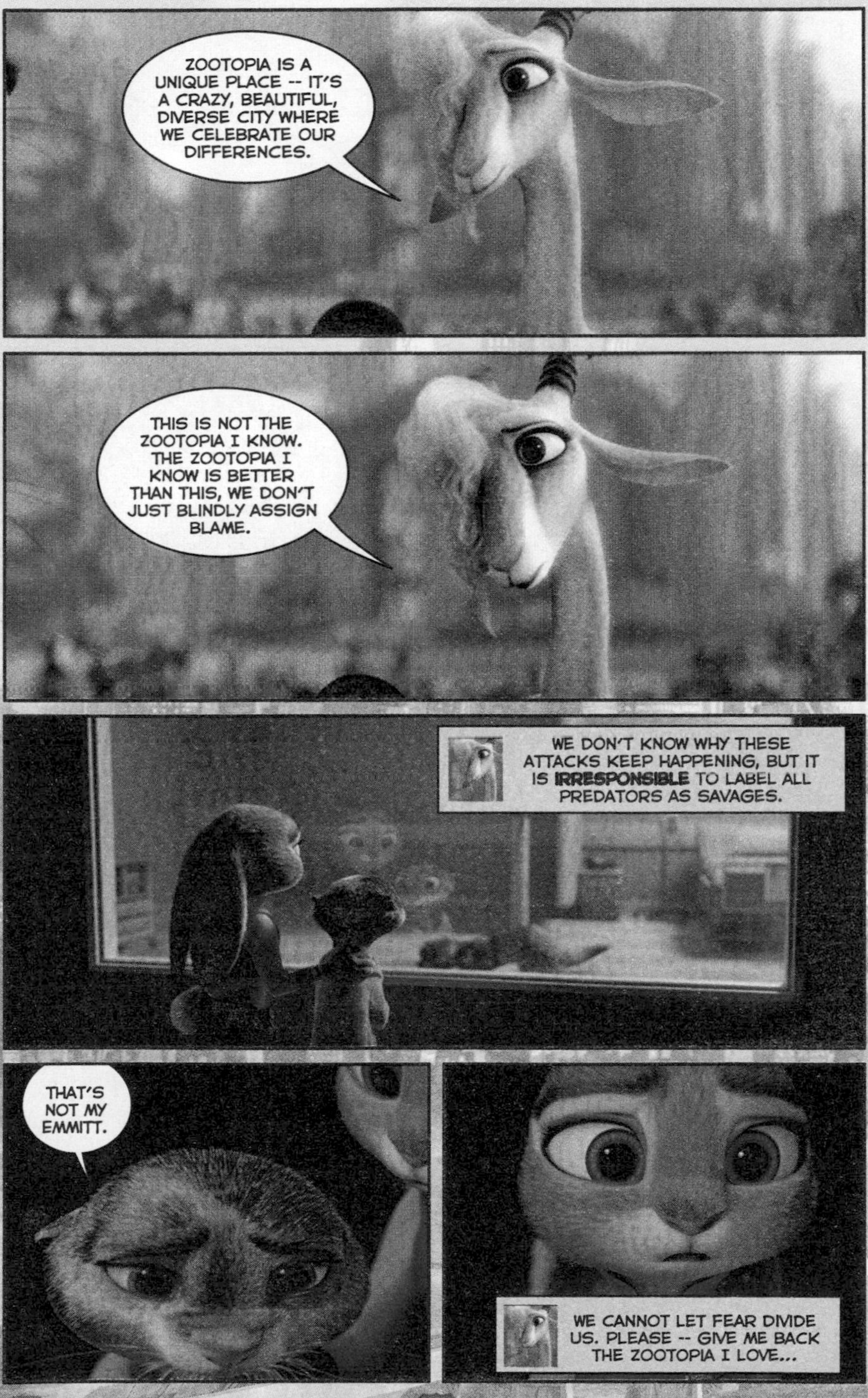
ZOOTOPIA IS A UNIQUE PLACE -- IT'S A CRAZY, BEAUTIFUL, DIVERSE CITY WHERE WE CELEBRATE OUR DIFFERENCES.
THIS IS NOT THE ZOOTOPIA I KNOW. THE ZOOTOPIA I KNOW IS BETTER THAN THIS, WE DON'T JUST BLINDLY ASSIGN BLAME.
WE DON'T KNOW WHY THESE ATTACKS KEEP HAPPENING, BUT IT IS IRRESPONSIBLE TO LABEL ALL PREDATORS AS SAVAGES.
THAT'S NOT MY EMMITT.
WE CANNOT LET FEAR DIVIDE US. PLEASE -- GIVE ME BACK THE ZOOTOPIA I LOVE...

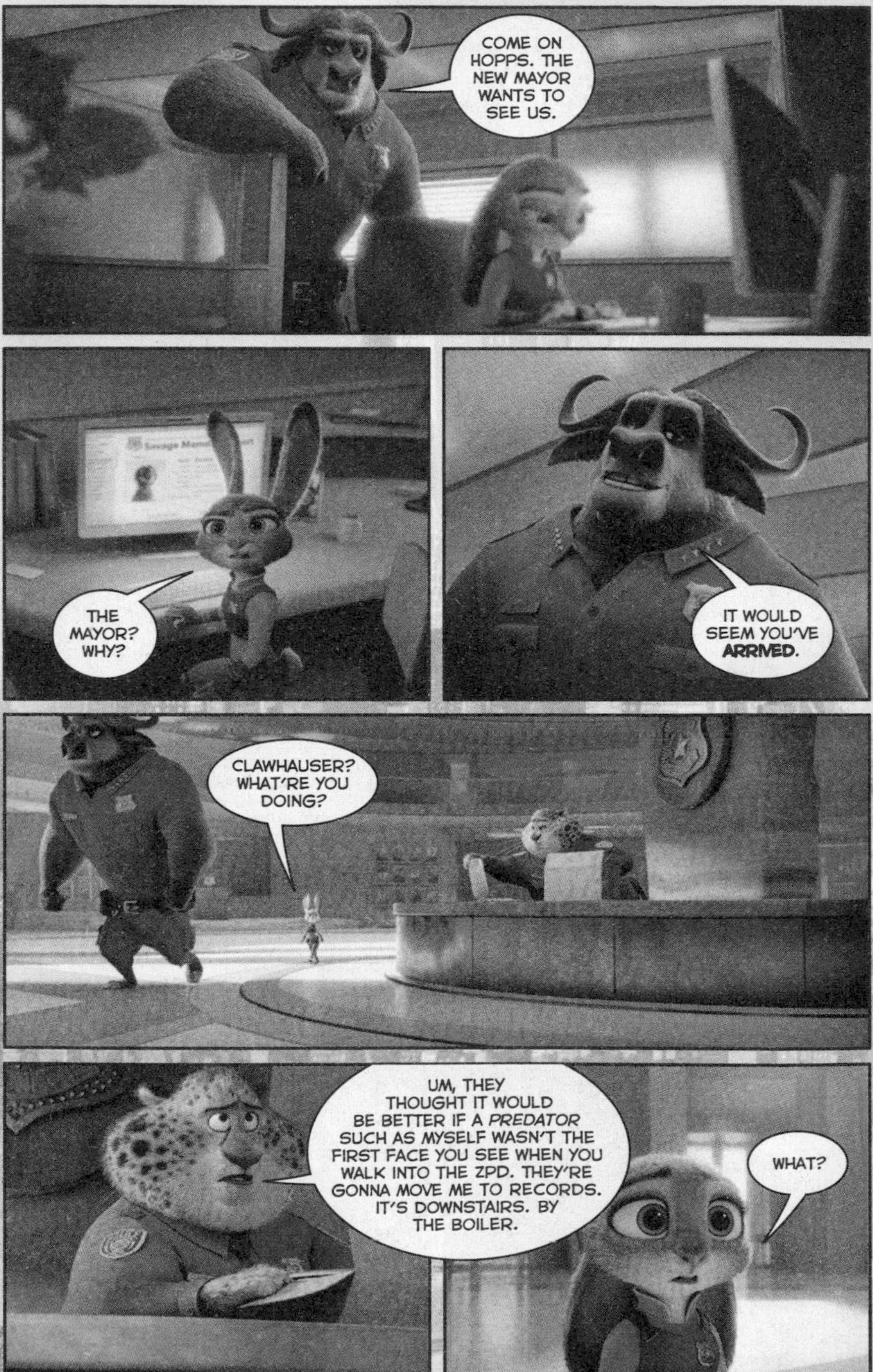
COME ON HOPPS. THE NEW MAYOR WANTS TO SEE US.
THE MAYOR? WHY?
IT WOULD SEEM YOU'VE **ARRIVED**.
CLAWHAUSER? WHAT'RE YOU DOING?
UM, THEY THOUGHT IT WOULD BE BETTER IF A *PREDATOR* SUCH AS MYSELF WASN'T THE FIRST FACE YOU SEE WHEN YOU WALK INTO THE ZPD. THEY'RE GONNA MOVE ME TO RECORDS. IT'S DOWNSTAIRS. BY THE BOILER.
WHAT?

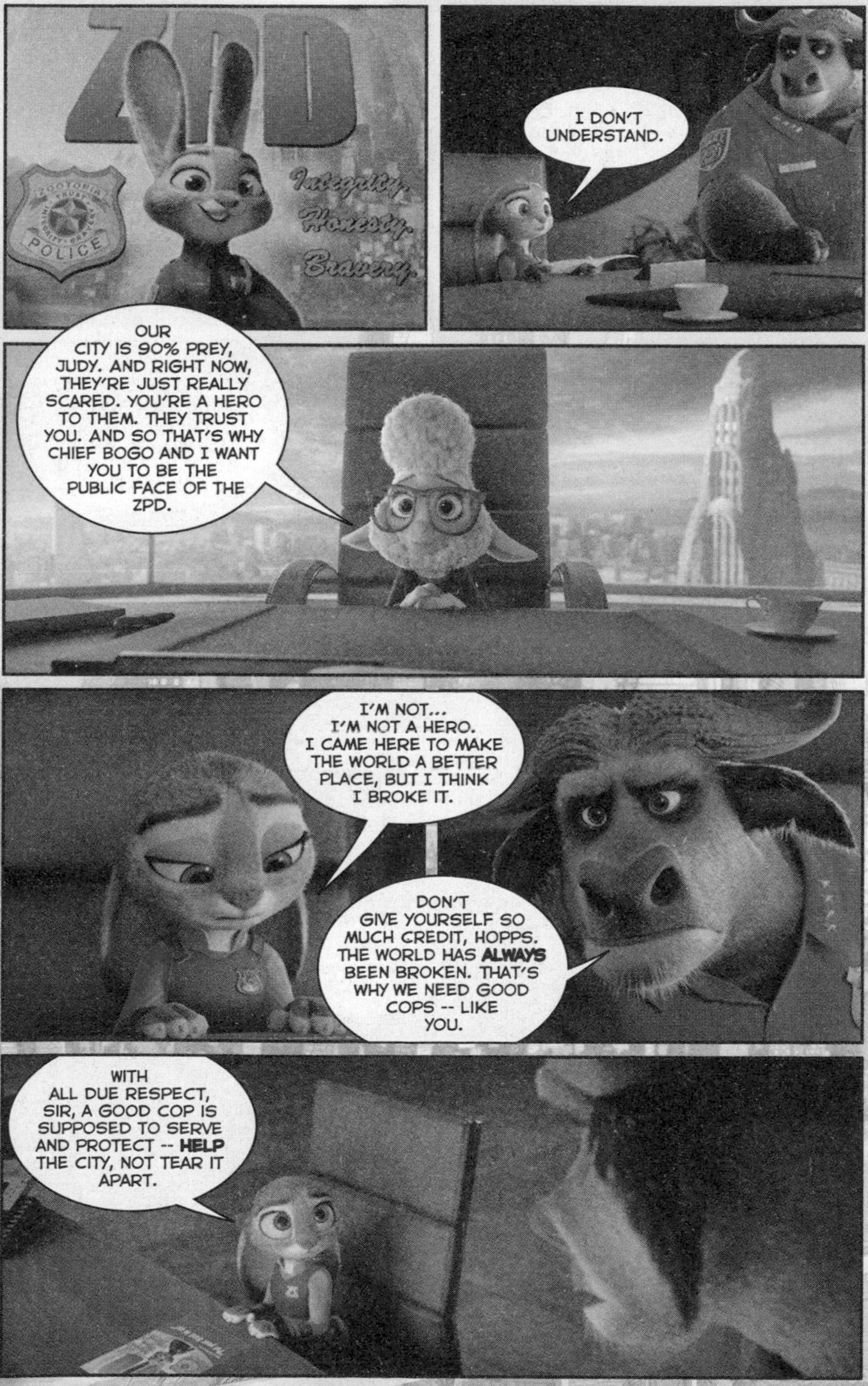
ZPD
Integrity. Honesty. Bravery.
POLICE
I DON'T UNDERSTAND.
OUR CITY IS 90% PREY, JUDY. AND RIGHT NOW, THEY'RE JUST REALLY SCARED. YOU'RE A HERO TO THEM. THEY TRUST YOU. AND SO THAT'S WHY CHIEF BOGO AND I WANT YOU TO BE THE PUBLIC FACE OF THE ZPD.
I'M NOT... I'M NOT A HERO. I CAME HERE TO MAKE THE WORLD A BETTER PLACE, BUT I THINK I BROKE IT.
DON'T GIVE YOURSELF SO MUCH CREDIT, HOPPS. THE WORLD HAS **ALWAYS** BEEN BROKEN. THAT'S WHY WE NEED GOOD COPS -- LIKE YOU.
WITH ALL DUE RESPECT, SIR, A GOOD COP IS SUPPOSED TO SERVE AND PROTECT -- **HELP** THE CITY, NOT TEAR IT APART.

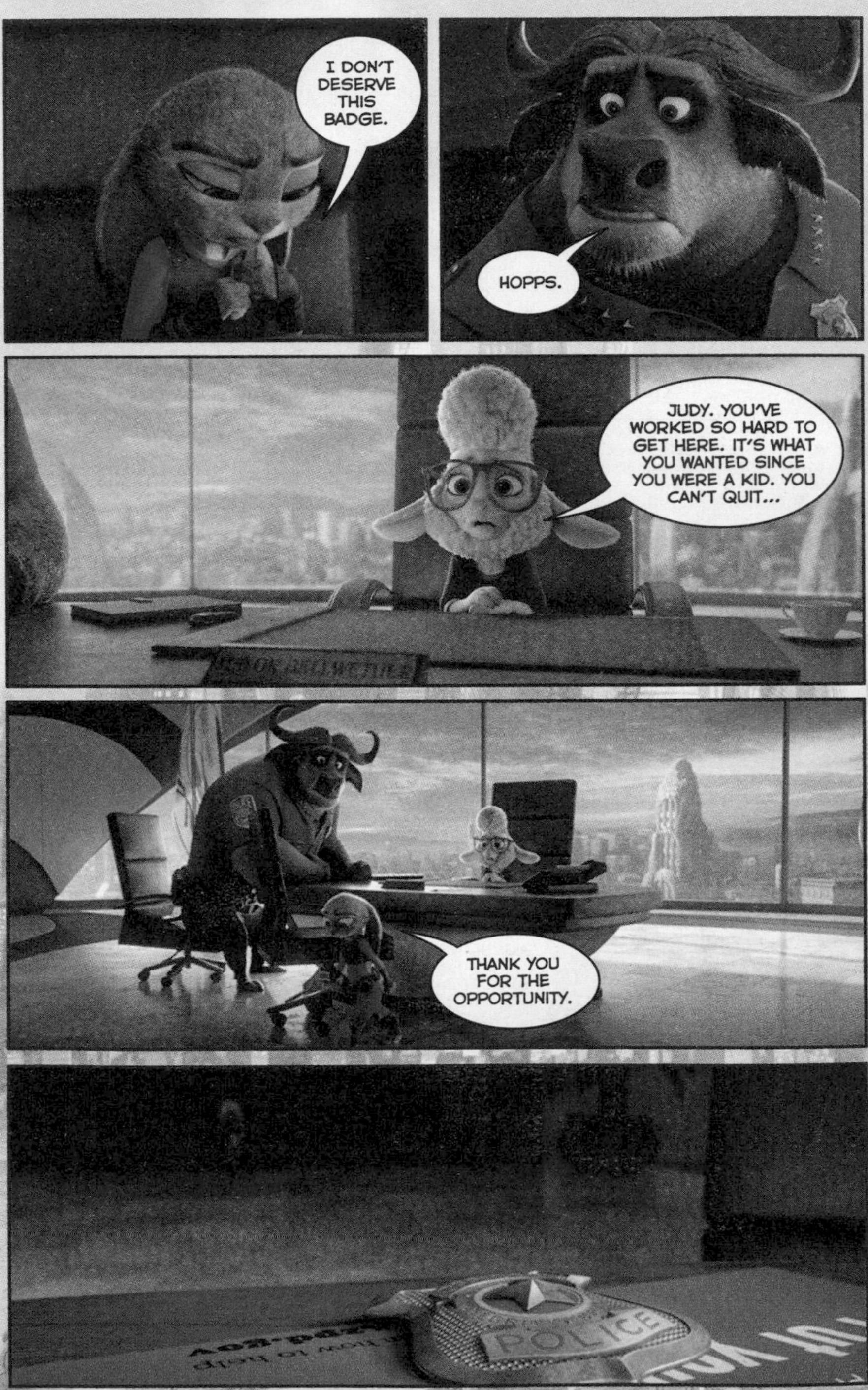
I DON'T DESERVE THIS BADGE.
HOPPS.
JUDY. YOU'VE WORKED SO HARD TO GET HERE. IT'S WHAT YOU WANTED SINCE YOU WERE A KID. YOU CAN'T QUIT...
THANK YOU FOR THE OPPORTUNITY.
POLICE

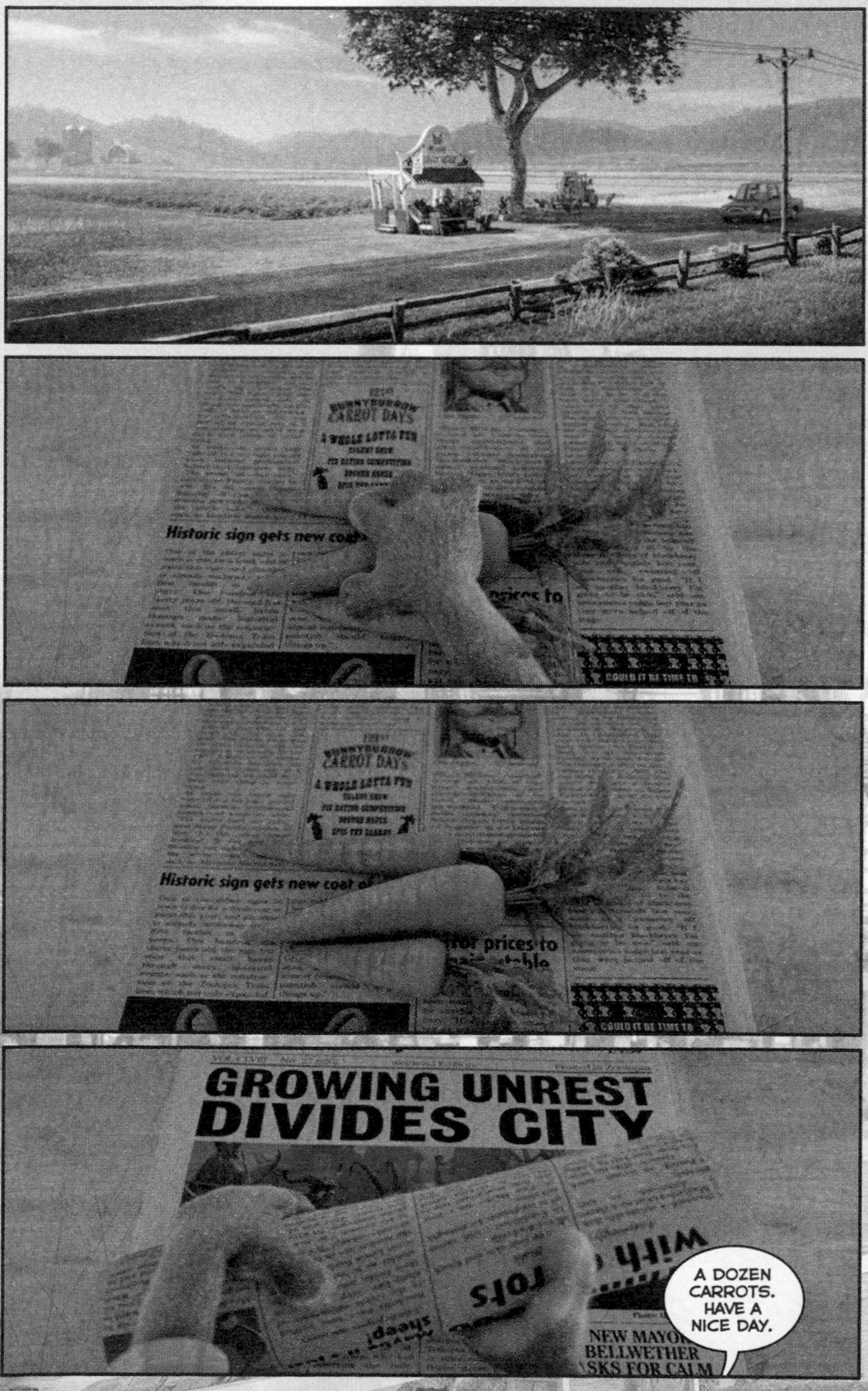
CARROT DAYS
Historic sign gets new coat
GROWING UNREST
DIVIDES CITY
NEW MAYOR
BELLWETHER
ASKS FOR CALM
A DOZEN CARROTS. HAVE A NICE DAY.

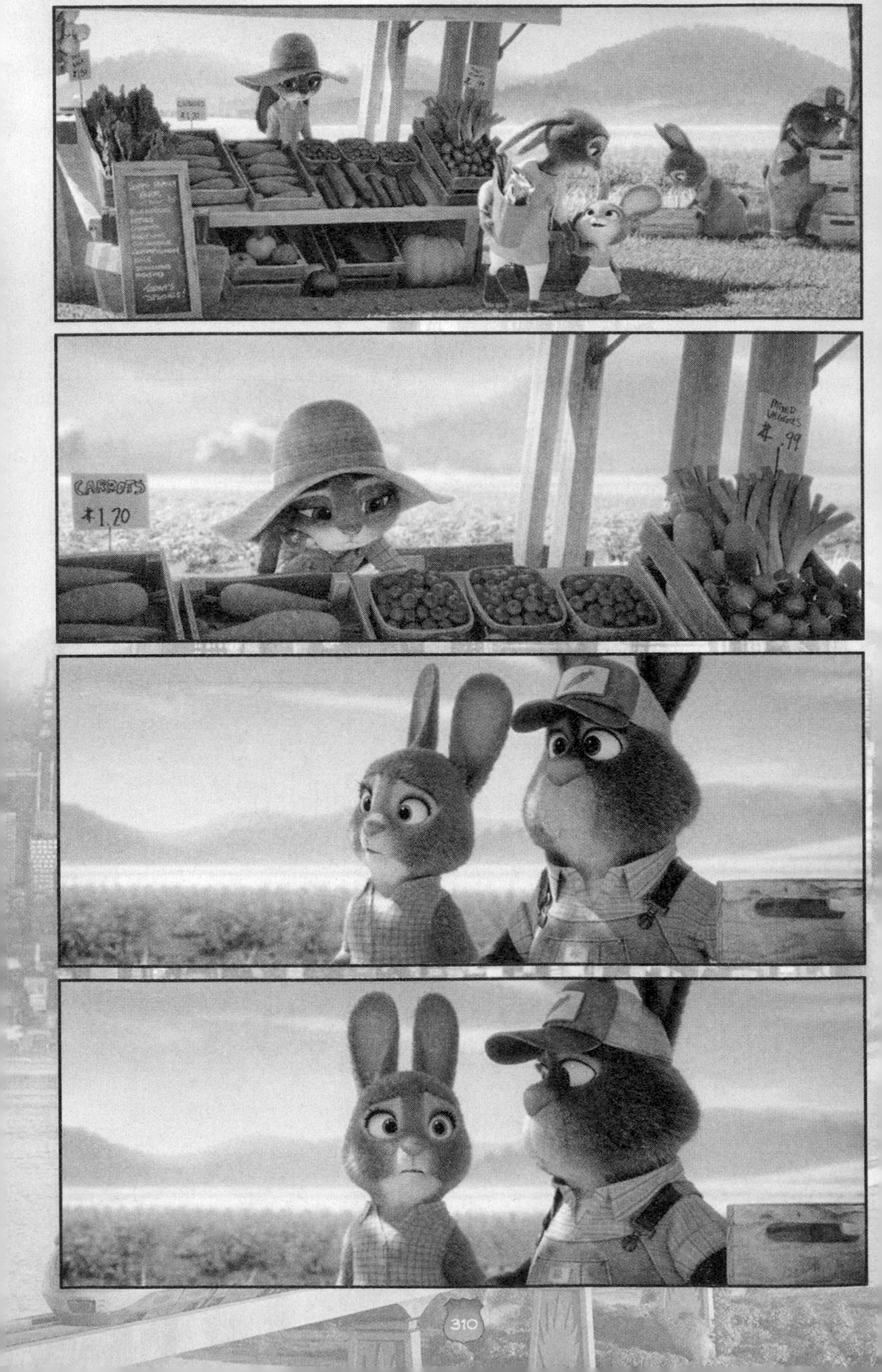
CARROTS
1.20
MIXED VEGGIES
4.99

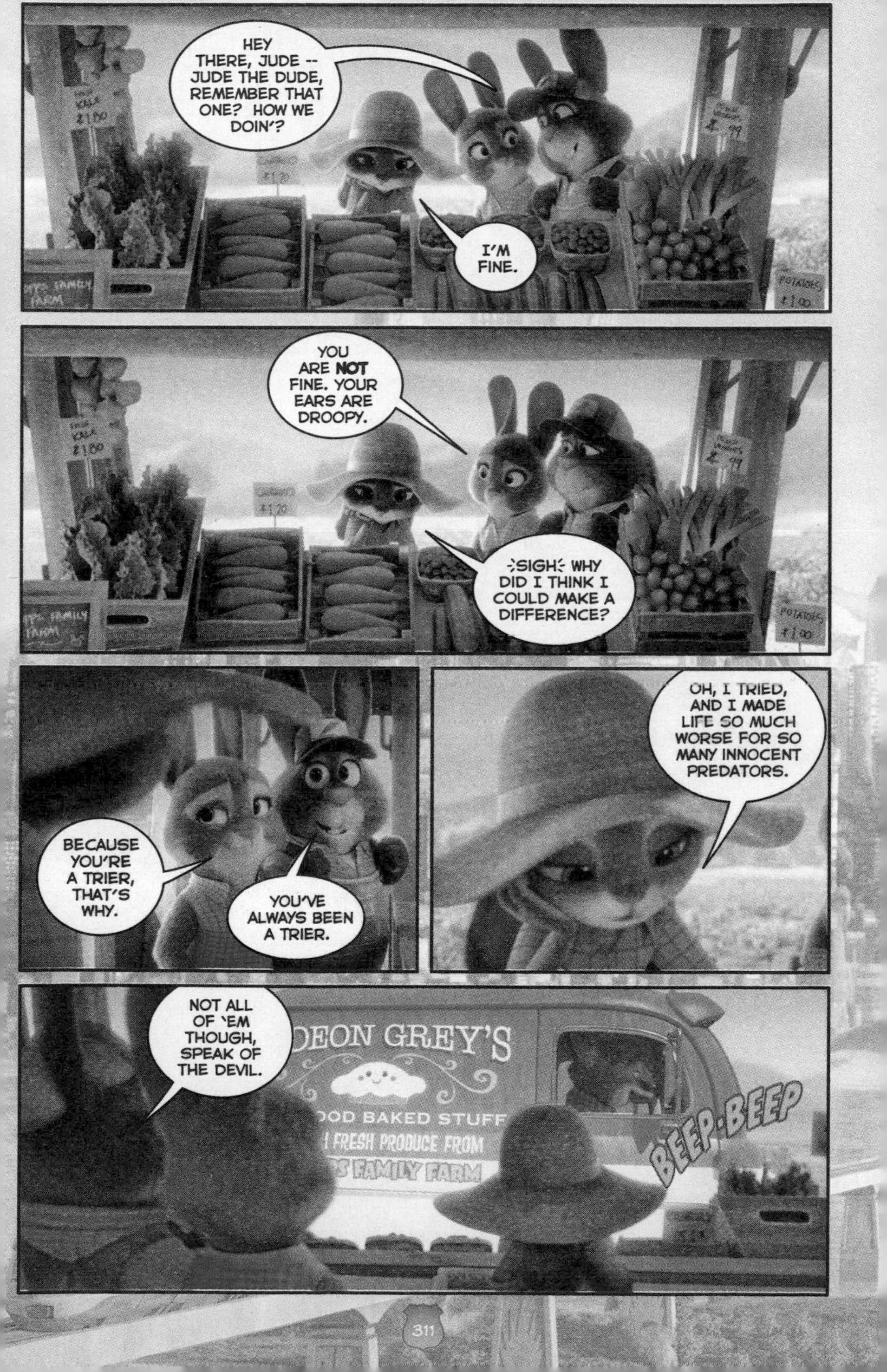

HEY THERE, JUDE -- JUDE THE DUDE, REMEMBER THAT ONE? HOW WE DOIN'?
I'M FINE.
YOU ARE **NOT** FINE. YOUR EARS ARE DROOPY.
SIGH WHY DID I THINK I COULD MAKE A DIFFERENCE?
BECAUSE YOU'RE A TRIER, THAT'S WHY.
YOU'VE ALWAYS BEEN A TRIER.
OH, I TRIED, AND I MADE LIFE SO MUCH WORSE FOR SO MANY INNOCENT PREDATORS.
NOT ALL OF 'EM THOUGH, SPEAK OF THE DEVIL.
DEON GREY'S
OOD BAKED STUFF
FRESH PRODUCE FROM
FAMILY FARM
BEEP-BEEP

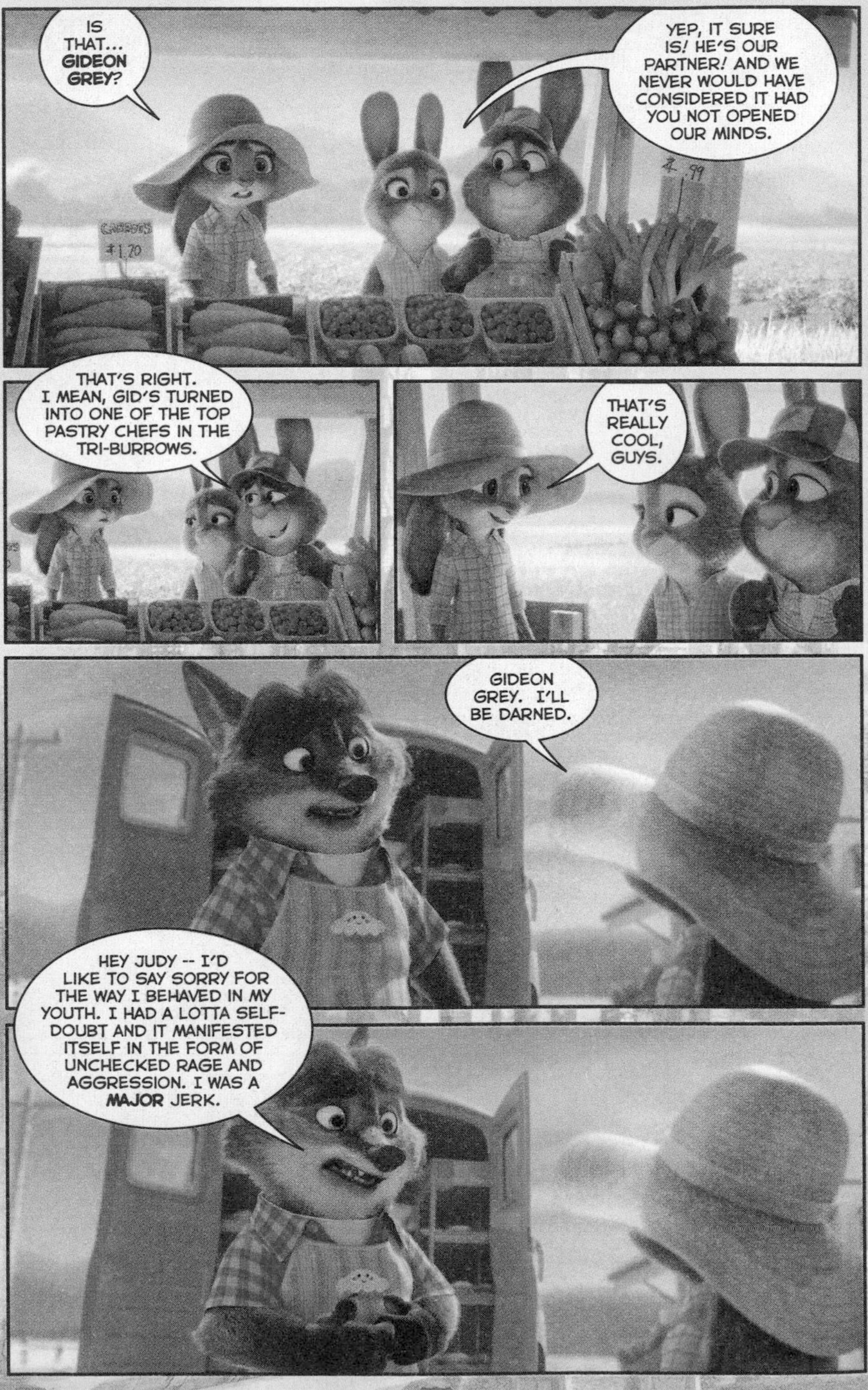
IS THAT... **GIDEON GREY?**
YEP, IT SURE IS! HE'S OUR PARTNER! AND WE NEVER WOULD HAVE CONSIDERED IT HAD YOU NOT OPENED OUR MINDS.
THAT'S RIGHT. I MEAN, GID'S TURNED INTO ONE OF THE TOP PASTRY CHEFS IN THE TRI-BURROWS.
THAT'S REALLY COOL, GUYS.
GIDEON GREY. I'LL BE DARNED.
HEY JUDY -- I'D LIKE TO SAY SORRY FOR THE WAY I BEHAVED IN MY YOUTH. I HAD A LOTTA SELF-DOUBT AND IT MANIFESTED ITSELF IN THE FORM OF UNCHECKED RAGE AND AGGRESSION. I WAS A **MAJOR** JERK.

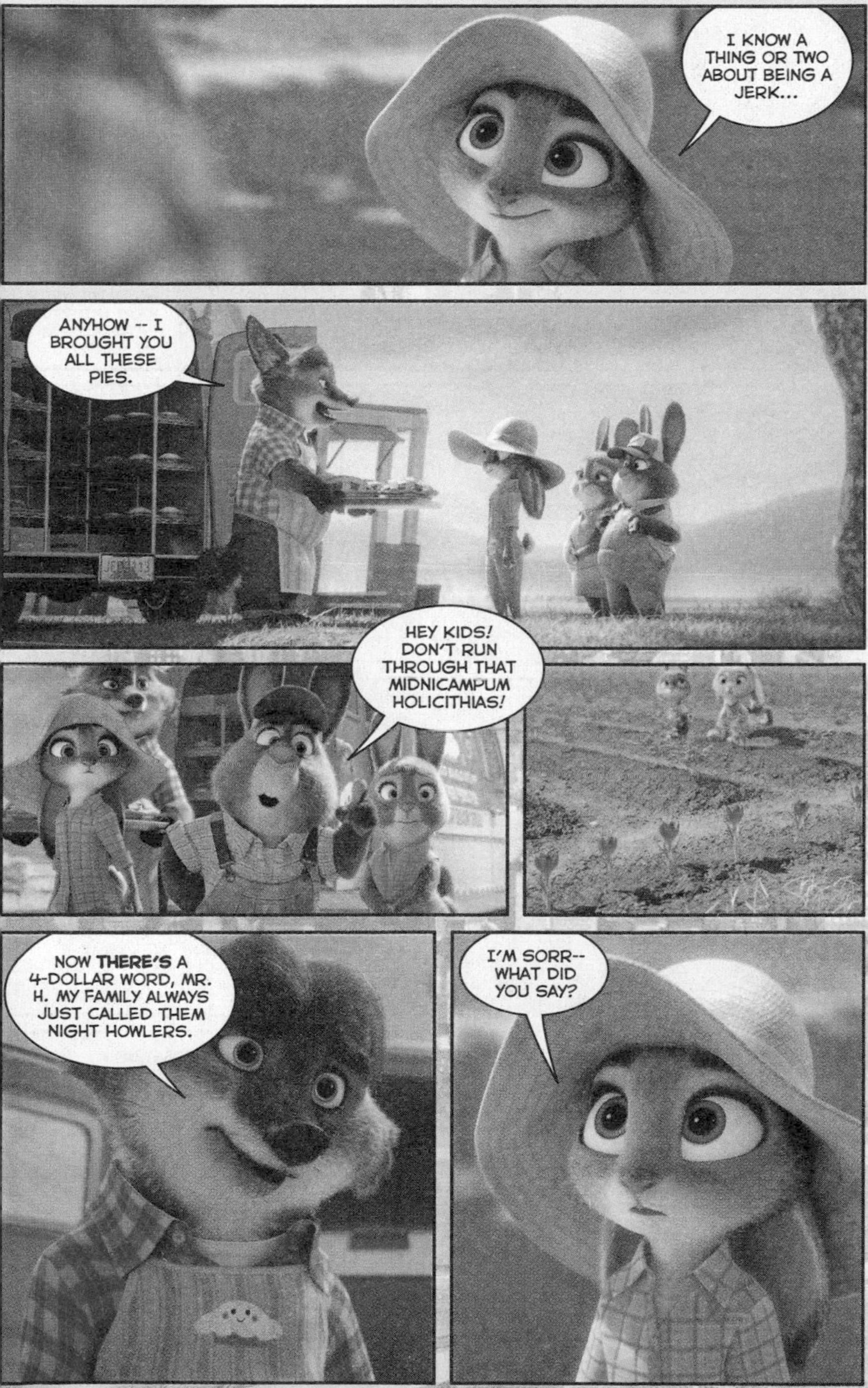
I KNOW A THING OR TWO ABOUT BEING A JERK...
ANYHOW -- I BROUGHT YOU ALL THESE PIES.
HEY KIDS! DON'T RUN THROUGH THAT MIDNICAMPUM HOLICITHIAS!
NOW **THERE'S** A 4-DOLLAR WORD, MR. H. MY FAMILY ALWAYS JUST CALLED THEM NIGHT HOWLERS.
I'M SORR-- WHAT DID YOU SAY?

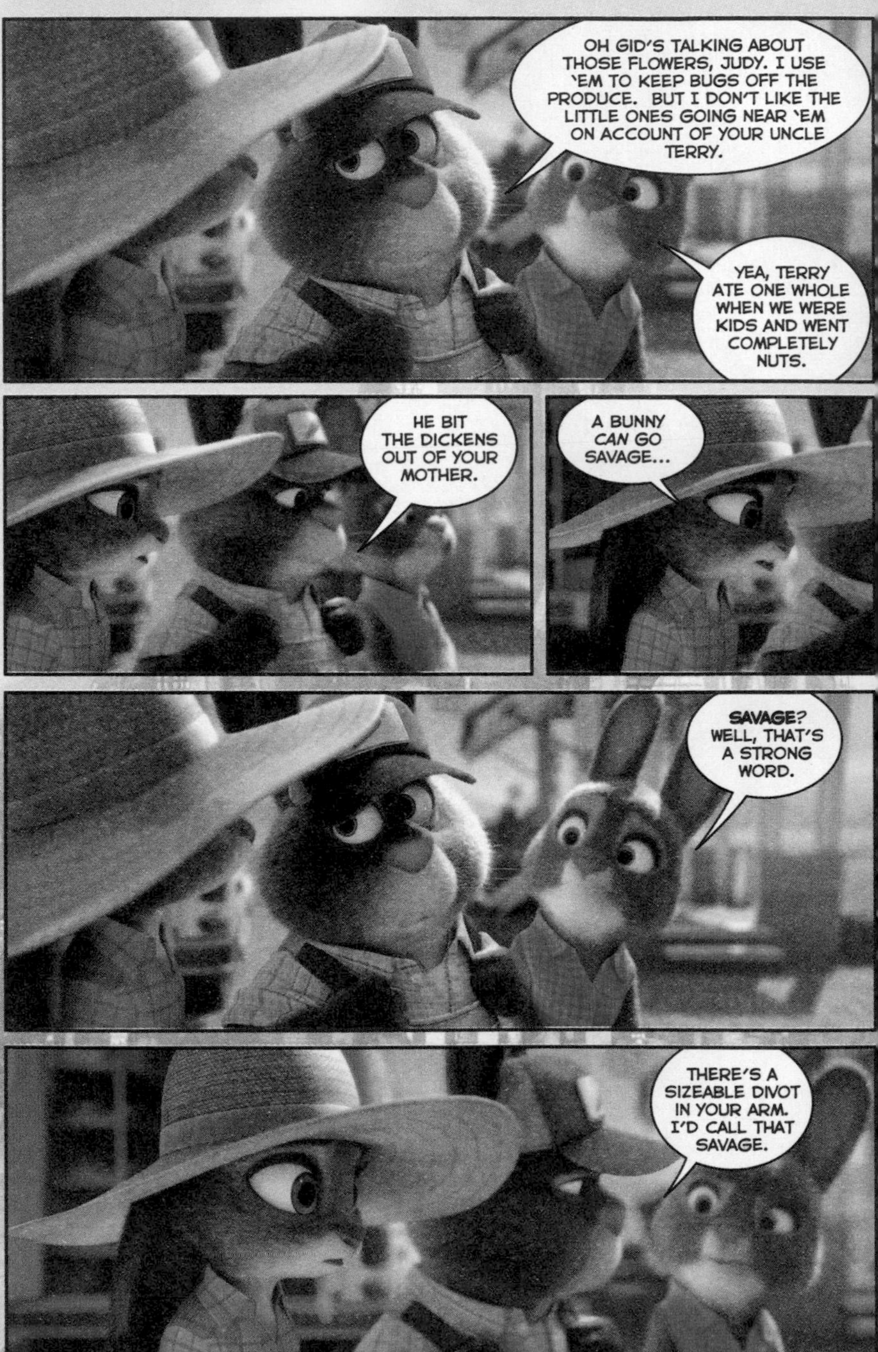
OH GID'S TALKING ABOUT THOSE FLOWERS, JUDY. I USE 'EM TO KEEP BUGS OFF THE PRODUCE. BUT I DON'T LIKE THE LITTLE ONES GOING NEAR 'EM ON ACCOUNT OF YOUR UNCLE TERRY.
YEA, TERRY ATE ONE WHOLE WHEN WE WERE KIDS AND WENT COMPLETELY NUTS.
HE BIT THE DICKENS OUT OF YOUR MOTHER.
A BUNNY *CAN* GO SAVAGE...
SAVAGE? WELL, THAT'S A STRONG WORD.
THERE'S A SIZEABLE DIVOT IN YOUR ARM. I'D CALL THAT SAVAGE.

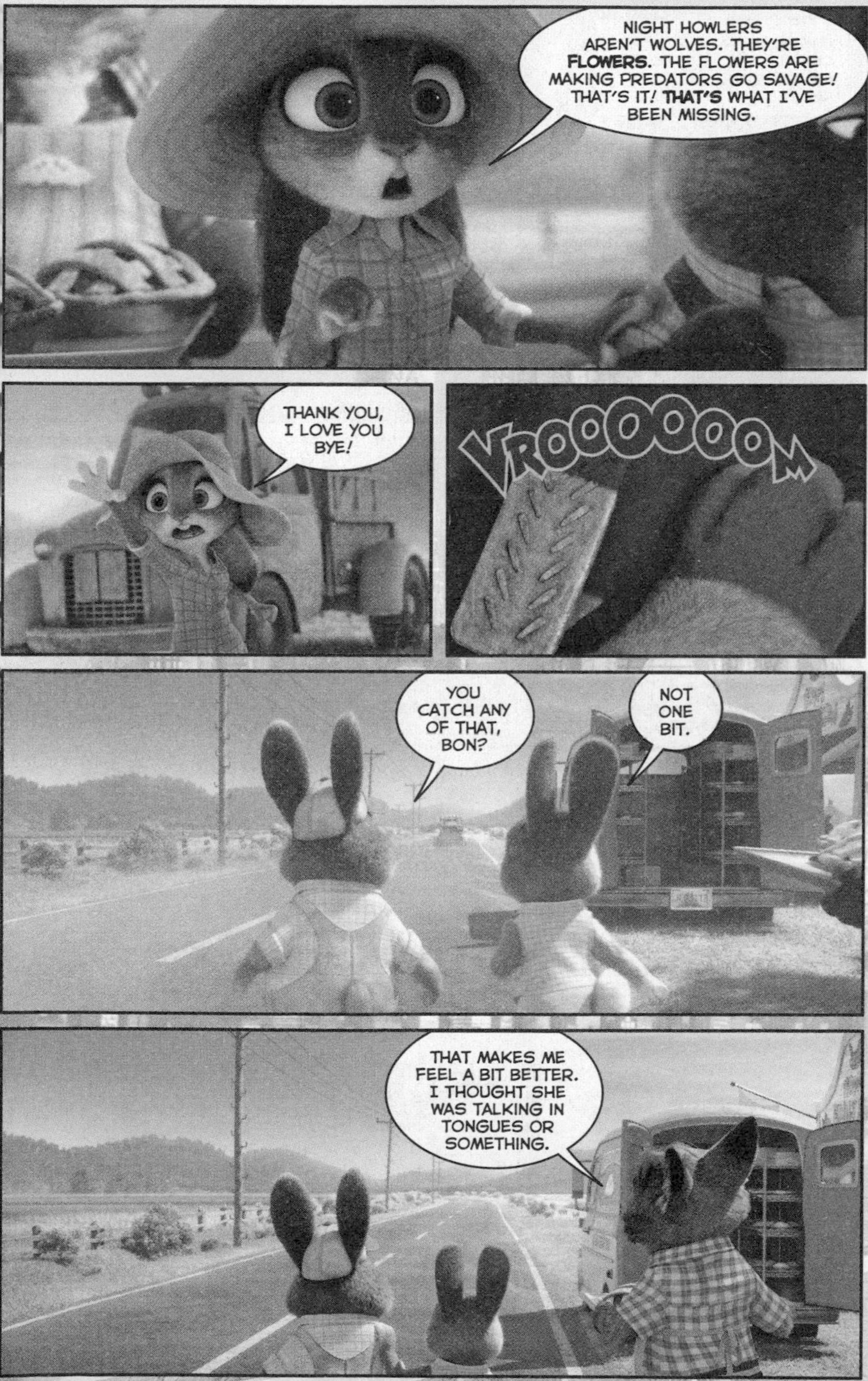
NIGHT HOWLERS AREN'T WOLVES. THEY'RE **FLOWERS.** THE FLOWERS ARE MAKING PREDATORS GO SAVAGE! THAT'S IT! **THAT'S** WHAT I'VE BEEN MISSING.
THANK YOU, I LOVE YOU BYE!
VROOOOOOOM
YOU CATCH ANY OF THAT, BON?
NOT ONE BIT.
THAT MAKES ME FEEL A BIT BETTER. I THOUGHT SHE WAS TALKING IN TONGUES OR SOMETHING.

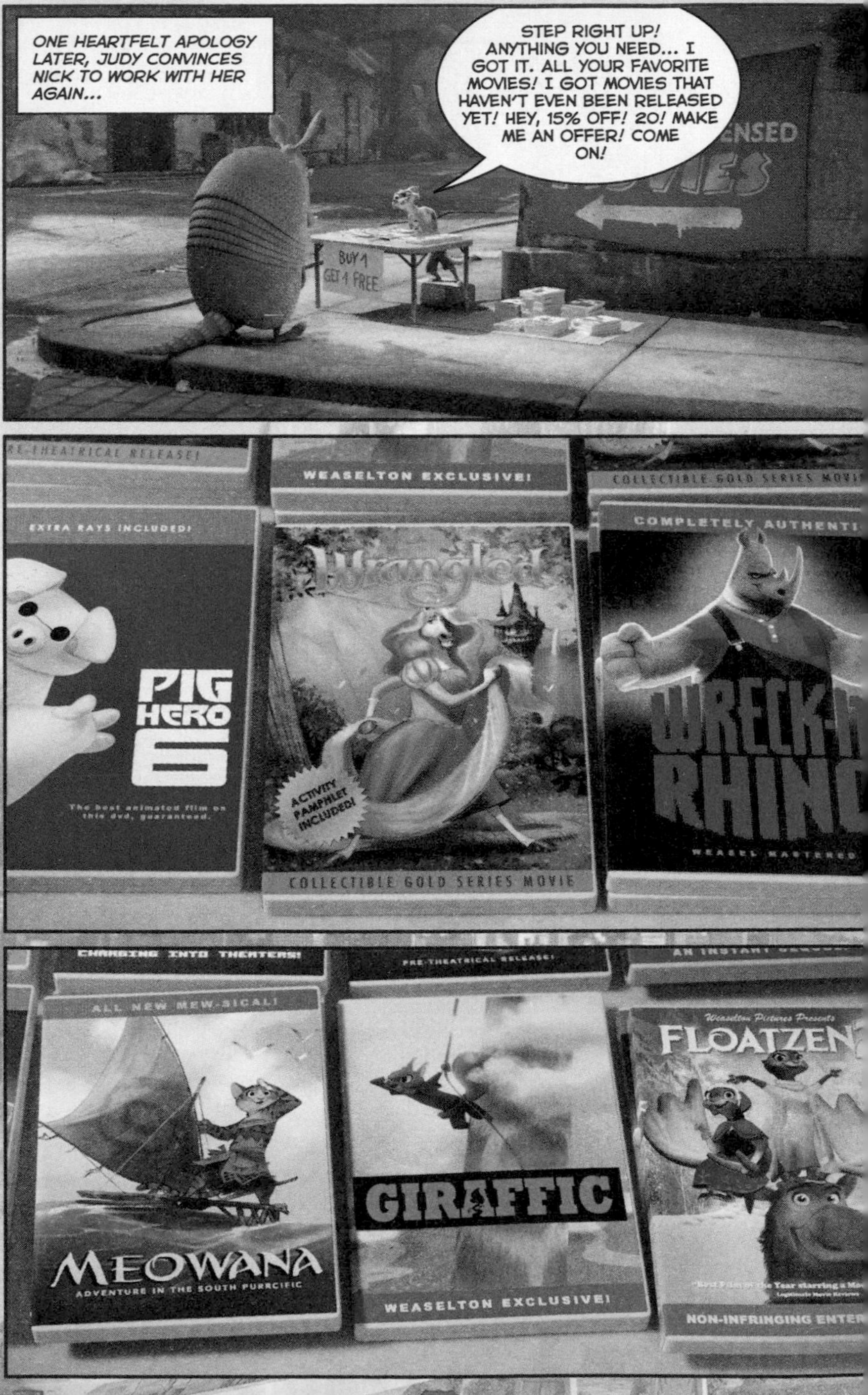
ONE HEARTFELT APOLOGY LATER, JUDY CONVINCES NICK TO WORK WITH HER AGAIN...
STEP RIGHT UP! ANYTHING YOU NEED... I GOT IT. ALL YOUR FAVORITE MOVIES! I GOT MOVIES THAT HAVEN'T EVEN BEEN RELEASED YET! HEY, 15% OFF! 20! MAKE ME AN OFFER! COME ON!
BUY 1 GET 1 FREE
WEASELTON EXCLUSIVE!
EXTRA RAYS INCLUDED!
PIG HERO 6
The best animated film on this dvd, guaranteed.
Wrangled
ACTIVITY PAMPHLET INCLUDED!
COLLECTIBLE GOLD SERIES MOVIE
CHARGING INTO THEATERS!
PRE-THEATRICAL RELEASE!
ALL NEW MEW-SICAL!
MEOWANA
ADVENTURE IN THE SOUTH PURRCIFIC
GIRAFFIC
WEASELTON EXCLUSIVE!
Weaselton Pictures Presents

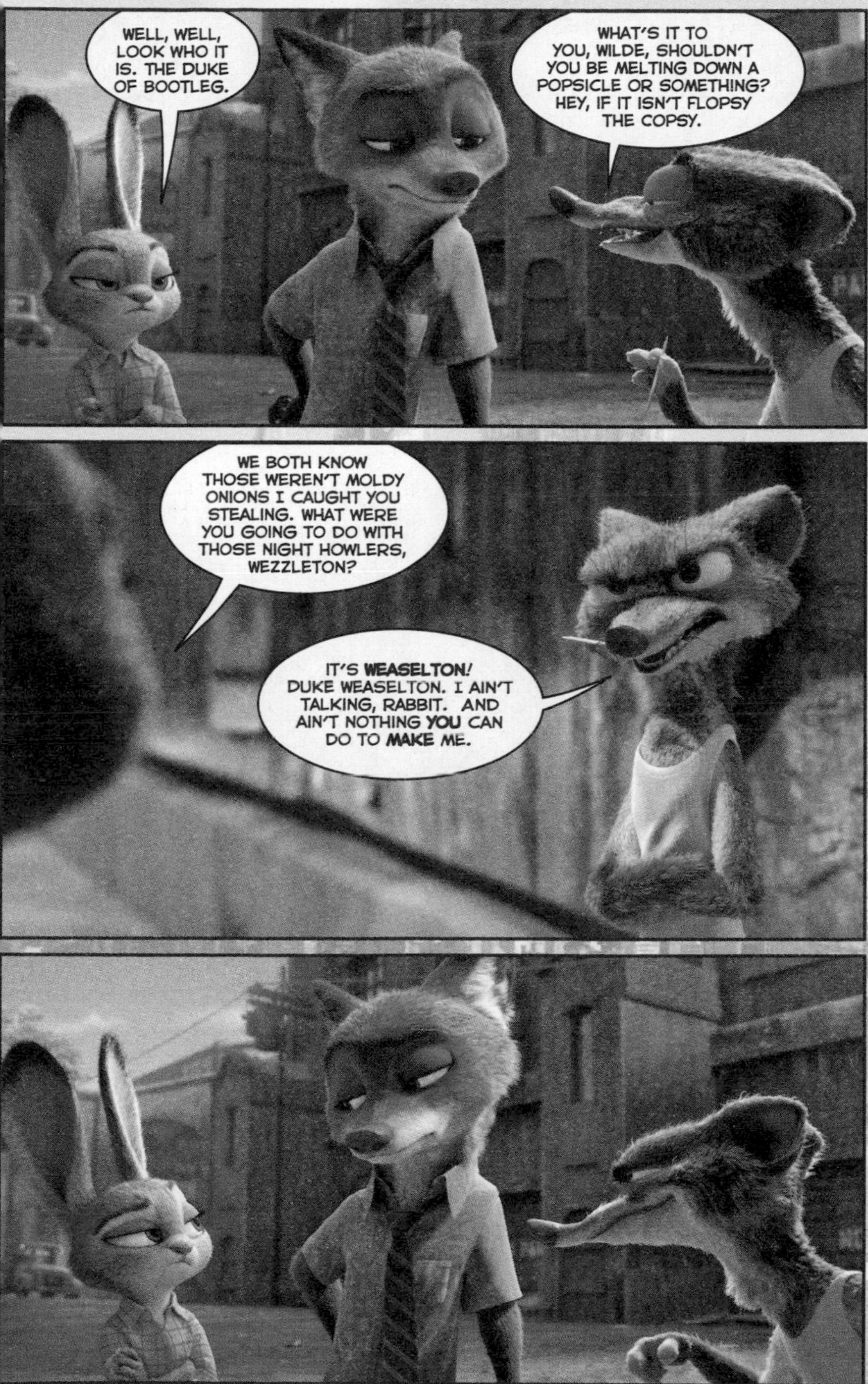
WELL, WELL, LOOK WHO IT IS. THE DUKE OF BOOTLEG.
WHAT'S IT TO YOU, WILDE, SHOULDN'T YOU BE MELTING DOWN A POPSICLE OR SOMETHING? HEY, IF IT ISN'T FLOPSY THE COPSY.
WE BOTH KNOW THOSE WEREN'T MOLDY ONIONS I CAUGHT YOU STEALING. WHAT WERE YOU GOING TO DO WITH THOSE NIGHT HOWLERS, WEZZLETON?
IT'S **WEASELTON!** DUKE WEASELTON. I AIN'T TALKING, RABBIT. AND AIN'T NOTHING **YOU** CAN DO TO **MAKE** ME.

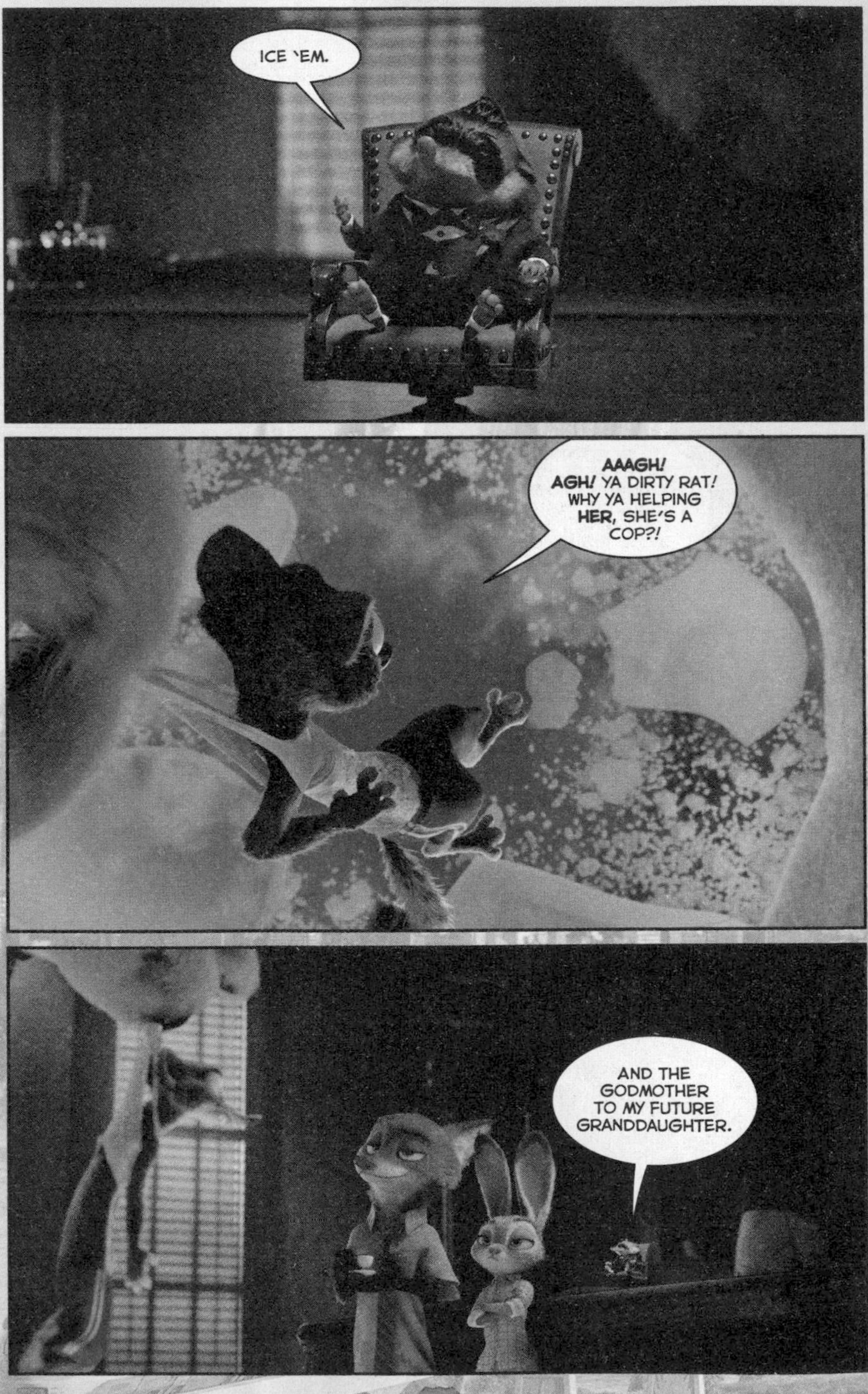
ICE 'EM.
AAAGH! AGH! YA DIRTY RAT! WHY YA HELPING HER, SHE'S A COP?!
AND THE GODMOTHER TO MY FUTURE GRANDDAUGHTER.

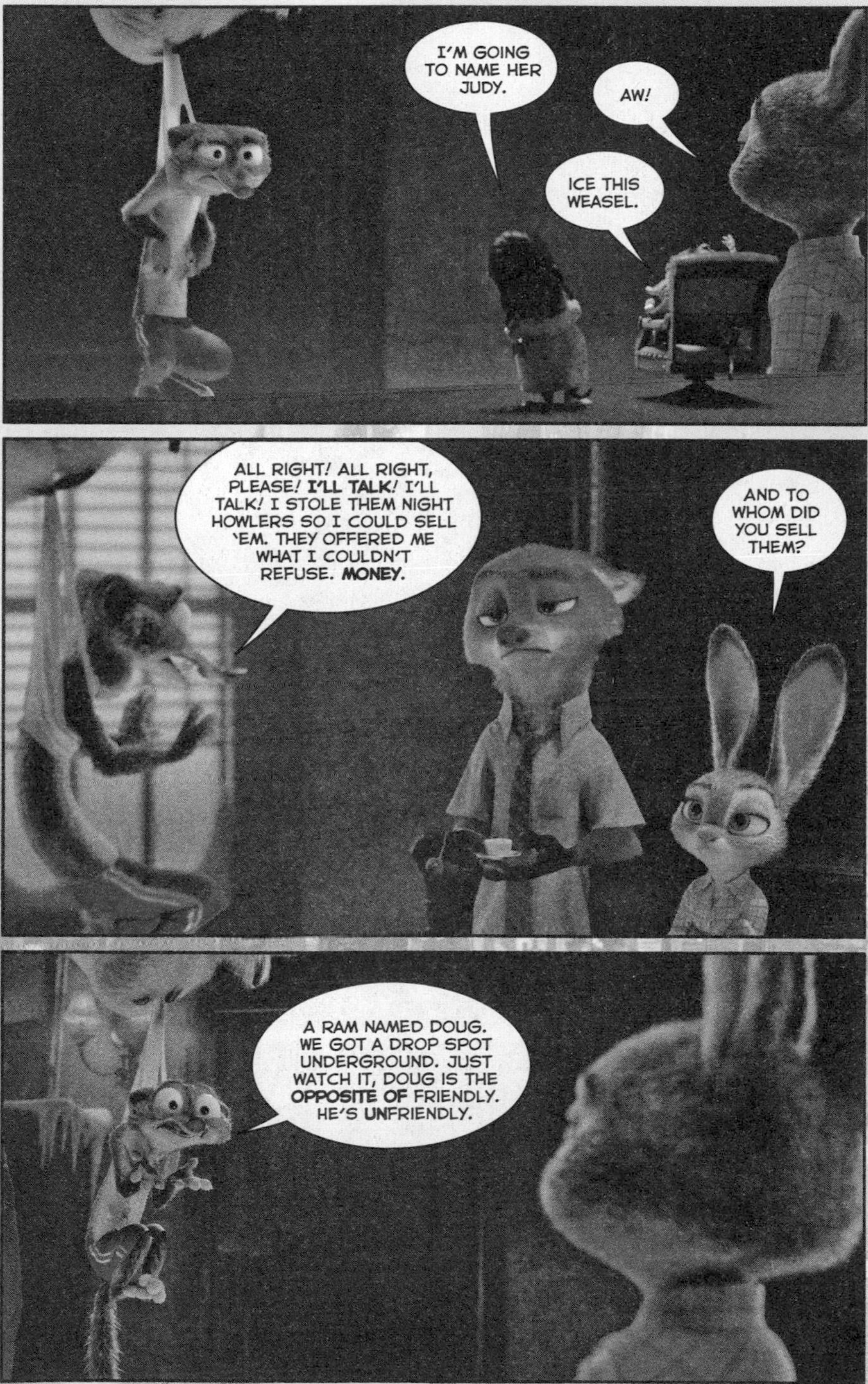
I'M GOING TO NAME HER JUDY.
AW!
ICE THIS WEASEL.
ALL RIGHT! ALL RIGHT, PLEASE! **I'LL TALK!** I'LL TALK! I STOLE THEM NIGHT HOWLERS SO I COULD SELL 'EM. THEY OFFERED ME WHAT I COULDN'T REFUSE. **MONEY.**
AND TO WHOM DID YOU SELL THEM?
A RAM NAMED DOUG. WE GOT A DROP SPOT UNDERGROUND. JUST WATCH IT, DOUG IS THE **OPPOSITE OF** FRIENDLY. HE'S **UN**FRIENDLY.

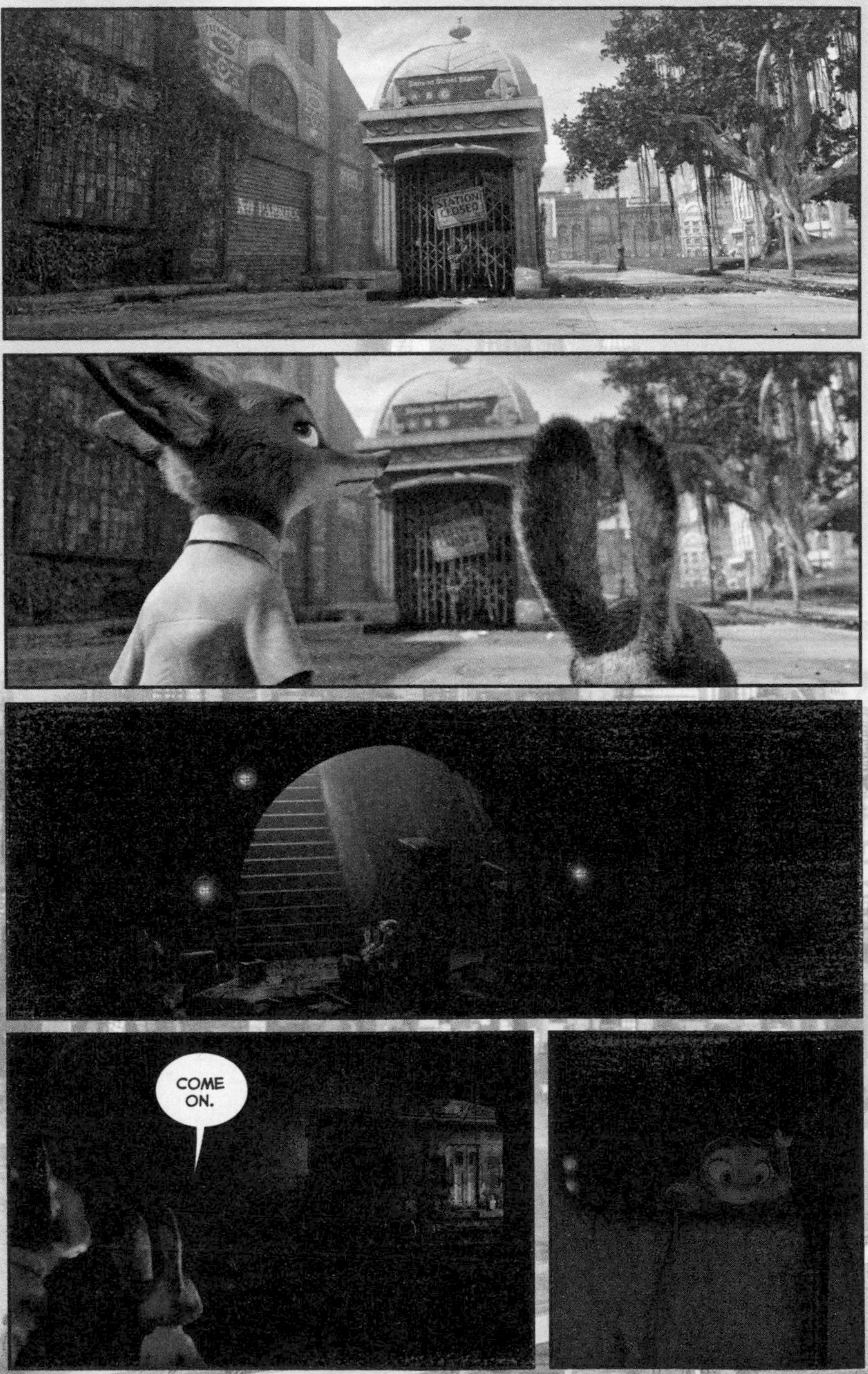
STATION CLOSED
COME ON.

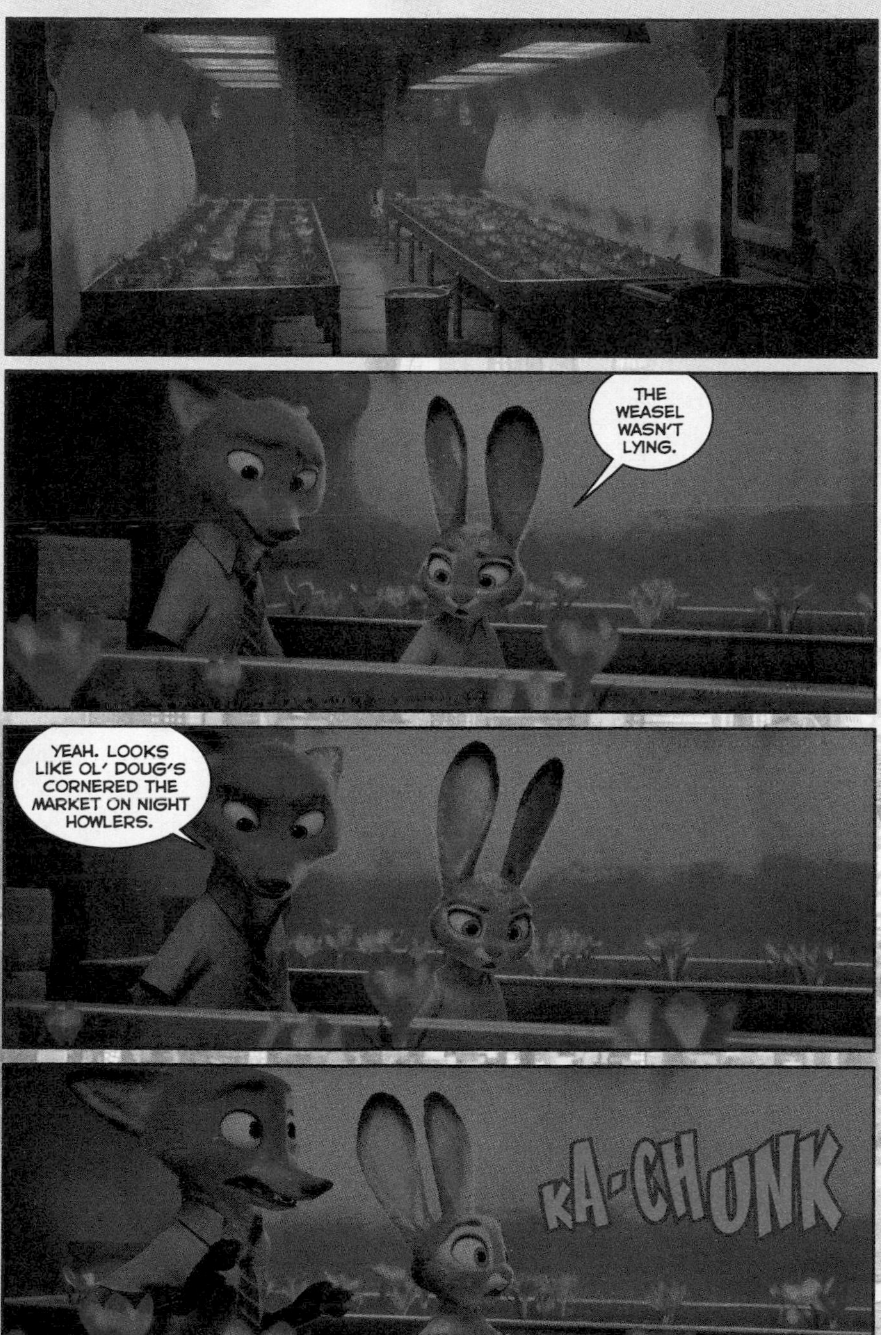
THE WEASEL WASN'T LYING.
YEAH. LOOKS LIKE OL' DOUG'S CORNERED THE MARKET ON NIGHT HOWLERS.
KA-CHUNK

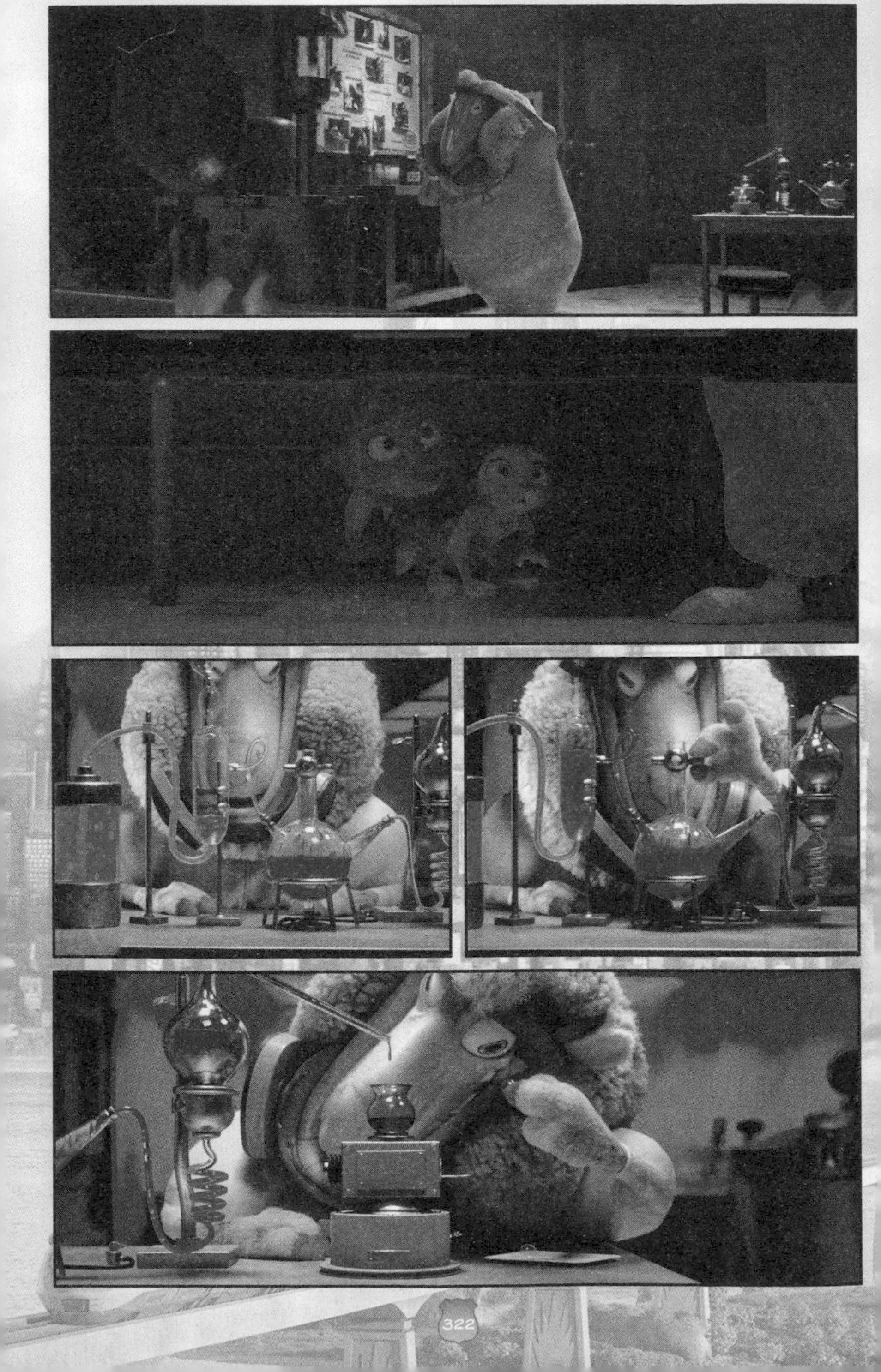

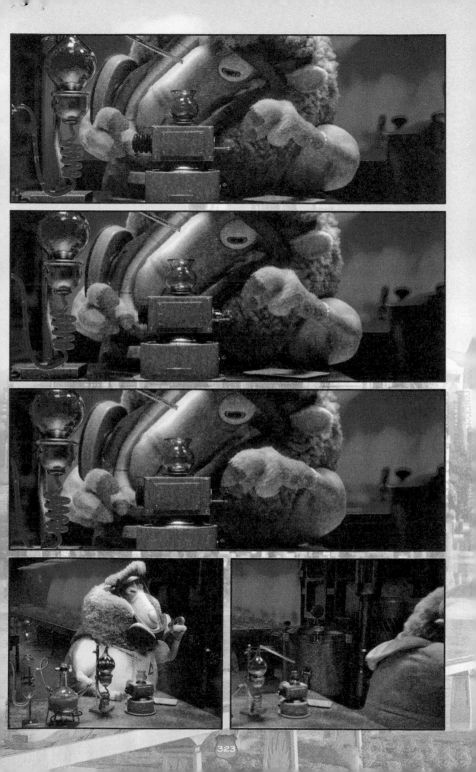

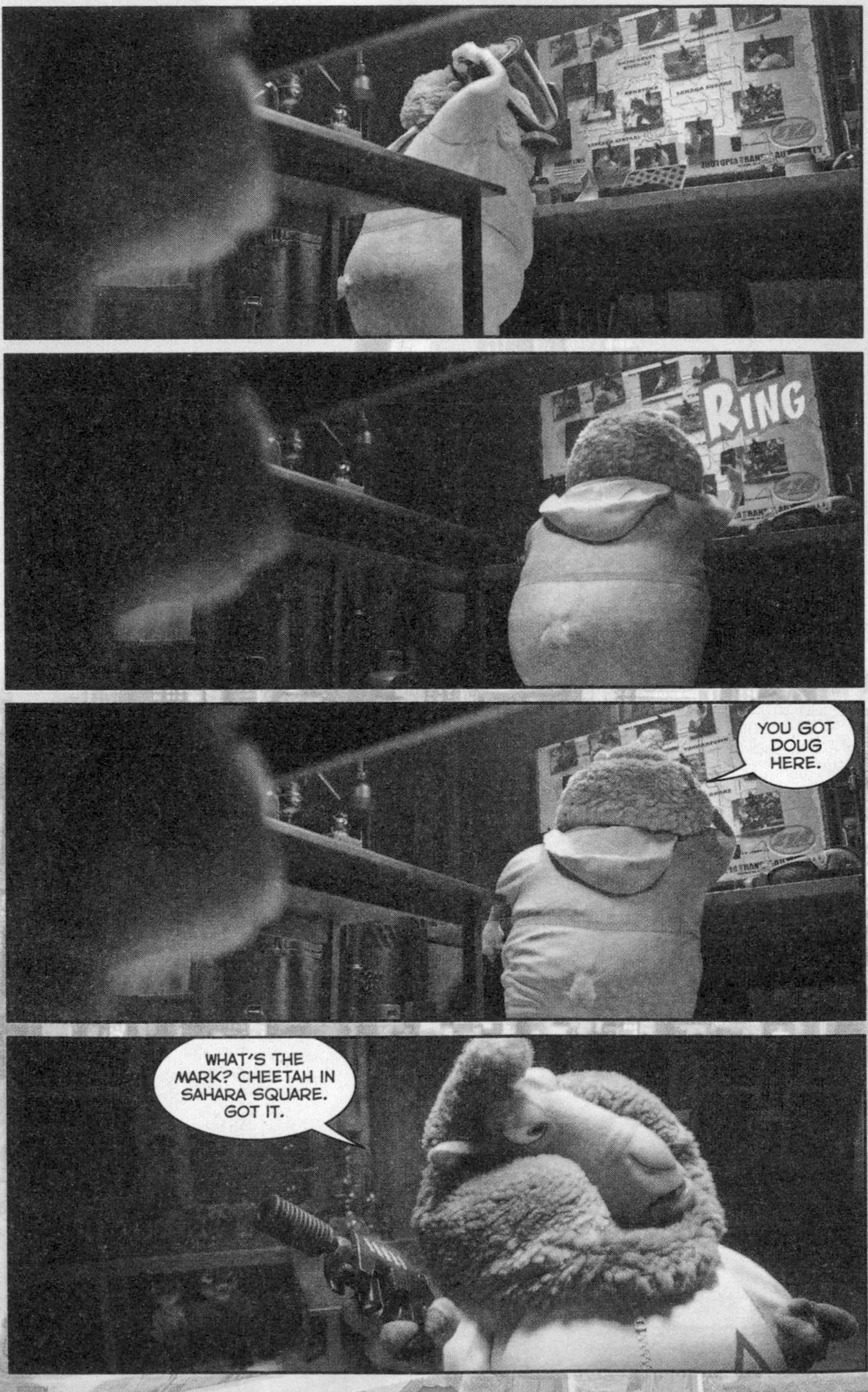
RING
YOU GOT DOUG HERE.
WHAT'S THE MARK? CHEETAH IN SAHARA SQUARE. GOT IT.

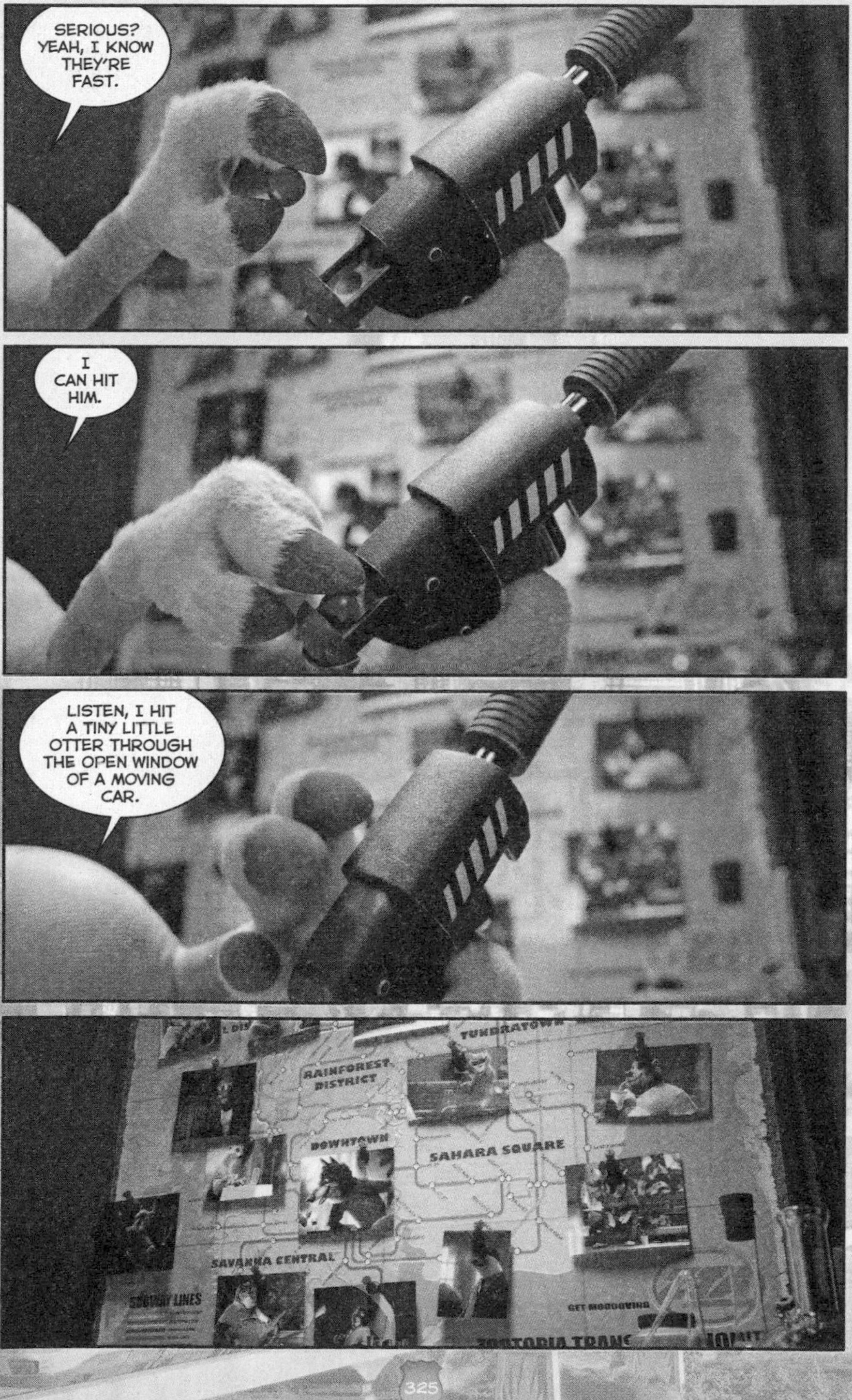
SERIOUS? YEAH, I KNOW THEY'RE FAST.
I CAN HIT HIM.
LISTEN, I HIT A TINY LITTLE OTTER THROUGH THE OPEN WINDOW OF A MOVING CAR.
TUNDRATOWN
RAINFOREST DISTRICT
DOWNTOWN
SAHARA SQUARE
SAVANNA CENTRAL
SUBWAY LINES
GET MOOOOVING

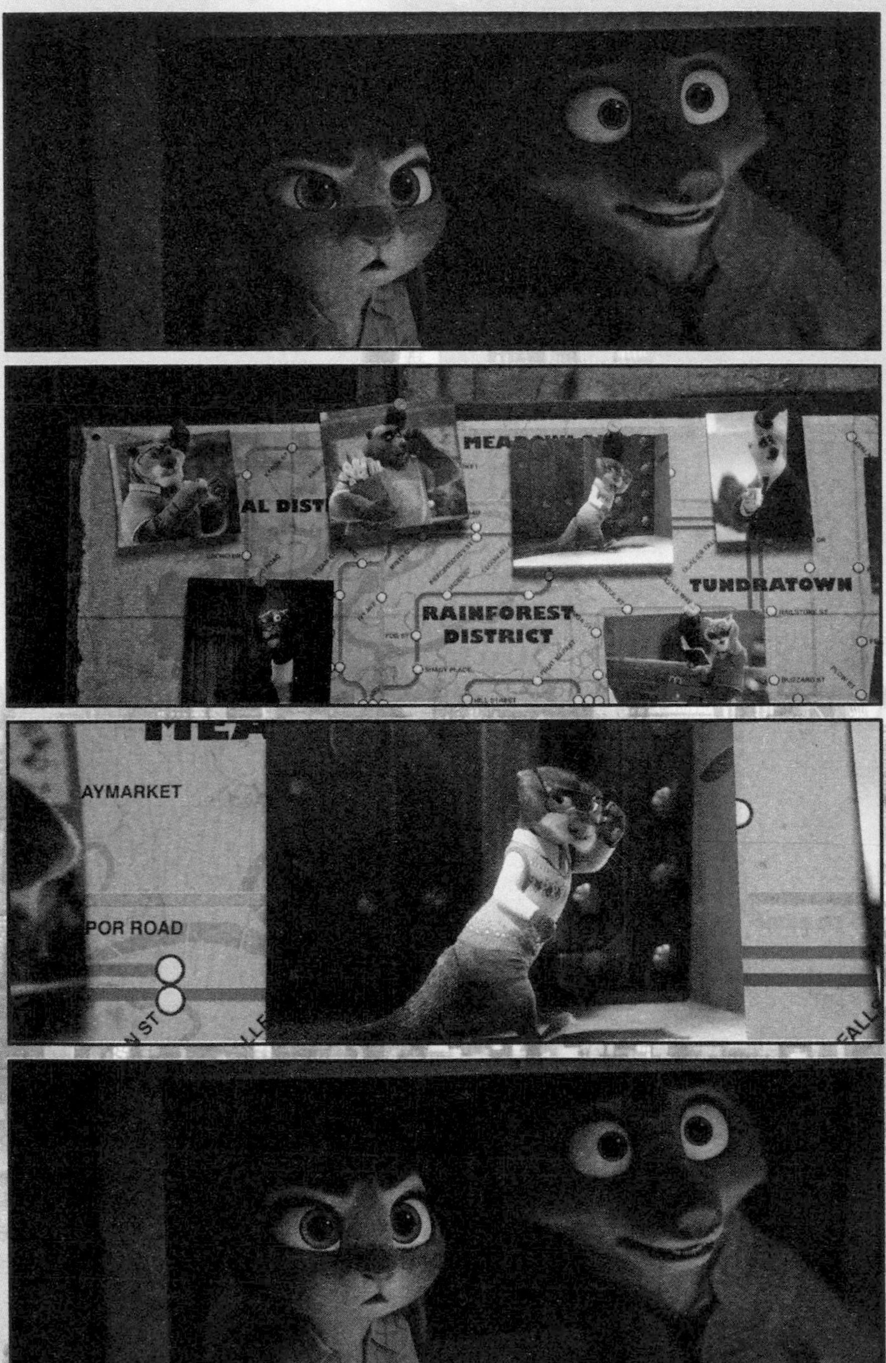
AL DIST
RAINFOREST
DISTRICT
TUNDRATOWN
AYMARKET
POR ROAD

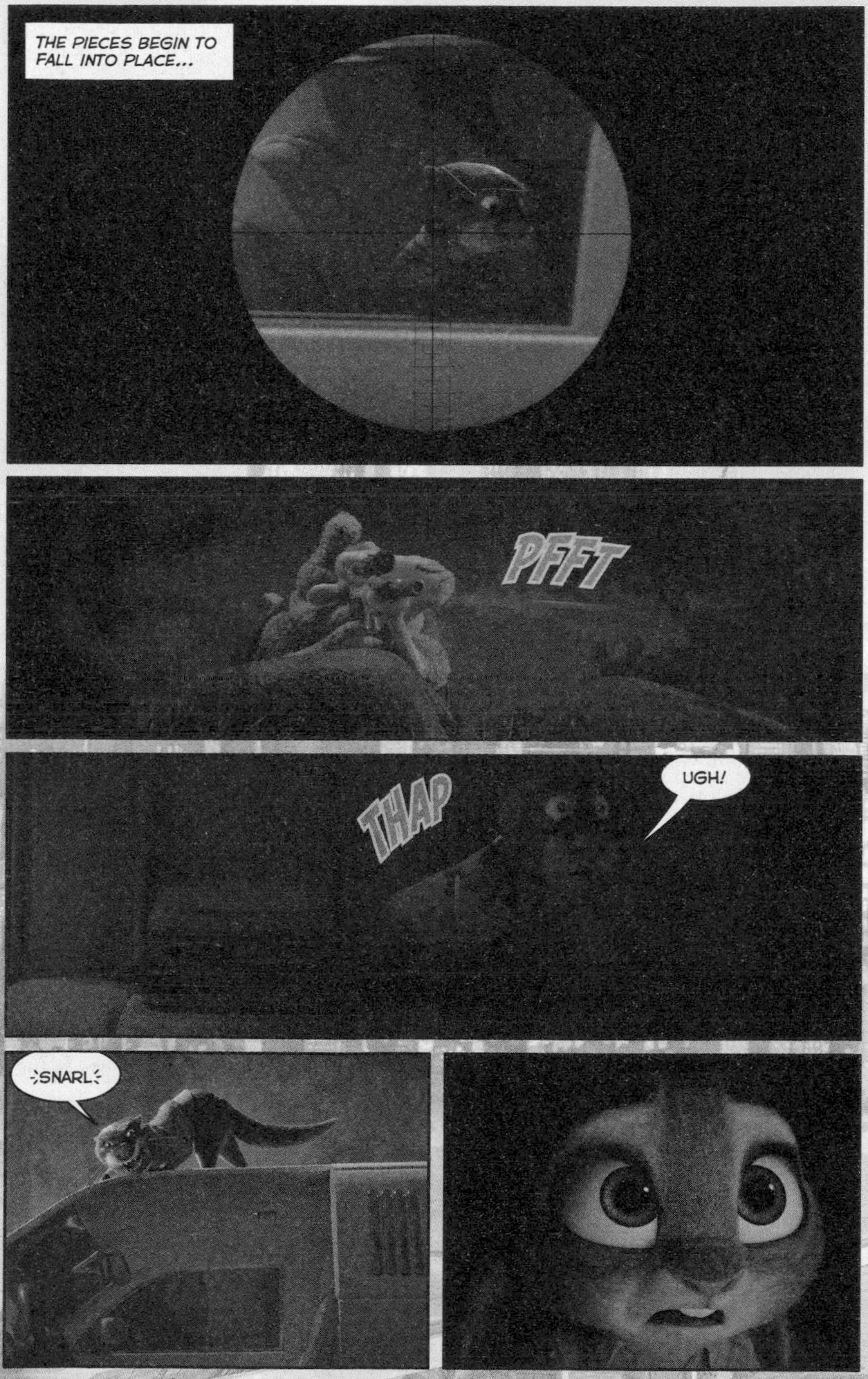
THE PIECES BEGIN TO FALL INTO PLACE...
PFFT
THAP
UGH!
SNARL

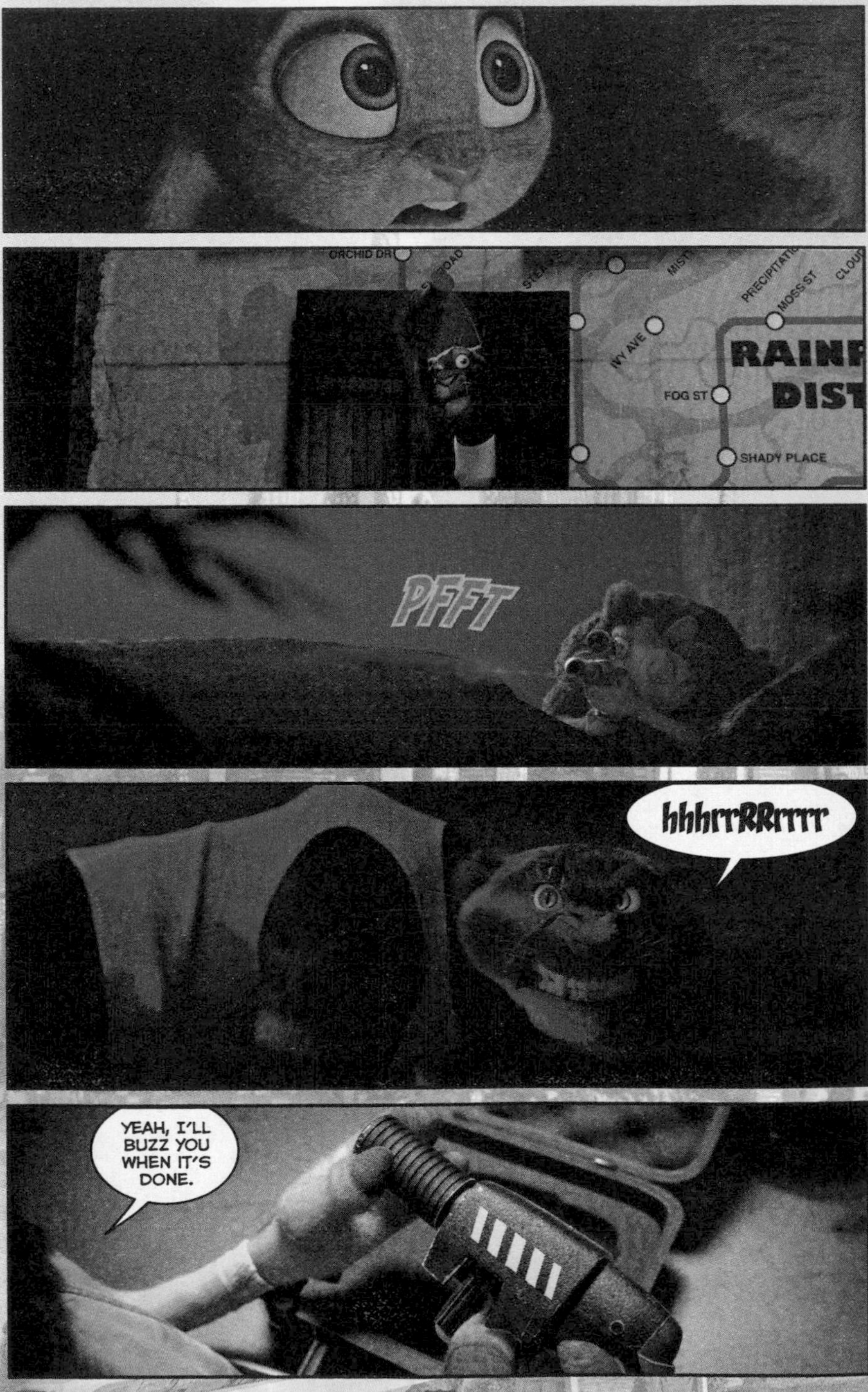
ORCHID DR
IVY AVE
FOG ST
SHADY PLACE
MOSS ST
RAIN
DIST
PFFT
hhhrrRRrrrr
YEAH, I'LL BUZZ YOU WHEN IT'S DONE.

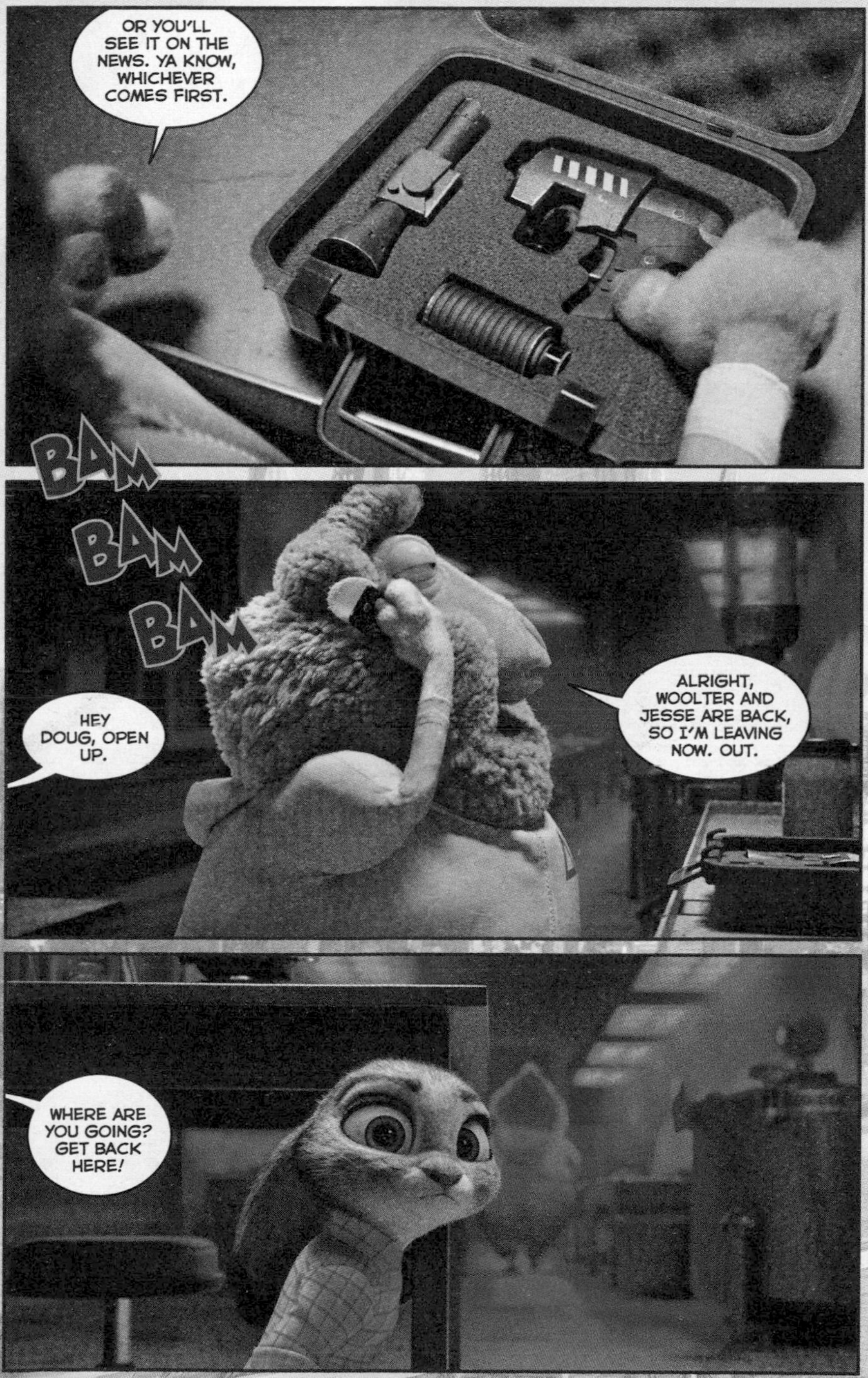
OR YOU'LL SEE IT ON THE NEWS. YA KNOW, WHICHEVER COMES FIRST.
BAM
BAM
BAM
HEY DOUG, OPEN UP.
ALRIGHT, WOOLTER AND JESSE ARE BACK, SO I'M LEAVING NOW. OUT.
WHERE ARE YOU GOING? GET BACK HERE!

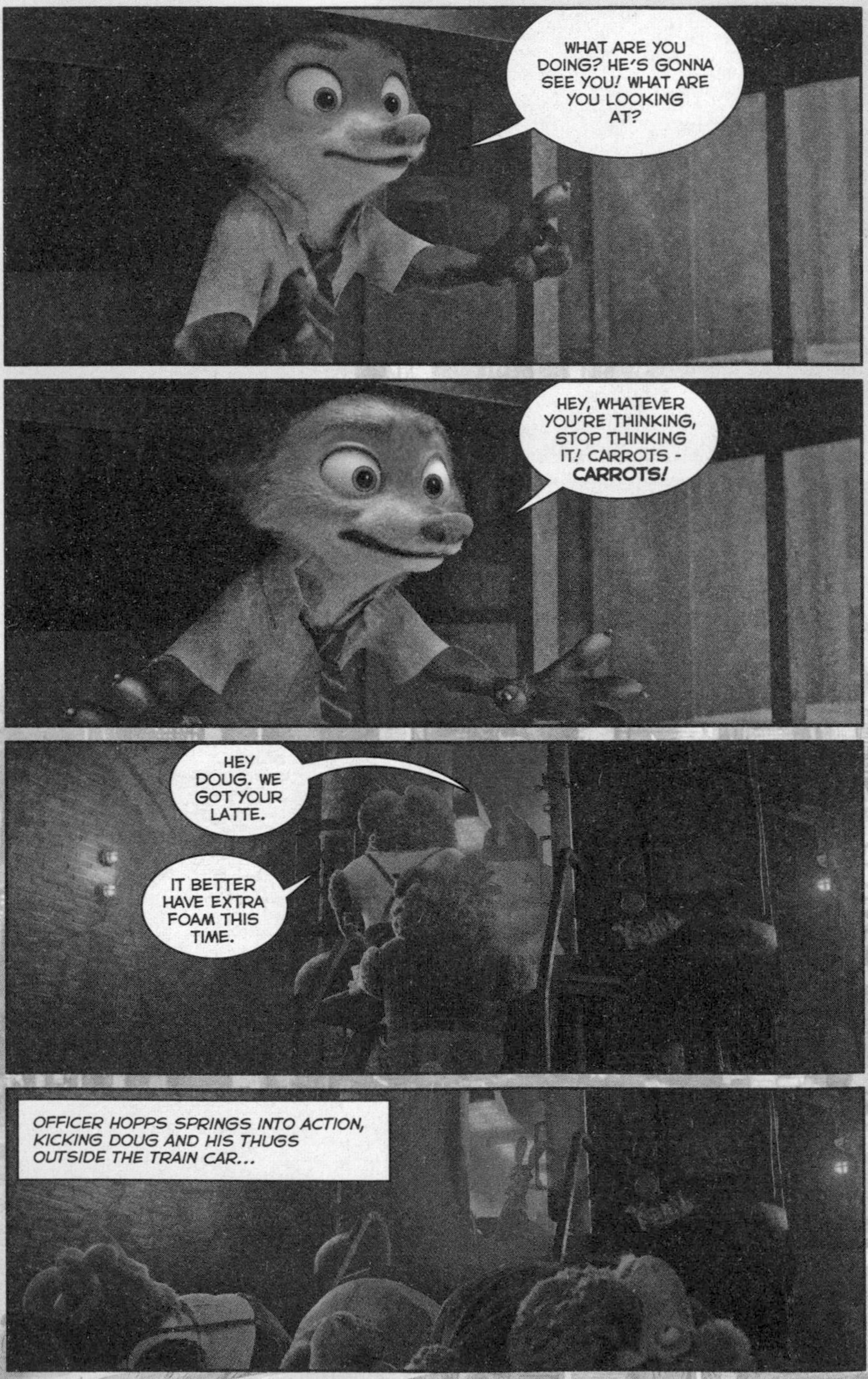
WHAT ARE YOU DOING? HE'S GONNA SEE YOU! WHAT ARE YOU LOOKING AT?
HEY, WHATEVER YOU'RE THINKING, STOP THINKING IT! CARROTS - **CARROTS!**
HEY DOUG. WE GOT YOUR LATTE.
IT BETTER HAVE EXTRA FOAM THIS TIME.
OFFICER HOPPS SPRINGS INTO ACTION, KICKING DOUG AND HIS THUGS OUTSIDE THE TRAIN CAR...

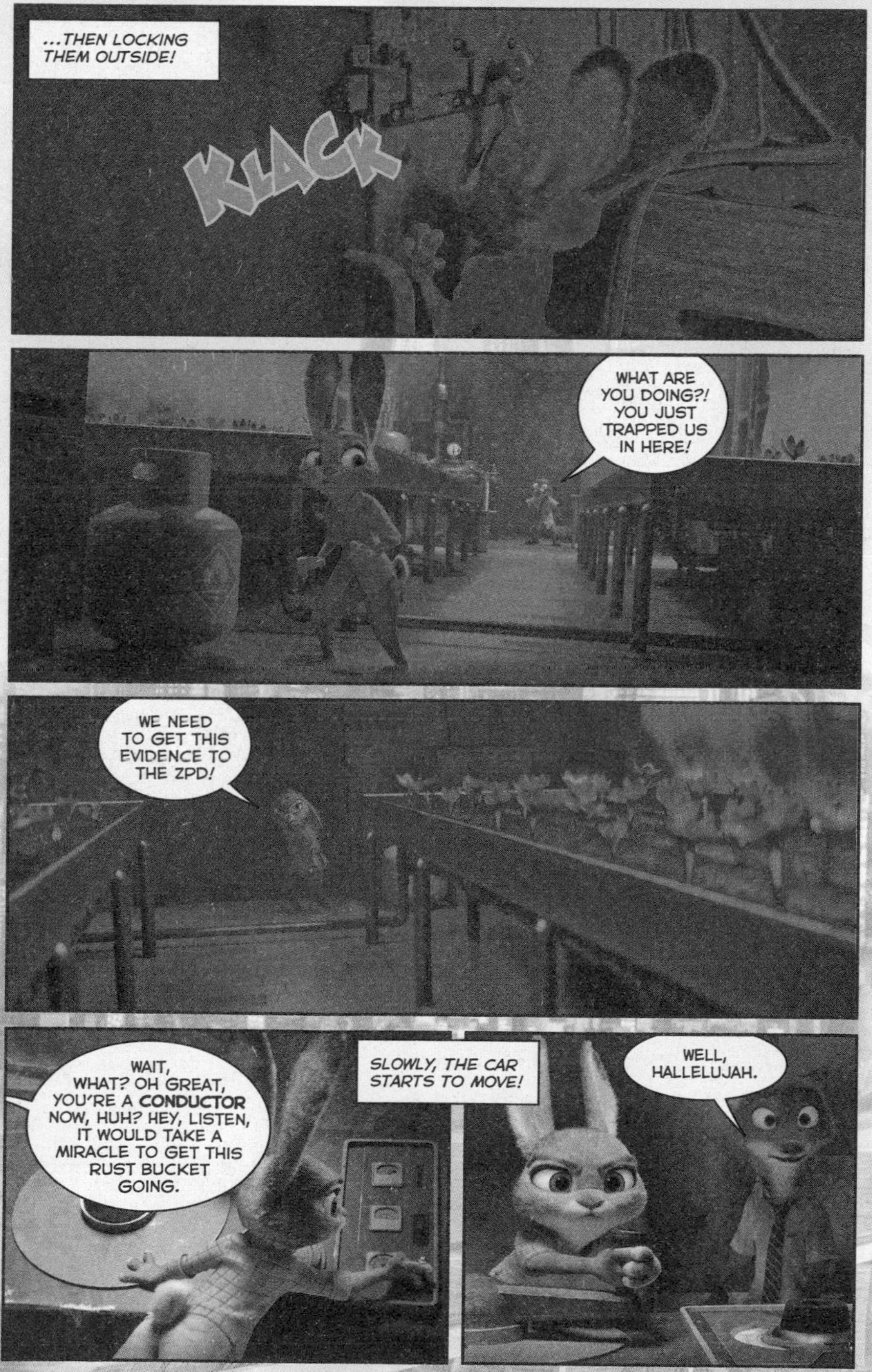
...THEN LOCKING THEM OUTSIDE!
KLACK
WHAT ARE YOU DOING?! YOU JUST TRAPPED US IN HERE!
WE NEED TO GET THIS EVIDENCE TO THE ZPD!
WAIT, WHAT? OH GREAT, YOU'RE A **CONDUCTOR** NOW, HUH? HEY, LISTEN, IT WOULD TAKE A MIRACLE TO GET THIS RUST BUCKET GOING.
SLOWLY, THE CAR STARTS TO MOVE!
WELL, HALLELUJAH.

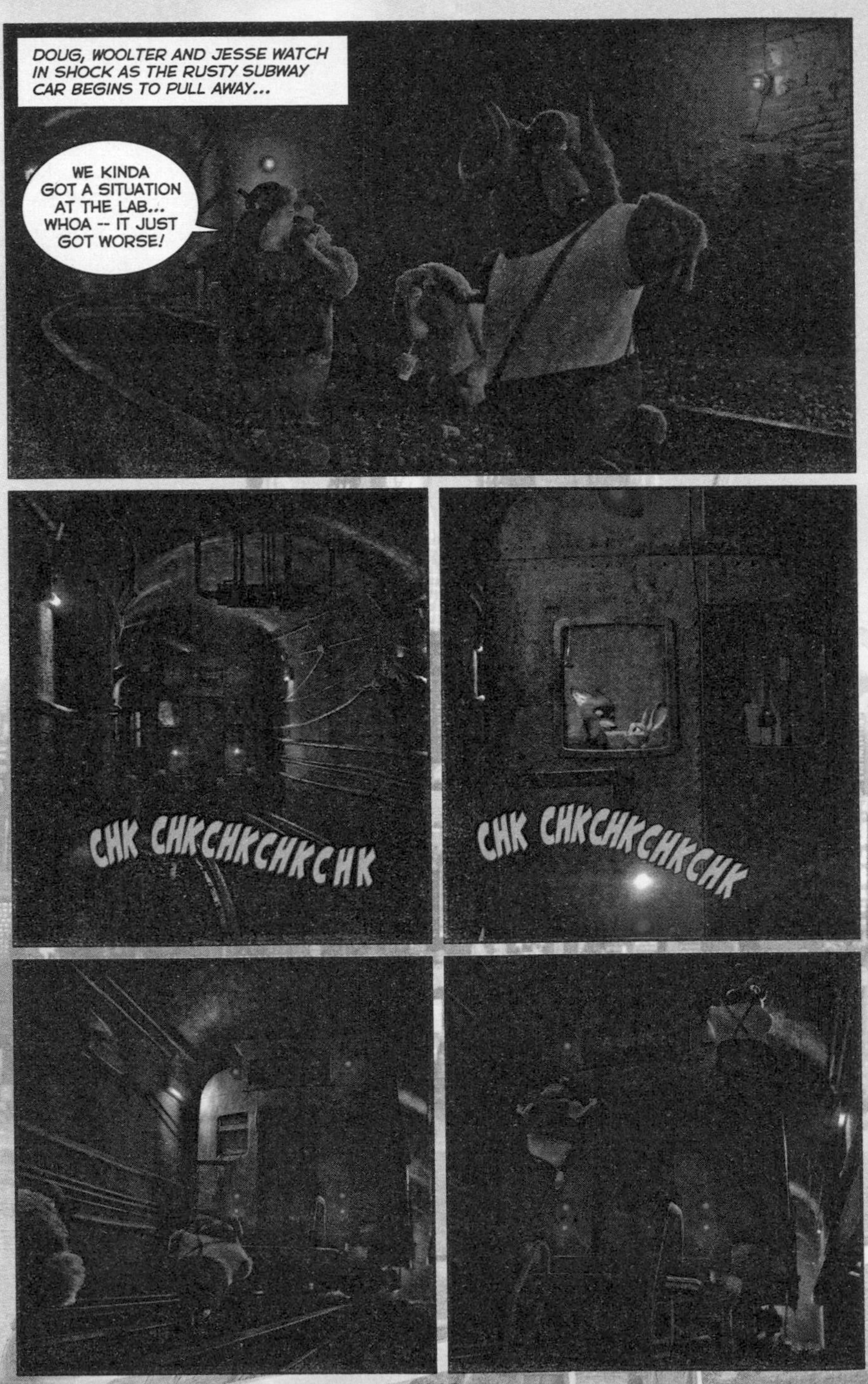
DOUG, WOOLTER AND JESSE WATCH IN SHOCK AS THE RUSTY SUBWAY CAR BEGINS TO PULL AWAY...
WE KINDA GOT A SITUATION AT THE LAB... WHOA -- IT JUST GOT WORSE!
CHK CHKCHKCHKCHK
CHK CHKCHKCHKCHK

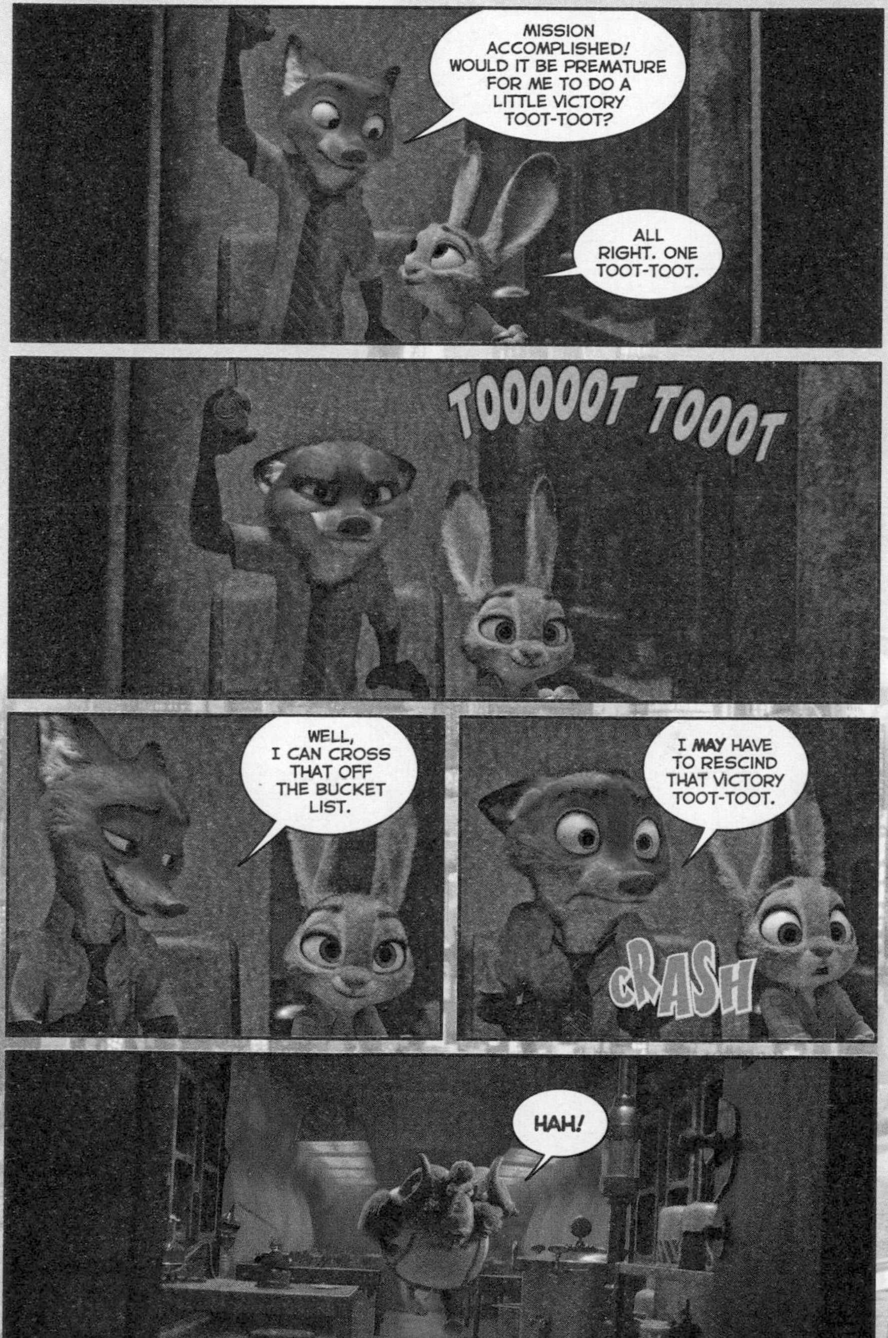
MISSION ACCOMPLISHED! WOULD IT BE PREMATURE FOR ME TO DO A LITTLE VICTORY TOOT-TOOT?
ALL RIGHT. ONE TOOT-TOOT.
TOOOOOT TOOOT
WELL, I CAN CROSS THAT OFF THE BUCKET LIST.
I MAY HAVE TO RESCIND THAT VICTORY TOOT-TOOT.
CRASH
HAH!

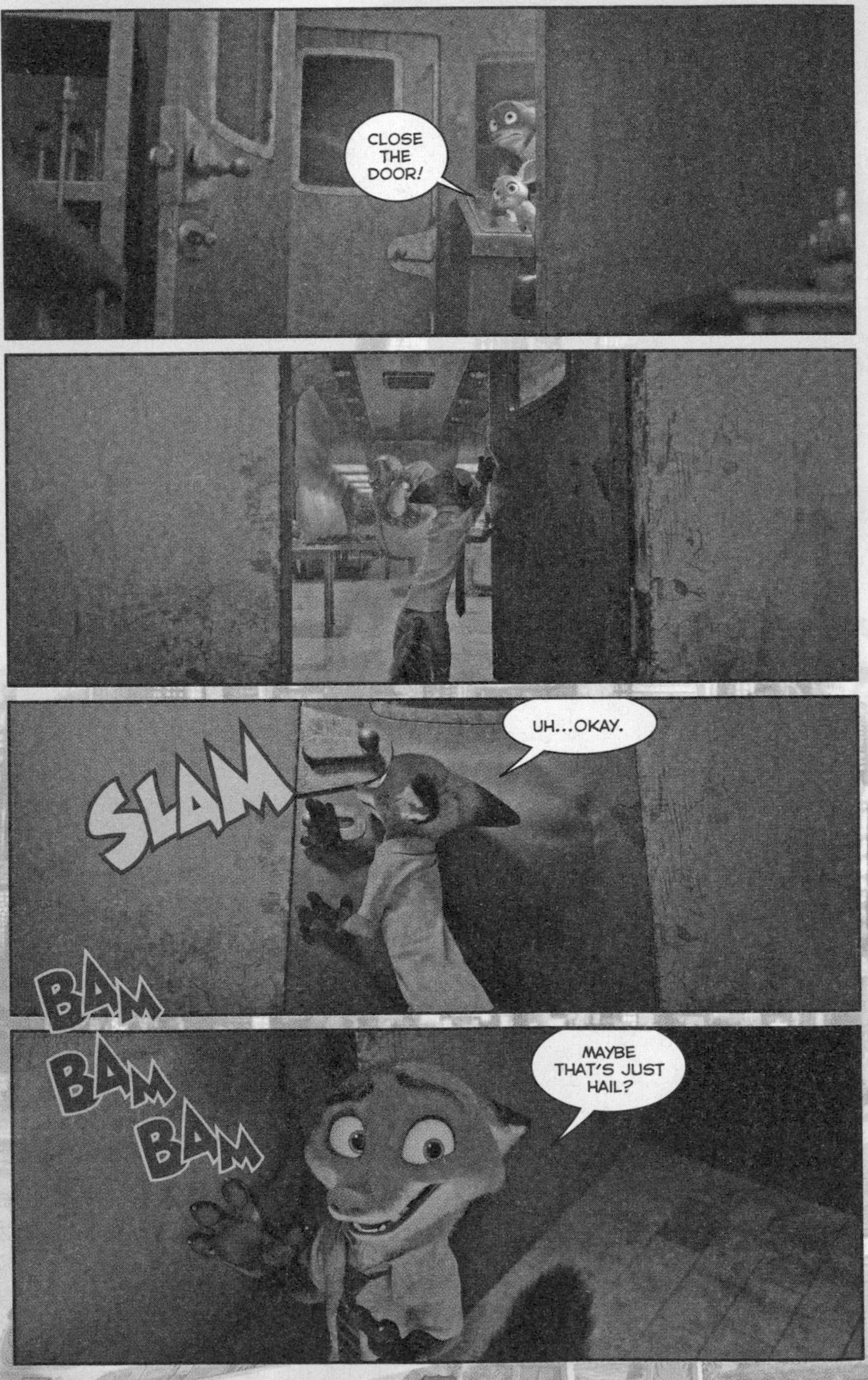
CLOSE THE DOOR!
UH...OKAY.
SLAM
BAM
BAM
BAM
MAYBE THAT'S JUST HAIL?

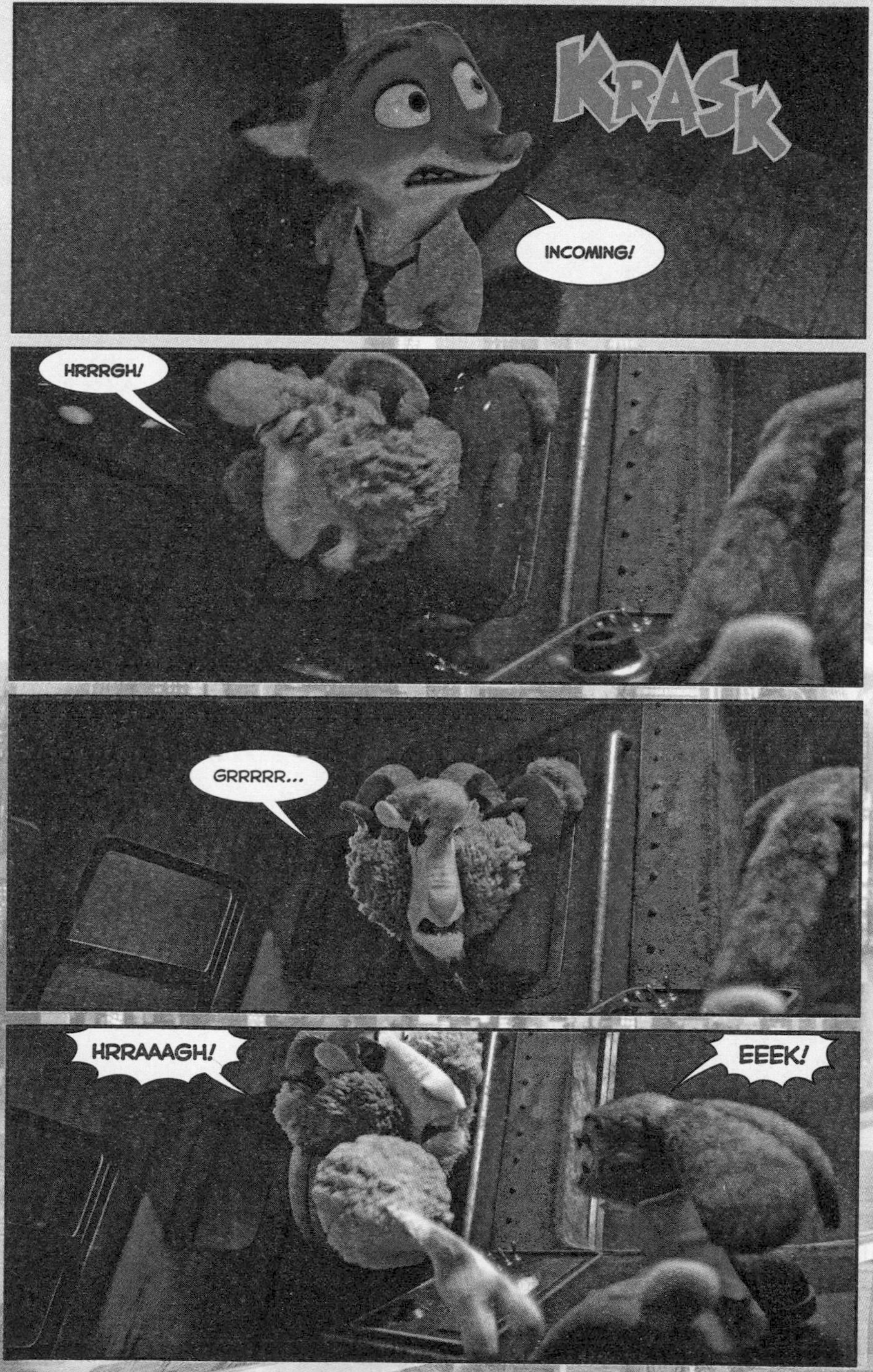
KRASK
INCOMING!
HRRRGH!
GRRRRR...
HRRAAAGH!
EEEK!

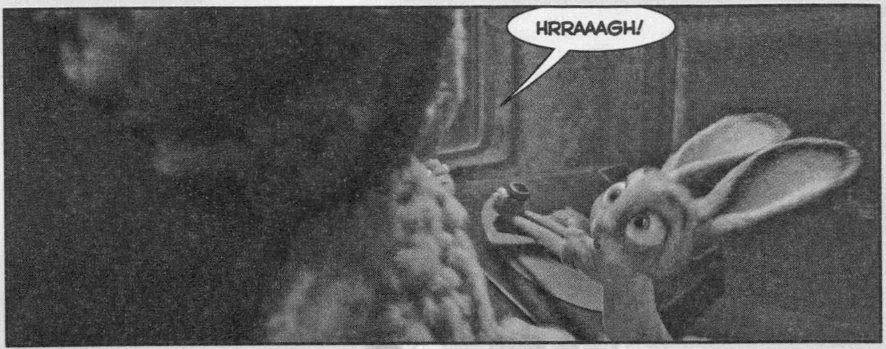
HRRAAAGH!

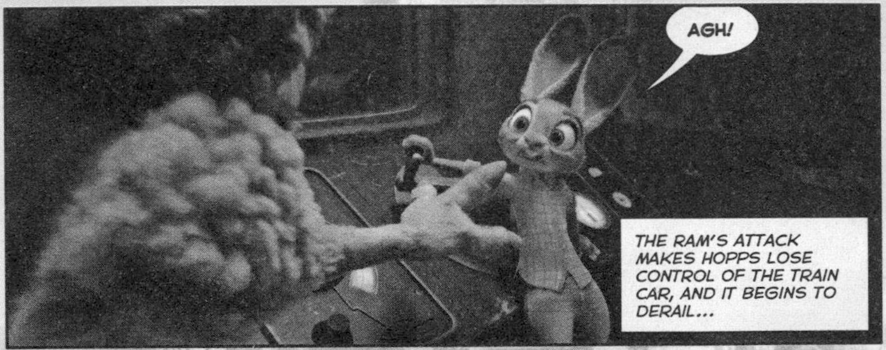
AGH!
THE RAM'S ATTACK MAKES HOPPS LOSE CONTROL OF THE TRAIN CAR, AND IT BEGINS TO DERAIL...

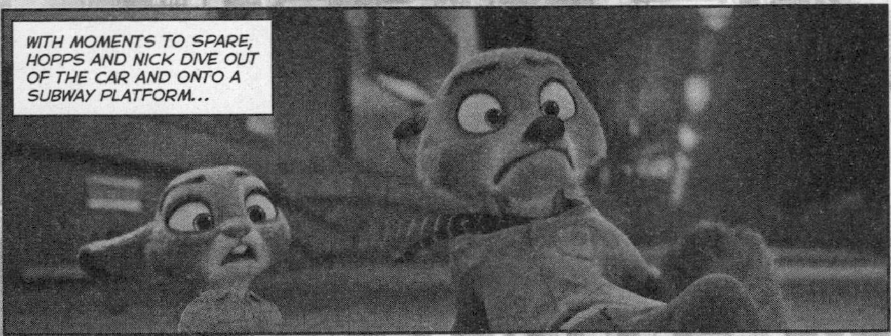
WITH MOMENTS TO SPARE, HOPPS AND NICK DIVE OUT OF THE CAR AND ONTO A SUBWAY PLATFORM...

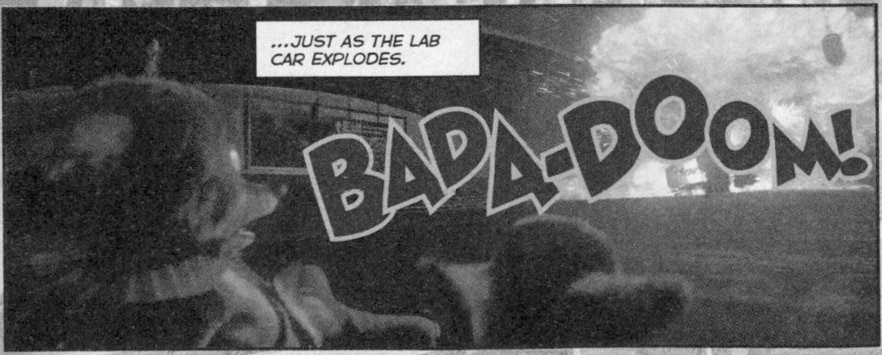
...JUST AS THE LAB CAR EXPLODES.
BADA-DOOM!

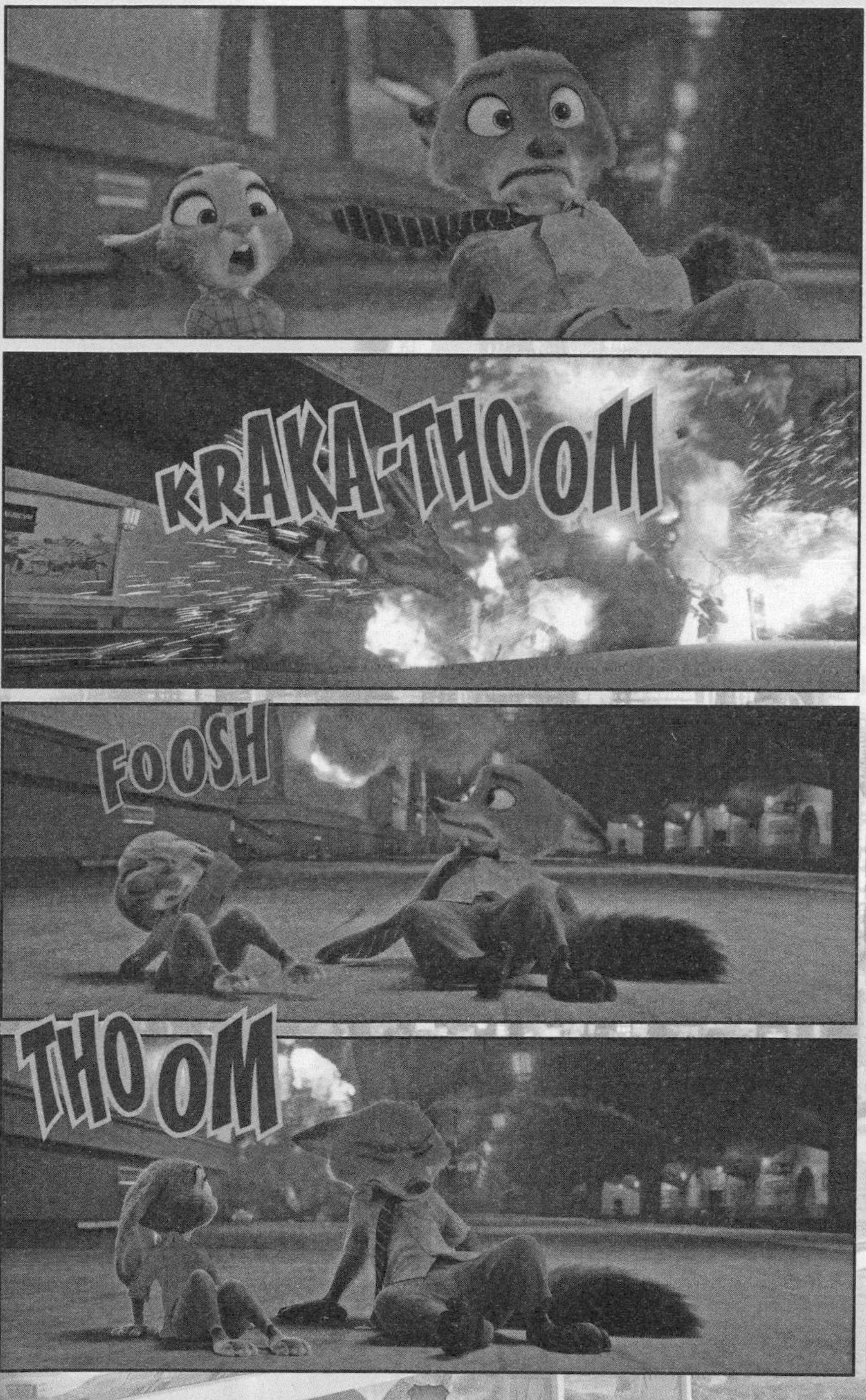
KRAKA-THOOM
FOOSH
THOOM

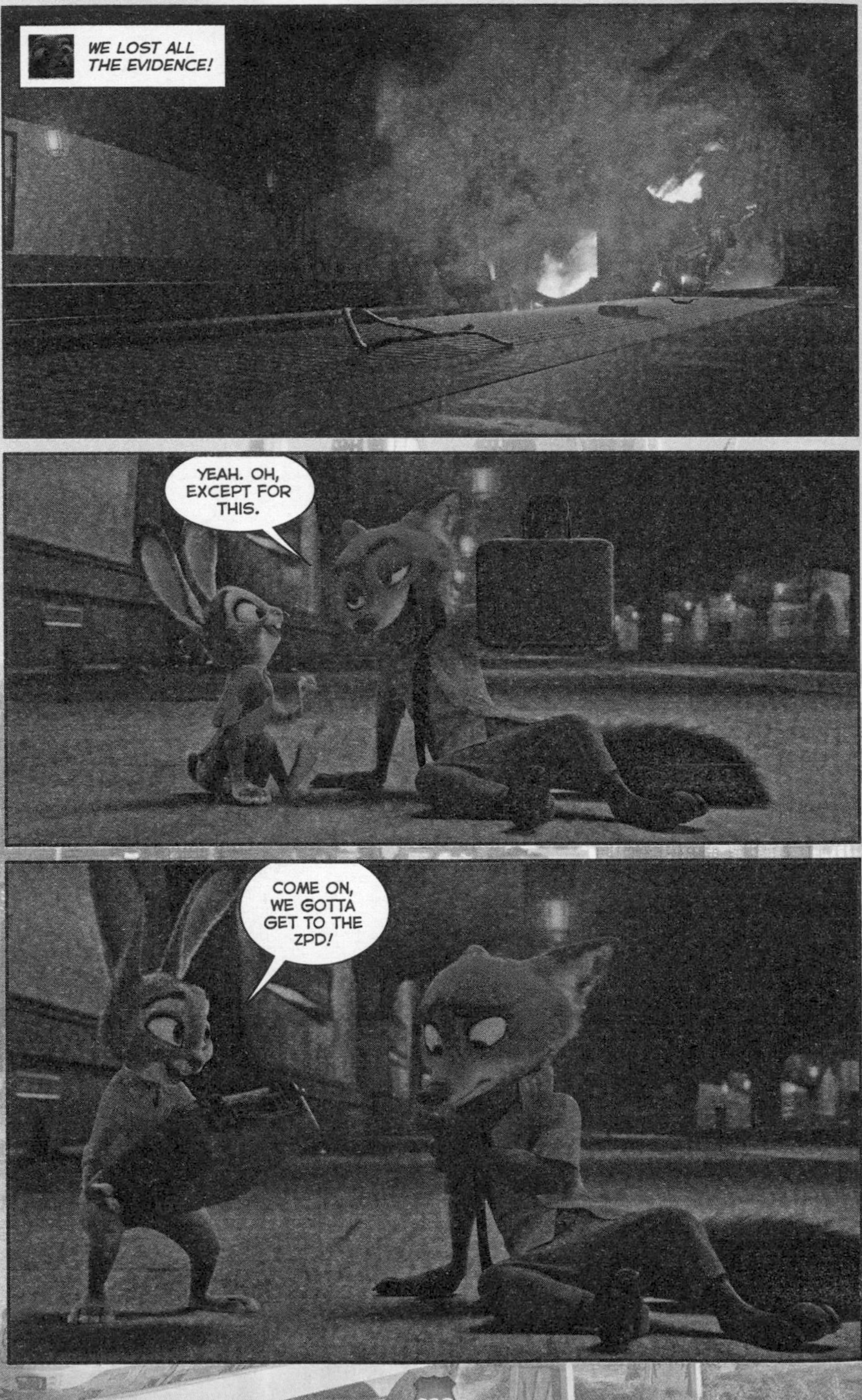
WE LOST ALL THE EVIDENCE!
YEAH. OH, EXCEPT FOR THIS.
COME ON, WE GOTTA GET TO THE ZPD!

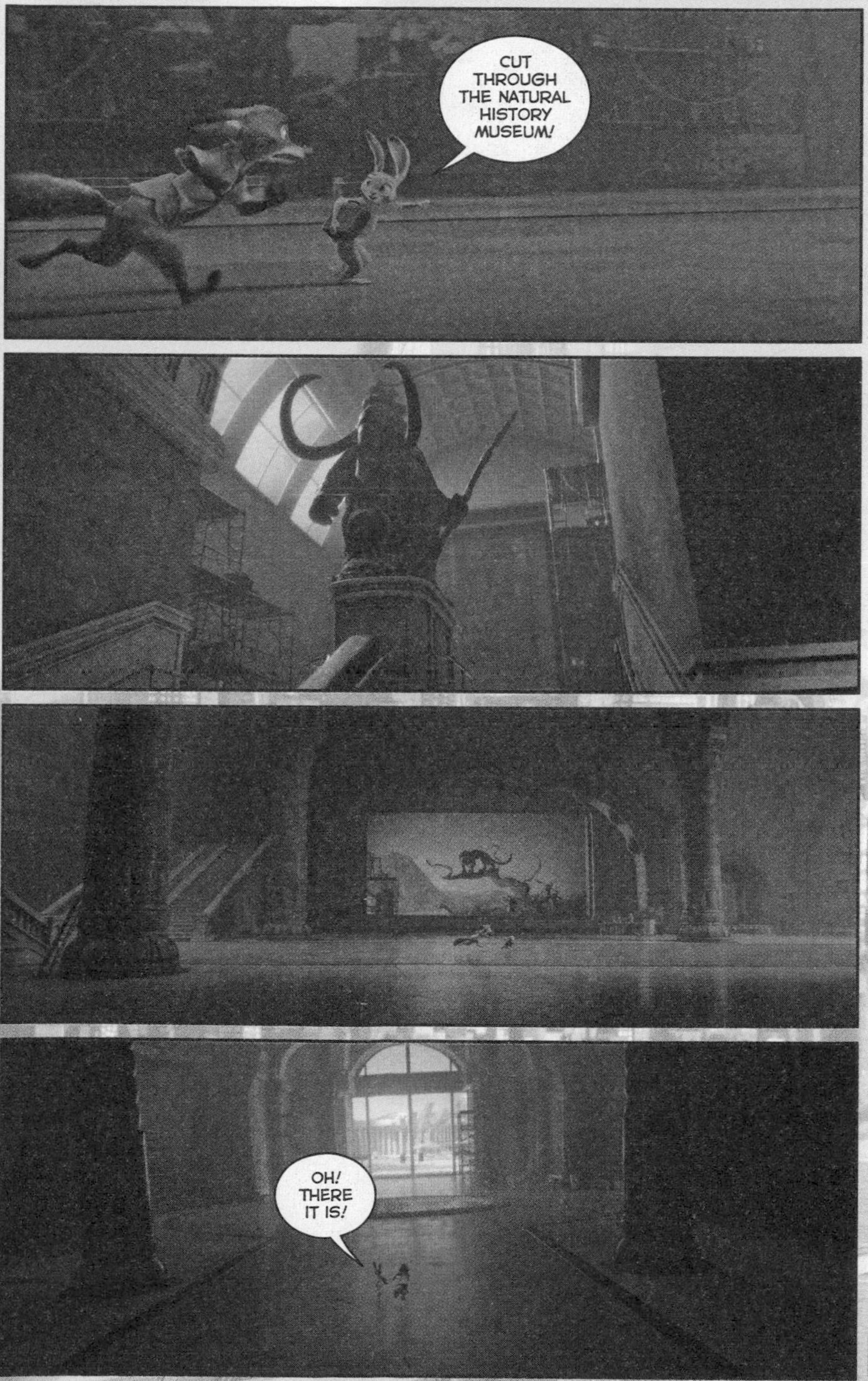
CUT THROUGH THE NATURAL HISTORY MUSEUM!
OH! THERE IT IS!

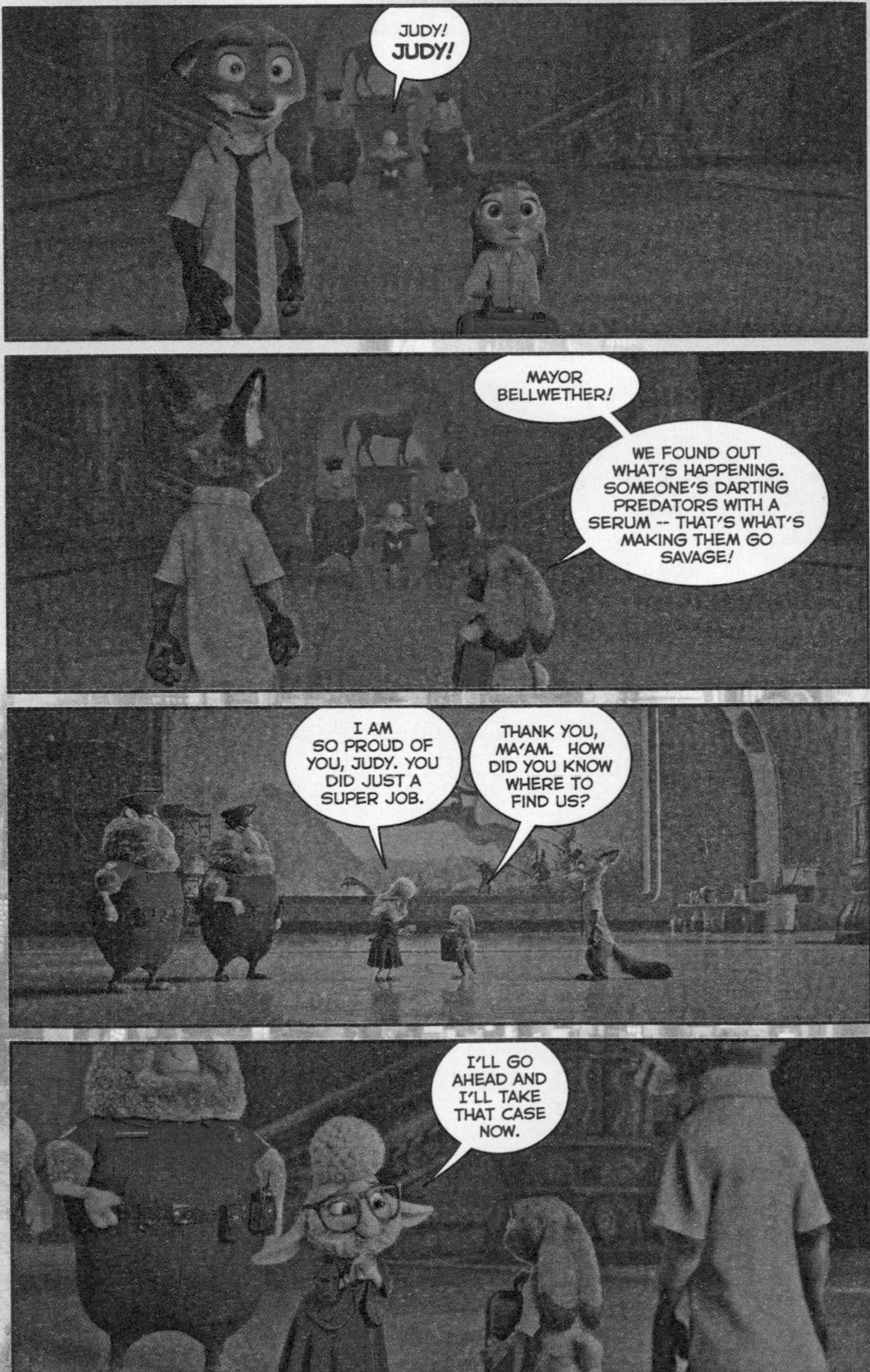
JUDY! JUDY!
MAYOR BELLWETHER!
WE FOUND OUT WHAT'S HAPPENING. SOMEONE'S DARTING PREDATORS WITH A SERUM -- THAT'S WHAT'S MAKING THEM GO SAVAGE!
I AM SO PROUD OF YOU, JUDY. YOU DID JUST A SUPER JOB.
THANK YOU, MA'AM. HOW DID YOU KNOW WHERE TO FIND US?
I'LL GO AHEAD AND I'LL TAKE THAT CASE NOW.

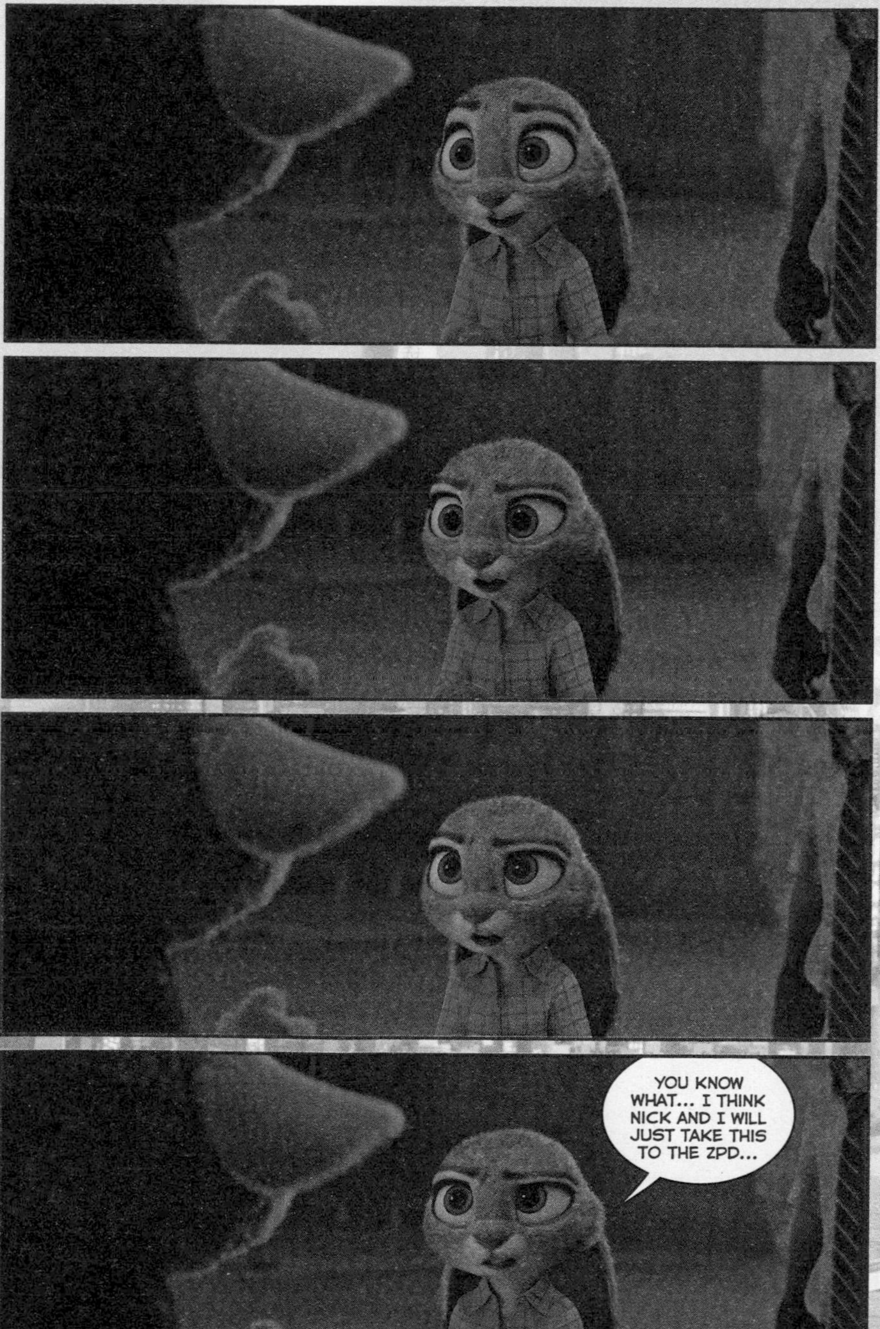
YOU KNOW WHAT... I THINK NICK AND I WILL JUST TAKE THIS TO THE ZPD...

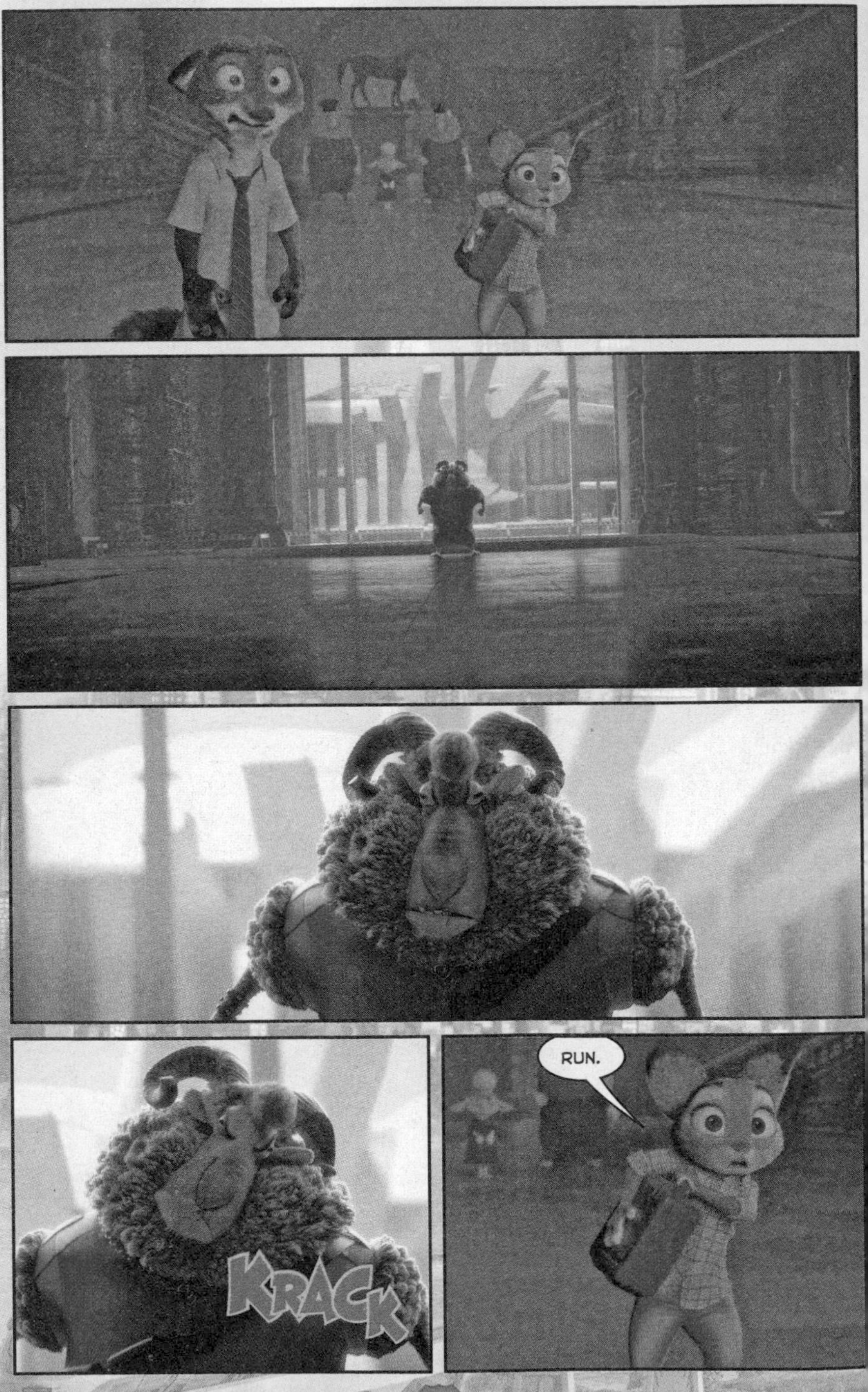
KRACK
RUN.

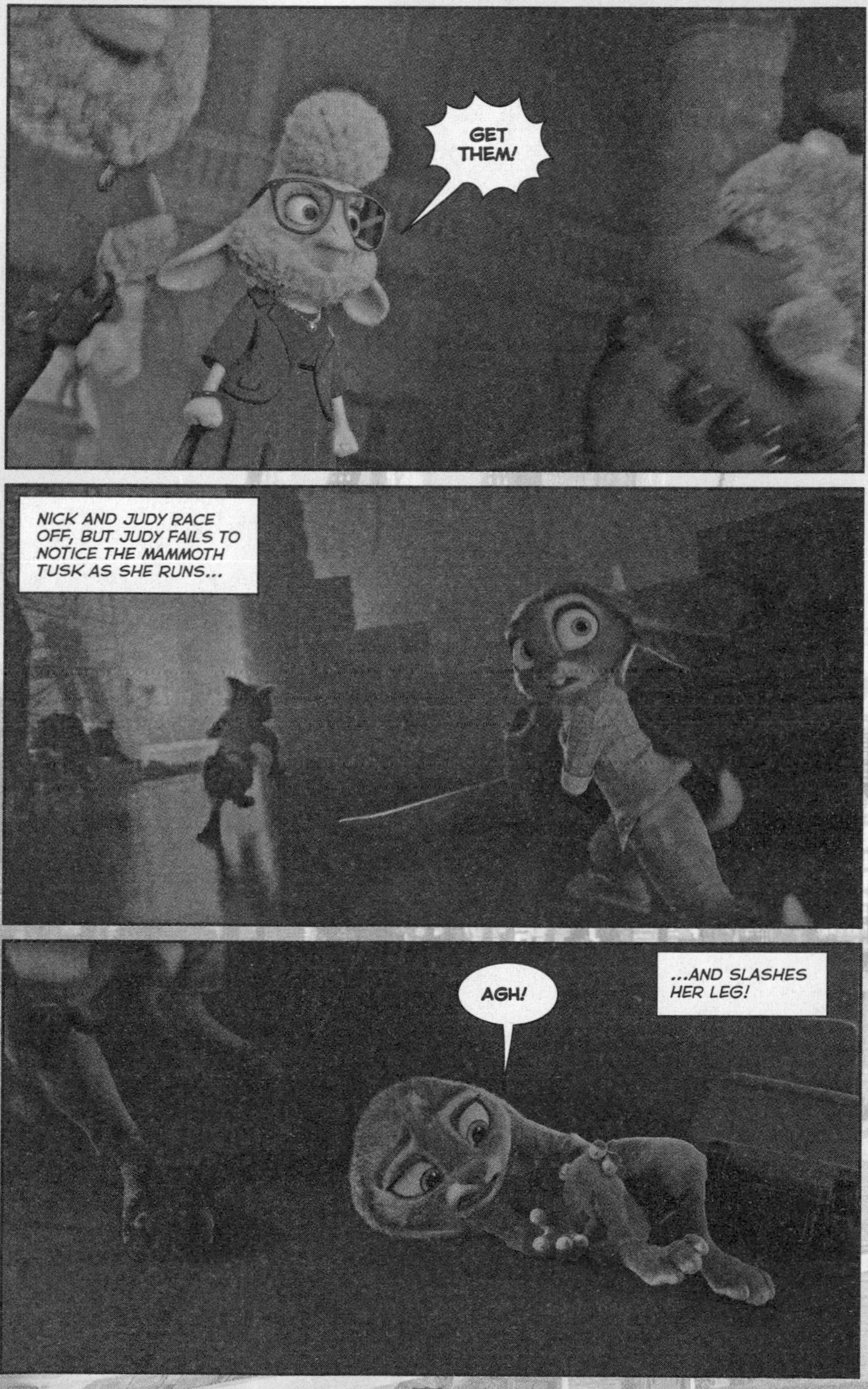
GET THEM!
NICK AND JUDY RACE OFF, BUT JUDY FAILS TO NOTICE THE MAMMOTH TUSK AS SHE RUNS...
AGH!
...AND SLASHES HER LEG!

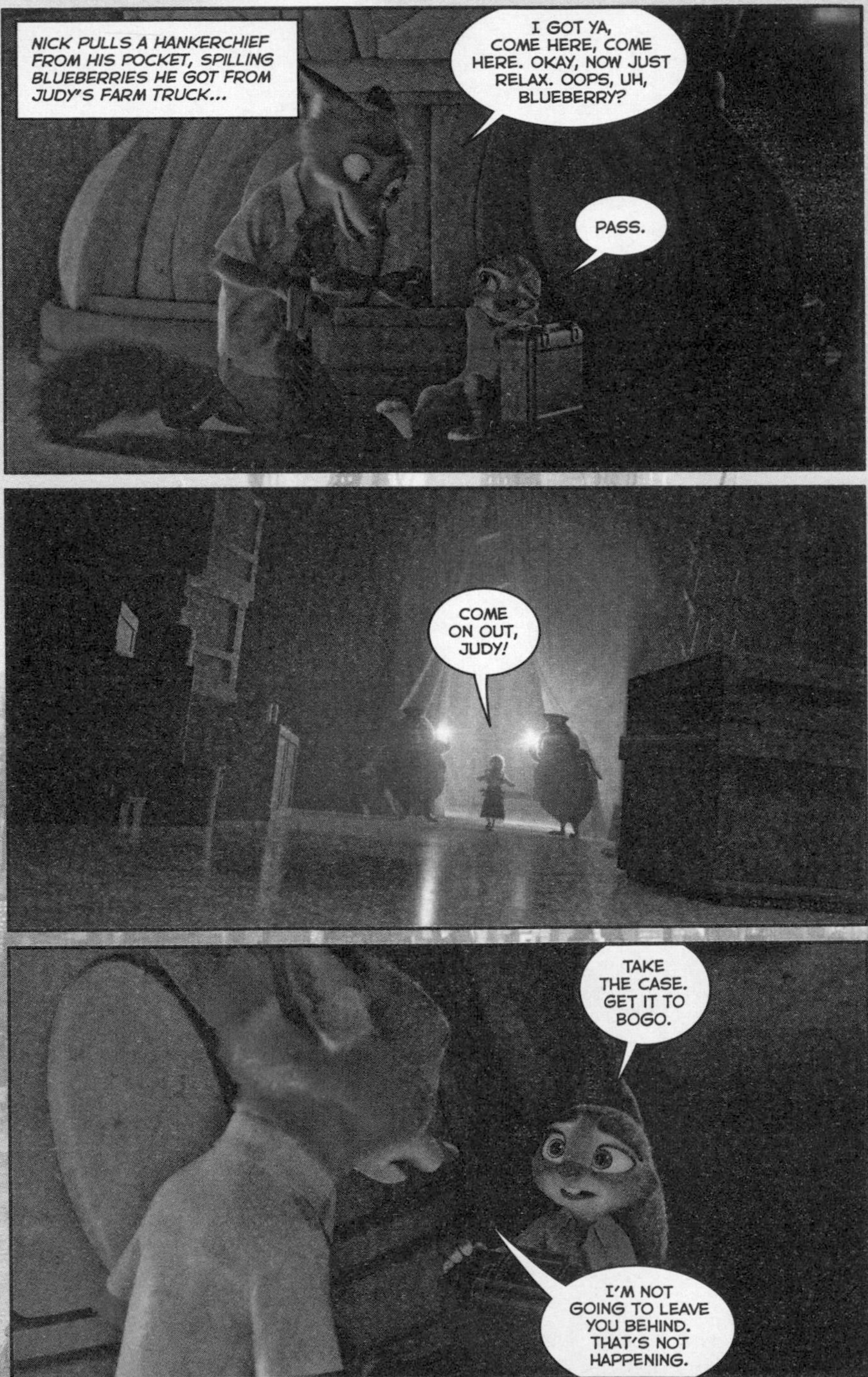
NICK PULLS A HANKERCHIEF FROM HIS POCKET, SPILLING BLUEBERRIES HE GOT FROM JUDY'S FARM TRUCK...
I GOT YA, COME HERE, COME HERE. OKAY, NOW JUST RELAX. OOPS, UH, BLUEBERRY?
PASS.
COME ON OUT, JUDY!
TAKE THE CASE. GET IT TO BOGO.
I'M NOT GOING TO LEAVE YOU BEHIND. THAT'S NOT HAPPENING.

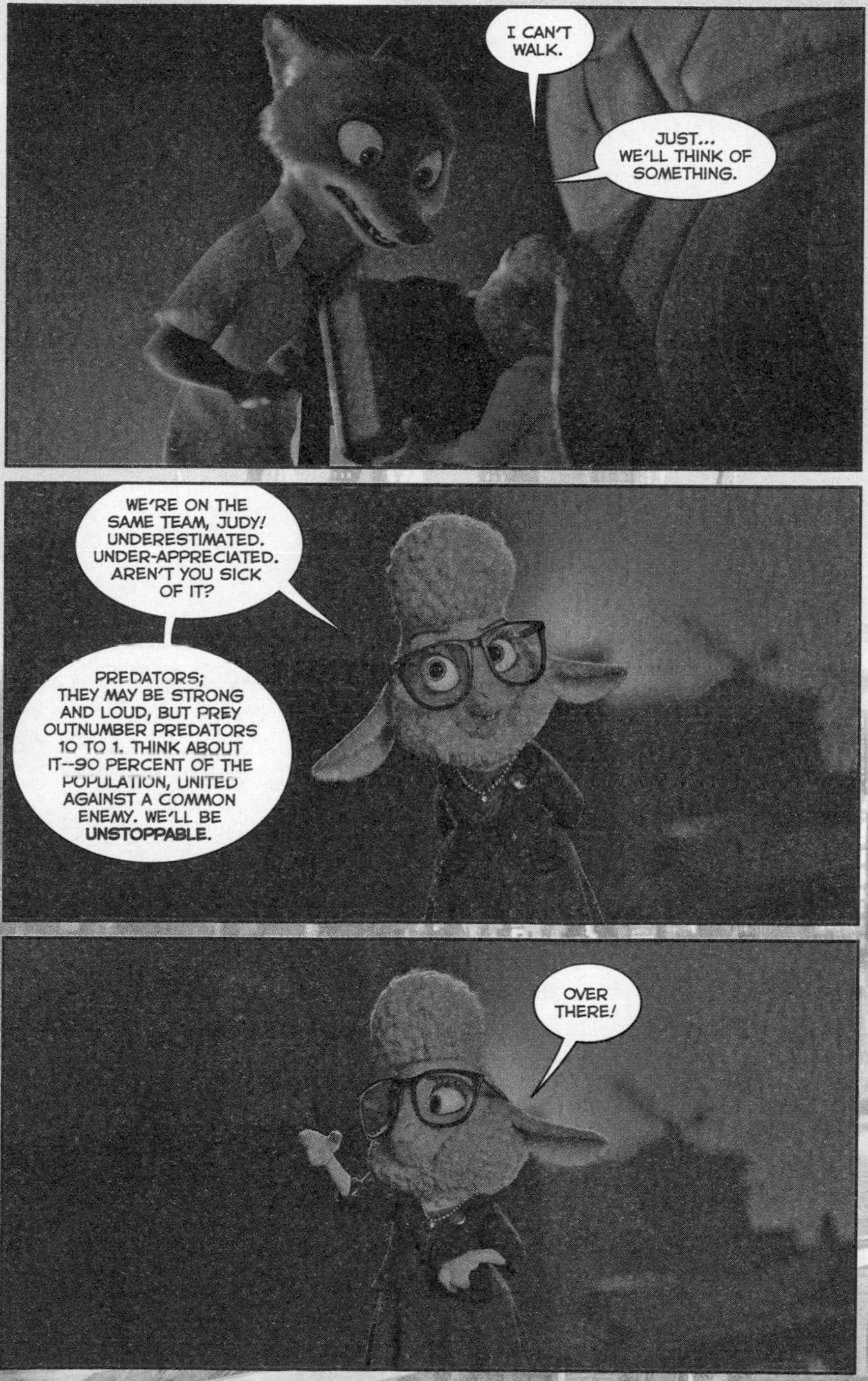
I CAN'T WALK.
JUST... WE'LL THINK OF SOMETHING.
WE'RE ON THE SAME TEAM, JUDY! UNDERESTIMATED. UNDER-APPRECIATED. AREN'T YOU SICK OF IT?
PREDATORS; THEY MAY BE STRONG AND LOUD, BUT PREY OUTNUMBER PREDATORS 10 TO 1. THINK ABOUT IT--90 PERCENT OF THE POPULATION, UNITED AGAINST A COMMON ENEMY. WE'LL BE **UNSTOPPABLE.**
OVER THERE!

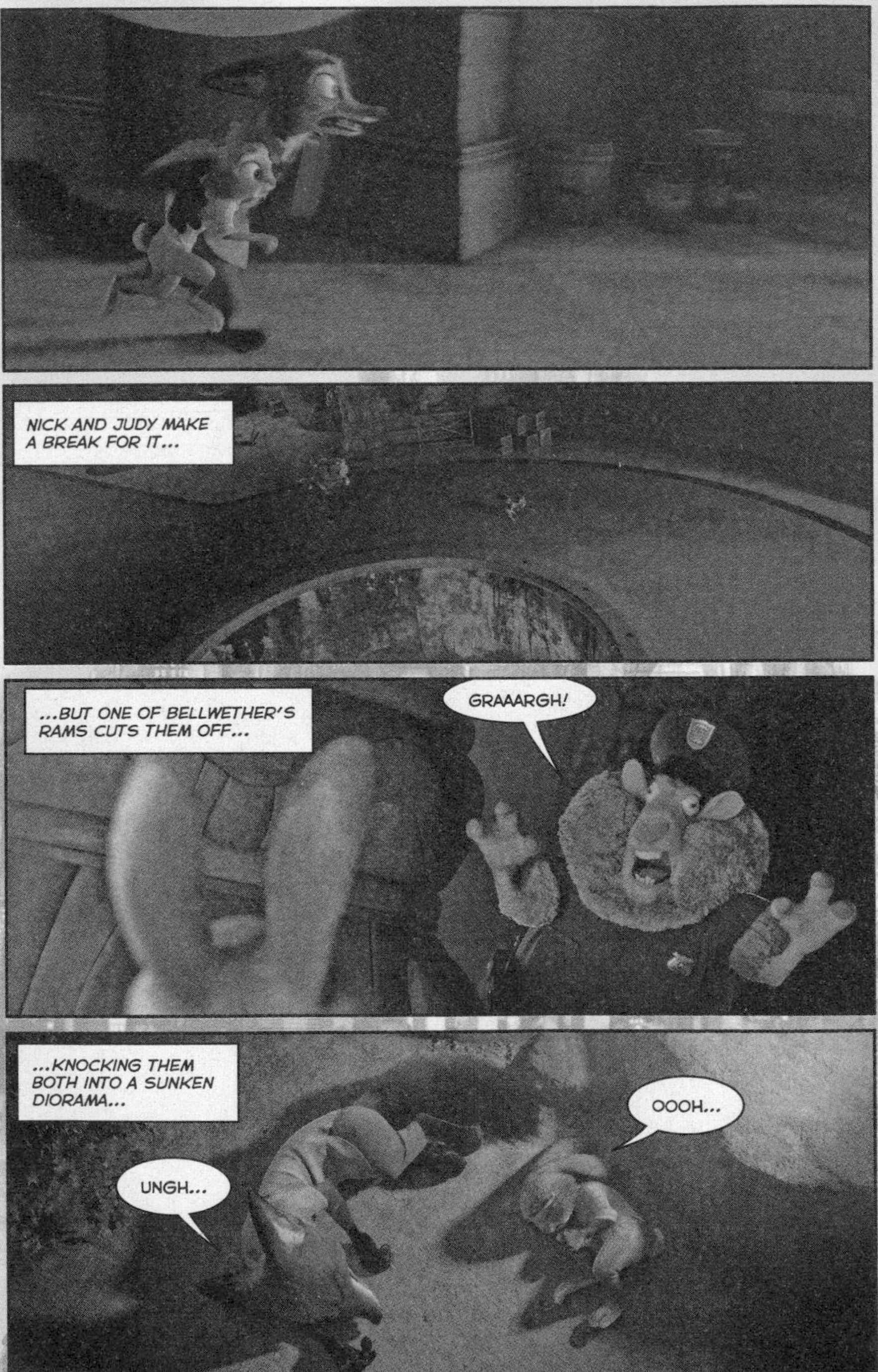
NICK AND JUDY MAKE A BREAK FOR IT...
...BUT ONE OF BELLWETHER'S RAMS CUTS THEM OFF...
GRAAARGH!
...KNOCKING THEM BOTH INTO A SUNKEN DIORAMA...
OOOH...
UNGH...

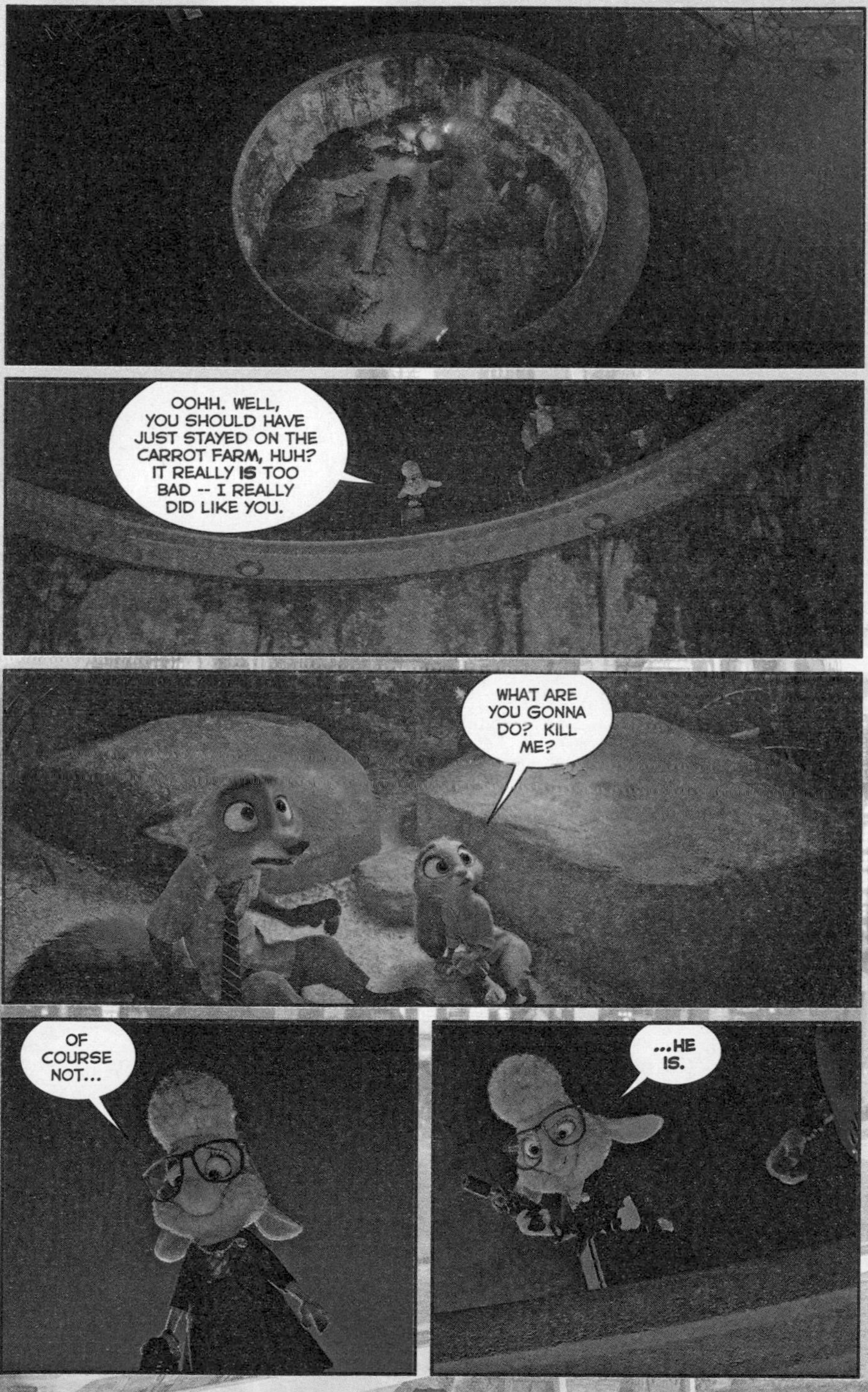
OOHH. WELL, YOU SHOULD HAVE JUST STAYED ON THE CARROT FARM, HUH? IT REALLY IS TOO BAD -- I REALLY DID LIKE YOU.
WHAT ARE YOU GONNA DO? KILL ME?
OF COURSE NOT...
...HE IS.

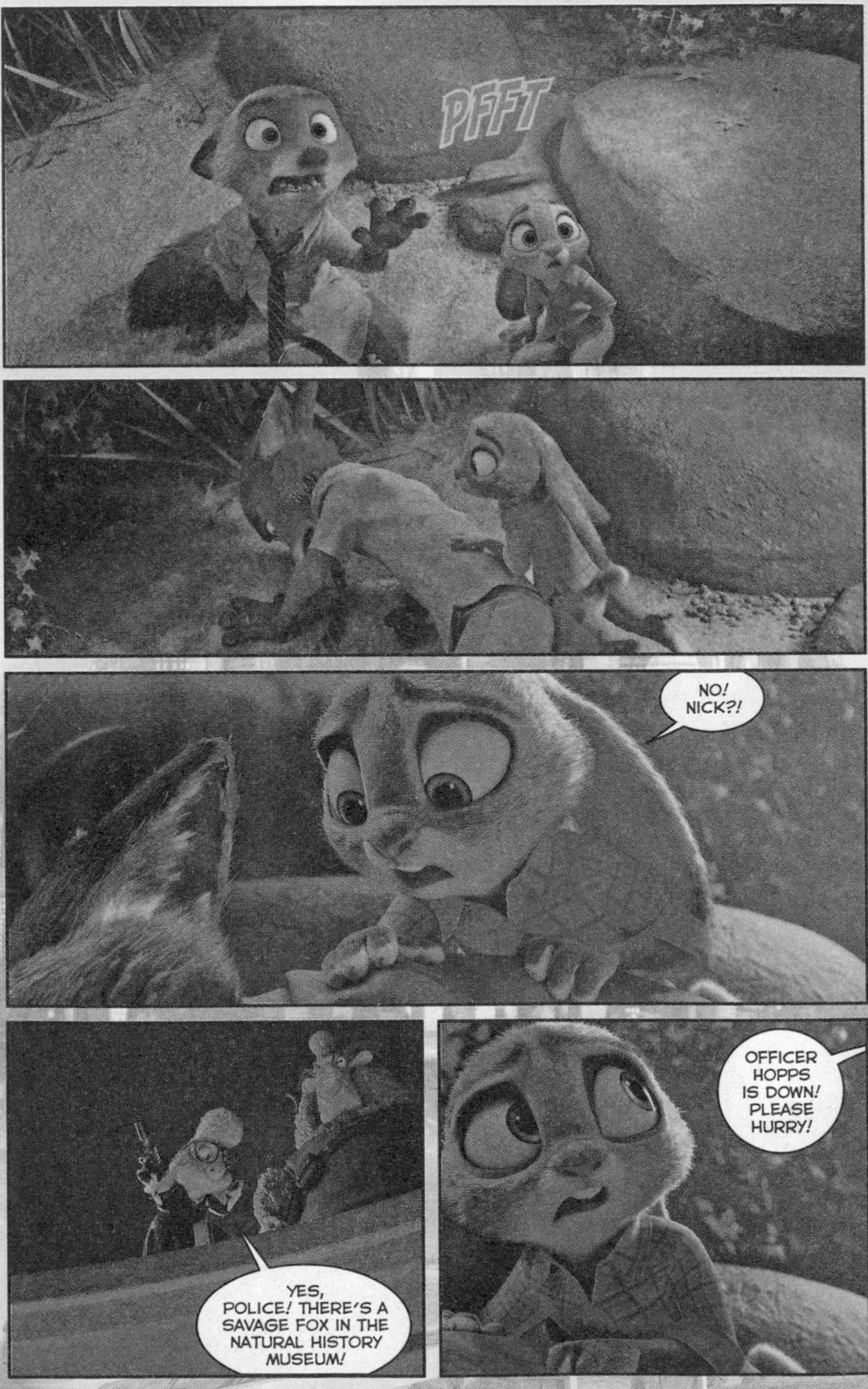
PFFT
NO! NICK?!
YES, POLICE! THERE'S A SAVAGE FOX IN THE NATURAL HISTORY MUSEUM!
OFFICER HOPPS IS DOWN! PLEASE HURRY!

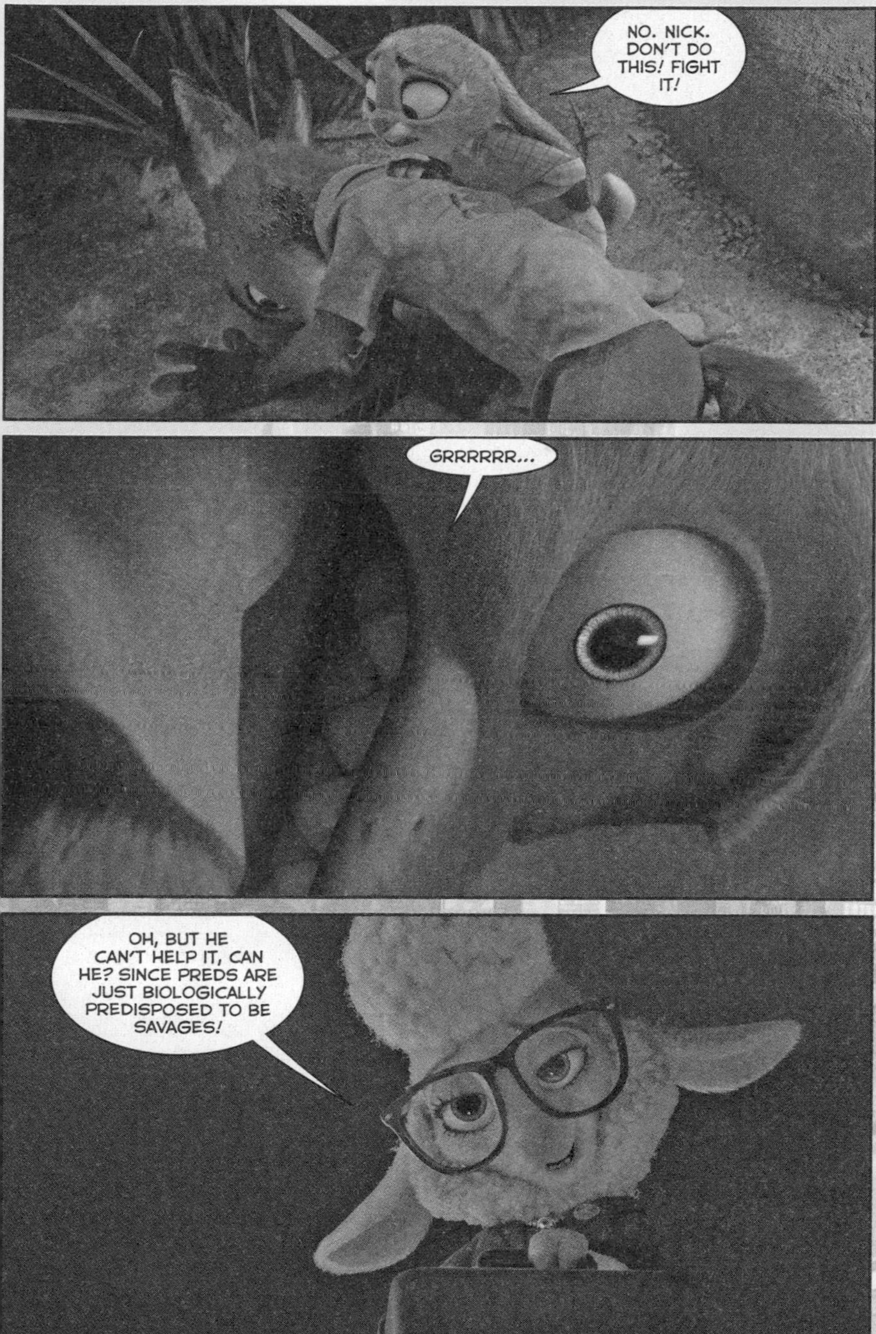
NO. NICK. DON'T DO THIS! FIGHT IT!
GRRRRRR...
OH, BUT HE CAN'T HELP IT, CAN HE? SINCE PREDS ARE JUST BIOLOGICALLY PREDISPOSED TO BE SAVAGES!

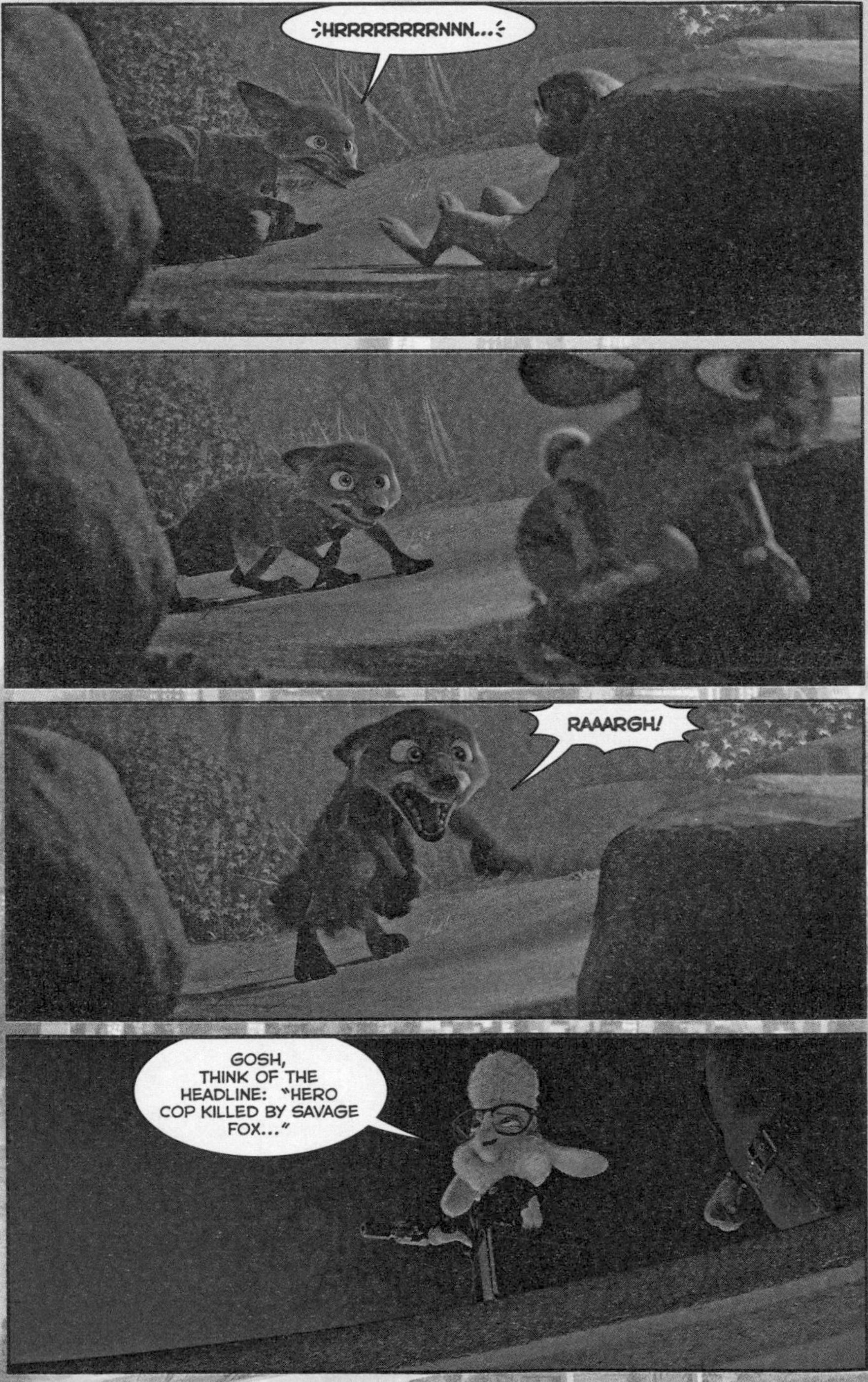
HRRRRRRRRNNN...
RAAARGH!
GOSH, THINK OF THE HEADLINE: "HERO COP KILLED BY SAVAGE FOX..."

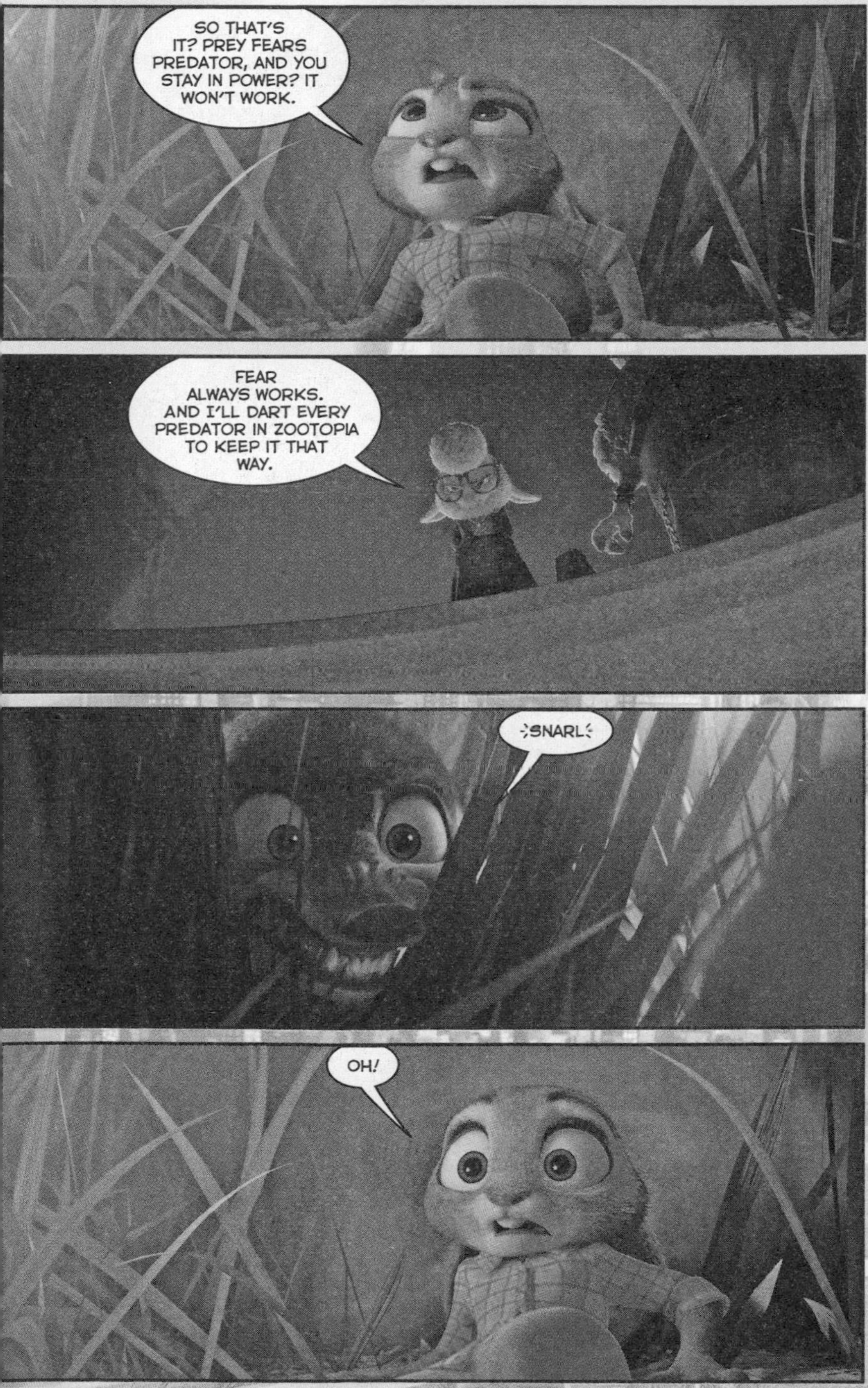
SO THAT'S IT? PREY FEARS PREDATOR, AND YOU STAY IN POWER? IT WON'T WORK.
FEAR ALWAYS WORKS. AND I'LL DART EVERY PREDATOR IN ZOOTOPIA TO KEEP IT THAT WAY.
SNARL
OH!

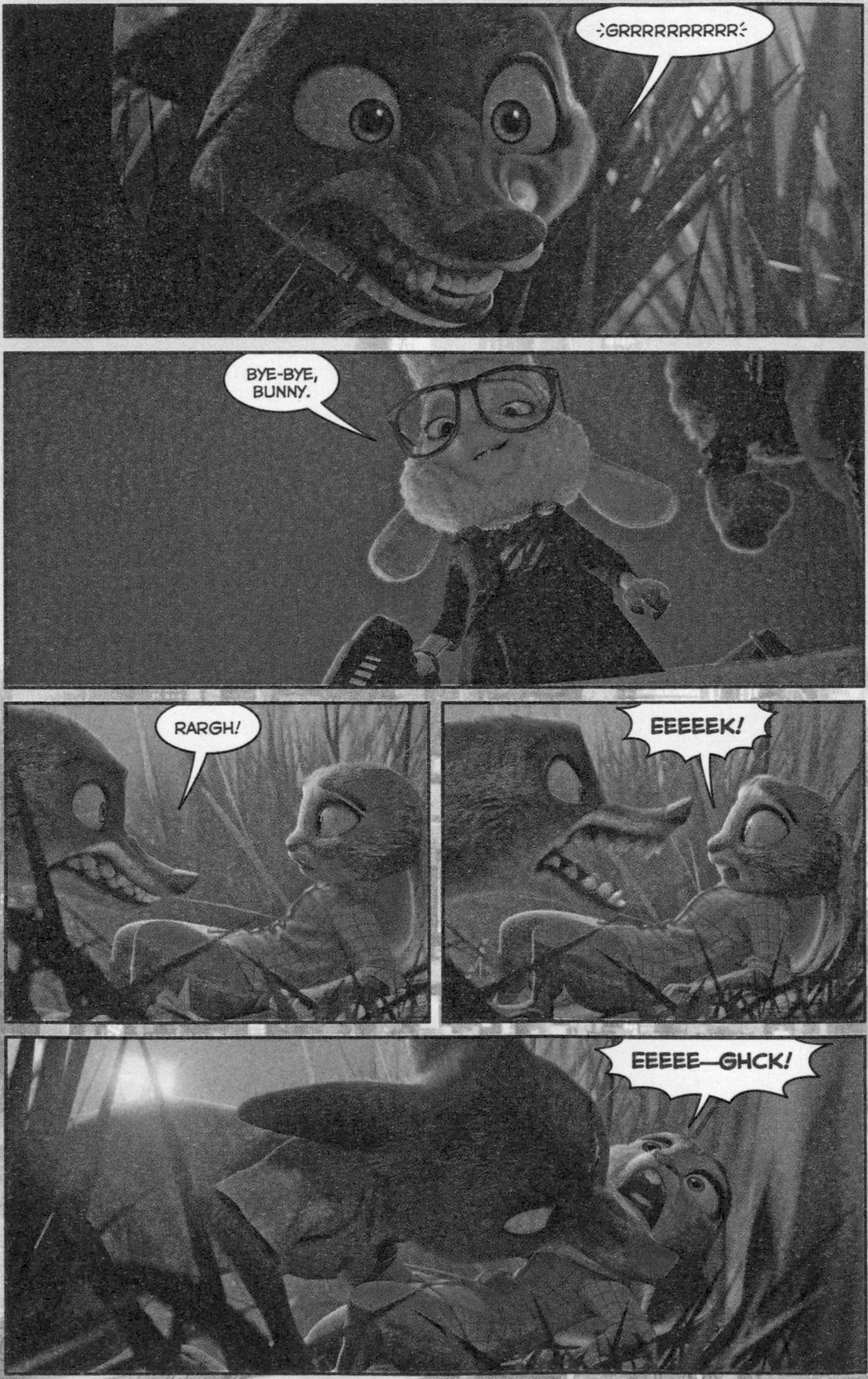
GRRRRRRRRRR
BYE-BYE, BUNNY.
RARGH!
EEEEEK!
EEEEE—GHCK!

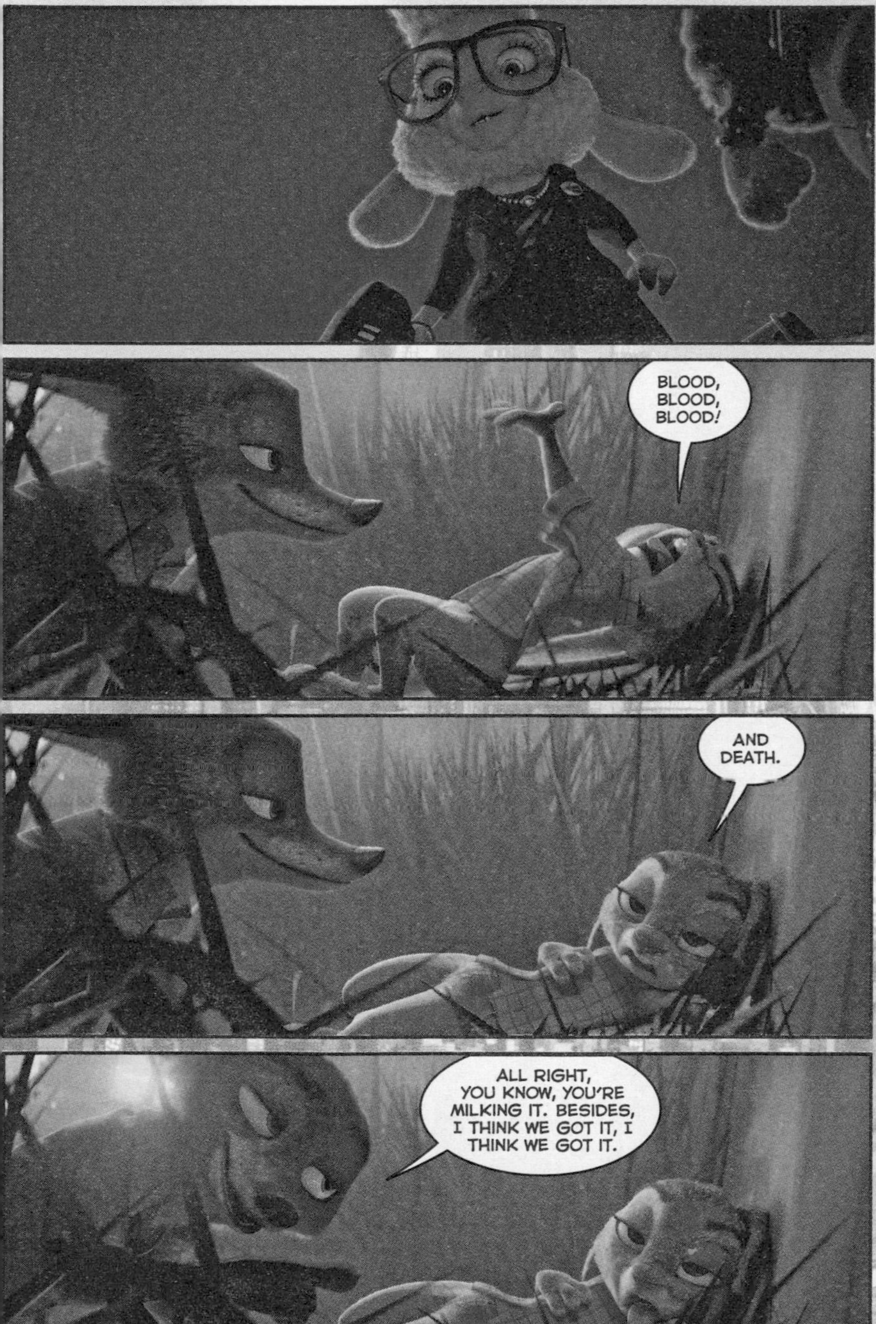
BLOOD, BLOOD, BLOOD!
AND DEATH.
ALL RIGHT, YOU KNOW, YOU'RE MILKING IT. BESIDES, I THINK WE GOT IT, I THINK WE GOT IT.

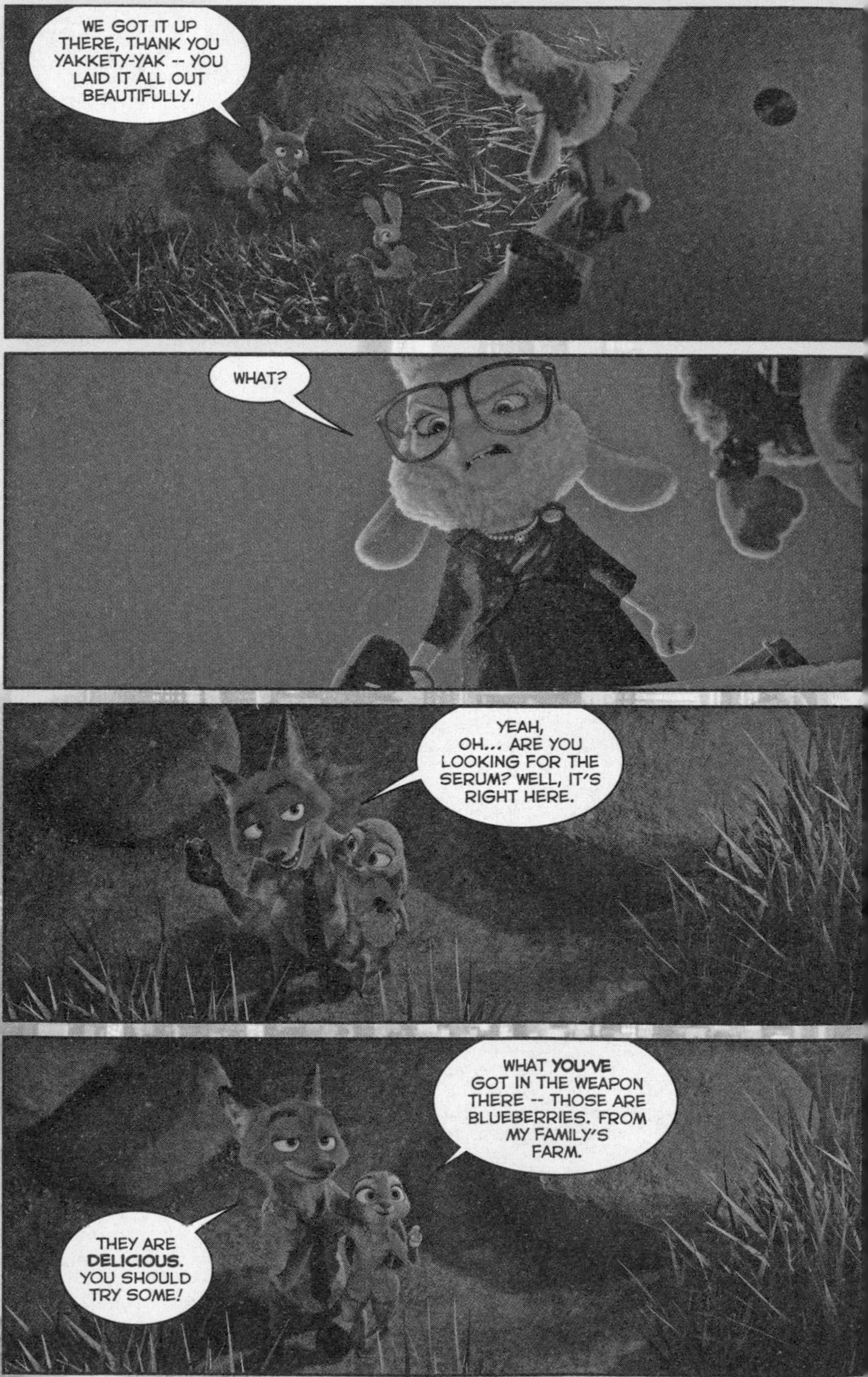
WE GOT IT UP THERE, THANK YOU YAKKETY-YAK -- YOU LAID IT ALL OUT BEAUTIFULLY.
WHAT?
YEAH, OH... ARE YOU LOOKING FOR THE SERUM? WELL, IT'S RIGHT HERE.
WHAT **YOU'VE** GOT IN THE WEAPON THERE -- THOSE ARE BLUEBERRIES. FROM MY FAMILY'S FARM.
THEY ARE **DELICIOUS.** YOU SHOULD TRY SOME!

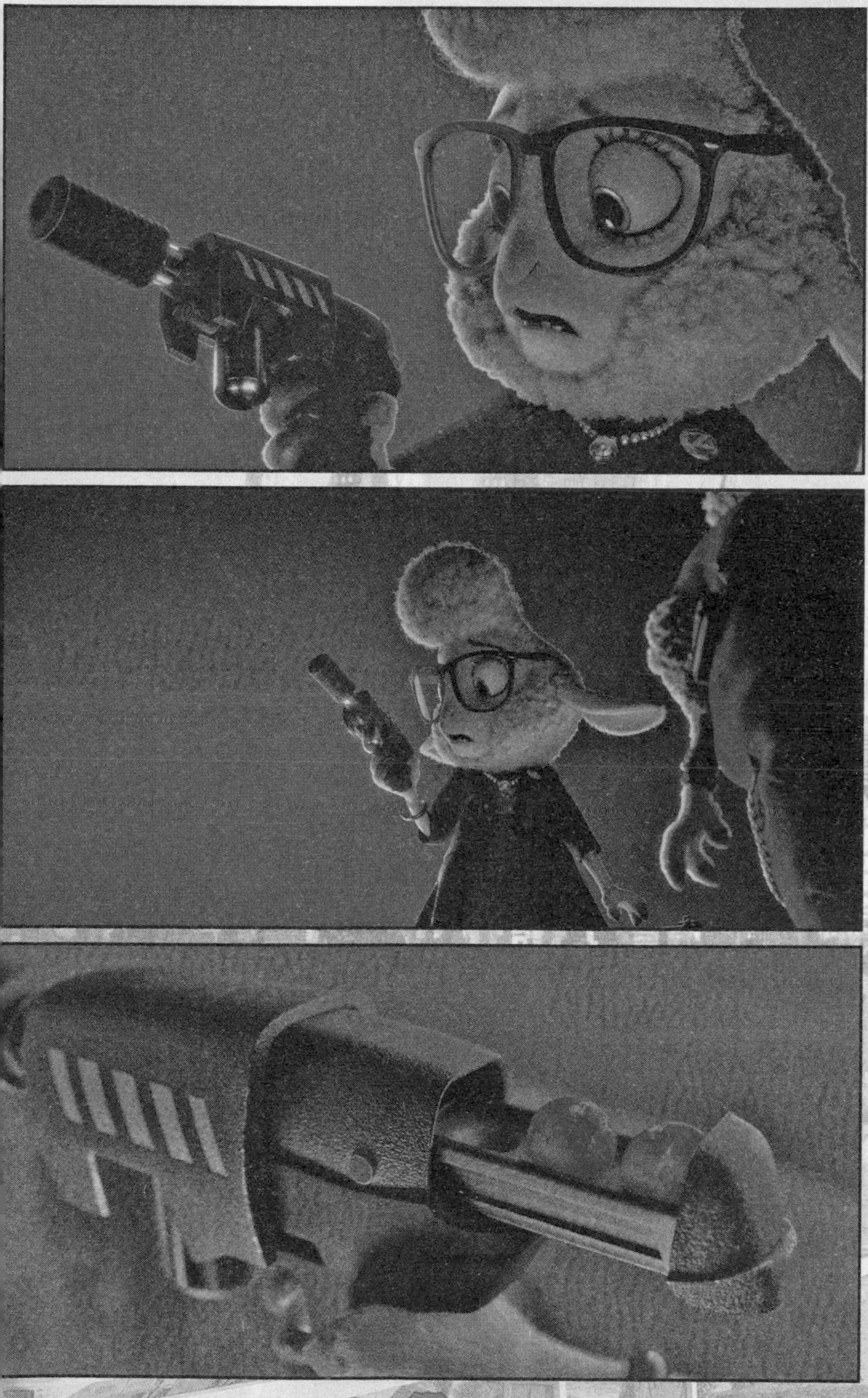

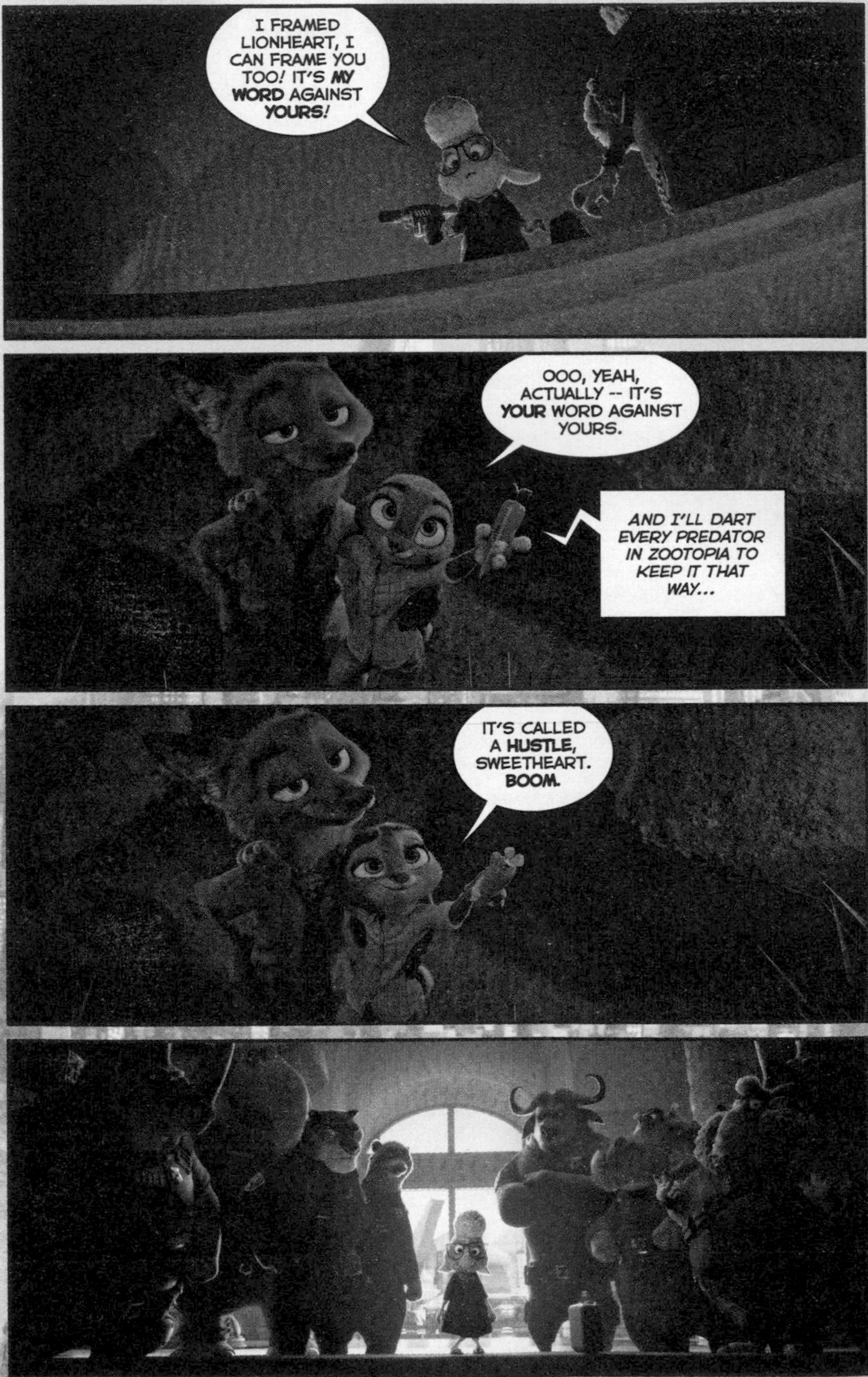
I FRAMED LIONHEART, I CAN FRAME YOU TOO! IT'S MY WORD AGAINST YOURS!
OOO, YEAH, ACTUALLY -- IT'S YOUR WORD AGAINST YOURS.
AND I'LL DART EVERY PREDATOR IN ZOOTOPIA TO KEEP IT THAT WAY...
IT'S CALLED A HUSTLE, SWEETHEART. BOOM.

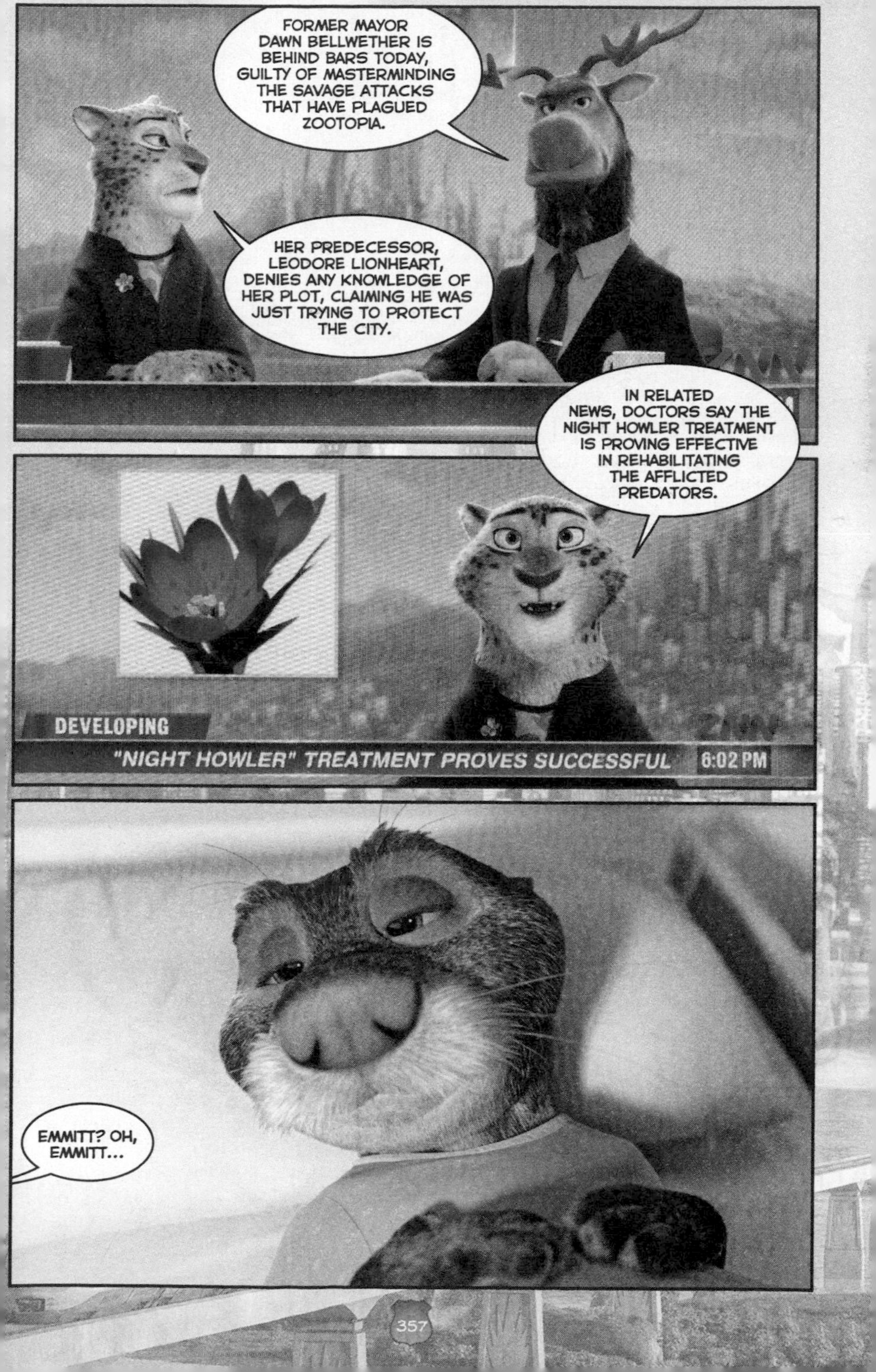
FORMER MAYOR DAWN BELLWETHER IS BEHIND BARS TODAY, GUILTY OF MASTERMINDING THE SAVAGE ATTACKS THAT HAVE PLAGUED ZOOTOPIA.
HER PREDECESSOR, LEODORE LIONHEART, DENIES ANY KNOWLEDGE OF HER PLOT, CLAIMING HE WAS JUST TRYING TO PROTECT THE CITY.
IN RELATED NEWS, DOCTORS SAY THE NIGHT HOWLER TREATMENT IS PROVING EFFECTIVE IN REHABILITATING THE AFFLICTED PREDATORS.
DEVELOPING
"NIGHT HOWLER" TREATMENT PROVES SUCCESSFUL
6:02 PM
EMMITT? OH, EMMITT...

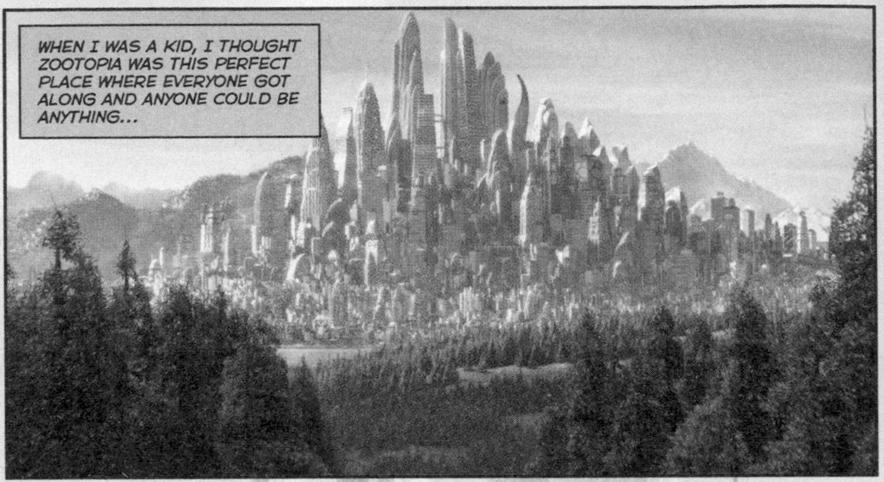
WHEN I WAS A KID, I THOUGHT ZOOTOPIA WAS THIS PERFECT PLACE WHERE EVERYONE GOT ALONG AND ANYONE COULD BE ANYTHING...

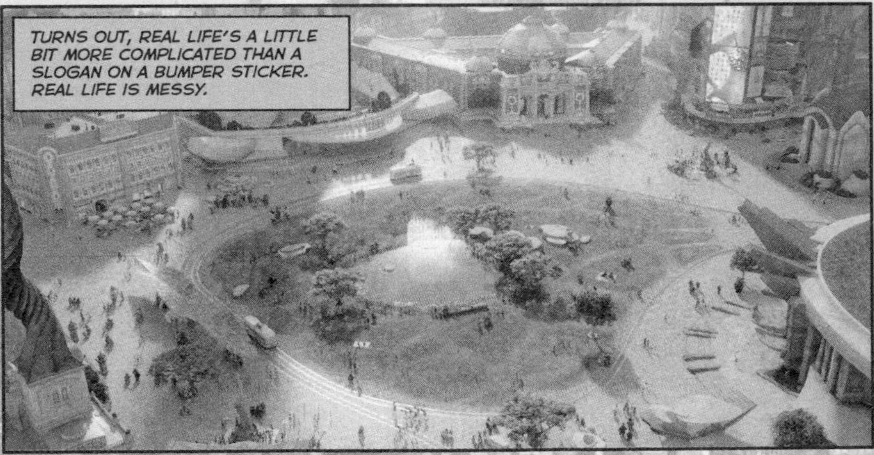
TURNS OUT, REAL LIFE'S A LITTLE BIT MORE COMPLICATED THAN A SLOGAN ON A BUMPER STICKER. REAL LIFE IS MESSY.

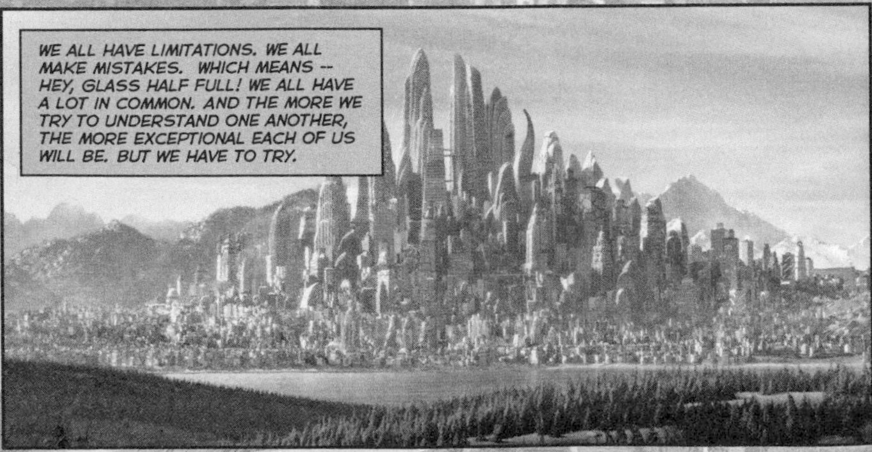
WE ALL HAVE LIMITATIONS. WE ALL MAKE MISTAKES. WHICH MEANS -- HEY, GLASS HALF FULL! WE ALL HAVE A LOT IN COMMON. AND THE MORE WE TRY TO UNDERSTAND ONE ANOTHER, THE MORE EXCEPTIONAL EACH OF US WILL BE. BUT WE HAVE TO TRY.

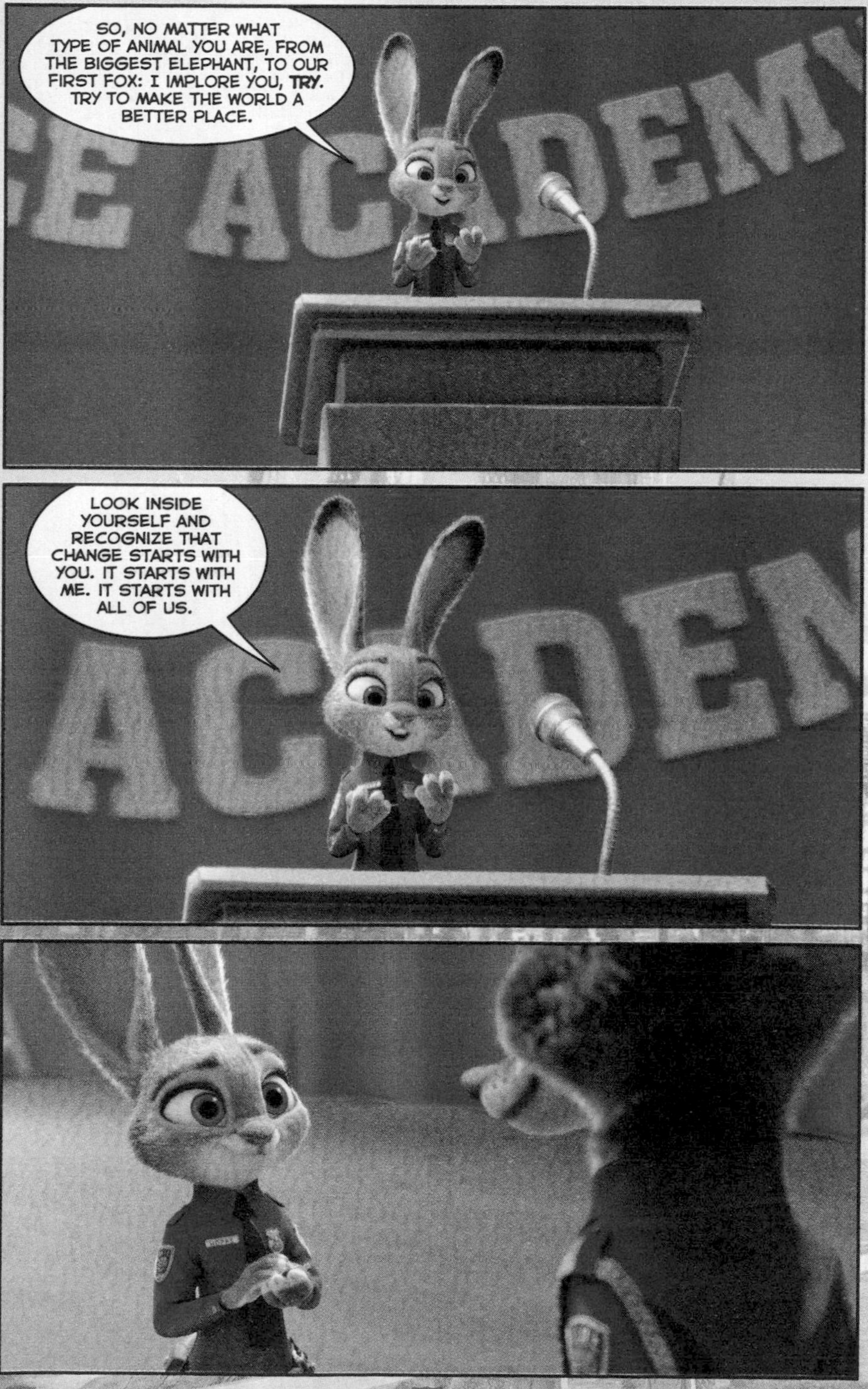
SO, NO MATTER WHAT TYPE OF ANIMAL YOU ARE, FROM THE BIGGEST ELEPHANT, TO OUR FIRST FOX: I IMPLORE YOU, **TRY**. TRY TO MAKE THE WORLD A BETTER PLACE.
LOOK INSIDE YOURSELF AND RECOGNIZE THAT CHANGE STARTS WITH YOU. IT STARTS WITH ME. IT STARTS WITH ALL OF US.

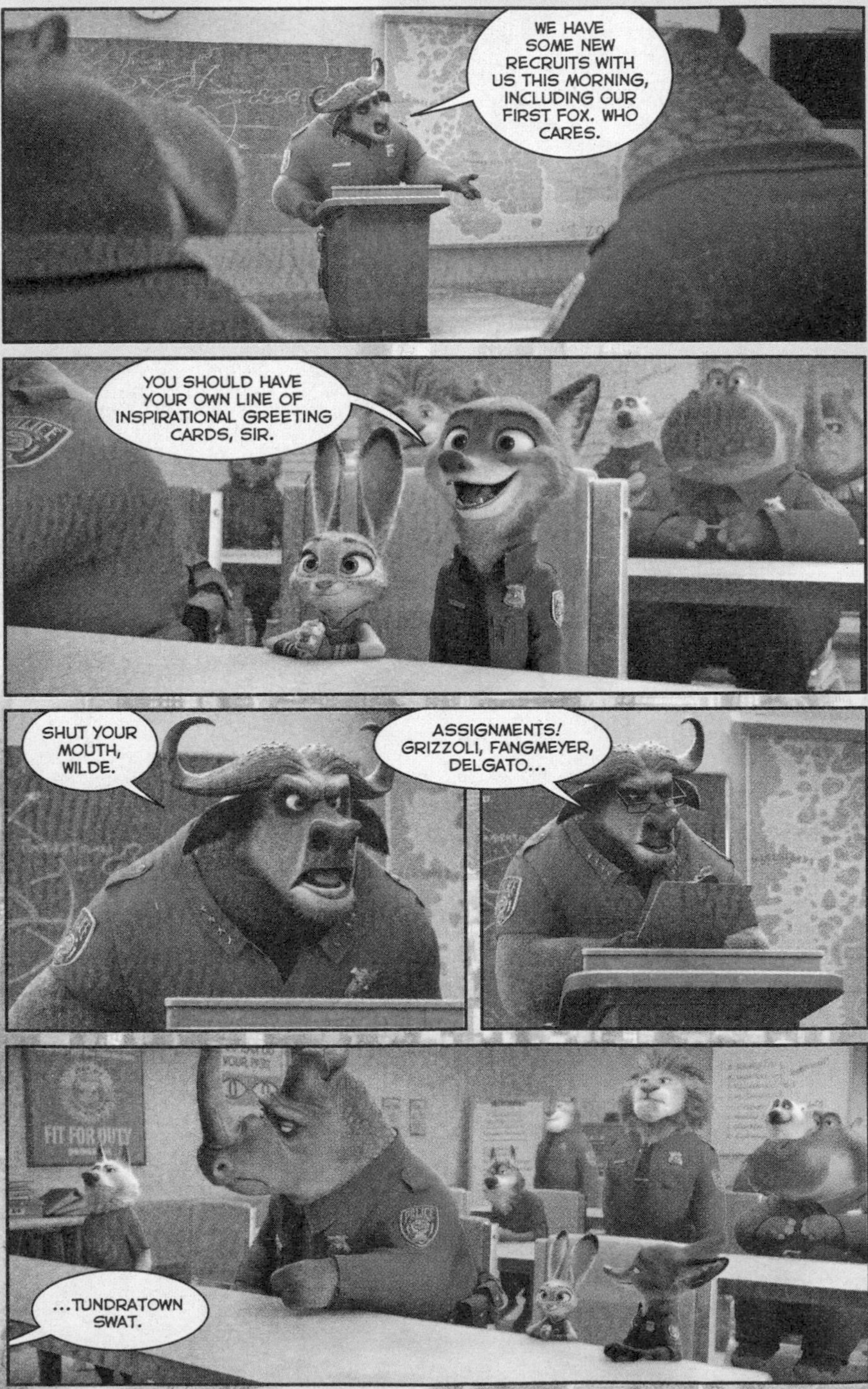
WE HAVE SOME NEW RECRUITS WITH US THIS MORNING, INCLUDING OUR FIRST FOX. WHO CARES.
YOU SHOULD HAVE YOUR OWN LINE OF INSPIRATIONAL GREETING CARDS, SIR.
SHUT YOUR MOUTH, WILDE.
ASSIGNMENTS! GRIZZOLI, FANGMEYER, DELGATO...
...TUNDRATOWN SWAT.

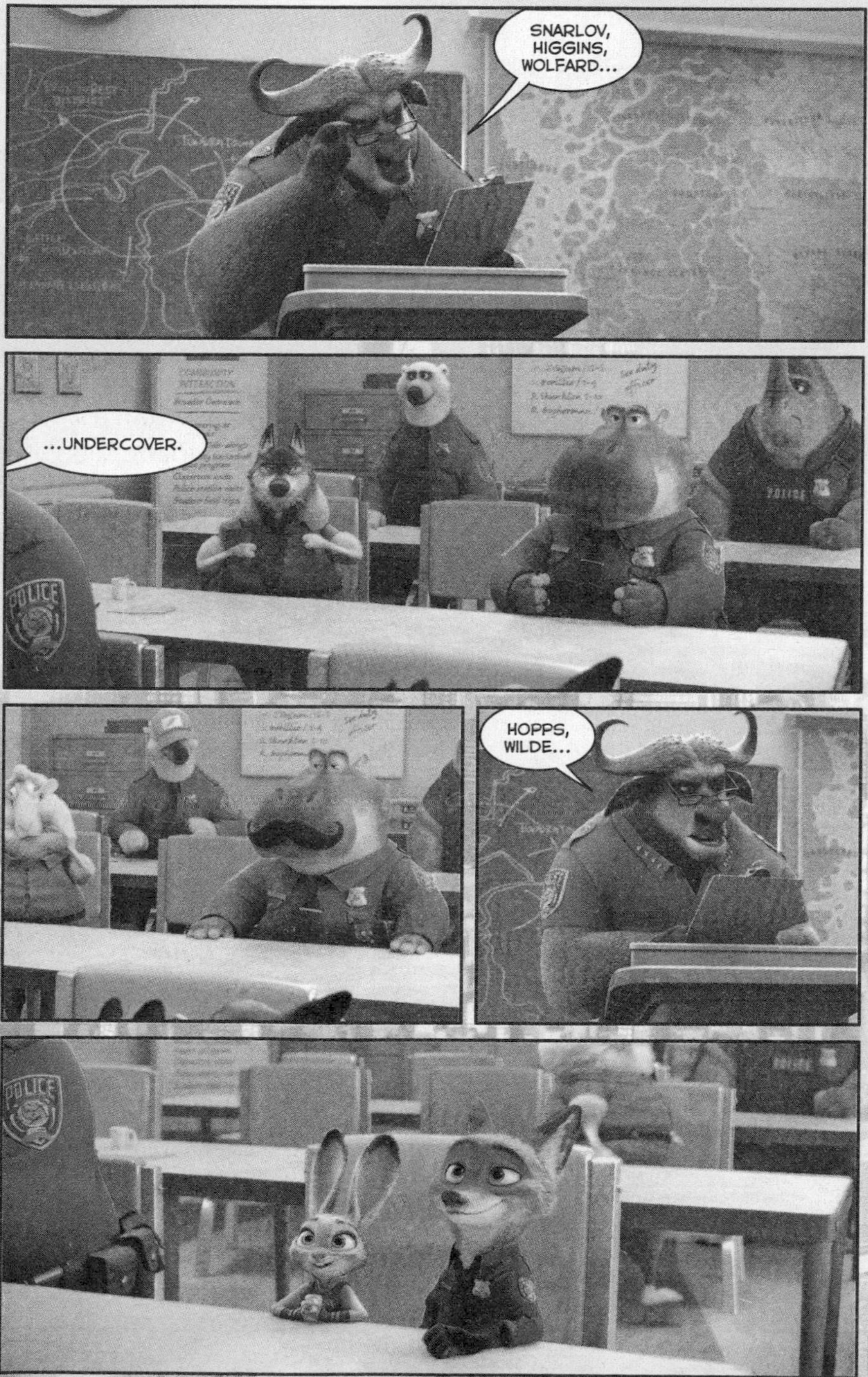
SNARLOV, HIGGINS, WOLFARD...
...UNDERCOVER.
HOPPS, WILDE...

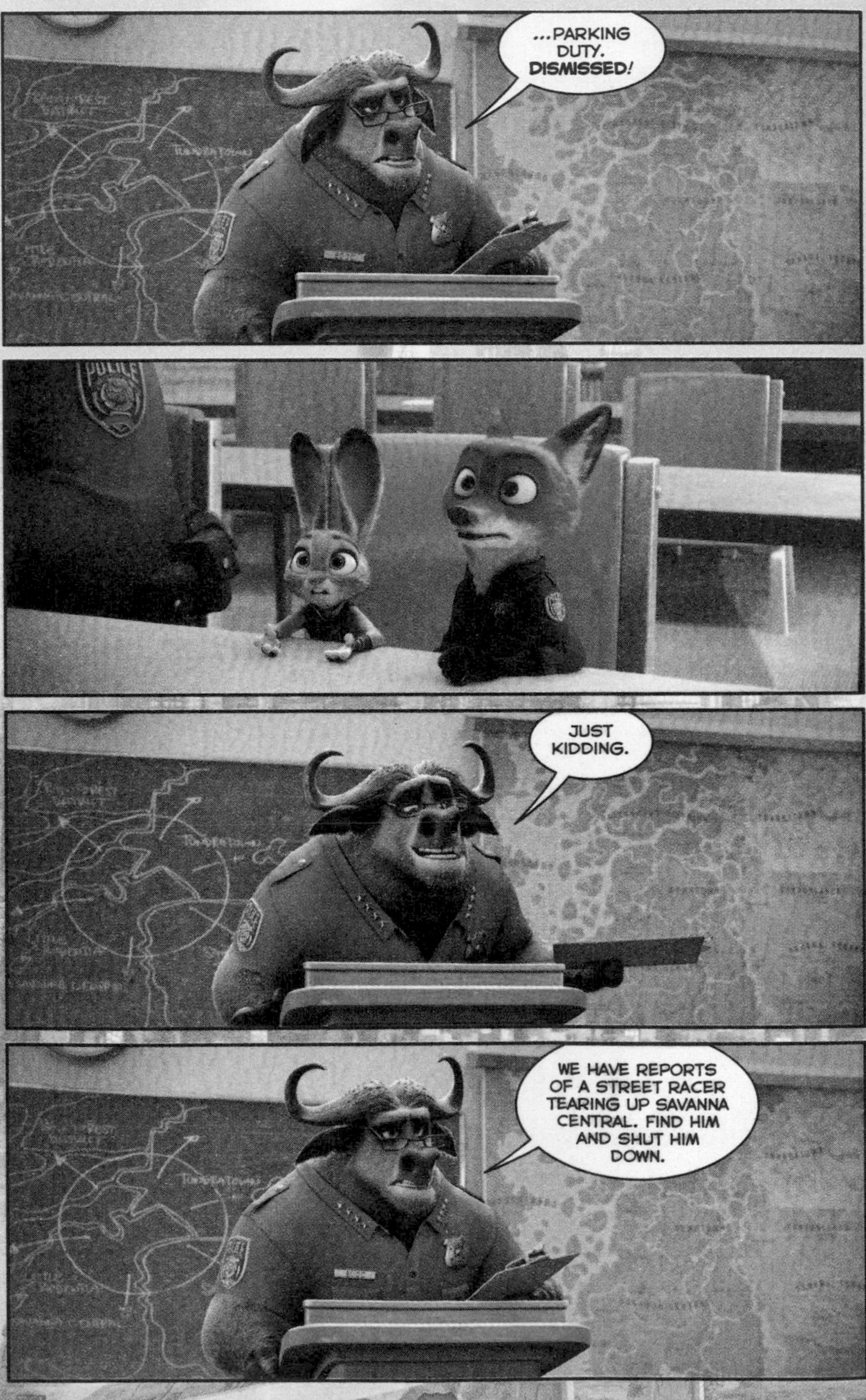
...PARKING DUTY. DISMISSED!
JUST KIDDING.
WE HAVE REPORTS OF A STREET RACER TEARING UP SAVANNA CENTRAL. FIND HIM AND SHUT HIM DOWN.

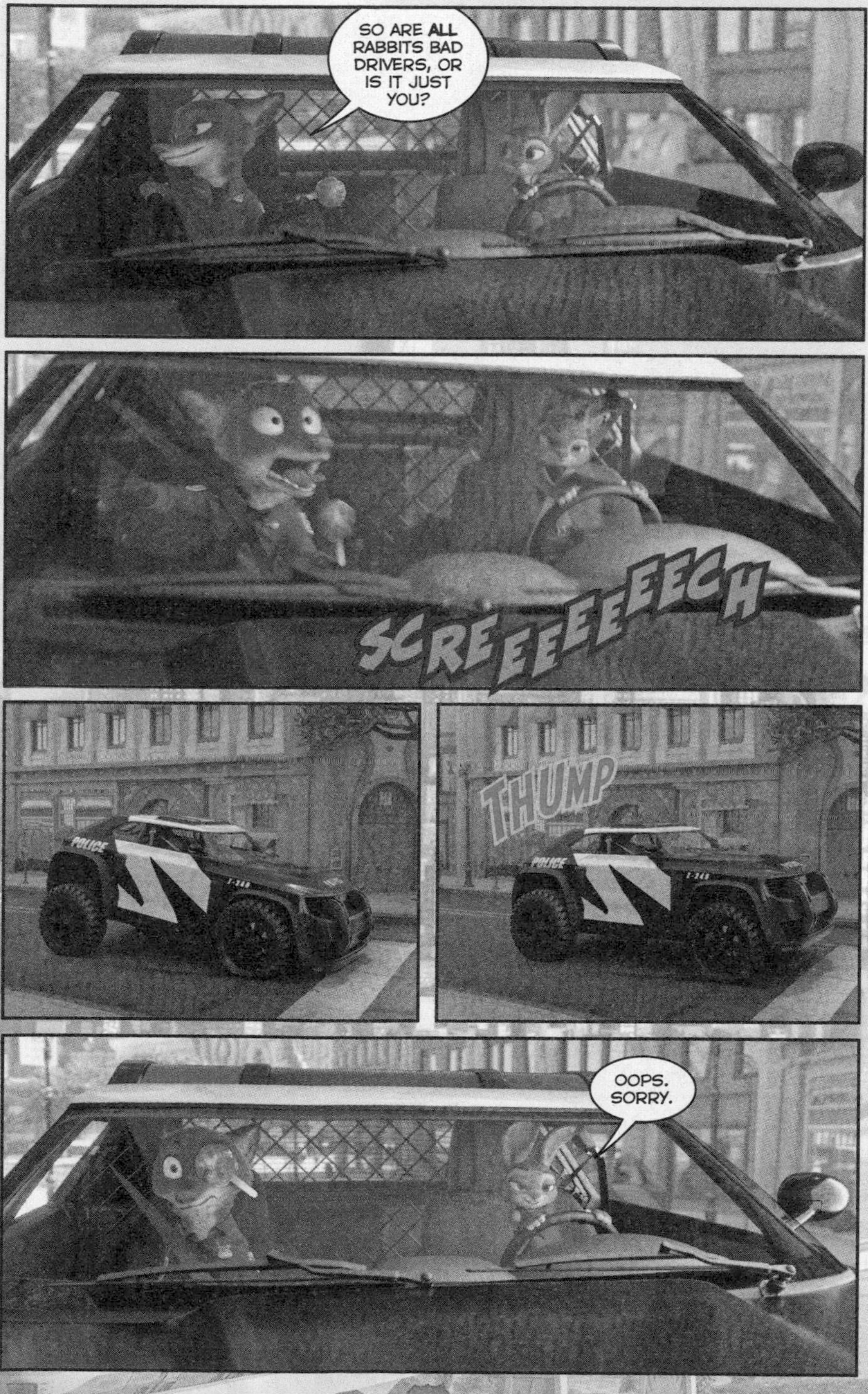
SO ARE ALL RABBITS BAD DRIVERS, OR IS IT JUST YOU?
SCREEEEEEECH
THUMP
OOPS. SORRY.

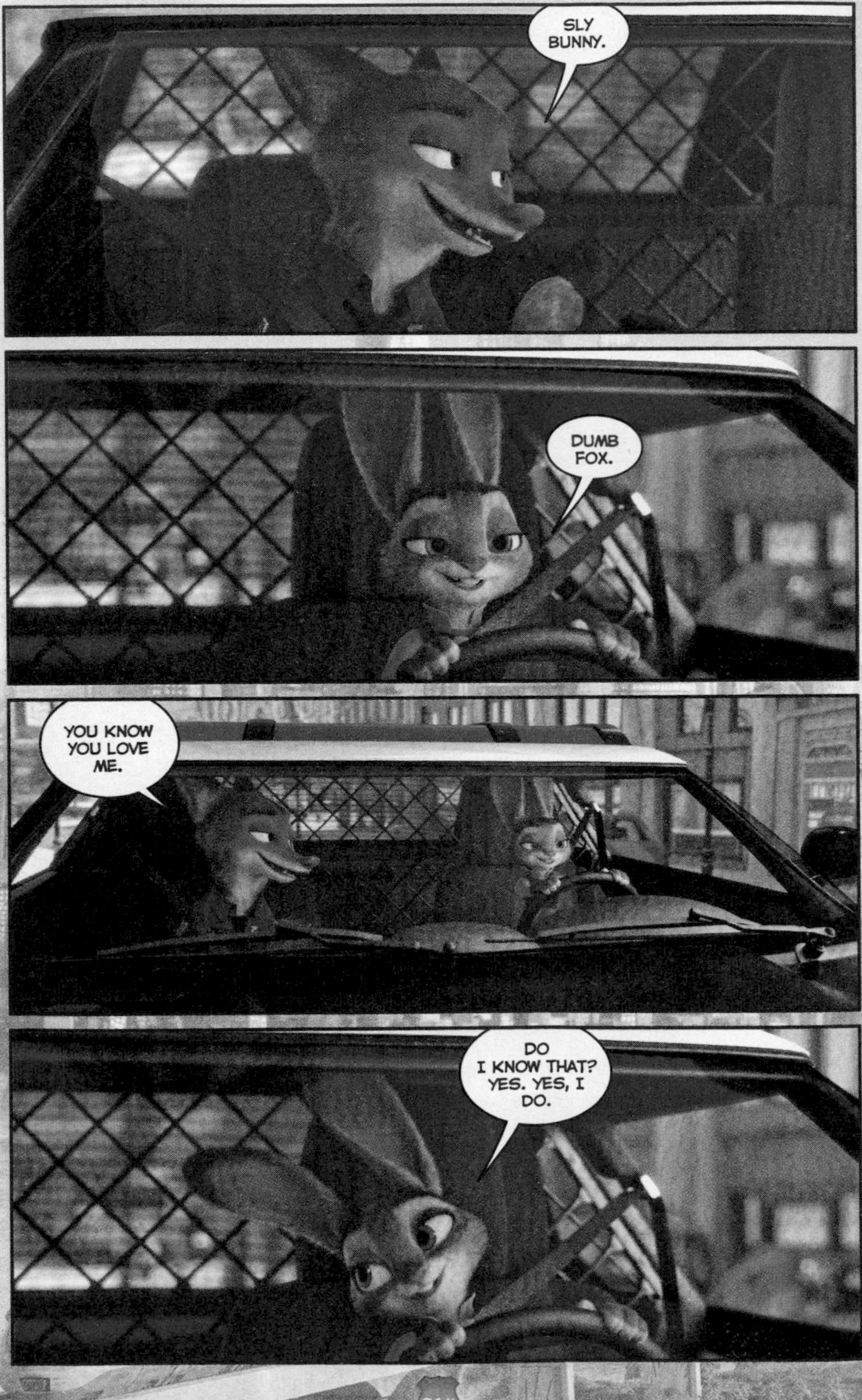
SLY BUNNY.
DUMB FOX.
YOU KNOW YOU LOVE ME.
DO I KNOW THAT? YES. YES, I DO.

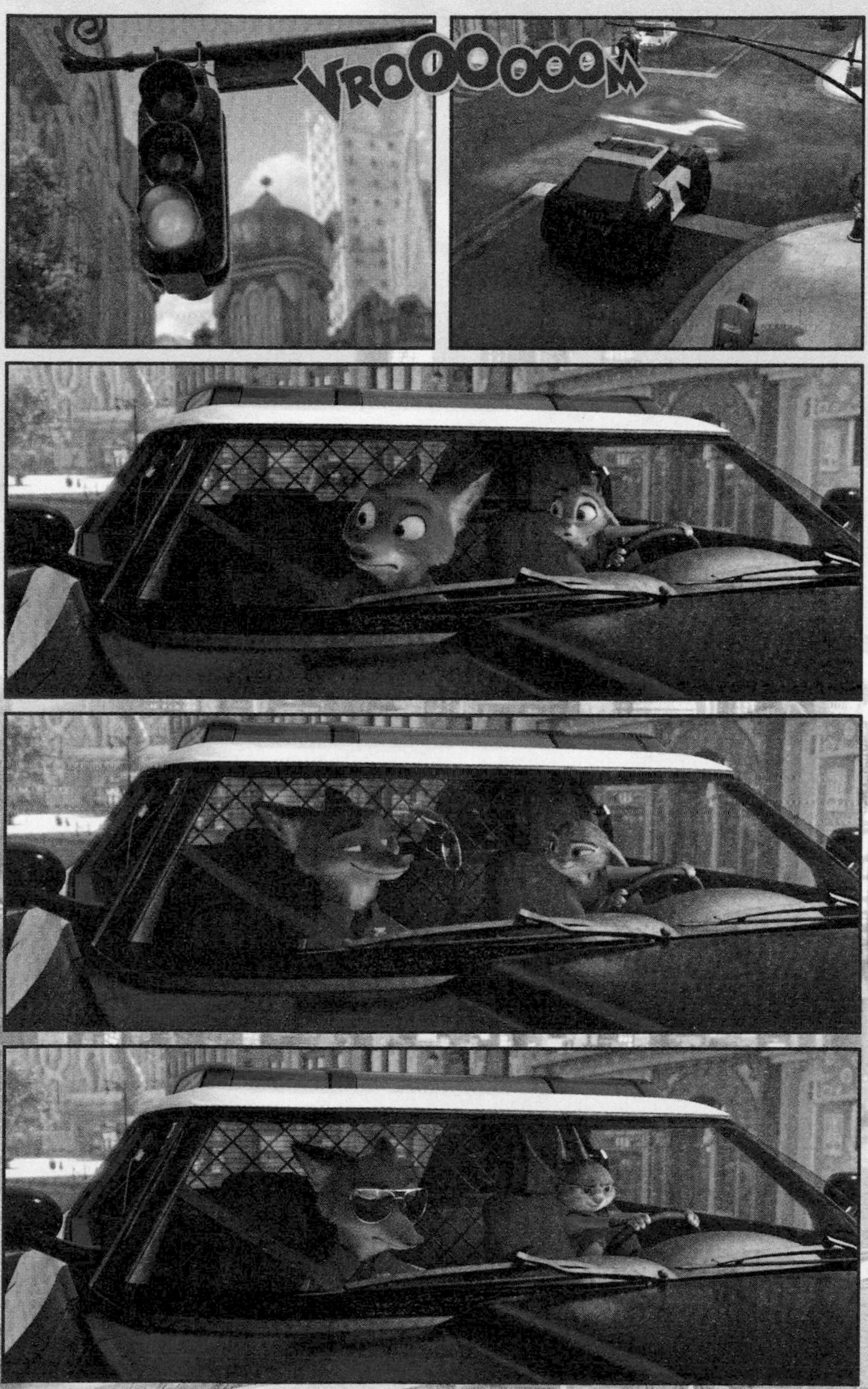
VROOOOOOM

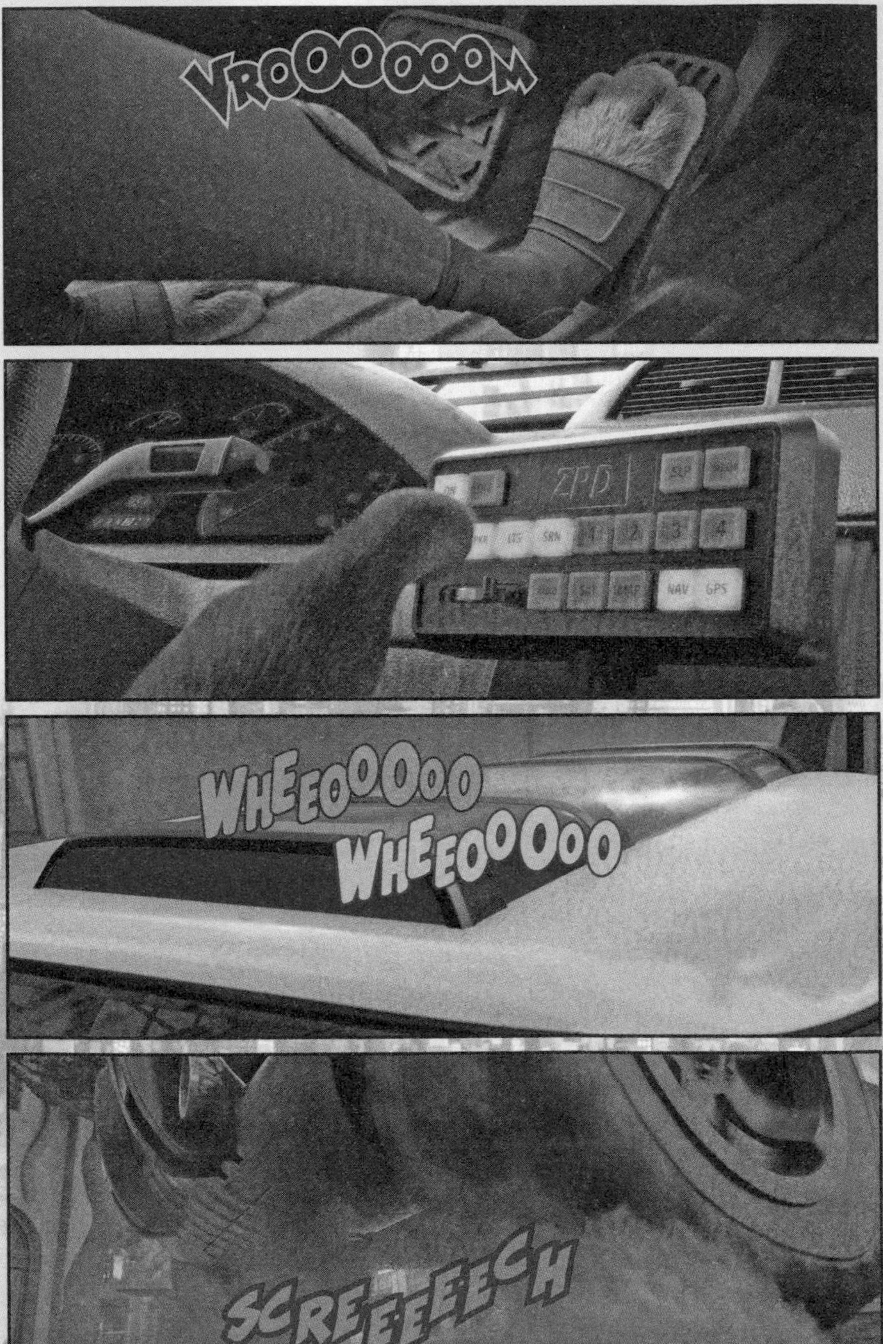
VROOOOOOM
ZPD
SLP
SRN
1
2
3
4
NAV
GPS
WHEEOOOOO
WHEEOOOOO
SCREEEEECH

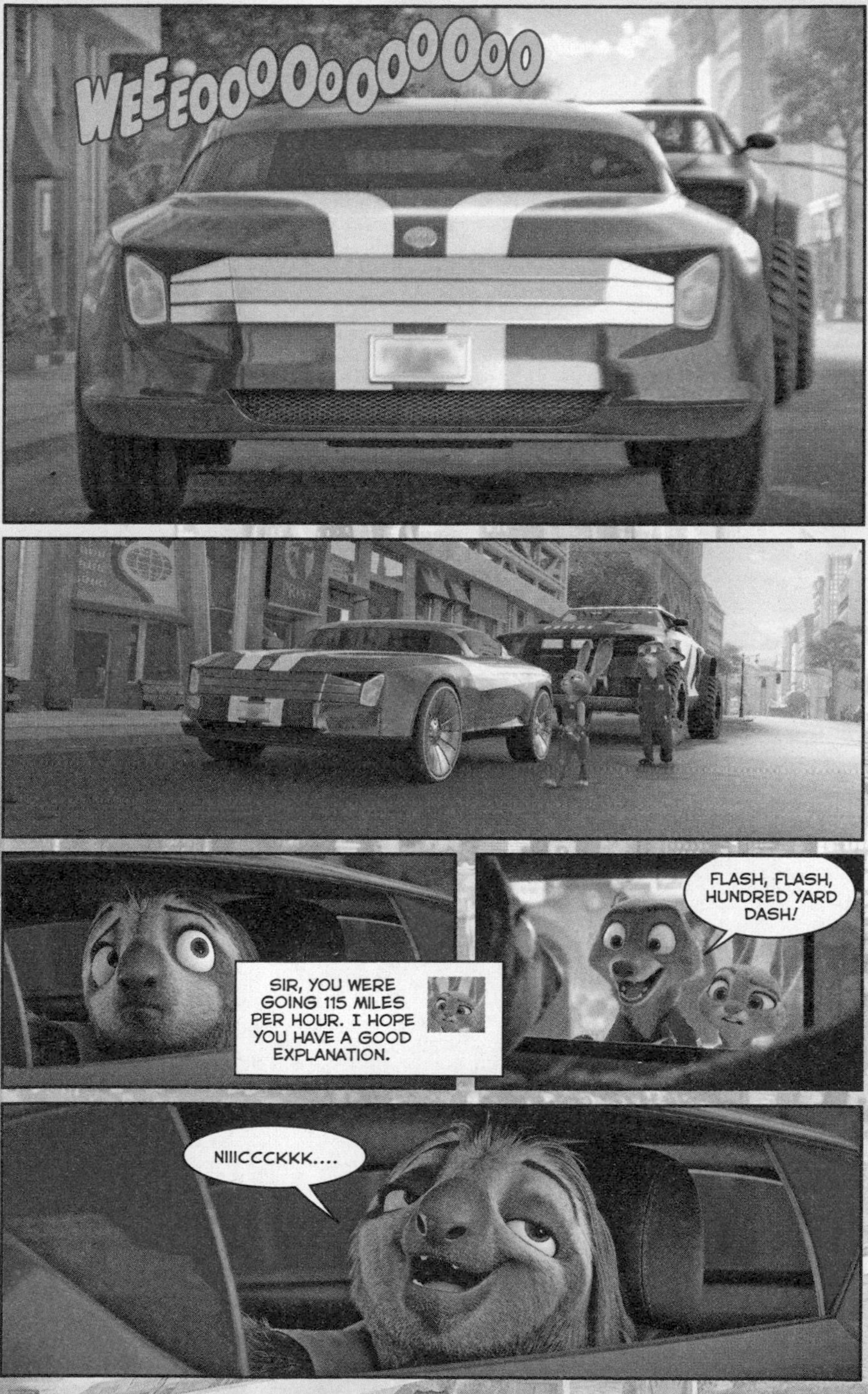
WEEEOOOOOOOOOOO
SIR, YOU WERE GOING 115 MILES PER HOUR. I HOPE YOU HAVE A GOOD EXPLANATION.
FLASH, FLASH, HUNDRED YARD DASH!
NIIICCCKKK....

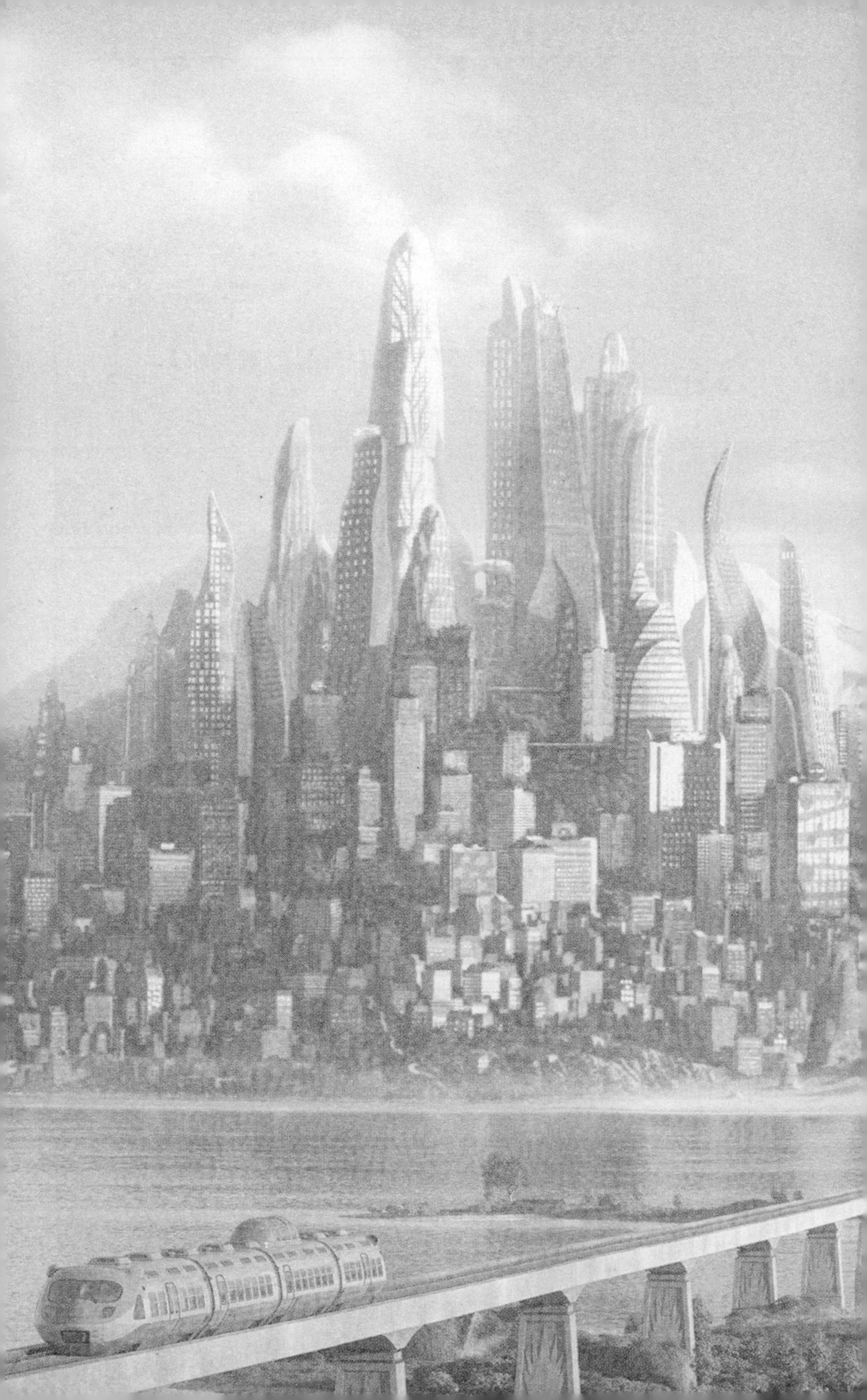

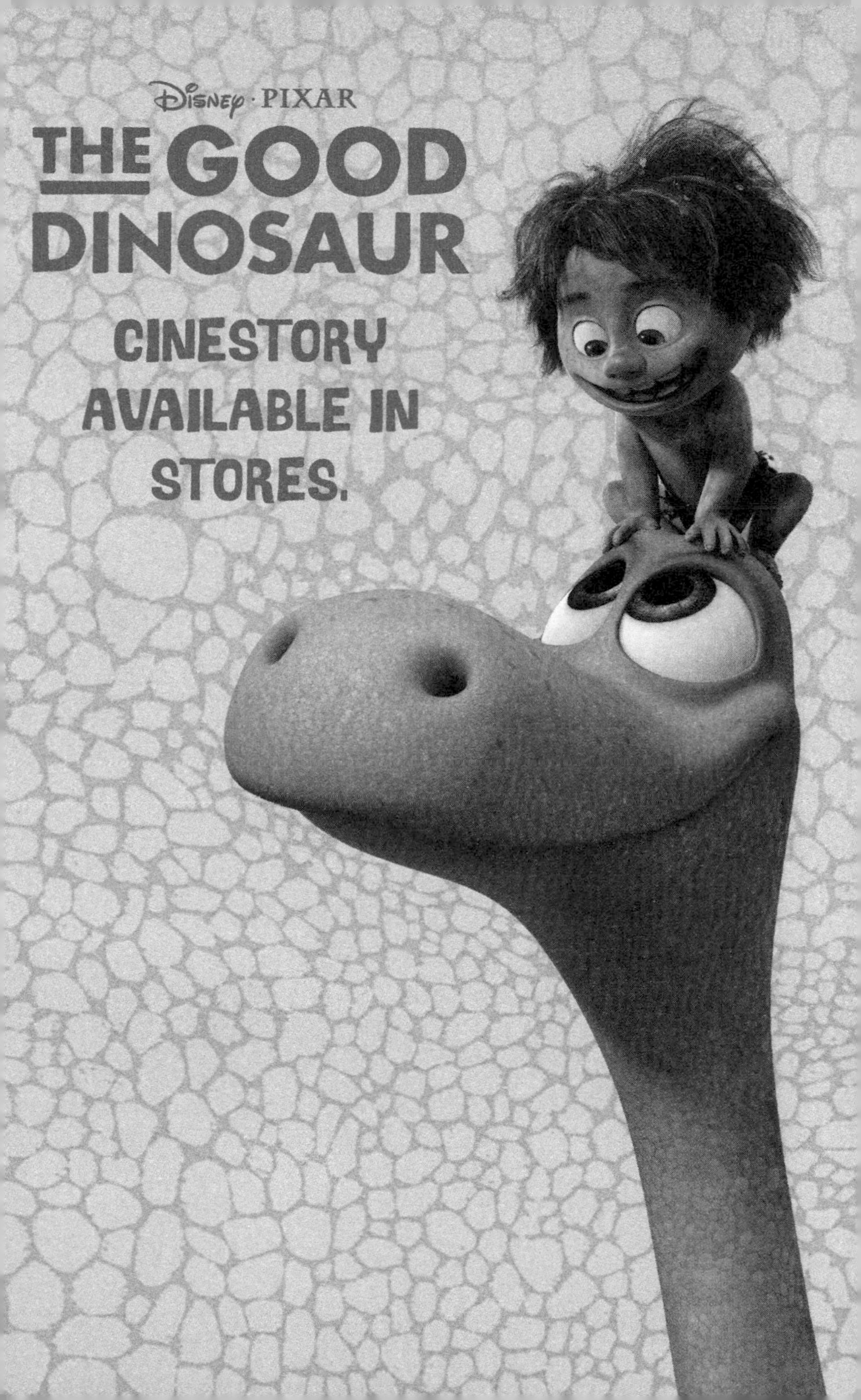
Disney · PIXAR
THE GOOD DINOSAUR
CINESTORY AVAILABLE IN STORES.

65 MILLION YEARS AGO

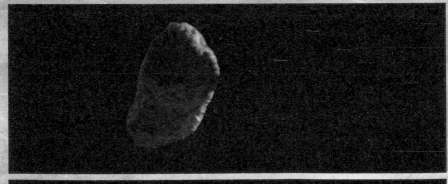

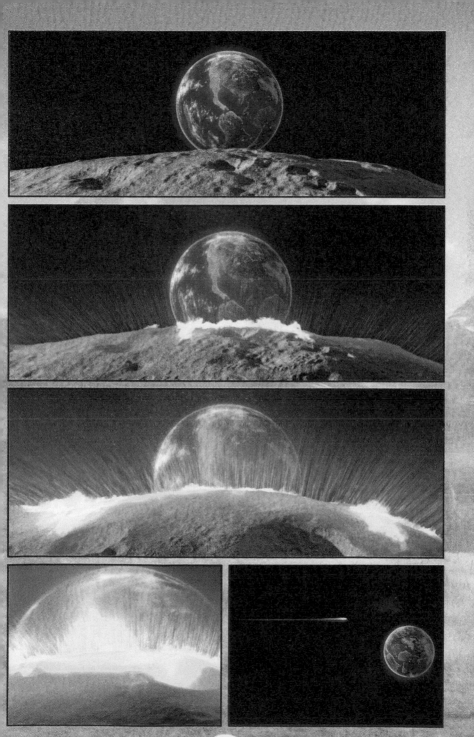

...AND MISSES EARTH.

MILLIONS OF YEARS LATER

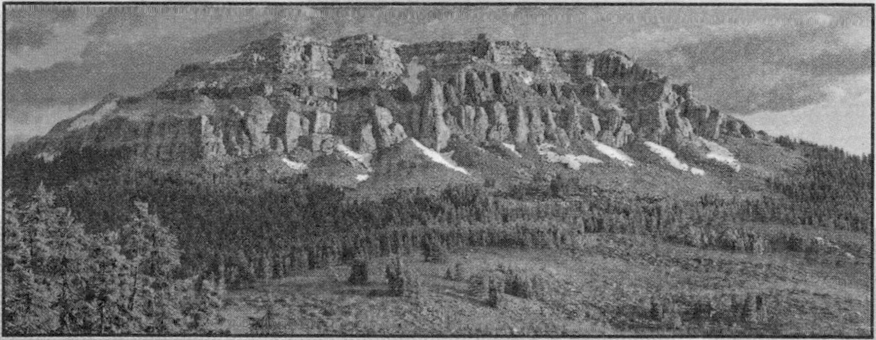

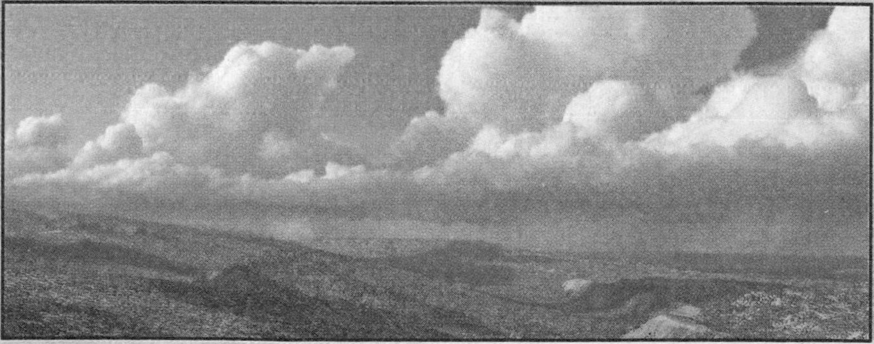

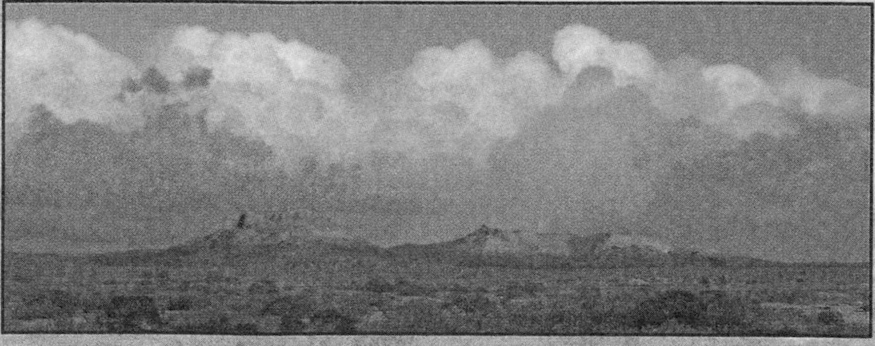

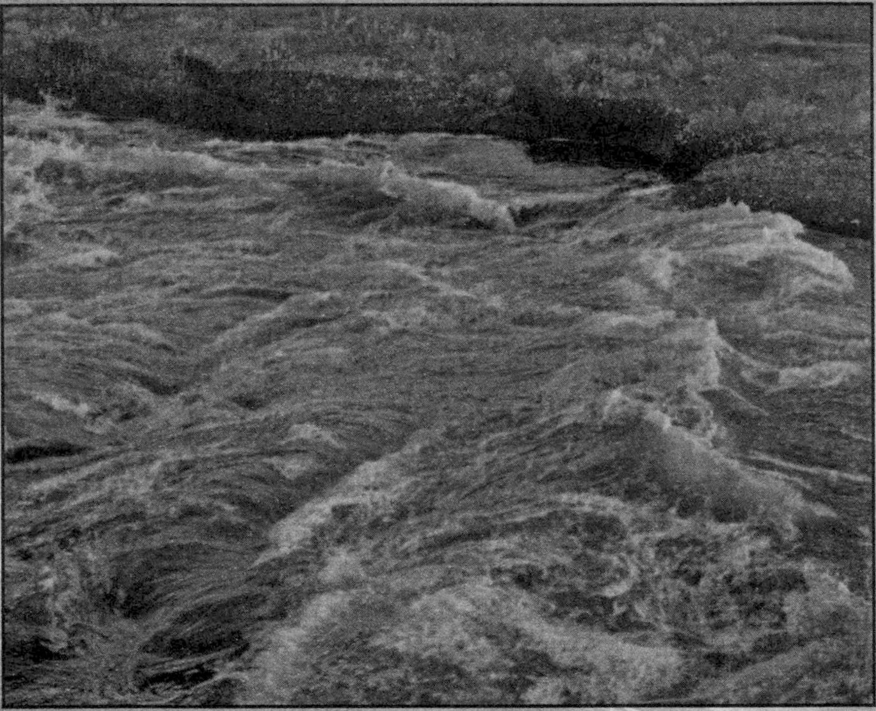

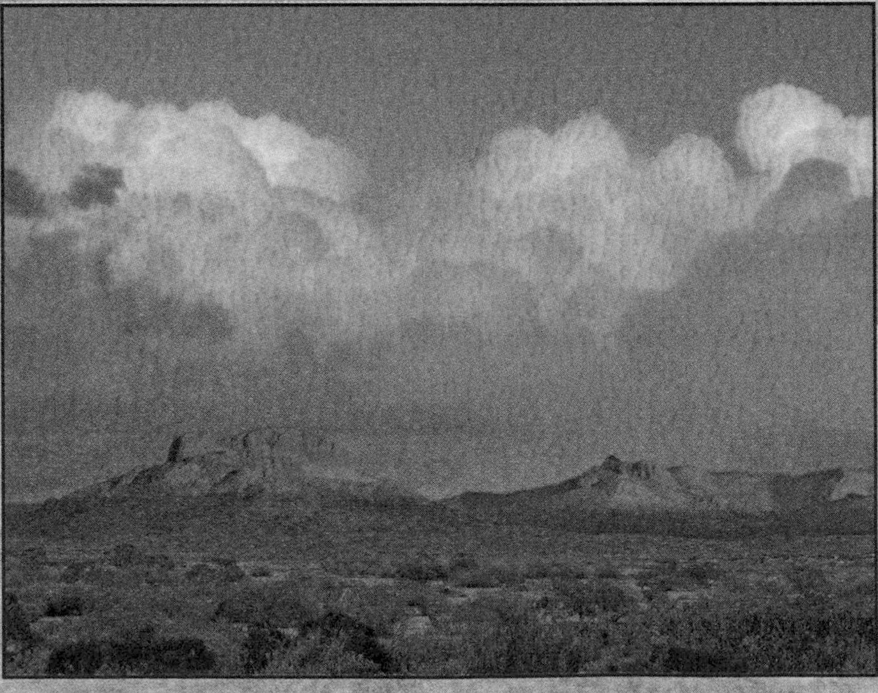

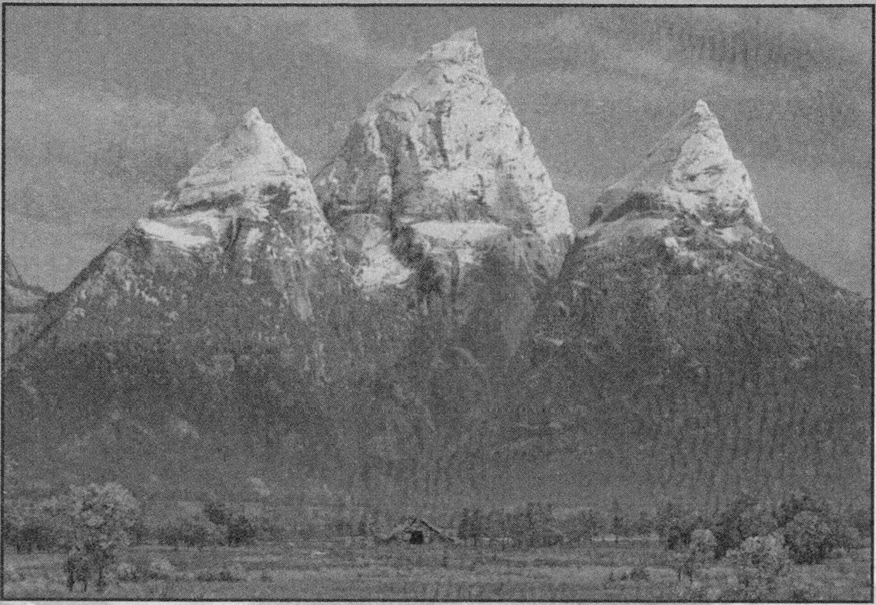

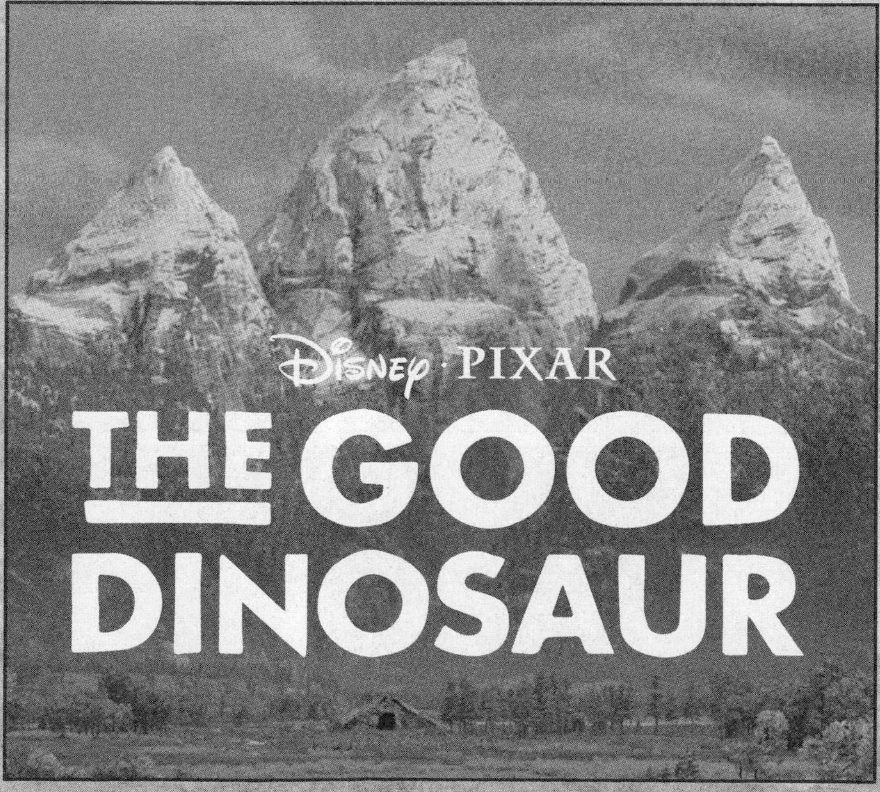
Disney · PIXAR
THE GOOD
DINOSAUR

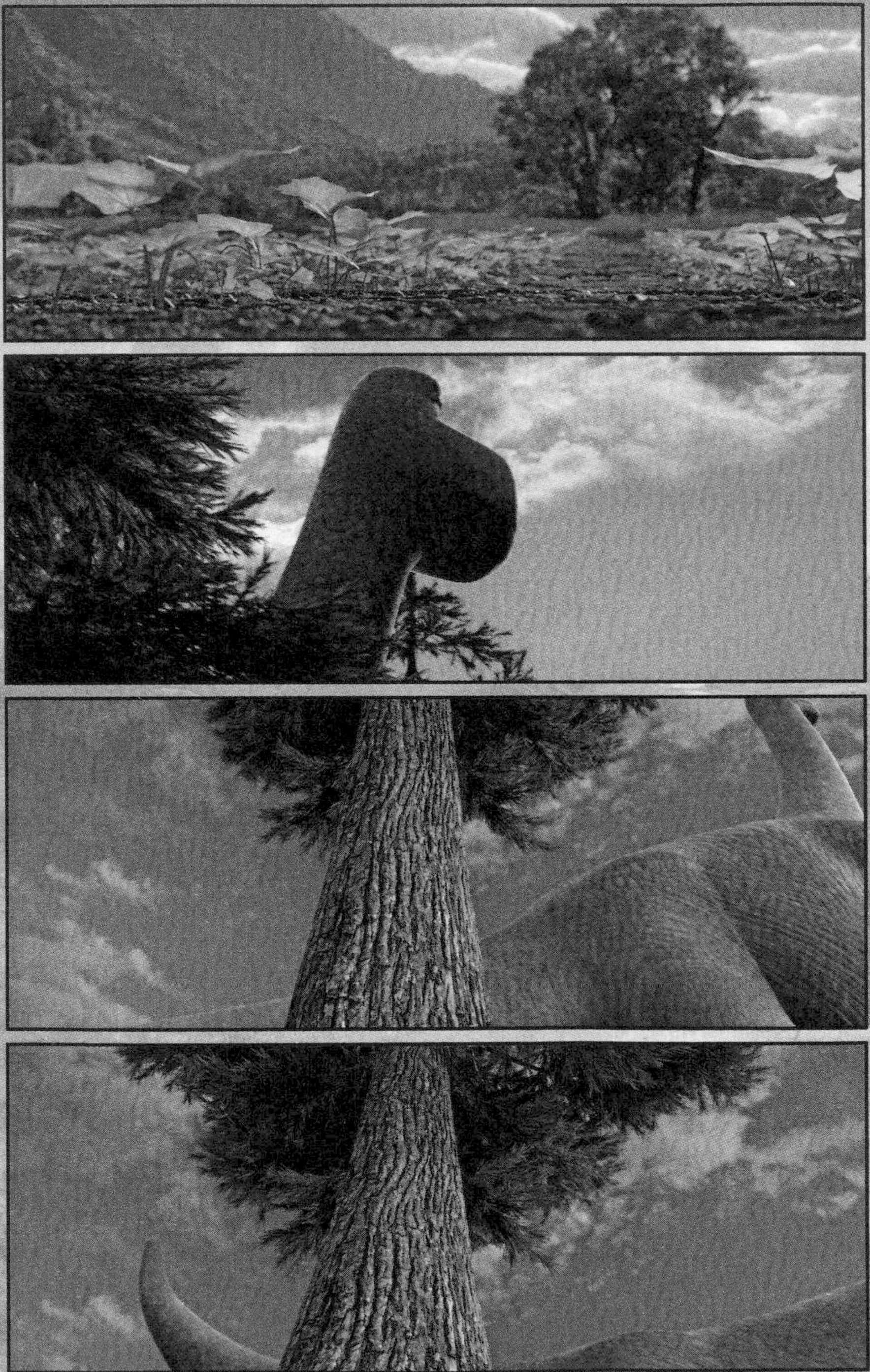

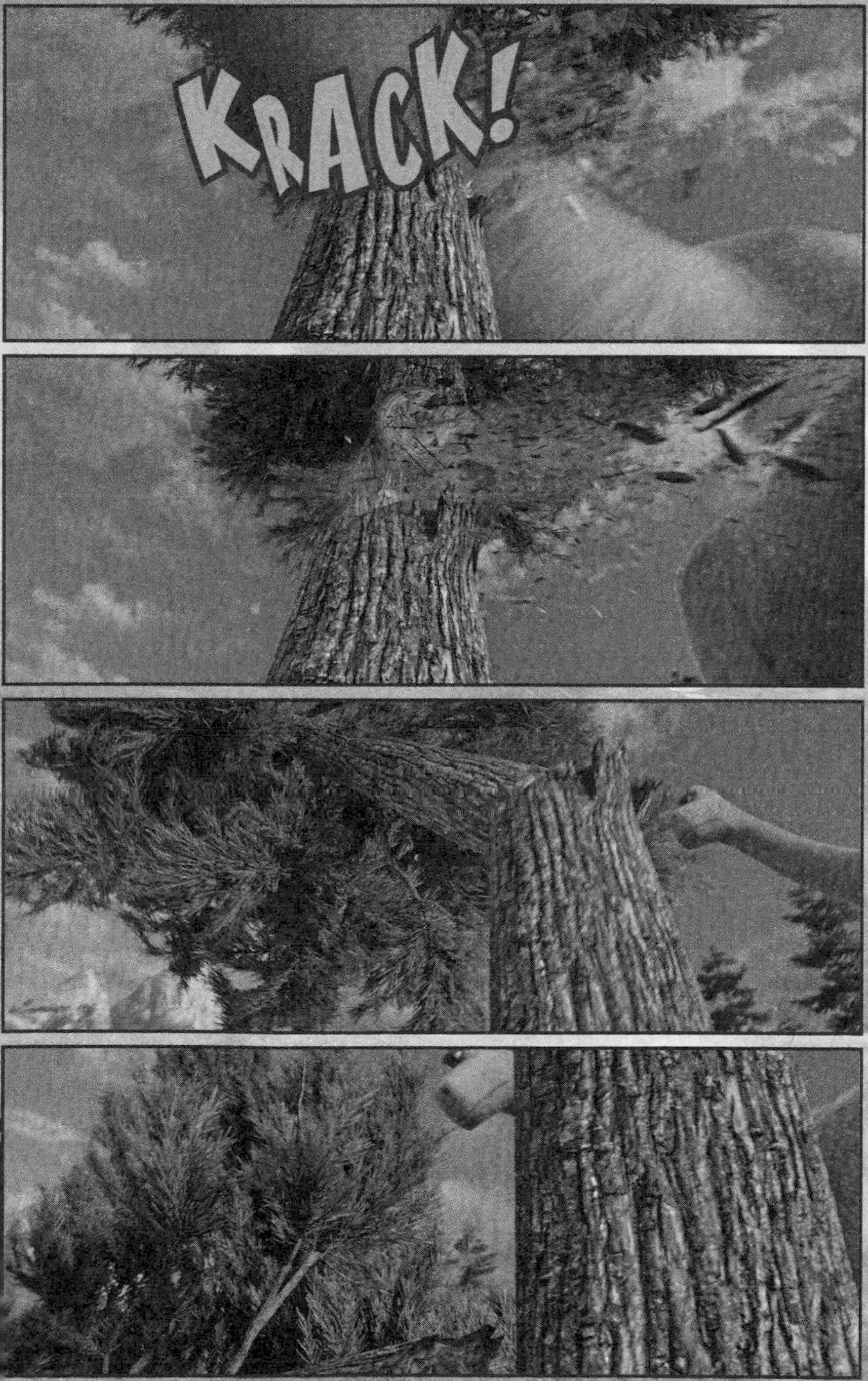
KRACK!

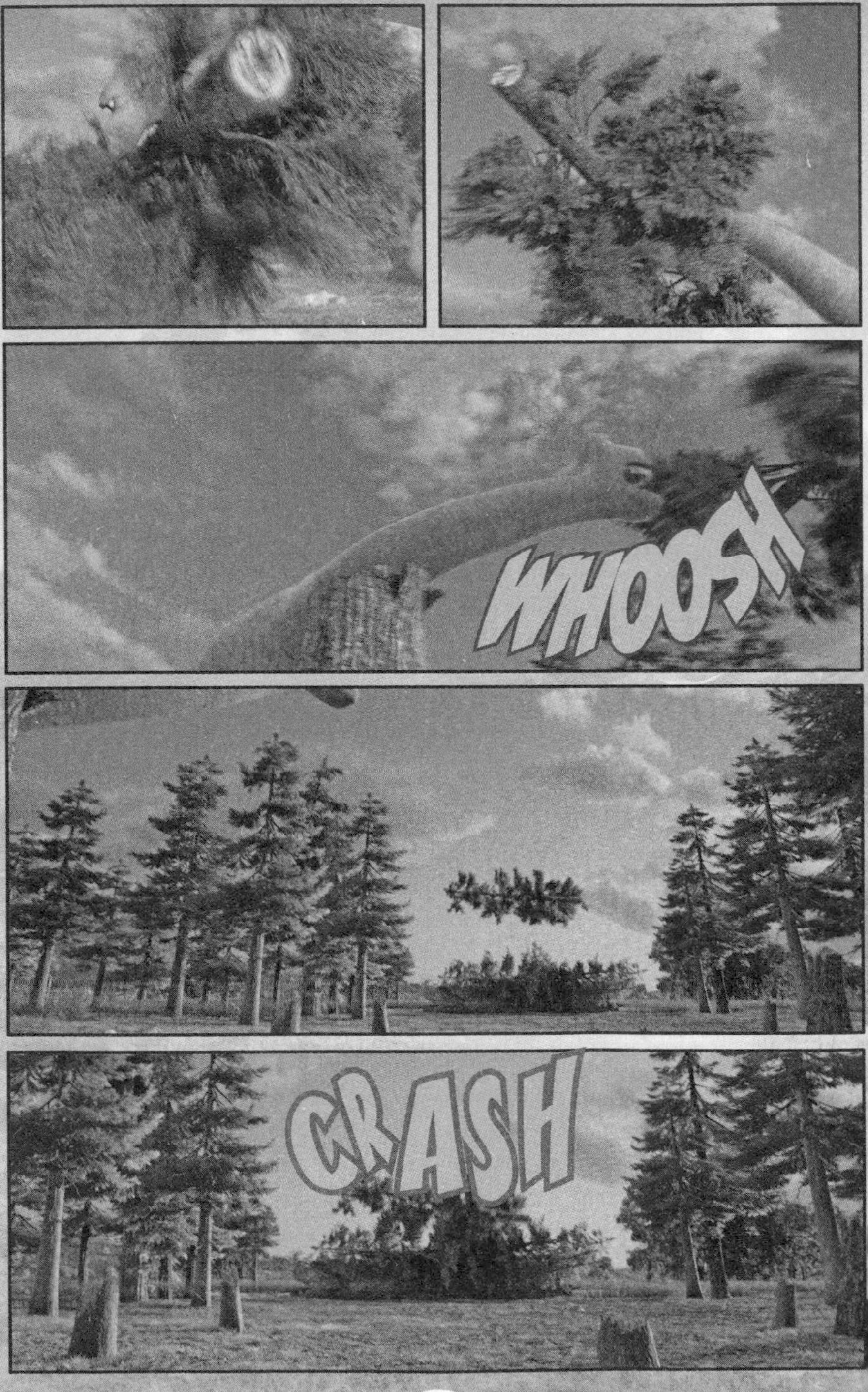
WHOOSH
CRASH